ALSO BY MELISSA GOOD

Dar and Kerry Series
Tropical Storm
Hurricane Watch
Eye of the Storm
Red Sky At Morning
Thicker Than Water
Terrors of the High Seas
Tropical Convergence

Storm Surge

Melissa Good

Yellow Rose Books

Port Arthur, Texas

ISBN 978-1-935053-28-6

First Printing 2010

9 8 7 6 5 4 3 2 1

Cover design by Angel Grewe

Published by:

Regal Crest Enterprises, LLC
4700 Highway 365, Suite A
PMB 210
Port Arthur, Texas 77642

Find us on the World Wide Web at
http://www.regalcrest.biz

Printed in the United States of America

New York has played a frequent part in my stories and not always in a flattering light. Many natives have accused me of being mean and not liking the Big Apple but the fact is it's the hometown I just never lived in and a place that has always held a piece of my heart. Not long ago I crossed the Atlantic and came into NY harbor by sea as both of my sets of grandparents did and realized at some level it would always be home.

~ Melissa Good

Chapter One

THE SUN PEEKED over the horizon lighting up an already coral pink sky with the bland yellows of morning. Its rays spread over the flat calm water, faint ripples brushing only lightly against the hull of a motor yacht bobbing quietly at anchor.

A seagull circled overhead, its white wings outstretched to catch the slight breeze as it watched the water's surface hoping for an easy breakfast while the air was still comfortable, and before the sun started really heating things up.

Inside the boat's cabin it was equally quiet and peaceful. The main living space was dark and cool, sprinkles of light coming in past the curtained windows to illuminate a blue and tan interior, and splashing over the body of a half asleep woman meandering around the counter into the kitchen.

Blond, sun bronzed, and dressed in a sleeveless shirt that came to her mid thigh, the woman stopped to yawn and stretch, rubbing her eyes as the boat rocked a little. She leaned against the counter waiting for it to stop.

"Hope that wasn't some dude with a couple of wave riders and a six pack." Kerry paused to peek out one of the windows, drawing aside the curtain to let the light in before she ambled over to the small refrigerator and removed a bottle of juice from it.

"Did you just say you wanted a six pack for breakfast?"

Kerry turned and leaned against the kitchen counter as she watched her tall, dark haired partner climb the steps from the forward cabin into the living area. "Have you ever seen me have beer for breakfast?"

"Always a first time." Dar squeezed into the kitchen area with her and ducked her head taking a drink from the bottle Kerry offered her. "Besides, it has grain or wheat or whatever in it, doesn't it?"

"Hm." Kerry took a sip from the bottle herself. "You know it's probably healthier than those Frosted Flakes you're about to pour in a bowl." She bumped Dar with her hip. "Glad it's Sunday?"

"Always." Dar leaned back and gazed around the interior of the boat. "Sometimes I think my parents had the right idea."

"Living on the boat?"

"Mm."

Kerry felt the motion as the boat rocked gently under her. "Well, now that you got that satellite dish installed and we can get TV and internet..."

"Slow internet."

"Still."

"It'd be tough on Chino," Dar mused. "Think we could teach her to use the head?"

Kerry took another swallow of juice. "She's a Labrador. Anything is possible. I keep expecting to walk into my office and see her sitting at my desk sending email."

Dar chuckled. "Maybe we should try taking her out on one of these overnights first." She eased past Kerry and went over to the door that led to the back deck. "I'm going to kick over the engines to charge the batteries."

"Want me to bring your coffee up there? I may jump in before breakfast."

"In my coffee? Fabulous. Bring it up then." Dar winked at her on the way out the door, letting it close behind her as a shaft of bright sunlight appeared and then disappeared.

"Punk." Kerry chuckled to herself, as she put her bottle down and turned to the coffee pot, hearing the rumble of the diesel engine and the vibration of it through her feet as Dar settled it into idle. She whistled softly under her breath as she scooped fragrant ground beans into the basket and poured water into the machine.

She turned as the coffee started dripping and headed down the steps into the front part of the boat. She ducked into the comfortable master cabin and pulled off her shirt trading it for a one piece swimsuit. "Living on the boat. Hm."

Kerry regarded her reflection in the wall mounted mirror and paused to imagine what that would be like. "It sounds good," she informed herself, "but I think I'd miss the broadband." She wrapped a towel around her neck and went back up into the main cabin where the coffee was almost finished dripping. "Not to mention Starbucks."

She took two cups, appropriately milked and sugared, and went out onto the back deck to find Dar loitering there, bathed in the early sunlight of a late August day. "Rats. I wanted to climb the ladder with this tray in my teeth."

Dar tipped her head back and watched as her partner set the tray down on the outside counter. "Nice morning," she commented. "Want to go down near Pennecamp later for a few dives?"

"Sure." Kerry handed Dar her coffee, then took the seat next to her with her own cup, putting her bare feet up against the transom.

It was warm, and humid expected weather for the time of year. On the edge of the horizon she could see the faint gathering of clouds that toward the afternoon would likely result in a thunderstorm.

Expected. Very normal. Kerry exhaled and flexed her toes. "So, how did the meeting with Hans go? I never asked you about that on Friday."

Dar had her sunglasses on, and was sprawled in the chair in a tank top and a pair of cotton shorts. "Pretty good. I really wanted to be there when those ships got into port, but now I'm glad I postponed going over until week after next."

"Big scene?"

Dar chuckled. "Hans said it was the most excitement in those parts since World War II, and not in a good way. I'd rather wait and meet with their executive board. A lot more fish to fry, and the European sales team is drooling so badly we had to send them three cases of old lobster bibs."

Kerry sipped her coffee. "Well, you get one week to shake them all up, and then I'm heading over there. That's a lot of infrastructure we're going to need."

"No kidding." Dar wiggled her toes. "Sure you don't want to come with me?"

Kerry sighed. "Stop teasing me, Dar. I told Angie I'd go up there and help her pack up to move. I can't back out on her now."

"I know. Sorry."

"It's not like I want to go to Michigan, you know."

"I know," Dar repeated. "Hey, it'll give me a week to scope out the best beer spots for you," she added, resting her elbows on the deck chair arms. "Hey, what do you think about softball?"

Kerry nearly choked on a mouthful of coffee. "Bw..." She swallowed. "Huh?" She turned her head and looked at her partner. "What brought that on?"

The taller woman shrugged. "I bumped into Mariana in the hall Thursday, and she said she had a bunch of people asking her if we could form a softball team to play in some half assed corporate softball league or something around here."

"Ah."

"I didn't think it sounded all that stupid, and the league raises money for charity," Dar reasoned, "and we're done with that other stuff for now."

"So, she asked you because she expected you to play?" Kerry put her cup down and half turned resting her chin on her fist.

"Us."

"Ah."

"The other choice was bowling," Dar said. "I don't know about you, but for me the biggest draw of the bowling alley is the cheese fries."

"Hmm." Kerry wrinkled her nose. "I think I'd like to try softball. I never played it in school and I wanted to."

"You said that once," Dar remarked. "I think you look really cute in a baseball cap. Sounds like it might be fun."

"You want to do it?" A little surprised at her anti-social partner's sudden interest in team sports, Kerry watched her profile out of the corner of her eye. "I didn't think you were into that sort of thing."

Dar blew bubbles into her coffee making a very odd gurgling noise. "Yeah, I know, but I've never tried this, so what the hell. Why not?"

"Works for me." Kerry got up and went over to the transom, sitting on it and swiveling so her legs were on the outside of the low wall above the platform they stepped off of when diving. "Tattoo, motorcycle, wife, softball." She glanced over her shoulder at Dar. "I think my rebellion is complete." She turned around and dove into the dark blue water.

Dar smiled and toasted Kerry with her coffee cup, content to remain in her deck chair as the sun slowly lifted higher over the horizon. She could hear Kerry splashing and after a moment, she moved the deck chair closer to the back of the boat so she could keep an eye on her.

Kerry was doing the backstroke, swimming a few body lengths away from the boat and then coasting, putting her hands behind her head and floating like an otter in the warm water.

"How is it?" Dar asked.

"Bathtub." Kerry stretched her body out. "Big enough for two." She gazed up at the pink tinged fluffy clouds overhead as she floated on the surface, enjoying the peace and quiet for about ten seconds when a wall of water swept over her. "Hey!"

Dar bobbed up a moment later shaking her dark hair out of her eyes. "You invited me into your bathtub." She grinned at Kerry stroking through the water toward her. She ducked under the surface as she came closer grabbing Kerry as she back peddled rapidly through the water.

"Hey, hey, hey!" Kerry twisted and reached out to grab Dar's shirt, but found only smooth skin under her fingertips. "Holy pooters, Dar! You're naked!"

Blue eyes appeared above the waterline, blinking innocently.

"You are naked!" Kerry hissed, glancing around. "What if one of those fishing charters comes by? Or a dive boat?"

Completely submerged aside from the top of her head, Dar started moving toward her partner.

"Dar."

A puckish grin appeared.

"Shit." Kerry ducked her head under the water and swam forward frog kicking with her hands outstretched to grab whatever they had a mind to.

She found them clasped, and the next thing she knew she was being hauled up half out of the water, landing on top of Dar as her partner flipped over and came up under her.

Abruptly, Kerry wished she'd forgotten her suit as well. She could feel skin everywhere she touched and she almost breathed in a mouthful of salt water as her body reacted.

She was flipped over again and dunked, and could only manage a quick breath before she was under the water again and being pinched on the butt. She flailed around and tried to grab Dar's arm, but as she surfaced, she found herself alone as she turned in a circle. "Hey!"

Dar surfaced on the other side of the boat, snickering.

"You're such a punk." Kerry let her catch up and they were nose to nose near the stern of the boat. "Just for that, I hope a cuttlefish nibbles you."

"Ready for breakfast?" Dar batted a piece of seaweed away.

"Well, now," Kerry laid one hand on her cheek and leaned forward to let their lips brush, "depends on who's cooking."

Dar licked a drop of salt water off her nose. "G'wan." She indicated the ladder.

"Oh no." Kerry shook her head and smiled. "You first." She rolled onto her back and put her hands back under her head, watching her with a wicked twinkle. "Little Miss Exhibitionist."

Dar stuck her tongue out.

"You're so lucky I didn't take my camera in the water."

"HI, KERRY."

Kerry looked up from her computer screen, and waved a few fingers. "Hey Mari," she greeted the Vice President of Human Resources for ILS. "What's up?"

Mariana entered and crossed over to Kerry's desk, taking a seat in her visitor's chair and settling herself. "Good morning, Kerry."

"Uh oh. What did I do?" Kerry turned away from her monitor and rested her elbows on her desk.

"You? Not a thing." Mariana smiled.

"What did Dar do that I have to explain?"

"She volunteered you to be captain of our new softball team, and before I sent out a memo with that delightful information I thought I'd check with you first."

Kerry leaned back in her chair and chuckled. "Nah, that's fine. I actually did volunteer for that," she told Mari. "I figured if I was going to do this, I'd do it right. So what's the deal with all this? I didn't know we had such a demand for inter-corporate sports in the company."

"Well," Mari sighed, "I don't know, really." She crossed her ankles. "You know the suggestion box down in the café?"

"Uh huh."

"Well, we usually get the usual. Less chicken in the café, lower the air conditioning on the sixth floor, raise the air conditioning on the ninth floor, change the dress code...you know."

Kerry nodded. She did, in fact, know as she was the representative from Operations to the employee working group sessions that took place monthly. "Change the coffee, don't change the coffee, bring bottled water in, and stop using bottled water because of the environment, yeah."

"Exactly," Mari said. "So anyway, the last couple of times I opened the box, we had requests for more group activities, more employee activities, and stuff getting involved in the community. So I put out feelers, and this league's what I came up with."

"Ah."

"People activity, sports activity, charity activity, all rolled into one. I figured it was at least worth mentioning." Mari went on, "However..."

"Yeah?"

"When I mentioned it, everyone went batty bonkers on me."

Kerry blinked. "Really?"

"You'd think I was suggesting we go to the Olympics." Mari shook her head. "So anyway, I thought I'd ask the poobah if she wanted to participate, since we all know you both are big into sports."

"We're...ah..." Kerry paused. "Yeah, okay," she said. "We're not really into sports, per se, but we do like being active, and I think Dar's intrigued since she's never done team sports before." She considered, "and I never got to play in school, so I have to admit I'm kinda looking forward to it too."

Mari's face split into a pleased smile. "Great. I know Dar can speak for you, but I just wanted to make sure this wasn't something you felt obligated to do. We've got so much of that around here. You know?"

"I know." Kerry played with one of her colorful pencils. A stack of them were in a cup on her desk in every color of the rainbow, and she'd selected her favorite, purple, to mess with. "So where do we start?"

Mari got up and straightened her skirt. "Remember you volunteered," she warned. "The first team meeting is tomorrow night after work, at the Biscayne ballpark down the street."

Kerry held up her pencil. "No problem for tomorrow, but you know we're out of town for a couple weeks after that, right?"

"I know," Mari said. "Tomorrow is just a kick-off meeting. We've got to get everyone shirts, hats, and the shoes...and get bats...Practices don't start until the third week in September. You should be back by then, right?"

"Right." Kerry saluted. "I'll be there," she said. "We're providing the shirts and hats?"

"Of course," Mari waggled her fingers, "see you later."

"Bye." Kerry watched the older woman leave. She chuckled and set her pencil down, getting up and grabbing her cup as she headed for the door. She poked her head into her assistant's office on the way out to the kitchen. "Hey Mayte."

The slim young Latin woman looked up. "Oh!" She smiled. "Good morning, Kerry," she said. "How was your weekend?"

"Great," Kerry said, pausing when she heard her cell phone ring. "Hold that thought." She unclipped the phone from her waistband and opened it, gazing at the caller ID before she half shrugged and pressed the answer button. "Hello?"

"Hello," a woman's voice responded. "May I speak with Kerrison

Stuart?"

Uh oh. Kerry winced in pure reflex. "Speaking," she reluctantly admitted, glancing at Mayte. She held her coffee cup out to her and mimed filling it.

"Of course." Mayte leaped to her feet with gentle grace and took the cup from her. "No problem!"

"Yes, my name is Allison Barker," the woman said. "I doubt you remember me."

Five seconds. Kerry closed her eyes and put her early training to use. "Actually I do," she managed to produce after a count of four. "You were the class president the year I graduated high school."

"Yes, yes I was." The woman sounded pleased. "I'm so glad you remember. This makes things a lot easier."

For you. Kerry sighed and took a seat on the edge of Mayte's desk, not wanting to take this unwanted phone call back into her office. "What can I do for you?" She glanced up and smiled in response to two accounting clerks who waved at her as they passed by.

"I bumped into your sister at church today."

Kerry tipped her head back and gazed at the ceiling, hard pressed to come up with a scarier statement than what she'd just heard. "Really?"

"Yes. She told me you were going to be in town next week, and you know, we're having our school reunion."

Kerry was silent.

"Hello?"

"Sorry." Kerry cleared her throat. "I was trying to remember what the penalty was for fratricide in Michigan."

"Excuse me?"

"Never mind. Yes, that's true. I will be in town next week, but I'll be very busy helping Angie move. I don't really have time to attend the reunion." Kerry looked up as Mayte returned holding out a steaming cup to her. "Thanks."

"Well, yes, she told me that," Allison responded, not at all put off. "And I'm sure you'll be very busy, but you see, I've been asked to contact you and see if you could make some time to stop by during the banquet and give the keynote speech."

Kerry had just taken a sip of her café con leche and stopped, holding it in her mouth as she stared at her cell phone.

"Kerry?" Mayte saw the expression on her face. "Are you all right?"

Kerry swallowed. "Excuse me," she said into the phone. "you want me to what?"

"I know this seems odd," Allison apologized, "and I do understand, really, but the senior class is participating in the reunion and they asked for you."

Kerry put her coffee cup down and shifted the phone from her right to her left hand. "Okay," she said. "Are you saying the senior class of my all Christian girls' high school wants me to speak to them?"

"Well...yes. I mean, after all, you're a very successful businesswoman," Allison said.

"Have you read the newspapers in the last few years?" Kerry covered her eyes. "Listen, Ms. Barker, I knew about the reunion. I decided not to attend. Please respect that."

Mayte's eyes widened.

Allison sighed. "Ms. Stuart, believe me, I do understand what you're saying, and yes, I know very well what's been going on around your family the last few years. But you know..."

Kerry mouthed a curse, making Mayte's eyes widen even further.

"I think you have a modern, relevant message, and the girls here, they want to hear what you have to say." Allison went on, "we didn't solicit this and, believe me when I tell you, I had my reservations before I decided to call you, but I thought it was important."

Kerry took a breath to answer, then paused.

As though sensing an opening, "You don't have to be at the whole reunion. I know that would probably be uncomfortable for you."

"For me or for the rest of you?" Kerry's mouth twitched into a faint, wry smile.

It was Allison's turn to be silent for a moment. "Well, we're not all that uptight."

Kerry looked over at Mayte, who had her mouth covered by one hand and was watching her in fascination. "So, the senior class wants to hear what I have to say, huh?"

"That's what they said."

What would it take, twenty minutes? She could probably stop by there between packing and getting some dinner with Angie and after all, she had talked Dar into going to hers, now hadn't she? Hypocrisy stunted your growth sometimes. "All right," she said.

"All right?"

"I'll stop by and give a piece of my mind," Kerry said. "But let me just warn you, Ms. Barker, I take a lot less bullshit now than I used to."

A sigh of what might have been either relief or resignation sounded on the phone. "Fair deal, Ms. Stuart. I'll tell the committee," Allison said. "So we'll see you the night of the 10th. The get together starts at eight p.m., we'll have dinner, then the speakers."

"Okay." Kerry gave in with a bemused shrug. "See you then. Bye." She waited for the click on the other end, then closed her phone and leaned over Mayte's desk to punch her phone pad.

A ring, then Dar's voice growled through the speaker. "Yes, Mayte?"

"Sorry, honey, it's just me."

Dar chuckled softly.

"Do me a favor?" Kerry tapped her cell phone against her jaw.

"Sure."

"Turn around and look out the window and tell me if it's snowing."

There was a moment of dead silence on the phone, and then the squeak of Dar's chair sounded clearly. Kerry waited patiently, listening to soft scuffles and sounds of the air conditioning cycling on and off. "The window behind you, hon."

"Is it SNOWING?"

The answer came right into her ear accompanied by the sudden warmth of Dar's body against her shoulder, making her jump nearly off the desk. "Yeek." Kerry cut off the intercom. "Well, after what I just got asked, it damn well should be." She picked up her coffee. "C'mon. You won't believe it."

Dar followed her into her office, pushing her sleeves up after exchanging puzzled looks with Mayte. "I can't wait to hear this."

Mayte watched the door close and went back to her work, muffling a smile.

"UGH." KERRY TOSSED the mail on the dining room table as she passed it scrubbing her fingers through her hair as she headed for the back door to let Chino out. "Yes, honey. I'm coming," she told her excited pet, who was whirling around in circles near the door. "Cheebles, you're going to smack your head against the wall one of these days."

She unlocked the door and watched the dog ramble down the steps into the small outdoor garden. She then headed back across the living room and trotted up the stairs to her bedroom.

As she entered, she glanced at the big doors leading out to the balcony, where the early evening light was still drenching the stucco surface. "I like summers," she announced, as she stripped out of her business suit, hanging the skirt and blazer neatly on hangers inside her closet. "You still get home as late, but you feel like you've got some day left."

Kerry changed into a pair of shorts and tank top, and retreated back down the stairs just as Chino came bouncing in from outside. "Hey Cheebles." She knelt and gave the Labrador a hug. "Are you glad to see me?"

Naturally, the dog was. Chino's tail wagged furiously as she licked Kerry's face, only stopping when Kerry stood up and made her way over to the cabinet that held the all important dog food supply.

"Gruff!" Chino sat down next to her bowl, tail sweeping the floor.

Kerry turned and put a hand on her hip. "Excuse me, madame."

Chino's tongue lolled out happily.

"Dar taught you that look, didn't she?" Kerry had to smile, as the dog looked back at her with those utterly unquestioning brown eyes, as steadfast and honest as her beloved partner's. "Little punklet." She opened up the dog food and filled Chino's bowl with both wet and dry, setting it down and watching her wolf it down. "Glad I don't eat that fast."

"Gruff?" Chino looked up at her, and went back to eating.

"I'd bite my fingers off." Kerry chuckled. She leaned back against the counter and considered the question of her own dinner, or more precisely, her's and Dar's, since Dar was stuck on a late conference call and wouldn't be home for at least an hour.

Dar would be totally happy if she offered her a bowl of cereal and some ice cream, and Kerry knew it. She also knew she probably would be happy with the same thing, and, on occasion, that's what they ended up with when they came home very late.

If she wanted to order something from the club for them, that would be okay too. Kerry peeked inside the refrigerator, pondered her choices, then she removed a premade pizza crust from the fridge and pulled the flat pan it went on from the oven.

She removed the crust from its wrapper, and went back to the fridge and removed a small jar of marinara sauce, a small jar of olives, some jalapeno peppers, a package of pepperoni, several slices of ham, a bag of mozzarella cheese, and a can of peaches, taking them back over and setting them on the counter.

Whistling softly, she assembled the pizza, putting down a layer of the sauce, a handful of cheese, then scattering the rest of the items indiscriminately over the surface before she covered it all over with more cheese.

Only then did she carefully place peach halves on one half of the pie, her face twitching a little.

Once she was done, she popped it in the oven and dusted her hands off, returning the fixings to the fridge and removing a bottle of ice tea. She wandered out onto the porch with the tea, settling on the two person swing as Chino joined her. "You finished already, Cheebles?"

Chino licked her lips, and sat down.

"I guess so." Kerry popped open her tea and sipped it, as she gazed out across the Atlantic Ocean. Pushed aside all day, the memory of her conversation and unexpected request now surfaced, and she nibbled her lip, thinking about what on earth she was going to say to a bunch of...

Kids? Like she'd been?

Kerry frowned. The kid she'd been, and the girls she'd gone to school with, probably would not have stepped outside the carefully constructed conservative box they'd grown up with to request who she'd become speak at their event.

Just would not have happened. Maybe they'd have talked about it, though she doubted even that much, but to demand it?

So what in the hell was she supposed to say to them? And if they were that confident already, why even ask her to give a speech? Kerry sighed. "Maybe they are interested because I'm a successful businesswoman," she reasoned. "I mean, I am."

That idea seemed a lot more appealing than thinking the girls wanted her just for the scandal it would cause the school. Kerry appreciated a good scandal, and she had to admit she was a little bit amused at the request, but she decided she'd come up with a respectable presentation and take the opportunity to visit her hometown without causing any headlines. She was still going to kick Angie's ass though.

Kerry relaxed against the back of the swing chair, a little ambivalent about the prospect of her sister's moving. On the one hand, she was glad Angie was getting out of the big house she'd lived in with her ex-husband, but disappointed she was moving in with their mother.

She'd half dreaded Angie's idea of moving down to Miami for very selfish reasons. But she understood that by moving back with Mom, the chances of Angie's son's father joining her were pretty much done. Brian's reluctance had disappointed her profoundly and she, truthfully, wasn't looking forward to meeting up with him during the move.

She knew she wasn't going to be kind. Kerry managed a wry smile. Brian probably knew that too. But you never knew about people, and maybe he'd end up surprising her.

Maybe she'd end up surprising him with a punch to the jaw. You just never knew. Kerry glanced down as her cell phone buzzed. She put the cap on her tea and answered it, smiling when she saw the name on the caller ID. "Hello, oh love of my life."

"Boy I'd love to have patched you into that goddamned conference call," Dar answered, "that sure would have livened things up."

"Anytime." Kerry could hear the sound of the ferry in the background. "You get out early?"

"Yeah," Dar replied. "I told them I had to go get fitted for cleats. That pretty much stopped the conversation and everyone said they had to leave."

Kerry started laughing in reflex. "Oh no."

"Hehehe," Dar chortled along with her. "I can't wait to send Maria around the building tomorrow to see what rumors *that* stirred up."

"How about if I use my red pencil to put little dots across my forehead," Kerry suggested. "Like mini train tracks. I can pretend not to be wondering why everyone's looking at me."

"Everyone looks at you anyway," Dar said. "All right, let me get off the phone so I can drive. Be home in a minute."

"Cool. I made pizza."

"Remember the peaches?" Dar asked, in a hopeful tone.

Kerry grimaced. "Yes." She cleared her throat. "Honey, couldn't you be hooked on something more normal, like anchovies?"

"Yuk."

"Okay." Kerry sighed. "Let me go see how it's doing. See you in a few."

"Bye."

Dar clicked off. Kerry spent a moment more watching the water before she got up and went back inside, trading the muggy warmth of the patio for the brisk chill of the air conditioning as she slid the door shut behind Chino and walked into the kitchen.

She could smell the pizza. She put a glove on her hand and opened the stove, peeking at her creation and judging the bubble factor of the cheese. Satisfied, she removed the pan and set it down on the stone cutting board, dusting the top with a bit of parmesan. "There."

"Gruff." Chino was sitting near her bowl, watching Kerry expectantly.

"Oh no. Don't even think about getting pizza for dinner, madam." Kerry pointed the can of cheese at her. "Go get mommy Dar."

Chino's head swiveled toward the front door immediately, as they both heard the sound of Dar's car door closing. "G'wan, go get her."

The Labrador raced for the front of the living room just as Dar entered, plowing excitedly into her knees and knocking her backwards. "Hey!" Dar grabbed for the door frame. "Watch it, you furball!"

"Aww...she loves you." Kerry watched from the doorway, leaning against one side of it as Dar got the door closed and tossed her briefcase on the loveseat, followed by her linen jacket. She had a white shirt on with the sleeves rolled up partway to expose her tanned forearms. The ends of the shirt were already untucked from her skirt in an appealingly rakish picture. "So do I."

Dar looked up from petting Chino, and smiled. "I have a surprise for you."

Kerry's brows lifted a little, seeing the warmth and the mischief in Dar's eyes. "Oh oh." She pushed off from the doorway and went over to where Dar was, bumping against her and then wrapping her arms around her and giving her a hug. "That's all the surprise I ever need."

"Aww." Dar echoed Kerry's earlier speech. "But don't you want to see the Swiss Alps?"

Kerry peered up at her, a look of surprised delight on her face. "Huh? Are you serious?"

"As a heart attack." Dar grinned. "I figured after we lock up this deal with the old man, we take a week and go see how the other half lives."

"What other half?" Kerry's mind tumbled into overdrive, the possibilities crowding onto themselves like pushy tourists.

"The half that takes vacations." Dar leaned over and kissed her. "You in?"

"Hell yes." Kerry bounced up and down. "Can you fast forward us a couple weeks, please? Now it's going to seem like a year getting through Angie's moving and my damn high school reunion."

Dar bounced a few times with her, making Chino bark in surprise. "Now where's my peach pizza?"

"C'mon." Kerry slipped an arm around her. "Let's get you undressed, before I have to suffer watching you eat that."

"That's what you used to say about grits."

"Not the same thing."

"THAR SHE BLOWS." Dar pulled her Lexus into the weed studded parking lot that ringed the small ballpark. "Nothing like a scroungy dirt pit on a muggy evening here in the thunderstorm and lightning capital of the world."

As if to punctuate her speech, a low rumble of thunder sounded in the distance.

"How did you do that?" Kerry asked, leaning back in the passenger seat and enjoying the last few minutes of air conditioning before she had to get out and face the humidity.

"Practice."

Kerry eased herself upright, studying the half filled parking lot where she spotted quite a number of familiar faces. "Hm. A lot of people are here."

Dar pulled into an empty spot. She was dressed in a pair of shorts and a tank top, and she paused a moment to pull her dark hair back into a pony tail and fasten it before she turned the car off. "Nice crowd," she agreed. "Wish we had stopped for dinner first."

Kerry got up and half turned, reaching into the back seat. "I've got a granola bar here."

Dar eyed her. "I'll wait thanks. You said this wasn't going to be a long session."

"That's what Mari said." Kerry straightened back up, holding her bar in one hand. "Share?" She ripped the plastic off the snack and broke it in half, handing one part over to her reluctant companion. "It's the peanut butter one you like, Dar. C'mon."

Dar's brows lifted, and she accepted the offering, sniffing it. "Mm. Okay." She bit into the bar. "Ready?" She indicated the gathering crowd, some of whom were looking curiously at the Lexus. "Before we become the entertainment?"

"Aren't we always?" Kerry stuck her granola bar in her mouth and opened the door, hopping out and taking a breath of the hot air. "Whoo boy." She tugged her sleeveless muscle shirt away from her body and spared a grateful thank you to Dar's suggestion they change into shorts before coming out to the park.

Dar joined her, sticking the door opener in her front pocket and letting the key hang down outside it. She munched her half of their snack as they walked toward the group of people. "You up for a swim after this?"

Kerry made a small groan of agreement. "Hi Mari. Looks like you had a great turnout."

"Sure does," Mari agreed. "However, it was forcefully brought home to me that if you call a meeting at dinner time you're obligated to provide dinner." She gazed pointedly at Kerry's granola bar. "I don't suppose you brought enough to share, did you?"

Caught in mid chew, Kerry shook her head slightly. She swallowed hastily. "Sorry."

"Hmph." Mari sighed.

"Hey, she shared with me." Dar licked the last crumb off her fingertips. "Tell everyone to go out and find a pizzeria after this. No one's gonna starve."

Kerry gave her a wry look, receiving an innocent bat of Dar's dark lashes in return. She chuckled and shook her head, as she followed Dar over to the big group, feeling the sweat start to gather on her skin.

"Hey Kerry!" Mark waved at her as they approached. "Hey big D."

"Hey." Kerry glanced around, seeing quite a number of people from their own department mixed with others from the office. "Hey guys." She wiggled her fingers at two of the junior accountants. "So here we are."

"Hello, Kerry." Mayte appeared. "I am glad you were able to come here. This should be fun. No?" She had her hair pulled back into a neat tail like Dar's and she was smiling. "I have never played softball."

"Me either, but I think it'll be a blast." Her boss went over to the rows of wooden, weathered, bench seating and paused, leaning against the boards.

"Really? You never did?" Mayte sounded surprised. "Mama thought surely you were a superstar at the least!" She took a seat next to Kerry.

"Really." Kerry rubbed her temple, trying to stifle the blush she could feel coming on, not being helped at all by her snickering partner. "Your mama is way too nice, sometimes. Actually, Dar was, and is, the superstar athlete in the family."

Mayte peeked past her to smile at Dar, who shrugged modestly. "I've never played softball either," Dar clarified. "But I've done other things."

"Did you know Dar still holds her high school's record in the broad jump?" Kerry asked, split seconds before her mind realized what she'd said and she nearly fell off the bench when Mayte's eyes widened almost into the size of golf balls. "Not...ah...it's a track and field event."

Dar put her head down on her folded arms resting on the plank and started laughing.

"Jesu." Mayte covered her eyes. "I was thinking schools have changed so much it is amazing."

Kerry sighed. "Sorry about that. If it's any consolation, I went to an all girl Christian high school, and we didn't have that event either...that I know of."

The rest of the crowd joined her and settled on the ominously creaking structure. Dar eyed it, and then decided to remain standing next to Kerry leaning an elbow on one of the planks.

"Thank you all for showing up on time." Mari took up her familiar role standing on the dusty ground in front of the stadium seats. "I really appreciate it. This won't take too much time. I wanted to go over what the schedule is going to be, and what's expected of us."

"And give out hats." Dar supplied, after she stopped speaking.

"Do you have a fixation on those hats?" Mari gave her an exasperated look. "I'll have cows horns put on them in a minute."

The crowd chuckled, a lot of heads turning to look at Dar's distinctive profile.

"Moo," Dar promptly responded. "I like cows. They produce my two favorite foods, cheeseburgers and milk."

Mari cleared her throat conspicuously. "Ahem." She went back to her clipboard. "As I was saying...thank you for being here on time, I really appreciate it. One of the first things I want to tell you is that we're all here to have fun, okay? This isn't major league baseball."

The crowd chuckled a little.

"Kerry Stuart has volunteered to be our captain." Mari smiled, looking over at Kerry as applause broke out. "So I'm sure we'll end up having a great time, and doing good things for a good cause."

"Mariana, how many other teams are in this league?" one of the accountants spoke up.

"About twenty." Mari was glad to turn her attention from her hecklers. "The games are played in a round robin tournament style. Where the charity comes in is that the company will contribute a certain amount to the charity fund for every employee who participates."

"So it doesn't matter if we win or not?" the man asked with a frown.

A little buzz went up at that.

"Well." Mariana lifted her hands a little. "It is about the charity, really..."

"It matters to us if we do," Dar spoke up again from her corner. "But the charity gets the bucks no matter what, is that how it is, Mari?"'

"Exactly." Mari nodded. "There are many things to strive for in the contest. There are trophies and awards and so on, and also several things donated by the various corporations that will be given to those who complete the tournament."

"What did we give?" Kerry whispered. "Please don't tell me a lifetime supply of Cat 5e cabling."

"Cool!" Mark spoke up. "So we can get some swag, huh?"

"Nerd gift certificate I think," Dar whispered back, "for one of the big online places. Enough for a nice system,"she added."Hm." Kerry grunted approvingly. "Nice."

"So," Mari got everyone's attention back, "here are the rules. Games will be on Friday nights here at the park. All the other companies are more or less in the area around Miami, so there is no home and no away or anything like that. Each team has to have enough players to play the game or they forfeit."

"That means everyone shows up or she posts it on the company bulletin board on Monday," Dar announced. "If you're gonna do this, do it, or stay the hell home."

Everyone swiveled to look at their boss, who raised one eyebrow and gave them all a stern glare. Silence fell briefly until Mark cleared his throat.

"Yes, boss," he said, in a mild tone.

"Ahem!" Mari put her hands on her hips. "Do you want to run this?"

"Do you want me to run this?" Dar returned the volley neatly. "Bet the other teams end up regretting it like everyone else here who just realized they're going to be sharing space with me and a softball bat."

After a second's pause everyone laughed, even Dar. Kerry reached over and tweaked her nose, giving her a look of loving exasperation.

"Hats? Anyone want hats?" Mari chuckled herself. "How about pizza?"

That got everyone's attention, and all heads turned as though the crowd were a collection of spaniels at dinnertime.

"I thought that might work." Mari lifted her hands. "Okay, everyone to Santorini's after this, on me. But as for the team–for every game you show up for your name gets entered into the drawings for the donated prizes," she said. "So, the more games you attend, the better your chance to win some pretty nice stuff. "

"Like what?" someone asked.

"Ah, altruism." Dar chuckled softly under her breath.

"At least it's not some thousand bucks a plate dinner so you can put your mug in front of some politician," Kerry reminded her. "It's a good incentive."

"Mm."

"Well, we have a three night stay in Cozumel..." Mari was drowned out by oohs and aaahs. "A cruise to Bermuda, shopping spree at Macy's...some crazy tech company threw in a certificate for a new computer..."

"Did we ever decide if we really wanted to do a cruise?" Kerry asked. "Or did we finally decide we wanted to sail on one of those things about as much as we wanted a root canal?"

Dar glanced at the cloudy sky, and breathed in a lungful of air deeply tinged with ions. "We dropped the question," she said. "Hey Mari."

"And that...what?" Mari put her hands on her hips and gave Dar a look.

Dar pointed up at the sky, then held her hand out as she felt the first droplets of rain bringing a cool down that was worth the dampness. "Take it up at the pizza shack?" she suggested, as the rest of the crowd started to scramble down from the benches.

"Sure." Mari raced by her shielding her head with her clipboard, as the rain started to come down in earnest. "You can grab the damn hats!" She pointed behind her. "Ahhhhh!"

Kerry hopped off the bench and started for the bag with Dar right at her heels. "How do we get ourselves into stuff like this?" she yelled over the thunder. "Jesus, Dar we're going to be soaked!"

"We volunteer." Dar grabbed the bag and got it and its contents over their head as they ran back toward the parking lot. "Bet Mari didn't figure on this being a wet T-shirt contest."

"Oh. Don't you even go there."

Chapter Two

KERRY RESTED HER head on her fist, tapping her pen on the pad of paper on her desk. She wrote a few words, then paused and studied them with a frown on her face. "What in the hell am I supposed to talk about?"

She heard a soft ding and turned to see a new mail alert on her computer. She clicked it and brought up her personal mail folder to find a note from Angie. "Ah." She clicked on it.

Hi sis.

Please don't hate me too much. I realized after I talked to that woman that I probably should have asked you first. It just sounded pretty innocuous, you know? She kind of tricked me. She started to talk about knowing you and the reunion and all that and, before I knew it, I spilled the beans. Sorry about tha...but hey, how bad could a little speech be? Remember your senior event?

Kerry grimaced. "Oh yes. I sure do."

Anyway, I'll take you to that brewpub you like afterward to make it up to you, okay?

"Eeeehhhh...okay."

Mom said she wants to have dinner with us. That I didn't commit to. I told her we'd be really busy moving stuff, and she got pissed off because she thinks I should have just hired the movers to pack up everything. Can you believe that?
Looking forward to seeing you–
Angie

Kerry scratched the side of her nose with her pen. Her last meeting with her mother hadn't been the most cordial, and though she'd spoken to her since, she didn't really want to spend that much time in the house. She hit reply, and started typing.

Hey Ang...eh, I got over being pissed. It is what it is, and Dar thinks it might be funny for me to do a speech there, so whatever.
I can do dinner with Mom, but let's go out. I don't want to sit at that table if I don't have to. I'm not looking for lectures and if she really pisses me off it's not going to be fun for any of us. If we're out in a restaurant, she'll probably behave.

See you on Saturday.

K.

Kerry turned back to her pad, but after a few more minutes of staring at it, she gave up and dropped the pen on it, getting up and stretching before she left her office and trotted off down the steps to the lower level.

She crossed the tile floor and entered the bedroom she and Dar shared, the soothing blue walls already making her feel more relaxed. "Dar?"

"Uh?" Dar was stretched out on their waterbed.

"Do we actually know how to play softball?" Kerry trudged over, and dropped onto the waterbed, making Dar's body rock back and forth. "Boy that hot tub felt good," she added, "but it gave me time to think about what we've gotten ourselves into here."

"Well." Dar folded her hands over her stomach. "It can't be that hard, Kerry. Someone throws a ball at you, and you hit it with a bat and then you run like hell."

"True." Kerry squirmed over and put her head on Dar's stomach, extending her body at right angles to her. "But tennis looks pretty easy too, and I really suck at it. And don't you tell me I don't just to be nice."

Dar chuckled softly. "I wasn't going to. You really do suck at tennis, but then again, so do I. So what does that say about tennis?" She laid her arm over Kerry's midriff. "I'm sure we can handle it."

"We should practice."

"Now?"

Kerry rolled onto her side, looking up at Dar. "You're so silly sometimes," she said. "I meant, before we go and make fools of ourselves out there. I, at least, want to know what I'm supposed to be doing," she explained. "We can practice here, can't we?"

"We can practice over near the golf course, sure," Dar agreed. "Tomorrow we can go get some gloves and balls and whatever, and work it out," she said. "Did you decide what position you want to play on defense?"

Kerry's green eyes narrowed. "If you even start to suggest shortstop I'm going to bite you."

Dar's lips twitched. "Actually, I think I'm better for that," she admitted. "Long arms, fast reflexes." She studied Kerry for a moment. "I bet you'd be a good pitcher."

Kerry snickered. "You never saw me throw anything other than a Frisbee," she said. "How about I try outfield first?" she suggested. "I think I can manage to catch the ball out there."

"We'll see." Dar ran her fingers through Kerry's hair. "Looks like a decent bunch showed up for it. If they keep showing up, this should turn out all right."

"Yep." Kerry exhaled, closing her eyes. "I'm tired."

"Long day."

"Long day, plus having to chase you all over the hot tub at the end of it." Kerry opened one eye and winked at her. "One of these days a night vision camera tape of us is going to end up in the hands of Panic 7 and boy, are we going to have our fifteen minutes of fame."

"Hmm...that will make for an interesting intro to the next board meeting," Dar mused. "I think at this point, they look forward to stuff like that."

Kerry chuckled and closed her eyes again, exhaling in contentment. "We have to pack," she said. "I'm trying to figure out what I should wear for the speech."

"Clothes?"

Kerry bounced her head against Dar's stomach twice. "Punk," she moaned. "C'mon, Dar. I thought about just wearing a suit."

Dar yawned.

"Business suit, not bathing suit," Kerry clarified. "I figure if they really want to hear from some business chick I can do that."

"You really think they want to hear from some business chick?" Dar asked, lacing her fingers and putting her hands behind her head. "I think they're looking for some crazy rebel who used to be who they are." She studied the ceiling, as she felt Kerry's hand come to rest on her shoulder, her thumb rubbing against the bone. "Rebellion sort of thing."

Kerry had to admit she suspected the same thing. She remembered, vaguely, being that senior in high school, and the last thing she'd have wanted to hear was some boring old lady in a suit talking about career paths. "I still don't know what the hell I'm going to say to them."

"Why not ask them?" Dar suggested. "Get up there and say, 'okay, you asked for me. I'm here. What the hell do you want?'"

Kerry laughed, her breath warming the skin under Dar's shirt. "Sweetie, that works for you. Not for me." She sighed. "Oh well. I'll think of something."

"Wear something sophisticated and sexy," Dar spoke up after a moment's quiet. "And if you can't think of anything to tell them, just open it up for questions. They know more about you than you do about them."

Sometimes, Kerry reflected, Dar had a knack for bringing home to her in sudden, vivid ways the reason she'd been so successful in life. Aside from her being smart, she had a lot of what Kerry's aunt would have called 'good horse sense'. "I love you," she replied simply, turning her head to kiss Dar's chest through her shirt. "Everyone else has Google. I have Dar."

"I love you too." Dar smiled. She unfolded her hands from behind her and half sat up, resting on her elbows. She waited for Kerry to lift her head up, then she rolled over and stretched out lengthwise on the bed as her partner squirmed around to join her. "I'm sorry I'm going to miss that speech, by the way."

Kerry pulled the covers up over them and sighed as Dar turned off the bedside light and the twilight shadows settled over them. It wasn't quite dark in the room. The blinds let in moonlight and the outside lighting, but it was comfortable and familiar.

She eased over and snuggled up next to Dar. "Are you going to miss it? I'm probably going to end up sounding either boring or crazy."

"You think I'd want to miss that?" Dar inquired. "I love watching you give speeches. I duck into the back of the presentation room when you do them at the office."

Kerry blinked invisible in the darkness. "You do?"

"Sure."

"How come you never told me that?"

Dar put her arms around Kerry and half turned onto her side. "Didn't want to make you nervous," she said. "The setup staff started leaving me chocolate cupcakes back there."

Kerry started laughing silently.

"Maybe I can have a little refrigerator installed with milk chugs. You think?"

"I'll order one tomorrow," Kerry assured her. "Now go to bed, cupcake. We've got a long day ahead of us tomorrow."

KERRY SAT DOWN on the carved wooden bench and studied her new toys, as she waited for Dar to come out of the condo and join her. On the bench next to her was a bucket with six balls in it, and in her lap was a leather glove, the new hide smell making her nose twitch as she examined it.

A softball glove. She fitted her left hand into it, pausing when the edge of the glove caught on her ring. "Ah." She put the glove down and removed the ring, unlatching the chain she had around her neck and stringing the ring on it. "There. "

She put the glove on again and flexed her hand, feeling the strange constriction as she tensed her fingers and made the leather move. It felt stiff and awkward, and she reasoned that she'd have to work it a little to get it more flexible.

At least, that's what Dar had said.

Experimentally, she picked up one of the balls in the bucket and dropped it into the glove, examining how the leather fit around the object as she closed her hand around it. She held her hand up and turned it upside down, agreeably surprised when the ball stayed in the glove and didn't fall out.

She opened her fingers and the ball fell out, dropping to land in her other hand. She reversed the position of her arms and dropped the ball into the glove again. "Hm."

The far off sound of a door closing made Kerry look up, and across the short grass sward to where the condos were nestled. She immediately spotted Dar trotting down the stairs, and leaned back against the bench to watch her cross the road and head toward her.

She was carrying her own glove, with a bat resting on her shoulder, and an expression that could best be described as 'here we go again'. Kerry stood up as she approached and held her hand up in its glove, flexing the fingers like a leather crab. "Hey."

"Hey," Dar greeted her. "Got it on, huh?" She tucked her own glove under her arm and examined Kerry's, tugging the back of it to make sure her fingers were all the way in. "Fits all right. How's it feel?"

"It feels like I have a honking chunk of leather on my hand," Kerry responded with a cheeky grin. "How's yours?"

"Mm." Dar put the glove on. It was a bit larger than Kerry's and a deep russet color. "Hm."

Kerry glanced at her partner's throat in reflex, seeing the slight bulge under the fabric of her shirt that meant Dar had, as usual, thought ahead to remove her ring. "What's wrong?"

"Nothing." Dar turned her hand around. "It just feels weird." She left the bat near the bench and picked up a ball. "Want to start with some catch?"

"Sure." Kerry walked with her onto the grass and they faced each other. Dar tossed the ball at her without much preamble, and instinctively Kerry put up her free hand, the one without the glove on it, and caught it. "Yow!" She dropped the ball and shook her hand out. "That stung!"

Dar put her hands on her hips, best as she could with the glove on. "Ker, you're supposed to use this." She held up her gloved hand.

"I know that." Kerry picked the ball up and examined it. Then she faced Dar and tossed it back to her, not surprised when her partner caught it in her glove. "You surprised me."

"Okay." Dar put the ball in her free hand. "Ready?"

"Ready." Kerry watched Dar toss the ball back, and she concentrated on grabbing it with her glove, finding the thing awkward and clumsy but managing to clamp it around the round target anyway. "Ugh."

"What's wrong?"

"This is hard." Kerry frowned at the glove. "Dar, a billion children do this every year, why does it seem so weird to me?"

Dar walked over to her. "Hon, you've only done it once. Give it a few minutes." She pulled her own glove off and adjusted Kerry's again. "It's stiff."

"Yeah."

"Stiffer than mine." Dar removed the glove and handed it over. "Trade."

"I think that one's too small for you," Kerry protested, but she fitted the new glove on her hand and found it to be a lot more comfortable. "Oh," she murmured in surprise. "That feels nice."

"Okay, let's try that now." Dar retreated, putting on Kerry's glove before she turned around and held the ball up. "Ready?"

"Ready." Kerry held her hand up, and when the ball came at her, she reached out and grabbed it, feeling the round surface hit the palm of the glove in a very satisfying way. "Lots better!" she yelled back, removing the ball and tossing it to Dar.

The new glove seemed to fit her hand better, and it was easier to close her fingers. It felt like a more natural extension of her arm and not quite so much of a club hanging off the end of it.

Weird. Kerry caught the next throw, already getting used to the feel of the ball hitting the glove. She tossed the ball back, pitching it overhand instead of underhand. "Catch that, Dixiecup!"

Dar stretched out one arm and snagged it, barely. "Hey!"

Kerry grinned.

"Told you you'd make a pitcher." Dar tossed it back to her with a grin of her own. "Ker, this is going to be a lot of fun." She tossed the ball back at her partner, watching it get caught with a touch of nascent confidence. "Atta girl."

Kerry felt better about the whole thing too. The last thing she really wanted to do was make a fool of herself in front of half the office, so it was a little reassuring that she could at least handle the basics of softball.

So far, anyway. She dropped the ball into her hand and tensed her fingers around it. She then faced Dar and whipped it back at her, aiming as close as she could to her partner's midsection.

Dar caught it and returned it. They spent the next half hour playing catch with each other as the sun slowly dipped behind the trees and brought a bit of relief to the warm, muggy air.

They took a break, and met back at the bench. Kerry sat down and picked up the water bottle she'd brought with her, taking a swig from it as Dar traded her glove for the bat. "That's the hard part, isn't it?"

Dar put her hands around the bat and took a step back, away from the bench before she extended her arms and took a few tentative swings.

Kerry leaned back and watched. "I thought you said you never played softball."

"I didn't." Dar swung a few more times. "Not on a team, but we played catch and sand lot ball on the base when I was growing up, and I played a little with Dad."

Duh. Kerry smiled wryly. Of course she did. "I can't imagine for a second my father playing a sport.. Well, maybe golf."

Dar's face wrinkled up into a scowl.

"Yeah, me either," Kerry admitted. "Golf was acceptable for girls, in a 'let's ride in the cart and sip ice tea while gossiping' sort of way. Or tennis."

"I played football with the guys."

Kerry tipped her head back and gazed fondly at Dar. "Of course you did, honey. So I guess you know how to use that thing?" She set her water bottle down and picked up a ball, walking out into the grass and turning to face her partner. "Ready?"

Dar assumed a very credible batters' position, setting her feet at shoulder width and cocking the bat. "G'wan, toss."

Amiably, Kerry complied, throwing the ball at her partner. A second and a soft crack later, a white missile was coming right at her face and she only barely evaded it by diving for the grass with a startled yelp. "Dar!"

"Whoops." Dar let the bat rest on her shoulder. "Sorry about that."

"Jesus!" Kerry got to her hands and knees then stood up, brushing the grass of her. "What in the hell was that?"

Dar actually looked mildly abashed. "Um…" She shrugged her shoulders. "A hit?" She walked over to Kerry. "Didn't mean to buzz you with it." She handed Kerry the bat and trotted over to where the ball had landed on the other side of the green space.

Kerry recovered her breath and removed her glove, tossing it onto the bench and giving her attention to the wooden pole she now held in her hands.

It felt weird. She wrapped her fingers around the handle and swung it. "Yow." She just kept from hitting herself in the knee. It was top heavy and awkward, and heavier than she'd expected. She looked up as Dar came back with the ball. "Show me how you did that."

Dar came around behind her and pressed up against her back, wrapping her arms around Kerry and taking hold of the bat. "Okay, now…"

She paused to reposition her hands, suddenly becoming aware of Kerry's warm body pressed against hers. "Um…now," she repeated, a bit bemused.

Kerry leaned against her, tipping her head back and batting her eyelashes. "Now what?" she asked. "Did you say something?"

It was an interestingly sensual moment, unexpected and public and Dar had to force herself not to do what had become natural for both of them. Instead, she nibbled a bit of Kerry's hair and bumped her with her nose. "Do you want to learn this or…"

"Or?" The green eyes took on a warm twinkle.

"Or do you want to get another homeowner complaint letter?" Dar reminded her. "There are some guys behind us driving a golf cart. Want to cause an accident?"

Kerry sighed melodramatically. "Oh, all right." She turned back around and focused on the bat again. "Now where were we?" She felt Dar move her hands back. "Oh."

"Okay. Stand like this." Dar nudged Kerry's feet apart a little. "Hold your arms like this." She shifted her grip and the bat lifted a bit.

"Now, the thing is, you can't look at the bat."

"No," Kerry agreed. "I have to look out for the ball, or I'll be taking the helmets off anyone in the vicinity." She let Dar swing her arms through a stroke, twisting her body around to the right as she imagined connecting with the ball. "Right."

Dar released her, and picked up the ball. She walked twenty feet or so away and turned. "Ready? Watch the ball."

"Watching." Kerry focused intently on the ball, watching it as it left Dar's hand and headed her way. She swung at it, but it didn't connect and the force of her swing turned her all the way around and made her sit down abruptly on her butt. "Ow!"

She looked up quickly at her partner. Dar's face had that stony expression she often used in important board meetings when she didn't want everyone in the room to really know what she was thinking. Kerry accepted that as the compliment it was, and got to her feet. "Thanks for not cracking up."

Dar's lips twitched.

Kerry picked up another ball from the bucket and tossed it to her. "C'mon. It's getting dark." She took up her position again, gripping the bat tightly.

Dar tossed the ball at her, and she swung at it again, this time catching a small piece of the ball and sending it ricocheting off the bench, nearly beaning herself in the kneecap with it. "Yow!"

"Ker?"

"Yes?" Kerry peered over at her, a touch frustrated. "Dar, this is ridiculous. Little kids do this."

"Stop trying so damn hard," Dar told her. "Just relax."

Kerry put the bat end on the ground and wrapped her hands around the top of it, taking a deep breath and letting it out. Twilight was coming on in earnest, and she had an abrupt desire to trade the muggy, gnat filled air for the cool of the condo, leaving this odd and frustrating activity behind.

Immediately, she was ashamed of herself. "Jerk."

"Ker?"

"Not you." Kerry lifted the bat and faced her. "Sorry, one more time?"

Dar waited, the ball held in her right hand, her left hand perched on her hip, watching Kerry's body posture until she saw her partner's shoulders drop just a bit, the muscles in the sides of her neck relaxing. Then she gently pitched the ball toward her. Kerry tracked its progress, and swung at it.

A soft crack split the gathering gloom, and Dar tipped her head back as the ball arched away from the bat and up into the sky. "Nice!"

Kerry blinked in surprise. "I hit it!"

Dar got herself under it and caught the ball as it fell. "Yep." She walked back over to where Kerry was standing and leaned forward, giving her a kiss on the lips. "You sure did." There was relief in her partner's eyes, and she bumped against her lightly. "Not bad for the first try."

It was really almost stupid. Kerry bumped Dar back. "Yeah, not bad," she agreed. "It's harder than I thought it would be though. I'm glad we got some stuff to practice with." She tugged Dar's shirt. "Let's go chase down those balls."

"Sounds good to me." Dar collected both of their gloves and the bucket. "We can play around the rest of the week before we travel."

Kerry walked along with her for a few steps. "I know no one expects us to be really great players," she said. "But...um...I don't know, I just..."

"Want to win." Dar finished her sentence.

"No, it's not really that," Kerry protested.

"You're competitive as hell, Kerry. Of course you want to win." Dar disagreed placidly. "There's nothing wrong with that." She collected the last ball and draped her arm around Kerry's shoulders as they headed back toward the condo.

"You make me sound like a soccer dad."

They both chuckled as they climbed the stairs to the door. "Better than a soccer mom," Dar said, as they went inside. "I can't even imagine what that would be like."

"If you had a minivan, it'd have a machine gun turret." Kerry closed the door behind them, and finally had to laugh. "And a satellite dish."

"And a beer keg for you."

KERRY SLOWLY OPENED her eyes, aware of the sun's warmth on the bare skin of her back. She was curled up in the waterbed, the condo around her quiet save for some muffled sounds in the living room.

She looked at the clock, yawned, and rolled over, reveling in the comfort, and working hard to ignore the fact she'd have to get up soon and drive to the airport. "Peh." She reviewed her schedule, glad she'd packed the night before.

A morning flight had been an option. However, Dar had an afternoon flight. She decided to match her partner's itinerary so they could go to the airport together. Silly, really. They were on separate airlines and different terminals, but hell, she wasn't looking to spend more time in Michigan than necessary.

A Saturday afternoon flight. Kerry smiled. They would pack Angie up on Sunday and Monday and probably Tuesday. She'd do her speech on Monday night, one more day of messing with her family, and then on Thursday she'd head out to Europe to meet Dar as part of the integration team for their new agreement.

Not so bad, really. Just a couple of days.

"Hey."

Kerry turned her head to see Dar standing in the doorway of the bedroom. "Hey."

"Sure you don't want to change flights?"

Kerry rolled her eyes in mock exasperation. "Dar! Cut that out!" She pulled the covers back and got out of bed. "You're such a punk!"

Dar entered and intercepted her, putting her arms around Kerry's naked body and pulling her close in a hug. "Sorry." She kneaded her partner's neck. "I hate the thought of you being in that state and me being across an ocean," she said. "Last couple rounds with your family wasn't much fun."

Kerry returned the hug squeezing Dar so hard she could hear her bones creak. "Thanks. Don't think that hasn't crossed my mind. I'm glad I'm going to help Ang, and I want to spend a little time with her, but my hometown hasn't been a happy place for me for a very, very long time."

"I know." Dar rubbed her back. "So don't kill me for wanting to kidnap you from that."

Kerry smiled. "I don't. I'll be okay, Dar. I'm a big girl."

Dar peered down at her. "No you're not."

"Punk."

"Sometimes," Dar agreed. "But you're my one and only. I'm allowed."

The casual confidence in Dar's tone almost took Kerry's breath away. She had always felt a sense of confidence in their relationship but there had always been that shadow of uncertainty in her partner before.

Not anymore. The change had taken her a little by surprise, but in a good way. "Yes, I am, and yes, you are," Kerry agreed. "Thanks, hon."

They released each other, and Kerry continued on her path to the bathroom, removing a T-shirt from the hook behind the door and sliding it over her head. As she brushed her teeth, she glanced at her disheveled reflection, noting the slightly overlong bangs and the image of Yosemite Sam flipping everyone off plastered over her chest. "Maybe I can wear this to dinner with Mom. You think?" She watched Dar's eyebrows hike. "Yeah. Maybe not."

She finished up and wiped her lips with a tissue, the bathroom still feeling a little damp and scented with apricot scrub from Dar's shower. Then she headed for the kitchen, pausing to greet Chino along the way. "Hey, puppy. What's up?"

Chino presented her with a stuffed lamb and a hopeful expression. Obligingly, Kerry tossed it across the living room, escaping into the kitchen as their pet retrieved the toy. "What are you doing?" she asked Dar, who was standing next to the counter.

"Me?" Dar turned her head. "Making breakfast." She moved aside to display the fruits of her labor, which had fruits, but little else in the way of solid nutrition.

Kerry observed the platter, and sighed. "Cheesecake," she said. "Well, it has cheese in it. That's protein."

"And strawberries." Dar pointed.

"Yep." Kerry selected a strawberry half and popped it into her mouth. "Yum." She slid around Dar's tall form and poured coffee into her cup, already resting on the counter. "Actually, that's a perfect thing for breakfast considering where I'm going."

"Me too." Dar licked a bit of strawberry sauce off her fingers. "It's already almost dinner time there," she added, "but I figured having a beer with it would be pushing things."

Kerry paused in mid sip and looked at her. She put the cup down. "How long are you going to be in Europe before I get there?" she inquired, in a wry tone. "Angie's going to wonder why I'm duct taping her boxes and throwing everything into the back of that pickup."

"What pickup?" Dar inquired, getting her own cup of coffee. "Your sister has a pickup truck?" Her voice rose in disbelief.

"No. I rented a pickup truck." Kerry's eyes twinkled. "I figure I can pick my mother up for dinner in it and start the trip off right." She picked up the plate of cheesecake and settled it onto the nearby breakfast counter. "Sit."

Dar took the stool next to her and they shared their breakfast in silence for a few minutes. Then Dar sucked on her fork tines, and gave Kerry a look. "What color pickup truck?"

"Bright red."

"Nice." Dar chuckled. "Now I really wish I was going just to see that." She rested her head on her hand, waiting for Kerry to finish her cheesecake, content to merely watch the morning light bring out the golden highlights in her partner's hair.

"Well." Kerry neatly cut a bit of cake and ate it, pausing to swallow before she continued. "I figured it would be useful to move things, and it's what they had. Either that or a sedan and you know, I just wasn't into a sedan."

"Uh huh," Dar murmured in sympathy. "Kind of like when I rented the motorcycle to drive to headquarters in Houston."

Kerry looked up and grinned. "Exactly," she said. "I know it's really silly and a little juvenile," she admitted. "And I know my mother was really pretty cool about us the last time we were there, it's just that this time you *won't* be there and I don't want any crap from her. "

"Maybe she caught a clue from the last time," Dar suggested. "After you told her off."

"Mm." Kerry sipped her coffee. "Maybe," she conceded. "She's been all right on the phone. It's just that she gets these family idea things and doesn't understand where I'm coming from." She went back to finishing her breakfast, leaving Dar to study her in silence.

"Y'know," Dar said, after a long pause.

Kerry put her fork down and wiped her lips neatly with a napkin.

"I know." Her lips twitched into a reluctant smile. "I know that I was the one who was all over you to reconcile with your mother, and did my damndest to aid and abet that by any means I could think of."

Dar's eyes warmed.

"But your mother didn't stand by while your father threw you in the loony bin, Dar." Kerry went on in a more serious tone, "and even though you had issues, they weren't those kind of issues, were they?"

Dar didn't immediately answer. She sat quietly for a few minutes, sipping the remainder of her coffee, a thoughtful expression on her face while Kerry finished up. "At the time," she said, as Kerry stood to take the plates back over to the sink, "they felt like a lot worse issues."

She got up and took Kerry's cup, following her over to the counter. "But I was young, and clueless, and looking back, yeah." She set the cups in the sink and gave Kerry a kiss on the back of her neck. "I didn't have those kinds of problems."

Kerry waited. "But?" she asked, after a pause.

"But nothing." Dar reached around her to wash off the dishes, trapping her neatly. "Gonna show her your tattoo?"

Kerry chuckled, a low throaty sound while she wiped off the dishes as Dar washed them. "Pick her up for dinner in my red pickup truck in a leather, no strap bustier. How's that?" She smiled, her good humor restored. "Actually, I'll show it to my sister. She'll tell my mother because she can't keep her mouth shut about stuff like that."

"Here we go with that sibling thing again." Dar put the plates up and they walked back through the living room, Chino trotting behind them. "You want to grab a shower? I threw the bags in the car already."

"Sure." Kerry stifled a yawn. "When are your folks due by?"

"Six," Dar said. "Assuming Dad doesn't cause chaos in Government Cut again."

"Uh oh."

AIRPORTS GENERALLY SUCKED. Kerry shouldered her carry on and eased her way through the crowded terminal, assaulted on all sides by loud voices in many languages echoing off the terrazzo floor. The Miami airport was large, sprawling, disorganized, and difficult to navigate at times around the groups of travelers standing with what seemed like month's worth of luggage.

She'd left Dar by the International gates, their extended hug completely unnoticed by the surging crowd as they parted and she'd continued on to her domestic gate further down the concourse. Announcements echoed overhead, but she let them bypass her as she got in line for the security check and tried to pretend she wasn't bummed.

She put her backpack on the belt pulling her laptop out and placing it in a tray along with her cell phone and her PDA. Then she watched it disappear into the X-ray before she walked through the portal as a bored looking guard waved her on. "Thanks." She picked her things up and restored the laptop to its place, then she shouldered the bag and headed down a long, badly carpeted slope toward the waiting area.

Her gate was crowded. Apparently the flight before hers was late getting out. So Kerry bypassed it and went to the small brewpub at the end of the terminal and claimed a seat, letting out a long breath as she eased her pack to the floor.

"Can I get you something?" The bartender stopped by, glancing around the mostly empty space.

"Amber, and a plate of wings," Kerry answered, after reviewing her options. "Thanks."

"No problem."

The bartender moved on, and she turned sideways in her high bar chair, resting her elbows on the back and the bar top and hooking her feet on the rungs.

She was bummed. Kerry flexed her hand, rubbing the edge of her thumb against the ring on her finger. She wasn't really sure why, since she and Dar often traveled independently and anyway, she'd be joining her in a week.

She really wanted to get on Dar's airplane and not her own, and that was sort of pissing her off. "Thanks." She accepted the cold glass of beer from the bartender, and took a sip. Her PDA alert light stuttered red and she put the beer down and picked it up.

Hey. Why the hell would they put a Budweiser Brew House in the international terminal?

Kerry chuckled in reflex and typed out an answer. *Are you in there?* She was glad of the distraction, her unease calmed by this disassociated communication that had become their way of staying in each other's pockets when they were separated.

It was either that, Burger King, or a health food place. What do you think?

Kerry thought that the fact they'd both ended up in the same bar in two different terminals was pretty funny and also predictable, but she only chuckled and sent back *Enjoy your wings.*

You too.

"Now, why can't we both be having wings together?" Kerry sighed. "Ah well. Stop being a jerk," she reminded herself, taking another sip of her beer, and forcibly putting aside her gloom. The bartender came back and deposited her plate of wings. She nibbled on one leaned back watched as her gate cleared, and things around her started to settle down.

After a moment, she put her wing down, divested of its flesh, and licked her lips. "Should have packed that damn bustier."

"Ma'am?" The bartender looked up from cleaning his glasses.

"Just talking to myself," Kerry said. "You know us crazy travelers."

"Yeah." The bartender eyed her, moving a little ways away to continue his cleaning. "Have a great trip."

A loud sound made them both turn and look out into the concourse to see a woman racing across the carpet, her arms outstretched, her voice panicked as she chased a white chicken across the hall. Kerry watched the crowd dodge out of the way of the women and bird, then she turned and looked at the bartender.

He shrugged. "It's Miami."

Kerry picked up her beer and took a healthy swig, and then she toasted the terminal. "It's Miami."

DAR CLIMBED THE spiral stairs up to the first class section of the big 747 giving the flight attendant a brief smile as she went down the aisle and put her briefcase in the overhead, settling into her seat and leaning back to observe the space around her.

It was quiet. Two other travelers had taken seats, on the other side of the plane from her, but it didn't look like the section was going to be very full. Dar was glad for that. Even though she certainly had a decent amount of space and a seat that reclined into a bed, she still didn't like people crowding in around her.

Well, except for Kerry.

"Can I bring you a water?" The flight attendant stopped by her. "Or perhaps a glass of wine?"

Dar considered, glancing up at the woman. "Got any milk?"

The woman's eyelashes blinked. "Yes of course," she rallied. "One moment."

"Thanks." Dar watched her move off in search of her requested beverage. After a moment, she got up and opened the overhead, rooting in her backpack for two magazines, then sitting back down and tucking them into the pocket on the side of her seat.

Flying bored her. Dar folded her hands in her lap and studied the tops of her thumbs, wishing she could fall asleep and wake up on the other side of the world. No matter how comfortable her seat, it still meant she had to stay relatively still for eight or nine hours and suffer the dry air and incessant drone of the engines for all that time.

"Here you go." The flight attendant returned with a goblet of milk and a cocktail napkin, depositing both in the tray next to Dar's right hand. "Enjoy."

"Thanks." Dar picked up the glass and sipped from it. Her tongue was still tingling a little from the extremely spicy chicken wings, and the cool, rich milk both tasted and felt good in her mouth. She got halfway through it before her ears popped slightly, and the flight attendant came over the PA system announcing the door had been closed and everyone should get ready for departure.

Dar put her milk down and fastened her seat belt, noticing her PDA flashing as she did so. With a glance to see where the flight attendant was, she opened it and peeked at the screen.

AC in the plane's not working. Can I take my shirt off?

Dar spent a pleasurable moment imagining Kerry scandalizing the first class cabin in her short haul jetliner, then she sighed. *Only if you give me a chance to pop the door on this one and come over to watch.* She paused and then sent it, closing the cover on the PDA and folding her hands over it as the flight attendant walked by checking that her seatbelt was fastened.

"Nice and quiet tonight," the woman said, gazing at her three passengers. "It will be good flight."

Dar had to admit being pretty much alone in the upper cabin with no one next to her and a lack of noise and people would be very nice. "Easy for you," she said, with a smile for the flight attendant.

The woman inclined her head in agreement, then went to the service area and busied herself getting ready for takeoff.

Dar went back to her PDA that was, in fact, flashing again. She opened it up. *Waaa! There's a bigmouthed salesman with more gold rings than a carnival yelling on his cell phone in here!*

Dar winced, having been there, and done that. *Put in your earplugs,* she advised. *See? Toldja you should have come with me. It's almost empty on my flight.*

Punk! Kerry answered back immediately. *Just wait till I catch up to you in Europe. You're toast!*

The plane started to move, pushing back from the gate, and the bright lights in the cabin dimmed as the late afternoon sunlight poured in the windows. Dar scribbled an answer for several minutes, long enough for them to taxi out to the runway and pause, waiting for permission to take off.

As the engines spooled up, Dar finished and sent the message tucking the stylus away and putting the PDA in her pocket as the sound rose around her and gravity shoved her back into her seat. She laced her fingers together and closed her eyes, willing the plane into the air and the trip to begin.

She hoped Kerry's flight would end on a better note than it had started on.

KERRY FOLDED HER hands together with her PDA between them, exchanging a brief smile with the harried looking flight attendant at the front of the plane. The clammy, hot air wafted over her, ripe with perfume, sweat, and aviation kerosene. "Hell isn't fire and brimstone," she mused. "It's a perpetual 757 on a hot tropical afternoon."

"Ma'am?" The flight attendant bent over her, "Can I get you something?"

"Ice cream. I'll share with you," Kerry suggested. "Or how about a pina colada?"

"Oh honey," the woman sighed, giving Kerry a pat on the shoulder. "Don't I wish. Give me a few minutes and I'll see if we have anything cold in the back, okay?"

"Thanks." Kerry took a deep breath and exhaled, hoping they got the air conditioning issue fixed before they started flying to Michigan. She could hear screaming children behind her, and far from resenting them, she found herself in sympathy with their frustration and almost let out a squawk of her own before she recalled her upbringing and merely sighed instead.

Her PDA flashed. She eagerly flipped the lid up and tilted her head to read the message. Her eyes slowly traveled across the words and then down to the next line in what was-for Dar-a very long note.

I got stuck on an airplane like that once. I had just started traveling for the company and I was on this late night flight to Pittsburgh with a load of high school girls going to a cheerleading convention.

At this point, Kerry had to stop, and put her hand up to cover her mouth, stifling a giggle. "Oh my gosh there are so many things going through my mind right now."

She knew her beloved partner hadn't been the most patient person in her younger years. She could picture Dar slumped in her seat, scowling at the girls with that dour glare and those narrowed blue eyes.

They would not shut up the whole damn flight. By the time we were close to landing the crew, the rest of the passengers, me, and even the co pilot were ready to open the door at altitude and let the little nitwads get sucked right out of the damn airplane.

Kerry tried to imagine the scene. Then she grimaced a little, as a brief memory of being a high school student on the way to Washington for a class trip made her blush.

I finally stood up and yelled there was a rat between the seats. They all took off for the back of the plane and the damn flight attendant nearly kissed me.

Kerry blinked. "Was it a guy or a girl?" she muttered.

After that, I figured out how to hack into the airline database and find out who else was on the flight before I booked it.

"You little hacker," Kerry chuckled, shaking her head.

We're outta here. Talk to you in eight hours or so. ILY. DD.

Kerry extended her denim covered legs and crossed her ankles, resting her elbows on the arms of her seat as the crew struggled to get the last of the unwilling passengers onboard and deal with the environmental annoyances.

"Are we going to have to suffer like this the whole flight?" a woman standing in the aisle asked, loudly. "This is unacceptable! I paid good money for this damn ticket!"

What, Kerry wondered, constituted bad money? Did the woman think anyone on the plane had just walked on for free? She rested her head on her hand and tried to block the noise out, flinching as the woman slammed the back of her seat in the middle of her tirade.

"Ma'am, please sit down. They're working on the problem. Yelling about it doesn't help." The flight attendant came forward and forced the woman to take a step back. "And please stop banging the seats. People are sitting in them."

Kerry looked up at her with a grateful smile.

"Horrible airline!" the woman said, but she retreated to the back part of the plane, grumbling loudly all the way. "I'll sue!"

The flight attendant sighed. "Boy it's going to be a long flight." She turned and looked at the people in the small first class section at the front of the plane. "We're about to close the door, ladies and gentlemen. Once we get up at altitude, we can adjust the temperature so it's more comfortable." She went on down the aisle, looking right and left as one of her coworkers accepted a sheaf of paperwork and helped the airport workers close the front door.

On one hand, that meant they were leaving. On the other, without even the little air that was getting in from the jetway, the heat started building and Kerry felt herself start to sweat under her light cotton shirt.

"Here you go." The flight attendant reappeared suddenly, handing Kerry a glass. "I didn't forget about you."

"Thanks," Kerry said, glancing at her name tag, "Ann." She met the woman's eyes. "I really appreciate it, and I appreciate you getting that woman to stop whacking my seat."

The woman smiled at her. "No problem, Ms. Stuart. Be patient, we'll try to get going as soon as we can."

She was about to move on, but Kerry held her hand up. "How did you know my name?" she asked, curiously. "Have we met?"

Ann chuckled. "No, ma'am, your boss called and gave us a few special requests for you...like that. "She indicated the glass. "It must be nice to have your company value you like that, I have to say."

Kerry glanced at the glass, which she realized was full of chocolate milk. "Ah," she murmured. "My boss." She looked up at the woman. "You know, I love my boss."

"Wish I did." The flight attendant chuckled, and patted her on the shoulder. She moved off down the aisle leaving Kerry to ponder her unexpected gift.

She sipped the milk, finding it cold, and very chocolaty. The annoyance of the heat faded a little, as she focused her thoughts on Dar, the little bit of thoughtfulness making her feel a tiny bit giddy inside. It wasn't at all unusual. They both tended to do soppy little things for each other, but for Dar to do it in such a public way was somewhat new.

Nice.

She wondered what else she had in store, suspecting perhaps she'd even be spared the chicken Florentine or three cheese vegetable lasagna for dinner.

Hot planes, screaming women, and her mother notwithstanding, life was good. Kerry smiled. Life was very good indeed.

Chapter Three

KERRY FLICKED ON the high beams for a brief moment before she returned the lights to their usual position and settled back in her seat.

It was in the mid fifties, cool enough for her to have dug her sweatshirt out of her bag, but comfortable as she walked to the car rental lot and picked up her buggy.

Ahead of her lay the bland drive to Angie's house. She turned on the radio, punching the buttons and finding a station she could listen to, then turning the sound down a little as her cell phone rang. She checked the caller ID, and then keyed the speakerphone. "Hey Ang."

"Hey." Her sister's said. "Where are you?"

"About twenty minutes out," Kerry responded. "Need anything?"

"Nah, we're good," Angie said. "Andrew's sleeping tight. I'm looking forward to hanging out with my sister."

Kerry smiled. "Yeah, it's been a while," she admitted. "Glad I made it up here."

"Me too," Angie said, warmly. "So much has gone on the last year it's hard to take in sometimes. Anyway, let me let you off the line, sis. See ya in twenty."

"See ya." Kerry hung up the phone and turned up the radio. Now that she was here, she was glad to be getting a chance to spend a little time with Angie. Her brother Michael said he'd be over to help too.

Not that Kerry had any illusions that Michael would do as much as pick up a book to put in a box, but she was looking forward to seeing him anyway. There were parts of him that she understood so much better now.

There were parts of herself she was starting to understand a lot better now too. Kerry smiled, and shifted her hands on the wheel, her eye catching the faint reflection of the streetlights on her ring. The visit might turn out to be interesting after all.

She let the miles slip by until it was time to turn off the main road, and onto the sloping one that led up a gentle hill to the house her sister had, until recently, shared with her ex-husband, Richard, who had sued her for divorce upon finding out her second child wasn't his.

Finding out her sister was an adulterer was almost as surprising to Kerry as finding out her sister was sleeping with the man Kerry was supposed to marry. Though finding out Kerry was gay had apparently been no surprise at all to Angie, who had seemingly known it all along.

Life was funny that way. Kerry chuckled under her breath as she pulled into the stately curved driveway of the house her sister lived in and seeing Angie's Mercedes parked along the front curb. With a grin, she parked her little red pickup right behind it, shutting the engine off and opening the door.

She drew in a breath of air and paused, aware of the scent of pine and honeysuckle so completely different from her adopted southern home. It tasted strange on the back of her tongue, and she had to shake her head as she closed the driver's side door and opened the extended cab door to retrieve her bag.

One of her bags, anyway. She shouldered the overnighter leaving her suit bag inside and circled the truck as the door to the house opened and she spotted her sister's outline in the light streaming out of it. "Hey."

Angie came out of the house and stood on the porch as Kerry walked up the sloping path. "Hey stranger." She held her arms out and greeted Kerry with a hug that her older sister returned promptly. "C'mon inside."

Angie was taller than Kerry, and had dark hair and their mother's hazel eyes. Even though Kerry was the elder of them, Angie's conservatively coiffed hair and clothing made the opposite seem true.

They entered the house, the hallway brightly lit and smelling of wood wax and chocolate. Angie shut the door behind them and joined Kerry as they walked across the marble tile. "Elana, can you take this, please?" Angie addressed a middle aged woman in a neat uniform standing nearby. "You remember my sister Kerrison, don't you?"

"Yes ma'am, I sure do." Elana took Kerry's bag. "Welcome back, Miss Kerry." Elana's face was mild with no hint of approval or disapproval at this invasion by their family's blond haired black sheep.

Kerry felt her nostrils flare, but she smiled anyway. "Thanks Elana. Nice to see you again." She watched the woman leave, and turned to her sister. "Hi."

"Hi," Angie responded agreeably, stepping back and looking her over head to toe. "You look great,and it's really good to see you," she said grinning. "Feels like it's been way too long."

Kerry grinned. "Right back at you. Got a cup of something hot around? It's been a long day."

"Absolutely, c'mon." Angie led the way back into the large kitchen. She was dressed in a pair of slacks and a red pullover, casually elegant and a definite contrast to Kerry's worn jeans and sweatshirt. "Did you have a decent flight at least?"

"Eh." Kerry took one of the seats around the kitchen table, everything around her clean and spotless, but in some disarray due to the impending move. "No AC on the way up."

"Ugh." Angie brought an already prepared tray over. It had two cups on it, and a plate of chocolate cookies. She set it down and sat down across from her sister. "How's Dar?" She watched Kerry's face, seeing her expression shift into a grin as warmth erupted into her eyes at the question.

"Great," Kerry responded. "We both had flights out today. She's on her way to England." She picked up her cup and sipped from it. "Mm."

"Did I get it right?" Angie's eyes twinkled. "You haven't stopped being a chocolate addict, have you?"

"Nope." Kerry relaxed, leaning back in the chair and resting her elbows on the arms as she cradled the cup in her hands. "Dar and I both are. It's hopeless," she admitted. "I've given up worrying about it I figure if I'm going go to hell, might as well enjoy it."

Angie laughed. "Kerry, you're not going to hell. You look fantastic. Last time I saw you it was such a stress fest I was worried about you, but looks like you bounced back just fine."

Stress fest. Mild way of putting it. "Yeah." Kerry remembered how she'd felt coming back from Michigan the last time, and how long it had taken her to throw off the effects. "I felt like crap when I got home. They almost had to put me in the hospital for my blood pressure."

Angie's eyes opened wide. "What?" She leaned forward. "Are you kidding me?"

Her sister shook her head.

"Ker, that's awful. Are you taking anything for that?" Angie looked concerned. "That's not anything to joke about, you know?"

"I know," Kerry said. "But no, I've got it under control. I cut down on my salt, and we went out on the boat for a week to chill out. Did wonders." She sidestepped the issue. "We went down to the Caribbean and got involved with pirates. It was crazy."

"Pirates!"

"Well, we can't have normal vacations, you know? Dar and I could walk to the grocery store and we'd end up causing a riot without meaning to." Kerry chuckled. "We have the damnedest stuff happen to us. Anyway, so what's up with you?" She regarded her sister. "Glad you're moving?"

Angie gazed shrewdly at her for a moment, and then allowed herself to be sidetracked. "I am," she admitted. "I don't really feel bad about what happened with Richard, you know? It was my choice and I knew what could happen. At least we ended up with split custody of Sally."

"Mm." Kerry selected a cookie from the plate and nibbled on it.

"That's a lot of why I decided to move in with Mom." Angie studied her cup. "It's just easier."

Kerry understood that. She remembered being both elated and scared when she'd moved out after so many years of having everything in her life taken care of for her and provided without question. "Yeah, I know what you mean," she agreed.

"No you don't." Angie burst into laughter. "You never did anything the easy way the entire time I've known you."

Kerry had to grin at that and raise her cup in her sister's direction in acknowledgement of the truth. "Touche." The only easy thing I've ever really done was fall in love with Dar. That was fast and painless.

Everything else...eh." She shrugged her shoulders. "I don't think I'd change anything though."

"I bet you wouldn't," Angie agreed. "Anyway, thanks for coming up to give me a hand packing up all this stuff. I really need help deciding what to get rid of. I didn't think I was a packrat until I started looking in the closets here."

Kerry finished her hot chocolate and dusted the cookie crumbs off her fingers. "I got off sort of lucky. When I moved in with Dar, it was over a couple months, so I moved stuff a little at a time. I still think I've got like three times the junk she does though."

"Not a keeper?"

The green eyes twinkled. "She's definitely a keeper, she doesn't collect frivolously."

"Ahh." Angie stood up. "C'mon, let's get you settled in." She waited for Kerry to join her and they walked through the hall, their footsteps echoing against the marble as they got to the wide, wood tread stairs and climbed upward. "I won't miss these stairs."

Kerry felt the slight strain as she climbed. "They're steeper than Mom's." She noted. "I think you've got higher ceilings."

"Yes. Richard's point of pride." Angie's voice took on a sharper note. "He made a point of mentioning that whenever he could."

Kerry rolled her eyes. "Sorry Ang, he's an ass. The only thing he had going for him was our father liked him, and that should have told you something right there." She looked around as they got to the second floor, trying to remember if she'd ever really paid attention to the inside of her sister's house before.

"Well," Angie sighed, "I was glad to get past that whole approval thing. I'm not a renegade like you."

Renegade. Kerry pondered that title as Angie led her over to an open door, and they entered a nicely proportioned, robin's egg blue room with a canopied bed and a bay window. "I don't think I ever thought of myself like that."

"We did." Angie went over to a rocking chair in the room and sat down on its padded surface. "Mike and me, anyway. Especially when we got older."

Kerry went to her bag that was resting on a low bench near the window. She unzipped the top of the leather case and removed her sundry kit and a long T-shirt, setting it down on the bench before she pulled her sweatshirt off and folded it. "I don't think I felt like a renegade until I told our father about Dar." She turned and faced Angie. "That night is when I crossed the line between being a passive aggressive milquetoast and being my own person."

Angie slowly nodded.

"Until then, I was trying to have it both ways." Kerry put her hands on her hips. "You can't, you know?"

"I know." Her sister sighed. "But that's why you're different than we are, Ker. I was just grateful he was already dead before Richard filed for divorce. I can't take that. I can't handle being that strong."

Kerry came over to sit on the edge of the bed. "How's Brian doing?"

Angie's expression grew wry. "Scared spitless to see you," she confessed. "Ker, he's just not ready to settle down. I'm not sure I'm even mad at him, or," her lips pursed, "that I even want to be in a relationship right now."

It was Kerry's turn to shrewdly study her sister's face. She half suspected Angie really wanted to keep the peace over the days she was there, but after all, it was her relationship wasn't it? Maybe Angie really wasn't ready to rush into anything, much less force Brian to.

Kerry could respect that. Even if it was a farce for her benefit. "Whatever makes you happy, sis. I'm the last person on earth to preach conformity, remember?" She straightened and reached down to grab the hem of her T-shirt and pull it up and over her head. "Speaking of which, let me get this out of the way."

"What are you...oh my god!" Angie bolted upright in her chair. "Are you kidding me? Is that really a tattoo?"

Kerry let the shirt rest on her denim covered knees and glanced at her chest. She drew her bra strap aside a little to give a better view of her artwork. "Yep."

"How could you do that?" Her sister got up and came closer to look. "Oh my god, Kerry."

Kerry studied her face with some interest, not expecting her sister to be as shocked as she obviously was. "Are you freaked out?"

Angie looked up from examining the design on Kerry's chest, the colors standing out in muted brilliance against her tan. "I can't believe you did this. Kerry, what were you thinking?"

What was I thinking? Kerry looked at the tattoo, then back up at her sister. "I was thinking that I wanted something I felt so strongly about to be visible on the outside of me like it was on the inside," she said. "Talk's cheap. Tattoos are expensive and painful."

Angie sat down next to her on the bed, still studying Kerry's skin. "Wow," she finally murmured. "Well, it's beautiful, at any rate. What did Dar say?"

"Nothing."

"Nothing?" Angie's brows shot up.

Kerry shook her head. "She just started crying. She didn't have to say anything." She rested her elbows on her thighs. "It was worth the pain."

Her sister sighed. "Wow," she repeated. "I really didn't think you'd do something like that."

Kerry felt obscurely satisfied at shocking her sister. Angie seemed to take anything and everything she did in stride, so it was oddly nice to provide her with a truly radical change she hadn't anticipated. "Well, I love it. A couple of days after I got it I wore a strapless gown to Radio City in New York and it felt great!"

Angie covered her eyes. "Oh my god."

"Maybe I can talk you into one. "

Angie got up and retreated to the door. "Go to sleep," she suggested, as she escaped from her surprisingly dangerous sibling. "You obviously need the rest if you think I'd get anywhere near some guy with a bunch of needles."

"Night." Kerry chuckled, as she disappeared, leaving her in splendid isolation in her pretty room with her colorful tattoo. She got up and took her jeans off, tossing them over her bag as she put her sleep shirt on. "I knew I should have brought that damn bustier."

"DAR!"

Hearing her name, Dar turned from signing her registration card and spotted a familiar figure moving toward her. "Morning, Alastair." She turned and met his outstretched hand with her own. "Good flight?"

"Not bad." Alastair, the CEO of ILS, Dar's boss, was dressed in what was for him an astonishingly casual pair of corduroys and a chain knit pullover sweater. "Yours?"

"Decent." Dar put her corporate credit card back in her wallet and returned that to her jeans pocket. "A little rough leaving, but I got some sleep." She looked around at the stately confines of the hotel, its tall ceilings and antique furniture giving an air of a well kept castle that she was sure was quite intentional. "This is fun."

"Have you had breakfast?" Alastair asked. "They've got a nice joint in here for that, or so I'm told by the locals."

Dar handed over her bag to a quietly waiting bellman. "Lead on," she told Alastair. "Last thing I had was cookies on the plane." She followed her boss through the lobby and into a mahogany trimmed dining room, giving the host a brief smile as he picked up two menus and motioned for them to move on.

It was 9:00 a.m., and the room was reasonably full of well dressed men and women enjoying their breakfasts amidst the soft tinkle of china and the hum of quite conversation.

"If it's any consolation, the trip from Houston wasn't any better, just a couple hours longer." Alastair commiserated with her. "I gotta tell you, even in first class these days it's like being back in the school cafeteria sometimes. What in the hell are we paying all that damn money for?"

"Leg room," Dar answered succinctly. "For me it's worth it even if it was on my dime."

Her boss turned and regarded her length, Dar's head topping his by a few inches, and lifted one hand in concession. "Point taken." He smiled. "And even if you were two feet shorter it'd be worth it to lose the aggravation. We get enough of that as it is."

The host led them to their table, and gestured for them to sit, giving them both a smile as they eased past. "Enjoy your breakfast."

Dar settled into a comfortable chair at a table for four across from Alastair, and leaned on one arm of it as she studied the menu. "Funny how this all worked out, huh?"

"Funny?" Alastair glanced around, and lowered his voice. "Lady, I've seen a lot of pulling furry woodland animals out of one's ass before, but this has to be the best one ever." He removed his reading glasses as a waiter came by and stood next to the table diffidently. "Could I get a couple of poached eggs and toast with some coffee, please?"

"Sir, of course," the man said, turning to Dar. "Madame?"

Alastair winced in reflex as Dar looked up, but his often tempestuous employee merely folded her menu shut and put it down on the table.

"Eggs over easy, sausage, and potatoes," Dar said, "and coffee."

The waiter nodded and left.

Dar turned her attention back to her boss. "Anyone else joining us for this?"

"David and Francois," Alastair responded. "They're due in tonight, said they'd join us for dinner. Meeting is at ten tomorrow morning?"

"Ten," Dar confirmed as the waiter returned with a pair of cups, a sugar caddy, and a silver pot of coffee. She waited for the man to pour out the beverage and leave before she continued. "Hans said he'd join us tonight too, so we can touch base."

"Lucky meeting the two of you, eh?" Alastair sipped his coffee. "Sometimes I think the gods of commerce have a crush on you, Dar. Things happen around you that are damned unpredictable." He smiled at Dar. "And always to our advantage."

Dar shrugged. "This was a tough one," she admitted. "To be honest, I didn't think we were going to get a damn thing other than a black eye out of it. It really was just dumb luck this time."

"I'll take it." Alastair leaned back and folded his hands on the table. "But it wasn't dumb luck for you to come up with a pitch and an end around using that new contact, Dar. That was good thinking, no matter how it worked out."

"Seat of my pants," she disagreed. "I couldn't let it go. Couldn't let them win after all that crap. Bastards. They're lucky I wasn't here when those ships got in or I'd have found that jackass and smacked him."

Alastair regarded his companion with a look of healthy respect. Dar had a sharp intellect, a lot of business sense, and an iron will, but behind it all he knew there was a potent temper. Though she was a woman and a nerd, and not crazy there was a danger about her he recognized.

Not entirely safe. But he knew it was a price he'd decided to pay when he chose to take advantage of that intelligence and take the risk on the rest. So far, it had paid off in spades. "Hell, Dar. If I'd have seen the little creep I'd have probably kicked him. Gave me indigestion for weeks."

They made small talk until the waiter returned with two steaming plates that he put down in front of them. "Is there anything else I can get for you?"

"Nothing for me." Dar picked up her fork. "Thanks."

"More coffee here," Alastair said. "Hey, Dar, did I hear right that you were going to hire that gal from Synergenics? What's her name, Graver?"

"Thinking about it." Dar neatly cut her sausage patty into squares and ate them.

Alastair fiddled with his eggs for a moment. "Isn't she the one who sent me those pictures?"

"Uh huh."

Alastair paused to study his dining companion. Dar was munching on a mouthful of sausage, gazing back at him with those big blue eyes so full of completely fake innocence. Though Dar had a mercurial temperament, he'd discovered she also had an unexpected puckish side that had arisen in the last year or so. "Ah huh."

"Can't beat em, buy em?" Dar finished her sausage and started on her potatoes. "Nah, Michelle's pretty sharp, and we banged heads enough over the ship disaster to get her viewpoint changed." She chased her mouthful down with a sip of coffee. "We'll see if she bites."

Alastair wisely decided to simply nod in response and change the subject. "That's a nice ring," he commented, stifling a smile as Dar's hand stopped in mid motion, and her already sun darkened skin darkened just a shade further. "Don't think I noticed it before."

"I've had it for a while." Dar recovered her composure from the unexpected question. "Remember that damn disaster up in Charlotte? When we lost the network?"

Her boss made a whining, groaning sound.

"Yeah, well, we took a few days off after that up in the mountains and got engaged." Dar paused and thought about that, and then she chuckled and shook her head. "Ever been in London before, Alastair?"

Bemused, he cleared his throat before answering. "Sure, once or twice. We had a few international board meetings here. Just a day up and back. You know." He dipped his toast into his eggs and took a bite of it. "Why?"

"Want to go do one of those double decker bus tours?" Dar asked. "I've never been here but I don't feel like walking around all day."

Alastair blinked at her. "Wh...ah, you mean us? You and I?"

Dar looked around. "Was there someone else here you think I was talking to? How often do I get to hang out with you?"

Her boss stared at her for a long moment. "Well, absolutely, Dar," he finally said. "I'd love to. The missus always dings me for not seeing a damn thing when I travel. Last thing I brought her back was a bottle of jalapeno jelly from Tijuana and let me tell you she didn't much appreciate it."

"Great." Dar returned her concentration to her eggs. "Keep me from falling asleep and screwing up my body clock too."

"Isn't that the truth, "Alastair agreed. "Isn't that just the absolute truth."

KERRY BRUSHED HER teeth, leaning on the marble sink as she regarded her reflection in the mirror. It was early. The sun was rising outside, and she was glad that she hadn't overslept since they had a lot to do and she really had no desire to get kidded about sleeping in.

She finished up in the bathroom and walked back into the bedroom, rolling up the sleeves on her T-shirt as she crossed to the window and looked outside. The slope Angie lived on gave her a view of Lake Michigan in the distance and it brought back memories of her childhood.

Not altogether bad ones, really Kerry had to admit, as she watched a flock of birds fly toward the huge body of water. She decided to take time out for a walk down to the lake before she left, wanting to recover a few of those better times from the place she'd spent most of her life.

Her PDA beeped softly and she turned and picked it up, flipping the top open to find a message from Dar waiting for her. "Hey honey!" She tapped the message, bending her head to read it.

Hey Ker.

Damn, I miss you.

Kerry's eyes closed briefly, and she smiled.

I just had a decent breakfast with Alastair and talked him into going sightseeing with me. I think I freaked him out by asking.

Kerry snickered.

So we're going to grab one of those buses and go see the sights. Want anything?

"You," Kerry answered. She pulled out her stylus and scribbled an answer, checking the time of the message and seeing a few hours had passed.

Hey sweetie! How's the sightseeing going? I just got up and found your message waiting. Tell Alastair I said hello, and don't do any shopping until I get there! Have fun. It's going pretty good here except I think I freaked Angie out with my tat.

She tapped the stylus against her chin.

Maybe you could come up here with me sometime and we can stay by the lake and go sailing. Aside from my family it's not really so bad.

K

A soft knock came at the door, and she turned. "Yeah?" She closed the PDA cover and stuck the device in the mid leg pocket of her carpenter's pants

The door opened, and Angie poked her head inside. "Hey, you up?"

"Believe it or not," Kerry turned and walked toward the door, "I am." She smiled at her sister. "Ready for breakfast?"

"Let's go." Angie opened the door all the way to let Kerry out. "Those are cute pants." She studied her sister's clothing. "They look comfortable."

"They are," Kerry agreed, as she followed Angie down the hallway. "How's Andrew? He up?"

"Downstairs waiting on us. You don't catch him missing a meal." Angie chuckled as they walked down the stairs together. Today she herself was dressed more casually in deference to their impending packing, a pair of sweatpants and a cotton shirt. She had her hair pulled back into a ponytail as well.

"Ah, we must be related." Kerry smiled easily as they reached the bottom of the steps and headed into the kitchen. "Looks like it's going to be a rainy one outside, perfect day for packing." She looked around as they entered and spotted her nephew in his highchair, and immediately headed in his direction. "Hey cutie!"

Andrew looked up from his tray, his eyes opening wide at this new distraction. He pointed at Kerry with his spoon and gurgled, his head tipping back to follow her as she approached. "Gah!"

Kerry crouched down next to the high chair and offered him a finger to squeeze, his dark cap of hair and blue eyes making her smile. "What are you up to, little man?" she inquired. "Is that good stuff there?"

Angie motioned for the quietly waiting cook to put their food down, and she took a seat on one side of the table, watching her sister with an indulgent smile. "You're a natural with kids," she observed, as her son giggled in delight, dropping his spoon and slapping at his aunt's wiggling fingers.

Kerry looked up from playing patty cake with the baby. "He's adorable," she said, then turned back to the chair as the cook came back with two plates. "Tell you what, Tiger, let's both eat, then we can play some more, okay?"

She got to her feet and ruffled Andrew's hair, and then joined her sister at the table, taking a seat and putting the crisply pressed linen napkin over her lap. "I love kids," she said, as she picked up her fork. "Long as they aren't mine."

Angie cut off a bit of her egg white omelet and put it on her toast. "Really?"

"Yup." Kerry tasted a bit of the egg, finding it as bland as she'd feared. "Tell you what," she said, "I'll do all the heavy lifting today but you have to let me cook breakfast tomorrow."

Her sister chuckled. "I forgot to warn them we had a chow hound descending on us. You still do the cooking down in Miami?"

"Sure." Kerry got up and went to the sideboard, evading the cook's belated attempt to intercept her and using the container of milk meant for the coffee to provide her with a glassful instead. "Dar doesn't mind cooking, but when she does, we either get something scientifically bizarre or like breakfast the other morning. She sat down with her milk. "Strawberry cheesecake."

"Yikes." Angie watched her sister tear into her breakfast with some bemusement. "So you don't want kids? Have you talked to Dar about it?"

Kerry looked across the table, for a moment, her eyes narrowing slightly.

"Ooo," Angie waved a fork at her, "sorry. Didn't mean to piss you off. I was just asking."

After a moment, Kerry relaxed, and she gave her sister an apologetic look. "Sorry. Usually people who ask me invasive personal questions don't have any good reason to," she admitted. "Dar and I have talked about it, sure."

"Ah."

"Dar thinks she doesn't have the patience for it," Kerry said. "I, on the other hand, know damn well I don't have the patience for it, and I just don't want to be a parent." She went back to her plate.. "It may sound selfish, but I like my life the way it is, and I like the freedom of being able to go and do what I want to do when we want to do it."

"I don't blame you," Angie interjected mildly. "I was just curious Ker, because you really seem to like kids that's all. You always said you never wanted to end up a soccer mom."

Which was true. "We have a dog," Kerry said. "That's enough for us, though I do have to admit I once told Dar she had to have kids so the gene pool wouldn't lose out on hers." She paused as she heard a beep from her pocket. "Speaking of." She pulled the PDA out and opened it. "I have no desire to perpetuate mine."

Angie motioned for more coffee, prudently letting the subject drop. Her sister had, without a doubt, certainly grown up a lot in the last couple of years and taken on more than a hint of the steely will Angie remembered all too well from their father.

Definitely not the time to bring **that** up either.

"YOU KNOW, DAR." Alastair politely held the door open for her as they re-entered the hotel. "I have to say, going to a medieval torture show in the Tower of London with you has to be one of the most unique experiences I've ever had."

"Glad you enjoyed it." Dar strolled into the lobby, a bag slung over her shoulder and a relaxed grin on her face. "Gonna hang that flail up in your office?"

"Erm…"

"Tell everyone I gave it to you," Dar cheerfully suggested. "That'll stop people in their tracks."

Alastair looked at her sideways for a long moment, and then burst out laughing. "Do you have any idea what my wife would say?"

"Where's mine?" Dar bantered right back. "Hey, it beats a jar of jalapeno jelly."

Her boss clucked his tongue and shook his head. "I can see this trip is going to get me in a world of trouble." He sighed, as they walked through the lobby to the elevators, entering one of the narrow, wood lined cars and pressing the old fashioned round button for the top floor.

Dar leaned against the back wall of the lift and folded her arms over her chest watching the floor indicator rise slowly. "What time are we doing dinner?" she asked. "Are they late or early here, I forget."

Alastair folded his hands in front of him his back against the side wall. "Early, I think," he said. "I think we're set to meet at seven. They've got a car arranged to take us somewhere or other." He glanced sideways at Dar. "Anything you don't care to eat? I'm not sure what they have in mind."

"Vegetables," Dar said, succinctly. "Anything else I'm all right with. I want to check in with the office, and get a shower, so seven sounds fine." She stifled a yawn with one hand, as the doors opened. For a moment, neither of them moved. Dar gave her boss a wry look and exited the lift. "Sorry."

"Not into the old courtesies, Dar?" Alastair chuckled.

"I'm usually the one holding the door," she admitted. "Learned it from my Dad."

"Me too," the older man agreed cheerfully. "He was a proper Southern gentleman who brought his sons up to be courteous to ladies and respectful to men even if you didn't like 'em."

Dar grinned. "My father's Southern also, but he played by a little different rules," she admitted, as they both left the elevator and exited into the hall. The space had sedate carpet and, surprisingly, striped wall paper, but the lighting was dim, and it made the hall a little dingy.

"So I remember," Alastair murmured. "I think we finally did get all the mildew out of the carpet up in the kitchen near my office. "He really did mix it up with Ankow, didn't he?"

"Oh yeah," Dar said. "Bastard was lucky he got out of there in one piece. Whatever happened to him, anyway?"

"Went to work for his father," Alastair replied succinctly. "Bad egg. Good riddance," he added. "Though, the world has gotten more conservative lately. "

"Mm." Dar grunted.

"Well, meet you in the lobby at seven, Dar. Get yourself some rest." He paused at the door to his room, as Dar went down two doors past him. "Thanks for the entertaining afternoon."

time." Dar opened her door and pushed it inward, giving
wave as she entered and let the portal shut behind her. Inside
as sitting on a luggage rack, and the room was dim and
peaceful. The sounds of the city below were muted by the thick glass of
the window.

She checked her watch, and she went over to her bag, unzipping it
and removing the inset that held her dress suits. Tomorrow she'd have
to slip into her corporate persona, but she was glad enough to put the
suit bag in the closet, giving it a shake to loosen the wrinkles, and
remain casual for the night.

She took her sundry kit from her suitcase and went into the
bathroom, setting the leather case on the marble counter and opening it.
She removed her various toiletries and set them up neatly, feeling the
jet lag starting to catch up with her.

Dar exhaled and glanced at her reflection. She turned the water on
and splashed some of the cold liquid on her face. It had a rich mineral
tang very different from the water at home, and she experimentally
licked a few droplets, finding it as brassy tasting as it smelled. "Peh."

She wiped her face with one of the thick hand towels and retreated
back into the bedroom, bypassing the danger of the bed and going to the
small desk near the window instead, pulling her laptop out of her
backpack and sitting down to open it.

Her cell phone rang. She glanced at the caller ID, keyed the answer
button and set the speakerphone on. "Hey cute stuff."

"Hey hon." Kerry's voice echoed slightly from the speaker.
"Whatcha up to?"

Dar was very glad of the distraction. "About to check office email,"
she replied. "You?"

"Lugging boxes," Kerry said. "Did you go sightseeing?"

"Sure." Dar booted her laptop resting her head on one hand. "Took
Alastair to a torture exhibit and then shopping in a whip and chain
shop."

Dead silence.

"Ker?"

"Honey, we do actually work for him, you know?"

Dar chuckled. "He enjoyed it. He bought a flail."

Kerry's flaring nostrils and blinking eyes were clearly audible
through the phone. "For w...no, never mind. Forget I asked that," she
muttered. "Flush cache. Flush cache. Flush cache," she paused, "okay,
better now. Please don't reload."

"Okay," Dar agreed. "How's the packing going?" She could hear
birds in the background, and guessed her partner was taking a break
from the work and possibly her family. "Everyone there being nice to
you or do I have to have a case of live gerbils delivered there to distract
people?"

Kerry laughed. "Nerd. Everyone's being fine. I'm having fun

playing with my nephew, and Mike's on his way over now, so I'm sure whatever progress we're making will grind to a complete halt. And hon, if I ever become as big a packrat as my sister you need to kick me to the curb."

Dar gazed at the phone. "Over my dead body."

"What?"

"You get kicked to the curb over my dead body no matter what junk you collect," Dar informed her. "I don't care if you pile crap up to the ceiling as long as there's a couple of square feet open in the bed for us to sleep in."

Kerry sighed. "I love you."

Dar chuckled as her laptop booted up and she plugged into the internet port in the room. "So did your sister really freak out about your tat?"

"Yeah," Kerry said. "She was like, how could you do that? Which is sort of what I asked myself the morning after I did it, but I love it now."

"Me too."

Kerry sighed. "Well, back to digging through boxes," she said, reluctantly. "You going out to dinner tonight?" she asked. "I think we are."

"With your Mom?"

"Uh huh."

Dar could read the several levels of commentary in the single grunt without much effort. She could also picture Kerry's face. "Send me a text if you want me to invent a tech nightmare for you to come save the day on, huh?"

Kerry chuckled. "I'll make them go to a barbeque joint. I'm in the mood for ribs and a nice loaded baked potato."

"Hedonist."

"Takes one to love one." Kerry's voice sounded a lot more cheerful. "Okay, hon, talk to you later. Have fun at dinner, and watch out for the haggis."

Dar closed the phone and went back to her laptop, smiling as she reviewed the mail careening wildly into her inbox and whistling softly under her breath.

KERRY CLIPPED HER phone back onto her belt and took a last long breath of cool air before she turned and re-entered Angie's house to be greeted by her brother coming in the other door. "Hey Mike."

"Kerry!" Michael rambled across the tile floor and flung his arms around her. "Good to see ya!"

"Oof." Kerry returned the hug. "Glad you see you too." She released him. "Nice haircut."

Mike ran his hand through what was almost a mohawk, the sides shorn close to his skull and the top longer. "Like it?" He looked at her.

"Hey, you got a short cut too!"

"Not that short." Kerry shook her finger at him. "I thought you were working for some big shot company. They let you look like that?"

Her brother put his hands on his hips. "Oh now look who's talking," he said. "I'm working for a marketing company, sis. They like outrageous. Hey...want a job?"

"I have a job," Kerry replied. "And besides, your company probably couldn't afford me."

"Ooo..." Mike stuck his tongue out at her. "Listen to the big shot." He turned as Angie entered, carrying a tray. "I can't believe you dragged her all the way up here just to carry boxes for you!"

Angie put the tray down and put her hands on her hips, giving her brother a withering look. "She volunteered," she said. "Just like you did. It's not my fault she didn't come up to help you move the last six times this year."

"Now now." Kerry maneuvered her way through the lines of boxes on the floor of the living room, most partially filled with various things. "No fighting, children." She accepted a glass from the tray and took a sip of it, agreeably surprised to find it lemonade. "So now that all three of us arehere, I'm sure we'll get even less done."

Angie took a seat on one of the stools. "Probably," she admitted, scrubbing her hair out of her eyes. "Boy, this is a lot of crap." She glanced at her sister who was leaning against the bar. "Maybe I should have hired someone to pack it all up and take it."

Kerry studied the living room floor. They'd been working since breakfast to sort out a lifetime of memories, trinkets, and items that even Angie had some trouble identifying. There were fifteen boxes on the ground, and thirty or forty plastic bags piled haphazardly around full of trash and things her sister could bear to give up. "You'd have ended up having to sort it out over at the house. You know that place. It's got no closets and this stuff won't fit in the attic."

"Mm."

Mike surveyed their work. "Holy cow," he said, after a moment. "What is all this stuff?"

Angie sighed. "Stuff," she admitted. "Stuff from when we were kids. Stuff from my kids." She gazed quietly at the boxes. "Letters."

Kerry rested her chin on her fist. "We'll get through it," she said. "Now that we're started, and Mike will help. Right?"

"Um..." Mike looked at his older sister seeing her brow arch. "Yep! I sure will," he hastily agreed. "Besides, I hear we get dinner out of all this."

Kerry rolled her eyes.

Angie snorted. "Oh, yeah," she addressed Kerry. "Mom called. She's got reservations at the Clearbrook. Are you going to freak?"

The Clearbrook Golf Club. Kerry remembered so many Sunday dinners at the Clearbrook, a stuffy and conservative bastion of very decent food she had been unable to fully enjoy. It had been her father's favorite 'neighborhood' place to show off his family and hold a very informal court. "Hm."

"Food isn't bad," Mike said. "If you get past all the frilly crap on the plate."

"Ker?" Angie moved closer to her. "I didn't say yes or no. You worked your ass off all day, if you want to go get pizza, I'm there."

Kerry gazed quietly past the boxes for a moment. "Nah," she finally said. "Let's get it over with." She straightened up. "Like Mike said, they've got decent food and I can shock three quarters of the town if I start a belching competition with him in the middle of dinner."

"Ker." Angie covered her eyes, while her brother snickered. "Please don't make me have to listen to her bitch for six months."

Kerry chuckled and patted her sister on the shoulder. "I'll be good." She promised. "Now c'mon. Let's get through this side of the room at least before dinner." She circled the counter and pushed Mike ahead of her. "Grab that box."

"Uh...shouldn't I watch for a while to get clued in on your system, sister?"

"Clue this, you lazy punk." Kerry lazily turned and roundhouse kicked him in the ass, sending him nearly head over heels across the room. "C'mon, the faster we do this, the faster it's done."

"Ow!" Mike yelped. "Bet you wouldn't talk like that to Dar!"

"Bet she'd kick you a lot harder."

Chapter Four

DAR LEANED BACK in her chair, the soft murmur of conversation around her as she watched Alastair order a bottle of wine from a very deferential waiter.

Hans was seated next to her looking pleased. Across the table, David McMichael and Francois Aubron were in obvious high spirits bestowing happy looks in her direction, as they waited for the server to leave and conversation to resume.

"Dar, I'm very glad you chose to join us for this meeting," David said. "It's so nice to finally meet you after all these years."

"Nice?" Dar's eyebrows lifted, but she smiled to take the edge off. "Wouldn't have missed it."

"I am thinking we would not be having this meeting if not for you in any case," Hans chimed in. "Or for me either, in fact," he added, after a pause.

"Without a doubt, without a doubt," David said. "It's a great opportunity for us to gain brilliant new partners, and investigate new business avenues."

"Do you talk to these people regularly?" Hans asked Dar in German.

Dar nodded. "On the phone," she clarified.

"Do you make faces at them?"

"Constantly."

"Gut." Hans smiled benignly at his new colleagues.

Dar steepled her fingers and tapped the edges against her lips, hiding a smile. "What do you recommend here, David?"

"Everything," David answered without hesitation. "If you eat the napkin you'll be fine," he advised. "I'm for the ox tongue, myself."

Dar eyed the menu, and wondered if she could get away with having a rabbit appetizer without having to admit that to Kerry. After a brief wrestle with her conscience, she folded her arms and looked up to see the waiter patiently waiting for her.

Huh? Dar started to frown, and then realized it was because she was the only woman at the table. Heroically managing not to roll her eyes, she gave the bunny a last regretful thought and glanced at the menu one last time. "I'll take the scallops and the lamb roast, please."

"Excellent," the waiter responded immediately. "Sir?" He turned next to Alastair.

Dar picked up her glass of white wine and sipped cautiously, finding it mild and a little sweet. "Nice." She lifted the glass toward David.

He beamed at her.

"So," Alastair said as he put his reading glasses into his pocket, "are we all ready for tomorrow? Hans, I understand you have a well established relationship with our new partner in this venture."

"I do," Hans agreed. "He is uncompromising, but he is fair."

"You brushed up on your English since the last time we met," Dar remarked dryly in German, chuckling under her breath when he blinked innocently at her. "Prussian fraud."

"Ah, we all have our secrets," Hans acknowledged. "And speaking of this how is your charming wife?"

"Doing fine, thanks." Dar smiled. "Alastair, let's make sure we put together a comprehensive package for this one. No ala carte."

The two sales executives looked at their boss, who pursed his lips for a moment before he answered.

"I don't want to be hasty," Alastair said. "If that's the plan, and I think it's a good one, Dar, then we need to take enough time to make sure we get all the wants and needs crossed and tied up." He picked up his wine glass and swirled it, then took a sip. "This is a big deal, and I want to be sure we can deliver what we promise."

Hans grunted and nodded, but didn't say anything.

"There's a lot riding on this. Lots of people watching," David spoke up. "You know, we've always been reasonably successful here, but that whole American company thing is tough to get past in a lot of places."

Dar lifted her hand, and let it drop. "We can't change that," she said, "and besides, we're high technology. It's not like America doesn't have a history of that."

"True," David said. "And that's why we've been as successful as we have, because that's exactly where a lot of this starts, and a lot of it generates from. "

"It also helps," Francois spoke up, "that the offices here are all local people."

Alastair sniffed and sipped his wine. "Well, just because I grew up on a farm outside Houston doesn't mean I'm dumb," he said. "Of course people want to deal with folks they can talk to, who understand their culture and share the same views and values."

"You grew up on a farm?" Dar interrupted. "Alastair I can't imagine you in overalls."

Everyone around the table laughed, as Alastair gazed drolly at Dar. "Thanks, Dar." He sighed. "Remind me to swap donkey tales with you later on."

They paused, as the waiter returned with a busboy and a tray and their first courses were delivered. Dar studied the three dimensional food artwork in front of her and picked up her fork, not entirely sure where she was supposed to stick it.

Oh well. There was always room service if she couldn't figure it out.

KERRY GOT OUT of the truck, closing the door and brushing a bit of cardboard scrap off the sleeve of her blue sweater as she waited for Angie and Mike to join her.

It was soft and cashmere, and had a casual elegance about it that she liked, especially when paired with her jeans and leather boots.

"Mom's gonna croak." Angie indicated her sister's denims.

"Not my fault," Kerry said. "I came up here to move boxes. She picked the pretentious place for dinner." She adjusted the three quarter sleeves and ran her fingers through her hair. "Let's go get this over with."

"Y'know," Mike spoke up, "I don't think she wants to piss you off again, Ker." He walked next to his older sister as they crossed the parking lot and approached the entrance of the club, where valets were busy handling a parade of well dressed diners. "It didn't sound that way to me."

"Me either," Angie chimed in. "Honestly Ker, he's right. I think she wants to make peace."

"Well," Kerry grunted as they reached the sidewalk and headed for the double doors, "that's up to her. I hope you're both right." She politely edged around a group of three older women standing on the stairs, ignoring the looks she got as she pinned the doorman with her eyes and dared him to say anything. "Good evening, Charles."

Caught by surprise, the elderly man gaped at her for a second, and then collected himself and reached for the door handle. "Good evening, Miss Kerry. It's been such a long time."

Kerry gave him several points. One for recognizing her, and two for smiling, with a bonus added on for treating her as though she was a very welcome guest. She returned his smile and gave him a pat on the arm as they entered. "Is my mother here yet?"

"Yes ma'am, inside," the doorman answered briskly. "Have a great evening."

"Thanks," Angie said, as she followed Kerry and her brother inside. "I'm sure we will."

Kerry paused for a moment as she cleared the door, sweeping her eyes over the interior and finding it had not changed much since she'd been gone from her hometown. A fresh coat of white paint and some new pieces of furniture appeared to be the only difference. She continued confidently toward the dining room.

The hall was moderately crowded. Kerry caught a few familiar faces in her peripheral vision, not unusual for a small town such as this one. She kept her focus forward though, and spotted a man in a suit hovering near the Maitre D station who had the air of a political aide.

Accordingly, she changed her path slightly, and addressed the man in the suit as he watched them approach. "Are you waiting for us?"

The man blinked. "Ah..." He spotted Angie and Mike behind her, and his face relaxed in relief. "Yes, absolutely. We have a table waiting, won't you come with me?" He waited for her to nod, then turned and started into the large dining room.

Angie poked her. "Stop scaring people!"

"Me?" Kerry looked over her shoulder innocently. "I haven't done anything. Yet."

"I should have brought my camera," Mike lamented. "This is probably going to be the first and only time I have a good time in this dusty old place." He caught up with Kerry as they turned a corner and entered a more or less secluded cul-de-sac, where a beautifully set table was waiting, and their mother standing at the head of it.

There were three aides milling behind her, and Mike realized everyone was more than a little freaked out. He saw the guy who had met them scurry out of the way, and then Kerry took control of everything with a manner that made him cover his mouth not to laugh.

"Mother." Kerry went to the head of the table and extended her hands, giving the aides a brief nod of greeting. "Good to see you."

Cynthia Stuart was caught faintly aback, but she rallied. "Kerrison, it's lovely to see you as well." She took Kerry's hands and clasped them. "I am so glad you were all able to come tonight." Her eyes flicked over Kerry's outfit, but to her credit, she sailed right past it. "Won't you sit down? Let's have some wine and celebrate being together."

Kerry allowed a real smile to appear, seating herself to her mother's right hand side as Angie and Mike took seats next to her and the serving staff replaced the hovering aides. "That sounds wonderful." She took her napkin and flicked it open expertly, settling it over her lap as her crystal goblet was filled. "They haven't started serving chili dogs here, have they?"

"Ah..."

"Too bad. I wonder if they'll make me one."

DAR WAS PATHETICALLY grateful to close the door to her hotel room behind her and trudge across the carpet, tossing her jacket down on the chair and continuing on through the room to the bathroom.

Inside, she stripped off all the clothing she'd been wearing, and put it into the linen laundry bag hanging neatly on a hook beside the door. Then she turned the water on, waiting for it to come to a reasonable temperature before she stepped in and simply stood there, letting it rinse over her.

After a minute, she picked up her scrubbie and body wash, and scrubbed her skin all over, sneezing a few times as she soaped her face, then following that with three washes of her hair with as much shampoo as she could fit in the palm of her larger than average hand.

After a good rinse, she shut the water off and stepped out of the shower, grabbing a towel to dry herself with. She opened the door, wrapping the towel around her as she picked up the laundry bag and took it with her back to the door. She unlocked it and dropped the bag outside, then went to the phone and dialed the number for the concierge.

"Good, ah, morning," a polite, male voice answered. "Ms. Roberts, what can I do for you?"

Nothing. Dar was convinced nothing was better than a hotel with a 24 hour concierge. "I have a laundry bag outside my room. Can you get it picked up and taken care of?"

"Of course," the man answered. "I'll send someone right up."

Dar considered. "And could you get me some warm milk and honey sent up as well?"

"Absolutely," the concierge said. "Right away."

"Thanks." Dar hung up the phone and went back to toweling her now, thankfully, smoke free self off. It was after 1:00 a.m. local time, but her body still thought it was 8:00 p.m. She hoped the warm milk would let her get to sleep. "All I need is to be a zombie tomorrow," she muttered under her breath, looking up as a knock came at the door.

Was it physically possible for anyone to come up that many flights of stairs that fast? Dar wrapped her towel around her again and tucked the ends in then ran her fingers through her wet hair before she went to the door and opened it.

"Ah." Alastair's eyes widened. "Listen, Dar..."

"Listen, Alastair," Dar cut him off. "Let's get this clear. The next time you drag me into a bar full of cigarette smoke and drunk assholes and force me to stay there, consider my resignation on your desk."

Alastair's mouth closed with a click.

"I am not bullshitting."

"Never would have thought you'd bullshit about that." Alastair recovered. "Sorry about that, Dar," he said in a more conciliatory tone. "I know the boys are so thrilled about the opportunity here they went a little overboard."

"Grr." Dar glanced at the man from housekeeping who sidled up and took the bag as quickly as he could and ducked back out of the way again. "Thanks." She turned and looked at Alastair. "I appreciate it's a cultural thing, Alastair, but next time, leave me out of it. I can't stand being in places like that, no matter how good the beer is."

"I forgot....well, no, really, I never even thought to ask, but you don't smoke, do you?" Her boss mused. "Or Kerry, I suppose. I guess it's what you get used to, and with all the new laws on our side, you don't bump into that as often."

"Yeah, well." Dar glanced down the hall. "That's true, I guess," she conceded. "Well, let me get back inside and try and get some sleep before we have to go act like world killers tomorrow morning."

Her boss lifted a hand and started off toward his own room. "Good idea, Dar." He turned at the door and looked back at her. "But you know you play a mean game of darts."

Dar paused before she shut her door. "It could have been a lot meaner," she said, giving Alastair a brief smile, before she ducked inside and left the hallway in stately silence again.

The knock at the door made her turn and grab the handle, yanking it open as she started to yell, only to swallow her outrage and muster a smile instead for the young woman holding a silver tray. "Oh. Sorry. Hi. Come on in."

She backed away from the door and the server entered, placing the tray down and removing a soft, quilted cover from the pot on it. "Thanks."

"You're very welcome." The woman presented the billfold to her, and Dar signed it, handing it back. "Will there be anything else you need this evening?"

Dar glanced at the clock. "I hope not." She sighed.

"Well then, have a good night." The server disappeared out the door, and Dar sat down next to the table holding the tray as it got blessedly quiet again. She picked up one of the nice, big stoneware cups and poured a glob of honey into it, then added steaming milk and stirred.

It smelled wonderful. Her throat, scratchy and sore from the night spent yelling over bad music and breathing in smoke was aching for the sweet taste. She picked up the cup and took it over to the bedside table, setting it down and going back to her bag to get her sleep shirt.

She picked up her PDA on the way and brought it back to bed with her, setting it down as she replaced her towel with the worn baseball shirt and shorts she seldom wore anymore. They smelled like home, though, and she sat down and picked up the PDA, flipping it open and checking for messages before she took out the stylus and scribed one of her own.

Hey.

I'm alone in my hotel with a pot of hot milk and a bad attitude. Where are you?

D

She set the PDA down and stretched out on the bed, picking up the cup and sipping from it. The milk tasted a little different than she was used to, but not in a bad way, and she, at last, allowed the stress and aggravation of the day to dissipate.

Just like the old days. She glanced at the PDA, waiting impatiently for the red flash to appear. Well, almost just like the old days.

"ARE THESE SOME of your new staff, Mother?" Kerry put down her glass relaxing a trifle as the servers gently interrupted the stilted conversation by placing salad plates in front of them.

"Hm?" Her mother glanced around. "Oh, yes. Yes they are," she said. "A nice bunch of young people. I will introduce you to them

58

Melissa Good

tomorrow. Angela says you all have been very busy today."

"Yes." Kerry sliced up her salad and decorated it with appropriate amounts of dressing. "Sorting through things, packing, you know."

"Well, I really don't understand why you didn't have someone take care of that for you, Angela. Having Kerrison come here for that seems very silly to me." Cynthia frowned. "Very silly."

Kerry took a moment to eat a big mouthful of the salad because it would take some time for her to chew it, and because she knew if she answered right at the moment the dinner probably would start sliding downhill faster than she'd anticipated. She swallowed, and washed down the crisp lettuce and greens with a sip of wine. "How could some hired firm decide what to keep and what to throw away?" She asked. "I don't understand that."

"Yes." Angela stepped up. "Really, Mother, you didn't want me bringing a lifetime worth of old plastic cups and shopping lists back, did you?"

"Well." Cynthia paused, and frowned. "I suppose not," she conceded. "But really, all that hard work."

"Definitely worth it," Angie said. "Besides, it's been fun spending some time with my sister just hanging out."

"Yeah," Mike added. "It's hard catching up in email or on the phone. You can't see her goofy faces."

Kerry looked across at him, her eyes twinkling a little. "Ah, my secret's out. Now you know why I do all those conference calls."

"I'm sure, I'm sure," their mother replied. "But surely you don't need the excuse of rummaging through all that to speak to one another. I'm positive Kerrison was glad to visit, just to see you. Isn't that so?" She looked at Kerry.

"Of course," Kerry replied quietly.

"There, see." Cynthia said. "So to have you endure this manual labor is senseless, really."

"Eh." Kerry made a noncommittal sound. "It's not that bad." She went back for a second mouthful of salad, pausing when her ear caught the faint beep from her PDA. She put her fork down and unclipped the device from her belt, opening it and peering at its screen. "Excuse me."

"What on earth is that?" her mother asked. "A calculator?"

"A personal digital assistant," Kerry replied absently, as she scanned Dar's message. "With a note from Dar inside it." She extracted the stylus and started answering her partner's note, a smile tugging at her lips.

Honey, if I could click my cowboy booted heels three times and disappear from having dinner with my mother just to share your milk and your attitude I'd be there in a heartbeat."

K

"How strange."

Kerry covered the PDA and put it on the table. "Not really." She picked up her fork again. "We use many different types of communications in our line of work. This is just one of them." She selected a wedge of tomato and ate it.

"Dar's in London right now, isn't she?" Angie spoke up. "It's late there."

Kerry nodded, and swallowed. "She is. She got there this morning. She just finished meeting with our international team there, and she has a client meeting tomorrow morning."

"London? How lovely." Cynthia took back the conversational ball. "I've always wanted to see London and Paris. So lovely and cultured." She looked past Kerry to where Angie was seated. "Isn't that something you'd be interested in, Angela? To see the continent?"

Angie put her glass down. "Well, sure I guess. Who wouldn't?"

"Perhaps we can plan a visit there," Cynthia said, with a glance at Kerry. "I would invite you as well Kerrison, but I know how busy you are with your work."

Mike snorted. "Too late. She's going there next week." He was plowing through a bowl of soup and rolls, having turned away the salad. "London, Paris, some place in Germany...then what was it, Ker, a vacation in the Swiss Alps?"

Kerry wiped her lips. "That's the plan, yep," she said, mentally making a note to give her brother a hug for the quick response. "We've got business meetings for the first week, and then I think we're taking some time and doing some touring around the Alps, maybe hang around for Oktoberfest."

"Well," Cynthia said, "isn't that lovely?"

"Sure is," Mike said. "Hey, can I come work for you, Kerry? I can carry your briefcase around and pretend I understand one word in ten you're saying."

The PDA beeped softly. Kerry opened it, and glanced at the screen.
Tell your mother to kiss my ass.

Kerry looked up from the screen, directly at her mother.

"Yes, Kerrison?" Cynthia peered back at her. "Did you want to say something?"

It was tempting. But Kerry knew she couldn't, not like that. Not yet, anyway. "Dar says hello," she reported. "She's sorry the timing of our travel worked out like it did. I know she would have liked to have been here to help too."

"Now," her mother smiled, "isn't that so gracious of her. I am certainly glad she's enjoying her travels. Do you know where you're staying in London? Some friends of ours just got back from there."

Kerry looked back at the note.

I've just spent the night in a dive bar with twisted English karaoke going on in the middle of a smoke pit with darts added into the bargain. I told Alastair if he did that to me again I was quitting.

"I think she's enjoying the culture," Kerry commented mildly.

"They're at the Stafford. Dar said it was nice."

These people are pissing me off. You better get over here fast, before I cause an international incident.

D

"And she's looking forward to me joining her." Kerry scribbled a reply and closed the lid. "The feeling's mutual." She wiped her lips as the waiter removed her salad plate. "So, Mike. What's up with your new job? You started telling us about it before we left for dinner."

"Well..."

KERRY WELCOMED THE cool breeze as they stepped outside into the wide entranceway. She moved to one side to let her family emerge behind her, and stood on the top of the drive, her hands shoved casually in her front pockets.

"That really wasn't too awful." Angie murmured in her ear. "Was it?"

"Nah." Kerry licked her lips. "That was great crème brulee." She drew in a breath of air tinged with pine and waited as her mother's aides attended to bringing her car around. Mike came up to stand next to her, and she bumped him with idle affection. "Hey."

"Hey," Mike responded. "I'm glad you're here, even if you aren't."

"Eh." His sister shrugged her shoulders a trifle. "Actually I don't mind it. It's great to see you guys." She glanced past Mike as her mother approached them. "Being the black sheep's not so bad."

"Kerrison." Cynthia was fussing with her bag. "I'm very upset with you!"

News flash. "For what?" Kerry turned to face her. "Paying for dinner?"

"Of course. So inappropriate." Her mother frowned. "My staff had it taken care of."

Kerry rolled her eyes a trifle. "I'm the vice president of a multinational corporation. I can afford it," she said, in a mild tone. "I think I actually get paid more than a Senator does," she added.

"Kerrison!"

Mike made a sound like a duck being shot at. He shuffled a step away from Kerry, while Angela merely covered her eyes with one hand.

"Well, we're a public company. It's published in our annual report." Kerry shrugged. "Anyway, it's no big deal, Mother. I was glad to do it. How often do I get to take my family out for dinner?"

Cynthia took a breath, and then merely pursed her lips.

"I'm glad I'm in a position where I can do that," Kerry continued, in a quieter tone. "I'm not sure why that's upsetting."

"Ma'am?" One of her mother's aides approached. "Your car is ready."

"One moment." Cynthia held a hand up. "Of course, I understand," she said. "Forgive me, Kerrison. It was a generous gesture, and I do appreciate it."

Kerry smiled at her. "No problem." I guess we'll see you at the house tomorrow, once we get all those boxes packed up."

"Indeed, yes." Her mother looked happier. "It will be so nice to have you all there. I'm very much looking forward to it."

There was a truth there, Kerry felt. "I'm looking forward to it too."

Satisfied, her mother lifted her hand and then followed the aide toward the limo waiting for her. She got in the car, and waved at them, and they waved back.

"It would have been funny if you offered her a ride home in the back of the truck," Mike commented, smiling as he waved. "Or even in the front seat."

"Mike." Angie chuckled. "You're a bigger troublemaker than Kerry."

"I gotta be better than her at something," Mike replied, as they descended the steps and crossed the parking lot, dodging between the cars trying to leave. "Thanks for dinner, sis!" He put his arm around Kerry's shoulders. "You rock."

Kerry chuckled wryly. "Actually you guys are cheap dates," she told her siblings. "You should see the bill when Dar and I go out for a night on the town." Her lips twitched into a grin.

"Party city?" Angie asked. "I don't know, Dar didn't seem the type to me."

"Well...no, not really that kind of stuff," Kerry said. "We go out for dinner, maybe a little bit of dancing. Dar doesn't drink much, but she likes champagne."

"Hm," Mike mused. "I figured her for a Jack Daniels woman."

"No way." Kerry beeped open the doors to the trunk. "Bubbly and the good stuff too. We've got a few seafood restaurants we like to hit." She opened the driver's side door. "It doesn't take much stone crab and Cristal to beat what we had in there, let me tell you."

"Fancy fancy." Mike got in the back and sprawled across the bench seat.

"Yeah." Kerry closed the door and started the truck. "Then the next night we stop at Burger King. My life's a study in eclectic."

Her siblings laughed. "You actually eat Burger King?" Angie asked.

"Sure." Kerry carefully pulled out of the parking lot, waiting until she saw her mother's limo drive off in the other direction. "Wendy's is my favorite fast food though. They have killer spicy chicken sandwiches." She settled back into the seat and concentrated on driving, the roads not quite as familiar as they used to be.

All in all, she had to admit, it hadn't been that bad. Her mother, after those first few jabs, had kept her conversation to superficial matters and they'd talked mostly about Mike's new job, the weather, local news, and a light mention of the conservative rumblings at the national level.

Having her mother as a Senator was very strange, and Kerry found herself almost unable to wrap her mind around it. In a way though, it gave her some small insight on how perhaps her mother felt about her, since her life in Miami and with Dar was so outside her experience as well.

So odd.

"Hey Ker?" Angle half turned in her seat to face her sister. "Do you really get paid more than Mom?"

Kerry laughed. "Oh, hell yes," she said. "Any bets she has her goons google our annual report when she gets home to find that out?"

Mike snorted.

"Well." Angie chuckled. "At least this bunch is a lot nicer than the old ones were. They don't give me the creeps, and they stay out of the way, mostly."

"Yeah, they're okay," Mike agreed. "I think one of them is gay, but don't tell Mom," he advised. "I caught him and one of the cleaning staff out behind the kitchen door the last time I was at the house."

"What were you doing back behind the kitchen?" Angie asked, her brows arching. "Mr. Nosy Butt."

"Uh oh." Kerry could hear a very familiar argument starting. "Here we go."

"Hey, it's not my fault you never see the fun stuff," Mike retorted. "If you'd get your butt out of the library once in a while you would."

"Library this monkey face."

Kerry smiled, keeping her eyes on the darkened road as she let the good natured trading of insults go on around her. It felt like home used to be, back when they were all running around on the second floor of the big house, when the biggest thing they had to worry about was knocking over one of the alabaster statues near the stairs.

George Washington had toppled to his demise from an ill judged tackle on her part. She could almost see his white head tumbling down the steps, thumping and cranking all the way down until he reached the bottom, and the marble floor, and shattered into dozens and dozens of pieces.

She chuckled.

"You think that's funny?" Mike poked her. "Hah! And I thought you were on my side!" He poked her again. "Holy crap." He grabbed her shoulder and squeezed it.

"Mike!" Kerry hissed. "I'm driving! What the heck's your problem?"

"You've got muscles like a wrestler!" Her brother accused her.

"How would you know?" Angie jibed him, giving him a shove back against the seat. "Leave her alone, you weirdo."

Kerry suddenly felt fifteen years younger. "Stop pawing at me and

I'll take my shirt off and show them to you back at Angie's." She warned her brother.

"And your tattoo." Angie teased.

"What?" Mike squealed, crawling up from the back seat and up halfway into the front of the truck. "You got one? You did?" He slid forward and almost landed on his head, between his sisters. "Bowah..."

"Oh for the love of..." Kerry released one hand off the wheel and grabbed him. "Mike, if I have an accident driving this damn thing I will never hear the end of it so cut that out! Sit still!" She checked her mirrors, glad to see she was almost alone on the road. "You want us to get pulled over by the cops?"

Mike twisted around and hung his legs over the seat back, his head almost hitting the console. "That would be funny as hell," he said. "Can you see the headlines in the Sentinel? We'd be the talk in the coffee shop for a month."

"Oh god." Kerry heard her cell phone go off. "Now what? Shh, both of you." She pulled it off her belt and keyed the speaker. "Kerry Stuart."

"Hey," Dar said.

"Hey." Kerry glanced quickly at the display. "Why are you up? It's 3:00 a.m. there, isn't it?"

"I can't sleep." Dar complained. "You're not here in bed with me."

Oh god. Kerry felt a sudden rush of blood to her face, as her siblings burst into laughter. "Thanks, hon." She sighed. "Things weren't chaotic enough in the cab of this pickup with my nutcase family here."

Dar chuckled. "Hey, it's the truth," she said. "How'd dinner go? Did you guys scandalize the town?"

"No, we didn't." Angie spoke up. "How are you Dar? How's England?"

"Annoying the crap out of me. Thanks for asking," Dar answered. "Other than that, I'm fine thanks, Angela. How's the packing going?"

"Ugh. Hard work." Mike announced, folding his hands over his stomach.

"Like you've done any." Kerry gave him a withering look.

"Everything's going fine, thanks for asking Dar." Angie covered her brother's mouth. "Thanks for lending me your significant other for a few days to help."

Dar chuckled again. "Well, she wouldn't let me rent her." She sighed. "But you better take good care of her or I'll reroute your paychecks to feed starving wolves in Oregon."

Mike was laughing so hard he was making the seat shake.

"You're so romantic," Kerry said, affectionately. "That's one of the things I adore the most about you, Dardar. Dinner went fine. We're headed back to Angie's house now." She slowed before the turn up to her sister's road. "You should try and get some sleep."

"Okay," Dar agreed. "Just wanted to find out how things went.

Talk to you later, Ker. Love you."

"Love you too." Kerry closed the phone and put it on the seat next to her, aware of the sudden and almost awkward silence from her siblings. She let that go on for a few minutes, and then she glanced at them right before she pulled into Angie's driveway. "Least she got you two to stop fighting."

"Yeah." Angie sighed. "You guys sound so storybook married."

Kerry smiled, as she parked the truck turning off the engine and popping the door open. "That's probably the nicest thing you've ever said to me, sis. Thanks." She got out and Angie hopped out on the other side.

They looked at each other, and then they both slammed their respective doors, leaving Michael hanging upside down in the front seat.

"Hey!" he yelled through the door. "Hey! Help me out of here!"

Kerry and Angie bolted for the house, running up the sidewalk toward the front door as the horn started honking behind them, laughing as they headed for the door.

DAR WOKE UP as the early light shone through the window, her internal clock as dependable as it was at home despite the five hour time difference. She studied the outline of the sill, content to lay there wrapped around her pillow as sleep slowly receded.

Softly, far off, she could hear the sounds of the city. Horns and the sounds of machinery, no different than any other city she'd ever woken up in save the one where she lived. Out on the island, there was no real traffic, and if anything penetrated the soundproofed walls of the condo it was the roar of the ocean and the occasional hoot of a barge.

Or sometimes a mating peacock.

The peace there was something she'd come to appreciate. It gave her a period of space in which to live, and get ready for the day before she had to cross the water, and enter the insanity of Miami traffic and head to work.

Spending the morning with Kerry, going through their routine, the gentle banter, the morning run, or walking over to the gym in bad weather, talking together, or being silent together–she found with a start like that, her entire attitude at work had completely changed.

People used to absolutely avoid her. Dar realized that. She knew that she'd done a lot to foster the notion that she was likely to bite people's head off in the morning unless she'd at least gotten a gallon or two of café con leche into her, and that if you wanted anything, you'd better wait until after lunch.

Now? People actually approached her in the damned elevator on the way up to the fourteenth floor. Dar rolled over and stretched her body out. Sometimes some of them even smiled at her, and occasionally, when she was in a particularly mellow mood after one of their long joint showers, she smiled back.

Less coffee, less stress, less screaming, more fun. Dar smiled at the ceiling. Life was charming the hell out of her at the moment despite the fact she'd had to spend the previous night in a smoky pub. Stifling a yawn, she pulled the covers back and rolled up out of the bed and onto her feet, stretching her limbs out as she wandered over to the window and peered out.

Raining. Dar pondered the gray exterior glad she had her long coat handy. The meeting was not that far away, perhaps ten minutes. She reveled in the notion that she had a reasonable amount of time to order breakfast and shower before she had to get ready.

Nice.

She sat down at the sleek desk near the window and flipped open the room service menu, propping her head up on one hand as she studied its contents. After a minute she closed the book and touched the speakerphone keypad, dialing room service and placing her order with the amiable and cheery voice on the other end.

With that done, she opened the screen to her laptop and started it up, leaning back in the chair as she waited for it to boot. Since it was in the middle of the night back at the office, she really didn't expect there to be much mail but you never knew, and anyway, sometimes Maria forwarded her unintentionally funny jokes she'd come to enjoy.

The room was pleasantly cool, and she felt a sense of contentment as she watched some birds fly past outside the window, turning her head back only when her laptop beeped wanting attention. She keyed in her password and let it continue starting up her secured session to the office.

Mark had found them biometric laptops. They had a scanner attached that took fingerprints. Dar had tried one for a period of a week and ended up almost tossing it off the balcony on the 14th floor as the technology was just not ready for her.

Either that or she had weird fingerprints. Mark swore it worked for him. They were going to try retinal scanners next, but she figured if the stupid thing couldn't even read her index finger, they had scant chance of being able to read her eyeball.

"Technology sucks sometimes," she informed her laptop. "It's never where we want it to be, is it?"

The laptop bleeped back at her.

"Shut up." Dar leaned forward and reviewed her mail. As expected, there was nothing too urgent and she picked through them with casual interest, pausing to smile at a forwarded picture of a sunbathing cat from Kerry, and to shake her head at yet another request from Mariana for people to stop cooking fish in the building.

"Ah." She saw another one from the Mariana, and opened it. It was the softball team lineup, listing Kerry as captain and laying out the game schedule. She reviewed it, nibbling her lip as she realized they'd only be back from Europe a few days before the opening night. "Hm."

Mariana had told everyone that winning wasn't as important as participating. Dar understood that intellectually, but she knew full well that no one wanted to lose, least of all her, and really least of all her curiously competitive partner.

So. She opened a message and addressed it to Mark.

Hey. Make sure everyone shows up for those practice games since we'll be out here. I don't want to look like a jerk when we play the first one.
D

She reviewed it then sent the mail. That left the problem of when she and Kerry were going to practice, and she frowned. Maybe getting involved in the softball thing when they were traveling wasn't the best idea.

On one hand, she figured she could probably handle a game without much preamble, trusting what she thought of as a reasonable set of athletic skills and a cursory memory of the sport to carry her through.

Kerry, however, though she had good reflexes and could handle her body, really had nothing to go by in terms of knowing what to do in the game, and Dar had gone and volunteered her as captain.

"That was idiotic," she remarked to herself.

A knock came at the door, and she left the problem to sit as she went and answered it, letting in the room service waiter complete with a little wooden cart full of her selected breakfast. She signed the check and handed it back, then sat down as the waiter left and closed the door.

In the midst of opening her cereal box, her cell phone rang. Dar cursed, launching herself over the bed to the nightstand where the device was rattling, and grabbing it. She opened it and managed to get it to one ear without falling off the bed, but without time to see who it was. "Yes?"

"Hey honey."

Dar stuck her tongue out and stifled a laugh. "Hey."

"You okay? You sound weird."

"I'm upside down." Dar squirmed into a more comfortable position and relaxed. "What are you doing up? It's late."

"I can't sleep," Kerry told her. "You're not here in bed with me."

Dar chuckled. "Sorry about that. I didn't realize you had me on speaker until it was too late."

"No problem I absolutely loved having my brother and sister hear what you said to me. Angie said we sounded so married."

"Aw."

"So how's it really going? I almost threw peas at my mother here. She finally stopped with the snarky BS about halfway through dinner."

"It's fine." Dar assured her. "I was pissed off about the bar, but that's no one's fault. I'm looking forward to the meeting at ten. You got more packing to do?"

"Yeah," Kerry agreed mournfully. "Then we're going over to the house and haul everything in there. I'm having fun with Ang and Mike, but boy I'm not looking forward to hanging out with my mother."

"Want me to invent a disaster for you to fix?"

"You keep teasing me with that offer," Kerry reminded her dryly. "Don't jinx us, hon. We're both out of the office and we don't really need something to crash, y'know?"

"Mm."

"We'd just have to fly back to Miami and fix it."

"Hm." Dar's low grunt grew far more cheerful. "We'd be in the same place then," she offered. "That can't be all bad, can it?"

Kerry laughed softly, for at least thirty seconds. "Let's see," she said. "It's been what... two days now? That must be a record for us before we start whining about being apart. We're so nuts."

"But in a nice way."

Kerry was silent for a brief moment. "In a very beautiful way," she said. "Being with my mother, and my sister, and my brother, who is on his fourth girlfriend this year, made me realize all over again how blessed my life is."

Dar studied the ceiling, feeling a stupid grin stretch her lips. "You're better than Frosted Flakes for breakfast, you know that? Ah, Ker. Go back to sleep. You're going to be toast tomorrow if you don't and you'll end up going off on everyone."

Kerry made a small, grunting sound.

"Won't you?"

"Probably." Kerry sighed. "This bed's not comfortable, and I miss my dog, and I want some chocolate milk," she admitted. "And you're the only one I can say that to who won't look at me funny or tell me to grow the hell up."

Dar chuckled.

"I'm not sure I even know who these people are anymore," Kerry added. "I feel like I hardly know them."

"They hardly know you," Dar said. "Give it a few days. You sounded pretty rambunctious with them in the car."

A small silence. "Yeah, I guess I did. It's all right. I think I just keep freaking them out. "

Dar's eyes flicked over the ceiling, her sensitive ears catching the change in her partner's tone. "Hey."

"Hey."

"Just be who you are, Ker," Dar advised gently. "They'll get used to it. Don't be afraid to not pretend, you know?"

Kerry sighed. "That's exactly what I'm afraid of," she confessed. "It's hard to make everyone change the way they see me. It's easier for me to pretend I'm someone else. It always was," she paused, "but you know something, I don't think I can do it anymore."

"Would it help if I sent you flowers at your Mom's house?" Dar asked, with a hint of a wry chuckle. "You know I always get you the most expensive ones."

Finally, Kerry chuckled. "I can do this," she said. "I'll be fine. I just needed a Dar time out."

Talk about freaking out. "Anytime, sweetheart," Dar assured her. "I'll always be there for you." She heard the slight inhale, and the faint sound of Kerry swallowing. "Now go to bed, and let me eat my English Frosted Flakes and weird tasting milk for breakfast."

"I love you," Kerry replied, simply. "Talk to you later, okay?"

"Later." Dar hung up the phone and let it sit on her chest for a few minutes. Then she chuckled and got up, taking her box of cereal with her back to the tray. "Dar time out." She shook her head and poured the cereal into the waiting bowl. "And she thinks **her** life's changed."

Chapter Five

KERRY HUMMED SOFTLY under her breath as she neatly flipped a set of pancakes. A plate of omelets and bacon were already waiting nearby. She had her back to her sister's servants, aware of their nervous anxiety, and wondered briefly if they were more worried about her getting burned or if that she was auditioning for their jobs.

Not really much danger of either. She'd cooked long enough and often enough to know how to avoid getting hurt and even when she'd been younger and willing to take about any job, short order cook had never been in her personal horizon.

She didn't mind cooking for herself, or for Dar, or for family. Cooking for strangers, however, was another story especially after a night of little sleep and a morning full of gray rain outside. Her ears pricked, as she heard footsteps in the hall, and she caught the nervous jerks from the staff as they heard them as well.

"Wh...Kerry!" Angie entered, spotting her at the stove. "What in blazes are you doing?"

Kerry looked at the pan, then she turned her head and looked at her sister, then she looked back at the pan. "You have done this, Ang. I know you have. I used to live with you, remember? Don't tell me you never told these guys about those banana brownies you used to make."

Angie came over and peered over her bare shoulder. "You're cooking," she said, avoiding the brownie issue.

"I am," her older sister confirmed. "I said I was going to. You didn't believe me?" She scooped the last of the pancakes into their dish and covered it, and then turned off the gas to the stove. "I didn't get much sleep last night so I figured I'd better make something I liked for breakfast so I didn't whine all day."

Angie picked up one of the dishes, a bemused but understanding look on her face. She gave her staff a wry smile as she turned and headed after Kerry to the dining room. "Don't worry about my sister. She's just got a mind of her own."

"Got that right." Kerry set the plates she had in her hands down. "Well, good morning." She greeted her brother, who was rubbing both eyes. "Fine state of affairs when I'm the early bird in the family." She took a seat near one end of the big table, the warm light bathing her tanned arms very visible in her tank top.

"Pissant," Mike grumbled, sitting down across from her before he peered at Kerry, and jerked upright. "Holy shit. You did get a tattoo." He scrambled out of his chair and came around the table, as Kerry continued to calmly butter her toast. "Wow."

"Eat breakfast first, gawk later," Kerry advised him. "It's not going anywhere." She dumped some pancakes, an omelet, and a slice of bacon on her plate.

"Did it hurt?" Mike asked.. "What made you get it?"

Angie motioned the staff to bring coffee over. "I think it's pretty."

"Can I touch it?" Mike asked.

Kerry put her fork down and half turned to face Mike. "Sure." She moved the strap of her tank top over to give him a better view. "Yes, it hurt," she said, as he bent closer. "It hurt a lot, but it was worth it."

"Wow," he repeated, putting a finger out hesitantly and touching the design. "Oh," he said. "It feels like skin."

Angie appeared on her other side, running her thumb over it. "It is," she said, in surprise. "I thought it would be raised up, like those inoculations."

Kerry felt herself twitch a little as they touched her. "Well, when he first did it, it was kinda," she said. "It was pretty swollen."

"It was?" Angie looked up at her at close quarters, nearly making her eyes cross. "Is it like a burn?"

"It's...yeah, I guess," Kerry said. "I mean, they take needles and jab them into your skin over and over again, so it kind of gets all sore and puffy. But it heals pretty fast." She went on. "It stops hurting really bad as soon as they stop sticking needles in you."

Mike shook his head and went back to his seat. "You are totally crazy," he announced. "But it is really nice looking, Ker. Did Dar like it? She should. It's her name there."

Kerry went back to sorting out her breakfast. "She did. I think one of the reasons, maybe, that I got it was because I knew it was something I could do that she probably wouldn't."

"She doesn't like tattoos?" Angie eased away from her and went back to her place at the head of the table.

"She's scared to death of needles." Kerry responded, with a wry grin. "Don't you remember in the hospital?"

Angie's eyes widened, as she helped herself to the plates. "Oh my gosh. I do. That's right!" She gave the woman at her shoulder a nod, and sat back as coffee was poured into her cup. "She almost went crazy there before everything got horrible."

They all fell briefly silent as they started breakfast, and Kerry was left in peace to think about Mike's first question.

Why. Why had she really gotten the tattoo? For herself? For Dar? Kerry chuckled a little under her breath and shook her head. She still really didn't know for sure. "So anyway." She broke the quiet. "I love the thing. Dar was in New York when I got it, and I had a day or so to let it heal before I showed it to her. I could see it was going back and forth in her mind if she wanted to get one too."

"Kerry?" Mike looked up. "Thanks for making breakfast. This rocks."

Angie looked around, but the two servant women had retreated back to the kitchen. "Yeah," she said. "Thanks. I know I used to make brownies, but I have no idea how to tell these people to make things I like."

Kerry waved a fork at them, busy chewing.

"Have you decided what you're going to speak about at the banquet tonight?" Angie asked. "You know, Marga Smithton called me last night and said she saw us in the restaurant with Mom and she said everyone's been talking about it."

Kerry rolled her eyes.

"Hey, slow news week," Her sister held a hand up. "C'mon, Kerry. You used to live here. How many weeks did duck racing make the front page?"

Kerry swallowed and wiped her lips with her napkin. "They need to get a life," she said. "I've figured out two different ways to go tonight, and it depends on how they react when I get there. Either they're going to get my professional presentation, or they're going to get the radical biker dyke. All up to them."

Both her siblings blinked at her.

"Ah. Forgot to tell you I got a motorcycle too." Kerry grinned, and took a sip of her coffee. "Actually, it was a joint purchase. Dar and I use it down at the cabin in the Keys," she explained. "Which by the way, you both have to come down and stay some time."

"I'll take you up on that," Mike said. "Can I ride the bike?"

"Sure." Kerry could still sense the faint waves of shock rolling around the table. "We go down on weekends a lot and just bum around there. It's quiet, and it's right on the water, I love chilling out on the beach in front."

"Sounds gorgeous." Angie recovered and picked up the conversation again. "Is it a long drive?"

"Well, it's about an hour and a half, I guess, but we also take the boat down there and that's a little longer. We don't care though because we stop and dive on the way down."

"Man," her brother shook his head, "what a life."

Kerry smiled and took a forkful of pancake to eat. She felt a faint buzz in her pocket and pulled out her phone, setting it on the table and opening it. "Excuse me." She put the forkful down and pressed the answer button. "Kerry Stuart."

"Hello, Ms. Stuart?" a male voice answered. "This is ops. We have kind of a situation here and we need someone to make a decision."

"Called the right person." Kerry regretfully glanced at her plate. "Go on. What's the problem?"

"There's a new sales account, the International Cellular group?" the tech ventured. "Do you know about them?"

"Sure," Kerry said.

"Okay, well, they were supposed to come live next week, but it turns out their stuff came early so they want to bring up the circuits into the network, but the change control's not ready."

Ah. Kerry leaned back and folded her arms, considering the issue. "Does Mark have the network provisioning ready?" she asked.

"He says he can have it."

Ah. Kerry almost laughed. That meant everyone really wanted to help out their new customer, and no one wanted to stand on procedure—but no one wanted to cross her strict insistence on documented change control either.

Only Dar would casually do that, and often did. But to be fair, if anyone else asked Dar if they could do it, Dar sent them to Kerry. She reserved the right to bypass the rules for herself and Kerry had accepted that without much qualm, not only because Dar was her boss, but because she trusted her instincts. "Okay, you have my verbal approval to proceed, so long as Mark files the paperwork in the system and it comes up after business hours."

"Right oh, ma'am." The tech sounded happier. "Mark's on the way to do that now. Thank you!"

"Anytime." Kerry hung up the phone and went back for her fork, glad the issue had been simple.

"So who was that?" Angie asked.

Kerry held up her finger, and managed to get a mouthful of her breakfast. She patiently chewed it and swallowed. "Our operations center in Miami," she said. "We put some new policies and procedures in place and they're determined to stick by them."

"So you really do run that place, huh?" Mike said.

Kerry nodded, but kept eating.

"She does," Angie said. "I don't know if Mom googled you last night, but I did. Holy bananas, Kerry. You're an executive vice president."

"Uh huh." Her sister nodded again.

"So, I have a question. "Angie leaned forward a little. "If you make what you do, and Dar makes what she does, and you live in a gillion dollar condo on some ritzy private island, and you own a boat, and a snazzy cabin in the Keys...why the heck do you cook for yourself and drive your own car?

Kerry stopped chewing and looked up at her, head tilted slightly to one side. After a second she hastily swallowed and picked up her coffee cup, washing her mouthful down. "Huh?"

"Yeah." Mike had no such worries. He plowed through his pancakes as he talked. "How come you don't have a half dozen people chasing after you holding your briefcase? I could be one of them."

How come? Kerry was honestly perplexed, never having even considered anything remotely like it. "Well," she said, after a long pause. "I like cooking, and I like driving. Why would I let someone else do it for me?"

She looked at her siblings, and they looked back at her, and she suddenly felt the gulf between them like it was a physical void. It was strange, and upsetting, since she'd grown up in this same type of home, in this same type of environment and yet living like her sister lived, like her mother lived, was as alien to her as winter had come to be.

"Huh." Mike grunted. "I like people doing things for me. Who likes to do laundry and stuff? I'd rather have clean clothes appear like magic."

"Me too," Angie agreed. "If I didn't have someone helping me with Andrew, I'd go crazy."

Kerry sucked on her fork tines then shook her head. "I don't have time in my life for that," she said. "It's way too complicated, dealing with people doing stuff for me. It's a lot easier to do it myself."

Angie looked at the plate, and then she chuckled and shrugged. "Well, no one can argue. You know what you're doing, sis. Whatever makes you happy."

"Right on," Mike agreed. "You can cook for me anytime."

"Thanks." Kerry went back to her breakfast, more than a little bemused. "Now can we shut up and eat? Before I have to get up and cook it all over again?"

"Oo...she's the boss."

DAR TOOK ADVANTAGE of being slightly behind Alastair to take a moment to pull her cuffs straight as they stood waiting to enter the sturdy oak doors to the conference room. She then put her hands together over her leather binder, shifting her shoulder a little under the weight of her laptop case as she listened to Alastair's cheerful chatter with their hosts.

She was the only one with a laptop, naturally. The rest of the team with them were sales executives, who had thick leather portfolios clasped under their arms, dark suits, light shirts, classy ties and appropriately confident, but reserved expressions.

Like theirs, Dar's business suit was a conservative charcoal grey, but that's where the resemblance stopped. She was wearing a knee length skirt and a creamy beige silk shirt, and her lapel was impudently decorated with a jewel encrusted microchip just to drive the point home that she wasn't one of the front of the house boys.

Nerd. Dar licked her lips and hid a smile, straightening her shoulders as she heard the doors start to open, and the chatter died down.

"Well, here we go." Alastair turned, glancing behind him as if to make sure Dar was there. "Ready, lady?"

Dar wrinkled her nose at him, and chuckled.

"Gentlemen," the polite man opening the door paused, "ah, and lady. Please come inside. Welcome."

"That's twice in sixty seconds," Dar muttered, as she followed

Alastair inside, the rest of the team deferring to her. She glanced around as she crossed the thick carpet, appreciating the high ceiling and expansive proportions of the conference room.

At the head of the table sat Sir Melthon Gilberthwaite, who was such a stereotypical forties movie style British magnate Dar half suspected there was a film crew around somewhere. Seated next to him was Hans, who solemnly winked at Dar as their group entered.

"Ah, Sir Melthon." Alastair advanced confidently. "It's good to see you again."

"McLean," the magnate barked gruffly. "Good start. You lot showed up on time. I hate slackers, like this godson of mine."

Hans smiled benignly.

Alastair reached the table and took Sir Melthon's extended hand in a firm grip. "We try not to slack, though I have to tell you this time difference smacks the heck out of us." He released the man's hand and turned. "Let me introduce my team here."

Dar stood quietly waiting, letting Alastair's genial introductions of the sales team roll past her as she waited her turn. She was pretty sure that he would introduce her last as he usually did when they were in a group. She wasn't sure if it was something to do with her being a woman, or just her being her, but she realized the magnate at the end of the table was waiting as well as he looked right at her the whole time.

"And of course, our Chief Information Officer, Dar Roberts," Alastair concluded, turning to give Dar a nod, "the architect of our infrastructure."

"Sir Melthon." Dar inclined her head in response, meeting his eyes. "It's good to meet you."

The magnate stood up and walked around the table to where she was standing, shooing the others out of the way. He stopped in front of her, his head nearly but not quite even with hers, and put his hands on his hips. "You the git who kicked my godson in the rear?"

"I am," Dar replied mildly, aware of Alastair's widening eyes behind him.

"You're one of those smart mouthed women, aren't you?" Sir Melthon accused. "One of them who think they know everything?"

"Absolutely," Dar agreed. "I wouldn't be here otherwise. I don't waste my time on small potatoes and two bit thinkers." She could hear the air being sucked out of the room around her, and wondered if the two European sales managers were going to pass out right on the conference room floor. "I don't think you do either."

Sir Melthon grunted. "Hah." He turned and went back to his chair. "What's the world coming to, hah? Foreign women in my boardroom. Scandalous!" He looked at the rest of them. "Well, you idiots! Sit down! You think I'm going to talk to you getting a crook in my neck? Especially that smart mouthed woman! Sit!"'

Everyone hastily grabbed for a chair except for Dar, who

meandered around to the other side of the table and set her laptop case down first before she took a seat in one of the comfortable leather chairs. "Nice," she commented to Hans in German.

"It will get better. He likes you," Hans advised her, in a low mutter. "I think perhaps he wants to take you to bed."

Dar nodded, steepling her fingers as the sales team prepared their presentation. "Did you tell him I was married?"

"I did so," Hans replied, in a regretful tone.

"To another woman?"

The German half shrugged. "Not so much."

Dar chuckled under her breath and removed her laptop from its case, opening it and starting it up. "This is going to be a party I can tell already. He's going to love it when Kerry gets here."

Hans smiled and folded his hands over his stomach, beaming contentedly at the room.

"THAT IT?" Kerry nudged the box she'd carried and lifted into the flatbed of the pickup into place. She stood up and dusted off her hands, glad she'd decided to keep her tank top on to work in as the afternoon sun warmed her skin.

"Ugh. I hope so." Mike sat down on the tailgate of the truck. "That was hard work."

"You carried three boxes." Kerry took a seat on the edge of the truck side, resting her elbows on her knees and removing the pair of leather work gloves she'd put on. "Give me a break."

Mike looked up at her. "Hey. We're not all athletic like you are." He swung his legs a little, watching his sister out of the corner of his eye as they waited for Angie to join them. As he'd expected, Kerry did in fact have visible muscles, but they weren't the kind you saw on sports shows or in those freaky infomercials.

They were just there, along her arms and shoulders, under the skin where you could see them move when she did. They didn't look bad, he decided, and they didn't look like a guy's, either. But with her cropped hair they presented a picture of her that didn't match the one he'd held in his head for a very long time.

She leaned back and crossed her ankles, resting her hands on the truck side and tipping her head back to look up at the sky, and Mike felt suddenly that this was a person he really didn't know that much about. "Hey Ker?"

"Hm?" She rolled her head to one side and looked at him. "Just kidding, Mike. I'm glad you showed up even if you didn't carry a box. It's good to see you."

He grinned. "I was gonna say pretty much the same thing. So much crap has gone on the last couple of years, it's been a bitch, you know?"

"I know," Kerry agreed. "It's been tough for me...all that stuff."

"Yeah."

"I'm glad I have Dar's family around," Kerry said, gazing at her work boots. "I don't think I was ready to not have anyone but me and her. I missed having people around me and her folks are amazing. They're at our place now, dog sitting."

"They seem really cool," Mike agreed. "Dar's mom scares me."

Kerry chuckled. "She's hilarious. There's so much of her in Dar, and neither of them will admit it. Dar looks like her Dad, but really her wit is just like her mom's."

Mike got up and climbed into the bed of the truck with her sitting down next to Kerry. "We had some fun before, though. It wasn't all bad, growing up together. I didn't think so, anyway."

"There were good times," Kerry said. "I had fun with you and Angie. I wish we could have stayed like...around ten. Once I started growing up is when things got weird." She pondered the boxes around them. "I'm really glad I didn't figure out I was gay until I left home."

"That didn't go over really well," Mike agreed. "Was it weird for you?"

Kerry thought about those long, confusing days, and after a moment of silence, she nodded. "It was really hard. For a while I wasn't sure. I knew if I had to tell the folks it would be the end of me being a part of the family." She paused. "I thought a lot about whether it was worth it."

"Telling them?"

"Living," Kerry answered briefly.

Mike turned and looked at her with a shocked expression.

Kerry looked back at him. "You have no idea what it's like," she said. "Being hated that much for something you can't change."

Mike was silent for a minute. Then he nodded. "You're right. I have no idea what that's like. I think...well, I know the folks thought you were just being stubborn, or rebelling or whatever." He frowned. "It was like, why did you have to do that?"

"For a long time I didn't. I lived with knowing I was going to have to say something sometime, but I was too scared to take the next step, until the day I met Dar." She studied her hands, her thumb rubbing against her ring. "Then I knew I couldn't pretend anymore. I had to fish or cut bait, as they say in the marina."

"Ang and I felt..." Mike paused, "well, we kind of felt like you picked Dar over us."

Kerry glanced up at him. "Actually what I did was pick me over the rest of you," she answered. "I decided my being happy was more important than my family, and you have no idea how much it hurt to have to make that choice."

Mike was quiet for a few minutes. They both looked up hearing the house door close, and saw Angie making her way toward them with one last box. "I'm glad you picked you, Ker," he said, in a serious tone.

"You're one of the few people I know who, honest to God, is happy."

"Hey you two." Angie thumped the box down. She was in jeans and a sweatshirt. "That's it. I'm over packing. Anything else goes to charity." She pushed the box into the truck and sat down on the tail. "Jesus, what was I thinking keeping all that stuff?"

"Eh." Kerry leaned back again, relaxing. "I have to admit, if I had to move now with all the toys and gear and what not Dar and I have, I probably would need to hire a moving company myself. So are we ready to get this stuff over to Mom's? I need some time to get changed for the shindig tonight."

"You going like that?" Angie pulled one knee up and wrapped her hands around it. "I have to bring the camera for Mom's face if you do."

Kerry considered it, then a cool draft hit her between the shoulder blades and she looked up at the sun. "Nah." She decided. "I'll throw a sleeved shirt on. I'm going to freeze my ass off if I don't and it's not worth the freak out." She got up and went to the other side of the truck, putting her hands on the side and vaulting over it to land with some grace on the other side.

"Okay, we'll wait out here for you," Angie agreed.

Kerry raised her hand and waved as she trotted off toward the house, taking her gloves off and stuffing them in her belt as she went.

Angie leaned back against the wall of the truck and reviewed her pile of stuff. "Not that Mom's not going to freak out as it is, us pulling up in a pickup in jeans," she remarked. "But what the hell. Kerry didn't rebel until her late twenties, maybe it's our turn."

Mike eyed her dubiously. "You're not going to get a tattoo are you?"

His sister gave him a look.

"Just asking."

KERRY DROPPED INTO the swing in the solarium, glad to get off her feet after a day of hauling boxes. She looked around at the quiet, glass lined room, the air rich with the scent of carefully tended plants around the borders of the room.

It was quiet here, though she could hear voices through the door coming from the direction of the hall where she'd left her sister getting her things arranged in their new surroundings. Surely though this house was almost as familiar to her as her own since she knew Angie spent a lot of time here.

Ah well. Kerry let her head rest against the chain holding the swing up, savoring the peace around her. She'd always loved the solarium, and now as she leaned back and gazed around her, she allowed memories of scampering around hiding behind the plants surface in her mind's eye.

It smelled so green, and there was so much for a small child to look at-plants with their big leaves, and the rich potting soil, and the occasional ladybug to capture and watch.

She glanced back into one corner, where there were now rose bushes, but once had been a stand of potted pines, clustered in a clump she'd learned to worm her way into and which had provided a haven for her. She could still, to this day, remember the Christmas tree scent.

She stretched her arms out along the back of the wooden bench seat, and rocked back and forth a little, looking up as she heard footsteps to see her mother approaching. Inwardly she bit off a curse, not really wanting to face an interaction with her at the moment.

"Ah, there you are, Kerrison," Cynthia Stuart said. "My goodness, what a lot of work you children did."

"It was," Kerry had to agree, as her mother seated herself on the bench across from her. "But we ended up with a lot of stuff that can go to charity, and I think Angie's happy to have her things the way she likes them."

Her mother smiled. "I think so too. I have to say it will be nice to have at least one of you back in the house. It's been so quiet."

Kerry relaxed a trifle. "You should have seen us last night. We ended up locking Mike in the truck and having a pillow fight in the living room. Sure you want that much excitement around?"

"Did you really?" her mother asked. "My goodness and you're all grown up."

"We're still brothers and sisters." A smile crossed Kerry's face. "We had fun."

"It certainly sounds like it," Cynthia said. "I'm very glad you have had some time to spend with Angela and Michael. I know they have both missed you."

"I'm glad too," Kerry answered.

Her mother cleared her throat. "So you're speaking at the reunion tonight?"

Kerry nodded. "They asked me to. I wasn't going to go."

"Why not? After all, you were going to be here this week."

"I just didn't want to." She'd gotten the invitation. Dar had even encouraged her to go, and had said she'd work around the Europe schedule to be there if Kerry wanted to, and wanted her there. "I don't much like being the celebrity freak show, I guess."

Her mother straightened. "Oh, but surely that's not the..." She paused, and frowned.

That, at least, made Kerry smile, if only a bit wryly. "Anyway, I'll do the speech then we're going out to the pub for dinner," she said. "So I guess we should get back to Angie's old place so I can change." She stood up, stretching her body out and reaching back to free her shortened hair from her polo shirt collar.

"Ah, yes of course," her mother said, rising hastily. "We thought perhaps we could all have brunch here tomorrow. Would that fit in your schedule?"

Kerry's ears twitched. "Sure," she answered, after a moment's hesitation. "I think we're done with packing. What time?"

Her mother looked pleased. "Eleven, I believe," she said. "Just the family, really. I want to get a chance to chat with all of you alone."

Uh oh. Kerry nodded. "Sounds like fun," she answered, reasoning that at least if they all were there, the subject could hardly be anything relating to her, personally. "Well, let me get going." She eased past her mother and ducked under an errant limb, heading back into the hall where she could see her brother standing.

"Kerrison?"

Urg. Kerry paused and turned, giving her mother a questioning look.

"I do like that haircut on you. It frames your face very nicely."

Kerry ran her fingers through the layers near her eyes and produced a brief grin. "Thanks. It got so hot this summer I had to get rid of some of it. I like it, though. I may keep it this way." She turned and slipped out of the door and back into the lit entryway, where Angie was now also waiting for her. "Hey. Ready to go?"

Angie glanced past her to see their mother emerging, and then gave her sister a wry look. "Ready if you are." She slid her small clasp purse under her arm. "Mom, see you tomorrow."

Cynthia waggled her fingers at them, as they stood together for a minute. "So nice to see the three of you together. We must get some pictures at brunch."

They got out the door, and Kerry realized a second later that not bringing a jacket wasn't the brightest thing she'd ever done. The cool air blew right through her polo shirt, and she was really glad she'd decided against wearing the tank. "Brr." She rubbed her arms with her hands. "Where'd the damn sun go?"

Mike snorted. "Boy did your blood thin."

Kerry didn't deny it. "Hey, it was ninety three degrees when I left," she protested. "I'm used to walking outside in a bathing suit in September." She scooted ahead of them and unlocked the truck door, sliding inside and shutting it after her to block the wind.

Angie got in the passenger seat, laughing, and Mike slid in the jump seat also chuckling. "It must be so bizarre not to have winter." Angie shut the door as Kerry started the engine. "I can't imagine it"

"We have winter." Kerry put the truck in gear and pulled around the big stately driveway. "We have at least two days where it drops below sixty. Dar and I make hot chocolate and wear our footie pajamas." She turned and waited for the big iron gates to open, and then eased out onto the road, looking both ways first. "I don't miss it. I like not having to think about putting layers of clothing on and being able to go swimming at midnight the whole year."

"Do you? " Mike poked his head over the seat. "Go swimming at midnight?"

Kerry had stopped at a traffic light, and now she turned and looked at him. "Yeah," she admitted. "When we get home from work sometimes, or in the ocean when we're down at the cabin. We've got a little cove all to ourselves."

"You guys swim naked?"

"MIKE!" Angie slapped him. "Of course they don't!"

"Well, actually we do." The light changed, and Kerry moved forward. "Sometimes," she answered, smothering a grin as she heard Angie nearly swallow her tongue while her brother chortled with glee. "Rebellion has its good points, y'know."

"Oh my god."

"Sweet!"

THE SALES PITCH over, it was time to get down to the real business.

"We understand that there are companies here with a lot more built out infrastructure." Dar faced the room, holding the remote for her presentation laptop in her right hand. "So your likely question for us is, how in the hell are we going to support this application until we can catch up."

Sir Melthon grunted.

"It's a good question." Dar clicked the control, and her laptop obediently responded with a lively, pulsing display, projected against a silver cased, insanely expensive screen set up at the far end of the table. It displayed a reasonably scaled diagram of their global network, long lines of green and blue tracing across the planet.

"Animated, eh. At least that's more interesting than the last idiots," Sir Melthon interrupted, "bloody boring the lot of them. You put me to sleep, woman, and you can go sell your slides out on the street."

"That's live, isn't it, Dar?" Alastair remarked from his seat next to Sir Melthon, drawing both the magnate's attention and that of the two men on the other side of him that had been introduced as his business leaders for the project. "That screen there?"

"Live?" One of the men leaned forward. "Do you mean to say that's showing a real time view of something?" He looked around. "What the devil are you connected to?"

"It is," Dar responded. "This is a reflection of the main operations console at our commercial headquarters in Miami, Florida." She went on. "I have a cellular link-up to our international gateway and we're backhauling the signal from there."

The man studied her. "Sorry, go on," he murmured.

She reviewed the screen. "As you can see, we are very built-out in North America, but we also have a significant presence in South America, India, Africa, and the Far East."

The man got up and walked around to get closer to the screen.

"We do have a basic set of pipes in Europe." Dar manipulated the control and a set of green lines grew brighter, across the European continent. "But since we size the infrastructure to the business, we haven't upgraded the port speed to provide a high capacity full mesh. Yet."

The man looked at her. "How long will it take you to do that?" he asked, sharply.

Dar studied the screen for a moment. "Two months," she answered.

"That's not possible," the other man next to Sir Melthon said. "We know it isn't, I'm not being a fly in the ointment here," he said, as Dar turned toward him. "We did a study to put our own network in. It would take over a year, and that's why we're looking to outsource."

"Two months, " Dar repeated, unmoved. "We have a certain degree of leverage."

The man looked at Sir Melthon, and shook his head.

"McLean, is this rot?" Melthon turned his head and peered at Alistair. "I don't need a load of hot air. I have a wife for that."

Alastair didn't turn a hair. "Nah," he said. "If Dar says two months, it's two months, and probably earlier," he said. "She rebuilt an entire networking center in one night, y'know. Reliable as the day is long."

The magnate snorted. "You willing to lay a bet on that?" he asked. "You do it in time or the whole deal is off, how's that for a bet?"

"Sure." The genial Texan didn't so much as glance at Dar. "But I'll tell you what, we do it in two months, and you toss in a contract for the rest of your network. How's that for a bet?"

Dar stood quietly waiting, gaining a new appreciation for her boss's always surprising wheeling and dealing side she didn't get to see very often. Usually she was pulling Alastair's ass out of the fire. This time, they were both playing a somewhat dangerous game of poker that was making the sales reps eyes bug out.

Sir Melthon studied the gray haired man sitting next to him, his hands resting relaxed on the table.

"Sir," the man next to him murmured, "this sounds dangerous."

"Hah!" the magnate barked suddenly. "Damn straight it does." He turned to Dar. "Well, smart mouthed woman, get to talking. We've got a bet on." He held a hand out to Alastair. "Good enough for you, McLean?"

"Absolutely." Alastair took his hand and gripped it firmly. "Dar? You were saying?"

Everyone turned back to Dar, and she collected her train of thought looking back at the screen. "As I was saying, the question is, how do we support this project until I can upgrade those pipes?" She illuminated two other lines, a pulsing blue one that landed in London, and another in Germany, with a heavy tracing of smaller, green lines between them. "Here's how."

"Wait." The man still standing near the screen held up a hand.

"This is our premier product. We can't rely on a single line back to the States. What if it goes down? Even for...ah...two months?" His voice expressed extreme doubt.

Dar walked over to her laptop and put the control down, trading it for her keyboard which she studied for a moment before she started typing. "Here's the average response time across that circuit to our London hub." She enhanced the display, showing the statistics of the two links. "Here's what happens when it goes down." She executed a few keystrokes, and the blue line landing in London went dark.

"B..." One of Dar's own sales reps started to stand up.

The rest of the map fluttered, and then the pulsing settled down, the link into Germany growing brighter, and the lacing of green lines expanding to take up the slack. The response time counter, in its small box, remained steady.

Dar let the silence go on for a moment, and then smiled. "I like to sleep at night." She reopened the link and it surged back into place, the map giving that little flutter again. She glanced over at Sir Melthon, catching him with his jaw slightly open. He scowled at her and shut his mouth with a click. "So our proposal is that we will support your infrastructure from our Miami offices until a local hub is in place."

"With local staff?" The man near the screen rallied weakly.

"Of course," Alastair said. "Do you know how much it costs to relocate people from Oklahoma?" He chuckled. "I've told the boys here to get ready to move fast, and bring in as many good people as they can find."

"Hmph."

"We're expecting to start up a support center with at least one hundred people," David spoke up. "And Francois here is handling the logistics and distribution facility near Nantes."

The men looked at Francois, who merely nodded, keeping his fingers pressed against his lip.

"Hah!" Sir Melthon barked again. "What a pack of smart alecks you lot are." He turned to Alastair. "Lunch. Then we'll get down to pen and paper. I've had enough egghead chatter for the morning." He stood up and headed for the door, clearly expecting them to follow.

Dar chuckled and went to her laptop to shut it down. "You know what this business is like sometimes Hans?"

"Pig's tail soup," he answered succinctly. "But he does like you, of that I am sure," he reassured her. "It is mostly an act, yes? That Lord of the British empire loudness."

Dar closed the lid on the machine. "Wait until he sees Alastair's contract terms," she advised him. "That's mostly an act too, that Texas good old boy stuff. "

"Ah." Hans got up and joined her as they walked to the door, the last to exit the room. "So it seems with the big shots acting, the truth of the situation then depends on you."

Dar held the door and smiled. "We'll soon find out."

"That we will."

KERRY TOWELED HER hair dry and paused in front of the bathroom mirror, regarding her reflection. She hung the towel around her neck and leaned on the marble countertop, wrestling with that age old question of women everywhere.

What to wear.

Normally, it wasn't much of an issue for her. She had work clothes, and she had casual clothes, and she had scroungy old rags in abundance. Twice as many as Dar, in fact, and she didn't often spend much time deciding which category to put on.

However, Kerry studied the pale, green eyes in the mirror.

"I think I feel like being a grown up tonight," she announced, putting aside the fleeting notion of wearing jeans to her speech. She finished drying herself off and put on her underwear, leaving the bathroom and crossing the carpet to where she'd laid out her choices.

Without hesitation, she lifted up the crisply pressed suit and hooked the hanger on the silent butler, sliding the jacket off and laying it across the seat as she loosened the silk, ice blue shirt and prepared to slip it over her shoulders.

A soft knock at the door made her eye the closed panel with some wariness. "Yes?"

"It's me," Angie's voice answered.

Slipping the shirt on, Kerry started buttoning the sleeves. "C'mon in." She glanced over as her sister entered, shutting the door behind her. "Hey."

"Hey." Angie dropped down onto the bed, leaning on one hand. "That's a nice blouse," she said. "So you're not going to go strapless?"

"No." Kerry smiled, finishing her sleeves and fastening the front closed. "I decided to present my professional side. Aside from not wanting to come off as a jerk, I always feel like I have a responsibility to encourage girls into IT."

"Really?" Angie's brows lifted. "Is it really that much a guy's world?"

Kerry removed her teal skirt from its hanger and stepped into it. "Well..." She tucked her shirt in and buttoned the skirt, then buckled the leather belt. "Yeah, it is," she admitted. "I think Dar is one of the few female CIO's, and our technical group is mostly guys, though we do try to recruit women."

"Try?"

Kerry went to her bag and removed her jewelry case. "Believe it or not, for some reason, women don't seem to gravitate to infrastructure." She took out a pair of favorite earrings and started to put them on. "I've seen great women programmers, project managers, service delivery reps, you name it. But high tech plumbers? Not so common."

Angie got up and came over, peeking at the earrings. "Ker, those are gorgeous," she said. "Can I see the other one?"

Her sister handed it over. She then retrieved her necklace and ring from the dresser and slid them into place. She brushed her hair out, glancing briefly in the mirror as the already drying, shortened strands settled around her face. "Sure is nice not to have to blow dry this stuff all the time."

"You like it short?"

Kerry took back the proffered earring and inserted it. "Yeah." She studied her reflection, and smiled. "I think it looks more sophisticated. Dar likes it. I keep trying to get her to cut her hair short, but she thinks she'll look like a punk."

"Mm." Angie got up and stood next to her. "Her hair's wavy, though. Your hair is straight. It might look weird unless it was really short," she pointed out. "I'm sure she doesn't want to look like a guy."

Kerry's eyebrow arched. She turned and looked at Angie. "Shaved bald she wouldn't look like a guy," she said, bluntly.

Her sister gave her a wry look.

Kerry made a face. "Sorry," she apologized. "I think I'm getting sensitive in my old age." She brushed her hair out again, feeling a little embarrassed. "Smack me."

"No way," Angie said immediately. "Are you kidding? I'm not hitting She-Ra. Not in this lifetime." She bumped Kerry with her shoulder. "Mind if I come along to the dinner? I know I wasn't in that class, but I'd love to hear you speak."

"I don't mind at all." Kerry was relieved. "I'd love the company." She finished her mild primping and reached for the jacket to her suit. "Thanks."

Angie followed her as she pulled the jacket on and tugged the lapels straight with an automatic gesture, reaching back to clear the short hairs in the back of her neck from the collar. "Is Mike meeting us after for dinner?"

"Actually..."

Kerry sensed a plot at hand. "Let me guess. He wants to come too."

"Well..." Her sister lifted both hands, as she watched Kerry slip into her mid heel shoes. "Why not? We know we don't have much time with you, Ker. Besides, if they start giving you a hard time, we'll gang up on them."

Kerry entertained herself with a mental vision of her siblings batting her old classmates around. She grinned. "Yeah sure, why not?" she said. "Let's go and get this over with." She clipped her Palm in its case to her belt and picked up the keys to the pickup. "Wanna drive?"

Angie chuckled, and then cleared her throat as they headed for the stairs. "Maybe."

KERRY FOLDED HER hands over her stomach and watched as the once familiar landscape whipped by, only half listening to her brother's chatter from the jump seat behind her. In her mind, she ran over what she might say at the dinner, reviewing a few different approaches depending on the reception she was given.

It would be the easiest if everything was at face value. She could talk about what was needed to enter the business world, and ramble on about the state of the technical industry for any length of time without any danger of either scandalizing anyone or being completely understood.

She scratched her nose, wrinkling the bridge of it a little as she acknowledged how stuffy and jaded that sounded even in the privacy of her own mind. It was true, though, that the world she worked in was full of over arching concepts and buzzwords that tried to describe in layman's terms what its functions were. Most of the time it ended up sounding like dystopian poetry.

"So Ker." Mike got her attention back. "You think this is a publicity stunt or something?"

On the other hand, Kerry smiled grimly, her brother had probably spoken aloud what her own primary suspicion was, that her school, always in search of funding, had used the opportunity of its class reunion to gain some press in an otherwise slow year.

What was that about any publicity being good publicity?

"Maybe," Kerry said. "I don't see what it really gets them though, except mention in the paper when the paper covers me." She glanced at her sister. "Did you say the paper was going to be there?"

"Of course," Angie said. She slowed, and then turned onto a busier road. "I'm surprised they didn't call the house looking for you, "she added. "A half dozen other people did."

Kerry blinked. "Huh? They did? Who?"

"Guys wanting dates. We told them off," Mike answered for her, reaching across the back of the seat and flicking Kerry on the back of her neck. "Then Oprah Winfrey called and we told her you were booked for the next two years already."

"Oh damn." Kerry had to laugh. "And here I really wanted to be on Oprah." She twiddled her thumbs a little. "Did I ever tell you guys that I got a call from Face the Nation after the hearing, wanting me to appear?"

"Oh my god you're kidding," Angie gasped. "They would have had a fit!"

"Face the Nation? They're used to weird political scandals." Kerry chuckled.

"Our parents," her sister clarified. "He hated that show."

"They roasted him the last time he was on it," Mike snorted. "Don't you remember that time, Kerry? I thought I sent you an email that he was going to be on. They nailed him on the offshore drilling crap he was supporting."

Kerry's brow creased a bit. "I must have been swamped with something," she admitted. "I don't remember seeing it. That's not something Dar and I usually watch." She spotted the beginning of the brick wall topped by wrought iron gating that marked her alma mater, and almost wished they would keep driving past now that it was here.

"Looks like it's busy." Angie eased the truck into the turn lane, reviewing the line of cars ahead of her. The truck was positively out of place, and she could see the people in the car ahead of her staring at it in their rearview mirror. "Can this go over the top of those little suckers?"

"Bet it can." Mike instigated immediately. "Creep up on that guy's bumper. Let's see if we can freak him out."

Kerry eyed her suddenly radical siblings. "What the heck's gotten into you two?"

"You're a bad influence," her brother informed her. "Everyone always said you would be." He reached over again and tugged Kerry's ear. "C'mon, you only live once. Let's get into trouble."

"Ah. Ah. ha!" Kerry grabbed his hand and held it. "It's not you two who'll get in trouble if we crash this thing. It's in my name," she pointed out. "Let's get inside. Then you can go around giving my old anything but pals wedgies if you want."

Angie chuckled. She eased the truck forward as the line moved, holding down the brake, and then giving the engine just enough gas to startle the car in front of her. "Vroom."

Kerry covered her eyes as she heard the crunch of the tires. She started thinking of what possible story she could come up with to explain why she'd totaled a rental car. At least Dar would probably find it funny. After no further sounds, she peeked out from between her fingers to see the car ahead of them pulling out of line, and heading off down the street. "What the heck?"

"We scared them," Mike said contentedly. "Weenie!"

Angie pulled the truck up to the next car in line. "Want to see if I can do that again?" she asked. "Get us through this queue in no time."

"Holy crap," Kerry sighed. "No, just chill, okay? Remember, you do live here. I get to go home in a day or so and I don't have to hear all the gossip."

"Screw that," Mike said. "If they want something to talk about, let's give them something. Otherwise they'll make stuff up about you and you know it. I'd rather have them saying we shoved some Lexus into the wall."

The line started moving again, much to Kerry's relief, and she rested her elbow on the doorframe as they made the turn into the entrance of the school and through the tall arched gates.

Mixed memories. She studied the name in the scrollwork as they went under it. She hadn't really disliked school, and she'd been more or less successful at navigating its social labyrinths since she'd been old enough to know better when she'd started attending.

Being Roger Stuart's oldest had brought both positive and negative attention, and now when she looked back on all the little things, the parties and invites, the snubs and the suck ups, she was content to acknowledge that, all in all, it could have been worse.

"Did Dar go to any type of...ah..."Angie paused. "No, probably not, huh?"

Kerry smiled. "Just regular school," she said. "But it wouldn't have mattered, I don't think. She's brilliant. They could never keep up with her down there, and I doubt they could have here either." She paused as Angie pulled up to the attendant, who peered inside with a doubtful expression. "Hi there. Is this Dominos Pizza?"

Mike fell back in the jump seat, chortling.

"Can I get a pepperoni and extra cheese?" Kerry continued pleasantly as the man frowned. "With a two liter of coke?"

"Ma'am, I don't think..." He hesitated, thrown off by the sport truck filled with unexpectedly well dressed people. "Ah..."

Angie removed the invitation from the sunshield and handed it to him. "Maybe this helps," she said. "Before my sister tells you we're hauling fertilizer for the dance hall."

The man looked at the invitation, then looked back at them. "Ah," he said. "No problem." He pointed to the left. "Valet parking's over there, ladies."

"Hey!" Mike popped his head up again. "Watch who you call lady, bub!"

"Thanks." Angie closed the window and got the truck moving before they could cause more chaos. "And you say **we're** causing trouble? Ker, you're the one who was going to show up in a tank top and jeans."

"Shoulda." Kerry chuckled, as they swung around the big, paved circle to the portal cachet, where valets were milling around, taking care of the well kept, expensive cars being dropped off. She had a moment to look at the crowd before it was their turn, her eyes spotting one or two people she was pretty sure she knew already.

Heads turned as the pickup pulled into the valet stand, and she was out of time to think about it. Kerry waited for the valet to hesitantly approach, then she opened the door from the inside and gathered herself to get out. "Okay, kids. Let's go."

As the door opened, the buzz of the crowd got louder, and she got that feeling she often did when she was about to enter a company they were acquiring and face the person she'd been once for the first time. She gave the valet a brief smile and turned to flip the seat forward so Mike could get out. "Evening."

"Ma'am." The valet reacted to her appearance and adjusted his attitude from seeing the truck. "Welcome to the homecoming."

Kerry saw heads turning nearby, and her peripheral view caught the flash of a camera. "Thanks," she said, as Angie came around to join them, and they walked as a group toward the steps. "Ready or not, here we come."

"Can I tell everyone I'm an alumnus too?" Mike asked.

"It's an all girl's school." Angie poked him. "What are you going to tell them, you had a sex change?"

Mike grinned evilly.

"Had to suggest that, didn't you?" Kerry said under her breath, as she saw a group of older women start in their direction. She recognized several as once upon a time teachers, and the lady in front, incredibly still there, as the headmistress in charge.

"Ms. Hauderthorn's coming right at you," Angie whispered. "What a witch! She hated me!"

Kerry plastered a determined grin on her face. "Remind me to tell you later why." She gave herself a little shake, and squared her shoulders. "But not until we've both had a beer."

Chapter Six

"DAR?"

Dar opened her eyes, to see Alastair standing in front of her chair, holding out a glass. "What is that?" she asked, eyeing the dark liquid with some suspicion.

"Irish coffee," he said. "I figured you could use it."

Coffee. Dar took the offered mug without further preamble, and sipped gingerly from it. "Thanks. Time lag's still kicking my ass."

Alastair took a seat next to her. They were in a quiet lounge off the main meeting space, the soft buzz of conversation trickling in through the adjoining door. "Well, lady, it's late in anyone's time zone." He glanced at the door. "But I think we're close."

Dar checked her watch, and winced. "1:00 a.m. I sure as hell hope so." She stretched her legs out and crossed them. "Is he done asking me questions?"

Her boss brought one foot up onto its opposite knee and rested his hands on his ankle. "I think so. Actually I think he's more tired of getting your answers so I think he's decided to beat me over the head with the terms again."

"He's tough."

Alastair chuckled. "They all are. No one in there wants to give money to anyone, least of all a bunch of smartass Yanks. I think our boys here are starting to piddle."

Dar snorted.

"McLean!"

"Ah," Alastair sighed. "Hey, they're bringing in some dinner. C'mon, maybe if we go in there together he'll settle down some." He patted Dar on the arm.

"Sure." Dar obligingly got up. "I was out here because I was bored listening to all the sales crap," she said, as she followed the older man toward the double doors. She kept her coffee with her, though, sipping it as they entered the big conference room where Sir Melthon and his team, and their sales reps were going at it.

At this point, she figured, it was a chest beating contest. She had no intention of bruising her own infrastructure, so she'd been sitting around merely waiting for a technical question to come up since she'd already gone over their plan four times and had no intention of doing it a fifth.

"Right." Sir Melthon looked up as they entered. "Ah, there you are, and your little girl too."

Alastair stopped in his tracks, turned, and looked Dar up and down. He then turned back to the magnate. "Sir Melthon? I know this lady's father, and let me tell you neither you, nor I want to make that statement even in jest."

"None of that now, just get over here." Melthon waved a hand at them. "I want..."

"I mean that!" Alastair suddenly raised his voice in a loud bark, cutting off all other conversation and making himself the sudden, startling center of attention. After a moment of silence, "I expect my staff to be treated with the same respect we show to yours."

Sir Melthon leaned back in his chair and studied him. "You do say?"

Alastair stared back at him. "Damned right I do say."

Dar stood quietly, sipping her coffee, not wanting to do anything to either escalate or downplay the moment. It went against her instincts to allow anyone to take her part the way her boss was doing, but she was smart enough to know there were dynamics here her usual bull-in-a-china shop style would not mesh with.

Sir Melthon pondered a moment. "Well, then all right." He shrugged. "Sorry about that. Didn't think you were the sensitive type." He directed the last comment at Dar.

"I'm not." Dar put her cup down and settled into a soft leather seat across from him. "But Alastair is right. I'm the Chief Information Officer of the company. If you sign on, I hold your family jewels right here." She held up her hand and crooked the fingers. "If you don't respect me, how can you trust me not to send your business to hell, or get bored someday and reroute your data stream to Iran?"

Melthon and his team stared at her, as Alastair took a seat next to Dar. "Is that a threat?" the magnate asked, in a splutter. "McLean, what is this?"

"Now, I am sure," Francois started to break in hurriedly, stopping when Alastair held his hand up.

"This is who we are." Alastair folded his hands on the table. "So let me tell you now, if you can't deal with my people being anything other than white bread old men like me tell me now, and we'll just cut the deck and go home. I'm not making us both miserable signing a contract with you." He gazed steadily across at the magnate, his blue eyes open and guileless. "I do mean that."

Melthon actually gaped at him.

"You are one fish, in my very, very big ocean," Alastair went on placidly.

Even Dar was hard pressed not to react, keeping her eyebrows in their customary places and concentrating on not letting her eyes widen. She leaned back in her chair and laced her fingers together instead, appreciating for, perhaps, the first time how hardball her boss was willing to be when he felt he needed to.

Hans was watching both men, with a fascinated expression as he tapped his fingers on the table, everyone else in the room was seemingly frozen in place.

Finally Melthon turned and looked at Dar. "I don't like women in business!" He thumped his fist on the table.

Dar cocked her head, looking down at herself before she looked back up at him. "Too bad," she said. "I'm not going to change into a man anytime soon. Sorry."

"Hah!" Melthon turned back to Alastair. "She'll get married on you. See if she doesn't, McLean! Then what?"

Alastair smiled. "Dar's already married," he said. "Hasn't been an issue."

"And have brats! You know how they are!" Melthon shot right back.

Alastair turned and looked at Dar, one brow edging up a trifle.

"We have a dog," Dar could see the twinkle in his eyes. "The mainframe will have kids before I will." She leaned forward and picked up her cup. "Besides, can you imagine there being two of me?"

"No," her boss replied instantly. "I can't afford two of you. My heart would give out." He turned back to Sir Melthon. "So what's it to be? It's late, you know. We can call it off now and I can get my people some rest before we move on to the next opportunity."

Melthon eyed him shrewdly. "You've got brass ones," he said. "This is not a small contract."

"It isn't," Alastair agreed. "It's got huge potential for us, and I think we can do a good job for you. But I'm not interested if it exposes my people, especially one of our single most valuable resources to being treated like an afterthought. It's not worth it to me."

"Indeed."

"Yup."

The magnate leaned back, most of his irascible attitude fading. "Valuing people is very old fashioned, you know. In this day and age, we are all expendable, or so they say."

"People who say that are the only expendable ones," Alastair replied quietly. "I've lived long enough in this business to have learned that the hard way."

After a moment's silence, Melthon nodded. "All right then. Fair enough," he said. "I have long been accused by many..." he turned and deliberately looked at Hans, who smiled, "of being old fashioned myself. I didn't think I'd find an American who had any interest in anything but the dollar. You surprise me, McLean."

"The missus says that on occasion to me too," Alastair replied. "But that usually involves tacky Mexican jewelry and never comes with good brandy like this." He held up his glass, tipping it slightly in Sir Melthon's direction.

The magnate burst into laughter. He lifted his own cup and inclined it. "We will do business, McLean. I like a man who knows how to stand up for himself." He glanced aside. "And for a woman!"

The sales execs relaxed and so did Sir Methon's minions, as nicely tuxedoed servers entered from the far door with mahogany serving trays. The first one of them paused and looked at the table, timidly eyeing the magnate before moving any further.

"Bring that in." Their host waved a hand. "Bring that, and bring me a couple bottles of that rotgut my godson forced on me the other week. Might as well get rid of it with this lot."

Dar eased back into her chair and drank her cooling coffee, the rich taste of the liquor in it burning her stomach as it settled. She watched the servers bustle around putting out plates and dishes and only after the noise in the room dispelled some of the tension did she glance over at Alastair.

Solemnly, he winked at her.

Dar lifted her mug up and behind it, poked the tip of her tongue out at him. She then glanced at her watch, and unclipped her PDA, opening it and tapping on the screen with the stylus.

Hey Ker.

You missed an eyeball busting moment here. It's possible I might not leave this place tonight without kissing Alastair.

Hope your speech is knocking them dead. Buy your family a beer for me when it's all over with and make sure someone took pictures.

DD

"So."

Dar closed the Palm and turned to find Sir Melthon now sitting in the seat right next to her. "So," she repeated.

"My godson there," the magnate spoke conversationally, as though the preceding standoff with Alastair had never happened. "Tells me you can do some very tricky stuff. Is that on the up and up?"

Dar peered over at Hans, who studiously avoided her gaze. "Maybe. We have some very proprietary technology that I developed, to help us provide the best services to our customers. If that's what he meant, then yes. "

Her PDA beeped. Dar resisted the urge to look at it while she waited for the magnate to continue, aware of someone putting a plate down in front of her on the table.

"You own it then, eh?" Melthon asked.

"He owns it." Dar indicated Alastair, who was sitting by quietly watching and listening. "Or, more to the point, ILS owns it because I developed it on their time and their gear."

"Ah hah." Melthon got up and went back around the table. "All right, let's get a bite to eat, and then we'll carry on," he said. "Hope none of you enlightened Americans are vegetarians." He looked around the table, his bushy eyebrows hiking.

Dar studied the slab of beef in front of her. "Looks good to me." She put the PDA down on the table and casually flipped it open. "Got any catsup?"

The men across the table stopped, and stared at her.

"Just kidding." Dar smiled. She waited for them to start working on their plates again before she looked down at the Palm.

Get pictures. What the heck, give him a kiss for me too. I am about to go on stage and I've already had two confrontations with women older than my mother, and just about kept my brother from kicking one of them in the shins. If I end up in jail, will you come home and bail me out?

Wish you were here. I have a headache.

K.

"Excuse me." Dar got up and tucked the PDA into her hand. "I need to make a phone call." She ducked past the chair next to her and headed for the small antechamber, pulling her cell phone out as she cleared the door and keying the speed dial without looking.

It rang twice, then picked up. "Hey."

"Hey." Kerry's voice sounded stressed, but also wry. "Was the whining that loud?"

"Tell me some old witch gave you a hard time. What's her name? I'll hack into her pension and send it to the ASPCA," Dar said. "I knew I should have co-opted you out of this."

After a brief pause, Kerry chuckled. "Nah, it's not that bad really," she demurred. "I ran into a few of my old teachers, that's all." She paused. "And..."

Ah.

"I don't know. I just want to get out of here," Kerry admitted, in a quieter voice. "It's weirding me out. Too many memories."

Dar exhaled, sensing the turmoil. "Hang in there," she said. "One more day, Ker. Just blow through this and go have a plate of wings and a beer. I'll be there with you in spirit."

There was a brief pause on the other end. "Know something?" Kerry finally said. "When I get to Europe, I'm going to buy you a tiara."

Dar's nostrils flared and her eyes widened. "Huh?"

"You rule my world. Gotta go, sweetie. Love you." Kerry hung up, leaving a faint echo behind her.

Dar tapped her cell phone against her jaw before she turned to head back into the meeting room. "I'd look stupid as hell in one of those," she sighed. "But I'd love to see her try it."

"WAS THAT DAR?" Angie asked, leaning against an unused podium as they waited behind the small stage.

"Yeah." Kerry tucked her cell phone away. "How'd you know?" She glanced up in question.

"You're smiling," her sister replied. "I haven't seen you do that all night." She put a sympathetic hand on Kerry's back. "Listen, I'm really sorry I got you into this," she added, softly. "I didn't think it would be such a big deal."

"Neither did I, but I probably should have." Kerry admitted. "Anyway, we're here now. I just want to get it done."

Angie patted her shoulder. "Just think about the brewpub. If it gets too obnoxious out there, I'll call Mike and have him moon the crowd and we can escape out the back."

The thought was startlingly appealing. Kerry smothered a grin, and ran her fingers through her hair again, feeling the dryness in the back of her mouth and wishing she had a tall glass of ice tea. "We're a family full of scandal, huh?"

"Hey, it beats reading about the flower show in tomorrow's paper."

"Yeah, well." Kerry sighed, as she spotted one of the event organizers heading her way through the small backstage area. She straightened up and twitched her sleeves out a little, taking a deep breath and exhaling it as she'd often seen Dar do before she presented. "Are we ready?"

The woman hesitated, glancing over her shoulder. "I think we are. Everyone's seated."

Kerry felt her nerves settle, as the waiting was over and now, at least, she could do it and get it over with. "Okay, let's go then," she said. "Hope I don't cause a riot."

The organizer's face twitched. "Let me go introduce you and...oh."

Kerry brushed by her. "You don't need to. I'll take it from here." She unabashedly stole a page from Dar's 'do the unexpected' book and slipped past the curtains, emerging into a pool of typically wishy-washy school auditorium lighting.

She crossed to the small podium, mahogany wood and long worn with the forearms of decades of speakers before her, and rested her hands on it, simply standing there and waiting to be noticed.

It gave her a long few seconds to look out over the room. She'd last been in it for graduation, and her mind flashed back to long hours spent there listening to religious instruction and lectures on morality and her place in the world.

The sudden absurdity of the contrast made her smile, and she felt her shoulders relax as she let her eyes scan the crowd as they began to realize she was standing there. It was a full house, a mixture of current students, her old classmates, and teachers, and she allowed herself a moment of surprised gratification that at least someone wanted to hear whatever it was she had to say.

The buzz settled down quickly, as all eyes turned to her. Unlike Dar, however, Kerry didn't find this intimidating. "Good evening." She injected her voice into the room, making sure to project a quiet confidence she almost actually felt.

"My name is Kerrison Stuart." She hadn't consciously intended to use her real name, but as it came off her tongue, it sounded right. "Some of you know me. Some of you only know of me, and some of you wish you'd never heard of me, but since you asked me to speak here, you get what you get so let's get started."

She paused, and after a long moment of startled silence, the crowd applauded. "Mph," she muttered under her breath. "Can't be worse than that women in business seminar last year, now could it?"

Kerry waited for the noise to die down, and studied the crowd for a few beats. Then she removed the microphone from the podium and came around from behind it. "Putting aside what's mostly public knowledge about me, I'm going to take a minute to briefly introduce myself for the benefit of those of you who are wondering who the heck I am."

Angie watched from behind the curtain, bemused at the confident figure that had so recently been nervous and withdrawn back stage with her. She could see Kerry's profile, and her sister had seemingly transformed herself now that the moment was on her.

Kerry had always been funny that way. Shy and reserved, Angie remembered her keeping her own council when they were teenagers. Part of that had been their parents, of course. By then Kerry had gone through the early stages of questioning their father and suffered the consequences.

Part of it hadn't been though. Kerry had once told her that it was too bad she understood as much as she did. That she'd have been a happier person if she'd been dumber. At the time Angie had thought she was being dissed, but now, knowing her sister a little better, she'd come to realize that it was just the truth.

Just the truth, that Kerry was smart, and though she didn't want to see or admit it, she had their father's calculating shrewdness and a certain toughness that she could hear echoing in Kerry's voice when she probably wasn't even aware of it.

Angie sighed. She and Michael had been 'the children', but Kerry had always been something special to their father. Aside from being smart, and good looking, girl or not, she'd been his firstborn and no matter how rough he'd made it on her, and no matter how awful things had gotten at the end, there were parts of him that had been proud of her.

Seeing her here, now-in front of this crowd-Angie knew he'd be proud of her again.

"So now that we're past the fact that I went to school here, and lived in town most of my life, let me tell you what it is I do now." Kerry paused and considered, aware of all the eyes on her. "The company I work for is ILS. We're the largest IT services company in the world."

Angie blinked a little. She hadn't known that, though she knew Kerry's company was large and she'd spent a few minutes reading about it on ILS's website when she'd hunted down their public filings. Seeing Kerry's name in them had seemed very weird, almost like she was reading about a stranger.

With a shake of her head, she turned her attention back to the stage.

"I'm glad I've gotten a chance to use the education I started here, and continued in college in the work I do now. " Kerry was saying. "As Operations Vice President, I've had the opportunity to take what I learned and apply it in an industry that engages me mentally, and provides me with an exciting work environment that I'm happy to go back to every day."

Kerry paused, evaluating the crowd. "So now that I got that far, any questions?" she prompted, seeing the startled reaction from her old instructors. The crowd didn't respond at first, and she felt a wry grin trying to appear. "C'mon," she said. "I can think of one question I know someone out there wants to ask."

Angie stifled a laugh, covering her mouth with one hand as she heard the audience react, and a low hoot, definitively male, she knew was their brother.

Kerry heard it too. She managed to suppress a grin, then she turned as she saw first one, then a few hesitant hands go up. Questions were a risk. She figured she'd probably get at least one that would make her wish she hadn't done it, but Dar had been right. The crowd knew more about her than she did about them, and she wasn't in the mood to preach the IT line tonight. "All right, go on."

One of the current students, a dark haired girl stood up. "What made you pick high tech?"

Delightful surprise. "Why did I pick high tech?" Kerry repeated the question into the microphone. "Well." She thought about it. "It was a lot sexier than law and it was like being on the frontier of something really new."

Another hand went up. "How much money is there in that?"

Even more delightful. Kerry smiled. "In my job specifically or in the tech industry?" she replied. "As I was telling my mother the other night, my compensation is public knowledge." She felt the slightly startled reaction. "Our executive salary structure is equal or better than the industry average." Her eyes twinkled a little. "But in terms of high technology, our lowest entry level is at least twice what the minimum wage is."

"Not really something you find listed in exciting careers though," the girl suggested.

Kerry shrugged one shoulder. "Depends on how you look at it. We usually call the line teams button down blue collar staff because they do things like set up machines and run cabling, but they also qualify for mortgages and drive nice cars."

Another figure lifted a hand, this time older, one of her classmates. Kerry recognized her and almost ignored the motion.   Fairness overcame her though, and she turned and acknowledged it.

"Do you ever get tired of people making comments about you sleeping your way to the top?" the woman asked, making heads turn toward her in surprise.

Ah, yes. Kerry resisted the urge to throw the microphone at her. "C'mon, Stacey. Do you really think people say that to my face?" she asked, above the sudden murmur in the room. "Let me tell you something about what I do, and who I do it for. You can get a job like mine by sleeping with the boss, but you can't keep it that way in a competitive business like ours. "

One of the event organizers was heading purposefully down the aisle toward her old classmate. Kerry caught her eye and lifted a hand, waving her off. "Please, I've had tougher questions over croissants in Vermont."

The woman slowed, and hesitated, as the crowd looked around, and then back at Kerry with gathering interest. "We expect people to be respectful." She glared at the woman who had asked the question. "Or else we'll ask them to leave."

Kerry's heckler took a breath to answer, then the older woman's eyes narrowed and she put her hands on her hips and Stacey subsided. "Sorry about that. I was just asking a question," she apologized. "It's not like it's a deep dark secret," she paused, "these days."

Kerry's right brow lifted a little. She wondered what that was supposed to mean, then she saw her old teacher's face tighten in anger and realized the jibe possibly wasn't pointed at her.

Ah huh. She heard the crowd buzz, some of the current students snickering a little and it occurred to her that there might be some drama in the room that had nothing at all to do with her presence. Something Dar once said popped into her mind and she scanned the crowd thoughtfully.

Hm.

"It's always nice to see how our students mature," the organizer said. "Or not, as the case may be." She gave the room a severe look, before she returned to a small group of the older teachers and resumed her seat.

The murmurs died down. "You have to walk the walk," Kerry added, as her old adversary finally sat down and the attention swung back to her. "Besides, if it wasn't people saying that, they'd be saying my father got me the job. What's the difference?" she added, looking right at Stacey. "In the end, it doesn't matter how you get there, what matters is if you succeed," she said. "And I have."

Stacey looked away casually, ignoring her.

Another current student raised their hand. Kerry nodded at her. "Go on."

The blond girl stood. "Do you face a lot of bias when you deal with men in your same position?'

Kerry felt pretty good about this class, a lot better than she had about her own. "Sometimes," she answered candidly. "When I go out to consolidate a new account, I have to deal with that sometimes because that's usually an adversarial circumstance anyway and some people, both men and women, think they can take advantage of me."

She strolled around back to the podium. "If you decide to pursue a career though, you're going to face that pretty much anywhere. It's something you learn to deal with, and if you're smart you use it to your advantage."

"How?" the girl asked. "If people treat you without respect, how do you use that?"

Kerry leaned on the podium. "Let me tell you a little story," she said. "Maybe that will answer your question, because I wondered about that too, when I first started out."

"PENNY FOR YOUR thoughts, Dar?"

Dar looked up from her plate of beef. "Kerry's worth more than that," she answered Alastair candidly. "She's at her high school reunion tonight giving a speech."

Alastair's face squiggled between surprise and consternation. "Ah. Oh," he murmured. "Well, I'm sure she's having a good time."

Dar looked at him.

"Or maybe not," he said. "Did she have a tough time in school? I wasn't that fond of mine, now that I think of it."

"Christian all girls school," Dar said. "Actually, she's never spoken badly of it, but she's not that comfortable going back to her hometown after the last couple of times there, and she got roped into this speech at the last minute."

"Ahh." Alastair picked up his glass of red wine and swirled it a bit before he took a sip. "Yeah, she's had a tough time up there from what you said. Surprised you didn't go with her."

Dar paused in mid bite. She swallowed the bit of potato and cocked her head at him. "And miss this meeting?" she asked, in a quizzical tone. "I offered. Kerry told me to stop talking crazy."

Alastair smiled. "You know, I never figured you for a family woman, Dar, but you make a damn fine one," he said, putting his glass down and checking his watch. "Well, damn it all. Does this guy think people don't need to sleep? It's 2:00 a.m.!"

"Uh huh." Dar ate another bit of potato. "On the other hand, I'll be sick to my stomach if I fall asleep after I eat this so maybe staying up is better." She glanced across the table, where Sir Melthon was in consultation with his minions. "By the way, thanks for kicking him in the ass for me."

Her boss smiled as he neatly cut his steak into squares. "Figured I owed it to you," he said, in a conversational tone. "But you know, even if I didn't, I would have done it. Man was giving me an itch."

Dar frowned, her dark brows contracting across her forehead. "You owed me what?" she asked, puzzled. "Did I miss something?" She looked around, but the rest of the group was busy with their own dinners or talking amongst themselves–even Hans was leaning over talking to Sir Melthon in a low mutter.

"Ah well." Alastair chuckled softly. "Remember when that crazy feller Ankow was in our shorts?"

Dar snorted, and rolled her eyes. "Jackass."

"Mm," Alastair agreed. "But you know, I felt like I was the jackass in all that, Dar," he said. "I look back and I know I sat back and let you take heat you didn't deserve."

Dar blinked. "Well..."

Her boss looked over at her. "He was after me. And the only thing standing in his way was you."

Dar blinked again, caught utterly by surprise, and unsure of how to react.

"You could have given him what he wanted, Dar, and done well by it," Alastair said, his eyes watching her curiously. "Any particular reason you walked into a bear trap on my behalf?"

Was there? Dar felt a little bewildered by the question. "Alastair, it never occurred to me to do anything else," she muttered. "Besides, you asked me to help."

"I did. So you know, when I look back at that, and how you were treated at that meeting, I kick myself every single time."

Well. Dar ate a few pieces of her steak, and recalled that tense, angry few days when she'd been torn between the stress of the board's being prodded to fire her and her anxiety about Kerry, testifying at her father's hearing.

She paused, putting her fork down and taking a swallow of the wine that had been untouched in her glass. "You know, I almost walked away from it all in that meeting." She tasted the unfamiliar tang of the tannins on her tongue. "There was one minute there, when I almost said to hell with it."

"Glad you didn't," Alastair remarked.

"Me too." Dar smiled, and raised her glass toward him. "Alastair, you don't owe me anything. I just did what comes naturally to me."

Alastair lifted his glass and touched it to Dar's. "Exactly," he said. "I can't tell you how much of a pleasure it's been the last year or so getting to actually know you."

Unsure if that was a compliment or not, Dar decided to smile anyway. "Likewise." She covered her bases. "I just wish I'd seen my father kick his ass. I was incredibly pissed off that I missed that."

"Security cameras caught it," her boss said. "I'll send you copy." He winked at her, and went back to his steak.

Dar took another swallow of wine, deciding that her life was enduring an evening of new experiences. She only hoped Kerry's would turn out as pleasantly interesting.

"YOU KNOW, THE truth is that people don't get respect." Kerry moved around in front of the podium, taking her microphone with her as she closed in on the audience again. "Especially, if you grow up in the spotlight like I did. Everyone assumes the worst of you because in a quirky kind of way, that makes people feel better about themselves if they do, doesn't it?"

She scanned the crowd, finding a lot of very curious eyes mixed with those very full of disapproval. "So I knew that even before I started working for ILS," Kerry paused, and made eye contact with a few people, "I knew that before I left here."

Kerry walked over to one side of the stage. "I knew that, even though I was a good, smart student, and even though I went to college and got a degree, that no matter what I achieved, everyone would assume someone handed it to me on a plate."

The room had settled into silence.

"So I eventually decided that I couldn't worry about what other people thought. What mattered is what I thought about myself, and that's why I decided to leave here, leave my home and my family to try and achieve what would be success in my own eyes."

A hand lifted. Kerry pointed at the girl. "Go ahead."

"Couldn't you have done that here? Wouldn't it have been more impressive, if you had?"

Good question. "I might have been able to," Kerry conceded. "It would have been harder, staying here and being so close to everything that I felt was boxing me in. But the fact is I didn't."

She paused, and then continued. "What I did was take a job in the field of my major, in a city far away from home. It was scary," she said. "But the people who hired me had no idea who I was, only that I could speak English and construct compound sentences, so it was like starting from scratch in a way."

Another hand. "What job was it?"

"Manager of an IT department," Kerry said. "It was a small company, and I actually did well there until one day a much bigger company bought us." She nibbled her lower lip. "When that happened, the person in charge of their IT department came in and told me that we weren't wanted or needed, and we'd be getting pink slips in very short order."

The audience reacted, murmuring a little.

"In a way, that was pretty horrific," Kerry said. "But in a way, it's just reality. That's what it's like out there." She made eye contact again with a few of the watchers. "That does happen, every day. It's business. And one thing it meant to me was that I was being treated just like any other unwanted worker would have been. There was nothing personal about it."

It was hard not to smile as she said it, seeing she knew just how much of a lie they were both telling themselves at the time. "When you grow up in privilege like I did, like a lot of you did..." She paused meaningfully. "You don't expect that. You expect someone to come in and fix things don't you?'

She could tell at least some of them were thinking about it. It had taken her a long time to be able to. "So for me, it was a learning experience because I hadn't faced that kind of situation before."

"What did you do?" the same girl asked. "Go to another company?"

"Well." Kerry smothered a grin. "Not exactly. I worked hard to make the transition less painful for the people working for me. I wasn't worried about myself, but there were people there who really were depending week to week on that job to survive."

"Wait, wait." Her old friend stood up again, glancing behind her at the headmistress, before she continued. "You can't have it both ways, Kerry. Either you were on your own there, or you were just posing, in which case you're right, you had nothing to worry about."

Kerry smiled. "I was on my own," she clarified. "But I knew I was unattached, and I could get a job again fairly easily. Most of the people working for me had families and mortgages they had to worry about, which I didn't," she said. "But it was a very tough time for me, because the last thing I wanted was to have to come home, having failed."

Several of the girls in the front nodded.

"So then I had my second big learning experience," Kerry went on. "That same person in charge from the bigger company came to see me, and, not knowing me from Adam's housecat, told me 'Hey. You've got talent. We'll keep you'."

The crowd laughed, a bit hesitantly.

"Honestly," Kerry said. "It was the first time in my life that I'd been taken at face value and been told I was competent–by a virtual stranger," she added. "So the lesson there was you never know where your inspiration in life is going to come from. It could come at you from unexpected places."

"So you stayed," the blond girl in the front called out.

"The bigger company was ILS. So yes, I did." Kerry smiled. "And as you can see, it worked out very much in my favor, which is another lesson–sometimes bad things can lead to good results."

"Would you do the same thing again?"

Kerry's smile broadened. "In a heartbeat," she said. "Do yourselves a favor–whatever you do, wherever you choose to do it, follow your heart. Do what feels right to you and you'll end up being grateful for it."

She stepped back to the podium, and put the microphone back in its holder. "Now I think it's time to get this party started," she said. "Thanks for inviting me to speak, but this is about old friends getting together, and rediscovering what they left here, so let's let everyone get at it."

There was a brief pause, and then applause sounded. Kerry lifted a hand in acknowledgement, then turned and headed back to where Angie was waiting, resisting the urge to wipe her palms on her skirt.

"Wow," Angie greeted her. "That was impressive."

"Gag." Kerry made a face. "I wish I could have just kicked Stacey in the teeth. Now that would have been impressive in these heels." Privately though, she felt good about her presentation. It hadn't been her best, but it hadn't been her worst, and at least no one had tossed a balled up program at her.

"C'mon." Her sister gave her a hug. "Stop dissing yourself Ker. You were great."

"I'm just glad it's over. Let's get out of here." Her sister exhaled, rocking her head to either side to loosen up tense shoulders. "Boy am I looking forward to that beer."

Angie chuckled and turned to lead Kerry out from behind the stage. They'd only gotten three or four steps though, before a tall figure intercepted them. "Ah, Ms. Strickfield."

"Girls," the older woman said. "A word with you please."

Angie pulled up uncertaintly. Kerry, however, didn't hesitate.

"Sorry, Ms. Strickfield," Kerry said. "My brother and sister and I have a previous engagement. Thanks for your hospitality, but we need to be going."

The older woman seemed surprised. "You won't be staying for the reception then?" she asked. "I thought perhaps you would enjoy meeting with your classmates. I think your speech was very well received."

"No," Kerry said firmly. "I appreciate that, and I'm sure the reception will be just lovely, but unfortunately I have prior family commitments."

"Of course." The woman recovered. "I'm sure you want to spend time with your loved ones while you are here. Forgive me, and thank you for coming, Ms. Stuart. It really was a pleasure to listen to you speak."

Kerry blinked, caught a little off guard. "Thanks," she said. "Bit of a tough crowd, but I did my best."

Ms. Strickfield smiled at her. "Ms. Stuart, I had no fear of that. Your grace under pressure is very well recorded in recent years. At any rate, since we won't have the pleasure of your company at the reception, have a good evening, and enjoy your time with your family." She gave Angie a brief nod, and slipped out a side door to the auditorium.

"Wow," Angie murmured. "Who'd have guessed?"

Kerry scratched her nose. "Dar, actually," she muttered. "But that's another long story best told over lager. Let's get Mike before he starts kissing someone, and get out of here." She resumed her course for the door, straightening her jacket again before she put her hand on the knob to turn it.

"Why do I get a feeling I'm going to get more of an education tonight than I bargained for?" Angie followed her with a wry grin. "You know, Ker, life around you must never be boring."

"Hah."

Chapter Seven

"SO, IT IS agreed."

Dar watched in utter relief as Sir Melthon and Alastair clasped hands. She avoided looking at her watch, resting her chin against her fist instead as she waited for the rest of the niceties to be finished. The negotiations hadn't been that lengthy, but it was late, and she was tired, and she was very much looking forward to that nice big bed with its fluffily soft pillows.

"Good deal," Alastair said, briskly. "It's been a pleasure spending the evening with you good folks, but now it's time for me to get my team some rest so they can start planning the integration transition tomorrow."

Sir Melthon nodded, looking tired himself. "Right," he said. "We can pick up tomorrow at lunchtime. I will have my lot set up a workroom, and we'll put a spread on. Mimosas will start the day off right, eh?"

"Sounds great." Alastair waved at his group. "Let's go people." He picked up the signed contract paper in its folder and tucked it under his arm as the rest of the ILS team stood up and started their goodbyes.

Dar stretched her back out, and let her hand rest on the back of her chair. She waited for Alastair to move toward the door, then followed him with a casual wave toward the rest of the team. "Goodnight, gentlemen."

"Good night, Dar," Francois responded. "See you tomorrow."

Hans caught up with them as she reached the door. He smiled, as he opened it. "It was a good day, yes?" he asked Dar in German. "Long, but good."

"Long, but good," Dar agreed. "I think everyone pretty much got some of what they wanted."

"That is very true." Hans was at her shoulder as they walked down the long, curving staircase that led to the ground floor of the big mansion. "I think he is happy. He likes your boss."

"I like my boss." Dar smiled. "In fact, today he's on my A-list."

Hans chuckled.

They reached the outer door that was opened for them by a uniformed doorman. Another was standing by, holding their jackets. Dar took hers and escaped in the chilly, very early morning fall air and took a minute to shrug into the soft leather as they stood waiting for their cars.

"Damn good way to end the night," Alastair commented.

"Any way you'd have ended it would have been good at this point," Dar said, dryly. "I thought we were going to have breakfast over foxhounds or something at this rate."

Alastair chuckled. "He's a tough negotiator, but I think we'll do all right." He stepped forward as the first of the cars pulled up. "C"mon, Dar. We're in the same place."

Dar didn't argue. She settled in the back seat of the sedan and pulled out her cell phone, checking the time on it before she dialed.

It rang twice, and then was answered. "Hey." Dar listened, but heard only a quiet humming in the background.

"Hey, sweetie," Kerry responded. "Are you finally done?"

"Mmhm." Dar leaned back as Alastair shut the door on his side and the car started to pull away. "How'd it go?" She guessed not that bad, just from her partner's tone.

"Not bad," Kerry promptly confirmed. "We're on our way to the pub now."

"Glad to hear it."

"How'd your part go?" Kerry asked, after a moment of quiet.

"You've got your work cut out for you," Dar informed her. "Bring your pencils and a bucket of patience."

Kerry's smile was audible through the phone. "Don't worry, I will. Were they tough?"

"A little."

"Want anything from here?" Kerry asked. "I have some shopping time tomorrow."

"You."

"Anything else?"

"You."

Kerry chuckled. "Okay, you got it." She exhaled and there was a faint sound of traffic that floated through. "That really wasn't nearly as bad as I thought it was going to be," she admitted. "I think I worked myself into a lather for no reason."

"Well." Dar glanced at Alastair, who was peering out the window with deep and abiding interest. "It's a good thing for them they didn't give you a hard time," she said. "I'd hate to think I was stuck here babysitting Alastair when you needed me to kick some ass."

Her boss turned his head and looked over at her, eyebrows hiking. Dar grinned at him.

"Is he there?" Kerry asked. "You didn't say that in front of him did you?"

"Sure did," Dar cheerfully acknowledged. "What the hell. It's 2:00 a.m., and I'm so wiped if we had a problem I'd have to FedEx myself a box of brain cells to take care of it."

Alastair snorted, and leaned back, lacing his fingers behind his head. "Glad that fella didn't tell us to meet him for breakfast."

"Me too," Dar agreed. "Anyway, I just wanted to find out how your speech went," she addressed Kerry again. "Go have fun, and buy your sibs a round on me, okay?"

"Absolutely," Kerry said. "Bye hon, get some rest."

"I will. Later." Dar closed her phone and put it away. "I think he was trying to see if he could wear you down and get those last set of concessions."

Alastair snorted again. "Listen, he may be a big shot royal whatever, but lady, I've played poker with slicker men than he ever will be," he said. "They're big here, and I like their setup. Good properties, good business model, but in terms of volume it's one of our smaller contracts."

"I know," Dar said. "Didn't think it paid to mention that though."

"Not at all," her boss cheerfully agreed. "And besides, I like to think we give all our customers top notch service, no matter what size the contract." He glanced at Dar. "I don't recall you ever asking if any of your high wire act shenanigans were worth the size of the deal."

"Huh," Dar grunted in agreement. "Yeah, never really mattered to me," she said. "But all in all, it's been a good day."

"Sure has," Alastair said. "Everything go all right for Kerry?"

"Yep."

They were both quiet for the rest of the ride to the hotel, and they got out in the subdued quiet of early morning to a mostly empty street and a dim, very sleepy lobby.

"Evening," Alastair greeted the doorman as they entered. "Well, Dar, I think it's safe to say we can all sleep in. Give me a buzz if you want to do brunch before we go over. If his menu tonight is any indication we'll probably get whole pheasant or something for lunch."

"Sure." Dar got her key out as they rode the elevator up and walked down the stately hallway that held their rooms. She left Alastair at his and went gratefully to her own. She pushed the door open and let it shut behind her.

It was cool inside, and quiet, and smelled unnervingly like chocolate. Dar smiled as the scent hit her nose, and she rested her hand on the back of the chair in the room as she kicked her shoes off and looked around for its source.

Near the bed, she spotted it. A small tray was sitting on the table, a silver pot squarely in the center of it. Even from where she was, she could see the faint steam coming from the spout and as she walked over. She recognized little dishes of condiments meant to be added to the waiting cup.

Dar pushed these aside to retrieve a small, white card, turning it over to read the words on the back with an already knowing smile. "Thank you, Kerrison." She put the card down, and inspected the dishes, selecting a few mini marshmallows and a gummy bear, dropping them in the cup, then pouring the steaming hot chocolate over them.

She left the gooey tidbits to melt as she removed her suit and returned it to its hanger, trading it for her long T-shirt and bare feet.

She glanced at her laptop, then deliberately turned her back on it and went back to the bed, pulling aside the already turned down comforter and sliding under it, appreciating the smell of clean linen mixed with cocoa surrounding her.

She picked up the cup, lifting it toward the window. "Here's to you, Ker," she said. "Hope you like the cake at the pub." She took a sip and smiled, and wiggled her toes in contentment.

KERRY LEANED BACK in her bench seat, resting one arm along the back of it as she picked up her frosty mug and took a sip of her second beer.   Having traded her suit for a pair of jeans and a sweatshirt, and having her speech behind her, she found herself to be in a good mood, and happy with the world around her.

"What in the hell was that one chick's problem?" Mike asked, around a mouthful of jalapeno popper. "Did she have a tulip stuck up her butt or something?"

"Who, Stacey?" Kerry tried to remember just what had been Stacey's problem. Her first beer had put enough of a displacement between her and the event that it took an effort, and she used the arrival of her coconut shrimp appetizer as a delay tactic while she rummaged in her memory.

"She was the one you beat in that debating championship your senior year, wasn't she?" Angie spoke up. She had a luridly colorful fruit drink in front of her and she was happily sucking the pineapple from it. "I remember she pitched a hissy fit at the Palace afterward."

"You remember that?" Kerry found she did also, but very vaguely. She hadn't known Stacey that well. They'd gone in different social circles, just one of the many girls not too different from her and her sister that she'd known. "I sort of remember that debate." She put her beer down and selected a shrimp to nibble.

"I remember because I heard her mother yelling at her in the bathroom at the Palace that night." Angie sucked her daiquiri through the straw. "She was blaming the fact that Stacey had spent the night with her boyfriend before the debate on her losing it."

Kerry made a face. "Ah, yeah, now I remember," she said. "I forgot all about who I was debating because I was scared spitless having father in the audience," she recalled. "I could have been facing Ronald McDonald and it wouldn't have made an impression."

"Oh yeah." Mike reached over and stole one of Kerry's shrimp. "What a big deal he made out of being there. I think every freaking paper within a hundred miles was straggling in the back of that place taking pictures."

Kerry glanced casually around, but the pub was quiet, and she didn't see anyone she knew around them. Not really surprising given that it was a Monday night and it was fairly late. There were a few men at the bar, and two groups of younger people near the pool table, and there was a low strain of Celtic music playing she found familiar. "I think that was one of the few times we had our picture together in the paper."

She had a copy of it that she had saved. A slightly tattered bit of newspaper tucked in a protective sleeve she'd stuck in a scrapbook of her school years and ended up taking to Miami with her. She and her father standing next to the wooden school podium she'd only recently spoke at, her father with his hand resting on her shoulder, a pleased and satisfied expression on his face.

For once.

She wondered what he'd have thought hearing her tonight. Would he have been able to set aside all the crappiness between them and been glad for her success?

"Yeah, what a photo op that was," Mike said. "I remember him telling the paper he thought you might have a career in politics ahead of you."

"Oh gag," Kerry moaned, retreating to her beer. "I'd rather have flipped burgers for a living." She stretched her legs out and crossed her ankles. "We should get drunk and show up to Mother's hung over tomorrow."

Angie covered her eyes. "Let's not," she said. "As you reminded me, I've got to live with her now." She glanced up as the waiter sidled up. "Can I get another one of these?" She ignored Mike's snicker and held up her daiquiri glass.

"Sure." The waiter took the glass. "Your dinners will be coming out shortly, but remember to leave room for dessert."

"Well..." Angie waggled her hand.

"Trust me, you'll want to." The waiter grinned and sauntered off.

Kerry chuckled, taking another shrimp. "Worse comes to worse we can take it home for breakfast." She reminded them. "Cheesecake in the morning's great."

"Hedonist," Mike accused.

"If you think that's hedonism, you've got a lot to learn."

KERRY SAT CROSS legged on the bed writing longhand in a small cloth bound book propped up on one of the pillows.

It was quiet in her room, and in the rest of the house. A glance at the clock told her it was well after midnight, and she pondered a moment before she went back to writing.

Sept 10th, 2001.

Well, today went better than I expected it to. I keep saying that. What was I really expecting? Did I really think they were going to throw rotten apples at me?

I don't know. Maybe I did. I'm glad the younger crowd showed some brain cells and class, and to be honest I wouldn't have minded talking to them a little longer if all of my old classmates hadn't been at the reception.

Is that cowardly? I don't think so. I just think it's normal for someone not to like being insulted like what Stacey did there. What a jerk. But Angie was right. She was a jerk when we went to school here. She didn't become one just because it turned out I was gay.

That was the one thing the kids didn't ask about. They were more interested in how to succeed in business. That's amazingly cool. I may even have to join my alumni society and start tossing them a few bucks if they're turning out people with those kinds of goals.

Does it really matter that I'm gay? It's the 21st century. People shouldn't care at this point in humanity's history but you know, I think it does matter to the older crowd because I think they feel like they're not in control of things and life's accelerating out of control.

I'm used to it. Technology changes every minute. If you spend your life immersed in constant change, then when the world changes around you it just seems normal, doesn't it?

Hm.

I wonder if that's how Mom's coping with everything. Just invest in the change, and maybe you stop stressing about how things used to be, and how you wanted them to turn out, and you just start surfing the wave and living in the minute.

I think I like that. Life is never boring if it's full of change, is it?

I was worrying about what Mom was going to talk to us about tomorrow, but I've decided to just not get mad about whatever it is, assuming it's something I might get mad about. The only power to stress me out she has is the power I give her.

Isn't that great? Only took me how many years to figure that out? I bet Dar would crack up.

Kerry reviewed her words, and chuckled.

After a few minutes, she heard footsteps approaching, and then she looked up again to see Angie in the doorway to her room. "Hey. Thought you were sleeping."

"Andrew was fussing," Angie explained, entering the bedroom. "And I saw your light on when I came back upstairs. Why are you still up?"

"Oh." Kerry glanced at her little book. "I just...it sounds silly but I've started keeping a diary," she explained, a touch sheepishly. "I'm about done. Is Andy okay?"

"Oh sure." Her sister sat down on the edge of Kerry's bed. "He's teething. After you go through that the first time, like I did with Sally, you know what to look for and what to do, but boy, the first time it freaks you out."

Kerry closed her diary up and capped her pen. "How's Sally doing?"

Angie paused, then shrugged a little. "She's confused," she said. "She doesn't really understand what's going on, or why she sometimes is in one place with her Daddy, and sometimes here with me, but for all his other faults Richard doesn't play the blame game so I think she'll adjust after a while."

"Mm." Kerry tried to imagine what that would have been like, and found it hard. "We never had to deal with that," she said. "It would have been weird."

Her sister nodded. "It would have been. Fortunately for the kids, our divorce was a lot like our marriage was–passionless and businesslike."

Kerry winced.

"Hey, it's true," Angie said. "Ker, when I see you and Dar, and hear you talk to each other–you have something I have no clue about, you realize that right?" She cocked her head to one side and regarded her older sibling. "The whole bit with you sending each other notes, and for Pete's sake, sending fudge covered mousse cakes? Unreal."

Kerry made a wry face. "You know, we've always done that," she confessed. "I thought it was one of those things you do when you're...uh...dating. Or whatever." She cleared her throat. "But we just kept doing it. I guess we'll stop sometime. Most married couples I know don't do that."

"But?" Angie watched her, as her words slowed to a stop.

"Dar's parents still do." Kerry chuckled. "Oh well. It's nice though. That was killer cake." She licked her lips in memory. "I didn't even remember seeing that on the menu."

"It wasn't," Angie said. "The manager told me it was delivered from some bakery in Detroit, hand carried."

Kerry had the grace to look mildly embarrassed. "All I had was hot chocolate sent to her room," she muttered. "And you know what? She probably had that all planned way before I called her hotel."

Angie covered her eyes in mock despair.

"So." Kerry cleared her throat. "Are you going to stay with Mom long term?" She turned her pen in her fingers. "I know it's a lot quieter here now."

Her younger sister got up and wandered around the room, pausing to look out the darkened window. "You know, I wish I was you, Ker." She turned to see a pair of blond eyebrows hiked up. "You've got guts, you're successful, you're in a great relationship..."

Kerry remained quiet, since there was no denying any of that.

"But I'm not," Angie concluded. "I'm a typical second child, and you know what? I don't want to risk what I'll have to risk for a sexy, adventurous life. So yeah, I'll probably stay here with Mom, unless Brian decides to make a commitment and then we'll see. Even so, we'll probably end up living with her. She likes Brian."

"Even now?"

Angie chuckled dryly and sat back down on the bed. "With everything that's happened in the last few years, I think she's learned to take her successes where she finds them. She wanted Brian for a son-in-law, so if it turns out he becomes one, she'll take it even if it's not really what she envisioned before now."

Fair enough. Kerry sighed. "I hope that works out," she said. "But anyway, if you ever do decide you want a radical change, you know where to find me."

Angie smiled. "Sally wants to come down to see her Aunt Kerry's log cabin. Maybe we can visit for a couple of days near Christmas, when it's all snow here, and anything but there."

"You're on," Kerry agreed instantly. "The kids would love it down there. It's right on the beach, and there's a bunch of cool stuff to do all around there, like glass bottom boats and paddle boats and things."

"Great." Angie got up. "Let me let you get to sleep. It's going to be a long day for you tomorrow," she said. "And hey, maybe I can even get Mom to come down and visit for a day. Show her you really don't live in the middle of some third world country."

Eh. Kerry waved at her, as she left. "Actually..." Though she loved her adopted home, very often between the massively immigrant population and the overly graft ridden political scene it did sometimes seem like they lived on one of the nearby Caribbean islands.

However, she figured her mother would actually be pleasantly surprised with a visit to the condo so she was content to let the chips fall where they might on that subject. She got up and put her diary into her briefcase, turned the lamp off and climbed under the covers.

Somewhere, halfway across the planet, she knew Dar would be getting up soon, despite her late night and she wished suddenly that they would be sharing breakfast with each other. She wanted to talk to her partner about the interesting things she'd seen and felt the last few days, and she was already looking forward to her part in the new project and wanting to get started on it.

When she got there, there would be the initial meeting with Dar to find out what Alastair and she had promised as part of the contract. Kerry trusted her partner not to sell her down the river, but there were times when Dar would okay a concession if she thought the contract was important enough and then sometimes they scrambled.

This was an important contract. Not for the size of it, but for the visibility and the foothold it gave them in an area they hadn't really been that successful before now.

It tickled her to no end that she'd been a part of that win, even though she knew that it had been more pure luck than any real skill on her or Dar's part that had achieved it. Take truffles where you found them, Dar had said.

Yum. So she would. Kerry closed her eyes and relaxed her body, hearing the patter of leaves against the window and the soft creaks of the big house around her, until it lulled her into sleep.

DAR WAS GLAD enough to sleep in, spending most of the morning working off some of the mail overload that had built up in her inbox over the past few days. She was sprawled in the desk chair in her sleep shirt, the remnants of her breakfast tray nearby and a pot of coffee still handy.

It felt good to relax for a few hours. The trip had been very frenetic so far, and Dar appreciated the chance to sit back and get her act together before she had to meet with their new clients again. They had a meeting scheduled most of the afternoon, and then Alastair had arranged to host a dinner someplace in London for all of them.

Thursday, they'd meet with the local folks, hopefully all day to keep her mind occupied and off the fact that she'd be suffering the nine or ten hours of Kerry in the air and unreachable while she flew from Michigan through Chicago and then onward to London.

Of course, Dar realized she herself had been in the same state just the other day, but ever since Kerry's near miss in the storm, she'd found herself a nervous wreck whenever her partner flew. Kerry, on the other hand, had put the event in the past and didn't mind the travel and didn't seem to stress when Dar flew.

When they flew together, naturally, it didn't bother her. Dar decided not to think too much about why that was, and went back to her inbox instead. She clicked on a note from Mark, and opened it.

Hey boss!

Practice went good today. I think we'll do okay, so long as we don't have to do stuff like hit or catch softballs. So far, we're really good at wearing funny looking pants, and tripping on cleats.

We miss you guys. How's it going?

Mark.

Dar grimaced a little. She clicked on the little video embedded in the mail and waited for it to spool up, then watched as she got a Mark's eye view of two of her employees crashing full into each other and bouncing back at least four feet. "Nice."

She shook her head. "At least Ker and I won't be the worst ones out there. " She clicked on reply.

Hey Mark.

I hope the team can at least not knock each other over by the time Ker and I get back because if that's what's gonna happen we'll be laughing so hard we might as well just forfeit and go get drunk.

Meetings are going well–be ready to start this one up running because these people are skeptics. I hope that damn hub's going to come online soon because if there's one customer who's likely to push our SLA's to the limit it's this guy.

Throws decent meals though. We had prime rib of some creature or other for dinner and unlimited bottles of grog.

D

She went on to the next mail, glancing down at her news ticker piddling along at the bottom of her screen. "Slow morning." She flipped over to the network monitoring screen that always, from habit, ran in the background and she viewed the gauges she seldom saw at this hour of the Miami morning.

Nine o'clock in the morning here, four o'clock in the morning at home. She rested her chin on her fist, observing the traffic patterns. She could see the heavy usage fluttering across their internal networks both in Miami, and in the big data center in Houston. Backups, probably, unending streams of data being copied to their storage arrays, mirrored to make even that precaution redundant.

Dar respected that. She knew her team took the need to cover her ass very seriously, and she knew her peers in the company depended on that to make sure if something inevitably did happen, they could recover from it with no harm done.

A blinking blue light caught her attention, and she shifted her gaze to the Houston links, watching the big routers there chewing over a healthy size chunk of traffic, which she realized was the government financial data stream going through its nightly reconciliation.

Between the offices, the parallel tie lines were quiet. They didn't share much data, since Miami was the commercial hub and Houston the governmental one, but traffic like payroll and mail, corporate shares and intranet servers were quietly replicated so that the IT operation to most people was pretty much invisible.

Just how Dar liked it.

Just then, her messenger software popped up. Dar blinked at in surprise, half expecting it to be Kerry. It wasn't.

Ms. Roberts? Sorry to bother you.

Dar recognized one of their night net operators. *No problem.* She typed back. *What's up?*

We're having a little problem with the Niagara 3 node. We were going to call Mark but we saw you come online.

Dar cocked her head, marveling in the fact that the ops crew felt they could approach her now in so casual a manner. Respectful, but casual. She accessed a secure shell session and navigated through the net to the node in question, one of the three that surrounded the New York area to handle the stupendous amount of traffic there. *Yeah? What's the problem?*

We're seeing routes being injected and then squelched. We think it's a circuit issue but the local exchange up there swears no trouble found.

LECs lie like fish. Dar informed him. *Let me take a look.*

Node 3 was her newest, an interlink to Canada that had only been online a few weeks. She poked around in the router, pecking away happily at the device as she went through its configuration. She checked the logs, seeing nothing out of the ordinary, and then she went through all the interfaces one by one. *Ah hah.*

Ma'am?

Found it. Dar typed back. *Give me a sec.* She reviewed the flapping interface, a little surprised to find a timing mismatch coming in from one of their major service providers. She watched the errors for a minute, and then she experimentally changed a setting, watched, and then changed a second. The interface settled down and stopped its gyrations and after another minute the data commenced flowing normally.

It looks great now ma'am!

Dar smirked, and then cut and pasted the circuit information into her notepad and got out of the router. *Anytime.* She typed back. *Now I have to go find out why the damn vendor changed his clocking without telling us.*

So it wasn't the LEC?

Not this time. Dar confirmed. *Service provider.*

Well ma'am, sorry about that but you just won me a bet here, and now Chuck has to go out and get me Dunkin Donuts, so thanks!

Dar laughed out loud. She pasted the information into a new message, and addressed it to the vendor with a couple of snitty pecks and sent it on its way. *Have a Boston Crème for me. Later.*

Thanks again, Ms. Roberts. Have a great day.

Well, she'd certainly do her best. Dar glanced up as an incoming mail binged softly. She was very surprised to see it was from the provider she'd just yelled at. She opened it.

Ms. Roberts –

We were about to contact you about this issue. We had a service interrupt out of the 140 West Street facility in Manhattan that resulted in a non scheduled recycle of the switch servicing your account.

Dar translated that without difficulty. "So. Someone rebooted the thing accidentally. Sucks to be you."

There was a configuration anomaly that was under review.

"Uh huh, and someone forgot to write the memory before you rebooted it too."

However, the issue seemed to self-correct, so no further action was taken.

Dar hit reply.

The issue didn't self correct. I went into our router and matched your timing change. I don't mind leaving it that way, but get your goddamned procedures straightened out and tell your operations people to get their heads out of their asses and follow the rules next time.

She reviewed the note and hit send with a satisfied little grunt. "Nitwads." She lifted her cooling cup of coffee and sipped from it, then set it back down. With a touch of curiousness, she clicked back to the network map and went into the graphical view of the node again, reviewing the traffic, then checking the other two nodes in the area.

Tons of data, even at this hour. What was it they always said? New York never slept? Watching this she could believe it. With a shake of her head, she closed the monitoring tool and went back to her mail, realizing there was one there from Kerry she'd somehow managed to miss. "Hey!"

She clicked on it.

Dar –

Ah, business. Dar knew a moment of disappointment, but immediately chastised herself and read on. Even using the corporate mail system, Kerry often sent short personal notes to her, and those were always addressed as something other than her name, so seeing one addressed with it made her aware it was probably either a problem or a solution to one.

Reviewing the growth chart, I found a hole here, in the mid Atlantic interchange.

Dar's eyes widened. "Oo!" she said out loud. "Checking up on me, Kerrison? You little scoundrel!"

With the new backhaul contract for the cellular consortium I think we're going to run out of space within six to twelve if the curve maintains. What do you think?

"What do I think?" Dar propped her chin on her fist and reviewed the graphs Kerry had inserted in her email. Her brow creased as she studied the bandwidth usage, then she quickly hunted something up on her hard drive and looked at it, switching between the document and Kerry's mail with rapid-fire flicks of her eyes.

After a long moment of silence, she snorted again. "Well, I'll be damned," she said. "What in the hell are those people doing? They're overshooting their per connection bandwidth by fifty percent." She flipped through the original proposal, wondering if she'd made a wrong calculation somewhere.

"Did they sign up a billion new users or something?" She puzzled over the numbers. "What the hell did I do wrong here?" She went to her browser and clicked on it, calling up one of the consortium web pages. After a moment's studying, her expression cleared. "Ah." She came close to slapping her own head. "Data. Pictures. No wonder."

She clicked over to Kerry's note, and hit reply.

Kerry –
Nice catch. I'll add bandwidth. Looks like they put in new services right after they signed the contract–maybe they figured they could get away with it.
Good work.
D

Then she added two small GIFS, one of a sheep, and one of a rock, and clicked send.   Then she got up and stretched, leaving the laptop behind as she roamed over to the window and looked out.

Today, it was reasonably sunny outside, and the streets were full of walkers. Dar suddenly had the urge to be outside as well, and she put that plan immediately into motion, closing down her laptop and heading for the shower.

There was shopping to be had, and cute trinkets for Kerry to be bought, and she thought she saw a couple of street food vendors off in the distance.

Just the thing to start the day off right.

KERRY LAY FLAT on her back on her bed, her hands behind her head as the early morning sun poured into her window.   After a moment's rest, she continued her crunches, counting under her breath as she worked through her last set, ending up grimacing on the last few but getting through them.

"Ugh." She spread her arms out and stretched them, waiting for the burn to fade in her midsection.   Then she rolled over and got up, twisting her torso and making shadowboxing motions to shake her muscles out as she went to the dresser.

Her laptop was seated on it, whirring through its screen saver placidly until she touched the track pad and it presented her login screen. She rattled in her password and unlocked it, opening her mail program and watching the screen fill with dark lines.

"Aha!" She pounced on the one from Dar immediately, clicking it as the rest of the mail downloaded. She leaned on the counter and scanned the words, a relieved and happy grin appearing a moment later. "Yes!" She pumped her fist in the air. "Score!"

Finding Dar in a mistake was so rare that when it did happen, she spent hours and hours going over the data to make sure she was looking at it from the right point of view until she felt secure enough to mention it.

Dar never seemed to get pissed off about it. Kerry suspected if she approached her in public with the issue, her beloved partner wouldn't appreciate it but she never did, and Dar's reaction either was an explanation of why whatever it was happened to be that way, or else, like this time, a cheerful admission of guilt and an action plan to fix it.

Awesome. Kerry stepped away from the desk and went to the window, peering out through the teak wood slats at what was going to be a gorgeous day. Though just seven, it was already light outside and she could see a beautiful, almost cloudless sky through the tree branches.

Great day to go out on the lake. She sighed. "Oh well, next time." She turned and went back to the dresser, picking up her laptop and carrying it back to the bed with her. She sat down cross-legged, and studied her mail.

Relatively uneventful. She clicked over and opened her morning report from operations, scanning it lightly until she came across an entry for the northeast sector and saw the outage notation. One eyebrow lifted. "And I didn't get a page, why?" She clicked the report. "Oh, that's why."

Opportunistic of her night administrators. Kerry couldn't really argue with the logic of contacting her apparently available boss, but really, there was a process for that sort of thing. She blinked as a small box popped up next to her cursor.

Hey.

Ah. Speaking of the devil. *Hey cowboy. What's up?*

Cowboy?

Kerry smiled. *I saw the outage report from this morning.*

Ah. Dar seemed to reflect on that. *I sent a nasty gram to the vendor. I copied you. Looks like someone tripped over a power cable at their New York Corporate Office or something.*

Where are you? Kerry asked.

Just about to leave the hotel for the client site. I just got back from walking around outside. It's gorgeous here today.

Kerry smiled again. *Here too. I wish I could go out sailing instead of to mom's brunch. Oh well. Are you doing anything tonight?*

The sun winked in the window and striped across the bed, warming Kerry's bare legs. She wiggled her toes in it, and wished very briefly and pointlessly that she was having this conversation in person.

Waiting for you.

So apparently the feeling was mutual. *I'm not leaving until tomorrow morning, sweetie. I have to get through the day at moms then I talked Angie into going down to the shops near the lake so I can get goofy trinkets for everyone.* She paused. *Wish I were at the airport taking off right now though.*

<ROFL>

Kerry cocked her head at the screen. *What's so funny?*

Tell you when I see you. I have to head out. Tell your crazy family I say hi and try to have a good time, okay?

Okay. Kerry typed. *Have a good meeting. Love you.*

Love you too, later. DD

Kerry chuckled and closed the window, and then she ran her eye over her mail. Not finding anything really urgent, she closed the program and got up to put the laptop back on the dresser.

"Hey, you up?" Angie stuck her head in the door, blinking in surprise to find her older sister in a pair of shorts and a sports bra apparently wide awake. "Boy, you have become an early bird haven't you?"

Kerry chuckled. "I have," she admitted. "I was doing my traveling exercise routine and then chatting with Dar for a bit. C'mon in."

Angie entered, still in her nightgown. "What's a traveling exercise routine?" she asked. "Is that what you do every morning?"

"No." Kerry turned and leaned against the dresser. "At home, Dar and I usually either go for a run in the morning, or if it's too hot and sticky which is often, we go to the island gym or to the pool," she replied. "I just have a few things I do when I am out of town like some sit-ups and push-ups and stuff."

"You're nuts," Angie informed her.

"I am," her sister cheerfully agreed. "But it makes me feel good to do it, so who cares?" She spread her arms out. "Hey, I even joined a softball team. Our company's doing a league."

"Oh my god." Angie rolled her eyes. "You always wanted to do that. You used to bitch about it all the time I remember."

Kerry grinned. "Yeah, I know. But this was something that just came up. It should be fun though." She folded her arms over her chest. "Hey, want to go roust Mike up?"

Angie grinned back. "Actually, I was going to suggest we do that, and then we go out and grab some breakfast somewhere. I gave my cook the morning off because she had a dental appointment."

"I'm all for that," Kerry agreed instantly. "Let's go for it." She headed for the door. "We can get some ice cubes to get Mike awake."

"Ker?"

"Hm?" Kerry paused at the door, with her hand on the knob.

"You going to go wake him up like that?" Angie asked, pointing at her sister's lack of real clothing.

Kerry glanced down at herself, and then she shrugged. "This is what I go out jogging in," she said. "C'mon. You can't tell me Mike's more conservative than the ghost of Commodore Vanderbilt."

Angie followed her out, shaking her head. "Guess we'll find out in a minute."

DAR RESISTED THE urge to stick her hands in the pockets of her dress slacks as she entered the big dining room along with the rest of their team and Sir Melthon's people. There was a huge sideboard set up, and everyone was definitely in a much better mood today.

Deal was done. Papers were signed. Now they were partners, and as partners, they were no longer the bad guys so everyone was chilled out and a lot friendlier.

"Hello, Ms. Roberts." The man who had been pounding her mercilessly with questions yesterday was now all smiles. "John Status, by the way." He held a hand out. "No hard feelings, I hope?" He had a distinct, rolling accent that was almost musical.

"Not at all." Dar amiably gripped his hand and released it. "I like hard questions. People who don't ask them either aren't serious about dealing with us, or don't know what they're doing."

Status grinned. "Now there's a good solid saying." He took a seat next to Dar at the table. "I'm the lucky man who gets to be in charge of our company net."

Dar was mutely delighted to be sitting next to another nerd. She left Alastair on her other side discussing grouse hunting with two of the other men. "Gets to be, or is?" She was aware of the servers moving around them and the smell of something roasting.

"Is," John said. "Am. Whatever," he clarified. "I've been here for about a year, and the first thing I was asked to do is hook us up with a global network provider." He glanced around. "From this side of the Atlantic."

"Ah." Dar nodded. "We'd heard that." She gave the server a nod as he filled her glass with something that smelled like apples and cinnamon. "It's been tough for us to grow here because of the bias."

"Eh." John lifted his hands.

"I understand the bias. If the positions were reversed, it would be the same on our side," Dar said. "No one wants to work with people who are different and hard to understand. Our business methods are very polar."

The man sat back. "You know though, most Americans don't understand that," he observed. "They just come over here, and try to ride over people with high pressure sales jobs. They never come in and say, well, here's what we do. You interested?"

Dar smiled.

"Now, understand it helps that his nib's godson came in like a raving loony about you," John said. "We were all saying, if Hans has his knickers in that kind of an uproar must be something to it."

"Hey Dar, your admin people in yet?" Alastair interrupted them.

Dar checked her watch. "Quarter to nine? Sure. Mine is anyway. What do you need?"

"Can you get one of the big portfolios headed this way?" her boss asked. "The one that shows all the lines of business?"

"Sure." Dar opened her phone and dialed her office number.

"Excuse me." She apologized to John.

"No problem." John turned to his plate, which had just been delivered, complete with a selection from the sideboard. "Ahh...now that's the thing."

"Hey, Maria. Good morning."

"Ah, good morning Jefa," Maria replied. "How are you? How is the England?"

"So far, very interesting and successful," Dar said. "Need a favor."

"Of course."

Dar paused, as her PDA buzzed. "Hang on a second." She opened it and glanced at the screen. "Hm. Hey Maria, can you ask Mark to check out what's going on over near Boston? One of the supplemental links just came up and they're using some unusual bandwidth for the links."

"Surely," Maria said. "Is that all, Dar? How is Kerrisita? Is she having a good time with her familia?

Dar closed the PDA. "She's fine, and her speech went great," she told her assistant. "Alastair needs one of the circus tent displays sent over here, can you get that in the works?"

"I will call over to the Sales right away, Dar," Maria said. "Oh, and Senora Mariana has delivered some packages to the office here for you and Kerrisita. I think they are your softball costumes."

"What color are they?" Dar chuckled. "Please don't tell me they're either yellow or purple."

"No, no, it is a pretty blue," Maria said. "And the pants are white. Mayte was showing me hers last night, and they are very, very cute." She paused. "The shoes were very strange. They had nails in the bottom. Is that right, Dar?"

Her boss chuckled, and then glanced down as her PDA buzzed again. She opened it, and after a minute, her brows creased. "What the hell?"

"Como?"

"Maria, can you conference Mark on? I'm getting pages that aren't making any sense. I think the monitor's gone whacky again." Dar paged through the messages.

"Surely. Hold on for one moment, Dar." Maria put her on hold.

"Something wrong?" John asked.

"Ah." Dar shook her head a little. "I think it's just..."

Maria came back on the phone. "I have Mark, Dar, but..."

"Hey! Boss!" Mark's voice echoed through the phone, sharp with excitement. "Holy crap!"

Dar felt a surge of adrenaline, but she wasn't entirely sure why. "What's up?"

"A freaking plane just hit the side of the freaking World Trade Center!"

"Jesu!" Maria gasped. "Madre di Dios!"

Dar absorbed that in silence for a minute. "What? How in the hell did that happen? Someone get lost looking for LaGuardia?"

"I have no friggen clue," Mark said. "But they just put it up on CNN and it's crazy! Smoke all over the place! People freaking out! There's a hole in the side of that thing the size of the space shuttle!"

Dar pressed the mute button, and leaned over, touching Alastair on the sleeve. "Alastair."

Her boss turned and looked at her, his gaze sharpening immediately when he saw her expression. "What's up?"

"We need to find a television. Something's going on in New York."

Chapter Eight

KERRY STROLLED THROUGH the big atrium and paused, looking around and remembering the last time she'd spent time in this space. Her father's funeral reception. It was much quieter now; even the echoes of that tumultuous time were gone along with his presence.

She suppressed a smile, and continued on into the formal dining room where the rest of her family were gathered, getting ready to sit down to the promised brunch.

Kerry regarded the trays of salad and light sandwiches with a polite interest, since their early morning breakfast escapade had resulted in a visit to Pumpernickels, and an English Scramble that both satisfied her salute to where her partner was, and adequately satisfied her appetite before their visit.

"Well, Kerrison, I hear your speech went very well." Her mother took her customary seat, and the rest of them joined her. "Did you enjoy yourself?"

Kerry picked up her glass of orange juice and sipped it, her brows hiking as she realized there was champagne in the mix. "Mimosas, Mother?" She put the glass down. "I had a lot more fun at the pub afterward, but I think it went well."

"Well, I thought it would be festive," her mother said. "After all, it's a lovely occasion, having all of you here." She took a sip of her own beverage. "It seemed to me to be a good chance for a little celebration," she added. "Even at 9:00 a.m."

Kerry had to smile. She set her glass down, and then almost jumped as her cell phone buzzed against her side. "Yow." She unclipped it and glanced at the caller ID, her smile broadening. "Excuse me a minute." She answered the phone. "Hey hon."

Unintended, but she could almost imagine the grimace her mother was hiding.

"Where are you?" Dar's tone, however, wasn't what she'd expected.

"My mother's." Kerry said. "What's up?"

"Is she acting like anything's going on?"

Kerry's brow creased, and she looked across at her mother, who peered back at her with a puzzled expression. "No. Is there something?"

"A jet flew into the North Tower of the World Trade Center," Dar said. "There's a lot of confusion going on, and I've got some traffic alerts on our net up there."

"Oh no!" Kerry gasped. "That's horrible! Did it lose an engine, or..." She glanced up, finding her family now quiet, and listening to her. "There's been an accident in New York," she explained. "A plane hit the World Trade Center."

"Dear God!" Her mother straightened, her eyes widening. "How incredible!"

The doors opened, and one of her aides rushed in. "Senator." He got out. "Come quickly. Please." He indicated the door. Visibly confused, Cynthia stood and started toward him.

Instinctively Kerry got up, her body reacting to the sudden tension in the room and the edge in Dar's voice. She followed her mother as they crowded through the double doors and into the media room where a large screen television was on. "Oh, wow."

"Are you watching it now?" Dar asked. "We're all here at the client site. Alastair is trying to get hold of Bob."

"Our guy in Manhattan?" Kerry asked, her eyes studying the horror on the screen. "My god, Dar. Look at that hole!"

"He was supposed to be at a client meeting there at eight thirty."

"Good heavens," Cynthia Stuart finally spluttered. "How on earth could they have allowed a plane to hit that building? What was the pilot thinking? Why didn't they stop it?"

"Oh no," Kerry exhaled. "Hope he's okay..." She stopped speaking.

Everyone stopped speaking. There was a shocked moment of silence before Mike grabbed the back of a chair and leaned forward. "Holy shit!" he said. "There's another one!"

"Fuck." Dar's voice echoed softly down the line. "That's no accident."

Kerry was stunned. She was watching the screen. She'd seen a second plane appear and crash into the other tower. Her mind was unable to grasp what she was seeing, however, as she struggled to make sense of the smoke, and the fire, and the sound of screaming and sirens coming from the television's speakers.

"Oh my god," she finally said. She could hear exclamations in strange accents from Dar's end of the conversation and it reminded her suddenly of where her partner was. "I don't think we're going to see the Alps, Dar."

Dar exhaled. "Not this week. No."

"Oh my god," Kerry repeated. "Dar we've got people all over that area." She finally forced her mind into a different gear. "What are we going to do?"

"I don't know," Dar answered. "I've got to call my parents."

"I'll get my laptop. I'll call you back," Kerry said. "I'll call you back in ten minutes. "

"Okay," Dar said. "No, let me call my Dad, and then I'll call you back. See if you can get on net," she said.

"Talk to you in a few," Kerry said. "Tell Mom and Dad I love them."

"I will," Dar's said. "I don't know where this is going, Ker. It could get worse. Talk to you in a few." She hung up.

Worse? Kerry folded her phone shut, only to have it ring again immediately, the caller ID showing the distinctive number at her operations desk. "Mother, do you have an internet connection in the house?"

Her mother turned her eyes wide and staring. "W...what?" she said. "What do you mean?"

Kerry shook her head. "Never mind, I'll find it." She turned and started out of the room as she answered the phone. "Stuart." She paused as she passed Angie. "I'm going to get my briefcase."

"Okay," her sister answered softly. "Kerry, what's going on? What's happening there?"

Kerry looked at her. "People are flying airplanes into buildings, Angie," she said. "On purpose." She eased past her sister and headed for the door, putting the phone back to her ear. "Go on."

Angie watched her go, then turned around to look at the television again. "Why?" she asked. "Why would anyone want to do that?"

DAR HELD ONE hand over her free ear as she waited for the line to be answered. Behind her, the room was raucous with all the consternation over what they were watching; only Alastair wasn't joining in as he was still, as was Dar, on the phone.

The line picked up. "Hello?"

"Mom?" Dar said.

"Well. That's one checkbox off my list." Ceci sighed in relief. "By the Goddess, this world has gone completely insane."

For once, Dar found herself in complete and total agreement with her mother. "How's Dad?"

"Freaking out," Ceci said succinctly. "So am I. Did you see those poor people jumping?"

"Yeah," Dar said. "It's horrible. I was on the phone with Kerry when the second plane hit." She glanced up as Alastair approached one hand over the mouthpiece of his cell phone. "Did you get Bob?"

"No," her boss said. "But John Carmichael just got through to me and he says they think there's more." His face was set and grim. "We need to start getting our people under cover."

"Right." Dar turned back to the phone.

"I heard," Ceci said. "Dar, please be careful. You're the only child I have and believe me, there aren't going to be any more."

The moment of macabre humor set her back a step, but Dar smiled anyway. "You guys be careful too. Glad none of us is anywhere near New York," she said. "I'll call back in a while. Stay put, that condo's built like a bunker."

"So your father said. Talk to you later, Dar." Ceci hung up.

Dar closed her phone, and looked up as John approached his face ashen. "What a way to ruin a lunch. Huh?"

"Is there anything we can do?" John asked. "We've already sent word to our people in upper Manhattan to get out of town, but I know you probably have a much bigger presence there."

"We do," Dar said. "I need net access. Can I get it here?" She looked over at Alastair. "I'm going to activate global meeting place."

"Absolutely, just come with me." John led her out of the room and through a wide oak door. They went into a smaller room, with several desks positioned around its edges. John indicated one of them. "There, and give me a minute and I'll get a line run."

Dar put her briefcase down and got her laptop out, sitting it on the desk and opening the top. She started it booting, while she removed her power plug and added the adapter that would allow it to connect to the UK power strip fastened neatly to one desk leg.

It was all mechanical. Her mind was going seventeen ways to Sunday in every possible direction, a brain cell overload that wasn't really helped when John flipped on the television in the corner on his way back over with an Ethernet cable.

She sat down and took a deep breath, exhaling slowly.

John glanced at the screen, shaking his head. "Here you go." He handed over the end of the cable. "You have an office in one of those?"

Dar plugged the cable in and waited for her logon screen. "No," she said. "I had a three week long screaming argument with the New York office when I refused to rent space there, and put them in Rockefeller Center instead."

"Bet they're thanking you now," John remarked.

"Bet they are," Dar said. "But we have probably two dozen clients in the towers and a lot more in that area."

"Ah."

Alastair entered the room. "There you are," He said. "I can't reach anyone in the Northeast. Damn cell system says all lines are busy."

"I bet." Dar entered her password and watched her desktop appear. She triggered the VPN tunnel to the office, and watched as the authentication system ran its routine.

Alastair perched on the edge of the desk, watching the television. John sat down in a nearby chair, doing the same.

After a moment, Sir Melthon entered, his face grave. "McLean, how about you and your lot moving here until this is sorted out. We've got space, and better facilities than the damn hotel." He glanced at Dar. "Who knows where this mess is going to end."

Alastair looked at Dar, who nodded. "Sounds good. Thanks, Sir Melthon," he said quietly. "We've got things there."

"Right. I'll send a man over for them." The magnate left, all his air of country squire completely vanished. "Things can spread. We're closing the gates."

Dar felt a headache coming on. She rested her chin on her fist as her work desktop appeared, and there, in the corner, a violently blinking box.

Global Meeting has been initiated. Please sign in immediately.
"Someone beat me to it." Dar logged in. "Damn I hoped we'd never have to use this," she said, as Alastair came around the corner and sat down in a chair next to her. "Here we go."

"Here we go," Alastair murmured. "Damn it."

KERRY SHOULDERED OPEN the door to her father's inner office, flipping the overhead light on and scanning the walls as she crossed the carpet over to the wooden desk. Her mind was so packed with dealing with the situation she felt no emotional charge on entering, focusing intently on finding a connection instead.

No wall jacks. She went to the desk and dropped her laptop on it, pulling the chair back and dropping to her knees to investigate the space underneath. Seeing nothing, she frowned, and started to get up again. "Guess it's the cell card. Damn."

Halfway up, she paused, suddenly aware of a soft humming sound. She thought it was her laptop, but as she moved away from the back of the desk it got softer instead of louder. She looked around the top of the desk, but saw nothing mechanical.

Puzzled, she got back down on the floor and turned over to lay flat on her back, inching forward so she could look between the desk and the wall to see if perhaps that was where either the elusive sound or the equally elusive connection might be.

There wasn't much space, but she managed to get an eye into position to look up and she immediately blinked at a box with blinking lights and a familiar logo. "Huh." Kerry reached up and freed an Ethernet cable already connected and coiled neatly, and brought it back with her as she wriggled back into the light.

She got to her knees and plugged the end of the cable into her laptop, hoping she wasn't about to expose her equipment to anything. "For someone who said they didn't trust technology..." She got up and pulled the rolling chair back over, seating herself in it and starting to log in. "Pretty strange to find a router nailed to the back of your desk."

The door swung open and Angie appeared. "There you are." She approached with a nervous expression on her face. "Oh my god, Kerry. They threw me and Mike out of mom's office." She looked around. "Is it okay to turn the TV on? You look so weird in here."

Mike burst in. "Stupid assholes."

Kerry glanced up from typing in her password. She found her brain completely unable to process this multiplicity of inputs and went back to the screen instead.

Mike went over and put the TV on, then dropped into the leather couch against one wall. "These people suck," he said. "Freaking government secrets. The big secret is the government has no clue what's going on."

"Mike." Angie sat down and twisted her hands. "This is really serious."

Kerry checked the IP settings her laptop had received, and then started up her secure VPN session to the office. It wasn't completely safe. She really didn't know whose router that was, or who controlled it, but the line in the back was an Internet circuit and she didn't have a lot of other options.

She hoped her Dar designed firewall was up to snuff.

"See?" Mike said, pointing at the screen. "No one's sure what's going on, look at those news guys."

"Give them a break, Mike." Kerry started up her profile and watched as her desktop appeared. "There are planes crashing into skyscrapers; that doesn't happen every day." The background of her profile was a picture of the sunset from their cabin, and for a split second, the familiar sight made her feel better.

Only for a split second. She signed into her management console as she got a barrage of network popups, the little boxes multiplying like hamsters across one side of her screen.

"Oh!"

Kerry glanced up, to see a fresh plume of smoke issuing from one of the towers, and then a ground shot of people running amidst showering debris. She jerked her attention back to her screen and ignored the popups, calling up the administrator access that allowed her control of their various systems and processes.

Selecting the Global Meeting place application, she activated it, clicking three times on the "Are you really sure?" warning boxes then sending it on its way.

Simple act, complex program. Kerry then turned and selected Mark's box from the popups. "Hey."

Poqueto Boss!

Kerry smiled grimly. *I just triggered the disaster plan. You better assemble your team in the conference room and get the situation stuff on the screens.*

Gotcha.

For a moment, Kerry just watched the disaster program assemble itself on her screen, opening up tabbed layers that broke the company down into regions and offices, placing a barebones chat area in the background, and presenting her with a box asking for her corporate identification, location, status, and role in the process.

"Kerry Stuart, Saugatuck Michigan, safe, moderator." Kerry muttered, as she answered the questions.

"What was that, Ker?" Angie asked. "They shut the airports down. Isn't that like locking the barn after the horse left?"

"What if there are more planes out there?" Mike asked.

"Oh no," Angie gasped.

Kerry's cell phone and PDA beeped. She opened her phone first, seeing an SMS message on the screen that echoed the request on her desktop. She then checked her PDA, and found a copy of it there. "Okay," she said. "So we know the SMS and email alerts are working."

A soft crackle alerted her in the background, and she reached into her briefcase for a small headset in a back pocket she'd never had to use before. She settled the buds in her ears, clipped the microphone on her shirt collar and plugged it in.

Already, information was flowing across the screen. She could see the senior management dashboard, icons lighting as their scattered main offices logged in to the system. A box opened, with Mariana's icon flashing, the system reporting her status on the header bar and very different from the normal net pops. *Hey.* Kerry typed in the box.

Hey. Mariana answered. *Have you contacted Dar?*

She was the one who called me and told me what was going on. Kerry typed back, aware of the chaos on the television across the room. *She's fine; she's at the client site in England. Alastair's fine too.*

Do you know if he got hold of the people in the NY office?

Kerry took a slow breath. *No.*

In her ear, she heard a soft chime. "Virtual conferencing coming online." She typed quickly. *I'm going on the conference bridge, you joining? I don't really know what's going on but it's a good excuse to try the system out isn't it?*

Mari's answer was wry even in written form. *I'd rather be doing shredder comparisons again.*

"What the hell was the point of this?" Mike asked. "How are they going to put those fires out anyway, drag hoses up a hundred floors?"

"I guess," Angie said. "I don't think there are ladders that reach that far."

"Okay," Kerry said into her microphone. "I'm opening the bridge, this is Kerry Stuart. "

Cracklings and murmurs answered her. "Houston ops here." "Lansing." "Charlotte." "Los Angeles Earth Station."

Slowly, a map built in front of her, stretching out from one side of the screen to the other, an outline of the world with the United States in the center and circles of light that indicated all their major offices, installations, infrastructure and service centers.

"Kuala Lumpur calling in." The acknowledgements continued. "Dubai." "Sydney's on."

"Miami Ops on," Mark's voice echoed softly. "Kerry, I'm inserting the news crawler into the global desktop."

"Thanks." Kerry saw the ticker appear.

"Oh, there's the president," Angie said. "Kerry, look!"

Kerry glanced up at the television. The destruction had been replaced by their president with several aides standing in what appeared to be a schoolroom. "Where in the hell is he?"

"Florida," Mike said. "Some school."

"Great," Kerry muttered. "Like the air traffic isn't screwed up enough," she said. "Every time he visits I end up sitting at some gate for six hours."

"Kerry." Angie turned. "Maybe we'll find out what's going on."

"CNN's got the prez on," Mark commented. "See if the feed updates."

"Miami exec?"

Kerry turned back to the screen. "Kerry here."

"This is Danny Chambers, at the Joint Chief's office," a man's voice said, sounding stressed. "Ma'am, it's crazy here."

"I bet," Kerry murmured. "I'm sure everyone's upset."

"No ma'am, that's not it," Chambers said. "They think there's more out there. More hijacked planes! There are folks running up and down the hallways around here. No one knows where the planes are."

There was a moment of dead silence. Kerry stared at the blinking status lights in front of her, and then she looked over her screen to the television, where the president was talking.

"Hello? This is Sherren from the Manhattan office! Is anyone there?" A voice broke in. "Is anyone there? I can't find half our people, and there's sirens and smoke everywhere! They closed the bridges and tunnels and they're saying to evacuate Manhattan!"

Voices now burst in, startled and afraid. Kerry took a few deep breaths, and then she spoke up. "Okay, okay, people, please settle down," she said. "Let's not panic. I know it's really confusing out there, but a lot of things are getting said and we don't have all the facts."

"This is Michael Talmadge up at the air hub," a new voice spoke up. "Kerry, I have a landslide of requests for more voice and video bandwidth for the FAA and essential services. "

"You got it," Kerry said at once. "Whatever you need to link speed up there."

"This is Houston ops," another voice said. "We're getting reports of cell failures on the East Coast. The government support team here says they're seeing a lot of dropped calls."

"Everyone's using their phones," Mark said. "Can't handle it, probably what's going on in NY. I can't reach any of the staff there, only Sherren is on the VOIP conf."

"That's right," Sherren agreed immediately. "Most everyone who's here is outside, or up on the roof trying to see what's going on. Sirens are going off like crazy."

Kerry thought fast. "Mark, send an SMS blast to everyone in the New York node and tell them to evacuate north. I don't' know what's going on there either, but I think it's too dangerous where they are."

There was a blast of confused noise, overwhelming the call.

"What in the hell..." Mark said. "Kerry I got that and we're working it but half the damn...oh, crap! The secure Virginia nodes just went down!"

"Danny?" Kerry asked. "Danny, you still there?"

Silence.

"Oh wow!" Angie exclaimed. "Now they think a bomb went off in the capital!"

Kerry felt her breathing getting faster. She could see on her network grid that there were flashing yellow and red lines now where she was used to seeing sedate greens and blues, and they were centered around the three nodes they had that ringed the Pentagon military complex.

"Yeah look! What? Oh...crap!" Mike half stood. "I think...did it go off at the White House? Is that what they said?"

"Pentagon," Kerry corrected him. "I think something happened there." She keyed her mic back on. "Okay, Mark, get those SMS messages out to New York, and also to anyone in the area of DC, Maryland, and Virginia. Tell everyone to get the hell out of there and get under cover."

"Kerry," Mari's voice broke in. "They're telling us to evacuate here."

"There?" Kerry leaned closer to the screen. "Why?"

"Oh my god! They just said another plane is heading here!" Sherren screamed. "Oh my god!"

"They think...they're afraid there are more targets," Mari blurted out. "We're a tall building, in the glide path...the building management just called. They got a call from Metro Dade and they told them to get out. They're evacuating a lot of the buildings behind us."

Too many inputs. "Sherren, why don't you go ahead and log off, go home, and then either text us or login from there if you can, okay?" Kerry suggested. "Mark, did you get those texts off?"

"Done, boss."

"Okay, I'm getting out of this office," Sherren said. "How do I text? Oh, no, wait, I see here in my phone, it's the first address, right? At least I can use this for something! I can't get a line to anyone!"

"Kerry, I just heard from one of our techs. A plane plowed into the Pentagon," Mark said. "He's texting me like a crazy person. The damn thing came in almost at ground level and smacked into one side. He says it's on fire there, and walls are about to come down."

"Okay." Kerry considered. "Houston Ops, are you there?"

"Here, ma'am."

"Can you take all the monitoring from Miami ops?"

"We're setting up consoles now."

"Mari, go ahead and tell everyone to leave the building," Kerry said. "I honestly don't think Miami's a target, but who the hell knows, and it's better not to take a chance."

"You got it."

"Mark, see if the tech can find Danny," Kerry said. "Get a text blast out and see if we can get a count of people out there."

"Working it."

"This is Sufir in Dubai," a voice very quietly broke in. "I know there is not much that we can do, but we are all thinking about all of you there and wishing with all our hearts the danger stops quickly."

"Miami Financial," Duks' voice broke in. "Houston, please stand by we're syncing the accounting systems."

"Standing by," the Houston Ops tech said.

Kerry looked up at the television, aware that her sister and brother were half listening to it, and half to her as pictures continued to roll along the screen, more smoke, more screaming people, more destruction.

Where would it end?

What if it didn't?

"COFFEE?"

Dar glanced up from her screen to find a server there, standing with a tray of steaming cups. "Thank you." She accepted one, and set it down, nodding as the server placed a small dish with four sugar cubes next to it, and a container of cream.

Alastair was still sitting next to her, one hand cupped over his ear, the other pressed against his cell phone. The television was on and Hans, John, and Francois were seated at the nearby desks watching the screen with expressions of bewildered disbelief.

"All right, thanks." Alastair closed his phone and turned back to Dar. "So where are we?" He picked up a set of ear buds connected to the second jack on Dar's laptop and inserted one in his ear. "Kerry's doing a hell of a job."

Dar nodded.

"Never seen her work before. Very impressive."

Dar nodded again.

"Dar?"

She looked up at him. "Sorry," she murmured. "Aside from all our people, I'm worried about my friend Gerry Easton."

Alastair's face tensed. "Ah. That's right. He works at the Pentagon, doesn't he?" He studied the screen. "What a goddamned mess."

Dar reached over to drop three of the cubes into her coffee cup, stirring the liquid with the provided spoon before she added cream to it. "So many damn people unaccounted for."

Alastair sighed. "What do we have down in that area?"

"Mostly commercial," Dar said. "Closest net node is near Penn Station." She leaned closer to the screen, listening as voices now echoed again.

"Hello? Hello? This is Sherren again."

Kerry's voice answered. "Sherren? Did you get out of the office?

Where are you?"

"I did, but you can't get anywhere," Sherren said. "I'm near Central Park though, at a Starbucks."

"Miami ops," Mark's voice sounded. "Kerry, I've gotten the blasts out to DC and NY," he said. "I'm only getting about fifty percent positives."

Everyone went quiet, and Alastair briefly closed his eyes.

"Well," Kerry said, "you know the cell systems are pretty overloaded, Mark. Let's wait and see what happens before we assume anything."

"Oh!" Sherren suddenly said. "Hey, it's Larry. Larry! Over here! I'm online!"

Dar studied the traffic patterns on the network screen behind all the chatter. She could see the bare bones chat window filled with lines of talk, the employees online who were not participating in the conference bridge sharing with each other in this remarkable time.

"Network looks pretty stable," Alastair commented. "But that shouldn't surprise anyone."

Dar glanced at the keyboard, then turned her head and looked at him, one eyebrow lifted.

"Well, I have seen you work before," her boss said. "So what's our plan here? Can we send help out to Virginia and New York? I know it's early yet..."

"OH MY GOD!"

Both of them jerked upright as though they'd been shot, and turned back to the screen.

"Good lord!" John blurted. "Look!"

"It's falling! Oh my god! Oh my god!" Sherren was yelling at the top of her lungs. "Oh my god! The whole tower! It's falling down!"

Dar's heart rate shot up as she found herself unsure of where to look first. The television screen showed a scene of unreal destruction, hundreds of stories of the World Trade Center collapsing in on itself as though taken down by an expert demolition team.

People were running.

People were screaming.

The air was full of thick, choking gray dust filled with debris that flowed and rushed over everything, leaving a landscape behind that must have been what Pompeii had been like just before the end.

Lunar. Horrifying

She stood up behind the desk, staring at the screen, unable to imagine actually being there and realizing she had been, the cross streets now covered in debris, places she'd walked on her last visit. "Damn."

"Son of a bitch," Alastair added, standing at her shoulder.

Hans covered his eyes, and then shook his head, opening his fingers to look at the screen again. "Mein Gott," he said. "Die ganzen

Leute hinein."

Dar remembered, then, suddenly, the moment after the explosion in the hospital when she'd been on the floor, lying in something like that same gray dust, in a completely different world.

Slowly she sat down and rested her elbows on her knees, and after a moment, Alastair perched on the edge of the desk, gazing quietly down at his shoes.

"Miami ops," Mark said. "Kerry, we're almost evacuated here."

"Miami ops, this is Houston ops," the Houston group broke in. "We are showing large scale outages now in lower New York."

"Miami exec, this is Herndon." Another voice. "We've had a request to activate the emergency circuits for Cheyenne, and add seventy two more channels to the tie lines."

It took a second, and then Kerry answered. "Ah," she said. "Sorry. Herndon, go ahead. Take standby circuits 2105 through 2110 and shut down the failover."

"Miami HR." Mari's voice. "Sorry to break in, but we're out of the building except for a few people."

"Miami exec, Miami ops." Mark's voice. "I'm staying."

Sir Melthon entered his eyes wide. "Did you see that?" He pointed at the screen. "Never in my life have I seen the like of it." He turned. "Got your things from the hotel, and they're settled here. Anything else we can do?"

Alastair sat back down in the chair and rested his elbow on the arm of it, propping his head up on his fingertips. "Got any good Scotch?'

Melthon snorted with wry understanding. "Of course we do. What do you think this is, America?" He snapped his fingers at one of the servers. "Bring me a bottle of the Talisker and a couple of dirty glasses."

"Sir." The man inclined his head, and scooted off.

Dar turned back to the screen, and settled the bud more firmly in her ear as she heard her partner's voice, sounding more than a little stressed.

"Miami ops, Miami exec. Mark, please shut down the center and leave," Kerry said. "The last person we need something to happen to is you. Work from home."

"Miami exec, you're not here, and you can't make me leave," Mark said, in a firm voice.

Dar keyed her mic for the first time. "I can," she said. "Get your ass out of there before I have my father drive over and smack you over the head and drag you out."

Totally against protocol. However, Dar figured the two people involved would know who was speaking without her announcing who and where she was and, given that the apocalypse was showing on television at the moment, who really cared anyway?

There was a moment of somewhat shocked silence. Then Kerry

sighed audibly. "Boy, is it ever good to hear your voice," she said, in an achingly sincere tone.

Alastair chuckled softly under his breath as Dar's face tensed into a mildly embarrassed half grin.

"Uh...okay, boss, I'm leaving," Mark responded meekly. "I don't want your pop thumping me," he said. "Or you thumping me."

Dar cleared her throat. "Good job, Kerry," she said, mindful of the global audience. "Everyone please just stay as calm as you can, and follow the plans we've laid out as best you can. This is horrific." She paused and exhaled. "This is unprecedented, and there are a lot people out there, both in the company and our clients that are going to need our help."

"Miami exec, this is Herndon." The voice almost sounded apologetic. "Excuse me, Ms. Roberts, but I have one of the folks at the Pentagon on a land line and he said part of that building just collapsed. They're going to need infrastructure support there."

What next? Dar rubbed her temples.

"Let's get some mobile units assembled," Kerry said. "Lansing, are you on?"

"Lansing here," a voice answered. "We have four vans."

"Lansing, this is Houston ops." The Houston office stepped up. "We have portable satellite units here. Miami exec, can we roll them east?"

"Going to need those in New York too, I'm afraid," Alastair murmured.

"Miami exec? This is Halifax," a crisp male voice broke in. "We have heard all the inbound international flights are going to end up diverting to Canadian airports and they're worried about the phone and data backhaul."

"Houston, go ahead and roll the units toward Virginia right now," Kerry said. "Halifax–Dar, do we have any spare capacity in that area to shift?"

Kerry could, Dar knew, have looked it up in the painfully detailed dynamic utilization chart she designed, but she knew that Kerry knew, she would know off the top of her head and, in fact, she did. "Well, I've got spare capacity right now in the Niagara node. I'm getting pretty much nothing from New York."

A small silence.

"We can land the net traffic. The phone backhaul is going to depend on how much damage the interchanges took." Dar went on. "There's a three carrier interchange that holds most of the big international circuits that sits right under 2 World Trade."

Another silence. Then Mark cleared his throat. "I guess that's why we're seeing red across the board up there."

Alastair clicked his mic on. "Ah, Houston," he said. "Let's get the community support teams rounded up and headed out. Not sure they'll let anyone near Manhattan but we can get to DC." He paused, and then added. "This is Alastair. I realize I'm probably not as instantly recognizable as some other people."

"Houston ops, we copy sir."

A loud crackle and everyone jumped. "Hello? Anyone there?" A breathless voice came through. "Oh hell. This is Danny at the Pentagon. What a mess. We need some help. I just managed to get my cell connected but they took out one whole side of the building and they're evacuating."

"Danny, do they need a trunk for backup?" Kerry asked. "I'm glad you're all right."

"Well," the tech sighed. "I've got a broken arm or something. We got lucky though. The side they plowed into was the side they just finished the renovation on and we were just pulling cable. Not many people were there."

Dar closed her eyes and rubbed the back of her neck, feeling a little relieved.

"But they say there are more planes out there so everyone's scrambling," Danny concluded. "I don't know if they're thinking about backup. I'll find out and let you know."

"Just text us, Danny," Dar broke in. "You'll probably lose cell."

A crackle, and there was no answer.

"Miami, this is New York," a new voice spoke up. "It seems we've moved the office to the Central Park Starbucks, but there are ten of us here now. We can't get cell to pick up, even for SMS. Can we get someone to log us in as okay?"

"New York, this is Miami HR-go head," Mariana answered. "Glad to hear from you."

Alastair clicked off his mic. "What the hell's going to happen next? This is nuts!"

Dar merely nodded, and then shook her head.

KERRY SUCKED SLOWLY at a cup of tea, her throat already a touch sore from talking. There seemed to be a slight lull for the moment, or else everyone was just a little shell-shocked and holding their breaths that nothing else bad happened.

She was resisting the urge to ask Dar to explain something esoteric, like node density, just to hear her voice.

"Ker?"

Kerry looked up over the edge of her laptop screen at her sister. "Hey."

Angie took a seat in one of the leather chairs on the other side of the desk and leaned forward. "What are you doing?"

"My job," Kerry said. "We're on a...I guess you could call it a big conference call, sort of," she explained. "But it's on the computer. We can all talk, and text message each other, and we try to make sure everyone knows what's going on."

Angie got up and came around the desk. "Is it okay for me to watch?" she asked. "I can't look at that television anymore."

"Where's' Mike?" Kerry eased over. "You can watch, sure."

"Getting some food. I think he's getting some for us too." Angie settled down next to her sister and peered at the screen. "Wow. That's a lot of stuff."

"It's what we call our Global Desktop." Kerry found herself glad to be just talking about something that wasn't a catastrophe. "That's a chat room in the back. Those are people all around just talking to each other over the computer."

"Uh huh."

"These folders are all the offices we have, and those dots are the people in them." Kerry indicated the other side of the screen. "These three over here are for our New York and Washington staff, and the people at the Pentagon."

Angie peered at her. "People at the Pentagon?" she asked, in a puzzled tone. "Why do you have people there? Is your company part of the military?"

Kerry heard people starting to talk again on the conference bridge. She keyed the external speakers so Angie could hear also. "The Pentagon is really just a humongous office building," she said. "We do their IT. Just like we do the IT for lots of other companies. We have about two hundred people there."

"Wow."

"Yeah." Kerry rested her head on her hand. "We can only find about half of them."

"Oh."

"Miami exec, Houston ops." A new voice came on. "This is Harold. I'm taking over for this shift."

"Go ahead, Houston. This is Miami exec," Kerry answered. She leaned back and tried to ease the stiffness in her back.

"Ma'am, the satellite trucks are ready to roll," Harold said. "We dug up enough gear for six."

"Good work," Kerry said. "Get them on the road, and please send at least three people in each one so they can spell each other driving and get rest."

"Yes, ma'am," Harold said. "We've got a lot of volunteers. Everyone wants to help."

"Miami exec? This is Danny in Virginia."

"Go on Danny. How's your arm?" Kerry responded.

"Um...it's okay," the tech said. "We just heard here that another plane is heading toward us." He added. "Two of the guys who were off got through all the barricades and we're going to get away from here for a little while. I think I could use a coke."

"This is New York!" Sherren broke in. "We just heard a bomb went off at the White House!"

"Maybe that's where the plane hit!"

Kerry drew in a breath, and then released it. She turned her mic off. "I just had the most unchristian thought of my entire life." Then she clicked the mic back on. "This is Miami exec, let's try to take in what facts we can, and not react to what we're hearing on television or rumors until there's some substantiation, please. "

"Miami ops here," Mark said. "From home," he added hastily. "I'm going to start cataloging the down circuits."

"Miami ops, this is the air hub," an unhappy voice interrupted. "Another plane just went down, but they're not sure where. "

"Pentagon here," Danny said. "At least it wasn't us again."

"New York here. Us either." Sherren sounded profoundly relieved. "I have a great view of the Empire State Building from here and that's where everyone said it was headed."

Kerry exhaled. "This is Miami Exec–everyone check and advise if there is any indication of an attack in your areas," she said. "Air hub, do they think there's more?"

"Air hub, Miami exec–they have no idea," the voice answered. "There are a lot of people in tears around here. They just evacuated LAX."

"LAX?"

"Miami Exec, Air Hub, this is LA Earth Station," a voice answered immediately. "Local news is saying they're not evacuating LAX, but they are evacuating a lot of buildings in downtown and the studios."

"LA Earth, this is Seattle Netops," a new voice said. "We heard they were going to close down LAX and SFO also, they think that's where the planes that hit the towers were going."

"Seattle, this is Herndon control–that's confirmed," a woman responded. "American Flight 11, America flight 77, United flight 175. Those are confirmed so far as the planes that hit."

"LA Earth station, Miami exec," Kerry broke in. "Do you have transponder space for 24 channels? I have Newark Earth station on text, they're getting overloaded."

"Miami exec, we'll check. Hold on one please."

"Wow," Angie whispered. "This is unbelievable."

"What is?" Distracted, Kerry whispered back.

"You know more than CNN does," her sister said. "I've heard more about what's going on in the last five minutes than I've heard all day on the television."

"Well, I wish I didn't," Kerry replied, turning her mic off. "The only reason we know as much as we do is because we're in the middle of it. We have a lot of government contracts. I know you remember our father complaining about that."

Angie blinked. "Oh," she said. "Wow. Was that what he meant?"

"Miami exec, this is LA Earth, we're good to take 24 channels," the LA satellite center responded. "Tell Newark to switch to our coordinates."

Kerry turned her mic on. "La Earth Station, thanks." She typed into the text box open on her desktop.

"Miami exec, Miami HR," Mariana said. "Miami office confirmed closed. The management company has locked the doors and verified that the generator is tested and ready to go."

"Thank you, Miami HR," Kerry said. "Houston ops, Miami exec. Do you see everything stable at the moment?"

"Miami exec, Houston ops. Standby we're verifying."

"Macro level looks stable," Dar's voice broke in, deep and rich and reassuring all out of proportion to what she was saying. "The autonomic programming expanded bandwidth across the northeast and it's doing a decent job of handling the backhaul, but I can see retransmits at a very high rate from the cell services."

Kerry smiled. "Thanks boss."

"You're welcome, Kerrison."

Kerry felt like melting, just a little, at the warm affection so evident in Dar's voice. She knew the rest of the company could probably hear it too but heck, if they didn't know by now about them the hell with it. She caught a small box blinking at the corner of her screen, and she clicked on it.

I am so damned proud of you.

"Aw," Angie said. "She's so sweet, Ker."

"I'm sure she wouldn't agree with you." Kerry typed in a response. *Boy do I wish you didn't have to be right now. But thanks, honey. I'm doing the best I can.*

"Oh!" Sherren's voice cut in. "Oh! Oh, there it goes! Oh! Oh my god! The North tower's falling! Oh! Oh no!"

Kerry and Angie looked up at the television, and stared as the screen showed a shaking picture of the second big tower collapsing into itself, the stories just dropping down and down and down as smoke and dust went up and up and up, outlined by people running toward the camera as fast as they could being chased by a roiling, thundering cloud.

"Miami Exec, this is the Air Hub," the Air Hub called out. "We've got a confirmation that the fourth plane is down, but it's in Pennsylvania."

"This is Danny at the Pentagon. We're still here. Now we heard a bomb went off at the state department and some helicopters just took off fast from the yard here," Danny said. "I can hear fighter planes going overhead."

"Miami, this is Seattle Netops." Another voice. "Vancouver hub's asking for more bandwidth. They're taking the Pacific overseas flights."

"Miami exec, Miami ops, Newark Earth Station just went down,"

Mark said. "We just lost the international telecom links in the Northeast. Only the Miami ones are up."

"Confirmed," Dar's voice said. "Everything from New York is down. I'm shifting the overseas banking through Miami."

"This is Herndon, Miami exec. We just got word another plane is inbound to Washington."

"Herndon, this is the Air Hub–we heard the same thing."

Kerry looked up again as Mike entered, carrying a big tray. "How much more of this can we take?" she asked. "Jesus."

He walked over and set it down, looking over his shoulder at the television showing the collapse of the North Tower over and over and over again. "This just sucks."

"This is New York," Sherren said. "People are screaming all over Central Park," she reported. "Just screaming. Screaming. Crying."

"Miami exec, this is Mid Atlantic Operations," a new, female voice interrupted. "We've gotten word they're evacuating all of Washington DC."

"New York too!" Sherren said. "They've got the bridges and tunnels closed south. Everyone's trying to get out north. You can't move. You can't move. Everyone's crying. Oh my god."

Kerry took in a deep breath, and then released it. "Seattle, give Vancouver what they need," she said, quietly. "Mid Atlantic, are you in a position to shift control to Lansing? Lansing, can you take that?"

"Miami exec, this is Lansing, we're working it," the local to her center said. "We've got a lot on our plates."

"Miami exec, this is Charlotte, we can take it," the southern center replied. "Mid Atlantic, give us five minutes and we'll be set up."

A soft knock made Kerry and Angie look up at the door to find their mother there, peering back at them.

"Children," Cynthia Stuart said. "I don't want you to be alarmed, but some very serious things have happened. Everything is under control, and I don't want you to worry, but you should plan to stay here for a few days while everything gets sorted out."

Angie looked at her mother, then at Kerry, then at the screen in front of them. She looked back at her mother, and then she looked at Kerry.

Kerry merely shook her head, and went back to the screen. "Thank you, Charlotte. Herndon–have you heard any more about that last plane? Is it confirmed in Pennsylvania? Miami ops is seeing a trunk down in the west there, but we don't want to assume."

Cynthia took a step into the room. "Whom is she talking to?" she asked Angie.

"The rest of the planet," Angie said. "Do you think you could ask the kitchen to make some fresh coffee? I think Kerry's going to need it."

Chapter Nine

"DAR, DID YOU say all the transatlantic phone lines were down?" Alastair pulled his seat a little closer to Dar.

"Alastair, don't talk to me for a minute," Dar said. "I'm rerouting traffic and you don't want me sending financial data streams to Tibet."

"Oh. Well, no, I sure don't."

Dar kept her eyes on the screen and her fingers on her keyboard, going through the somewhat delicate task of rerouting traffic across alternate paths they were never intended to travel. At stake were a lot of American tourists in Europe who needed to get to their ATM accounts, or use their credit cards.

Including herself and Alastair, of course.

There were four links across the Atlantic from New York, from four different providers, going to four different head ends in Europe. Absolutely rock solid redundancy unless you happened to lose the major landing point offices for all four providers on the same day.

What were the odds of that? Well. Dar exhaled, blinking a little as she peered at the screen. It was too bad she hadn't taken a bet on those odds, wasn't it? Probably could have paid off ILS's outstanding debt with the winnings.

She finished typing and reviewed the results, switching over to her network monitor to watch the lines out of Miami branching to South America, across to the Bahamas, and out to Africa. The traffic would have to take a back route across Africa to Europe, and the access would be hundreds of milliseconds slower.

A thousand milliseconds was a second though, and the end result would be an extra tap of someone's fingernails on the top of an ATM before it barfed out the local currency.

"Damn," Dar sighed. "The world's getting smaller every damn day."

"What's that, Dar?" Alastair turned around in his chair. "Can I talk to you now?"

Dar sat back and let her hands rest on her thighs. "I'm done," she said. "For now anyway, until the next damn thing happens." She flexed her fingers a little, reviewing in her head the details she knew she had to send over to the operations group soon.

Twenty changes that, in normal times, would have gone through four levels of approval, been scheduled weeks in advance with carefully coordinated validation from the individual banks and networks involved. No one except for Dar would have even considered doing it on the fly, but that was her role in this type of situation.

Anyone could have made the changes, one by one. Only Dar had the comprehensive understanding of the intricate spider web that was their network to do it without documentation, trusting her instincts and getting the moves done at the speed at which events were actually transpiring.

Had she not been there, or had net access, it still would have happened. Dar wasn't nearly so arrogant as to write a single point of failure into either her network design or their corporate processes. No one was indispensable.

Sir Melthon entered. He crossed over to Dar's borrowed desk and stuck his hands in his pockets. "My people are telling me it's no good trying to call over to the States. We've got resources in New York we can't contact, and it's a bit worrisome."

"The main trunks from overseas come into New York City," Dar said. "The termination point was underneath the World Trade Center."

"Ah," he grunted. "Putting a kink in your work, I'm guessing."

"Not really," Alastair said. "We've got a pretty comprehensive plan for this sort of thing."

Sir Melthon's head dropped forward a little, as he peered at Alastair. "For **this** sort of thing?"

"Well, disasters," he explained.

"Dar?" Kerry's voice echoed softly in her ear. "Can you cover for me for ten minutes?"

"Sure." Dar put her other ear bud back in. Then she removed it, and reached over to trigger the speakers in her laptop and half turned the machine so that their newest client could see the screen. "This is a system we developed to direct and coordinate a response to any kind of widespread disaster."

"We?" Alastair moved back so give Sir Melthon a better view. He folded his hands over his stomach and twiddled his thumbs. "Charmingly modest as always, Dar, but didn't you design this?"

Dar gave him a look from the corner of her eye. "Someone had to." She went on. "The system alerts everyone corporate wide where there is an event, either by sending them a network message..."

"Not much good if they're not in the building," Sir Melthon commented.

"Or via a PDA alert, SMS text message, or automated cell phone voice mail. Sometimes all four." Dar continued. "They're asked to respond in any of those methods, and the system logs their location, response and status."

Sir Melthon leaned closer. "Huh," he said. "How many people?"

"A quarter of a million," Alastair supplied. "It's a lot of people to keep track of."

"Those that can get on the net connect to this global desktop," Dar said, taking advantage of the slight lull in the chaos. "There's a chat area, a status tab for all the locations showing who's accounted for and who isn't, and the global conferencing system, which is a voice over IP bridge that lets us all talk to each other."

"Some folks call into that with their cell phones if they can, or a landline," Alastair supplied. "Keeps everyone informed, and lets us react to whatever we need to react to in real time."

"Miami exec? This is LA Earth station," a voice erupted suddenly. "Do we have a go to bring up the reserve transponders? We are not at capacity yet, but I bet we will be and we'd like to grab them before someone else does."

"LA Earth, this is Miami," Dar conceded to protocol, mostly for Sir Melthon's sake. "Go ahead and bring up whatever you have and hold it ready."

"LA, this is Seattle Netops. We're getting a request for additional uplink from Vancouver, can you take it? Four channels."

"Miami exec, this is Charlotte. Can you advise the status of Interbank? We have a text from London asking."

Dar cleared her throat a bit. "Charlotte, Interbank is routing via the southern links, approximately an extra seven hops, plus two hundred milliseconds, but stable," she reported.

"Uh, thank you ma'am."

"Miami exec, this is Miami ops, we're publishing the new routes on the big map," Mark said. "Be advised, we're assembling technical teams and checking inventory."

"What's that about?" Sir Melthon inquired. "Checking inventory?"

Dar checked the news ticker, and then looked up at the television screen. "Any word on how long the flights are grounded?" she asked. "They're getting teams ready to go and help all our customers get back onto service."

"Tomorrow noon, at the earliest I heard," Alastair said. "I've been exchanging mail with Bea. She's trying to see if she can get us international flights into Mexico and arrange a pickup if you don't mind going to Houston first."

"Huh." Sir Melthon got up and moved out of the way, strolling back across the room toward the door. "Not bloody bad, for Americans." He disappeared, leaving them to listen to the new voices coming from Dar's speakers.

"This is Tom Stanton from the New York office."

Dar recognized one of the senior salesmen's voice. "This is Miami, go ahead Tom," she said. "Good to hear you."

"I just made it up to our office on the Rock," the man said. "We were up in the South Tower."

Dar felt a chill run up and down her back, and Alastair leaned forward, his expression altering to one of grim seriousness. "Go on," she said, as the rest of the background chatter faded.

"What a nightmare," Tom said. "We were up on the ninetieth floor when the North Tower got hit. I saw the damn plane plow right into the side of the building and saw whatever was in its way come flying out the back side."

"Good lord," Alastair muttered.

"A lot of people stayed to watch," Tom said. "We started to head out of the place because it seemed to us the tower might lean over into the South. We couldn't get an elevator, so we started walking down and we were just past the sky lobby when that second bastard hit."

Dar caught a pop up box from the corner of her eye. She opened it.

I'm back, thanks sweetheart. Needed a bio break.

Dar flexed her fingers and typed back.

Anytime. I reported the Interbank reroute and told Seattle they could take four more sat channels from LA for Vancouver, and told LA they could bring up the cold reserve transponder space. She paused, glancing at Alastair who was typing on his PDA. *Wish we were home on our couch.*

"So we kept going," Tom said. "The stairs were full of dust and hot as hell. You could hardly breathe, and there were these firemen trying to go the other direction. What a mess. Pieces of concrete kept falling on everyone."

I wish we were too. My mother's here listening. I want my dog, and my PJ's and you, and all I have is my father's desk and my family not understanding what the hell I'm doing.

"Tom, this is Sherren," Sherren interrupted. "Are you all back? Are you at the office? We're up at Central Park, about a dozen of us."

There was a silence. "Just me and Nancy are here right now," Tom answered. "I don't know where everyone else is. We lost them. Bob stopped to help this lady, and two of the other guys did too, and then part of the stairwell caved in."

"Jesus," Alastair whispered.

"Oh no," Sherren said. "Maybe we should go back to the office and wait there, maybe they'll show up next."

"Anyway," Tom continued, tiredly. "We got down to the bottom floor and out into the plaza. There were bodies all over the place. People jumping, I guess. The firemen were trying to move them but they kept getting called to go this way, then the other way. They were going crazy."

Dar closed her eyes. She was aware that someone had muted the television, and the room they were in was totally silent.

Alastair clicked his mic on. "Tom, this is Alastair. I'm glad you made it out. I know it was rough."

"Thank you sir," Tom answered. "We were just past the plaza when everyone started screaming, and I heard this rumbling in back of me. It sounded like a big plane, you know, a seven forty seven. That rumbling when they're going to take off? And these huge bangs. I never heard anything like it." He took a breath. "There were cops in front of us and they just started yelling for us to run, run, run–they shoved us down the street and I looked behind me and saw it coming down."

"Oh no," Sherren murmured.

"We started running, but there were these firemen..." Tom stopped, and then went on again. "They started yelling and running the other way, toward the building, and the cops were trying to catch hold of them and stop them, and then the cloud was on top of us and all we could do was get behind some trucks and lay down and pray we didn't die from it."

At the end of the sentence his voice broke, and they could hear him crying. Dar bit her own lip and looked down at her keyboard. She folded her hands and rubbed the tips of her thumbs together, unable to truly fathom what it must have been like to have been there.

Alastair keyed his mic again. "Tom. Is there anything you need done? What can we do to help out?"

Tom drew a shaky breath. "We're okay," he said. "We both live down in Greenwich. We can't go home." He added "is Dar there?"

Startled, Dar looked up. "I'm here," she said, after a brief pause.

"God bless you," Tom said. "God bless you for not listening to us."

"Tom, we're all heading back to the office," Sherren said. "We'll stay together and help each other out. Okay? We'll see you soon."

Alastair put his hand on Dar's arm. "Do they have any kind of facilities there, at the office? Food?"

Dar nodded. "Showers, gym, kitchen, vending, yeah," she said. "They were so pissed at me for not putting them in the Trade Center I decided to throw in the works for them there."

"Hindsight," Alastair said, grimly.

"Yeah." Dar typed a response into the waiting message box. *On the flip side, at least we're both away from the trouble and safe instead of in the middle of it. One building collapsing on me in my lifetime was more than enough.*

Kerry's response was almost immediate. *You are so right. I'll stop my whining and get back to work now—talk about getting a new perspective.*

Definitely. Dar leaned back and looked around, finding the room full of both their team, and Sir Melthon's people, all quietly listening. "Damn." She shook her head. "Not a good day."

Not a good day at all.

"Scotch all round, I think." Sir Melthon turned to practical matters. "Think it's going to be a rather long night."

KERRY STOOD UP and stretched, twisting her body right and left. "Pentagon, Danny, this is Miami exec. Are you still out there?"

A soft crackle. "This is Roger, Miami exec. Danny is getting his arm taken care of finally." The voice that answered was hoarse. "Part of the wall, the outside, just fell down. Fires are still burning here, but a lot of the paramedics are around and taking care of people."

"Miami exec, this is Herndon. We believe the outage in Somerset is due to the United 93 crash near there. One of our techs reported it's in a large field about 80 miles southeast of Pittsburgh."

Kerry rubbed her neck. "Okay," she said. "Thanks Herndon. How many people are we looking at for the outage?"

"Ten major customers, Miami exec." The voice on the other end sounded apologetic. "And our backhaul to Houston."

"Ah." Kerry sighed. "Okay. How many transponder channels are we looking at? I want to send as many of the sat rigs to New York as we can, since they've got so much infrastructure down."

"We can probably do it with three megs, Miami exec"

Kerry considered. "Hang on." She glanced across the room, uncomfortably aware of her mother watching her like some match at Wimbledon. She keyed her mic again. "Tell you what, Herndon. If the lines aren't repaired by the time the trucks get to your area, I'll send two your way. Can you pressure the vendor?"

There was a moment of silence. "Uh...I don't think we've even called them," Herndon answered meekly. "Everyone's still freaking here."

Understandable. "No problem, Herndon," Kerry said. "Let's revisit the question in about ten hours. It'll take that long for the trucks to get out of Texas anyway."

"Will do, ma'am," the tech replied. "That sounds like forever. It feels like today is already twenty four hours gone."

Kerry looked at her watch. "And it's not even noon," she murmured. "You're right." So much had happened in so short a time it was hard to process it. Had it really been less than three hours? So short a time for the world to have changed so profoundly.

It seemed incredible. But at least they hadn't had any catastrophic news in the last fifteen minutes. Kerry wondered if there were more planes out there, heading to places further away. Could they have gotten them all?

What if there were other things planned? What if it was just the start?

"Miami exec, this is Miami HR," Mari's voice caught her attention. "I've just gotten off the phone with the community support team. We're working on sending assistance to Washington and New York, but we need some input on what the requirements are."

"Miami HR, this is Roger at the Pentagon. We sure could use a chuck wagon and a hot spot here."

"Roger, we already have the big bus headed your way," Mari said. "I'll tell them to stop and pick up food."

"I remember that big bus," Kerry commented to Angie. "It's what showed up outside the hospital the last time. I was so glad to see it I almost cried."

"I remember you told me about it," Angie said. "I think you mentioned leather couches and a beer tap."

"Oh, thanks ma'am." Roger did, truly sound grateful. "We'll tell the guys with guns to let us know when it gets here. They're really tight right now."

"I can well imagine," Mari said. "Which reminds me, Miami exec? Do we know when we can get relief teams into Manhattan? I heard the bridges and tunnels are all closed inbound."

Kerry's brow creased, and then she keyed her mic. "Hang on. Let me see what I can do." She turned to her mother. "Mother? Can you find that out for me?"

Caught utterly by surprise, Cynthia Stuart stared at her for a long moment. "I beg your pardon, Kerrison?" she finally spluttered. "What are you asking me?"

The irony was almost too much. Kerry felt uncannily like she wanted to sneeze. "We want to send community support trailers into New York to help our people, and anyone else," she explained. "I need to know when they'll let people into the city. Can you find that out for me?"

Her mother looked honestly perplexed. "Me?" she asked.

"You're a Senator, Mom," Angie supplied helpfully. "I think Kerry figures the government would probably tell you sooner than they'd tell her if she called." She ignored Mike, who had covered his mouth with one hand. "Right Ker?"

Kerry nodded. "I think our nearest ones are in Boston and Albany."

"Senator." One of Cynthia's aides poked his head in the door. "I think they are ready to start the conference call again, apparently the lines are working better now."

Cynthia regarded him. "Albert," she said. "I need you to find something out for me, urgently."

The aide blinked in surprise and entered all the way in the room, glancing at Kerry and her brother and sister briefly. "Yes, ma'am? Do you want to discuss it in your office?"

"No," Cynthia said. "Please find out at once when the roads into Manhattan will be reopened to allow assistance into the city."

"Senator?"

"Was I not clear?" Senator Stuart asked. "I realize there is much confusion in this situation, but there are resources ready and willing to help some of those poor people and we must assist. So please go at once."

"Ah, sure," the aide said. "We have resources?"

"Yes," the senator confirmed.

"Okay." The aide turned and headed for the door. "I'll start working on that right away. Do you want to come to your office for the conference call?"

Cynthia sniffed. "Based on the last one, I think my time is more valuably spent sitting here. I certainly have learned far more."

The aide looked puzzled. He merely nodded and left.

There was a brief, awkward silence. "Hey Ker." Angie got up.

"Want some ice tea? My throat's dry listening to you yak this whole time."

"Sure," Kerry said.

"I'll help." Mike followed his sister out the door, leaving Cynthia and Kerry alone in the room.

Kerry made a mental note to properly thank her siblings at a later time. She sat down and rested her elbows on the desk, half hoping for an interruption from the conference line. "Thanks," she said belatedly. "I know there's a lot going on but we want to help where we can."

Her mother folded her hands together. "I had no idea how involved you were with this sort of thing," she said. "Your company seems quite organized."

"We try to be," Kerry said. "I don't think you can ever prepare for something like what we're living through today, but we do have plans for different types of problems."

Her mother digested this. "You seem very competent." She looked up to see Kerry's expression. "I'm sorry. That must sound very patronizing," Cynthia said. "But to be truthful, I really had no idea until today what it is you actually did, Kerrison."

Kerry grunted.

"And, actually, I still don't really grasp what it is you were discussing on that machine." Her mother went on. "Except that it seems to be very involved with different parts of the government, which surprises me."

"It shouldn't," Kerry said. "Don't you remember father saying he wanted our company out of all the government contracts we hold?"

Cynthia studied her. "Extraordinary," she murmured. "I do remember him saying that. I just had no understanding of what he meant until now."

It almost made Kerry smile. But not quite. "Don't worry," she said. "You're in good hands." She turned hers over and exposed the palms of them. "We know what we're doing."

"It certainly sounds like you do," her mother said.

"Does that surprise you?" Kerry asked.

Her mother frowned. "Of course not," she said. "You've always been quite clever, Kerrison."

"Senator? The call's starting." Another one of the aides popped his head in. "They think they've gotten hold of someone at the Pentagon to give an update, and they're asking for all of Congress to go to Washington to be in session tomorrow."

Cynthia Stuart glanced at him. "Please put the call in here, to this phone." She indicated the console phone on the desk where Kerry was sitting. "I'll take it here."

"Ma'am?" the aide looked pointedly at Kerry. "It's a secure line."

"Yes, thank you for clarifying that for me," the senator said. "Now please just do as I asked, and while you are at it, tell the staff to bring coffee service in as well," she added. "I will need to evaluate if I can leave my family here before travel is arranged to Washington."

"All right, Senator. If you say so." The man still looked dubious, but he nodded and escaped out the door, shaking his head a little.

Cynthia waited a moment, and then she turned to Kerry. "I would rather we have all of the information in one place. I trust you understand how confidential it is."

"It's okay." Kerry rested her chin on her hand. "I've got a top secret clearance."

Her mother paused in mid breath, tilting her head to one side as she regarded her daughter. "You do?"

Kerry nodded.

"Miami exec? This is the Air Hub."

Kerry turned to her screen. "Go ahead, Air Hub, this is Miami exec."

"We've been alerted to possible power disruptions." The Air Hub tech sounded exhausted. "We've only got a four hour generator at the moment since the big one is on service."

"I'll take this one," Dar's voice broke in. "I'm just in the mood to scream at someone."

Now, Kerry couldn't help but smile. "Thanks boss." She keyed her mic. "My throat's giving out."

"Miami exec, this is LA Earth station. Any word on Newark Earth station? We're running out of transponder space here."

Kerry checked her text messages. "Miami ops, anything from Newark?"

"Nada," Mark answered. "I'll text them. See what I can find out. They probably lost the backhaul. It went through the 140 West station into the Niagara 3 hub."

"Everything's down on that hub," Dar said. "We lost a ton of facility."

"Miami, this is Sherren in New York. We're all back in the office at Rockefeller." She paused. "No one else has showed up from the Tower yet."

"Okay, thanks Sherren," Kerry said. "Are you sure you all don't want to leave and go home?"

"No." The woman sounded tired, but definite. "We want to stay together here and wait for the others. Anne's making some soup for us in the kitchen."

The aide returned, and went to the phone, picking up the receiver and punching some buttons on it. "They're a little late Senator."

"Mm," Cynthia said. "More than you possibly know."

"Ma'am?"

"ALL RIGHT, THANKS Bea." Alastair closed his PDA, and sighed.

"Well, damn it all. Bea said it's hard to even get the travel agents to talk to anyone. Everyone's packed to the gills busy with people stuck all over the place trying to get from point A to B."

"Mm?" Dar was chewing on a rib.

"Right now, there are zero planes flying," her boss said. "So everyone's trying to get around that, and Canada's not letting anything take off so a lot of people are looking to Mexico." He rubbed the back of his neck, looking more than a little stressed. "Mexico City and Guadalajara are booked solid. Cabo's open, but that's a hell of a trip."

Dar put her rib bone down and selected another from the plate in front of her. "Fly us into Cancun and I'll have my parents pick us up in the boat," she suggested. "They can drop you at Galveston and take me home."

Alastair pursed his lips. "Are you serious?" he asked. "That's an awful lot of trouble to go to."

Dar shrugged. "It'll take days, but it's going to take days to get home anyway," she said. "Dad's boat will go thirty five knots and he's got a small satellite onboard," she said. "Worth a try, anyway."

Her boss pondered a moment. "Well, let me let Bea look at that possibility." He opened his PDA gain, half turning away as he typed. "Beats driving up from Cabo I guess."

The idea was on the crazy side. Dar had one ear cocked in the direction of the laptop, and she was listening to the stream of chatter from the conference bridge while she worked her way through some unbelievably excellent barbeque. Everything today had been on the crazy side though, and she saw little advantage in not thinking as outside the box as she could.

The pictures on the large screen flat panel television were bleak. She'd watched the crashing of the planes and the falling of the buildings dozens and dozens of times and she found she was starting to get a little shell shocked from it.

The pictures of the men and women covered in gray dust were almost surreal, and she had to keep reminding herself that this wasn't a made for television disaster movie every time they showed the huge, billowing cloud chasing people down the street.

Hard to believe it was real, until she heard the counterpoint of Kerry's voice behind her acknowledging this outage and that, and taking reports from people who were really there, really experiencing the horror and trying to stay professional and work their way through it.

High point for the company. Bottom of a crater point for humanity.

Sir Melthon entered. "Well, things seem to have settled a bit."

"Planes are out of the sky," Dar agreed. "Who knows if that's the end of it though?"

The magnate sat down in the seat across the desk from her. "Hell of a thing," he said. "We've still got some missing people in New York.

Could I pass you along the names, and see if your fellows there have seen or heard of them?"

"Sure," Dar said. "We're missing some of our own."

"So I heard," he replied. "Dinner turn out all right for you? My second chef's from Dallas, and he insisted on making some of this stuff for you lot. Been cooking since last night."

"It's very good," Dar said. "I don't get to eat barbeque very often. Takes too long and the local joints are all chains," she admitted. "Miami's not really a part of the south."

Sir Melthon snorted. "The wife's been after me to visit there. Worth it?"

Dar shrugged one shoulder. "My hometown, so I think so. If you want to enjoy it, come in winter. If you want your wife to ask you to go somewhere else stop by in the summer."

"LA Earth Station, this is Miami exec." Kerry's voice sounded more than a bit hoarse. "We have Newark on text, they not only lost their backhaul, they have a total power outage and their plumbing backed up."

Dar turned all the way around and stared at the laptop in bemusement.

"Uh. Miami exec, this is LA Earth. We copy that," the Earth station replied. "Sorry to hear it. We'll keep squeezing everything we can up to the birds."

"Thanks," Kerry answered. "Okay, what's next?"

"That one of your people?" Sir Melthon asked. "That gal? Sounds like a sharp one. Been listening to her go on for a while now."

Dar put her rib bone down. "That's our vice president of operations," she replied. "Kerry Stuart." She picked up her napkin and wiped her lips. "She's very sharp." She caught sight of Alastair watching her out of the corner of her eye. "And yes, she's mine."

"Another one of those smart mouthed women?" But Sir Melthon smiled when he said it.

"I wouldn't have any other kind," Dar replied mildly. "Especially not in Kerry's position." She picked up a french fry and bit into it, aware of the faint shaking of Alastair's shoulders nearby.

"Well, to each their own," the magnate pronounced.

"Hey, Dar?" Alastair turned around and faced her. "Can you think of a reason why the government's looking for me?"

Dar stared at him in momentary bewilderment. "What?"

Her boss held up his PDA. "Bea just messaged me that she got a call from Washington asking where I was, and could they talk to me."

Sir Melthon held his silence, looking between his two guests with a look of absorbed interest.

Dar folded her hands together. "Well," she considered, "we do have a lot of accounts with them." Her brow creased. "But this is hardly the time for them to be asking about contracts and we're already doing everything possible and some things not possible to keep things rolling."

"Exactly," Alastair said. "Ah, maybe it was a mistake. Someone following up on something that doesn't really matter today, probably."

Dar nodded. "Happens sometimes. People focus on small stuff when they can't handle the big." She agreed. "We've got a lot of work to do, though. Those six sat trucks aren't even going to be a drop in the bucket with all the lines we lost."

Alastair exhaled, forking up a piece of brisket. "Should we even be worrying about that, Dar? Lot of people lost a lot of things, including their lives there today. What the hell do our circuits matter, really? Everyone's going to understand if things aren't back to normal by tomorrow." He looked uncharacteristically grim. "I feel like a bit of an ass listening to us go crazy there on the link when people are lying under tons of debris on the south end of Manhattan."

There was a small silence. Dar picked up a rib and bit into the side of it. "Alastair," she said, after she finished chewing. "What are our options? Do nothing and just watch CNN all day? We can't help those people."

"Well, yes but..."

"We can, however, work our asses off keeping people communicating with each other." Dar cut him off. "That's what our people are doing. That's what Kerry's doing, making space for people stuck in Canada trying to send mail home and make arrangements, or keeping the cell centers connected, or people's ATM cards working. We do what we do. We're doing more to help the damn country than ninety percent of the planet."

"Woman speaks the truth." Sir Melthon broke in. "It's been damned impressive to watch. Wasn't looking for a practical demonstration of your abilities, McLean, but I'm no idiot not to take advantage of the opportunity."

Alastair sighed. "Of course, and thanks," he said. "It's just such a rotten excuse for it."

Dar finished her rib and wiped her fingers, then picked up her glass of tea and took a swallow. She understood Alastair's frustration. At least she had something she could do, instead of just listen. "I'm going to give Kerry's throat a break," she said. "Last thing she needs is laryngitis."

Her boss managed a smile at that. "Bet she wishes you were there," he said.

"We both wish we were home." Dar answered, sliding her chair back to face the screen and keying her mic. "Ker?"

There was a scuffing noise. "Here."

"Go take a break," Dar said. "Drink some hot tea. You're starting to sound like a frog. I've got this for a little while."

Kerry cleared her throat. "Ah. Yeah." She sounded grateful.

"Thanks boss. Any word on flights?"

Dar had to smile. "Not so far," she said. "They're still working on it."

Her partner sighed. "Okay. I'll be back in a few." She clicked off and Dar settled down to watch the screen, consciously aware of how far she was from home. "One problem, Alastair." She glanced over at him. "We'll be in the air a hell of a long time."

"I know," Alastair said, rubbing his eyes. "I know."

Too much happening, too fast. Dar rested her chin on her hands. Now that the immediate threat seemed to be on hold for the moment and she had time to reflect, her mind was starting to churn over with all the problems she now had to worry about.

Getting home. Getting Kerry home. Finding out about their people. Finding out about Gerry.

Figuring out how this was going to change their world.

KERRY RETREATED TO the solarium with her big mug of tea and honey, curling up on the bench as she let the silence and the rich, green smell sooth her nerves. Her ears still felt like they were ringing with all the voices and the sounds from the television, and it took her a few minutes before her mind wound down and she could relax.

She hitched the knee of her jeans up and rested one socked foot on the opposite knee, comfortable in her T-shirt in the relatively warm air.

She sipped her tea, grateful for the warm sweetness as it slid down her throat, and more than grateful to her partner for taking over the reins for a while so she could have a chance to chill out and collect her scattered thoughts.

Thank goodness for Dar. What would she do without her? Kerry thought about some of the things that had gone on and how if just a few things had been different how they could have so easily been affected more dangerously.

It felt good to just sit quietly, out of the limelight, and away from the watching eyes of her family and her mother's aides. She thought she'd done a very credible job so far, but she felt exhausted from all the emotional and intellectual turmoil of the past few hours.

The television had just been showing shots of people being recovered from the Pentagon. Kerry had sat there watching with a sense of odd disconnection, knowing some of the people on the screen were surely known to her by name, but not by sight.

Then they'd shown a press conference from New York. How many were dead? No one knew. Or else, no one wanted to say, all the mayor kept repeating was that it was more than they could bear. People were shell shocked, literally.

Terrorism. Kerry remembered, vaguely, her father once talking about the country's tendency to serve its own best interests being good for business, but bad for politics and she wondered if that notion was finally coming home and proving him right.

Odd. Roger Stuart had never been a friend of the rest of the world. He'd been an America first supporter for as long as Kerry could remember, but now she had a sense that despite his views, he'd understood more of the truth of the world than he'd preached to his constituents.

She thought about how he'd have reacted to what had happened. She suspected he'd have been at the head of the line urging retaliation immediately. Eye for an eye. He'd been that kind of man, something that had always made her very uncomfortable and had led to him doing his best to interfere in her life.

It was internally very surprising to her to find she had more of an understanding of that viewpoint than she'd imagined. She could think about these people, who had destroyed so much and hurt so many, and knew in her heart what she felt for them wasn't anything close to compassion.

A little shocking.

"Hey Ker." Angie entered the solarium, and took a seat on the other swinging bench.

"Mm." Kerry lifted her mug in her sister's direction.

"I was just listening to Dar talk on the computer. She's got a little Southern accent, doesn't she? I never noticed it before."

Kerry was quite happy to focus her thoughts on her partner for a minute. "Hm." She considered the question. "A little, yeah," she agreed. "Not all the time. It comes and goes."

"I like it," Angie said.

"Me too." Kerry smiled. "When she's around her father a lot, it gets more pronounced because he has one, and sometimes when we spend time down in the keys, too." She spent a moment thinking about Dar's voice, hearing the faint drawl echoing in her imagination. "Wish she was here."

"I bet you do," Angie said. "Is Mom being in there freaking you out?"

Kerry swung back and forth a few times. "Not really," she finally said. "I mean, there are a lot of other people on there listening to me, you know?"

"Not in the same room."

"No," Kerry admitted. "I think it's freaking her out a little."

"It was freaking me out," Angie said. "It was all happening so fast. But you just handled everything like it was an everyday thing," she added. "It was such a weird contrast to that conference Mom was on. No one knew anything."

"Mm." Her sister grunted agreement, as she slowly sipped her tea. "Or didn't want to admit anything," she said. "After all, we have whole chunks of the government we pay a lot of money for that are supposed to keep this kind of thing from happening."

"Well, I'm sure they tried. I mean, who'd ever have thought someone would fly a plane into a building?" Angie asked. "I mean, you think about bombs and stuff, not things like that."

Maybe that was true. Kerry leaned back and let her head rest against the chain support of the swing. The sun was pouring in the windows of the solarium and it warmed her skin, providing her with some quiet peace as the silence lengthened between them.

"Richard's dropping Sally off here," Angie finally said after about five minutes. "He thinks he might have to go to Washington for his firm."

Kerry started back to alertness from the light haze she'd fallen into. "Oh," she said. "Well, it'll be nice to see her anyway," she said. "How long has he had her?"

"Only a week. He picked her up a few days before you got here," Angie said. "I'm glad. Not that he has to go to Washington but I'd feel better with her here. Things are so weird." She gazed at her sister with a smile. "And she can't wait to see her Aunt Kerry."

Kerry returned the smile. "Ah well." She finished her tea. "I'm going to go back in there and see what Dar is up to. She's the one who's under pressure, really. Alastair's right there next to her and they're in front of our new clients."

She got up, a little surprised at how tired she felt. She waited for Angie to precede her and then followed her sister out of the solarium and through the hallway, checking her watch as they entered the big entranceway where several of the Senator's aides were gathered talking.

The voices cut off as soon as they were recognized. Kerry and Angie exchanged wry looks. "Some things never change," Angie commented, as they walked past and pushed open the door to their father's former office.

"Isn't that the truth?" Kerry glanced around, spotting her mother talking with another aide near the far wall, while her laptop sat quietly on the desk, a soft murmur of voices coming from it. She went over and sat down behind the desk, reaching down to pull her socks up a little as she glanced at the screen to see if anything had radically changed.

"Kerrison?" Cynthia left the aide standing near the other door and came over to the desk. "It seems that it's felt we all, that is the Congress, should all go immediately to Washington to show our support in this horrible time."

Kerry rested her elbows on the desk. "Well, I guess that does make sense," she said. "But...is it safe?" she asked. "Weren't they evacuating Washington?"

Her mother perched on the edge of the desk. "Well, that did come up," she said. "But the general thought was, for that reason especially we should all go and show we aren't afraid," she explained. "Ah, I think the term was, show the flag."

Kerry stared at her for a long moment. "Mother," she said. "That's idiotic."

"Kerrison."

"I'm sorry, but it is. If you have people who are willing to fly airplanes into buildings, what's to say they're not also willing to drive trucks into the front of the Capitol?" Kerry asked. "They're not even sure who did it yet."

Her mother sighed. "That actually did occur to me, as well as to several others," she said. "However, as I say, the consensus is that we need to come together and show support and I am not entirely sure that's wrong either. We must set an example for the country, after all."

Kerry caught a motion out of the corner of her eye and she focused on the screen, surprised to see a familiar figure sitting in the corner of her desktop, holding up a sign. "Will work for hugs," she murmured. "Oh sweetie."

"Excuse me?" her mother asked.

"Sorry." Kerry tore her eyes from the forlorn looking Gopher Dar. "Mother, I understand what they mean. I just hope it turns out that everyone stays safe, and they're not part of another catastrophe."

Her mother looked more than a bit discomfited. "Yes, well..." She looked around, then looked back at her daughter. "You know it was so curious to me that really, you had so much more information than we did during this morning's horrible events."

A little surprised at the subject change, Kerry resisted the urge to return to her desktop and concentrated on paying attention to her mother instead. "Information is what we do," she said. "We have to know what's going on."

"Exactly," Cynthia Stuart said. "That's what I told some of my colleagues and they were also very surprised at how much better organized it all seemed for your company."

Kerry frowned. "Well, they do pay a good amount of money for our services, Mother. I'd like to think we give the American taxpayers their dollar's worth."

"They were very interested to hear about that," her mother said. "They would like you to accompany me to Washington," she added. "I was sure you'd be more than glad to go."

For a moment, Kerry sat very still, aware of a flush of cold anger that made her hands tingle and left her slightly lightheaded. "Number one," she said, after waiting long enough to make sure she wasn't going to stand up and yell. "You had no right to tell them that, and number two, no I would not be."

"Kerrison, I don't think that's called for."

Now, Kerry did stand up, aware her body was tensing and her hands were curling into fists. "I don't give damn what you think," she said. "And I certainly don't care what your friends in Congress think. I don't owe them any explanations."

Her mother got up off the edge of the desk. "I told them you'd come talk to them," she said.

"Too bad."

"Kerrison!" Her mother's voice now lifted in anger.

"No, Mother." Kerry managed, just barely, to keep her own temper from getting completely out of control. "I'm not going with you, and I'm not discussing our business with anyone." She folded her arms across her chest.

Cynthia Stuart stared at her, but Kerry's grim expression and truculent posture didn't alter and she finally looked away. "Well, if that's your decision," she said, after a pause. "But I think you should consider carefully, and then we will talk again." She motioned the aide out, and followed him to the door, going through it with as much dignity as she could muster.

No slammed doors, no yelling.

After a brief silence, Angie made a face, biting her lip as she approached the desk. "Sorry, Ker."

"Blech." Kerry finally relaxed, leaning her hands on the desk and letting her muscles unlock. "My own goddamned fault. I should have kept the ear buds in and not shown off." She looked down at the screen when she heard an odd sound, to find Gopher Dar knocking on the inside, peering at her. "Wait until Dar finds out. Just what we didn't need."

"Maybe she'll drop it. I think she knows you were pissed," Angie suggested. "That look you were giving her could have frozen hot coffee."

"Hmph." Kerry grunted, and sat down. "Got any Advil?" She sighed. "I'm gonna need a case of it."

Chapter Ten

"WELL, HELLO TO you too, Ham." Alastair had answered his cell phone in some surprise when it rang for the first time in hours. "I'm in London. Oh, what? Sure, of course you knew that."

Dar was half sprawled across the desk, her legs wrapped around the chair base and her head propped up on one hand. The other hand was wrapped around the mouse, but now it released the creature and rattled over a few keys instead.

Ker?

"Dar? She's right here."

Dar looked up over her screen, one eyebrow lifting.

"No, she's fine," Alastair went on. "Bea's been keeping my wife and the board filled in on what's going on. Have to say, this digital assistant thing Dar made me start using sure paid for itself today."

Dar's screen beeped softly. She looked back at it.

Hey. Need to talk to you.

Dar's brows knit. She unhooked her cell phone from her belt. "If you can get a call in, I'm going to try a call out."

"Hm?" Alastair put his hand over the phone. "Ham says he had to call over and over again for an hour to get through. Seems there's a lot of hullabaloo around his area."

Their corporate lawyer lived, Dar recalled, in Boston. "Tell him I say hello." She opened the phone and started to dial, then looked back at the screen when the speaker crackled.

"Miami exec, this is Miami ops," said Mark.

"Go ahead." Dar listened to her phone with her other ear, hearing a fast busy signal. She hit redial.

"Boss, we can't get a good handle on how many pipes we need to replace," Mark said. "We need to eyeball."

Dar released the button, and dialed again. Having someone onsite in both Washington and New York was probably a good idea, especially in Manhattan where most of their presence was business services. "You think we can wait for the planes to start flying again?"

"Hard to say," Mark said, honestly. "I'd rather jump on my bike and start up there."

Dar triggered the dial again, considering the request. "Tell you what." She heard the line start to ring. "Rent a van and take three or four people with you. Don't make me worry about you ending up wrapped around a tree on that Harley."

The phone was picked up. "Hello?"

"Hey," Dar said, only barely remembering to click off her mic. "What's up?"

"Hey." Kerry exhaled. "I love you."

Mark cleared his throat. "Okay, I can do that. I've got a bunch of guys here who just held up their hands to volunteer to go."

"I love you too," Dar replied, with a relieved smile. "Damn, it's good to hear your voice."

Kerry chuckled a tiny bit. "Honey, you've been hearing my voice all morning, "

"Not the same thing."

"Thanks for sending Gopher Dar to keep me company."

"That okay, boss?" Mark asked. "We can leave tonight."

"Hang on," Dar said.

"Nah, I'll answer," Kerry replied. "Miami ops, this is Miami exec, that's fine. Make sure you pack a case of Jolt. "

"Uh. Okay." Mark seemed caught off guard with this sudden change. "We'll get moving."

"Why don't you take as much spare gear as you can pack in the back while you're at it? I'm not sure when we'll be able to ship anything in there," Kerry suggested.

"Good call." Dar complimented her. "Alastair thinks you're the bomb, by the way."

"Will do," Mark said.

"Miami exec, this is the Air Hub."

Kerry sighed. "Air hub, hold on a minute, would you please? I need to take a call."

"Air hub, will do."

"Hey." Kerry's voice returned to the phone. "Where was I?"

"Saying you loved me." Dar was aware of the tiny, startled reactions from Alastair every time she mentioned the word. "What's up? You said you needed to talk."

Kerry sighed again. "My effing mother," she said. "Dar, she told someone else in...I guess another senator or something, about all the stuff we were talking about on the bridge and told them I'd come to Washington and talk to them."

"Dar, Ham says he needs the list of down customers as soon as we can get them, so he can head off any legal action," Alastair said.

Dar glanced over at Alastair, and nodded. "Well," she said. "How bad is that, Ker? You're doing a first class job. Maybe she's just proud of her kid."

Dead, absolute silence.

"Ker?" Dar asked, tentatively. "Granted the last thing we need to get distracted by is government bullshit but...I assume you said no, right?"

"I said no."

Dar could hear the tone. "Didn't mean to piss you off, sweetheart," she said, waiting until she heard the slight exhale. "I'd rather you go find a canoe and start paddling in this direction."

"Sorry," Kerry said, after a pause. "You just made my brain go somewhere I wasn't expecting," she admitted. "Dar, she has no right to go and tell people in the government the stuff we're doing. She was all freaked out about how we knew stuff she didn't. I think that's what she wants them to talk to me about. How did we know what we knew?"

"Hon." Dar almost chuckled, but thought better of it. "We get paid to know what we know."

"Yes, I know that," her partner said. "But I told her off. I was so pissed."

Dar felt a bit out of her league. She understood how Kerry felt about her family, and for sure she understood what it was like to be at odds with a mother. But she had always felt the evil in the family had rested with Kerry's father.

Maybe she'd been wrong. "Well," she said. "You don't need me to be the bad guy for you, but if you want to tell her Alastair and I said absolutely no way anyone from our company is going to go and chat with Congress, feel free."

"Huh?" Alastair craned his neck around and peered at her. "What was that?"

"Any luck on you heading this way?" Kerry asked, in a quiet voice.

"Miami exec, this is LA Earth Station," a voice interrupted. "We have the local FBI office demanding bandwidth we don't have. Need some help here."

Both Kerry and Dar keyed their mics at the same time. "Hold on a second," they said together. Then Dar released hers and cleared her throat. "Bea's trying, hon," she said. "Soon as I know anything I'll text you on it."

"Okay," Kerry said. "Is it okay if I go expense a hotel room?"

"Buy the hotel if you want," her boss said. "Put it on Alastair's credit card. I think I left the number on a sticky yellow pad by Maria's desk."

"What?" Alastair covered his phone again. "Dar, what trouble are you getting me into?"

Finally, Kerry chuckled. "Okay," she said. "It may not get that bad, but this is already so stressful I don't really need my family adding to it."

"No problem. Totally understand," Dar said. "Hang in there, okay?"

"Okay. Talk to you later. Let me go put a hose on this fire," Kerry said. "Bye Dardar."

"Bye." Dar closed her phone. "Sorry, Alastair. Kerry's mother's caused a problem and she's thinking of staying elsewhere."

"Ah hah." Her boss nodded. "My wife doesn't get along with her folks either. Wants to serve them the dog's kibble every time they stop by." He went back to the phone. "Ham? Yeah, I'm back. What's that? Well, sure, I understand the board is probably upset, Ham, but you know everyone is pitching in like gangbusters to keep things moving along."

"All right, LA Earth Station." Kerry came back on the bridge. "Give me a second to clear up the Air Hub's issue then we'll discuss the FBI request."

"Will do, Miami exec," the west coast facility said. "We told them we're carrying the East Coast right now so they backed off for a few minutes."

"Nice of them," Kerry said. "Air Hub, go ahead."

"Miami, we have some spare capacity if you need," the Air Hub said. "We aren't carrying any air traffic other than management layer. Everything's landed."

There was a moment of silence. "Well," Kerry finally said. "I'm sure we can use it somewhere, no matter how rotten the reason is. Thanks Air Hub."

"You're welcome, Miami exec."

"Okay. LA, who contacted you? Get me a name."

"Will do, Miami exec."

Dar rested her hands on the desk, her phone clasped lightly between her fingers. She looked across the room at the big screen television, her thoughts almost completely focused on her partner. "Alastair?"

"Eh?"

"Bea having any luck with flights?"

Her boss peered at her. "Haven't heard back yet."

Dar juggled her phone. "I'm going to call my folks. See what they think about taking a run to Cancun. Sooner we get back in the States the better."

"Funny," Alastair said. "That's exactly what Hamilton just said," he related. "He heard from a buddy of his that things are damned bad in New York. Worse than they're letting on the television."

"Yeah. Well." Dar opened her phone and started dialing again. "Tell Ham the FBI's trying to grab signal over on the west coast. See what he can do about that."

"Eh?"

KERRY SCRIBBLED DOWN the number, one hand holding her head up as she studied the computer screen. She was aware of her sister and brother entering and she heard the door shut quietly, but she focused on what was being carried over their stressed infrastructure and what she was going to say to the person on the other end of the phone when it answered.

Dar had a way of turning her viewpoint at different angles. Kerry tried to recapture her former indignation, but that calm voice kept intruding into it, forcing her to reassess what she was feeling and examine whether or not there wasn't a different way to look at it.

Ironic, since that's what she'd hoped to do for Dar when they'd first started working together, wasn't it? Change her perspective? Sometimes, Kerry admitted, she had, but more often she'd found herself pulling up short when faced with her new partner's internal logic and having to really think about where the right and the wrong was sometimes.

Dar didn't do or not do things because they were 'right' or 'wrong'-she did them because they made sense, or they didn't. It was a far more profound difference in their mental working than Kerry had ever suspected when they'd met, and it had taken both time and effort to get used to it.

Instinctive intellectualism- that odd sometimes disjointed instinct that Dar used to make business decisions, write her programs, and solve her problems. It was what led her to hire Kerry, or so she often claimed.

Kerry had enough ego to suspect that was only ninety percent true, the other ten percent being something a little more primal. Certainly it had been on her side of the question. "Okay." She opened her cell. "Let's call the FBI."

"Huh?" Mike said. "What did you do? Or what did we do? You calling the FBI on Mom? Holy crap!"

"No, I'm not." Kerry punched in the number, and waited. "They're just another customer of ours."

"For real?"

"Hello?" a man's voice answered.

"Hello, I'm looking for Robert Ervans. This is Kerry Stuart, from ILS. Our West coast facility advised some help was requested."

"Huh? Oh," the man said. "Yeah, okay, sorry. This is Agent Ervans," he added. "You're the computer people?"

"Yes," Kerry agreed. "What can I do for you?'

"Listen, we need to send a lot of pictures over to our Washington office. It's taking too long. We need more space so it can happen faster," the man said. "I know your guy there said you already had a lot of other things happening, but this needs to take over. It's important."

Kerry's nose wrinkled. "Mr. Ervans, I can review what traffic is on the line there, and certainly we can prioritize yours because I understand you must be working on critical items."

"That's right. Exactly right," the man sounded approving. "It's really important that we get these files to Washington."

"But the fact is, you're on our satellite link and the slowness there is due to the latency, the time it takes for the packets to get to the other side of the continent, rather than a lack of bandwidth." Kerry explained. "I can see if we can find more space, but I don't think the speed will get much better."

"Oh," Ervans said. "Well, what can we do about that, then? My boss said whatever it takes, just get it done."

Kerry sighed. "My boss usually says the same thing," she said. "In terms of the latency, there's not much we can do, since that's caused by the traffic having to go up to the satellite and back down. Other than shrinking the circumference of the planet, we're stuck with it."

"So you can't do anything?"

"Not with the satellite," Kerry said. "But let me see what other options we might have and I'll get back to you."

The line abruptly cut off, and Kerry gazed at her cell phone in bemusement for moment. "You're welcome." She closed the phone, and looked up at her siblings. "So," she said. "Am I in trouble?"

Mike snorted, throwing himself down on the couch and slinging one leg over the side of it. "Bunch of jerks."

Angie came over and sat down in the chair across the desk from her sister. "Mom's upset," she said. "But I think she's upset because you're upset more than she's upset about the whole going to Washington thing." She made a face at her sister. "Anyway, I think she's going to go with those aides to Washington tonight so once she's gone it should relax around here."

"Like they're all going to do anything there except yak," Mike said. "What are they going to say? Oh, this is terrible. We have to get the people who did this and make sure it never happens again." He lifted his hand and let it drop. "Bunch of self important little prick heads."

Angie looked at Kerry, and they both half turned to look at their younger brother.

"When, exactly, did you become a radical?" Kerry asked, in a quizzical tone. "We've lived as part of the government in this house for as long as any of us has been alive."

"Yeah, well," Mike said. "Now I can say how I feel and not worry I'll get thrown in the cellar."

"Miami exec, this is Herndon."

Kerry turned back to her computer. "Go ahead, Herndon." There wasn't much she could really say to Mike anyway and not sound completely hypocritical and she suspected he knew that. She'd kept her own silence in the house for how long? "Miami exec here."

Until life had handed her something more important to her than herself. That was exactly how long.

"Miami exec, we just had a visit from some people from the government. They want access to the center, ma'am. They want to put taps in place and I don't think they want to hear no from me."

"Taps?" Kerry's voice went sharp. "What kind of taps? On their own stuff?"

"Ma'am, I'm not sure," the tech said. "They weren't specific."

Kerry put her fingers on the keyboard and rattled a sentence into the open messenger application.

Did you hear that?

Dar's voice broke in. "Herndon, this is Dar Roberts," she said. "I have just locked out our entire infrastructure with my personal pass code. You tell those people from the government they need to contact Alastair McLean if they want to discuss tapping into anything."

"Oh boy, she sounds pissed," Angie said. "Can she do that?"

"I think she just did it," Mike said. "Good for her! Government jerks!"

"I hear you, Ms. Roberts," the Herndon tech sounded relieved. "I don't know what it was they were looking for ma'am, and to be honest I don't think they knew either, based on how they were asking."

Kerry glanced down at a soft beep.

I don't think they're going to take that from the local folks. They'll be back and that's a major commercial link not just a government one.

"She can do it," Kerry said, quietly. "Dar isn't someone who does something just because someone in authority tells her too. Believe me."

"Understood, Herndon," Dar said.

"I back that up completely," Alastair broke in. "I'll call our contacts in the government, and see if I can determine what's going on."

"Yes, sir."

"Is that your big boss?" Angie asked. "The one who's with Dar?"

Kerry nodded. *What do you think they're after? Could this be related to the terrorists, Dar? We don't want to be accused of obstructing anything.*

I don't know. Dar typed back. *We could be in a bad spot here.*

Kerry studied the string of text, starting with the first message. "Shit."

"What?" Mike sat up.

Kerry exhaled, and typed. *I should go there. All we have is an infrastructure manager. Not fair to put them on the front lines.*

Maybe flights will be allowed out tomorrow sometime.

Kerry had to smile, no matter how wryly. Dar knew perfectly well what her options were, and what was best for the company, but Dar also made no bones over whose priorities were more important to her. *Maybe I could go apologize and suck up to my mother and go out tonight.*

In no way am I asking or expecting you to do that. Let them wait. Let them call me. If they want it that bad, I'll make them send a damn bomber to pick our asses up here.

"God, I love her," Kerry said. *This could seriously be a matter of national security, Dar. We shouldn't screw around with this.*

"What's she saying?" Mike asked. "Did you just tell your whole company you loved Dar? That mic was on. I heard the reverb."

Kerry blinked, and looked at the mic in her hand, and felt the blood rush to her head. "Oh, crap."

Thanks hon. Love you too. Dar rattled back. *At least, I assume you were talking about me.*

"I'm pretty sure they already know." Angie watched her sister's face. "Whoops."

Of course I was talking about you. Kerry put the mic down to be safe.

"Jesus," she muttered. "Too much crap happening at once."

Anyway, I know it's serious, Dar responded. *It might be a matter of national security but you know what? Bottom line is, we're the experts, and that's our facility. We handle that data. If they need something from it, we and I mean Alastair too, we have no problem doing whatever we have to in order to help, but I'm not giving the people who let this happen carte blanche access into my network.*

"Wow," Kerry murmured, as she read. "I'm not sure we're going to get away with that."

"What?" Angie got up and went around the desk. "What's going on?"

"Dar's being Dar," Kerry said, picking up the mic again. "Okay, Herndon–if you get another request, let us know as soon as it happens, and you can tell them our senior management is contacting the government to find out what their requirements are so we can do our best to fulfill them."

"That sounds cheesy," Mike said.

"Are you really going to go suck up to Mom?" Angie whispered. "Wow!"

Kerry sighed. "We learned political compromise early, didn't we?" She tasted the smarminess on her tongue like a coating of stale fry oil. "Oh, lord I don't want to do that, but the bottom line is someone should be there and I'm closer than Dar is. "

"Isn't there someone else they can send? Surely you two can't be the only responsible people in that whole ginormous company," Angie pointed out. "For Pete's sake, Kerry."

"There are lots of people." Kerry typed back. *Can you see if Hamilton Baird can get someone over there from his department?* "The problem is, this is all operations and that's our division. Mine and Dar's. We don't have anyone else in the company that does that at an executive level."

"She and Dar are the only ones with balls, she means," Mike said from his perch on the couch. "Gorgeous women with bad attitudes scare the crap out of guys. Everyone knows that."

Angie turned around and stared at him. "How in the hell would you know?" she asked. "Your girlfriends are all empty headed bimbos."

"That's how I know."

Alastair's on the line with him now. Dar responded. *This is getting crazy.*

Crazier. Kerry responded. *Okay, I'm going to bite the bullet and go find my mother. Cover for me?*

You sure?

"I'm sure I'm going to be sick to my stomach," Kerry muttered. "Where's that bucket of Advil?"

KERRY DECIDED A glass of tea was in order to get her handful of pain killers down before she went in search of her mother. She crossed the dining room and pushed open the door to the kitchen, surprising the woman standing just inside. "Hey Mary."

"Ms Kerry," the cook greeted her. "Terrible things are going on."

"They are," Kerry agreed, going over to the cabinet and taking down a glass. "It's been a really tough day."

"What can I get you?" Mary asked. "I have to say it's going to be nice having your sister back in the house with the little ones. It's been too quiet around here."

"Some tea, if you don't mind." Kerry offered up the glass without protest. Mary had worked for her parents at least as long as she'd been alive, and this kitchen was her territory, no doubt about it. "How have you been, Mary?"

"Well thanks." The cook returned with the glass full and handed it to her. "And yourself? How's your sweetheart Dar?"

My sweetheart. Kerry had to smile at that. She swallowed her pills and washed them down with a mouthful of tea. "Dar's fine, thanks. She's in England right now. I think we'd both be better if we were home in Miami though."

"Just a good thing you were out of harm's way," Mary said. "And I was thanking the Lord that your mother was here too, and not in the way of those crazy people."

Kerry sipped her tea, leaning back against the counter. "I'm glad too," she said. "I tried to talk her out of going to Washington tonight."

"Crazy people," Mary repeated. "No sense to it at all. I wish she was staying here and not going out to be with the rest of those government people. It was fine for your papa, he was a strong man."

"He would have been very upset," Kerry said, quietly. "This would have made him very angry."

"Oh yes, ma'am. That's very true." Mary nodded. "Now, I know you didn't get on with him, Ms. Kerry, but he was a good man to have around when things were terrible like this."

And that, Kerry had to acknowledge, was true. "As long as he was mad at something other than you, yes," she said. "And he would have been furious at the people who did this. He'd have been trying to find out how it happened."

Mary nodded. "Would you like more tea, Ms. Kerry? I have to say I do like that haircut you have. It looks very nice on you."

"Sure." Kerry handed back her glass. "And thanks. I like it too." She ran her fingers through her hair, pausing to rub the back of her neck a little as she willed the Advil to start working. "I didn't think I'd like it at first, but it ended up being nicer than I thought."

Mary poured the glass full again. "Well, don't get upset at me for saying this , Ms. Kerry, but short like that, you do remind me just a bit of your papa."

Well. Kerry took the glass back. "How could I be upset at you,

Mary? He was my father. No matter how much we disagreed, that's not going to change."

Mary smiled at her. "Glad to hear you say that," she said, then fell silent as the door to the hall opened.

"Mary, I will need for you to..." Cynthia Stuart entered, then stopped as she saw who was visiting with her cook. "Ah. Kerrison."

Ah. Yikes. Kerry exhaled silently. "Mother." She returned the greeting in a mild tone.

Her mother's expression brightened just a trifle at that. "Mary, could you please see what we can arrange for a luncheon in perhaps an hour? I know it's late for it, but everything's so out of sorts today."

"Of course, ma'am." Mary gave Kerry a knowingly sympathetic look. "Nice talking to you, Ms. Kerry. Let me know if you need anything else." She ducked out the door into the pantry.

Kerry quickly considered her options. "Want some tea?" she finally asked. "I just had to take a handful of aspirin." She eased over a few feet and sat down at one of the chairs at the worktable.

Her mother relaxed a trifle. "Yes. It's been that kind of day hasn't it?" She went to the refrigerator and opened the door removing a small bottle and taking it over to the table in the corner along with a glass. "I've had to take some myself." She took a seat. "This was the kind of thing your father would say was a full bottle of whiskey day I believe."

"Yes," Kerry agreed. "I could use a beer."

Cynthia glanced furtively at her. "That does sound so odd," she said. "I don't think either of us was ever partial to beer."

"Probably why I am," her daughter admitted. "All part of that complete rebellion thing." She looked up and found her mother looking back at her in wary surprise. "I was rude before. I'm sorry," she said.

Cynthia looked momentarily overwhelmed, as though Kerry had gone in a direction she hadn't anticipated.

Which she had, Kerry realized. Straightforward apology was something she'd learned from Dar, not something she'd picked up growing up where admitting fault was never easy. "I've got a lot on my shoulders. I wasn't expecting complications from the government."

Her mother nodded at once. "It is I who should have apologized, Kerr...y." She bit off the last part of her daughter's name with visible difficulty. "It completely did not occur to me that I was speaking so far out of turn," she went gamely on. "I didn't mean to...cause you difficulty. I just saw an opportunity to help and thought your involvement would be a good thing. I should, in fact, have asked you before proceeding."

Kerry pondered her glass. "I probably would have reacted the same way, if you had asked," she replied honestly. "Being here is very uncomfortable for me. I don't trust you." She looked up again, to see her mother's eyes wide as saucers. "And given what happened, you probably shouldn't trust me either."

Way too much truth in one sentence, she realized. Her mother had no idea how to react, and merely sat there blinking at her. It was hard, and it was making her headache worse. "I'm not trying to be a jerk," Kerry said. "I just can't help how I feel."

"Well," Cynthia finally said. "I have no idea what to say to that."

"I know," her daughter said. "It's probably going to be easier for both of us if you try not to think of me as the little kid who used to run through this kitchen, and more like an adult you don't know that well."

Her mother set her glass down. "Do you have any idea whatsoever how impossible that is? I am your Mother."

"I know," Kerry said again. "And no, I have no idea at all how impossible that is. I just don't want to make this so hard on both of us."

Cynthia sat back and regarded her. "How can you still be so angry?" she asked, in a quiet voice. "I don't understand it."

Reasonable question, Kerry felt. From her mother's point of view at any rate. "I don't know," she said. "I guess maybe along with the eyes and the high blood pressure I inherited father's long grudges." Her eyes lifted again and met Cynthia's, watching several emotions cross her mother's face; first shock, then a touch of anger, and what might have been a flicker of grudging understanding.

Might have been.

"Well," her mother said. "Perhaps in time we can adjust," she concluded. "But at this time, I fear we cannot, since I do have an 8:00 p.m. flight, and I am sure you will be on your way home before I get back." She poured the rest of her bottle of juice into her glass and placed the bottle down with a slightly more than necessary force.

Kerry felt her headache start to ebb a little. "Actually," she said, "I do have to go to Washington tonight." She watched her mother's eyes start to blink again, this time in confusion.

"You...changed your mind?" Cynthia said, doubtfully. "I'm not sure..."

"No." Kerry decided honesty was the best route. "The government wants to take over some of our facilities in the area. I have to find out why, and give them a face to yell at with some authority," she said. "If you don't want me to ride with you, I understand. I'll drive."

Her mother's lips started twitching. "Well," she spluttered. "K...surely you aren't...you can't drive by yourself there. It's dangerous!"

Kerry propped her head up on one hand, a faint smile appearing on her face. "Wasn't I saying that to you earlier?"

Cynthia's mouth opened, and then closed. Then opened again, and then closed. Then she sat back and took a sip of her juice. "This is all very confusing," she said. "You said the government was trying to take over your things? Why would they do that?"

"I don't know, Mother. Why would they?" Kerry asked. "You are the government, remember? So maybe if you're going to talk to your committee...if you still want me to talk to them, we can ask them that first?"

Her mother frowned. "Are you going to be rude to them, and embarrass me?" she asked, directly.

"Possibly," her daughter answered just as honestly. "But that could have happened anyway." She sat back and regarded her mother. "Didn't you realize that when you told them about me in the first place?"

Cynthia met her eyes, a thoughtful expression on her face. "I should have," she conceded. "I think you're right, you know. I don't think you're the child I raised at all."

It was almost a relief. Kerry merely nodded.

"In fact, I'm not really sure who you are at all," her mother said. "I don't know that I want to find out."

"Fair enough," Kerry said. "We all make choices we have to live with. I know. I've had to make a few," she said. "Losing my family was one of the consequences of that."

Cynthia eyed her in somber silence for a minute. "Well." She got up and put her glass in the sink. "We do all have to make choices." She went to the door. "I will see about adding you to the flight."

She left, and Kerry tipped her head back and regarded the ceiling, unsure if the situation had just gotten marginally better or a lot worse.

Time would have to tell.

DAR CURLED HER arm around her bundled sweater, putting her head down and allowing her body to relax in the semi-darkened room. The rest of their team and most of the client's were in the media room next door, watching three or four different television screens and talking.

Dar had no desire to either join them or talk. She closed her eyes, just letting the chatter in the background of the computer go past her, trying to tune out enough to get a few minutes of rest before it was time for Kerry to go to the airport with her mother.

Kerry's only comment to Dar's question about how that worked out was 'Ugh.' It made her unhappy because she sensed her partner was unhappy and there wasn't a lot she could do about it. What was that Alastair had said earlier? She'd turned into a good family person?

Ugh.

Alastair had gone to the rooms Sir Melthon had prepared for them. He was waiting for a call back from one of their contract administrators from the government. Dar, frankly, didn't hold out much hope in that regard because she figured everyone was either glued to CNN or in the middle of the confusion, and didn't have much time to call back some CEO of some company.

Kerry's voice filtered softly into her awareness, and Dar opened her eyes to peer at the nearby screen. Then, after a moment's consideration she opened a browser and clicked over to their corporate travel website.

Kerry hadn't said if she was staying at the family townhouse she knew they had in Washington. She might, Dar reasoned, but she also might rather escape to one of the high end business hotels they used when they traveled.

She reached over and typed in the location, then reviewed the results as the website searched and disgorged its results. "Hm." Dar grunted. Hotels were packed, not unreasonable considering air travel was at a standstill. Everyone stuck at the airport had to stay somewhere.

There was, however, an obscenely expensive suite available and Dar clicked on it without hesitation. She pulled down the available profiles on the website and selected Kerry's, and watched as it filled in her information and obediently reserved the space.

Dar selected and copied the details, and then she pasted them into the open instant message box where Kerry's last "Ugh" was still blinking mournfully. She clicked send, and then settled her head back down on her sweater.

Kerry's voice, in the middle of acknowledging Mark's status update, stopped in mid word.

Dar smiled, watching as the message came back with a tiny graphic, a small beating red heart that was a complete, if charming, waste of bandwidth.

"As I was saying," Kerry's voice now had an audible grin in it. "I will be out of contact for a few hours in transit to Herndon this evening. Dar will be covering for me."

"Miami exec, this is Herndon. We're looking forward to seeing you," a voice answered. "Do you need a pickup?"

One blue eye opened and its dark brow lifted as Dar listened for her partner's answer.

"Ah." Kerry was muffling a laugh, she could tell. "I'm going to rent a car at the airport, thanks. I'll let you know if that doesn't work out. I'm sure it's crazy around there."

Dar reached over, and one handed, typed out a series of instructions into a console session, reviewing them before she compiled the results and sent the new little routine to run. A moment later, she heard a soft chuckle come through the mic.

"Hey Miami exec, this is Miami ops," Mark broke in. "Wouldn't that be god of the clock in England?"

"Yes," Kerry responded. "Dar's supposed to be getting some rest now so she can take over, but I just found out she's actually dealing with some petty details behind the scenes."

"Petty?" Dar murmured. "Wench."

"How about I burn minutes and watch stuff from the van?" Mark suggested. "It's not like we've got a lot else to do, you know?"

Dar frowned, considering the question. She trusted Mark

implicitly. He'd been working for the company nearly as long as she had, and his knowledge and loyalty were unquestioned.

Trust? Not trust? Dar reached over and picked up her mic, bringing it over to her head.

"I think that's a great idea, Mark," Kerry answered before she could click in. "Thanks. I appreciate it, and I know Dar will appreciate it since there's a lot going on over there too."

Touche. Dar knew rejecting the offer now would seriously embarrass her partner and make her look like a cad since it was made in her best interest. Kerry's little payback for her hotel reservations. She clicked the mic on. "I do appreciate it, Mark," she said. "Especially since now I can send Kerry off shift to get ready to leave and relax before she has to fly."

Kerry forgot to turn her mic off, and her laughter echoed through the speaker, a strangely light sound after so much tension. "Right Kerry?" Dar inquired.

"Right boss," Kerry surrendered. "You win this round."

Dar glanced down expectantly at the message box.

Hoisted, wasn't I? Kerry's typing popped up.

Figured you could use some time to decompress. Dar typed back. *You don't know what you're going to get into when you get to Herndon.*

True, her partner responded. *I'm going to go grab a shower and crash for a few hours. Thanks for the hotel reservations—I hadn't even started to look into that and I sure don't want to spend the night in DC.*

I figured, Dar said. *Sure you're okay with going?*

There was a moment's pause in the response. *Yeah,* Kerry finally answered. *I don't know. Maybe I'll get a chance to get this family thing worked out. I think you were right about the whole thing with my mother. I think she just wanted to have something to show her committee.*

Dar smiled. Hell *must be freezing over if I'm telling you not to think the worst of someone.*

Ah heh, Kerry responded. *Yeah. I know. Part of me wants to just move past it all and just drop the whole thing, and the other part of me just thinks about stuff they did and gets pissed off all over again. I just really wish I were home.*

Right there with you. Dar sighed, glancing around the room, pausing when the door opened fully and Alastair entered. *Hang on, Alastair just came back.*

"Well, we've got good news and bad news." Alastair came over and sat down. He looked tired. "Which do you want first?"

"I can't believe there's any good news. So bad first," Dar said.

"Okay," Her boss responded. "Bad news is, there's not one person in the government that can tell me why someone from some agency is knocking on our doors in Virginia. This group says they think that group may be doing it and when you ask that group, they don't know anything about it."

"Ugh." Dar wasn't surprised.

"Hamilton's working on trying to track the request down, but he's coming up against a lot of people who are in high gear with no brakes, if you catch my drift," Alastair said. "But on the bright side, we've got flights to Mexico City tomorrow morning."

Dar blinked in surprise. "They found seats?"

"The board instructed me to charter an airplane," Alastair looked a touch bemused. "Apparently you and I are considered a little important. We've got a transfer in Mexico City to an executive jet service out to Nuevo Laredo and we're being picked up there for the ride across the border."

"Wow," Dar said.

"Lucky for us, there's quite a number of airplanes that are hanging around here unable to fly to the U.S. Finding one to charter was easy, or so Bea tells me," Alastair said. "At any rate, sorry we'll have to end up in Houston, but at least we won't be on the other side of the world."

"I'll take it," Dar said. "Maybe by then domestic flights will be going again." She felt a sense of profound relief, regardless of the destination. "That is good news, Alastair. Thanks."

Her boss smiled. "I know you want to get back home. Me too." He slapped Dar on the shoulder and stood up. "You going to get some rest?"

Dar nodded. "Mark's covering for us," she said. "He's heading up to DC in the equipment van and has a lot of time on his hands. I sent Kerry off to get some down time before she goes to Herndon tonight."

Alastair nodded. "All right. I'm going to go get some rest myself," he said. "The devil only knows what we'll have to deal with tomorrow, if today was any indication."

"Night." Dar waited for him to leave. Then she turned back to the screen. *Ker?*

There was no response. Dar frowned, and then picked up her cell phone and dialed, getting a fast busy. She sighed, and sat back, then rocked forward again when her message was answered.

Hey. What's up? Kerry typed. *Sorry, Brian just showed up here, same time as Richard dropping off Sally.*

Dar winced. Nice. She typed. *Like it needed to be crazier.*

Uh huh, Kerry agreed. *Did Alastair find anything out?*

No, Hamilton's still trying. Dar rattled her keys. *But they chartered a plane for us to fly to Mexico tomorrow morning.* She hit enter, and waited.

Yahhooooo!

Dar smiled. *Yeah, well, then we fly local to the border and someone is picking us up to make the run into Houston. At least it's halfway home. And maybe by then I can just fly up to DC and meet you.*

There was a long silence. Dar almost decided to send a follow up, when a response came back.

Sorry. Yelling match outside the study here. For once, not involving me.

"Oops." Dar sighed.

Fly fast. Kerry typed, after a pause *I need you.*

There was a rawness there that made Dar's breath catch. She reached out in reflex to touch the screen with her fingertips, and then let them drop.

I'll try to hold things together in Herndon. Kerry went on. *But I've got a gut feeling this is going to be something more than a request to track some IP addresses.*

Dar nodded to herself. *Go with your instincts, Ker. You know what I'd go for and what I wouldn't. If it's something you know I wouldn't do, just tell them you can't do it and wait for me to land. I still have the systems locked down there.*

"Systems control is passing to Miami ops," Mark's voice interrupted. "We are heading north. We picked up a Trailrider RV hitched to my truck and we've got every spare piece of gear we had in inventory with us."

"Miami ops, this is Danny at the Pentagon. That's great to hear. We'll need some of it to get stuff spooled back up, and some facilities. Do you have WAN rigs with you?"

"We sure do. This thing has even got a sat hookup and we're pulling a generator."

We have good people. Kerry typed.

"It's still on fire here," Danny said. "But we just got asked when all the stuff is going to be back up. We can't get inside, but we think the cross connect room was burned up."

We have the best people. Dar replied.

"Okay, we'll stop for some sixty six blocks. Can you guys source some three quarter ply if we need to rebuild the d-marc?" Mark asked.

"We can do that," Danny said.

"Then go ahead and get a dozen sheets," Mark said. "We'll get there, and we'll get it done."

"Will do, Miami ops. We'll be ready for you."

Dar keyed her mic. "Sounds like a good plan, gentlemen," she said. "Miami exec signing off for the evening. If something happens that requires senior approval, try my cell phone first."

"Try mine second," Kerry added. "Let's all stay alert. We don't know what might happen next."

Go get some rest. Dar typed.

You too, Kerry responded. *Let's hope tomorrow's a much better day.*

Chapter Eleven

REST WASN'T IN her cards, apparently. Kerry almost decided to turn around and go take back over operations when she eased out of the study and found her sister and her ex husband facing off with an unhappy looking Sally in the middle of them.

Richard hadn't changed much. Tonight he was wearing a shockingly casual leather jacket and corduroys though, something he'd have never worn in her parent's house when her father had been alive. Kerry took a deep breath and forced herself to move forward toward them, hoping her presence would break up whatever the issue was.

"If you think I'm going to leave her here with him here you're crazy!" Richard was saying. "She's upset enough as it is, she doesn't need that to complicate her life!"

Angie's face was set and angry. "Stop being such a jerk, will you? He's not going to complicate anything. She's known him all her life, for Pete's sake."

"That's not the point!"

"Aunt Kerry!" Sally spotted her and bolted, distracting her parents just long enough for them to turn and see her target before she collided with her aunt's sturdy legs.

"Hey, kiddo." Kerry gave her sister a brief smile. "How about I take her into the library and tell her a story."

Angie looked utterly relieved. "Thanks, sis," she said. "That would be great."

"Would you like that?" Kerry held a hand out to her niece. "Want to come hear a story?"

"Yes!" Sally was hanging onto her leg, looking up at her. She reached up and grabbed Kerry's hand, swinging on it.

"Okay." Kerry gave her ex brother in law a nod of acknowledgment. "Richard."

"Kerry," Richard answered, stiffly. "You look well."

"You too." She escaped with her niece through the archway and headed for the library at the other end. They ducked inside the dim, quiet room and closed the door behind them. "All right, here we go."

"Aunt Kerry." Sally reached up for a hug, and Kerry gladly complied, picking her niece up and wrapping her arms around her. "You been gone a long time." She put her arms around her aunt's neck and gave her a kiss on the cheek.

"Yeah." Kerry walked over and sat down with her on the big leather couch. "I know. It has been a long time, huh?" She sat Sally down on her lap and studied her. "How old are you now, almost five, right?"

Sally nodded, her dark blond hair in childish curls bobbling with the motion. She was an engaging child with a rounded, cute face and a snub nose that Kerry had seen in the mirror once upon a time. She had hazel eyes and a dimpled smile, and she smiled now at her aunt. "Where you been?

"Well," Kerry said. "I don't live in Michigan anymore. I moved down to Florida. Do you know where that is?"

"How come you went there?" Sally swung her legs a little. "Mommy said you live far, far away."

"That's where I work," Kerry told her. "And it's warm there, and pretty. I like it a lot. Your mama came to see me there...where I live now."

"Oh."

"It's far from here, but I have lots of friends there, and even a dog," Kerry said. "Maybe you can visit and meet her."

Sally's eyes lit up. "You gotta doggy?" she squealed. "Oh wow!"

Kerry smiled at this unrestrained enthusiasm. "I sure do. Her name is Chino, and she's about as big as you." She bounced Sally up and down on her lap. "She's really cute, too."

"I wanna see her," Sally said. "Daddy won't let me get a doggy."

No, Kerry bet he wouldn't. "Oh, maybe when you get a little older," she said. "They're a lot to take care of you know," she added. "I didn't get to have a doggy when I was little either."

Sally pouted.

"Aw, cmon." Her aunt chuckled. "So you want to hear a story? I know a good one, about a bumblebee."

"I want a doggy!" Sally said. "Can I come to where you live and stay there?"

Kerry studied her for a minute. "You can come visit us, sure," she said. "I said so, right? Then you can play with Chino, and go the beach and see the ocean."

The little girl pouted again.

"Want to see pictures of my doggy?" Kerry suggested.

Sally nodded.

"Okay, c'mon." Kerry set her on the floor and stood up, leading the way into her late father's study, where her laptop was still resting on the desk. She sat down as Sally climbed up onto the chair next to her, and unlocked her screen saver. "Let's see what we have here."

She had a folder of pictures, specifically arranged together for the purpose she was using them for right now. Safe pictures of home, and work, of Chino and humorous ones of Dar. "Okay, see? Here's Chino."

Sally squealed. "She's so cuuuutte!"

"I told you." Kerry gazed fondly at her pet. "That's her favorite bed. She loves to swim in the ocean, too."

"I want a doggy," Sally lamented. "All I got is a stuffed chicken and it's stupid."

Kerry gave her a one armed hug. "Aw. You'll get one someday. I did, right?"

"I don't wanna wait till I'm old!"

Kerry started laughing. "Gee, thanks!" She made a face at her niece. "Tell you what, I'll ask your Mom to get you one, okay?"

Sally's eyes lit up. "For real?"

Paybacks were certainly, certainly a bitch. "For real," Kerry assured her. "I'll tell her to get you one just like Chino. She'll have plenty of room to run around and play here."

Sally looked around the room. "Mommy says we have to come stay here now."

"Mmhm," her aunt said. "You know, your Mommy and I grew up here," she said, seeing a sad look in the little girl's eyes. "We had lots of fun with your uncle Michael, playing hide and seek and running around."

Sally looked around. "You did?"

"We did," Kerry said. "I used to close my eyes, right over by the wall there, and your Mommy and Uncle Michael would find a place to hide and I'd have to track them down. One day, I thought they were hiding in the kitchen, and I thought I would surprise them in there."

Sally giggled.

"So I got a basket, and I filled it with dirt from the garden, and I crept along the hallway really quiet." Kerry lowered her voice. "And I crept, and crept, and when I was at the door, I threw the door open and ran inside, and threw the basket up in the air."

"Oh! They got dirty!"

"Not exactly," Kerry smiled. "Your grandma was in there talking to a stranger and they got dirty."

"Ooooo." Sally giggled, her sadness forgotten. "Did you get in trouble?"

"I ran really fast outside and they couldn't catch me. And then I climbed up a tree and got stuck and everyone got so scared about that they forgot about the dirt." She chuckled as her niece giggled harder.

"That was funny," Sally said. "Can we play hide and seek?"

'Sure," Kerry said. "I'll get your Mommy and Uncle Michael to play too, and we'll see how much trouble we can get into. Doesn't that sound like fun?"

"Yes!"

Kerry gave her another hug. "It'll be fun for you here. When your brother's a little older, you can play with him too, like I did with Uncle Michael."

Sally got quiet. "Did your Daddy live somewhere else too?"

"Well, sort of." Kerry turned her head and regarded her niece. "Do you remember Grandpa?"

Sally nodded. "He's not here no more."

"No," her aunt agreed softly. "Did you know Grandpa was my

Daddy?" she asked. "Mine, and your Mommy's, and Uncle Michael's?"

"Oh. He was?"

"Mm." Kerry nodded. "And Grandpa had to spend a lot of time in a different place because of his job. A lot of times we had to go there too, so sometimes we lived there, and sometimes we lived here, and a lot of times, he wasn't here because he had to do things."

Sally put her thumb in her mouth. "Mommy told me Grandpa went to Heaven."

Kerry just nodded. "I'm sure he didn't want to go, but I know he's happy there, and waiting for us to come too. Isn't that what your Mommy told you?"

Sally nodded emphatically. "I miss Grandpa." She was watching Kerry's expressive face intently and there was no way for her aunt to dissemble.

Kerry exhaled. "I think he misses us too, sweetheart," she said. "But we all have things we have to do, and he had something he had to do in Heaven, so he had to go there and wait for us."

The child threw her arms around Kerry's neck. "I miss you too, Aunt Kerry. I thought you went to Heaven too, but Mommy said you just went to Miami."

Kerry bit her lip to keep from laughing, despite the pang in her chest. "You'll have to come to Miami to visit me, honey. Then you can see if it's anything like Heaven."

Sally released her and sat up, looking back at the computer. "More pitchers?"

"Sure." Kerry was glad enough to leave that conversation alone. She opened up the folder and the pictures popped up, tiny little colorful chunks of her life spread out on the screen.

"Who's that?" Sally pointed at one of them.

Ah. Kerry found herself looking back into a familiar pair of very blue eyes. "That's my friend Dar," she said. "She lives in Florida too."

Sally studied the picture. "She's pretty."

The picture was Dar sitting behind her desk in the condo, chin propped up on one fist, and a look of bemused tolerance at what Kerry knew was a just showered, T-shirt covered camera wielder on the other side of the office snapping the shot.

Nothing really remarkable about it, save the smile, and the warmth in those eyes, which were looking right through the viewfinder into Kerry's.

"I think she is," Kerry said, with a smile. "Dar's my best friend. We have a lot of fun together."

"Do you play hide and see?" her niece asked.

"Sometimes." Kerry's eyes twinkled. "We do a lot of things together. " She pointed at another picture. "See that? It's a fish."

"Big fish!" Sally said.

"That's a shark," Kerry told her. "I took that picture, under the water."

Sally turned all the way around and looked at her. "No you didn't," she said. "You're not a fish!" She looked up as the door creaked open. "Mommy! Aunt Kerry isn't a fish, right?"

Angie entered, looking very stressed. She took a moment to relax, and then she shut the door behind her. "What's that, honey? What crazy story is Aunt Kerry telling you now?"

"I was showing her my diving pictures." Kerry turned the laptop so her sister could see them. "That one."

"That on...holy Christ, Kerry! That's a shark!" Angie came over and sat on the edge of the desk. "Tell me you didn't take that."

"I took that," her sister said. "Honestly they're not bad to swim with. You just have to remember not to stick any body parts near their mouths."

"Oh is that all." Angie peered at the pictures. "Well, you still have all your fingers anyway. That's a nice shot of Dar," she said. "So, what have you two been up to?"

"Mommy, Aunt Kerry says you'll get me a dog," Sally piped up. "Like that one!" She pointed at the picture of Chino. "Can I have one, huh? Please?"

Angie looked at the picture, and then she looked at Kerry, who smiled charmingly at her. "You're lucky you're my sister, and I love you."

"Can I Mom?"

DAR SPREAD HER arms out across the bed and let her body relax, wincing a little as the stiffness from sitting as long as she had eased.

It felt very, very good to just lie down and do nothing. The day had seemed to her to last at least a week, and to have it be quiet, and still with just the sound of a ticking wall clock around the corner was a wonderful thing.

Her neck ached. She debated if she should get up and go to her briefcase that held a supply of pain killers to address the problem along with her customary bottle of water.

Deciding that getting up and undressing while doing that instead of falling asleep was easy. Dar rolled over and pushed herself up to her feet, standing and trudging over to the mahogany sidebar where she'd tossed her case.

She unzipped it and took out the bottle of Advil and the water. She opened her suitcase and took out a long shirt to sleep in. She draped it over the nearby chair and turned, leaning against the wood as she opened the bottle and shook out a few pills.

The room was a relatively pleasant space to spend the night. It had a small bathroom with an old fashioned tub in it, a decent size bed long enough for her legs not to hang off, and a rich tapestry on the wall that featured dogs and horses in unlikely poses that made Dar smile.

She swallowed her pills and washed them down with a mouthful of water. Then she picked up the shirt and walked into the bathroom, glancing in the mirror as she unbuttoned her shirt. She pulled the fabric off and crossed her arms, studying her mostly naked upper half with a thoughtful expression.

A game she played with herself, lately.

Tattoo or no tattoo? That was the question. With a wry chuckle, Dar studied her tan skin, trying to imagine what it might look like with the sort of colorful decoration her partner now had spread across her upper chest.

It felt good to waste some brain cells on triviality after the long day. It was like a tiny slice of normality in what had become a morass of uncertain stress.

Would she do it? Dar rubbed her thumb over the skin on her chest where Kerry's mark was. She found the tattoo sexy, and not even because it incorporated her name. But if she had to choose her own, she knew it wouldn't be anything like what her partner had.

What would it be?

Dar studied her skin, and then shook her head and laughed. "I have no damn idea." She finished changing and brushed her teeth. She then went to her briefcase and pulled a diving magazine from it, settling down in the leather armchair near the window where the light from the lamp would allow her to comfortably read.

She was tired, but not sleepy yet. There was a small television set in the corner of the room, almost hidden, but she had no desire to turn it on and listen to yet another retelling and see again the terror and the destruction she'd lived with the entire day.

It was good just to sit, sipping her water, and looking at pictures of colorful fish and clear blue water, reading about live adventures and what the price of a good rum drink was in Roatan in the spring. She leaned back and turned the page, losing herself in the text as her mind remembered the rich tang of salt air and the deep, rumbling sound of underwater breathing.

A soft knock at the door made her jump. She put her water bottle down on the desk, and looked up at the door. "C'mon in."

The door pushed open, and Alastair's head poked around it. "Hey, Dar I...oh, my gosh. Sorry. Didn't realize you were...ah..."

"Wearing a T-shirt?" Dar gave her boss a wry look. "Relax. It's more than I wore to that damn Halloween party that time."

Alastair cautiously entered. "Just thought you'd like a nightcap." He held up a bottle. "Our host had this delivered. It's good stuff."

"Sure." Dar closed her magazine. "Last time I shared whisky with you I was resigning. We should find happier occasions."

Alastair walked over and sat down in the chair opposite Dar. He was still in his slacks, but had his shirt untucked and the sleeves unbuttoned and partly rolled up his forearms. "I do remember that," he said, pouring a measure of the golden liquor into one of the two glasses he'd brought and handing it to Dar. "Wasn't fond of how that day started."

"Me either." Dar waited for him to pour his own glass, and then lifted hers. "Here's to better times."

"Amen." Alastair reached over and touched his glass to hers, then sat back and sipped it. "I just talked to the missus," he said. "Seems a neighbor of ours was in the North Tower and can't be reached."

Dar shook her head.

"Nice feller," Alastair said. "His family's in tatters, of course. My wife said she'd never been so glad to have me out of the country as she was this morning." He studied the whiskey in the glass. "Could easily have been otherwise. I was in New York last week."

"Could have," Dar agreed quietly. "We all travel a lot. It was just a toss of the dice." She considered. "But then again, so is driving to work every morning in Miami." She sipped the whiskey, the unfamiliar burn making her nose twitch.

"Well, that's true, or so I've heard," Alastair said. "It's not so bad in Houston, but still." He leaned back. "You think though, so many of us work like dogs so we can retire and take it easy, and those boys in New York work harder than most, and then something like this happens."

"Sometimes it takes something like this happening to make you take a step back," Dar said, after a sip of the whiskey. "We get so damned focused sometimes." She held the glass up to the light, admiring the honey color. "Some times you have to stop and live. You miss out otherwise."

Alastair smiled. "Learned that relatively recently?"

Dar's eyes twinkled wryly. "You could say that."

Her boss chuckled. "What are you reading there?" He took the extended magazine and turned it around. "Ah...your crazy hobby." He flipped through the pages. "Those islands do look nice, but the missus won't hear of it. She wants to go see Niagara Falls on our next trip."

"I've seen them," Dar said. "Alastair, take her someplace you can spend more than ten minutes. The falls are nice, but unless you're going to go over them in a barrel they're not much fun."

"Have you?" Alastair asked. "Gone over them?"

Dar's brows shot up. "How nuts do you think I am?"

"Just asking." He chuckled again. "We usually end up at tourist central locations like Vegas. I don't mind exploration, but I like mine to come with a scotch and sour and a limo driver, I'm afraid."

"Well." Dar extended her legs and crossed her ankles. "We call our cabin down south Microsoft Rustic for a reason. Ker and I talk about going camping and hiking in the Grand Canyon, but I had my fill of that as a kid and I'd rather call room service myself if the truth be known."

"Camping in Florida?" Alastair asked. "And you lived to grow up?"

Dar smiled. "We were actually going to take a trip around Europe when we were done here. See the Alps. See if I'm as bad at skiing as I was the last time I tried, and maybe end up down in Italy." She exhaled. "Kerry was really looking forward to it. She never got the chance to travel much."

Alastair set the magazine down and cradled his glass in both hands. "Chance will come again soon enough," he said. "I know we've got a rough patch to get over now, but the world will keep turning, y'know? We'll get through it. Then you two can take a month and see the place the right way."

Dar cocked one eyebrow. "I'm going to hold you to that," she warned.

"Deal," her boss said. "Say, what do you think about Key West?" he asked. "That was the missus other idea. She got some brochures from a little place down there on the water. I'd like to try some fishing myself."

"That's the place for it." Dar turned her head as she heard her cell phone ring. "Uh oh." She got up and reached across to the sideboard, grabbing the phone and opening it. "Ah." She recognized the number. "Hey hon."

"Hey." Kerry's voice came through the phone. "Were you sleeping? Sorry if you were."

"Nah." Dar sat back down. "Alastair and I were having a nightcap and talking about our vacation plans. What's up?"

"I had to call you. Danny just called from the Pentagon, and he said one of the techs there came to find him, because someone wanted to get a message to you."

"Yeah?" Dar didn't hear any upset in her partner's tone, so she reasoned it was probably good news. "What was it?"

"General Easton," Kerry said. "He just said to say he said hello, and that he needs to talk to you when you can get through to him tomorrow."

Dar felt a sense of profound relief. "That's great news," she said, glancing at Alastair. "Gerry Easton's okay. He wants me to call him tomorrow." She turned back to the phone. "Why aren't you sleeping, by the way?"

Kerry cleared her throat. "Um... well, I was playing with my niece and then we got into a game of hide and seek."

"You and your niece?" Dar asked.

"Me and my brother and sister," Kerry muttered. "It ended up with a broken table leg. Don't ask."

"Um... okay."

"Listen, when you talk to the General, can you find out if his dog's had puppies again?" Kerry asked. "My sister wants one."

"She does?" Dar's brows knitted. "She didn't seem like a dog person to me."

"She isn't. Yet."

Dar decided ignorance was probably better at this point. "Okay," she said. "Listen, have a good flight, and let me know when you land," she said. "Be safe."

"I'll text you," Kerry promised. "It's a commuter plane. I'm sure we'll be fine. I just wish there was more room inside it."

Dar chuckled briefly. "Catching my claustrophobia?"

"Don't want to be that close to my mother," her partner said, succinctly. "Later hon."

"Later." Dar closed the phone, and smiled. "Well, that's good news at least."

Alastair stood up. "Sure is," he said. "Let me let you get some rest." He picked up his glass. "And let's hope that call tomorrow is just him wanting to catch up on you personally."

Dar blinked at him in surprise.

Her boss smiled wryly, lifting his glass in her direction then making his way to the door. "Nice fella, glad he's safe," he said, as he eased out. "But he's also a big customer," he reminded her, closing the door behind him.

True enough. Dar tossed back the rest of her whisky, grimacing as it burned its way down her throat and into her gut. Then she exhaled, puffing her dark hair up out of her eyes, and pulled her magazine back over. "Hope it's personal too." She opened the pages. "I'm not going to have time to call in any favors."

KERRY ZIPPED HER bag closed and set it on the floor, glancing around out of habit to make sure she hadn't forgotten anything. She'd left her share of travel alarm clocks, toothbrushes, and other sundries in hotels across the country and learned her lesson the hard way.

"Ker?" Angie stuck her head in the room. "You ready? I told Mom I'd take you down to the airport to meet her so we didn't have to swing back by the house."

"Yup." Kerry shouldered her overnight bag and picked up her laptop case. "Let's go," she said. "Am I safe letting Mike return the truck to the rental joint?"

Her sister chuckled.

"That's what I thought." Kerry sighed. "Oh well." She followed her sister out of the room. It was already dark outside, and the kids were tucked in bed in the half empty house already echoing with the impending move and a little sadder for it. "How much can one of those cost anyway?"

Angie led the way down the steps and over to the front door, picking up a handbag and slinging it over her shoulder and picking up her keys. "Marco, is the car ready?" she asked the man standing near the door.

"Yes, ma'am," Marco replied. "I filled the tank. Do you want me to drive you though? Roads are pretty dark."

Angie regarded her house manager with a smile. "Thanks, but I'll be okay," he said. "My brother's coming with us. He can keep me company on the way back."

Marco looked dubious at this proffered safety, and Kerry shifted her overnight back and reached up to scratch her nose.

Angie seemed to sense the unspoken doubt. "We'll be fine." She grabbed the strap of Kerry's bag and tugged her out the door. "We're in Saugatuck, for Pete's sake."

"Mm." Kerry followed without further comment, walking down the steps toward where Mike was waiting by her sister's big sedan as the cool air hit her face. She blinked into it, feeling the dryness against her eyeballs, and thought briefly of the sauna bath she lived in most of the year.

That had been hard to get used to. Now this was hard to get used to. Kerry shook her head as Angie opened the doors and went around to the driver's side.

"Here, gimme." Mike took her bag and tossed it in the back seat, sliding in after it.

Kerry got in the front passenger side and closed the door, glad enough to relax into the leather seat for the relatively short drive to the regional airport. "Think Mom's still pissed off?" she asked. "My shoulder's killing me where I hit that table."

Angie started the car and gave her sibling a wry look. "Your shoulder's killing you? Remember you bounced into me after you broke the furniture. I feel like I was hit by a truck."

"I was just glad it wasn't me for a change," Mike commented from the back seat. "It was worth it to see Mom's face when she came around that corner and saw you sitting there with all that broken china around you holding that stupid leg."

"I felt like I was six," Kerry admitted. "But it was funny."

"It was freaking hilarious," Mike said. "I mean after that whole lousy day it felt great to just be stupid and laugh and not worry about what building was falling down or if a plane was going to crash on my head."

They were all momentarily quiet. "Yeah," Angie finally said. "It sure was a horrible day." She looked at Kerry from the corner of her eye. "I think you and Mom are crazy to be flying tonight. I can't even believe they're letting you."

"I know," Kerry said. "But this is different. It's a private plane."

"A crappy, tiny commuter," Mike said. "I've seen the inside of it. I'd rather drive."

"I should have gotten a van, like that guy of yours did, Kerry, and thrown the kids in there and we could have all taken a road trip," Angie said. "Even Mom."

Kerry covered her eyes with silent eloquence.

"Ang, you're a retard," Mike said. "That didn't work when we were ten."

"Shut up," Angie said. "We're adults now. We could have made it work."

Mike slid around and extended his legs behind Kerry's seat. "Ah, maybe," he conceded. "I looked up that thing Kerry's guy got, it's not a van. It's an RV. It's pretty cool," he said. "It's got a kitchen and a bathroom and everything."

"It's a long trip from Miami," Kerry said. "I'm glad they found something comfortable. Last thing I'd want is for them to zonk out on the ride and have an accident. It takes...I think ten or twelve hours just to get out of the state."

"Have you driven that?" Angie asked.

Kerry shook her head. "Just to Orlando with Dar," she said. "But Dar has driven up the East Coast. She says unless you take the scenic route through the mountains it's a snore." Her eyes flicked to the dark countryside they were passing through.

"You staying with Mom?" Her sister asked. "Hotels must be crazy there."

"No." Kerry shook her head. "Dar made me reservations on the edge of town. I can pick up a car or have the office pick me up in the morning, then maybe stay out there after that." She let her head rest against the back of the seat. "I haven't told her yet. I think she assumes I'm going to the townhouse."

"She does," Mike supplied. "She was telling some dude over there to get a room ready, like you care what the view is."

"Sometimes I do," Kerry objected mildly. "But then again..." She pondered. "Usually I'm with Dar so the view inside the room is better anyway." She chuckled under her breath as her siblings both groaned. "I hope her flight goes okay tomorrow."

"She's flying into Mexico?" Mike asked. "I heard on the news that it's nuts there, the airports are crammed," he said. "Hope they don't give her a hard time coming back in the country."

Kerry extended her legs out and crossed her ankles. "I hope not," she said. "I can imagine they'll be pretty freaked out, and Dar does get touchy sometimes about official stuff. She gives the airport people grief when they want her to start up her laptop."

"Glad I don't travel much," Angie sighed, as she turned onto the access road for the small local airport. "Especially now. I'd be scared to death to get on an airplane."

Kerry thought about that. She remembered thinking once that you had no idea, really, who you were going to share a plane with, who was sitting next to you, what their motives were, or even what viruses they were going to gift the rest of the passengers with.

Scary. Now, it was a lot scarier. She imagined being on those planes that had taken off, and finding out that passenger sitting next to you was a killer.

Ugh.

Her flight, and Dar's, would at least be private this time. But the next? Kerry sighed, hoping that the domestic flights wouldn't start flying so soon that Dar needed to hop on the first one available to come out to meet her. Much as she wanted to see her partner, and she certainly did, she'd rather her be safe.

Was there a train from Texas to Washington? Kerry drummed her fingers on the armrest. Hmm. Dar might like a train ride.

"Wow, look at those lights," Angie interrupted her musing, "at the gate."

Kerry peered through the windshield to see the entrance to the field approaching, bracketed by a line of emergency vehicles with their flashing lights on. "What's that all about?" she wondered.

"Maybe mom's limo crashed into the guardhouse," Mike suggested.

"Michael," Angie scolded him. "That's not funny."

"Why?" he retorted. "That thing's built like a brick. I'd feel sorry for the guy in the guardhouse not anyone in that tank."

Angie slowed the car as they approached. Shadowy figures emerged from the vehicles blocking the entrance. "Oh. Wow."

"Guns," Kerry observed. "I hope it's the Michigan National Guard."

"Me too," Mike agreed, in a far meeker voice. "I don't like guns." He slid back against the back of the seat, moving over to Kerry's side of the car. "Bet Dar does."

"Bet she doesn't." Kerry watched as Angie rolled the window down. "I'm the registered gun owner in the family."

"This airport is closed, ma'am." The man was dressed in a guard uniform and sounded very stern, but polite. "Please turn around and go back the way you came."

Kerry heard a sound behind her. She glanced through the window and saw three more soldiers, standing with their rifles pointed not quite at the car, but not quite at the ground. "Oh boy." She fished for her identification in her briefcase.

"Thank you officer," Angie replied in her most polite voice. "I know the airport is closed. My mother, Senator Stuart, asked us to join her here. I am dropping my sister off to accompany her to Washington."

The soldier looked at her doubtfully.

Angie removed her wallet from her purse, and extracted her driver's license. She handed it over to the man. "Glad I had my name changed back," she muttered. "This doesn't need to be any more complicated."

Mike prudently just kept his mouth shut, for a change.

Kerry leaned slowly over and handed her own ID over, in a leather folder that held not only her driver's license, but her passport and corporate ID. "Here you go."

The soldier took both ID's and stepped back. Another man joined him and shone a flashlight on the documents.

"Got mom's cell phone number?" Kerry asked, keeping her voice low.

"Yep," Angie answered. "Hope we don't need it." She glanced behind her. "Give me your license Mike."

"I don't have it with me," he answered, in a small voice. "I left my wallet in my car."

Angie closed her eyes and exhaled. "And you called me a retard."

"Can you open the trunk please, ma'am?" the guard said.

Angie and Kerry exchanged looks. "Oh boy." Angie triggered the trunk lock. "I'm trying to remember what I have in there. Hope it wasn't the diapers."

Kerry faced forward and folded her arms over her chest, very aware of the men watching through the window. "I guess given what happened Ang, they don't have any choice. I'd rather be sure, even though this is creepy as hell."

"True." Angie looked out as the soldier came back. She heard the trunk slam.

The soldier handed her back her ID, then he leaned forward and handed Kerry hers with a little duck of his head. "Ma'am."

"Thanks." Kerry took the leather portfolio, and put it back in her briefcase. Then she gave the soldier a smile. "Long night?"

"Long day," the man responded. "Gonna be a lot of them." He looked back at Angie. "Go down the road there ma'am. There is a guard in front of that little terminal. They'll ask for ID again. The Senator's not here yet, but I got a radio call that she's on the way and will be here in a few minutes. Said she was expecting you."

"Thank you." Angie said. "Very, very much."

"You ladies be careful, okay?" the soldier said. "This is not a night to be out driving." He lifted his hand, and the other soldiers went over to pick up the barrier, moving it aside to let them through.

Angie put the car into drive and eased through the gates, passing the cluster of soldiers and their trucks and gaining the relative safety of the short road that led to the airport terminal building. "I don't think he noticed Mike."

"Not if he called me a lady he didn't." Mike finally scraped up the courage to lean forward and sling his arms over the seat. "I think he liked Kerry. He was nice to her."

"Yes, he was." Angie glanced at her sister, with a grin. "But then, she was always the magnet in the family."

Kerry eyed them. "He probably recognized the logo of the company that handles his paycheck," she remarked dryly. "But if it's like this here, what's it going to be like where we're going?"

Angie parked the car. "I don't know, but no matter how much it's needed, I don't like it." She indicated the squad of armed soldiers waiting for them, complete with helmets and side arms.

"Me either," Mike agreed. "Too forties movie-like."

Kerry zipped up her jacket and opened the door letting in a rush of pine scented cold air. "Well, let's just hope for the best." She got out of the car and picked up her briefcase, seeing the bright lights on the small plane in the field beyond. "Cause I'm not sure we've got a lot of choice right now."

"Crazy," Angie said, as they walked toward the line of armed soldiers. "Just crazy."

KERRY SLIPPED PAST the crowd of aides and found a seat near the front of the plane where it was quieter. The aircraft had eight seats, plush and comfortable, and she settled into the one nearest the cockpit and stowed her briefcase.

Her mother and her three aides were clustered toward the rear of the plane where the four seats were turned facing each other with small tables to work on.

Kerry leaned back and crossed her legs at the ankles, glancing at the two empty seats nearby and wishing her siblings weren't back in Angie's car waiting to watch them leave.

Safety in numbers? Kerry had to admit she'd always felt more comfortable and a bit more anonymous in the presence of her siblings at family events. Even though she tended to stick out with her fair hair and shorter stature, it still had diluted the attention.

Well. She folded her hands in her lap and twiddled her thumbs. Here she was.

"Kerrison?" Her mother was looking around the plane.

Kerry looked past the set of seats opposite her. "Over here." She lifted one hand and let it drop. "Thought I'd stay out of the way."

"Oh." Her mother studied her for a moment. "If you like, one of my aides can sit over there, and you can sit here with the rest of us."

Kerry smiled. "I'm sure you have work to do," she demurred. "I'm fine over here. After all, I'm just hitching a ride." She caught a look of relief out of the corner of her eye from the aides. "It's not that long a flight."

"True enough. Possibly two hours," Cynthia said. "Very well, we will continue our business." She went back to her discussion, dismissing Kerry to sit quietly in her corner.

That suited Kerry just fine. She fished in her briefcase and removed a magazine from it, laying the pages open on her lap and turning the reading light on.

Colorful fish faced her. She turned to an article on underwater photography and relaxed, leaning against the chair arm as she read.

She glanced at her watch, and then went back to the review of new models of underwater cameras. She had seen divers with rigs the size of small minivans taking pictures and she knew the results were often spectacular. She herself was more prone to moderation in her gear, preferring to trade off professional quality for ease of use and handling.

However, the enticing possibility of filming Dar swimming underwater in high resolution, now...

"Kerrison?"

"Huh?" Kerry looked up to find her mother looking back at her, two of the soldiers at her side. "Ah, yes?"

"This gentleman wishes a word with you." Her mother indicated one of the men. "I hope there's no problem."

Kerry wondered what problem her mother thought would involve her and the Michigan National Guard. "Sure, what can I do for you?" she asked, closing the magazine and setting it aside. "Sit down. " She indicated the seat across from her.

The man came over and sat down gingerly, moving his automatic rifle out of the way. "Sorry to bother you, Ms. Stuart," he said, "but I got a favor to ask."

Kerry was aware of a silence behind the man, as everyone else listened in. "If I can help, sure." She gave the soldier a smile. It was her friend from the gate, she realized, a tall man with sandy brown hair and a square, Midwestern face.

"My brother Joshua works for your company," he said, without preamble. "He works out in Manhattan. He runs cable for you all."

"Okay." Kerry nodded. "We have a service office there, yes."

"We haven't been able to talk to him since last night and my mother's having a heart attack," he said. "Do you know if he's okay?"

Yikes. Kerry took out her PDA. "Let me see if I can find out for you," she said. "His name is Joshua."

"Douglass," the man supplied. "He's my brother."

Kerry typed out a quick message to Mark. "I'll give that a minute, and if no answer I can log onto our systems and check," she said. "I know there are a lot of people that couldn't be contacted. The phones are jammed up and a lot of lines are down."

The soldier nodded. "That's what they said on the television." He glanced behind him. "Sorry to cut in here, ma'am," he addressed the Senator. "Uh, and you know–the press is here too, wanting to take pictures, I guess."

"Are they?" Cynthia asked, sharply. "Oh my. I didn't think we notified them we were leaving tonight, did we Charles?"

"I'll go see them." One of the aides immediately rose. "Shall I bring them onboard?"

"Well..."

"Let me see what their angle is," the aide said, scooting for the door. "It could be a good op."

"Guess I should have said that first," the soldier said to Cynthia. "Sorry about that Ma'am."

"Please." Cynthia held a hand up. "Your family is more important than the press, or I should hope!" She came over and took the seat on the other side of Kerry. "Let's hope for good news."

Kerry's PDA beeped and she opened it, crossing her toes as she scanned the note. "Hm." She picked up her cell phone and dialed a number. "Let's see what this is about...Mark?"

"Hey, Kerry."

Mark's voice sounded relaxed, which made the sudden knot in her gut relax. "What's up? Do we have anything on the name I sent you?"

"That's why I'm calling," Mark said. "I thought it was so completely freaking weird that you sent me that note when I was actually on the phone with that same guy," he said. "How did you do that?"

"You were?" Kerry asked. "Oh, wow!"

"Still am," Mark said. "So what's the deal with him? He's one of our line techs. Spent the whole damn day getting out of Manhattan and ended upstate near Buffalo," he said. "He got the alerts on his cell but couldn't answer and then turned it off for a while."

Kerry looked up to see her mother and the soldier watching her anxiously. Behind them, the sound of people approaching echoed. "Can you conference me in? I have his brother here."

"For sure," Mark said. "Hang on a sec." He clicked off, and then clicked back on. "Okay, we're here. Say hi to Kerry, Joshua."

"Uhhh...hi ma'am."

Kerry smiled. "Hang on." She held the phone out to the soldier. "Here. Want to say hello?"

The man stared at her, and then reached out for the phone, his eyes wide. "Are you kidding me?" He put the phone to his ear. "Hello?" He paused. "Josh, is that you? Yeah! Yeah it's Mike! I can't believe you're on the phone! Jesus Christ, bro, mama's about sick to death with you!"

Kerry leaned on her seat arm, a big grin on her face, very satisfied to have pulled this particular undeserved rabbit out of her navel in typical coincidental fashion. Across the aisle, her mother was also smiling as she listened, and behind them she caught the flash of a camera capturing it all.

"No, no man, I'm guarding the airport here." Mike was saying. "I saw that lady from your company come in and so I came and asked her what was up...what? Where are you? Buffalo?" He paused. "Well go have some damned chicken wings then!"

Kerry chuckled. "Mm," she said. "I love chicken wings." She saw her mother's eyebrows hike.

"Okay, okay, listen," Mike said. "Call mama. She's crying, man! Okay? Yeah, you used to make fun of me for being in the Guard, and look who was nearer the hard stuff, huh?" He glanced around. "Listen, I

gotta go. I'm holding these people up here. You call mama, okay? Bye!"
He hung up the phone and turned to face Kerry.

"Feel better?" She took the phone.

"Man that was cool," he said. "That was great. I can't believe you just called up and found him. We have been trying and trying all day long. We were so scared cause he was supposed to be downtown today." He wiped his forehead with the back of his hand. "Wow."

Kerry reached over and patted his arm. "I'm really glad we found him," she said. "It was really great timing that you asked right after he called us."

He grinned at her. "Sometimes you gotta have some luck," he said. "After a crappy day like this, man, that was just cool." He looked over at the Senator. "Thanks for letting me on the plane, ma'am."

"Oh! Of course," Senator Stuart said. "I'm so glad, so very glad it was good news, and my daughter could help. It's fabulous. Simply fabulous," she told him. "Worth every moment of the delay, without question."

The soldier stood up and carefully lifted his rifle so it didn't smack Kerry in the head. "I can go out there with a light heart now," he said. "You want everyone to be safe, but when it's family...man, that's just different, you know?"

"I do know." Kerry also stood up. "We had a lot of people in harm's way, and we care about all the people who work for us. It's not exactly like family, but it is close," she said. "I hope you have a quiet night after this."

"Me too," the soldier said. "Thanks again, ma'am. I really, really appreciate what you did," he said. "Let me get out of your way now." He edged into the aisle and headed for the door, ducking past the television camera and the man holding it with a third person ahead of them with a microphone. "Man that was the best."

Kerry tucked her cell phone back on its clip. "That was pretty awesome," she commented. "We have so many people unaccounted for in New York. I'm glad his brother wasn't one of them."

Her mother stood up and twitched her jacked sleeve straight. "Well, I shall go talk to the press," she said. "They might want to speak with you," she warned. "I believe they are looking for any bit of news in our area about this."

"Well." Kerry eyed the reporter. "They could also want to talk to me about a lot of other things. But that's fine." She put her hands on her denim clad hips. "I'm up for it if they want to." She took a deep breath, feeling the finely knit wool of her sweater tighten around her body.

"That is another lovely sweater," Cynthia remarked. "Just lovely. What are those designs — are they animals?"

"Beavers." Kerry's lips twitched as she muffled a grin. "Dar gave it to me."

"Ah," her mother said. "Is she a supporter of wildlife?"

"Yes," her daughter answered. "She loves wildlife. And beavers."

Her mother merely nodded, and then turned and walked down the narrow aisle to where the reporter was waiting. The television light went on immediately and the aides closed in on either side, blocking Kerry's view.

Which was fine. She sat back down in her seat and picked up her magazine, glancing at her watch again. "Should have kidnapped Angie and drove." She shook her head and started reading.

Chapter Twelve

DAR WOKE UP in complete darkness disoriented and not entirely sure of where she was. The smells and sounds were wrong for home, and she remembered light pouring in her window from the street in her London hotel.

Here, just darkness, and lots of quiet.

After a second of confusion, she remembered, and her tensed body relaxed back onto the goose down topper on the bed's mattress.

Sir Melthon's estate was set back from the road and surrounded by hedges and land, and thick gates. Far enough from the city sounds to be silent, much like it was in her condo back in Miami.

But no ocean sounds. If she concentrated, she could hear crickets though.

"Sheesh." Dar rolled over and lifted up her watch, pressing the side button and checking the digital display. "Ngh." She set it back down. "Four in the morning." She counted back, then reached over and picked up her PDA to check for messages.

Sure enough. Dar clicked contentedly and opened it.

Made it. Slept most of the way. Mother won't hear of my getting a cab this late so she's sending me in the car to the hotel once we drop her off at the townhouse. Lesser of two evils. I will end up being on the local late news in Michigan though. There was a press bunch that cornered us at the airport. Interview wasn't bad They were too busy with all the disaster news to ask me stupid questions about my sex life. Mom likes my sweater by the way. She thinks you have good taste if a rather odd fixation on small mammals. Love you. K.

Dar started laughing, the motion waking her up enough to make going back to sleep immediately out of the question. The tone of Kerry's note was a little resigned, but amused, so she figured things weren't going along too badly.

She sat up and crossed her legs up under her and leaning her elbows on her knees as she removed her stylus and started an answer.

Hey Ker–

I've commissioned a knitted pullover for you with the Gopher from my program in poses guaranteed to get you thrown out of Wal-Mart. Tell her that. Glad you made it okay. Hope everything is calm in the city. Mother or no mother I'd have rather you go directly to the border and not stay near anything white and colonnaded just in case. I know that sounds callous and obnoxious but I am sometimes.

Dar could almost hear Kerry's objection to that, but it was true, and she knew it.

Send me a note when you get to the hotel. I have no doubt the Mandarin

Oriental will have a room ready for you, but I'd sleep better if I knew you were in it.

DD.

Dar clicked send and lay back down, letting the PDA rest on her chest. Aside from the early waking, she'd slept pretty well, the quiet and comfort of the room allowing her to get more rest than she'd really expected to.

She wasn't really tired. She didn't want to spend hours lying in bed staring at the ceiling either. After a moment more of it, she sat up and swung her feet off the bed, reaching over to turn the lamp on. A soft, golden light filled the room and she took a moment to stand and shake her body out before she walked over to retrieve her laptop.

It was quiet enough that the zipper of the case sounded loud, and she glanced around a trifle guiltily, though she knew full well the sound wouldn't penetrate the walls.

At least she hoped it wouldn't. She removed the machine and its cable from the case and took it back with her to the bed, laying it down and then returning to the sideboard where there was a tray resting with cups and several bottles.

Reviewing her options, she poured a cup of still warm milk out of a very efficient thermal carafe and brought it back to the bed with her. She set it on the bedside table and sat down, opening the lid of the machine and pressing the power button.

Her PDA was blinking.

Dar smiled and opened it, bending her head slightly to read the message.

I would wear Gopher Dar on my chest any time, honey. But telling my mother that here in front of her little aides is not going to make this road trip any shorter if you catch my drift.

"Probably not," Dar had to agree. "And you'd have to explain it anyway."

And I'd have to explain it anyway. You know I would.

Dar started laughing.

Why are you up? It's four in the morning there. But if you are, after we drop Mom off, can I call you? I want to try and get through, and it would be nice to talk for a few minutes before all the crazy stuff starts up all over again. I'm sure tomorrow's going to be worse than today. I think everyone-the business people I mean-are in shock. Tomorrow it'll be...well, okay, but when will I be back up?

Dar nodded in agreement. "Yup."

It's so quiet here in the city. I know it's sort of late, but there's hardly a car on the street. It's almost spooky it's so quiet, and I realized just earlier how funny it was to not hear airplanes. You never think of that, but we have them all the time at home flying over head. I've been here a couple hours and not one except for fighters. So strange.

There are lots of soldiers around. It almost feels like we're at war. Are we?

Dar gazed thoughtfully at the message. "Good question," she said aloud. "Have we ever not been at war?"

Anyway, we're pretty close to the townhouse now. So hopefully I'll be calling soon. Hope you're up just because you're up and not because you're doing stuff.

Dar glanced guiltily at the laptop. Then she half shrugged and decided to look forward to talking to Kerry instead of worrying about it. She took a sip of her warm milk and logged in, waiting for the machine to present her desktop before she started the cellular card up and connected.

It wasn't nearly as quick a connection as she was used to, of course. The cellular service provided speed more or less like a fast modem though, and it was enough for Dar to start up her VPN session and connect to the office. "Might as well clear some mail," she decided. "With any luck, everyone will have been a lot busier with everything else than sending me a lot of it."

She took another sip of milk, licking her lips a little at the strange but not unpleasant taste. Different grass, maybe, or just a different way of processing the milk, she wasn't sure. She suspected she'd get used to it after a while.

The computer chimed softly, and she started up her mail program. "Of course, I'm not gonna get the chance." She sighed. "Bastards."

It wasn't logical for her to be upset, and she knew it, because given what so many others were going through her lack of a touring vacation was so petty she'd have been embarrassed to mention it to anyone other than herself.

But she was mad. She was pissed off her life had been disrupted. She was even more pissed off that she wasn't going to get to enjoy some simple wandering with Kerry that she'd looked very much forward to. "Bastards," she repeated. "They're damn lucky it's not my finger on the nuclear button cause if it was I'd have pressed it."

Self centered, shocking, and unworthy of even thinking it. Dar watched her inbox fill. A thought she wouldn't consider repeating to Kerry. But the venal stupidity of the act chewed at her, since the reasoning behind most of the world's ills right now was based in the unthinking animal tribal instinct that humanity had no real hope of getting rid of any time soon.

There was no logic there. The instinct to hate what you weren't was written so deeply, Dar felt that on some level it wasn't something you could address with words or thoughts. It was a burning in the gut. A fire in the brain that resisted any attempt at change.

It was easy for people, and she'd heard many of them in the last few hours, point at a particular group and act like those people were so alien and so isolated in their hatred. Easy, especially on a day like yesterday. But the truth was, the ravaging need to destroy what wasn't you was universal.

Dar sighed. "So I go and say something like, yeah, I want to blow them off the face of the earth, and thereby prove out my species." She shook her head. "Asshole."

She scanned the mail, seeing not a lot that wasn't either group sent mails or brief acknowledgements. Her brows raised in surprise. "I know I said I didn't expect much mail, but I did expect some."

But really, there wasn't any. Dar reasoned that maybe the fact they'd all be in a huge conference call all day accounted for that. She could imagine sitting down to write some mundane note and just stopping, and clicking the close button instead.

She minimized the mail program and called up her status screen instead waiting for it to appear and the counters to settle in and show what the latest was across the company. There was no audio, she wasn't about to trigger the voice link over the slow connection.

Instead, she studied the lists of employees, checking first the one from the Pentagon area, and then the one from New York.

Each person's name had a red, a green, or a yellow tag next to it. Green meant they'd been heard from, and were okay. Yellow meant they'd been heard from, but were having problems. Red...

Dar exhaled slowly, her eyes running over all those little red dots. A dozen in Washington, and three times that in New York. She studied the names, her stomach dropping when she saw Bob's name still stubbornly crimson.

They hadn't exactly gotten along. She hadn't exactly enjoyed his company. But he was an old friend of Alastair's and now, his proud enthusiasm about his city caused a pang in her chest as she remembered very clearly not wanting to hear a second of it.

She'd argued with him just the other day, over parking spaces at the office there. He wanted to spend money for covered parking.

Native Floridian Dar had thought that was crazy. Bob had gotten frustrated, and almost hung up, but then had gotten lucky in the form of Kerry's arriving and explaining to her tropical lover trying to get your door open in an ice storm.

Saved by the Midwest. Bob had almost seemed embarrassed, but they'd ended up splitting the cost and now, she was glad.

She was glad they'd ended the meeting not screaming at each other.

Her PDA flashed. Dar was glad enough to push aside the laptop and pull the smaller device over, opening it up to find another message from Kerry.

Streets full of soldiers, Dar. They blocked off most of the streets. I don't think we're going to be able to get close to the townhouse I'm not sure what's going on.

Dar sat up straight in alarm, feeling a surge of adrenaline hit her.
Something about a car bomb. Crap.

Dar reached over and grabbed her cell phone, hitting the speed dial button. Instead of a fast busy, the call went through and she heard it ring twice before it was answered. "Hey."

"Hey." Kerry cleared her throat.

Dar could hear Kerry's mother in the background, and a male voice, lower and official sounding. "Listen, you want me to call up the hotel and make reservations for the whole lot of you? Kerry, you are not going anywhere near a damn car bomb."

There was a moment of silence. "Yes, I would like you to do that. A lot."

Dar yanked the laptop over and rattled in the travel website. She stopped on hearing noises in the background on the phone. "Were those gunshots?"

"I don't know."

The website responded, and she typed in the information. "Hell, your suite's got three rooms you could probably cram everyone in there if you had to."

Kerry cleared her throat again, this time with a completely different inflection.

Dar scanned the response. "They have two rooms available," she said. "I'm grabbing them. Must be last minute cancels because they weren't there earlier."

"Okay, let me get things organized on this end." Kerry sounded resigned. "Wish me luck. Thanks sweetie. I'll call you back in a minute."

"You'd better." Dar clicked the reserve button. "And get away from those damn sounds!"

"MA'AM, I DO understand, but I can't let you go any further. It's dangerous. They have the road blocked off, and they called the bomb squad," the soldier said. "No telling when they'll get here. They've been all over the city tonight. People are real nervous."

Senator Stuart folded her hands in exasperation, turning to look at her aides. "This is ridiculous," she said. "I understand security, but what are we supposed to do, sleep here in the car?"

"Senator, please," the most senior of the aides, a middle age man with a bearded face said. "Let me arrange an alternative. I'm sure there's a hotel in the area we can go to. I have your overnight bag in the trunk."

"That's a good idea ma'am," the soldier added, respectfully. "Though you might need to call around, I hear it's pretty busy."

Cynthia sat back, distress apparent on her face. "Well, my goodness."

"Mother." Kerry leaned forward and touched her knee. "My hotel had two rooms left. I had them held."

Her Mother glanced around at the four aides. "I certainly do appreciate it, however..."

"My suite's got three rooms," Kerry accurately intercepted her concern. "You're more than welcome to share it with me." From the corner of her eye she saw the aides relax, their shoulders dropping and veiled looks of gratitude being nudged in her direction.

Her mother though, still hesitated.

"I mean," Kerry could feel the irony right down to her toes, "we are related."

That seemed to snap the Senator out of her reverie. "Of course we are," Cynthia said, briskly. "Of course, and that's a perfect solution. Thank you so very much, Kerry." She motioned to the window separating them from the driver. "Please tell him to drive on to..." She glanced at her daughter.

"Mandarin Oriental." Kerry supplied. "It's on the edge of town."

Her mother's eyes blinked. "Yes, it is," she agreed, in a mild tone. "Lovely hotel. I attended a banquet there just last month."

"Mandarin Oriental," one of the aides told the driver. "Let's get out of here."

The car turned, and headed away from the blockaded area and every one settled back in their seats as they moved through the almost deserted city.

"Well," Cynthia said, after a moment. "That was unexpected." She folded her hands in her lap. "I'm glad you had the forethought to call the hotel, Kerry. That was very proactive of you."

"I've been called that before." Kerry decided her boss wouldn't mind her taking credit for her quick thinking just this once. "I'm glad they had the space. It's been a really long day," she said. "I'm looking forward to just getting some rest."

The aides nodded. "You're right there, Ms. Stuart," the senior aide said. "It certainly has been a rough time today."

Kerry realized it was the first time the aide had addressed her directly. "This is one of those things where I think you'll remember where you were when it happened," she remarked. "I know I will."

The other aides nodded.

Cynthia pursed her lips for a moment. "I do honestly think I'm very glad I was at home when I did hear," she said. "And that all my children were there also. You do worry about your family at times such as this, and we had so much going on."

Surprisingly, Kerry found herself in agreement. "I'm glad too," she said. "I'm glad you weren't in Washington, and I'm glad I didn't have to chase around looking for Mike and Angie to make sure they were okay, and that Mike wasn't off in New York on some promotion or other."

"Absolutely," her mother murmured. "Do you still have people unaccounted for?"

Kerry nodded. "But we hope it's just because so much communication structure is not working," she said, quietly. "Maybe we'll hear from them tomorrow."

A pensive silence fell. Kerry let her head rest against the window.

Her eyes burned, and she checked her watch, seeing the hands pointing almost to midnight.

It had been a very long day. The time she'd spent doing crunches in the early morning light now seemed to be from a different time.

A different lifetime.

She glanced out the window seeing a blast of flashing lights. A line of police cars blazed past, heading in the opposite direction in an eerie, siren-less silence. She studied the buildings going past, most with darkened windows, some with entryways blocked by large, solid looking vehicles.

Under siege?

Kerry supposed that's what it must feel like. No one really knew if there would be more attacks, and if there were, what form they might take. Car bombs? Maybe. Human bombs? Happens in the Middle East every day.

"Crazy." One of the aides was also watching out the window. "What the hell's wrong with these people?"

"Well," Senator Stuart spoke up. "I would guess that they-whomever they are-probably are saying much the same about us, wherever they might be," she said. "There's just too much intolerance in the world. That's the real problem."

"Senator, these people are crazy. People who fly airplanes into buildings aren't intolerant, they're nuts," one of the younger aides said. "That's not human."

"They were celebrating over there. Did you see that on CNN?" the young woman aide said. "There were people over there cheering when they saw bodies dropping from the tower to their deaths."

Senator Stuart laced her fingers together. "Now, why would they do that?" she asked. "What kind of hatred can they have that makes them celebrate such a horrible thing?"

"I don't think I want to know why," the woman aide said. "There's no way to understand that. We should just send our own planes over there and get them back."

"Make them stop cheering," the young male aide agreed. "They're just animals."

Cynthia frowned. "I'm sure we will do something as a response." She sighed. "And yet, what will that bring in the long run? More disasters." She shook her head. "I fear though, you are correct. We have no common reference."

Kerry tilted her head to one side and poked her finger in her ear, wiggling it vigorously.

"Something wrong?" her mother asked.

"Sorry." Kerry gave her head a shake. "Thought I felt my brains leaking out there for a minute." She laced her fingers together in her lap. "Lack of tolerance and understanding is not unique to the people who drove those planes," she said. "I think it's something that's part of human nature, to not like, and fear things we don't really have a handle on."

Her mother's eyes narrowed slightly, but Kerry managed to retain a mild expression. "But still, there's no excuse for what those people did. There would be no excuse for us if we did it. Violence isn't the answer."

The senator nodded immediately. "Exactly what I meant."

"Especially not in this circumstance," Kerry went on. "Let's say we do send planes over and drop bombs. Then what? We don't know where the people who planned this are, so we drop a bomb and kill a couple thousand innocent people. How does that help? How does that make us any better than they are?"

"Well..." the woman aide said.

"So they just send more people to do more horrible things, and we send more bombs. What's the point? That doesn't get you anywhere." Kerry sighed. "My mother's right. We have no common frame of reference with this group of people who have been a civilization for twenty centuries at least. More than our country has even existed. They might as well be ET."

Cynthia looked a bit overwhelmed by the agreement. "Yes," she said, after a pause. "My point exactly."

Silence fell as they drove on past another block of police cars.

"That was a really good movie," the young male aide ventured. "ET, I mean."

It almost made Kerry giggle. She leaned against the arm of the limo door and rested her head against the glass again and hoped the hotel wasn't that far off. The conversation was veering toward the positively dangerous.

THE HOTEL LOBBY was definitely quiet. Kerry had her bag over her shoulder, and she headed for the reception desk where two receptionists were standing, backs turned to her, watching CNN on the television.

One of the aides hurried to catch up to her. "Listen, Ms. Stuart..."

"Hm?" Kerry turned her head and regarded him. He was a medium sort of person. Medium height, medium coloring, medium shade of brown hair. The only thing that stood out was a set of beautiful, long, well maintained eyelashes that looked very much like they were fake.

She hoped they weren't. "Yes?"

"Thanks for getting the rooms," the man said. "I wasn't looking forward to sleeping in the car."

Kerry's brows creased a little. "Don't you have an apartment here?" she asked. "You don't sleep in the townhouse garage, do you?"

The man chuckled. "No, there's a staffer's apartment building but it's right across the street from the Senator's place. We live there."

"Ah." Kerry removed her wallet as she approached the desk. "Good evening folks."

The two receptionists spun around. "Oh." The one on the left hurried forward. "Sorry about that. We were just..."

"We know." Kerry held a hand up. "It's okay. I have a reservation. Actually there are probably three of them under the name of either Stuart or Roberts."

The aide looked at her, his brows knitting over his outstanding eyelashes.

"My married name," Kerry was unable to resist, adding a smile as the man jerked a little. "I never know how Dar's going to book it."

"Yes, we do have them, Ms. Stuart," the receptionist interrupted. "I have two deluxe rooms with two beds, and the Presidential Suite." He glanced behind her. "Is there luggage we can take care of for you?"

"No." Kerry handed over her corporate card. "I have my overnight, and the rest of our party wasn't expecting to need a hotel. Do you have a sundry kit available for them?"

"Of course," the man said, instantly, handing back her card. "This is prepaid, ma'am."

Kerry rolled her eyes. "Of course it is." She chuckled under her breath. "Okay, we need two keys for each room, please." She tapped the card on the desk. "And could I get a pot of hot tea sent up to the suite? My head's pounding."

"Absolutely." The receptionist scribbled something on a pad. "Any particular type? We have a selection."

"Green Jasmine?" Kerry asked, hopefully. "With honey?"

"Not a problem."

"Do we want to mention..." The aide glanced behind them, into the depths of the spacious lobby where the Senator and the other aides waited

"Probably not," Kerry said. "No sense advertising, even if my mother's not really a hot potato on the international scene like my father was." She caught the receptionist's furtive glance, and smiled.

"Good point," the aide agreed. "Presidential Suite huh? I've seen pictures of that. It's swank."

Kerry collected the keys being handed to her. "After a while, they all just look like hotel rooms." She handed the aide the other keys. "No matter how nice, it's not home."

They walked back across the lobby floor to where the rest of the group was waiting. The other three aides stopped talking as they walked up and glanced at each other.

The female aide cleared her throat. "Basil, you want to share? We went to college together."

"Sure," the other younger aide said. "No problem."

The aide with Kerry passed out the keys. "That means I'll share with you, Robert," he said. "Ms. Stuart asked them to bring us up necessities."

"That was very thoughtful of you, Kerry," Senator Stuart said. "I am very glad I thought to bring my little overnight bag, myself."

Kerry hefted her own bag. "Okay, have a good night, folks. Time to get some rest." She herded them toward the big elevators, already imagining she could feel the softness of a bed under her back and the taste of hot tea on her tongue.

"Robert, please make sure my schedule is set for the morning," Senator Stuart said, as they entered the elevator and it started to rise. "I think we convene at 10:00 a.m. tomorrow."

"Yes, ma'am, that's correct," Robert said. "I'm sure the roads will be clear by breakfast tomorrow."

"I hope so."

The elevator doors opened on the fourth floor and the four aides got out. "Have a good night, Senator." Robert gave her and Kerry a little wave. "Ms. Stuart."

"You too." Kerry waved back, as the doors closed and they headed up to the top floor.

"Well," her mother said, as they exited and headed to the door of the suite. "This was certainly an unexpected end to a very unexpected day."

Kerry opened the door and entered, holding it for her mother. She detected the competing scents of fresh wax, steaming tea, and chocolate. Even she blinked at the grand entranceway and expansive stretch of the room they were staying in. "Wow."

"My goodness." Her mother stopped and peered around. "Is that a grand piano?"

"Is that a telescope? Kerry muttered in response. "Well, Mother, I think we've got enough space here."

"To play tennis, it seems," Cynthia remarked with surprising humor.

"I had them send up some tea." Kerry felt a little nervous and more than a little unsettled now that they were here and alone, and she realized it. "Have some if you like. My throat's a little sore." She moved past the ornate living room and found her way into one of the bedrooms.

"There's a large basket here. Is that from the hotel too?" her mother called in. "How nice of them."

"Is it fruit or chocolate?" Kerry responded.

"I believe it's...yes, some type of candy."

"Not the hotel. Dar." Kerry looked around the room. "Hm." She set her bag on the credenza and opened it. "Feel free to have some of that too." She pulled her shirt from her jeans and unbuttoned it, kicking off her sneakers at the same time.

The windows had an expansive view, and she turned to look out them as she removed her shirt. It was a little hard to believe she was here.

Okay. It was impossible to believe she was here. Kerry went back over to her bag and removed her bra , trading it for a long, soft T-shirt that she pulled over her head. She unbuttoned her jeans and slipped them off folding them in thirds and laying them down with her shirt on the dresser.

Then she squared her shoulders and faced the door, heading back out to where she could still smell the tea and hear her waiting parent. "Be good, Kerry," she muttered under her breath. "Be good."

THE BASKET WAS a typical Dar basket. Kerry studied it, loosening the ribbons as she pondered whether her partner had some cosmic internet shopping service with her favorite things predefined and simply pressed the correct button at the correct time. Or whether she took the time to select each item.

Knowing Dar, if she'd had the time, it was the latter. She was single minded about certain things, and Kerry knew she was one of them.

The basket held several types of chocolates, a pair of soft, fluffy socks, an aromatherapy eye shade that smelled of peaches, and a beanie baby that was the image of her pet Chino.

The crinkly plastic came off. She set it aside, glad her mother had decided to retreat into the second bedroom. "Hmm." She selected a wrapped Lindt chocolate ball and took it with her over to where the teapot was sitting along with the socks.

There were comfortable wing chairs to either side of the small table, and she sat down in one, putting the socks on her feet, then extending them across the marble floor and crossing her ankles. Dropping two sugar cubes in a cup, she poured out some of the steaming beverage, releasing a strong scent of jasmine in the air.

She unwrapped the chocolate and bit into it, enjoying the rich, creamy center. She washed it down with a sip of the hot, mildly astringent tasting tea, the clean freshness contrasting with the indulgence of the chocolate.

"That smells lovely." Her mother appeared wearing a plush robe and slippers. "Do you still favor tea? I remember you did always like it better than coffee." She walked over to the table and prepared a cup for herself.

"I do," Kerry said. "I'll drink a cup of coffee in the morning, but tea after that unless I'm doing an all nighter or that sort of thing." She took another bite of her chocolate. "This is pretty good."

Her mother sat down in the other chair on the other side of the table with her cup. She took a sip. "It's quite good. I prefer tea myself. I find it more delicate," she said. "I think it's calming."

Kerry thought so too. "Might be the illusion of Zen," she said. "But it works for me."

They were silent for a minute. Kerry got up and went over to the basket, picking up a couple more of the Lindt balls and bringing them back with her. She sat back down and stifled a yawn, unwrapping a chocolate.

"That was very kind of Dar," Cynthia ventured. "Very thoughtful. Does she do that often? I seem to remember Angela saying she'd gotten you a cake at the restaurant the other night or something like that."

Kerry rolled a Lindt ball over in her direction. "On special occasions, sure," she said. "When we're apart, we try to do little things for each other." She sipped her tea. "Not always baskets, but like reserving each other the nicest hotel room, or renting each other a fun car."

Her mother paused, and looked around the hotel room completely. Then she picked up the Lindt ball. "I would say she did well in this round," she commented. "It's nice to hear that you two get along so well. You're really quite unlike each other."

"Probably why we get along as well as we do," Kerry said, briefly. "We like a lot of the same things though, and naturally we've got our work in common."

"Of course," her mother said. "And you are both so clever," she said. "You know, I was listening to Dar speak earlier. What a charming voice she has."

Charming. There were lots of things about Dar Kerry found charming, but she half suspected her mother was trying to be a little over the top nice, to avoid any uncomfortable discussion between them. That was okay by her. It was very late, and she was both tired and emotionally overloaded from the day. "I could listen to her talk all day," she responded with a smile. "But really, you should hear her sing."

"Really?"

Kerry nodded, taking a sip of her tea. "We have a lot of fun together," she said. "I'm sorry she's going to be flying so long tomorrow. A lot can happen in ten hours."

"Goodness," her mother murmured. "Isn't that the truth. I don't really know what to expect, actually. I think everyone was just overwhelmed today, and tomorrow all the reactions will start," she said. "It's been very curious to be involved in the government, you know. After being a spectator for so long I mean."

"I bet it has," Kerry said. "From the interviews we were seeing on the news, it seems like most of the people in Congress are pretty much in agreement with each other though."

"Well." Cynthia curiously inspected the unwrapped chocolate, and then bit into it. "My, that is wonderful," she said. "In any case, there are the things one is expected to say to the press and in public, and then there are the things everyone says in private in the council chambers, and that is what made me understand just how much of a charade we do play here in Washington."

Kerry blinked a little in surprise. Not from the revelation that Congress often said different things to the press than to each other, but that her mother seemed so disapproving about it. "I just hope everyone sits down and thinks about what to do instead of just reacting."

"I hope so too," her mother agreed. "What will your plans be for tomorrow?"

The long day was now creeping over her. Kerry blinked a few times. "I have to go to our office in Virginia in the morning to see what the problem is with the government officials showing up wanting to tap our circuits," she said. "Then we'll probably go to the Pentagon. I want to visit my team there."

Cynthia pondered this for a minute. "Well, if there is anything I can help with on the government side," she offered diffidently, "please let me know."

Kerry nodded. "Thanks. Hopefully, it's just a misunderstanding," she replied. "I've gotten requests like that before, where people ask for things because they've either been told to, or someone mentioned a buzz word and there really isn't a full understanding of what they're asking."

Her mother finished her tea and set the cup down. "Well, it has been a long day, so I will leave you to get some rest. Perhaps you can join us for breakfast before you leave?"

"Sure." Kerry was too tired to even mind. "Good night...Oh." She felt a little sheepish. "Sorry about the table."

Her mother, already at the door to her bedroom, turned and peered at her, a faintly bemused expression on her face. "I have to admit," she said. "After all your talk about being this terribly different person, finding you under my dining room table amongst broken crockery was really quite amusing."

There wasn't really any defense to that. Kerry rested her head against her hand and gazed back at her mother through her somewhat disordered bangs. "Not everything's changed," she admitted, with a wry smile.

"No." Cynthia smiled back. "Not everything. Good night." She turned and went into the bedroom, shutting the door quietly behind her.

"Night." Kerry remained slouched in her chair, sipping her cooling tea. She finished her chocolate, then stood up and set the cup down, heading for the refuge of her room as the day's tension and discomfort started to rub against her like sandpaper.

She sat down on her bed, resting her hands on the mattress as she looked out the window.

She could see the Jefferson Memorial. It was shrouded in shadows, its normal brilliant lighting dimmed for safety she supposed, but she felt somehow that the somber sight reflected her attitude about the events of the day.

She felt like the world was overcast. With a sigh, she got up again and turned out the desk light, and went to the already turned down linens and started to get under them.

Her cell phone rang. Kerry cursed under her breath at it, then leaned over and grabbed the phone, turning and using her momentum to land back on the bed as she opened it. "Kerry Stuart."

"Hey sexy. You naked under the sheets yet?"

The mental whiplash made her sneeze. "Buh!" She rolled over onto her back, her gloomy thoughts lifting like magic. "I forgot to text you!"

"Is that a yes or a no?" Dar's voice sounded amused. "Or were you partying with your mother?"

Kerry started laughing. "Actually we had tea and chocolate together. Thank you, my love. The socks are warming my toes as we speak."

"I was just standing on my head for twenty minutes. My nose is throbbing," Dar informed her. "It's goddamn boring in a country mansion in England at five in the morning you know that?" she complained. "I'm afraid to go out and run in case they have foxhounds or something out there."

"Well." Kerry smiled. "You're a fox. It's a valid concern." She heard a conspicuous silence on the other end and her smiled grew wider. "Oooo...I gotcha."

Dar chuckled softly. "You did," she admitted. "So how's it going?" Her voice altered. "I'm stopping you from sleeping so I'll keep it short."

"Don't," Kerry said. "I could easily talk to you all night long," she added. "Even my mother thinks you have a charming voice."

"Huh?"

Kerry cleared her throat a bit. "It's not bad," she said. "This room you rented for me could hold our entire department with room for our dog. Mom's being okay. I think after that blowup she's just staying away from a lot of stuff. Which is fine by me."

"Yeah."

"I wasn't in the mood for a fight tonight anyway," Kerry said. "And after I made that whole speech about being grown up and everything we were playing hide and seek in the house and I knocked a freaking table over. Ended up breaking a bowl the size of our sink."

She could hear Dar muffling a snicker. "No, go ahead and laugh." Kerry sighed. "Talk about blowing my image. I could have smacked Mike. He tripped me right into the damn thing and I hit the legs sideways."

"Table didn't have a chance." Dar commiserated. "You've hit me in the knees. I know what that feels like."

"My sister was laughing so hard she was crying," Kerry admitted. "And the look on my mother's face when she came around the corner to see what the hell was going on was pretty much priceless." She paused.

"It reminded me of the fact that growing up in that house wasn't always a horror show."

Dar chuckled aloud.

"Anyway." Kerry sighed. "So it's not going too bad. How about you? Are you ready to fly?"

"Yeah. Actually, the timing is going to give me a problem trying to get hold of Gerry," Dar said. "If I don't get him before I take off, I might need you to call him," she said. "I'll message you if that's the case. It'll be really early your time when I leave."

"No problem," Kerry said. "I think I'm going over there in the afternoon so I can touch base with him. Shouldn't be an issue."

"Good," Dar said. "We can stop taking about business now. How did my voice come up in conversation?"

Kerry closed her eyes and smiled, narrowing her world down to the sound in her ear. She reached over and turned the bedside light off, leaving her in darkness that only made their conversation all the more private. "She was being nice. She was listening to you when you were on the conference call. Angie said something too, about your accent."

"My what?"

"Your cute little Southern twang," Kerry clarified. "I'm so used to hearing you I don't really hear it anymore, but they both noticed."

"I don't have an accent. My father has an accent," Dar said. "You have an accent."

"No I don't."

"Sure you do."

"I do not!"

"You do!" Dar insisted. "Everyone has an accent. Except me."

Kerry started laughing, "You're so funny. Thank you for calling me. I was starting to really get bummed out."

"Why?" Dar asked. "You said things were going okay."

"I know. I don't know," Kerry replied. "I just was. All the stuff going on and thinking about our people who are still missing, and not knowing what's going to happen with the government tomorrow... it was just bumming me out." She thought about that. "Do I sound like a weenie?"

"No." Dar's voice deepened a little, warming audibly. "I was getting bummed here too. I feel like I'm so far away from everything," she admitted. "I'm glad we're leaving today, but knowing I'll be out of touch for that long is driving me insane."

"Me too," Kerry agreed, in a wry tone.

They were both quiet for a moment. "We're a couple of goddamned idiots," Dar said. "We'd give Mr. Rogers diabetes." She sighed with exaggerated exasperation. "Wait. Let me go out and see if I can find a box of bonbons and a pair of pink fuzzy slippers."

Kerry started laughing. "I have the bonbons and fuzzy slippers here, honey. Come and get them."

"If I could," Dar said. "If I could close my eyes and will it, and be there, I would in a heartbeat." She sighed. "But unfortunately I'm not a refugee from a bad science fiction movie of the week. I did tell Alastair I'd need to head out to Washington as soon as we got in the States though. I'm hoping the planes will be flying by then."

"Me too." Kerry could feel the beginnings of a disassociation that meant she was falling asleep. "Would you do me a tiny favor?"

"You have to ask?"

"Sing to me. Just for a minute."

Dar hesitated. "Oh. Uh...okay. Sure."

"I just remembered when I was talking to Mom what that sounded like and I want to hear it. I love your singing voice." Kerry smiled, as she heard Dar clear her throat softly, and she took a deep breath and released it as her partner complied, easing her into sleep so gently she didn't even remember the tune.

Chapter Thirteen

DAR TURNED THE collar of her leather jacket up to protect her neck against the damp, chilly wind as she waited for Alastair to finish his goodbyes. She'd made the mistake of dropping off to sleep again after talking to Kerry and now she felt as foggy as the sky appeared, waking up again only ten minutes before they were supposed to leave.

The only thing that had saved her ass was that she'd grabbed a shower and packed while waiting for Kerry to get to her hotel. So she just had to throw her clothes on, brush her teeth and hair and try to pretend her brain wasn't somewhere in the southern Caribbean where her dreams had taken her before she woke.

On the boat, in the sun, Kerry's warm body curled up next to her and the late afternoon sky getting ready to set and provide them with an evening entertainment.

Goddamn she wished it hadn't been a dream.

Her cell phone rang. She unclipped it from her belt, glancing at the caller ID and hoping it was Gerry Easton. It wasn't, but she was glad to see the name anyway. "Morning, Mark."

"Hey Boss." Mark sounded absolutely exhausted. "We just crossed into North Carolina. What a bastard of a drive."

"It is. How are things going? I didn't have time to login to the desktop this morning. We're about to leave for the airport." Dar felt a distinct sense of embarrassment.

"For us, we're cool," Mark said. "Nothing big new on the board, and all that, since it's like 2:30 a.m. But we just heard they closed down NY again and found some truck bomb trying to cross one of the bridges."

"Shit." Dar exhaled. "Kerry's in Washington."

"Yeah, I know." Mark sounded unhappy. "But hey, she's probably safe someplace, right? She's not like, at the Pentagon, is she?"

"No." Dar caught motion of the corner of her eye, and saw Sir Melthon and his staff walking toward her, the magnate still in discussion with Alastair. "She's in a hotel, but I'm about to get on an airplane and be out of touch for ten hours. I'm going to lose my mind."

"Well, Dar, we ready?" Alastair said, as they closed in on her. "Everything all right?"

"Hang on Mark." Dar put her cell phone on mute. "Just getting a status," she said. "Sir Melthon, it's been a true pleasure working with your team, despite the circumstances."

"Likewise," the magnate said. "Now, I know this is not really the time to discuss this, but I have a schedule to meet. I need to know how this event is going to impact that." He held a hand up. "McLean, this does not change anything in our pact. I'm not an idiot. I know full well this disaster requires attention."

Alastair and Dar exchanged looks. "I'll know better once we get back to Houston,." Dar said. "The resources tied up normally in that side of our organization would not be dedicated to your project, but I'm going to have to pull people in so I need to assess."

The Englishman frowned, but he also nodded at the same time. "Fair enough," he said. "My godson tenders his regrets. He had to hurry back to Hamburg last night. An aunt of his was taken sick."

"Hope she's doing better," Alastair said. "As Dar said, let us get back and sort ourselves out, and we'll be back in touch soon as we can." He held his hand out, and the magnate gripped it. "Thanks for your hospitality. Hope I can return it sometime if you're in my neck of the woods."

"Could be I'll take you up on that," Sir Melthon said. "Wouldn't mind seeing your headquarters, but not until after all the broohah passes on." He extended his hand to Dar. "Ms. Roberts, believe me when I say it has truly been an honor."

Dar took his and traded strong grips with him. "I'm glad you're a customer," she said. "You're the kind I don't mind going two hundred percent for."

Sir Melthon smiled, looking for a moment as though twenty years had been erased from his face. "Have a good flight home, you lot. Let us know if you get in safely. My man here will get you to the airport fast as London traffic allows. Which means...hold on to the armrests and close your eyes if you're smart."

Dar waited until they were in the car before she unmuted the phone. "Sorry about that Mark."

"No problem boss, I got a grilled cheese sandwich and a Bawls out of it," Mark replied, in a somewhat muffled tone. "These RV's are awesome. We should keep one around the office."

Dar sighed. "I'll put it on the budget list," she said, in a distracted tone. "Now, where were we?"

Mark rustled some paper. "We were just talking about stuff going on," he said. "You were bitching about having to be out of touch for ten hours."

"Ah." Dar glanced at Alastair. "Hang on again." She waited for her boss to turn his head. "Mark says they reported a truck bomb in Manhattan."

"Damn it," Alastair exhaled. "Damn it all to hell, this has to stop."

"Sorry." Dar went back to the phone. "Just catching Alastair up." She braced her elbow against the door and rested her head against her hand. "I talked to Kerry earlier and there were bomb threats in Washington too."

"Yeah, they were saying," Mark murmured, "some place near the Capitol, and two other ones around there." He hesitated. "Listen, boss, you want me to go find her instead of heading through? If we keep driving, we'll probably make it before you land."

Dar was silent for a moment, weighing her personal desires against her judgement.

"Hey Dar?" Alastiar touched her arm. "You all right? You look a little pale."

Dar felt a little pale. "Yeah," she said. "Just woke up with a headache." She drew in a breath. "Keep going, Mark. I'm not sure where Ker's going to be by the time you get there, and it'll be a wild goose chase."

"You sure?" he asked.

"Yeah," Dar said, briefly. "She'll be all right. They're going to need you in the city."

"Okay," Mark said. "I'll drop her a note with my cell and remind her I'll be passing through though, okay?"

Dar managed a small grin. "Sure," she said. "At worst maybe she'll need you to rescue her from her mother."

"Uh."

"Hey, you volunteered." Dar felt her neck muscles relaxing a trifle. "What else is going on? We find any more of our folks?"

"Two in Washington," Mark replied. "They weren't even at the Pentagon, like they were supposed to be. They got sent on a run to get freaking doughnuts, and got in a car wreck."

"Oh," Dar murmured. "Hope they're okay."

"Sure," Mark said. "Numbskulls didn't have a cell with them, and decided to take the rest of the day off with a freaking doctor's note and went hiking."

She could hear the frustration in Mark's voice, a mixture of relief that the two workers were all right and anger at their desertion. "Did you talk to them?"

"Yeah."

Dar watched Alastair watch her, distracted by the realization that her boss had never really seen her exercise the management part of her position. It got her mind off Kerry and her discomfort, and she felt her concentration sharpen. "How old are they?"

Mark chuckled wryly. "Twenty," he admitted. "Freaking kids."

"Do you remember what you were like when you were twenty?" Dar asked him, suppressing a smile. "Hm?"

"Sure," Mark replied. "But that's squashed by the fact I also remember what **you** were like when you were twenty so I don't wanna cut them that much slack."

The unexpected retort made Dar laugh, despite everything. "Ahh, yeah," she said. "I was an anal retentive workaholic control freak, wasn't I?"

"Was?" Alastair asked, his blue eyes twinkling.

"Was?" Mark asked, at the same time.

"Hey." Dar growled. "You can't have it both ways, you two," she said. "Either I've mellowed or I haven't. Pick one." She knew the answer, though. She wasn't the asshole she had been back then, because if she had been she and Kerry would never have lasted together.

That was her yardstick. She could look back now on things she'd done and things she'd said, and she knew it wasn't in her to be like that anymore. "Well?"

"Now, Dar." Alastair patted her knee. "I'm just kidding you. For heaven's sake."

"Just messing with you, boss." Mark chuckled. "You sounded down," he added. "These guys pissed me off, but they're pretty good techs."

Dar was glad of the distraction. "They weren't in the right place at the wrong time," she said. "I think they probably know that, and they'll remember it."

"Yeah."

"Besides we're going to need every hand we've got. So make them feel guilty and get them back to work," Dar concluded.

"Okay. I'm cool with that," Mark said. "I think they'll be cool with it too."

"And if that doesn't work," Dar mused. "Tell them I'll show up there and spank their asses."

"Blurp." Alastair had been drinking from a bottle of water, and nearly sprayed it over the inside of the car. "Who approved that bonus plan?"

There was a moment of silence from Mark. "You want me to give them a perk after they pulled a stunt like that?" he queried. "Jeez, boss. I'll be hiking to Paris next week. Can I get in it?"

Dar actually felt herself blush. Fortunately, the car was too dark for it to be visible. "What a bunch of kinks I work with," she rallied, watching her boss chuckle. "All right. Let me let this line loose for someone else to get bad news on," she added. "Talk to you later, Mark. Drive safely."

"Will do, boss," he answered. "Have a good flight, okay?"

Ugh. "Okay. Bye." Dar closed the phone and let it rest in her hand as she leaned back in the car seat. "Damn it." Despite the levity, she couldn't dismiss the knot of worry in her guts. "Too much going on."

Alastair watched her quietly for a moment, as she rubbed her eyes. "Sure you're okay, Dar?" he asked. "I've got some aspirin if you want it."

"Nah." Dar tapped the briefcase by her right knee. "I've got some in there. I just woke up on the wrong side of the Atlantic this morning." She pressed her fingers against one throbbing temple. "You think those bomb threats are real, or just people being nervous?"

Alastair took in Dar's tense body posture. He'd seen Dar in a number of business situations now, and he knew how hard it was to rattle her. Being almost fired by the board hadn't. Standing up to new clients like Sir Melthon hadn't. Even being in a hospital collapse had produced nothing more than that cool, collected front that put forward total confidence and belief in self.

This was different, and he recognized that. This was personal. "Kerry make it to Washington?" he asked casually. "She doing okay?"

Dar went still for a minute, then she looked up, an openly vulnerable look on her face that probably surprised both of them. Then she took a breath and glanced out the window. "She's fine," she said, in an even voice. "I'm just not crazy about having her around things that might blow up."

"Well." Her boss folded his hands over his knee. "Tell her to get in a damn car, and start driving away from the place and keep going. Get the hell out of town or...hey, head back to Miami."

Dar refused to meet his eyes. "It's her job to be there."

"Oh, screw that," Alastair snorted. "Please. Give me a break, Dar. Do you really think this job or any job is worth harming a hair on her head, or yours, or mine for that matter?"

"No."

Alastair waited. "But?"

Dar took a breath. "I can't tell her not to do her job," she said. "Not if everyone else is doing theirs. She won't take that from me."

Her boss studied her in silence for a moment. "That's complicated," he said, eventually. "Dar, I don't envy your balancing act there." He reached over and clasped her shoulder. "Want me to tell her?"

She appreciated, truly, what Alastair was saying. However, she'd agreed with Kerry that she needed to go to Herndon to do what it was the company paid her for, and at this stage, it was all in motion. "No." She glanced up at him. "She's a big girl, and she can make her own choices. Sending her off to hide somewhere is only going to royally piss her off."

Alastair pondered that, then he nodded. "I can buy that," he said. "But lady, it's tough watching you sweat, know what I mean?"

Dar smiled faintly. Then she was saved by her cell phone ringing again. She opened it up and glanced at the screen, a prickle making her nape hairs stand when she saw Gerry's name. "Ah." She pressed the talk button. "Gerry??"

"Dar! Where in the hell are you?" the general asked.

"London," Dar said. "Glad to hear your voice."

"What? Oh." Gerald Easton paused. "Bastards."

"Mm," Dar agreed. "Ker said you were trying to get in touch with me. I'm on my way to the airport," she explained. "Everyone okay on your end?"

The General sighed. "The family's fine,"he said. "Listen, Dar, I need to speak with you right away." He cleared his throat. "You're in

London, are you? We can fly you back here."

Dar glanced at Alastair, whose brows were twitching. "We've already got a plane chartered, Gerry. But what did you have in mind?"

"Hang on." He clicked off.

Dar exhaled. "Wants to fly me back to the states. Says he needs to talk to me," she told her boss. "Doesn't sound good."

"Mm." Alastair grunted. "Depends what he wants to talk about, I suppose."

"Hello, Dar?" Gerry came back abruptly. "We can have a transport pick you up just near dinnertime there. How's that?"

"Our flight leaves at 10:00 a.m., Gerry. I think it'll be faster, but..." Dar considered. "We're flying into Mexico and driving to Houston. I could use a lift from there."

"Houston!" General Easton spluttered. "What in the hell's the...oh, that's right. That's where your paycheck's cut, isn't it? Okay, call me when you land in Mexico. We can swing that easier than the overseas flight."

"Okay," Dar said. "Kerry's in Washington. Anything she can help with?"

"Is she?" General Easton asked. "I think I should talk to you first, Dar. It's a little sticky."

"All right," she responded. "Gerry, this doesn't have anything to do with a bunch of suits showing up at our Herndon office does it?"

Long pause. "Eh?" Gerry grunted. "Well, to be honest, it's hard to tell from here right now what has to do with anything, Dar. Do yourself a favor though, will you? Don't say no to anything right off. There's a bit of a headless viper lashing around and I don't' want you to get bit."

Uh oh. "Okay," Dar said. "I'll call you from Mexico City then. I have a commuter scheduled for the border."

"Right. Gotta go, Dar. Good to hear your voice too. Glad you were out of harm's way." The line went dead, leaving a faint echo in the car.

"Hm." Dar closed the phone. "Headless viper." She looked at her boss. "That doesn't sound any good."

"Sure doesn't," Alastair murmured. "Sure doesn't."

CYNTHIA STUART SAT quietly, sipping her morning tea and watching the sky outside turn from black to gray with the coming dawn. She'd woken early, as she always did, and treasured the peace of the early morning to think about the coming day and go over her busy schedule.

She opened her organizer and flipped to the last page she'd updated from the day before, going over her notes, rereading again the horrors she'd put down in brief entries.

Only by reading the words was she really able to absorb the fact that all the terrible things had, in fact, happened. Sitting here in this lovely hotel room, it cut through the surrealness. After a moment, she closed the book and got up, walking silently across the floor to the door across from the table.

She pushed it in and peered inside, her eyes adjusting to the dim light as she studied the large bed inside with its still asleep occupant.

Kerry was curled on her side, her head on one pillow and her arm wrapped around a second. Relaxed in slumber, she was far less threatening a presence, and seeing the familiar position reluctantly made her mother smile.

Her eldest. Cynthia sighed and closed the door retreating back to the table and settling down to resume her notes. She picked up a pen and found her place and scribed a careful addition as she shook her head over the subject. "Terrible."

The world was still gripped in its peculiar insanity, it seemed. She picked up her morning news brief, delivered quietly by her staff, and reread it. If she looked out the big windows at the edge of the hotel room, she knew she would see flashing lights and the oddness of military transports in the streets and, for a moment, she honestly regretted her decision to complete her husband's government term.

It would indeed have been better to be home. There was Angela and her children to get settled and many small things requiring her attention. Perhaps she could have also had another day of Kerry and Michael's presence to make it seem as though her family wasn't quite as fractured as, in truth, it was.

Hard on the furniture that it might have been. Cynthia glanced up and smiled, hearing the echoes of that laughter the day before, and Kerry's exasperated "Michael!" that had brought back so many more pleasant memories.

"Good morning."

Cynthia jumped a little, not expecting the sound. She looked up to find Kerry in the door to her bedroom, still dressed in just a T-shirt. "Good morning," she replied. "Did the room service wake you? I'm sorry if it did. He was trying to be very quiet."

"No." Kerry came over and sat down at the table. "I've been up. I didn't really sleep that well." She rested her forearms on the table and laced her fingers together. "Too many things on my mind, I think."

The older woman studied her daughter. The tanned, serious face under it's mop of shaggy blond hair was a little unfamiliar to her now. The planes of her face had gotten a little longer, the jawline a touch more rounded, and there was a definite wariness shadowing the light green eyes that hadn't been there before.

The T-shirt she wore pulled tight over her shoulders as she leaned against the table, showing the outline of muscles Cynthia didn't find appealing. She didn't really approve of women working so hard and gaining the attributes she more properly applied to men.

Though it really wasn't terribly unattractive. When her daughter was properly dressed it lent her body a pleasantly tapered shape despite her carrying more weight on her frame than ever before. It wasn't really fat, and it wasn't really the slimness she preferred. It just seemed odd to her.

Cynthia supposed it gained her nothing to mention it. Kerry was obviously content with the way she looked and perhaps her own view was a little biased as she'd heard from friends around town how everyone else seemed to think she looked quite good, really.

Ah well.

She glanced at the strong hands on the table, her eye catching a glint as the light reflected off a ring on Kerry's third finger. It was attractive and refined, and it fit her well. "That's a lovely ring," Cynthia said. "Is it new?"

Kerry glanced at her hand. "No," she said. "Dar gave it to me at our commitment ceremony," she explained. "We exchanged rings."

Cynthia pondered over that. Commitment ceremony? "Is that..." She paused, not wanting to upset her daughter with any assumptions over breakfast. "What exactly is that? What does it mean?"

Kerry tapped her thumbs together. "What does that mean?" She mused. "I'm not sure what it means to everyone else, but to Dar and I, it means we belong to each other." Her fingers flexed a little. "We're married," she clarified.

She glanced up to gauge her mother's response, seeing mostly a mildly encouraging thoughtfulness there. "As legally as we can be, of course, since our government seems to think gay marriage is as dangerous as an unstable nuclear stockpile." She added a wry smile. "Dar and I had to spend a long time with a lawyer to get the same legal protection a five minute blood test and signature get for everyone else who isn't gay."

Cynthia's face twitched.

There was a soft knock at the door, and Kerry got up. "Room service," she said, as she went to the door and opened it. "Hello."

"Ma'am." The room service waiter, a slim woman, entered. "Your breakfast."

"Thanks." Kerry indicated the table. She followed the server over to the table, and waited for her to set the tray down. The woman did, then she turned, with a leather billfold in her hand, which Kerry held her hand out for, then signed.

"Do you need anything else, ma'am?" the woman asked, as she handed the bill back.

"Not right now." Kerry smiled at her. "Thank you."

The woman smiled back. "My pleasure." She gave Kerry's mother a respectful nod and left, closing the door quietly behind her.

Kerry opened a packet of raw sugar and poured it into her cup, filling it with hot coffee before she added some cream and sat down to enjoy it. She sipped from the cup, aware of the faintly pained look on her mother's face. "You don't like that word, do you?"

Cynthia looked up, startled. "I beg your pardon?"

"Gay," Kerry said. "You don't like it."

Her mother frowned, stirring her tea as she added a bit more hot water to it. "It makes me uncomfortable," she admitted finally. "Yes."

Kerry uncovered one of the dishes on her tray and picked up a cheerful looking cherry and cheese Danish. "Me too."

Cynthia blinked, and her brows creased again.

"I don't think I should have to define myself by who I sleep with." Kerrry studied the Danish and selected a spot, biting into it and chewing. She swallowed, and wiped her lips with her napkin. "It's kind of stupid."

"Well." Her mother took a sip of her tea. "You know, I think I agree with you on that subject." She watched her daughter chew her breakfast. "Really, it shouldn't matter, should it?"

Kerry looked up at her, eyes glinting with wry bemusement.

Cynthia seemed to appreciate the irony. She remained silent, fiddling with the teaspoon in obvious discomfort.

"It shouldn't," her daughter finally said. "So what's going on this morning?" She shoved the conversation onto a different track. "Anything new?"

Her mother sighed. "I'm afraid they stopped a bomb, a truck bomb from crossing into New York last night."

Kerry sat up, her brows creasing. "Good lord," she said. "So they're still doing things?"

Cynthia shook her head. "Apparently so," she said. "I was waiting to hear further details. Perhaps..." She hesitated. "Perhaps your people have heard more?"

"Let me get my laptop." Kerry set her cup down and got up. "And Dar's flying. I'm going to be a nervous wreck all day." She disappeared into her room, leaving the living space in silence.

Cynthia folded her hands in her lap and bowed her head for a moment, her lips moving as she whispered a short prayer. Then she straightened back up as she heard Kerry coming back in the room, taking a deep breath as her daughter reappeared holding her computer in her hands.

It was exhausting, dealing with this child of hers. Though Kerry was certainly being civil, the hostility she felt just under the surface was obvious to Cynthia, and she wondered when, not if, that simmering anger would erupt again.

Very difficult. Hard to know where to start, really. She didn't want to be so much at odds with her eldest daughter, but everything she'd tried so far to smooth the waters between them had ended badly and she wasn't truly sure why.

She knew Kerry was angry about all that had happened before, but really now it was in the past. Couldn't be changed.

"What about what we ran into last night?" Kerry asked, as she opened the device and started it up. "Was that real? Mother, honestly, if there are bombs in the city, it's insanity to go into the center of it." She sat down and glanced across the table. "What if they already planted something at the Capitol?"

Her mother pursed her lips. "It's a concern, certainly," she agreed. "My staff was calling around to find out what the rest of my colleagues are intending on doing."

Kerry leaned on the table with both hands, waiting for her laptop to boot up. Then she straightened. "Let me go throw some clothes on," she said. "I've got a feeling it's going to be a busy morning and your staff probably won't appreciate my nerdish pajamas."

She left the laptop where it was and went back into the bedroom, rubbing the back of her neck to work the crick out of it from her night of tossing and turning. She went into the bathroom and stripped out of her shirt, turning on the shower and taking the sponge and bottle of body scrub from her kit bag.

Ignoring her reflection in the mirror, she ducked under the spray and squeezed a blob of wash onto the scrubbie and started using it. The faintly rough texture felt good against her skin, and the pounding of the water across the back of her neck was working to loosen the muscles there.

She felt a little anxious. She wasn't sure if it was the situation she was in, or some subliminal worry about Dar, or perhaps even a reflection of Dar worrying about her, but it was rubbing her nerves raw. She really wished she was alone in her palatial hotel room and didn't have to deal with her mother.

"Now," she muttered to herself over the water, "I'm guessing she probably feels the same way." She glanced at the reflection of her eyes in the small, surprisingly unsteamy mirror fixed to the wall. "Cause I know I'm not being little miss sunshine."

She got a handful of shampoo and soaped her hair, scrubbing above her ears and standing under the water to rinse the suds out. Then she let her arms drop and simply stood, appreciating the powerful pulse of the water against her body.

A bad dream had woken her this last time. She couldn't even remember now what the dream was, except that she could recall feeling sad, and scared and alone in some strange otherworld of her sleeping imagination.

Now she felt tired, irritated, and anxious with a day of conflict and confrontation with the government ahead of her. "Rats." Kerry folded her arms across her wet body. Then she exhaled and reluctantly left the warmth, shutting off the water and grabbing a towel hanging on a rod nearby.

She dried herself off, her ears picking up low voices in the room next door that made her glad she'd decided to get changed when she did. Unlike Dar, who pretty much completely lacked body consciousness, she really had no comfort level in facing fully dressed people in her sleepware.

Crazy really, since she walked around in less at home all the time. On the island, either a pair of shorts and a tank, or shorts and a bathing suit, or just her bathing suit which was absolutely more revealing than a damn T-shirt.

Just a weird crick in her brain. Kerry studied her choice of clothing, then pulled on a pair of jeans buttoning them before she added a bright red polo with their company logo on it. She ran a brush through her damp hair and studied the results.

Hm. She set the brush down and tucked in the polo, reaching into her bag and adding a braided leather belt and buckling it around her waist. With a satisfied grunt, she clipped her phone to the belt and slid her PDA in her pocket, and headed back out to face the world.

DAR WOKE TO the smell of sizzling steak nearby. The dichotomy of the view around her, the drone of the engines, and the scent made her look around in utter bewilderment before she remembered where she was.

"Feeling better?"

Dar glanced to her right across the wide aisle where Alastair was ensconced in a leather lounger much like hers, a reading light glowing dimly on the sheaf of papers he was reviewing. "I was until someone started roasting a steer somewhere," she said. "Where the hell did the barbeque come from?"

He removed his reading glasses and peered back at her, a bemused expression on his face. "You know, I've been on private jets before, but I bet you haven't."

"No," she readily admitted.

"They asked Bea how to cater the plane when she reserved it." Alastair put his glasses back on and went back to his papers. "I took the liberty of ordering for you. I've been traveling with you long enough that I figured I could guess right on what you eat."

Dar glanced at her watch, surprised to see they'd been flying for four hours and she'd slept for three of them. "Ah, okay," she said. "Yeah, the nap helped." She eased a little more upright, running her fingers through her hair. "What's so interesting?"

Alastair picked up a glass with ice and liquid in it and took a sip. "Our SEC pre-filing report for quarter three," he said. "Want to read it?"

Dar eyed him. "I just woke up," she said. "You want me to go back to sleep? You'll have a lot of dinner to eat by yourself."

Alastair chuckled. "I was trying to put myself to sleep, to be honest." He set the report to one side, and tossed his glasses on top of it.

"Sometimes I look forward to retiring, when the most urgent thing I have to look at is an LL Bean catalog," he admitted. "You get tired of all the fine print, y'know?" He put his hands behind his head and stretched out.

"Do you?" Dar half turned onto her side, drawing one knee up as she faced her boss. "What would you do if you retired?"

Alastair tilted his head back and regarded the ceiling of the private jet, pondering the question.

Dar took a moment while he was thinking to look around the jet she hadn't paid much attention to when they'd boarded. It was reasonably large inside, but had two single lines of fully reclining leather couches on either side of a wide aisle instead of the usual rows of upright chairs.

It was quiet, the drone of the engines muted, and it felt expensive. Dar realized this was what it was like for the truly elite when they traveled.

She liked it. It meshed well with her view of appropriate personal space and comfort, and the leather loungers were just big enough that she and Kerry could possibly squish together on one.

That thought made her wish Kerry was on the plane with her and she frowned, turning back to Alastair as he cleared his throat and started to answer.

"Well you know I have the ranch," Alastair said. "I'd love to spend more time with the horses. I've got a granddaughter who's learning to ride the circuit and it would be great to watch her out there instead of sit on my ass in my office in Houston."

"Sounds nice," Dar said. "I like horses. I saw the pictures in your office. Those are beautiful animals."

"Good blood." He turned his head a little. "What about you? What would you do if you retired, Dar? I know it sounds crazy for you given how old you are, but you've got fifteen plus years in. Ever think about it?"

"Sure," Dar responded, with a smile. "I'd move down to the Keys and spend my days diving and bumming around on the beach, with an occasional consulting stint to pay the bills."

Alastair smiled. "Ah, the child of the sea. How could I forget."

"Which is exactly what I'd do if you decide to retire. By the way," Dar continued, her smile widening as she caught the look of honest surprise on her boss's face, "I have no intention of doing this for anyone else."

Alastair looked at her in silence for a long moment. "Are you serious?"

Dar nodded. "As a heart attack."

Her boss's eyes twinkled. "That might be the nicest thing you ever said to me," he said. "Thank you, Paladar." He paused. "Now let me tell you something. You remember when you sent me that resignation letter?"

Dar nodded.

"Had mine written out too, stapled to it," Alastair said. "So it's probably a pretty good thing for the company you decided to stay." He considered. "Though, gotta admit there have been times lately I almost wish you hadn't."

"Yeah," Dar said. "I know what you mean." She hoisted herself out of her chair and stood, stretching her body out before she crossed the aisle and knelt next to where her boss was sprawled. "Thanks, Alastair. I know I've been a pain in the ass over the years." She held her hand out, and as he reached over, she clasped his in a powerful grip. "Hope it was worth it."

He chuckled again. "Bet your ass it was." He released her hand. "You know, the one bright spot of that whole mess with Steven and you was getting to meet Kerry for the first time."

Predictably, that made Dar grin. She got up and strolled down the aisle, exploring their little world. "She was so pissed at me for quitting."

"She's a firecracker," Alastair said. "You know she called me up and told me I had to get my ass on an airplane and get over there because everyone in that office was an idiot who didn't have a clue."

Dar turned and looked at him, both eyebrows lifted up to her hairline.

"Not in so many words," her boss admitted. "But that was the gist couched in soft, gentile Midwestern politeness, and it was at that point I realized you were gone hook line and sinker for very good reason." He smiled at Dar's sheepish expression. "She was your match."

Dar leaned back against the wall of the cabin. "She is," she said quietly. "She changed my life."

"She up for being a beach bum too?" Alastair asked. "I thought she likes the craziness."

"After this last cluster, she's open to it," Dar responded. "She does like the job. She likes the energy of it."

"But?"

Dar looked mildly embarrassed. "She'll go wherever I go."

"Loyal kinda gal." Alastair commented, with a smile. "But then, you're two of a kind in that regard so I'm guessing the company's in for a world of hurt some day."

"Mmph."

The door to the front of the plane opened, and a tall, lanky, young man entered. He was dressed in a pair of pressed black slacks and a ribbed black pullover, with striped epaulets on his shoulders. "Ma'am, sir," the man said. "We've run into a weather issue and wanted to advise you on it. A tropical depression has formed in the Gulf, and the outflow is going to extrude into our course and make it a very rough ride."

"Can we go around it?" Alastair asked. "My kidneys are not in the mood to be rattled tonight."

"I can certainly ask, sir," the man replied. "It might make us need to change our flight plan though," he said. "We're taking a very long route over the Southern Caribbean to avoid US airspace and this would mean a shift nearer to the coast of South America."

Dar and Alastair exchanged looks. "Depression look like it's going get worse?" Dar asked. "Strengthen?"

The man nodded. "They expect it to become Tropical storm Gabrielle tomorrow."

"Let's avoid it if we can," Dar said. "Nothing against your pilot's skills but I'm not in the mood for a swim off Tortola today."

"I'm not up for a swim off Tortola any day," Alastair chimed in. "Even though I do float like a cork."

The man nodded, and disappeared again.

Alastair grunted. "Figures."

Dar leaned back against the wall again. "That time of year," she said. "Wish I'd taken Gerry up on his offer now," she admitted. "He sounded like he had a thousand irons in the fire though."

Alastair regarded her. "Lady, if you think these old bones wanted to spend eight hours crossing the pond in an Airborne jumpseat you're nutty as a fruitcake without any rum in it."

Dar chuckled, and started to roam again, walking to the front of the cabin past the service bulkhead she'd been leaning against, then turning and moving along the rows of chairs to the back where a small suite of bathrooms were tucked. "I'm pretty sure he meant a civilian transport, Alastair. I'm sure they had other people that needed a ride home, diplomats and whatever."

"Let them ride in a steel bucket seat," Alastair said. "Damn politicians spend most of their time busting my chops anyway."

Dar went over to where their carry on baggage was stowed and dug in hers, removing her bathroom kit and retreating with it into the typically small airplane facility.

For shorter people, it was bearable. For Dar, the experience usually left her with a crick in her neck and so she brushed her teeth and splashed some water on her face as quickly as she could. The nap had definitely cleared her head, but now that she was awake, the uncertainty of what was going on below was starting to gnaw at her again.

She checked her watch. Kerry was up and working by now, she was sure. It was maddening to know her partner was in the middle of who knows what and not be able to help. Not that she thought Kerry needed her in order to do her job–her performance the day before amply demonstrated that–but they were in uncharted territory right now and she had the greater experience.

Dar gazed at her reflection in the mirror, seeing the somber furrow in her brow. "She's going to be fine," she told herself. "She's just going to Herndon, and she knows how to deflect someone if she has to."

Kerry did. She could politely, charmingly, and warmly tell the most demanding, insistent customer they weren't going to get what they wanted and leave them unable to voice a complaint about it. Dar had seen her do it on more than one occasion, and she had no doubt she could handle whatever request awaited her there.

She studied the blue eyes reflected in the glass surface. "So why are you chewing nails?"

Was she afraid Kerry would do so well, she'd show how much she didn't need the support? Dar's nose wrinkled. "Yeesh I hope not." She really didn't think so, though. It was actually a pleasure to be able to count on someone and not have to worry about babysitting them at work.

Was she worried her prolonged contact with her family would change the way she felt about anything? About anyone? Dar watched her own eyebrow lift, and her lips curve into a smile. No. She was not worried about that.

She was, she reasoned, worried about the person she loved most in the world simply because that's what people in love did. They worried.

She packed up her kit and bumped the door open, emerging into the main cabin of the plane and restoring her sundries to her bag. Alastair had turned his reading light off, and was standing near the front of the plane, peering out the window in the boarding door. "See any good birds?"

"I see a lot of ocean," Alastair responded. "Imagine what it was like for the first fellas who crossed that thing in a boat. That took a lot of guts."

"It's a big ocean," Dar agreed, coming over to stand by him. "I've only sailed part of it, and those long stretches of only water really hit you sometimes," she said. "And I've been caught in storms that made me wonder how sun and star navigators ever made it across."

"Ah yes. Captain Roberts, isn't it?" Alastair glanced at her, with a grin.

She smiled back. "Yes, it is"

The door behind them opened and the steward came back in. "Oh." He turned, evidently surprised not to see them sitting in their seats. "The captain says he's filing an amendment to our flight plan, that'll bring us just north of the Grenadines, and along the south coast of Cuba and then across to Mexico. It means adding an hour to the flight, but it will end up being a lot smoother. We were intending on slipping between Cuba and Florida before.

An hour. Dar sighed inwardly. "Damn I wish we could just land in Miami."

The steward looked sympathetic. "Us too," he agreed. "We'll try to make it as comfortable as possible." He gave them a brief smile. "We're about ready to serve, if you want to freshen up." He slipped out again, closing the door behind him.

"Well," Alastair said. "That's a damn shame." He eased past Dar and went back to his seat. "But I think it's better than flying through a storm."

Dar gazed out the small window, feeling more than a little trapped. She hoped things were going well for Kerry, and that the company plan was proceeding.

She hoped there were no more attacks.

"Dar?"

"Hm?" Dar turned and pushed off from the window, walking back down the aisle and stopping by her seat. She sat down on the arm of it, and rested her elbows on her knees. "Guess all we can do is put up with it."

"It'll be fine," he reassured her. "We've got good people running the show, don't we?"

Dar nodded.

"Want a drink?"

Dar slid backwards into her chair, leaving one leg slung over the arm of it. "Not yet."

"How about a tranquilizer? Got a bottle of em."

Dar turned her head and looked at him, her eyebrows lifting.

"If you don't take one, I'm gonna have to," Alastair informed her. "If you're going to pace like a cat for the rest of the flight."

Dar chuckled wryly. "Let me see if they have chocolate milk first." She sighed. "That'll probably be less destructive for both of us."

Chapter Fourteen

"OKAY." KERRY HAD her headset on. She checked her watch as she glanced over the screen of her laptop to see her mother come out from her room. "So what's the status there before we go any further."

Senator Stuart paused as she fastened her earring. She was dressed in a well fitted business suit, and an aide was standing quietly by holding her briefcase. "Are you sure we can't offer you a ride?"

Kerry covered the mic with her hand. "I'm fine. Our office is sending a someone to pick me up,"she said. "I'll rent a car out there." She paused. "But thanks."

Her mother hesitated, then nodded. "Well, take care in that case. Things are very unsettled," she warned her daughter. "Please let my staff know if there is anything you need."

"Hold on." Kerry hit her mute button. "Thanks. I think we have it covered. Take care yourself." She watched her mother follow the aide out, feeling a sense of relief as the door closed behind them. "Okay." She went back to the line. "Listen, I've got about ten minutes before I go mobile. So give it to me fast."

"Boy," the male voice answered her. "That's going to be tough, Ms. Stuart because it's more like, what isn't going on? We've got a ton of stuff hitting now because of deliverables that were missed yesterday."

As she'd expected, the world that had stopped turning the day before had now started up again. "Okay," Kerry said. "Well, obviously we need to put out the message that we're in a holding pattern ourselves for a lot of things."

She sat down and picked up her third cup of coffee, sipping it as she reviewed the laptop screen. On her status map large chunks of the Northeast were blinking red, and to one side, she now had a list of accounts with stoplights by them most of them also red, though with a few yellows sprinkled in here and there.

"Miami exec, this is Houston ops."

Kerry checked her watch again. "Go ahead, Houston."

"Miami, we've got a list of demands from the government groups here," the voice answered. "More circuits, more bandwidth, some extra processors...and they want it all right now."

"Miami exec, this is LA Earthstation," a very tired voice broke in. "We're getting the same kinds of requests too. I've explained transponder space about three hundred times already and it's only 6:00 a.m. here."

Kerry thought a minute. "Okay," she said. "Let's just start gathering up requirements, and getting a list together of our available resources. We can't give everyone everything."

Her cell phone rang. "Hang on," she said, then muted, as she answered the phone. "Kerry Stuart."

"Ms. Stuart? This is Daniel Green. I work for the NSA."

Yikes. Lovely. "What can I do for you?" Kerry asked. "It's a pretty busy morning."

"I can appreciate that," the man said. "As I am sure you can appreciate it's the same for us," he added. "My department has been trying to secure the cooperation of your facility in Virginia since yesterday, and we've had some problems. I was told you could help."

Kerry paused to draw in a steadying breath. "Okay. Hold on one moment, please. I am in the middle of a conference call. I'll be right back to you." She put the call on hold. "Folks, I need to duck out. I have the government on the line here."

"Great," the voice from the Earth Station sighed.

"Okay. Listen up." Kerry stood. "Right now, no one gets anything," she decided. "Just take detailed notes of what is being asked for, and post that to the desktop workspace. Miami ops, are you on?"

"Right here, boss," Mark's voice answered. "We're rolling up the road past you right now."

"Can you please get me an updated resource list and post it on the desktop?" Kerry asked. "I don't want to start pulling circuits until I know what the real priorities are."

"Everyone thinks theirs are, Miami exec," Houston replied. "You know how it is."

"I know," Kerry agreed. "Maybe this guy I've got on the phone can get me to someone who can tell me what the real first in lines are," she said. "Until then, we just listen. Everyone understand?"

"Understood," Houston said.

"Fine by us," LA answered. "We don't have any spare capacity anyway."

"Okay," Kerry said. "I'm signing off until I pick up on mobile. Mark, cover me."

"Covering," Mark replied. "If you need anything, text me boss. We can pull over."

"I'll be back on shortly. I'm off." Kerry hung up the connection and started to close down her laptop, while she took her cell phone call off hold. "Mr. Green?"

"I'm here," the man answered. "Ms. Stuart, I really don't have much time to discuss this with you."

Kerry closed her laptop and maneuvered it into its case one handed. "Well, Mr. Green, let me tell you something," she said. "I have hundreds of customers, including the government, all having all kinds of problems all over the country and halfway across the planet right now."

"I'm sure you do."

"So I don't have much time to talk to you either. I would like to help you," Kerry said. "I would like to understand what it is you need from us. I am on my way to our offices in Virginia right now, would you like to meet there?"

She waited for him to answer, draining her coffee and picking up the last bite of the danish her mother had professed to be horrified by and popping it into her mouth.

"That will be good," Green finally said. "Two of my men are already there, but they aren't being allowed inside the building."

"It's a secure facility." Kerry came perilously close to having to speak with her mouth full, swallowing just in time. "So that sounds right."

Green sighed. "I will meet you there," he said. "I hope we can come to an understanding, Ms. Stuart, without me having to get my upper echelons involved. You won't like dealing with them."

Kerry licked her lips. "Likewise," she said. "See you there." She hung up the phone and clipped it to her belt. She scanned the tray for any remaining edibles, then she lifted her jacket off the back of the chair and slipped into it.

It wasn't really cold enough to need a jacket, but it gave her a place to clip her identification badge, and she felt it was just slightly more formal than her jeans and polo shirt. Technically, since she was making an official visit to the office, she should be wearing a business suit, but she hadn't brought it, leaving the folded suit bag she'd intended on bringing to Europe with her with Angie instead.

So they had to deal with her in casual clothes. Kerry spared a moment to wonder if it would put her at a serious disadvantage, then she shrugged and decided if it did, there were plenty of stores in the capital where she could remedy the situation.

No time to worry about it now at any rate. She pocketed her room key and shouldered her bag, heading for the door to the room. The conference call would wait until she was in the car, and the few moments silence as she rode the elevator gave her a space of time to think about what Dar was up to.

Besides 35,000 feet, that is. Kerry's eyes flicked around the inside of the elevator, noting the advertisements for the hotel's spa and making a mental note to investigate it after what she was sure would be a long, painful day.

She hoped Dar was getting some rest on her trip across the Atlantic. At least the private flight would be quiet, and she was sure her partner would be well taken care of by the professional crew. Maybe she'd have picked up some new magazines to read on the way.

Her PDA beeped and she jumped, grabbing at it and wondering if her clever partner had found some way to send messages from the sky. Opening it, she was profoundly disappointed to find that was not the case, and in fact, the message was doubly unwelcome since it bore the address of the National Hurricane Center on it. "Oh please."

000
WTNT44 KNHC 131458
TCDAT8
TROPICAL DEPRESSION EIGHT DISCUSSION NUMBER 4
  NWS   TPC/NATIONAL   HURRICANE   CENTER   MIAMI   FL
AL042001
  0900 AM EDT MON SEP 12 2001
"Just what we need." Kerry read the rest of the advisory as she exited the elevator and crossed the lobby, keeping an eye on the path with her peripheral vision in an odd, disjointed sort of way common to nerds who had to learn to communicate and walk at the same time.

She studied the coordinates, giving the doorman who opened the door for her an absent greeting as she came into the hotel's front entranceway, her brows creasing as she pictured where the storm was forming. "Shit."

"Madame?" The doorman looked at her, his head cocked to one side.

"Sorry." Kerry tucked her PDA away and glanced around, seeing no obviously waiting cars. "Just got some bad news."

The man nodded and stepped away.

Kerry rummaged in her briefcase and pulled out her cellphone earbuds. She set the case down and untangled them, trying not to be impatient as the slim cables knotted stubbornly. It required a more intense concentration than she'd anticipated, and so she was surprised when someone cleared their throat unexpectedly close to her.

"Excuse me, Ms. Stuart?"

Kerry looked up, to find a young, slim, dark haired woman standing at the curb. "Hello." She glanced at the ID clipped to the woman's crisply pressed shirt. "Nan? I don't think we've ever met."

"No, we haven't," the woman replied with a smile. "I thought I recognized you but wasn't sure."

"Well, you guessed right." Kerry held a hand out. "You my ride?"

"Yes, ma'am." The woman smiled, and returned her grip. "Sorry if I startled you. They made me park the car down the slope."

Kerry got her buds sorted out and shouldered her briefcase. "Lead on." She followed the woman down toward where the standard issue company SUV was parked. Nan was a technical supervisor at the Herndon center and Kerry had both spoken to and emailed her on countless occasions.

Laid back and competent. Kerry had formed a favorable opinion of her from their previous interaction and nothing so far had contradicted that. She had a fine boned face and a well shaped profile and a slender build that matched her relatively short stature.

"It's been frantic crazy," Nan said, after a brief silence. "I know the powers that be are really glad you're here though. We're running out of excuses and coffee for the government guys."

"I bet," Kerry said. "Their boss is meeting me out at the office. I'm sure we'll get it straightened out." She opened the passenger side door of the SUV and settled into the seat, putting her case down between her boots.

Leather boots, jeans, leather jacket. There was nothing western about any of them, but Kerry had to smile privately at just how much her taste in clothing had changed, and the look of dubious surprise on her mother's face.

She didn't look bad in it. One glance in a mirror attested to that. Dar had told her in fact that she actually looked really sexy in the clothes and Kerry was fully willing to bow to her opinion in the matter.

It was, however, probably not what her colleagues here expected.

Nan got in the driver's seat and started up the SUV. "Seat goes back if you need," she said. "I adjusted it before I left but you're taller than I expected you to be."

Huh? Kerry stopped in mid motion and turned her head, both eyebrows shooting up. "Well, that's the first time I ever heard THAT comment before," she blurted. "Excuse me?"

Nan chuckled wanly. "Beg your pardon," she said. "I know we've emailed a lot but the only pictures I've seen of you are on the intranet."

"Ahh." Kerry started chuckling. "Where I'm always standing next to Dar. Yeah. I'm surprised most people don't think I'm a circus midget." She extended her denim covered legs and crossed her ankles. "Let me get back on the conference call. Sounds like things are going to hell this morning."

She pulled her earbuds from her pocket and put one in her right ear, then dialed the conference line. "How long have the NSA people been there today?'

Nan glanced quickly at her, then back at the road. "Is that who they are?" she asked. "Wow. They wouldn't tell us. They were there when the admins opened the guest center at seven."

"Nice." Kerry exhaled, shaking her head as she typed in the conference code. "Do you know what it is they're asking for, or are they still being vague?" She heard the call connect, but she left her mic on mute for the time being, electing to listen to Nan instead.

Nan paused at a light, and waited for it to turn. "They were pretty obscure. They have some big black box with them," she said. "And they told us they wanted to put it in the center, and have our core switch hooked up to it."

Kerry eyed her. "You have got to be kidding me," she said. "Do they realize what goes through that center? What do they think they're looking for? Those are internal government systems."

"We told them that," Nan agreed. "They think they can see traffic coming in from the outside to them. They say they're looking for terrorist hackers," she continued. "They seem to be convinced that the whole attack thing isn't over and they'll be making an attempt at our systems next."

Kerry folded her arms over her chest, her brows contracting. "What in the hell do they think connecting something to our core switch is going to do to stop that?" she asked, in a puzzled tone.

Nan shrugged. "It's the government. You know how they are. Someone tells them to do something and whether or not it makes sense goes out the window. I talked to their lead tech guy," she confided. "He told me we have to do it, or else we'll get in really big trouble."

Hm. Kerry pulled out her PDA and glanced at the next to last message, one from Dar.

Sweetheart.

I'm about to get on this damn plane. I talked to Gerry, and something's up but not something he wants to talk about over the phone, and not to anyone but me. Sounds screwy. He doesn't know anything about what's going on where you are, but says not to automatically say no to anything because everyone's flying blind and there's a lot of knee jerking going on.

Nothing goes in our facility. Feel comfortable about saying that to them, because hon, it's locked under my login and though you know it, you've got a perfectly good reason not to. Let them wait for me and Alastair. We're legally responsible for the contracts anyway.

Love you. Wish I could fly right to DC to be with you. Hang tight.
DD

"Wish you could too," Kerry muttered under her breath. "We can talk to them, and try to find out specifically what they're looking for," she told Nan. "If I can't convince them they're barking up the wrong tree, then we just have to tell them to wait until Dar lands."

Nan nodded. "They said the systems were all locked," she said. "It's making the network guys nervous," she added. "Like I said, they'll all be glad to see you. No one minds making decisions but man, when you've got the dark side of the government camped on the doorstep it's freak city time."

"Yeah." Kerry rested her head against the back of the seat, listening with one ear to the chatter on the call. "Freak city? We're living on Freak Planet right now." She shifted and drew one knee up a little, resting her hand on it as she cupped the other over her ear. "That's for damn sure."

Nan leaned back in her seat, watching Kerry from the corner of her eye.

"What?" Kerry caught the look.

The dark haired woman appeared to be suppressing a smile. "You're really not what I expected," she explained.

"In a good way or a bad way?" Kerry asked, wryly.

"Oh. Good way," Nan said. "Definitely."

Now what, Kerry wondered, did that actually mean? "Well, glad to hear it." She clicked her mic on. "Scuse me a minute...Miami ops, this is Miami exec back on. What was that about a power outage?"

Nan drove on in silence, passing quickly through unusually empty streets, for once the lack of traffic causing no one any cheer.

DAR LEAFED THROUGH her magazine, reading the technical articles then amusing herself by viewing the ads that luridly bracketed them.

"Whatcha reading?" Alastair asked.

Dar held up the front page.

Her boss rolled his eyes. "Jesus, lady." He folded his hands across his stomach. "Don't you ever go off duty?"

"I like technology," Dar protested mildly. "Shit, Alastair, what do you think you pay me for? My typing skills?" She had one leg slung over the arm of the chair and now she leaned on her knee a little. "This stuff changes every damn second. You have to keep up."

Alastair chuckled. "I don't have to keep up. That's why I have you." He put his hands behind his head and stretched. "Wasn't bad dinner, eh?"'

"Very good, matter of fact," Dar agreed. "Sure beats chicken Florentine or three cheese pasta, which would have been our choices otherwise." She put the magazine down and got up to wander to the back of the cabin and stretch her legs.

There was an open space there, enough for her to stand and extend her arms. She did so, and twisted her body back and forth to loosen up the stiff muscles in her back.

"Now what are you doing?" Alastair asked.

"Jumping jacks," Dar replied. "Wanna join me?"

Her boss leaned on his chair arm and craned around to watch her. "My last jumping jack was in basic training when I was eighteen years old, way before you were born," he informed her. "My idea of strenuous exercise is letting the caddy drive the cart on the golf course."

"Ugh." Dar tested the luggage rack's strength, then she gripped them and let her body drop back, tensing her shoulders as they took her weight. "I can't handle golf," she said. "I don't have the patience for it. I end up hunting for grasshoppers and losing track of what hole I'm on."

Alastair snickered. "Y'know, I can picture that," he said. "You do sports though, don't you? I thought I remember seeing some pictures of you winning some karate tournament or something, and Bea said you were all joining a softball league down there."

Dar lowered herself to the ground and decided on a few pushups. "I do sports," she conceded. "I've been doing martial arts since I was a kid." She settled into a smooth rhythm, glad for the distraction. "Lets me let off some steam." She paused, her body held up off the floor and peered up at Alastair. "You saw pictures?"

"Sure," Alastair said. "Kerry's quite a photographer." He watched

Dar as she merely looked at him, remaining in place. "How long can you stay like that?"

"Long as I have to." Dar pressed herself up into a handstand and felt her back relax as gravity inverted. "I'd forgotten she put that in the department news blurb." She crossed her ankles and pondered the matter. "They wanted me to continue in that circuit, but I figured I'd quit while I was ahead and not push my luck."

"Mm." Her boss got up and sat on his chair arm to better watch her, extending his legs across the aisle.

"Yeah, I'd rather you didn't risk getting kicked in the head," he said. "You get into enough damned situations as it is."

Dar bent her elbows, then pushed off gently from the floor of the aircraft and flipped herself upright, shaking her arms as blood returned from her head to the rest of her where it belonged. "It's been a little crazy the last year or so," she conceded. "Maybe I'm just doing more."

"Maybe you actually got a life." Alastair's eyes twinkled. "I used to worry about you sleeping under your desk down in that office."

Dar snorted softly. "I've got a perfectly good couch in there. What kind of a nitwit do you think I am?" But she smiled to take the sting from the words. "But yeah, maybe." She sat down on the arm of the chair across from Alastair. "Feels like it's been busier."

"Been good for you," her boss concluded. "Hasn't it?"

"Hell yeah. Wouldn't have traded a minute of it." She stuck her hands in the pockets of her cargo pants. "But I don't think what we're going through now counts."

Alastair's face grew serious. "No," he said. "I'm sure this is going to have a lot of consequences." He folded his arms over his chest. "You can bet on a military response. I sent a note to Ham to review our contracts with the service branches to see what we're obligated for."

Dar nodded. "I thought of that," she said. "I'm having Mark spool up the new tech groups to start reviewing everything they can get their hands on. I don't know what they'll ask for. I have a feeling Gerry's need to talk to me is something along those lines."

"I figured the same."

Dar exhaled and looked around the plane, then back at Alastair. "Are we there yet?"

Her boss chuckled wryly.

They turned as the forward door opened, and the steward appeared. "The captain wanted me to tell you he's submitted the new flight plan, but he's been told it needs to be cleared by the U.S. Government, even though we're not going to encroach on U.S. airspace."

"Ah."

"It's very tense," the steward explained. "We had to forward a manifest to them. I hope neither of you has any outstanding issues in the States, because that could be a problem."

Alastair and Dar glanced at each other. "Well," Alastair said. "We both have dozens of outstanding issues but they're not personal ones. I believe they'll be glad enough to let us by." He thought a moment. "Maybe we can ask them for permission to land, while we're at it."

"I don't know about that sir," the steward looked mildly alarmed. "The people I heard the captain talking to really didn't sound very friendly. We really don't want trouble. We didn't contract for that."

Alastair held a hand up. "Hold on there, son. We're not looking for trouble either. We work for a company with a lot of government contracts, and it's possible they'd make an exception because there are issues they're looking to us to solve. Chances are when they put our names into their system..."

"Which I wrote," Dar commented, in a mild tone, peering back at her boss when he looked at her in surprise. "That was before I got a life," she clarified, her eyes glinting with amusement. "I had more time back then."

Alastair scratched the back of his neck, and shook his head. "Anyway, when they call us up, they might say something about it."

The steward didn't look reassured. "Well, I'll let the captain handle all that," he said. "Is there anything I can get you in the meantime?"

"Got any ice cream?" Dar inquired.

"Ah, yes. I think we do." The steward nodded. "Sir?" He turned to Alastair. "Would you like some as well?"

Alastair reseated himself. "Not for me, thanks." He lifted a hand. "I'll take a glass of cognac though."

"Very good, sir, I'll be right back." The steward disappeared again behind the service door, leaving them in solitude.

Dar fell backwards into her seat, sprawling sideways across the chair with her legs over one arm and her head resting on the other. She studied the ceiling of the airplane and wished the time would just go damned faster. "Hope they don't give them trouble."

"Got a lot of scared folks down there," Alastair said. "Did you really write that system?"

"Uh huh," she said. "It's just a flexible relational database with a custom index. Not that big a deal," she said. "The biggest pain in the ass was writing the API they wanted so they could connect it up to other government systems and exchange data."

"Mm. What other systems did they hook up to?"

"None." Dar crossed her ankles. "That's why it was a pain in the ass. I wrote it so it was a standard data exchange interface, and every other god damned system in the government was a) different, and b) proprietary, so no one could talk to them anyway."

"Oh, for Pete's sake," he said. "So what do they do?"

"Export to a flat file and re-import." Dar folded her hands across her stomach. "Know how long that takes?"

"Especially in a situation like this? Too long." Alastair shook his head. "We should do something about that." He took out his PDA. "I'll have Ivan work up a white paper to pass around after this is settled down a little."

Dar considered that as she waited for the steward to return with her much needed dessert. "Wonder what's going on in Herndon?" she asked. "Hope they're not giving Kerry too hard a time. "

Alastair gave her a wry look, which she missed. "I'm sure she can handle it."

"I'm sure she can too. It's just that people try to take advantage of her because she's not a big mean looking macho dude," Dar said. "Then she has to kick them in the ass a few times before she gets their respect and frankly, that sucks."

The steward slipped back in with a tray. "The captain will be coming back to speak with you both in a few minutes. We've got some additional questions from the U.S. government." He moved forward, pausing as Dar shifted her position to a more normal one and swung her tray out in place. "Right now, they aren't clearing us to fly south of Florida."

"I thought they only control their local airspace?" Dar asked. "How in the hell can they stop someone from flying to Central America?"

The steward put a bowl down on her tray. "Ma'am, I don't' know. You can ask the captain." He turned and put Alastair's snifter down, filled halfway with a clear golden liquid. "Right now, we're considering just withdrawing the request and continuing on our original flight plan, which was approved. It will be a rough ride, but at least we'll get there."

Alastair sighed, and picked up the glass. "Well." He swirled it. "Sorry if it caused a hassle. If that's what we need to do, then we do. Got any seasick pills? I don't tolerate turbulence well and I'd hate to hand you back your nice dinner."

"We can provide some, of course," the steward looked relieved. "Ma'am, I can get you some as well."

Dar waved her hand no as she was busy with a mouthful of ice cream.

"Captain Roberts sails the bounding main on a regular basis," Alastair chuckled. "I don't think she needs any help."

The door opened again and the captain stuck his head in. "Folks, we've got trouble," he said seriously. "I'm being instructed to land in Nassau. The U.S. military are grounding us for inspection."

Dar licked off her spoon. "What?"

"That's crazy." Alastair put his glass down and got up. "C'mon, son. Let me go talk to these people." He headed for the door to the service area. "I'll throw some names around. We'll get it sorted out."

"Sir I..." The pilot had to either back out of the way, or get hit by Alastair's forward motion, and he chose the better part of valor and moved. "We can see if they'll talk to you, but they were pretty explicit."

"I'll be explicit, too." Alastair shooed him toward the cockpit. He glanced back at Dar. "Now let me see if I can go earn **my** paycheck."

Dar shook her head. "Crazy."

"I hope the gentleman knows what he's doing," the steward said, unhappily. "I heard those people on the other end, and I don't think they're going to appreciate someone questioning them." He looked at Dar. "This is very intimidating."

Dar found herself caught in the dilemma of both being concerned about the situation, and guiltily happy about the possibility of being on the ground with the ability to get hold of Kerry. "I'm sure it'll work out," she told the man. "It's probably just a misunderstanding."

"I sure hope so," the steward muttered. "I knew I should have called in sick today."

KERRY WAS GLAD enough to bypass the stately main entrance to their Herndon office and use the staff door instead. There were two big, black, ominous looking SUVs parked near the front and she wanted a few minutes to get herself settled before she had to interact with the people who'd come in them.

"This way." Nan led her through the door pausing to scan her badge, then her handprint at the glass double door inside. "Wait for me to go through, then scan. It should validate you." She waited, nodding her head a little bit as the system pondered for a while then clicked and turned green. "Eventually."

"Guess we'll find out." Kerry waited for the door to close behind her guide before she removed her badge from her lapel and held it against the sensor, then presented her palm on the glass plate when it glowed.

It turned green instantly and the door opened. Kerry's brow twitched a little, but she pushed the door open and let it close, then opened the inner door which clicked when the outer locked. She rejoined Nan and glanced around, finding the sedate gray and maroon interior weirdly familiar. "I see we had the same interior decorators."

Nan chuckled. "You mean here and Miami?" she asked. "Is it the same?"

"Pretty much." Kerry followed her down a long hallway inset with cherry wood doors. It was thickly carpeted and quiet, despite all the unsettled chaos. "I'll need a workspace," she said. "But I'd like to stop in at Operations first."

"Right." Nan nodded. "Bob Willingsly is getting an office set up for you. He said it would be about five more minutes." She indicated a large security door just ahead in the corridor. "That's ops." She stood back to let Kerry pass her. "I'm not credentialed for that."

Kerry gave her a brief smile. "Well, thanks. I appreciate the ride, and the tour," she said. "I'll be back shortly. I want to check things out."

She went over to the door and pressed her badge against the sensor, then offered her palm to the reader. The door clicked without hesitation, and she pushed it open.

"Hey, Ms. Stuart?" Nan called after her. "You do something special to your badge to get it to clear that fast? We'd love to copy whatever it is. Takes ours forever."

Kerry glanced back. "I know the designer," she admitted. "I'll see what I can do." She entered the ops center and let the door close behind her, turning to face the operations staff who were standing as they spotted her. "Morning guys."

The operations center, like the one in Miami, was a half circle of admin stations behind a heavy desk spaced with chairs on the inside curve. Unlike the one she was familiar with though, behind the console there was a big, intimidating plate glass double wall separating the operators from the data center equipment they managed.

"Ms. Stuart!" A man hurried forward, extending his hand. "Dave Draper. We've talked many times."

"We have." Kerry smiled at him. "It's good to meet you, Dave, but I wish it wasn't for this reason," she said. "I hear we have visitors already."

"Sure do," Dave said. He was a man in his mid forties, with thinning dark hair and a square jaw. "We're real glad you're here. Those folks are getting pretty mean," he told her. "My boss, Ken, is with them, but I know he'll be glad to see you too."

"I bet." Kerry put her briefcase down on a nearby chair. "Okay, before I go mess with them give me the five cent and bring me up to speed on what the status is."

"Sure." Dave turned and faced the room. The console operators were all busy at their desks, but each had turned their chair just a bit so they could watch what was going on.

Kerry could see the global meeting place screen on their monitors, split with various console ops applications that monitored the traffic and data that ran through the center.

"Y'know we've got a mix here," Dave said, pointing to the secured space. "One side is the government racks, they're green, and the other side is the commercial ones. They are that flat gray color. We keep the cabling and everything color marked so no one gets confused and connects the wrong thing to the wrong infrastructure."

Kerry nodded. "Looks very good," she complimented him. "Dar would approve."

Dave managed a grin at that. "Anyway," he said, "The only thing they share is the net d-marc. Ms. Roberts put in a parallel infrastructure, but they all terminate to the same blocks in the back. That's where this guy wanted to put his thing."

Kerry folded her arms. "What did he want to connect it to?"

"That's just it," Dave said. "He wanted us to let his guys in there, and let them connect it to whatever they wanted to."

"Oh hell no," Kerry said. "What are they nuts?"

"I heard them, ma'am." The nearest of the console ops had turned around. "They said they were trying to find the terrorists, and we had to let them."

"That's right," Dave said. "So we have console ops here, split into two sides. The left side is government, the right side is commercial, and John here was the man on ops when it all came down yesterday on the government side."

Kerry remembered the voice. "Hello, John." She extended her hand to the tech. "Thanks for the great job."

The lanky, blond man blinked and accepted her grip. His eyes had shadows under them, and he looked tired. "Thank you ma'am. I hope I never, ever have to do that again."

"Me too," Kerry agreed. She looked up at all the operators, who were now openly watching her. "Everyone did a good job. Everyone's doing a great job today, and we're just beginning. I think everyone here knows that the hard part's just starting."

The men all nodded.

"Show me the big board." Kerry turned to Dave. "I want to see what we're up against in bringing services back before I talk to those folks in the guest center."

"Sure." Dave walked over to the other side of the ops console and turned, pointing at the large screen display with the trace work of connectivity for the resources the office was responsible for.

Kerry exhaled, seeing the big red circle around the Pentagon, and the scattering of outages around that area due to the loss of infrastructure. "Boy, that's a lot of damage."

"Problem was we were using one drop room," Dave said. "Cause the other one was in the section that got taken out." He sighed. "So you'd figure we'd be fine, but the other drop room was at the inner edge of the area and it got trashed, and the one under construction is...well..."

"Still under construction," Kerry finished for him.

"Yes ma'am."

"Okay." Kerry knew there wasn't much she could do from the office. "I'm going to need a ride out there after I finish with these guys. I have resources coming up, but I want to see the lay of the land firsthand."

"Nan will take you," Dave said. "She's all yours whatever you need."

Kerry retrieved her briefcase. "Then let's get this over with." She motioned for him to precede her. "Lead on. I could guess where the guest conference room is based on the floor plan, but you probably don't want me wandering around knocking on doors."

Dave managed a smile at that and led the way out the door. He opened the door with his badge. "You'll have to clear through after me. We have a scan in, scan out policy."

"Sure." Kerry waited for him to pass through then followed. She took the few minutes the walk through the halls afforded her to concentrate on relaxing as much as she could, and preparing herself mentally for what she suspected was not going to be a pleasant confrontation.

She didn't really mind confrontation any more. She hadn't liked it much when she'd first started with ILS, but over the months she'd gradually gotten herself used to the stress of it, getting her mind around the fact that it wasn't so very different than her debating challenges had been way back when.

"Hope they're not too pissed," Dave said. "I'd hate to have them just go off at you, ma'am."

"I'm used to it," Kerry said. "I've done a lot of new client consolidations and contract challenges," she assured him. "And my very first confrontation with ILS was with Dar Roberts. It kind of goes downhill from there, you know what I mean?"

Dave produced a surprised little laugh. "Ms. Roberts sure is something."

"She sure is," Kerry readily agreed.

They passed through a larger hallway, and came around a corner where a security door blocked the way. "Guest sections past there," Dave said. "You want me to go with you?"

Kerry was pretty good at reading body language, but in this case she had no need do. Dave's voice told her everything she needed to know. "Nah." She patted him on the shoulder. "Hang in there, Dave. Just try to keep what we have working, running as smoothly as possible, and call me if anything starts going to hell, okay?"

"You got it," Dave said, watching as she held her badge to the door. "Good luck."

"Thanks." Kerry went through the door, now finding herself in the two level, stately lobby that featured a big reception desk on one side, and a glassed in conference space on the other. She could see several people inside the conference hall, and she paused to settle her nerves before she headed for them.

"Oh, Ms. Stuart?" the receptionist spotted her. "Sorry, didn't realize you were here. The gentlemen were asking for you."

"I bet." Kerry gave her a wry smile.

"Would you like some coffee brought in? We've been holding off," the woman said, her nose wrinkling. "They weren't really very nice."

"Go ahead." Kerry patted the desk. "Let me go see what I can do with them." She shouldered her briefcase and approached the entrance to the conference center, pausing at the door way just long enough to interrupt the heated conversation inside before she entered. "Good morning."

The men had been caught by surprise. They turned and watched her as she made her way around the table to the head of it, setting down her brief case and leaning her fingertips on the polished wood surface. "Okay. Let's start with who you gentlemen are, what department of the government you work for, and who your bosses are."

The men glanced at each other in some slight puzzlement.

"I'll start. My name's Kerrison Stuart. I'm the Vice President of operations for ILS," Kerry said. "I think you can appreciate that I have a slate of issues to deal with taller than I am so if we can discuss what your issue is quickly and efficiently, I'd really appreciate it."

Now they all looked at one of the men, an older gentleman of middling height, with copper curly hair. They all had dark suits on, and Bluetooth earpieces and Kerry suspected their jacket pockets held identical pairs of dark sunglasses they had no use for at the moment.

"Okay," the ginger haired man said. "I'm Dan Cutter. I'm the agent in charge for this area for the Secret Service."

"Okay," Kerry said. "So, I guess you're different people who want something from us than the gentleman from the NSA who is on his way here."

"NSA." one of the other men said. "What do they want?"

"The NSA's on the way here? Who?" Cutter asked. "This is not their jurisdiction."

Oh Jesus. "Please sit down." Kerry did so, folding her hands on the table. "Suppose you tell me what you need, before they get here and confuse things."

Cutter did. "Listen, Ms. Stuart. No offense but your people here don't seem to know there's a crisis going on."

"They know," Kerry said. "Every single person in this corporation knows."

"Well, then they don't seem to want to cooperate," Cutter said. "We have a surveillance appliance we need to install here, and they won't let us."

"I won't let you," Kerry corrected him. "The people here don't have the authority to either grant or deny that request."

"What?" Cutter stood up. "Listen, lady, who in the hell do you think you are?" I'm a Treasury officer! You've been blocking my men since yesterday and I'm not going to put up with it a minute more!"

Kerry remained seated. "I am the vice president of operations for this company," she repeated. "I am under no legal obligation to allow you to enter this facility. In fact, I have a mandate to not allow anyone unauthorized from entering it, and please don't try to browbeat me." She merely gazed up at him. "Why don't you start by explaining to me what exactly you need to do, and what information you're looking for?"

"I don't have to do that."

Kerry shrugged. "I don't have to continue speaking to you. This facility is secured. There are high level government accounting systems that process through it. If you seriously think I am going to let some people from some agency with some unknown device come in and connect to that frankly sir, you are nuts."

"I can arrest you," Cutter said. "For obstruction."

"You can," Kerry agreed. "But that's not going to get you your information. These people here not only will not help you, they cannot. Our systems are in security lock down mode."

Cutter stared at her.

Kerry gazed back at him. "Would you like to tell me what you gentlemen are looking for? Before you go off arresting me and causing yourself a lot of trouble, it would help to know if what you need is even in here."

"Cutter, sit." The man seated at the far end of the table spoke up. He was tall, and dark, and had a Latin accent. "Ms. Stuart, my name is Lopez." He stood up and came around the table. "I know you have your responsibilities to take care of, but so do we."

Kerry decided this apparent bait and switch was legitimate, and that this was the actual boss of the group. She and Dar played that game sometimes with new companies. "Mr. Lopez." She tapped her thumbs together. "No, I don't think you really do understand what kind of responsibilities I have here." She stood and opened the whiteboard at the back of the room.

Lopez stopped and waited.

She turned and faced them. "I have a quarter of a million employees," she said. "I have two dozen of them missing in New York, and a dozen missing in Washington." She turned and scribbled on the board. "I have most of the infrastructure for communications down in Manhattan. I have an entire secure multipoint structure to restore in the Pentagon." She scribbled again. "I have overseas links down, a major satellite uplink used by the Navy down, bandwidth shifted in gigabits to cover planes in Newfoundland and Vancouver, satellite endpoints to establish, cellular backhaul to rebuild, and last by not least, several hundred major financial and banking customers who are depending on us to put them back in operation and prevent a major financial crisis."

She turned and faced him. "Now explain to me again why I am in this room, listening to you bitch at me for something you won't explain instead of letting me go and do my job bringing this country back from crisis?"

Lopez blinked at her.

"As my late father would have said, put it on the table, or take a hike." Kerry found the irony almost painful, but the quote fit. "I don't have time to play games with you." She could feel an exquisite tension in her guts, and knew she was playing with fire. She could see in Lopez's face that he wasn't a goon, and he could, in fact, drag her ass off to jail and might very well do so.

"This is a matter of national security," Lopez said.

"I have a top secret clearance," Kerry shot right back. "Next excuse?"

Lopez sat down in the chair next to hers. "Okay."

Kerry sat down, and folded her hands.

"Close the door." Lopez looked at Cutter. "Is this room secure?"

"It is," Kerry said. "We had them sweep for security yesterday after you first got here." She paused. "Though, I would still love to know where the NSA fits in."

Lopez frowned. "First things first." He waited for the door to be shut, and glanced up as the air compressed a little around them. "Soundproofed?"

"Yes," Kerry said, quietly.

"Okay." Lopez looked a little more relaxed. "I'm sorry," he said. "I didn't realize the extent of your company's involvement in all this. I was told you were simply a service provider."

Kerry nodded. "Then I understand your approach," she said. "Please go on."

"This device," Lopez said. "We suspect that the people who planned and executed the atrocities yesterday are still here, still planning, still executing more horrible things. We have to find them. Do you understand how critical that is? We have very little time."

Kerry nodded again. "Okay, what exactly is this device looking for?" She held a hand up when he started to protest. "I don't want to know specifics. I need to know what type of data stream you're hoping to intercept. Are you thinking these people will be trying to attack the government financial systems?"

"They could be," Lopez nodded. "This device analyzes conversations and determines if they are of interest to us."

"Conversations from where? Inside the government?"

"No. From the public."

Kerry sighed. "Then you're in the wrong place," she said. "There's no public access here."

Lopez frowned. "There isn't?"

"No," Kerry said. "These are all closed systems. Isolated."

Lopez turned to Cutter. "Didn't you say they had internet access from here?"

"That's what I was told," Cutter said. "The guys in accounting said they had internet." He looked accusingly at Kerry. "You saying they're lying?"

"No," Kerry said. "They get internet via our secure gateway," she said. "But that's not here. They go out to the internet via three different nodes-in New York, Chicago, and Dallas." She got up and drew a rough circle, with three points on it, then put an X near one edge. "The request goes through two NATS and three different gateways. There's no outside access."

"Shit," Cutter muttered.

Kerry could see the consternation around the table. She almost felt sorry for the men. "If it's any consolation, the systems here are protected. I won't quote my boss and say they're un-crackable because it gets us into trouble, but they are secure. Feel free to run tests against them."

"Shit," Cutter repeated. "We wasted a whole fucking day."

Lopez rubbed his temples. "Ms. Stuart, are you telling us the truth?" He looked up into Kerry's eyes. "People's lives can depend on your answer. We have to find these people."

Kerry gazed gravely back at him. "I'm telling the truth," she said. "If you really want to tap public access, you need to go to the tier 1 providers, and put your appliance there," she said. "We provide our own access for our customers, but the rest of the country uses one of them.

"Tier 1?" Lopez got out a pad and scribbled that down. "Can you give me the names?"

Kerry promptly provided them. "There are lots of smaller companies, but those three form the public backbone," she told him. "Now I will tell you that we maintain a lot of filtering capability on our net access nodes. If there's something, some phrase or type of information you are looking for specifically, I would be glad to put a scanning routine in place and output the results to you."

"You would?" Lopez lost some of his menace. "You can do that?"

"Just let us know," Kerry said. "The security of the country is very important to us. The government is one of our biggest clients."

Now the men were nodding, and the whole atmosphere had completely changed. "Okay." Lopez handed her his business card. "We'll be in touch, Ms. Stuart. Thanks for the info."

Kerry selected one of her own cards and handed it over. "Good luck," she said sincerely. "Now if you'll excuse me, I've got to head out to the Pentagon."

Lopez extended a hand. "Sorry about this whole thing, Ms. Stuart." He shook Kerry's hand. "Everything's in a lot of flux right now. We're all scrambling."

"Us too." Kerry felt a sense of relief, and more than a little pride. "Gentlemen?"

They filed out, and headed for the door, walking quickly and bending their heads together as they left the building. Kerry watched through the smoked glass as they got into their SUVs and pulled away, and shook her head. "Wow."

The receptionist looked over at her. "Are they gone?" she said, as a service person arrived with a cart of coffee. "Wow. That was fast."

Kerry shrugged modestly. "Bring that up to wherever they've stuck me." She told the service person. "I'm sure I'll need it." She turned to the receptionist. "I'm expecting someone else from the government looking for me. I'll be here for another thirty minutes or so, and if they're not here by then, I'm heading for the Pentagon."

"Yes ma'am." The receptionist scribbled a note. "Good to have you here."

Kerry smiled and headed for the security door, her shoulders straightening. "Wish Dar had seen that one," she muttered to herself as she swiped through. "She'd have loved it."

Chapter Fifteen

THE SMALL COCKPIT was getting very crowded. Dar stood just outside the door, her hands braced on the frame as she listened to Alastair arguing somewhat forcefully on the radio.

The steward had edged back out of the way and was busy in the galley, seemingly glad not to be involved in what was going on.

Dar didn't blame him. In front of her, Alastair was perched on a small jump seat behind the seats that the pilots were in, crammed in next to the slim, dark haired navigator.

Everyone was nervous. She could see the pilots all trading off watching their instruments with looking back at Alastair, as the intractable voices on the other end of the radio got angrier and more belligerent.

Not good. "Alastair." Dar leaned forward and put a hand on his shoulder. "Should I try to get Gerry involved?"

Alastair glanced back at her. "Hold that thought." He turned back to the radio. "Lieutenant? Are you there?"

The radio crackled. "Listen mister, I don't know who you think you are but you better just listen to instructions and shut the hell up before I send planes up there to blow you out of the sky."

"Nice," Dar said. "Sad to say, I grew up with jerks like that."

"Son." Alastair kept his voice reasonable and even. "You don't really need to know who I am. If you've got your last paycheck stub, just pull it out and look at the logo in blue on the right hand side on the bottom. That's the company I work for. We're not terrorists," he said. "So stop threatening us."

The radio was silent for a bit. Alastair let the mic rest against his leg, and shook his head. "What a mess," he said. "I appreciate things are in chaos down there, but for Pete's sake we don't even want to land in the damn country."

The pilot nodded. "That's what I tried to explain to him," he said. "He just kept saying security threat, security threat. I couldn't get a word in edgewise." He glanced back at Dar. "Are you in the military, ma'am?"

"No." Dar felt a surprising sense of relief at the admission. "My father was career Navy. I grew up on base."

The radio crackled. A different voice came on though. "This is Commander Wirkins. Is this Mr. McLean?"

"Ah." Alastair picked the mic up. "Maybe we're getting somewhere." He clicked it. "It is," he said. "Go ahead, Commander."

"Mr. McLean, we've established who you are. We understand you are trying to file an amended flight plan," the commander said. "Due to a situation in the area, I have to ask you to please instruct your pilot to land in Nassau. This is not negotiable."

"Something's going on." Dar shook her head. "Damn."

"Commander." Alastair gathered his thoughts. "I appreciate that you have your own issues," he said. "So let me ask you this. If we land in Nassau and your people are satisfied we're not going to hurt anyone, can we get cleared to fly into the States so your pit stop doesn't cause a delay in what we have to do?"

"Mr. McLean, you're not in a position to bargain with us."

Alastair sighed. "All right then, please put your ass in your chair and call the Joint Chiefs of Staff. Get Gerald Easton on the line," he said. "I'm about out of patience with you too. He was going to send a plane for us, damn well shoulda let him."

Silence on the radio.

"If they force us down," Dar said. "Chances are they're not going to let the plane take off again."

The pilot glanced over his shoulder at her. "We'll be out of air time anyway," he said. "No offense folks, but the storm would have been a better option."

"Agreed," Alastair held his hand up. "My fault. Sorry about that."

The radio remained silent.

"It's only about four, five hours from Miami by sea," Dar said. "We can charter a boat to get there."

The co pilot turned and looked at her. "Ma'am, are you crazy? That's not a trivial trip across the Gulfstream."

Dar didn't take offense. "I know," she said. "Been there, done that."

"I've been to the Bahamas. You won't get a captain to take you over like it is now. They're not stupid," the co pilot said. "They don't like risk."

"I'll captain it myself." Dar shrugged. "Pay enough money and they'll rent us a tub."

Both flyers looked at each other, then shook their heads. Alastair merely chuckled wryly.

Finally the radio buzzed. "Mr. McLean, this is Commander Wirkins."

"Go ahead," Alastair said. "At least we've got a plan B," he added, in an aside to Dar. "Though spending four hours bouncing over the Atlantic ain't my idea of fun."

"Mr. McLean, we're in a state of national emergency here and I do not appreciate, and my command does not appreciate you asking for special dispensation."

"Too bad," Alastair said, in a genial tone. "We have a job to do, mister, and you're keeping me from it. You may think it's got nothing to do with you, but if you do about ten minutes research on who we are, you'll catch a clue that's not the case."

The commander cleared his throat into the open mic. "I have done that research, or believe me, buddy there'd be two fighters up there blowing your ass out of the sky right now," he said. "So like I said, I don't appreciate you dropping names, no matter how justified you think you are."

Dar held her hand out. "Gimme."

"C"mon Dar." Alastair bumped her knee with his elbow. "He's about to cave. He's just pissing all over the wall so everyone knows what a big guy he is first." He clicked the mic. "Fish or cut bait, Commander."

"Well, Mr. McLean, sorry to tell you, but you're not getting to where you want to go today," the commander said, a note of smugness in his voice that made both Dar and Alastair's lips twitch. "You can call me an asshole if you want to, and report me to whoever you want to, but I've got a job to do too, and I'm going to do it."

"Shoulda given me the mic," Dar sighed. "At least we'd have gotten some laughs out of it."

"So my controller is going to instruct your pilot to land that plane at the Opa Locka airport, where we're going to have you met with a security team so that I can get my job done. I don't much care about yours."

"Whooho." Dar laughed. "Score!" She lifted her hand and Alastair smacked it with his own, surprising the crew.

"How you get your affairs in order after that isn't my concern," the commander said. "But it's a nice long drive to Texas. So have a great day."

"Well. How do you like that?" Alastair chuckled. "First time I had someone's sand up their ass work to my favor. "If that's what your decision is, Commander, then we'll have to take it," he said, mildly. "It sure is a long drive from there to Texas."

The radio clicked off with a snitty hiss, and Alastair handed the mic back to the navigator. "Well, gentlemen, after all that crap in a hand basket I think we ended up winning that round."

"You didn't want to go to Texas?" the co pilot half turned. "I don't get it."

"Well," Dar said. "Houston is where our main offices are, and where Alastair here lives," she said. "On the other hand, Miami is where our main operations center is, and where I live, and we both need to end up in Washington and New York so this guy just did us a big favor trying to screw us over."

"Yep." Alastair nodded. "Be sorry not to see the wife and the kids, but this cuts what, two days travel for you?" He nodded. "That cloud sure had a silver lining. Maybe by the time we sort things out we can get a flight up from your friend the General."

"Otherwise I'll go pick up my truck at the airport and we can drive," Dar said. "But that gives us a lot more options. You can even stay in the Miami office and run things if you want, while I head up."

Alastair nodded. "So, sirs, please do what the nice men want and land us in Miami." He chuckled. "Bea's gonna kill me after all the arrangements she had to make."

The pilot nodded in relief. "You got it," he said. "Get us out of the air faster, we don't have to fly around a storm, and if we're all still grounded I get a layover on South Beach. Doesn't get any better than that." He looked at his co pilot. "You up for that Jon?"

The co pilot shook his head and laughed. "I'm up for that," he said. "Man, I thought this was really going to end up like crap." He looked back at Alastair. "You sure have brass ones, sir."

The older man chuckled. "Live as long as I have, you learn to figure out how much you can poke the stick at the bear, if you get my drift. Once that fellah knew who we..." He indicated Dar and himself, "were, I figured he knew better than to be serious about shooting us down."

"I don't know. He sounded pretty aggressive," the co pilot said. "We've heard from other pilots that the attitude is they've got carte blanche to do whatever they want in the name of national security."

"Someone still has to be accountable," Dar said.

"Do they?" the co pilot asked. "I sure hope they do. I've been on the wrong side of an INS officer in a bad mood. Almost cost me a paid flight."

The pilot half turned in his seat and addressed the navigator. "Egar, you okay with us landing there? I forgot to ask you."

The tall, slim man nodded. "I have family in Miami," he said. "I am very happy we're going there. It's good." He smiled. "I achieved my pilot's license at that airport. It's very nice."

Alastair stood up and waited for Dar to clear out of the way so he could exit the cockpit. "What a relief. No offense to your boating skills, Paladar, but I'm no yachtsman." He slapped Dar on the shoulder as they retreated back down the aisle to the passenger compartment. "Besides, fella was probably right. We'd have to end up buying the damn boat and then what? Be tough to explain a motor yacht on our inventory list."

Dar chuckled. "We could have auctioned it off." She was, however relieved. Much as she would have stepped up to sail an unfamiliar craft across what were sometimes very treacherous waters, she was damned glad she wasn't going to have that particular bluff called.

Silver lining. Absolutely. "We lucked out."

"Sure did," her boss agreed. "Well, sometimes we have to, y'know?" he added, as they resumed their seats. "Wish it hadn't gotten so nasty, though. I know the fella has a lot of issues he's contending with but my god."

Dar pushed her seat back. "They teach you to do that," she said. "Be a bastard, I mean. You try to overwhelm whoever your opponent is with loud, aggressive talk to knock them off balance and put them on the defensive."

"They teach you that in the military?" Alastair asked, in a quizzical tone. "I thought you never went through that."

"They teach you that in most of the negotiating and ninja management classes these days," Dar informed him dryly. "But a friend of ours, who's a cop in Miami, says taking the offensive when you're confronting someone is a well used tactic of theirs too."

"You use that, yourself," her boss commented.

"Sometimes," Dar admitted. "If someone knows you're going to be an asshole, they usually do what you want, faster. Like our vendors. They know if they don't do what I'm asking, I'll just keep going up their ladder and get louder and louder until they do."

"Like what I just did to that fellah."

Dar nodded. "That's why they like dealing with Kerry better." Her eyes twinkled a little. "She's got the best of both worlds. She gets to be nice, and they like her, and she's got me in her back pocket to threaten them with."

Alastair laughed. "Well, all in all, I guess I can forgive that guy. I know he must be dealing with a thousand different problems. I was just his most annoying one that minute." He folded his hands over his stomach. "He must be laughing his head off thinking about how he showed us though."

Dar suspected he was. Probably cursing about them, and telling everyone around him how he showed these damn jerks who was boss. Dar couldn't really blame him either, since they had asked for special treatment, and had threatened him with going up the chain, and in fact, were the jerky pain in the asses he actually considered them to be.

However, it had gotten them what they wanted, in a rather classic case of the end justifying the means. Dar checked her watch. So they'd end up in a few hours in Miami. Awesome. "I'll send him a note telling him how much he helped us out after this is all over," she said. "My body's so screwed up I can't figure out whether to take you out to breakfast or dinner when we get there though."

"Well, it'll be different than burritos in Mexico City." Alastair put his hands behind his head. "Wasn't looking forward to all that, or the drive to Houston."

Dar smiled at the ceiling, relaxing for the first time since she'd woken up. She was already looking forward to landing, her mind flipping ahead to the messages she'd need to send, and more importantly, how happy she knew Kerry would be to hear from her. "I'll have someone go to MIA and bring my car down." She decided. "Figure it'll take a while for them to get through the paperwork once we land."

"Take me a few minutes to call Bea and get everything squared away anyway," her boss said. "It's going to feel good to be back home."

Dar exhaled. "Sure is," she said. "Sure damn is."

KERRY SETTLED HER ear buds in and peered at her laptop screen. "Okay, Mark, did we get inventory availability from the vendors yet? I know you've got everything we had with you, but from what they're telling me here we lost the whole WAN room."

"They got," Mark said. "But they can't get it to us faster than a truck. The distributor's in California."

Kerry looked down at the pad on the desk. "Well, tell them to start driving," she said. "By my count here, rebuilding that will take most of the inventory on your truck, and we're not even started yet."

"Will do."

"Miami exec, this is the Air Hub."

Kerry blinked. "Go ahead Air Hub."

"We're hearing rumors that they might let some flights up tomorrow, ma'am," the voice answered. "Sorry we can't be more specific. It's pretty quiet here."

"Miami, hello? This is Sherren in New York. We've got good news! Six people just showed up here. I'm logging them in now!"

"That's great, Sherren." Kerry exhaled slowly. "Do they know about any of the others? Have they seen them?"

"No, no they don't," Sherren said. "Everyone got separated, they said. They're all taking showers. They're covered in that white stuff. They said a lot of people went south, too, toward the battery."

Kerry watched the red led's slowly change to green. Too few. "I'm really glad to hear that, Sherren. How are you all doing? Are you all right? Do you need anything?"

Sherren's voice sounded calmer today. "We're doing okay, you know? We needed some clothes so we went out and got some. We got bagels. The dog carts are there. People are out there. You can't stop this city. People are in shock, but we keep going."

Kerry thought about the empty streets she'd traveled through the night before. "You sure do."

"I'm sure the rest of the office will be here any time now," Sherren said, confidently. "We're going to get some coffee on. I wish we could get the phones working," she added. "I know some of our customers need us."

"Miami exec, this is Miami telecom," a new voice broke in. "We're handling the inbound 800 service trunks for New York. We can get messages to the people there, if you can get us a mailing list built."

"Oh, that would be great!" Sherren said. "You can get calls out, if you try hard enough. Or maybe if they have email, we can email them. That works a lot better than the phones."

Kerry nodded. "Good idea." She glanced at the screen. "Miami server ops, are you on?"

"Yes, ma'am," a quiet voice answered. "We're here."

"Build a list based on the reported list onscreen." Kerry said, after a brief pause. "And get that to telecom."

"Will do."

"Miami exec, this is LA Earth station. I have Newark Earth station on landline. They need generators. They've got a seven day estimate on repairs to the power station there. Someone told them it was sabotaged."

"Oh my god," Sherren said.

"Miami exec, this is Miami ops," Mark's voice replied. "That needs industrial. That little trick you and I pulled ain't gonna cut it."

Kerry tapped her pen on the desk. "Shouldn't their facilities operator be handling that?"

"Miami, no one's doing anything there. Everyone's been sent to staging to go into the city." LA Earth station reported. "If we want help, we need to do it ourselves, that's what they were told."

"Right." Kerry scribbled a note on her pad. "Let me get in touch with APC. Everyone's going to be hitting the usual providers let's try the high tech ones."

"Ms. Stuart?" Nan stuck her head in the door. "I have some president or other of AT&T on the line for you."

"Tell them hang on a minute." Kerry finished writing.

"Miami exec, this is Danny. The bus is here." Danny sounded relieved. "Man, are we glad to see that," he added. "We're waiting for clearance to start going in there, but we're going to need some help."

"Danny, we're almost there," Mark said. "Hang in there, buddy. I got ten people with me."

Ten? Kerry glanced at the screen, then back at her paper. "Hope that's a big RV," she muttered under her breath. She looked up. "Okay, you can transfer whoever it is from AT&T here." She pointed at the phone. "Thanks."

Nan disappeared.

"Mark, we're looking for you man," Danny answered. "Did you say you have a truck? We haven't been able to shake loose and get that plywood yet."

"No prob," Mark said. "Miami exec, any word on when we can get into lower NY?"

Kerry keyed her mic. "Let's concentrate on DC for now since we have access to the facility. With all the damage in Manhattan it could be a while."

"Miami exec, this is Lansing," the Michigan center broke in.

"Hold on, Lansing. I have to take a call." Kerry put her mic on mute and hit the speaker phone. "Kerry Stuart."

"Ms. Stuart?" a man's voice answered. "This is Charles Gant from AT&T. I think we met at that technical conference in Orlando a few months back."

"We did." Kerry nodded. "What can I do for you? I assume this is something critical."

Gant sighed. "Much as I'd rather be asking you to meet me for coffee and chat about high end routers, it is a critical issue. I just want to bounce a question off you, since I know of all the private providers you guys are the biggest."

"Okay." Kerry picked up her bottle of water and took a sip. "I'm listening."

"We lost everything in lower Manhattan," he said. "I think you probably know that, since we had a lot of tie-ins to you."

"We know," Kerry said. "We have almost nothing at all coming in to our three nodes in the region. A lot of customers are affected."

"Well, let me give you the laundry list," Gant said. "We lost the triple pop. Verizon said nothing's recoverable. They also lost their West office. Power's out for the area, including all the cell towers and the ones that do have power either don't have backhaul or are overloaded."

"Wow," Kerry murmured.

"I got my counterpart at Sprint on the other line. Between us, we lost everything overseas, and so did MCI."

"We realized that," Kerry said. "We had to backhaul a lot of overseas financial via our southern circuits."

There was momentary silence. "So how badly are you affected?"

Kerry took another sip of water. "We obviously can't service the local accounts in lower Manhattan, and we lost our major switching office in the Pentagon." Then she stopped speaking.

There was another moment of silence. "So you have service otherwise? Transatlantic?"

"We have data service, yes," Kerry confirmed. "We rely on your interchanges, and the other Telco's for phone service, naturally, so that's down, but we're backhauling everything else across our redundant links, or sending it up to the birds."

"Interested in renting some bandwidth?" Gant asked, in a wry tone. "We've got nothing between New York and our main service centers. I can't even guess what's down because our systems can't connect." He cleared his throat. "I figured I'd ask you before everyone else does."

Kerry thought about all the times she'd had to browbeat the Telco vendors for everything from bad circuits to late ones. "How much do you need?" she asked. "And what would it take for you to get a tie into our Roosevelt Island node?"

"I'll take ten meg if you have it." His voice sounded utterly relived. "I think our substation on the island can carry the traffic over. I can check but my notes here show we're in the same building."

Mentally, Kerry did a quick calculation. Dar had provisioned a larger than normal spare of bandwidth in the area, thankfully, but she knew there'd be more requests to come. This was just the first. "We can do that," she said. "Get me your LOA and I'll send it to my internal provisioning group."

"God bless you." Gant sighed. "Sorry if I sound overwhelmed, but damn it, I am," he said. "My brother is missing in that mess and I can't think straight."

"Charles, I'm glad we can help," Kerry said gently. "We have some people missing ourselves. Most of our office in Manhattan was in the Towers for business meetings yesterday morning."

"My god."

"So we're sweating right along with you," Kerry said. "And speaking of that, could you possibly do me a favor?"

"If I can, for sure," Charles said.

"My Rockefeller Center office is down hard," Kerry said. "Any chance of getting one of our lines up?"

"Give me the circuit ID," he answered instantly. "We've got service near the Rock. You probably are just terminated closer to the triple…to where the triple was."

Kerry typed a question into her search applet, and was rewarded with a number. "Here it is." She gave it to him. "It would help the people left there. Most of them lived down in the affected area and can't go home."

"You got it, Kerry," Charles said. "Expect that LOA in the next five minutes."

"Call me if you need anything else," Kerry said. "Talk to you later." She hung the phone up, and went back to her screen. She clicked her mic on. "Miami exec to New York, you still on Sherren?"

"I'm here," Sherren responded promptly. "Two more people just showed up! We're all like kids here, screaming."

Kerry smiled. "I'm very glad. We're working on getting you some phones there, too."

"Oh, that's great!" Sherren said.

"Ma'am?" Nan poked her head back in. "Do you want a CNN feed in here?" She indicated a dark panel on the wall. "We've got one running in ops."

"Sure," Kerry said. "Any sign of more government visitors?"

"None yet." Nan shook her dark head. "When did you want to leave for the Pentagon?"

Kerry checked her watch. "I think I need to spend a little more time here, maybe an hour. Let's say eleven? Mark's almost at the Pentagon and he's going to be tied up for a while when he gets there."

"Okay, I'll be around," Nan said. "We'll push the feed in here." She ducked out and closed the door behind her.

Kerry scribbled a few more notes, listening with one ear bud in to the conversation going on in the background. A flash of motion caught her eye, and she looked up at the screen just in time to see a shot of the inside of the Capitol, where the hall was full of men and women all milling around.

Her mother was there, she realized. She spotted her immediately off to one side of the chamber, with two other senators who were vaguely familiar to her. "Hi Mom." She briefly waved at the screen, remembering the odd occasion when she'd flip past CSPAN2 and find her father talking.

She always stopped and listened.

"Miami exec, this is Miami HR."

"Go ahead." Kerry keyed her mic. "Good morning, Mari."

"Good morning," Mariana replied. "Not sure if you caught the news, but it's all over the local here that they've issued search warrants for a bunch of locations in Miami."

Kerry's head jerked up and she stared at the screen. "What?"

"No one's really sure what's going on. Duks says one of his people had a police raid in their apartment complex around four a.m.," Mari said. "We heard something about some of the hijackers coming from here."

"From Miami?" Kerry found this hard to believe.

"That's what they're saying."

Holy crap. Kerry stared in bewilderment at the television, reading the crawl on the bottom that repeated what Mari had just said. Hijackers from Miami? "But didn't they say yesterday this was something from the Middle East?"

"I don't know," Mari said. "Just wanted to give you the heads up since believe me, there's a lot of crazy, nervous people down here at the moment. We have about half the office in. A lot of people stayed home."

"Wow," Kerry said. "Okay, thanks for the warning." She scanned the lists again then sighed. "I'm going on hold for a minute, to call APC."

"Good luck, Miami exec," the LA Earth station chimed in. "Those guys sound pretty tapped."

"Mari, can you find out how close our community support teams are to Newark?" Kerry asked, as she searched her address applet for the phone number of their racking vendor. "Make sure they stop for a cold keg of beer."

Silence. "I don't think that's spec, Kerry," Mari said.

"Don't give damn. They've been there all night," Kerry said. "It's as muggy there as it is here. Have them bring fans and make sure they've got six volt to 110 converter lines so they can run them."

"Okay, will do," Mari said. "You're the boss."

"Until 3:30 p.m. I sure am." Kerry sighed. "Someone turn the planet faster please."

KERRY CHECKED THE time, then put her pen down on her pad. "Okay folks," she said. "I have to head out of here. Mark, I'll see you in about thirty."

"Gotcha, boss," Mark replied. "We're waiting for clearance to pull this rig in. "

"Mark, this is Danny," Danny said. "We'll come over there and talk to them. Give me five."

"Will do. Kerry, I've got it."

"All right. Miami exec off. " Kerry pulled out her ear buds and stood up, walking around in a circle to shake the cramps out of her body from the tension of dealing with issue after issue for a solid hour. She had a headache from it, and even two cups of tea hadn't prevented her throat from gaining a painful rasp.

The door cracked open, and Nan stuck her head in. "Ready to go? Sally at the front said no one else showed up for you."

"Well, good." Kerry flexed her hands and walked back over to the desk, picking up her jacket and slipping it on. "Maybe they changed their mind, or figured out something else to do, or talked to the Secret Service. Either way, I'm outta here."

She shut down her laptop. "Is there a Wendy's between here and the Pentagon?" she asked. "Love my hotel, but they have seriously deficient continental breakfasts."

Nan smiled. "Yeah, there is. You sure you don't want to stop somewhere else? There's some great restaurants around there."

"Nah." Kerry buckled her briefcase and slid the strap over her shoulder. "So little time, so many fubars." She followed Nan out the door and down the hallway. "I've got my fingers crossed hoping I get a call back from APC. They have a manufacturing plant in Pennsylvania."

"APC...the rack people?" Nan asked. "Do they need that many new ones for the Pentagon?"

"Well, they need some, but I called them for a couple of UPSs." Kerry shouldered the staff door open and held it as Nan went through. "For the Earthstation."

"Ah, yeah. Right." Nan pulled her keys from her jacket pocket. "Those poor guys. They were being pounded yesterday. I think they were almost glad they lost power because everyone stopped bugging them for space."

Kerry slid into the passenger side seat. "Right now, I need to get the pressure off the station on the other coast, so hopefully we can get them some power and get them running again."

Nan started the SUV and pulled out of the parking lot, pausing at the gate as the security guards waved and the big iron portal slowly slid aside to let them out. The big doors were set into well made concrete and stone walls that stretched around the facility to an impressive height and came complete with a set of serious looking security guards whose bulk and stance were staunchly professional.

Kerry liked the guards in Miami, but most of them were what Dar called domesticated tabbies, nice men and women, and very competent, but they focused on watching the building and checking for fire alarms, helping the staff out when they locked their keys in their car, and manning the badge issuing equipment.

They weren't the ILS police. Most of them were far less intimidating than some of the marketing reps were with their big white teeth and aggressive tactics.

These guys here, on the other hand, looked like they were ready to turn back a platoon of Marines. Kerry was pretty sure she didn't want to swap them for her uniformed friends down south, but it was nice to have them here, especially given the shifting uncertainties of the situation they were in. "Nice guys?" she asked, as they waved on the way out.

"Oh, absolutely," Nan said. "In a no neck, space ranger kind of way." She pulled out of the entry road and onto the main street. "They really take themselves very seriously, if you know what I mean. Most of them are ex military."

"Mm." Kerry remembered her time at the Navy base with Dar. "Are they reserve?" she asked. "I have a feeling this situation is going to end up with us fighting someplace again."

"Well, I don't know that much about them," Nan said." But I thought I heard someone saying that they had to be completely retired, not in the reserves to be hired. Someone was complaining that it wasn't fair, because being a reservist or National Guard is supposed to be a good thing."

Kerry considered that. She rested her elbow on the armrest and leaned back, watching the buildings flash by. "Boy, I can see both parts of that," she admitted. "I do think serving your country is an admirable thing, and shouldn't be a reason to block someone from employment."

"That's what that person was saying," Nan said.

"On the other hand, if my whole security department was reserve and guard, and they all got called up, I'd be a pickle," Kerry said. "It's a really tough question, especially these days. Used to be if you were guard, the worst thing you'd have to deal with is helping with a flood, or being asked to patrol streets during a riot."

"Well, yeah."

"Now, it's not like that," Kerry said. "Before, employers didn't really worry about hiring someone who had that commitment, because it wasn't likely to impact them more than that one weekend a month or whatever. Nowadays, you've got a reasonable chance of being sent overseas for six months, a year, who knows?"

"We shouldn't stop people who want to do it though," Nan said, with a frown. "That seems selfish, I guess."

"Business very often is," Kerry agreed. "It's all what's in the company's best interest." She had to smile wryly at this. "Sometimes. But actually I agree, you shouldn't stop people from serving and it shouldn't be a bar to employment, so I am going to find out from Mariana why that's so for this group since it doesn't apply to anyone else that I know of. "

Nan nodded. "That's cool," she said. "My brother's in the guard. He didn't have to go the last time, but his boss pretty much told him he'd never promote him to anything really critical because he just couldn't afford to have to replace him on short notice, and it was too much of a hassle."

Well. Kerry felt very ambivalent. She thought about how she'd feel if someone, say, Mark, had decided to join the Guard and what that would mean for them if he had to leave and go overseas. "Well, you know, you have to deal with that all the time in business. I mean, people get sick or they quit and find other jobs," she commented. "I'm not sure that's fair of his boss, though. I have to admit I do see the man's point."

"That's what my brother said, pretty much," Nan sighed. "He understands, but it still sucks. He really likes being in the Guard, and he has a lot of friends there. But he's also got a kid on the way, and he also needs to make more money."

Kerry folded her arms. "What does he do?" She gazed out the window, watching trees flash by that had the first tinges of leaves losing their green color.

"Java developer," Nan said, succinctly. "There's the Wendy's. Sure you want that?"

"Yep." Kerry could already taste the spicy chicken. "Tell your brother to send me his resume," she added. "Mariana was saying last week she was desperately looking for more developers for two or three new projects we're doing."

Nan slowed, and pulled into the driveway of the fast food restaurant. "Are you serious?"

"Sure." Kerry reached down and removed her wallet from her briefcase. "Dar once hired an out of work police receptionist with a nose ring off the streets in New York who now runs the data entry department at our largest payment processor in Queens," she said, straightening up. "What?"

Nan was looking at her as though she'd grown a horn. "Really?"

"Really," Kerry assured her. "We look for talent everywhere. It's a bitch trying to keep up with the turnover on a quarter of a million people, you know? So if he's interested, have him email me his resume. Most of the developers are flexible work space, so they can work from home, or here, or go to one of the local centers."

Nan studied her for a brief moment, then she smiled. "Um... you want to get this to go or eat in?" she asked, after a second. "And thanks. That wasn't my motive in mentioning it, but I'll tell him. He's always asking me to get him into ILS, but I never felt comfortable recommending my own family."

"Drive through is fine," Kerry said, opening the wallet and flipping past her driver's license to her corporate credit cards. She selected one and waited, as Nan pulled the car up to the ordering kiosk. "Spicy chicken sandwich with cheese, sour cream and chive baked potato, and a medium Frosty. Get whatever you want, lunch is on me."

Nan took the card she held out, then she rolled down the window to place their order.

Kerry had a moment's peace, then her cell phone rang. She put her earphones back in and answered it. "Kerry Stuart."

"Kerry? This is Michael from APC, we spoke earlier?"

Never had she been so glad to hear from a salesman. "Hi, Michael, you got good news for me?"

"Well, I think I do," Michael said. "We've got two big units, the EPS model, that we'd just finished fitting out for a road show, you know? To show the capabilities? Anyway, they're truck mounted, with a diesel generator and we can have them over to your Newark location by tonight."

Kerry did a little nerd dance in her seat. "Michael, that's awesome. Doesn't even matter how much it is, just send me the bill."

"Do you one better," Michael said, sounding pleased. "We'll do it for the promotion, since the names all over the truck, but in return give me a shot at providing the racking and power for everything you rebuild."

"You got it," Kerry answered instantly. "I'll tell Mark to start sending you a list of what we'll need."

"Great. I'll get the guys rolling," Michael said. "I'll let you go. I know you must be swamped. Call me if you need anything else, okay?"

"Will do. Talk to you later, Michael and thanks again." Kerry hung up, chortling softly under her breath. "One down, a hundred to go." She finished dialing in and waited, as the phone connected to the global conferencing system.

They pulled forward to the delivery window. "Guess that was good news?" Nan handed Kerry's card over to the cashier. "Thanks for lunch, by the way. It beats heating up pizza in the data center."

Kerry held up her hand. "Miami ops? This is Miami exec," she said. "Someone please get Newark on the landline or text, tell them we'll have power generators there around dinnertime." She listened to the ragged cheers. "Okay, I'm off again. Mark, see you in a few. You inside yet?"

"Just let us in, boss. We're driving over to the far side," Mark said. "I can see part of it. Holy crap."

Kerry considered. "Thanks Mark. Be there shortly." She closed her phone and turned in her seat. "You know what, we'd better pull over here and munch before we get there."

Nan nodded, as she handed over Kerry's bag. "Yeah, it's probably going to be pretty busy. That's a good idea."

"Right." Kerry waited until Nan pulled the big SUV into a nearby spot, and parked it. She then opened her bag and removed her sandwich, settling her frosty in the cup holder and unwrapping her chicken. "Actually," she said. "I've been around a collapsed building.

It's not some place you want to have a picnic near."

Nan took a sip of her drink, setting her taco salad down on her lap. "Was that the hospital thing from last year?"

Kerry nodded. She took a bite of her sandwich, enjoying the spicy taste.

"That was scary as hell. I was at project management training in New Mexico that week, but I saw it on the television, and the papers were full of stories about it for days after I got back." Nan speared her salad with a fork. "You must have been scared in there."

Kerry chewed thoughtfully, and then swallowed. She wiped her lips with a lurid yellow napkin and reached for her frosty. "I sure should have been," she said. "But I was too freaked out to be scared. I know that sounds bizarre, but I just wasn't. I was pissed off and wanted out of there that was for sure."

"Did you get hurt?"

Kerry nodded. "Dislocated my shoulder." She swallowed a spoonful of her frosty and went back to her sandwich.

"Ow."

Kerry nodded again, but remained silent as she chewed.

"How in the heck did you climb out that window with a dislocated shoulder?" Nan asked, suddenly, after they'd eaten quietly for a minute.

"Dar put it back in place after it happened," Kerry explained.

"Good thing she knew how," Nan spluttered. "That's no joke! I've seen someone dislocate a shoulder on the football field and they were screaming!"

Kerry chuckled softly. "Her list of talents never ends." She finished up her sandwich and folded the foil wrapper, putting it neatly inside her bag before she removed the container with her baked potato. She'd gotten the top off, and the sour cream applied when her phone rang again.

"Niblets." Kerry got the mic clipped into place and answered it. "Kerry Stuart."

Nan glanced at her, eyebrows hiking briefly, then she put the cover on her now empty container and put it away in its bag. "I'll get us moving again," she said, starting the car and releasing the brake.

"Hello, Kerrison?"

Kerry sighed. "Hello Mother, how are the meetings going? I saw you on TV this morning." She mixed her potato up and ingested a forkful as they pulled out of the parking lot and back out onto the main street.

"Did you? Ah, well, things are about as expected," Cynthia Stuart responded. "Everyone is terribly upset, of course. But my committee would really like to speak with you if it can be arranged."

"Which committee is it?" Kerry asked.

"The intelligence committee," her mother replied. "They were very interested in how much more information was available to you yesterday, and I know you were upset when I mentioned it, but really, I cannot take that back now."

No, she couldn't. Kerry had to admit.

"I did tell them I would ask you if you could arrange a little time to speak with them, but could not promise anything."

Fair enough. "Okay," Kerry decided. "I'm on my way to the Pentagon now. I have to do a situational analysis there, and see what needs to be done to get everyone back up and running. Once that's done, I'll give you a call and we can arrange something."

"Excellent." Her mother sounded profoundly relieved. "Are things going well for you today?"

Kerry peered through the windscreen as she spotted the unmistakable bulk of the Pentagon looming in front of them. "So far, yes," she said. "We found some of our people in New York, and my staff made it up here from Miami safely."

There was heavy traffic around the entrance to the crash site, backing up onto the roadway. Nan slowed to a stop and they both looked through the trees at the building. "Holy Moses." Nan breathed. "That looks totally different than it did on CNN."

"I'm glad to hear that," Cynthia said. "Perhaps we can have dinner together tonight?"

Kerry's eyes were fixed on the huge black hole, smoke still drifting from it. "Sure," she answered absently, her mind trying to sort out the horror. "I'll call you later. Okay?"

"Excellent. Until later then." The phone clicked off and Kerry merely closed it and put it on her lap, still peering out the window. "My God." She closed up the remnants of her lunch and put it into its bag, rolling up the opening and putting it down between her boots.

It was shocking. She had a clear, though somewhat dim memory of the building in all its imposing, concrete glory and somehow seeing it squatting there in the grass, a black gouge taken out of it seemed completely unreal. "It's like a bad movie."

They inched up, toward the police guarding the entrance until they were even with them, tired, harried looking men trying to move cars past with impatient gestures. Nan rolled the window down and visibly braced herself for the argument she was sure was coming.

"Please move along, ladies," the man said. "C'mon, we have to get emergency people in here."

Nan took a breath, but Kerry put a hand on her arm, and leaned over. "Hello, officer," she said, already holding out her badge in her hand. "I'll make this quick because I know the last thing you need is a stopped car out here."

The police officer leaned on the door and peered in at her. "Yes?"

"My company handles the IT for the building," Kerry said, nodding toward the Pentagon. "We want to get things rolling again."

The officer looked at her ID, glancing over it to look at Kerry. "One of your guys just went in there."

"Our equipment van." Kerry nodded. "With generators."

The officer nodded. "You people don't waste time. Go on in, Ms. Stuart. They told us you'd be here." He stepped back and motioned to the next officer, who dragged aside a barrier blocking the entrance to the big inside parking lot.

"Thanks," Kerry said, taking back her badge. "Tell your guys to come by our truck later. We've got food and coffee there. I bet you could use some."

The policeman managed a smile. "Thanks," he said.

Nan rolled the window up and maneuvered the SUV through the opening in the barriers, the wheels bumping up over debris as she edged into the parking area.

"Over there." Kerry spotted Mark's truck, with the RV behind it, not far from the company courtesy bus. "That's our area." Already there were techs surrounding the spot, in jeans and company polos. They were in the back part of the lot. The front was filled with emergency vehicles and military ones, with a huge cluster of press tents behind the lot and separated by a fence.

Nan parked and they got out. Kerry stepped away from the SUV and faced the building, her eyes taking in the smoking, gaping hole in disbelief.

She could smell the smoke. Mixed with that was the tinge of fractured concrete, the smell of burning electrical and shot through, with every other breath, a darker hint of decay and ruin. She took a few more steps toward the building, and stood, arms crossed as her eyes slowly scanned the area, seeing wreckage, and people, and exhausted faces.

Anger. Grief. Sadness.

To one side, a huge American flag was draped, as though in defiance. Kerry felt tears sting her eyes as she saw it and knew a moment of solemn kinship with everyone around her.

"Sucks." Mark came to stand shoulder to shoulder with her.

"Yeah." Kerry drew in a long breath. "Fifty states, right and left, Yankee and redneck, two billion opinions and twice as many assholes but right now we're all Americans." She turned and gave him a brief hug. "Let's get to work."

Chapter Sixteen

DAR WAS SIDEWAYS in her chair again. She had both legs over one arm of her seat, and her head resting on the opposite padded rest. She had her eyes closed and her hands folded over her stomach, the drone of the engines filling her ears.

Her anxiety had faded, buoyed by the knowledge that she'd be landing hours before she'd expected to, and be in a position to immediately jump back into the problems she knew were waiting rather than facing international immigration, a second flight, a cross border drive, and a long haul up into Houston.

Across the aisle from her, Alastair was finally napping, and the lights had been lowered in the cabin along with the window shades producing a dim, peaceful atmosphere. Dar was content to sprawl where she was in a state of half waking, half sleeping.

She'd started out by trying to think ahead to what was going on down on the ground, but the long day and the stress had caught up to her and now she was merely daydreaming. Her mind running free with thoughts of where she'd wander with Kerry in Europe after world events calmed down.

Where would Kerry really like to go? She'd seemed enthusiastic about the Alps, Dar mused. Would she rather go to one of the ritzy winter resorts? Dar opened her eyes and looked around the inside of the private plane. She reluctantly admitted, privately, that she wouldn't mind spending time in someplace nice. She suspected that-though Kerry poo poo'd high society trimmings-she wouldn't argue too hard against a room with a marble Jacuzzi or chocolate dipped strawberries before bed either.

But would she rather be in some nice lodge somewhere quiet, where they could go outside and simply sit on a hill and look at the stars? Or would she rather go outside and sit in a café looking at other kinds of stars living the high life?

Maybe they could find a compromise, like their cabin. She loved the comforts of it and the contrast of the raw, weatherworn dock outside and the proximity of the wildness of the sea. She and Kerry could go out and get as sandy and seaweed ridden as they pleased, and then relax on the couch in the air conditioning with a bowl of microwave popcorn.

Were they wimps? Maybe. Did she care?

Hmm.

Dar let that thought drift for a moment, then pondered the notion that it might work out that they were on vacation during Kerry's birthday. What would she like to do for that? Dar decided her partner would probably want to do something special, maybe something exciting and new to her for her birthday.

Maybe they could go to Venice. Or Rome. Dar smiled. Or maybe the Greek Isles.

A soft sound made her open her eyes, and she turned her head to see the door opening quietly allowing the steward to enter. He paused when he saw her somewhat odd position, but then continued moving, shutting the door behind him.

"It looks like we picked up an escort," the man said, quietly, as he stopped next to Dar's seat. "I don't think it is anything to worry about. They seem to be keeping their distance."

"Fighters?" Dar asked.

"I guess," the man agreed. "Not my area of expertise. But the captain is okay with it," he continued. "They called him and just told him to keep on course, which is exactly what we want to do."

Dar smiled. "Yep," she said. "I'll be damn glad to be home, even if it's just for a little while."

"I can well imagine," the steward smiled back. "I'm going to go get my passport. I'm sure they'll want to see it when we land." He moved past Dar and went into the back of the plane, leaving her to resume studying the woven cloth ceiling.

After a moment, though, she sat up and reached across to the window shade, opening it to peer outside. Off the wing, at a reasonable distance, was a Navy fighter. "Ah. Hornet." Dar put the shade back down and extended her seat out again.

She wasn't sure how she felt about the escort. On one hand, she suspected they'd rattled more than one cage and no one was taking chances. On the other hand, she knew damn well there was a good chance whoever had sent the planes up recognized her name.

That was arrogant. Dar acknowledged it with a smile. But it was also true that there were a lot of people who would remember her either for better or for worse.   Some now, for a lot worse.   Her smile disappeared as she remembered Chuckie and what a mess that had turned out to be.

She wished again, for the nth time, that she could go back and do that all over. She thought maybe her father did too.

Her father. Dar found her thoughts moving to a different track. What would this mean for him? Would the Navy try to get him to come back?

No way.

Would he?

Dar was troubled to realize she honestly didn't know the answer to that question. She knew her father was very much invested in how he'd spent his life for all those years, and he had friends by the hundreds and probably thousands still in service.

But then there was her mother. After what he went through, Dar had to think that at the very least he had to seriously consider the question if they asked.

And if they did ask, she knew she'd go to the wall to convince him to say no. For her mother, for herself, damned if she was going to lose her family again. She'd get Kerry to help her if she had to.

She picked up the bottle of orange soda on the table and took a swig of it, and checked her watch, wondering what Kerry was up to. She'd probably made it to the Pentagon already, and Dar was sure she'd have plenty to tell her when she called.

Once she got the squeal out of the way.

She felt a faint pressure change against her ears, and let the thoughts go as the steward came back through the cabin, giving her a smile as he passed. "Heading down?"

"We are." The steward nodded. "Boy, I'll be glad to get on the ground." He went to the front of the cabin and started preparing it for landing, bringing up the lights a little and fastening the curtains back.

Dar reached across the aisle and gave her boss's sleeve a tug. "Alastair?"

"Eh?" Alastair blinked and lifted his head. "What? More people need yelling at?"

Dar chuckled. "No. We're starting down." She moved her seat upright and reached for her briefcase, digging in it to retrieve her leather ID holder, which had her passport and her company badges in it. She also got her PDA and cellphone out, and set them on the small table next to her seat.

"Ah. We're there." Alastair stretched. "Damn, that's great. But I could definitely use a cup of coffee." He rubbed his eyes and rummaged around, getting his things together. "This is the tough end of the jet lag. We've got a whole damn day to get through now."

"True." Dar sighed. "Ah well, there's always Cuban coffee."

Alastair eyed her. "I heard about that the last time I was in the office here. What exactly is it?"

Dar settled back in her chair. "Strong espresso coffee, essentially, not that different from Italian but when they make it right, they take a pyrex mixing cup, put a half pound of sugar in it, and a half cup of the coffee then they whip it in to a froth, before they put the rest of the coffee in, mix it, and there you go."

Her boss's eyebrows knitted. "Are you telling me it's coffee and sugar one to one? Half and half?"

Dar nodded.

"And you actually drink that?"

Dar nodded again. "I like it," she said. "You can also mix hot milk with it, and then it's café con leche."

Alastair covered his eyes with one hand. "When was the last time you had your blood pressure checked?"

"One ten over sixty six." she replied, her eyes twinkling a little.

"Disgusting."

Dar chuckled. "Stress does more to you than coffee," she said. "Best thing I did for my health in the last couple of years was get an assistant." She held up a hand as Alastair started to laugh. "Ah ah...not a joke. Aside from everything else."

"I told you for years to get an assistant. "Alastair shook his finger at her.

"I couldn't," Dar said, swallowing a few times as the air pressure started to increase. "Everyone I interviewed either drove me crazy, or was out to knife me in the back. Do you know how many of them were brought in by other people inside the company?"

Alastair sighed. "Yeah, I'm glad those days are behind us," he admitted. "But you're not going to BS me and tell me the only reason you hired Kerry was her business skills."

Dar was silent for a few minutes. Then she turned and regarded Alastair. "The only reason I hired her as my assistant was her business skills," she said. "I wasn't about to screw either of us over by putting her in a spot where she'd end up looking like a jackass."

"Really?"

"Really," Dar said. "Oh, I won't say I wouldn't have brought her in to some other position. I liked her. I knew we were attracted to each other. I knew there wasn't much else she could do in that pissant little company she was in."

"Uh huh."

"But she had brains, and the guts to stand up to me. I could tell by how she kept changing her game depending on what I threw at her that she'd be able to step in and handle us at an executive level in ops." Dar rested her elbows on her chair arms and laced her fingers together. "And I was right."

"You sure were," Alastair agreed cheerfully. "She does a damn fine job. If that wasn't true, your ass would still be back in London on the conference call because I wouldn't have risked having you in the air with me for this whole time."

Dar nodded. "Yep."

"And it was a good opportunity for her. I'm sure she appreciated that," he went on. "Seems like she has ambition. I'm not surprised she jumped at the offer."

All very true. Dar acknowledged. "I'm just glad she did." She rubbed the edge of her thumb against the cool band of her ring. She swallowed again, and leaned over to pull the shade up. The Hornet was no longer visible outside, but the ground was, and she smiled as she recognized the very familiar outlines of the Everglades passing under the wings. "Landing from the west."

"How can you tell?" Alastair lifted his own shade and peered out. "What in the hell is that?"

"The River of Grass," Dar said. "The Florida Everglades," she added. "In reality, one whomping big ass swamp."

"Ah."

The steward poked his head into the cabin. "We're about to land. Please stay in your seats until we do, and try to keep your seat belts fastened. It's not a lot of fun bouncing off the inside walls if we have to stop short."

Dar obediently clicked her seatbelt in place and tugged it snug. She was already looking forward to feeling the ground hit their tires. She flipped open her PDA, tapping it open to a new message and writing it as she heard the landing gear extend, and felt the distinctive motion as the plane moved from a nose down, to a nose up posture for landing.

"Ever wanted to learn to fly, Dar?" Alastair asked, suddenly. "One of these things?"

"No." Dar shook her head. "I'll stick to boats, thanks. You?"

"Have my pilot's license."

Dar stopped what she was doing and looked over at her boss, in real surprise. "You do?"

Alastair nodded. "Bunch of fellas and I went in on two of the little single engine putterbouts," he said. "It's a nice way to spend a Sunday, when you get tired of golf." He fastened his seat belt and folded his hands, letting them rest on one knee. "I buzzed the country club last time I flew and scared two ladies right into the lake. I'm living in fear they'll find out it was me."

Dar started laughing.

"All those years in the boardroom sure came in handy when the wife came telling me all about it." Her boss chuckled, glancing out the window as they approached the landing strip. "Well, here we go."

The plane slowed, its wings drifting to one side and the other as the edges slid down to cup the air. Outside the windows, clouds were replaced by buildings and trees, flashing by as they settled down through the atmosphere and lined up with the runway.

A shocking sound made both of them jump, and look, but it was only the Hornets breaking off and roaring past, their engines sounding like a brass thunder that rattled the interior of the cabin and made Dar's ears itch.

"Thanks for stopping by, fellas," Alastair remarked. "Good to see my tax dollars at work."

Dar finished her message and hit send, waiting until the wheels of the plane touched down with a thump and a bounce before she activated the PDA's comm link. Then she picked up her phone and opened it, dialing the first speed dial number on the list.

Home. She could almost feel the humidity and the smell of rain tinged hot air already.

KERRY BLINKED IN the thick dusty air, sucking in breath through a white mask that covered her mouth and nose. In front of her was a door hanging off its hinges, and half a wall. Past that was a mass of concrete and metal, fused into unrecognizable lumps with a scattering of cables drooping out of it.

"Shit," Mark exhaled, directing the beam of his flashlight into the wreckage.

"Well, that's a total loss," Kerry concluded. She folded her arms over her chest. "Someone just needs to confirm the inventory list for that room so I can have legal claim it against our insurance."

"I don't have nearly enough crap to replace this," Mark said. "There were at least ten racks of gear in there."

"It was just a fluke," another masked man said on her left side. "You see this corridor is pretty okay."

Kerry looked around. "I see." The hallway was broad and mostly silent, only a few ceiling panels and bits of concrete knocked out near where they were, and then nothing but long expanses of carpet and concrete walls further off. "So we were duplicating this on the other side, Danny, with a link between them?" She glanced at the man on her left.

"Yes, ma'am," Danny nodded. His arm was in a sling, but it was encased in a thick compression bandage rather than a cast. He was a fairly short man, with a gymnast's build and thick curly brown hair. "But there's nothing in it yet. Not even racks.

"Do we have runs in there from the distribution closets?" Mark asked. "They were really doing duplex? Not just runs from half to this room and half to that one with a crossover?"

Danny shook his head solemnly. "Runs from each distribution to each core room," he said "Ms. Roberts told them to, and you know whatever Ms. Roberts says..."

"Yes we know," Kerry and Mark said at the same time. "God bless Dar's forethought again." Kerry went on, with a sigh. "All right. Let's go over to the new room and get a list started." She turned and waited for Mark to precede her with his flashlight. "I'm not going to be able to count the favors I'm going to have to call in on this one, and we're nowhere near Manhattan yet."

"No shit." Mark shook his head. "I can start having everyone get their spare stuff ready to ship, but I heard from the office today they won't even let FedEx or UPS pick up."

Kerry thought about that. "Well, how do you make sure all those brown packages aren't bombs?"

"They want to blow up FedEx trucks?" Mark's brows knitted.

"Maybe they want to blow up FedEx trucks delivering last minute bouquets to Pro Player Stadium."

"Oh," Mark said. "Yeah."

Yeah. Kerry tried not to think about Dar, flying over the Atlantic in a potentially enticing to terrorist plane since it was coming so close to the U.S. She was sure the company had chartered the plane from someplace reputable, but after yesterday, anything could happen.

She didn't want anything to happen. "Just get down, and have a margarita," she muttered under her breath.

"Ma'am?" Danny leaned toward her. "Did you say something?"

"No, just clearing my throat." There was no power, and the smell of crushed concrete and burning debris brought back surprisingly strong memories of the hospital collapse. "How's the roll call doing, Danny?" Kerry asked to get her mind off that.

"We're still down three, ma'am," Danny said. "Ken Burrows, our lead punch down guy, his assistant Charlie, and Lee Chan, our WAN specialist." He wiped the dust out of his eyes with his free hand. "They were all in the section that took the hit, we think."

Kerry involuntarily glanced behind her, at the crushed room. Then she turned her head and looked resolutely ahead, picking her way carefully through the fallen ceiling debris. "And you said five people are in the hospital?"

"Yes, ma'am," Danny said. "We logged them in yellow, though. The other four we were missing turned up last night. Said they were helping people get out all day and didn't get a chance to get online," he explained. "It was really crazy here yesterday."

They moved through inner hallways, mostly empty, the air still and almost stale. Kerry felt sweat gathering under her shirt and she fought the urge to pull the mask off her face as she followed the group along one wall.

Everyone was pretty quiet. The masks muffled speech and the lack of power and air conditioning let them hear creaks and pops in the walls around them. Kerry felt anxious, and she walked a little faster even though they'd been told several times the building was safe.

Inside, it was hard to picture the destruction she'd faced on the outside of the building. The walls of the structure looked very much like some huge giant had taken a hatchet and whacked the top side of one of the five sections, cutting right through the concrete and exposing inner offices as it collapsed inward.

Chillingly bizarre. At the edge, you could see file cabinets. Chairs. The beige inevitability of computer monitors.

It felt so unreal. Just as it had when she'd been in the hospital collapse, the familiar turned strange and frightening, making her want to get past it, get out, and feel cool, fresh air again. She heard voices ahead, and she looked up and past Mark's shoulders to see a cluster of men in work clothes ahead at the junction of two hallways.

"Uh oh," Danny said. "Those are the electrical guys."

Kerry patted him on his uninjured shoulder and eased past, coming up even with Mark as they approached the crowd. There were men in fatigues mixed in with the workers, she now realized, and several others were in more formal military uniforms. "Damn."

"What?" Mark whispered. "What's wrong?"

"Wish Dar was here."

Mark eyed her wryly. "44 75 68, boss."

Kerry's brows knit, as she allowed herself to be briefly distracted. "Hex?" she finally hazarded a guess. "No, not for the reason you're thinking. She's just a lot better at relating to the guys in uniforms than I am."

"Uh huh." Mark slowed and came to a halt since the crowd was blocking the hallway. "Let's see what's up with this now." He removed his mask. "Driving me nuts."

Kerry had about enough herself. She eased the mask off and sniffed the air, relieved to smell nothing more ominous than a little dust, this far from the destruction. The rest of the crew did the same, clustering warily behind Kerry and Mark as they eased closer to listen.

"Okay, here's the plan. Everyone has their clipboard?" one of the men in uniform was saying. "You have your sectors. I need to know the power, status, ability to work in, and damage in every square inch of the four sections not involved in the crash."

He glanced up as he sensed motion and spotted Kerry and her group standing there. "Excuse me," he said, in a stern tone. "Who are you people, and what are you doing in here?"

Kerry nudged her way to the front and met his eyes. "We're from ILS."

The man looked blank.

"Those are the IT people, chief," one of the men in fatigues supplied. "The computer guys."

"Oh." The officer nodded at them. "Well, none of the computers are working."

"We know," Kerry agreed. "That's what we're here for. To get them working again." She stuck her hands in her pockets.

The officer looked at her with interest. "Okay, hang on a second." He turned to the group. "Move out, gentlemen. I expect you to report back here in four hours."

The men dispersed, easing around Kerry and her crew and moving down the hallways in groups of three or four. They led the way with flashlights, the beams flickering around the half darkened walls in an odd and disjointed rhythm.

"Now." The officer faced Kerry. "Sorry, let's start this again. I'm Billy Chaseten." He held a hand out, which Kerry gripped firmly. "You said you were from what company now?"

"ILS," Kerry said. "My name is Kerry Stuart. My team and I are here to start the process of restoring communications to the facility." She glanced at his name plate. "For starters, do you know when they're going to turn the power back on, Captain?"

"Still got people cutting the live lines into the bad section," the captain said. "They can't turn the juice on until that's secure," he added.

"You all the ones who handle the internet, and the phones and all that too?"

"That's right," Kerry said. "Our main core space was destroyed. We need to get rolling on replacing it." She smiled at the captain. He was tall, and had a handsome face under a brown buzz cut. "I know everyone's scrambling."

"That we are, and I don't want to get in your way, ma'am." The officer smiled back at her. "Anything I can do to help you?"

"Well," Kerry cleared her throat gently, "actually you can get out of our way. You're standing in front of the door to our backup core center."

The man blinked, then he turned, shining his flashlight on the big metal door he'd been leaning against. "Well, shoot. I am." He moved aside. "Sorry about that."

"I've got the keys." Danny moved forward, going to the door and fishing a set of thick silver keys from his pocket. "They hadn't even put the scan locks in yet."

The soldier sidled over closer to Kerry as Danny sorted amongst the keys. "You folks lose a lot of stuff? I was talking to the security system people and they said they had a ton of rewiring to do."

"Got it." Danny unlocked the door and opened the room, pulling the metal portal toward him and back against the wall.

The inside of the room was dimly lit with emergency lighting, and they all shuffled inside, Mark and one of the other local techs shining their flashlights around to illuminate the space.

"Well," Kerry sighed, "We lost enough equipment to fill this room." She glanced at the captain, who was still at her side. "Unfortunately."

"Ouch." The captain shook his head. "I heard my CO going on or really, going off about nothing working in the rest of the building. He know you all are here?"

"Probably not," Kerry admitted. "We...well, my team came up from Miami with our equipment truck and I...just got here from Michigan. We didn't talk to anyone first."

The captain looked at her strangely.

"We know what to do." Kerry smiled briefly. "It's not like someone had to call us to tell us there was a problem."

"Hey boss?" Mark called over. "This room wasn't near ready for occupancy. They haven't run the power, or the environ."

"Ah." Kerry removed her hands from her pockets. "Excuse me." She eased between two of the local techs and went to Mark's side. His flashlight was shining on a very un-terminated power distribution box and a set of wires hanging from the ceiling. "Oh, boy. Nothing easy here."

"They were supposed to put that stuff in next week," Danny agreed glumly. "We didn't even have storage yet, that's why we told them to hold delivery of the gear."

Damn. Kerry exhaled and took a step back, somewhat at a loss. What was that Dar was always telling her? Think out of the box?

Think out of the box. "I think this box just got slammed over our heads," she muttered. "Danny, can you take me to whoever's in charge of the building electrical?"

"Uh. Sure." Danny nodded.

"Mark, start calling in a list of PDU's and racks to APC," Kerry said. "Bring what you can in here. Let's just do what we can to start."

"Got it, boss," Mark said. "Okay guys, go get the lanterns, and get the trolleys out and unfolded. Let's get moving."

The techs trooped out. Kerry and Danny were the last ones out, and he turned to close the door and lock it behind him. The captain was still standing there, leaning against the wall.

"Ah, hey. Ms. Stuart?" The captain pushed off as she cleared the door. "Heard you say you needed to talk to the building people. Maybe I can help with that? My CO's got some push."

Kerry patted his arm. "I'll take any help I can get. C'mon with us." She motioned Danny ahead of her and they trooped off down the hallway. "Thanks for the offer, Captain."

"Call me Billy," the officer said. "All my friends do."

"Ma'am?" Danny cleared his throat. "Maybe we could invite the facilities chief to the bus for lunch?" he suggested. "He's been here all night." He peeked over at the captain. "Maybe we could all go?"

Kerry chuckled wryly. "Hungry?" she asked. "Sure. I think that's a great idea. We can meet in the bus if the chief is up for it. You're invited too, Billy."

"Sounds good to me." Billy was more than willing to go along. "Let's take a shortcut through here." He indicated a guarded hallway. "I'll stop and give my CO a heads up. I know for sure he's very interested in this whole computer thing."

"Lead on." Kerry checked her watch. "Jesus...half past one already?"

"Day's flying," Billy said. "Not like yesterday," he added. "Every minute yesterday lasted an hour."

They all sobered, as the guards opened the doors on their approach and they entered a cooler, grayer hallway, with metal doors on either side of it. Billy headed for one, his hand on the knob as Kerry's cell phone rang.

"Hang on." Kerry unclipped the phone and glanced at the caller ID, stopping and staring at it for a long moment before she hastily opened it. "Dar?"

"Hey, love of my life."

Kerry felt like she had electrical prickles heating her skin. "You guys go on. I need to take this," she told Billy and Danny. "I'll catch up with you."

"Yes ma'am." Danny went over to where the captain had paused. "That's our big boss," he explained, as they entered the office and closed the door behind them.

Kerry leaned against the wall. "Where are you?" She was glad the hall was empty. "Are you in the air?"

"Nope," Dar said. "Just landed in Miami."

Another surge of prickling across her skin. "Miami?" Kerry squealed. "Are you kidding me? You're really home? What happened to Mexico? They let you land? Did you call Gerry?"

"Long story," Dar said. "Bottom line is, we just landed at Opa Locka. I figure we've got some explaining to do to the local officials then they should let us out of here."

"Explaining?"

"Like I said, long story," Dar replied, in a wry tone. "I'm just glad to be on the ground."

Kerry felt unexpected tears stinging her eyes. "I'm glad too," she said, lowering her voice. "I feel like fifty pounds just came off my shoulders. I was worried about you."

"Back at you," her partner said. "Where are you?"

"Pentagon." Kerry sniffled and wiped her eyes.

"Bad?"

"Yeah."

"What do you need me to do?"

Kerry sighed. "Where do I start?" She tried to put her thoughts in order, squirming through the emotion with some difficulty. "Can you lean on Justin and get us gear?" she asked. "I'm trying to deal with facilities here."

"You got it," Dar said. "I know what was in that room. I'll get it out there."

"The black box thing...that was just a foul up. They were looking for something we didn't have," Kerry said. "I sent them to the Tier one's."

"Good girl."

"I want to squeeze you so hard your eyeballs pop out."

Dar started chuckling.

"I'm not kidding."

"I know. I wish I could have wangled them into letting us land in Dulles. Hang in there, hon," Dar said. "We're getting surrounded by tin soldiers. I have to go be me. I'll call you back once I'm getting a café con leche with Alastair, and we figure out the next twenty minutes of the plan."

"Okay." Kerry relaxed against the wall, smiling whole heartedly. "Love you."

"Love you too."

Kerry closed the phone, letting out a long, heartfelt sigh. Then she clipped the phone to her belt, squared her shoulders, and headed for the

CO's office. "Let's hope my lucky streak keeps hauling its ass right on down the road." She pushed the door open. "But it's going to be hard as hell to beat that."

DAR GOT UP and clipped her phone onto her front pocket, stripping off the pullover she'd worn and leaving herself in just a T-shirt. She folded the pullover and tucked it into her briefcase, as Alastair closed his own phone and sighed. "Bea pissed?"

"Relieved, actually." Alastair pulled his own briefcase over and started to gather his things. "She said at least she knows my landing here means I probably won't be dancing on some table with a bottle of tequila."

Dar paused, and glanced over her shoulder. "We could arrange for that if you really wanted to."

"Ha hah," he said. "Bea seems to think you'd be a good influence. I don't think we have any pictures in the archives of you with a flowerpot on your head."

"I'm sure you don't."

Alastair chuckled. "How's Kerry?" He watched Dar's face crease into a brief grin. "She doing all right?"

"Yeah," Dar said. "She's at the Pentagon. She needs me to take care of some things but we'd better wait to get off this tub."

"Waiting till then to call the wife, myself," her boss said. "I can hang up on Bea and not get in too much trouble."

Dar chuckled.

The steward came in and went over to the door to the cabin. "Folks, please take your seats until we get the plane fully secured here. They're going to come inside."

Dar dropped into her chair, setting her briefcase down by her feet as she tucked her passport and identification into one hand. She looked out the window, not surprised to see several military transports pulling up. "Ah. C'mon."

"What?" Alastair looked up from rooting out his passport.

"I have too much to do with too few energized brain cells to deal with pissed off officials," Dar sighed, bracing her foot up against the small desk as the steward opened the door and carefully lowered it with its attached stairs. "Alastair, just cut them a check."

Her boss chuckled and shook his head, then straightened as three men in uniform came into the plane, with machine guns pointed right at them. "Ah."

"Everyone stay where you are and don't move," the first man said, in a firm voice.

Dar took in the tense posture, and the flicking eyes, and had the sense to stay still, just watching as two of the men came down the aisle and the third slammed the steward against the wall. "Don't move,

Alastair," she said. "That's loaded and he's jacked enough to pull the trigger."

The lead soldier swung his muzzle around and pointed it at her, his face obscured behind a gas mask.

Dar met his gaze evenly. "My father taught me not to point at something unless I'm going to shoot it," she remarked. "Especially civs."

He stared at her briefly, moving the muzzle of his gun away from her, then just continued on down the aisle, moving to the back of the plane and kicking open the bathroom door.

The second man, after sweeping the area around them turned and headed for the cockpit. "Get him secured, and come with me," he instructed the third man. "They said these people are all right."

The third man hustled the steward out to hands they could see reaching in the door, then whirled and ducked through the door and headed up to the front of the plane.

"Well." Alastair folded his hands on his lap. "Ain't this nice."

"At least we're all right." Dar got out her PDA and started typing on it. "I was definitely not in the mood to be body slammed."

"You were pretty cool in front of a gun," he commented. "Not that you're not pretty cool in most situations."

"I was hoping I was talking to a pro," Dar admitted. "They really do know how to do this. Military training is not the oxymoron most people think it is."

"Ah."

The third man came back down the aisle and passed them without comment. He went to the door and motioned to someone, then he too, headed for the cockpit.

Heavy steps sounded on the stairs and two men entered, dressed in dark uniforms complete with gun belt and mace cans. They approached Alastair and Dar with very no nonsense expressions.

"Hi," Alastair greeted them. "How're you doing, fellas?" He held up his passport. "Want to start with this?"

The man in the lead did take the passport, opening it to study the contents while his companion held out his hand to Dar for hers. "Ma'am?"

Dar obliged. She watched him flip through the pages. She noticed behind him that two more soldiers had come in and were standing in the aisle, blocking her view of the front of the plane. They weren't facing toward her though. They were facing away.

Hm.

"You folks say you boarded in England?" the first man asked Alastair.

"That we did," Alastair agreed. "Little airfield in London. Nice place. Nice folks."

"Where did you expect to land?" the man asked.

"Mexico City," Dar answered.

The customs officer turned. "I didn't ask you."

Dar merely looked at him, one eyebrow lifting.

"Mexico City," Alastair spoke up, in a dry tone.

The customs officer turned back to him. "Did you know your pilot asked for a course change?"

"Sure. I told him to." Alastair leaned on his chair arm. "I didn't feel like flying into a storm and spending a couple hours losing my lunch," he added. "So yes, I knew. I asked him to fly south, and go around the storm. For some reason, that wasn't appreciated."

"No, it wasn't," the man said. "What was your business in Mexico?"

"It's the closest place I could land to Houston," Alastair said. "That's where we actually were going."

"Houston? You live there?"

"I live there," Alastair confirmed. "Our corporate offices are there."

There was a hustle of motion near the front, and Dar got a glimpse of the crew being crowded out the door, surrounded by the soldiers. She got a look at the pilot's face, and saw utter fear there. "What's going on there?" she asked, pointing at the door.

"That's not your concern ma'am." The other customs officer studied the rest of her ID. "I see you have a Florida driver's license in here." He glanced up at her. "Can I ask what that's for?"

"Driving," Dar answered. "You need one. It's the law."

The officer looked hard at her. "You need a Florida license in Texas? That's news to me. What about you, Roger?"

"News to me too," the other officer said. "Can you explain why you have a Florida license if you live in Texas?"

"I don't live in Texas." Dar was starting to find the conversation irritating. "I live in Florida, at the address on the license." She pointed at the passport. "That's why the passport was issued in Miami, too. Flying to Texas to get one would have been pointless."

"But you were going to Texas?" The man ignored her sarcasm.

"We were going to Texas because it has a country on its border we could fly into." Dar explained. "And we were trying to get home. But trust me, I would be a lot happier to be in Miami." She paused. "Where I live. At the address on the license."

"I'm not, given this conversation," Alastair said. "I'd rather have played poker with the agents in Laredo."

The first officer swung around to him. "You may think this is funny, but I can assure you it's not."

"I don't find it funny at all," Alastair shot back. "Considering you've had our names for four hours and a five second visit to Google would have identified us and the company we work for, and since we've got to now go bust our asses fixing things for the government I'd just appreciate it if you agree we are who the passports say we are and let us get on with it."

"Alastair, you're getting grumpy in your old age," Dar remarked. "C'mon, the only pressing thing we have to deal with is getting the government payroll out and bringing the systems back up for the Pentagon. I'm sure they'll understand we had to spend time with customs."

Alastair sighed again. "Bring back the fellas with the guns."

The customs officer studied Alastair's passport. "Do you have anything to declare?" he asked. "I assume they didn't get you entry cards."

"Nope, and nope," Alastair said. "Didn't even stop for a bottle of Scotch."

The second man handed her back her identification. "Ma'am, anything to declare?"

Dar took her passport and tucked it into her briefcase. "No...wait, yes," she said. "About four hundred bucks worth of stuff I got for friends before the planet crashed in on us."

The customs agent nodded somberly. "Souvenirs?" He watched Dar nod in response. "Did you bring in any tobacco, alcohol, or prohibited products?"

"No."

"Roger?" Another man stuck his head in the door. "We need you guys over here. We may have something with these pilots."

Roger handed Alastair back his passport. "Welcome home," he said, briefly. "No one wants to give you a hard time, Mr. McLean. We just have a job to do."

"I appreciate that," Alastair said, sincerely. "It's just been a very long day, and it's only half over. I'm sure yours is too," he added. "And I realize it's not our affair, but is there a problem with the fellas who flew us here?"

Roger hesitated, then shook his head. "I can't discuss that," he answered. "They're being investigated. They may be allowed to go on their way. They may not." He motioned his companion to move toward the door. "Have a good day, folks. Watch your step on the way down."

They rattled down the steps and there was a sound of engines revving outside, then silence.

Alastair looked at Dar, as a gust of hot air blew in the door. "So that's it?"

Dar got up and went to the door, peering out. The tarmac was now empty, the cars disappearing into the distance where a big hangar was abuzz with military activity. There were no other planes anywhere near them, and they were alone. "Guess so."

"Lord." Alastair sighed. He got up out of his seat and came over to where she was standing, poking his head out to look around. "Y'know Dar? I'm not getting much out of today."

"C'mon." Dar went to the back of the plane and unlatched their luggage. "Glad they didn't put this underneath. I've lost my chops for breaking into aircraft."

Her boss came over to claim his rolling bag. "Did you used to do that?" he asked curiously. "I didn't think you had a larcenous youth, Dar."

"I didn't." Dar followed him down the aisle, pulling her own bag behind her. "Just a wild one. We used to run all over the base getting into things. Personnel carriers. Old airplanes."

"Ah."

"Tanks."

They climbed down out of the airplane, awkwardly dragging the luggage behind them. Outside it was a very typical muggy Miami afternoon, and after about ten seconds Dar was direly grateful she'd stripped down to her T.

She paused, something odd niggling at her senses. The airfield was dead quiet, and there was a warm breeze that moved the muggy air and the thick foliage of the trees at the perimeter of the field. It was partly cloudy, and everything seemed normal.

"Dar?"

"Hang on." Dar turned all the way around, then slowly tipped her head back and scanned the sky. It wasn't something odd, she realized, it was something missing. "It's so quiet."

Alastair looked at the sky, then at her. "No planes?"

"No planes," she answered. "The only time before this I remember there were no planes is when Andrew hit. And it sure as hell wasn't quiet."

"Huh." Alastair shaded his eyes. "Well..."

"Yeah." Dar turned and started walking. "Where were we?"

"Tanks?" Alastair asked, as they trudged across the steamy tarmac toward the terminal.

"Tanks," she confirmed. "Ask my father. He loves to tell people how I took out the dining hall with one."

"Did you?"

"Not on purpose," Dar admitted. "I ordered a car for us."

"Are those two statements related?" Alastair asked. "We could take a cab, y'know."

"Only if you'd be amused at me knocking the driver out and taking control of the air conditioning and the radio. I lost my love for sweat and someone else's taste in music years ago."

"Well, all righty then."

"Besides, with our cab drivers the car's cheaper." Dar opened the door, standing back to let Alastair enter. The inside of the terminal was cool and empty, only a single security guard slouched in a bored posture at the entrance desk. He looked up and studied them, then went back to reading his magazine.

"Ah," Alastair mumbled. "High security."

"Guess he figures if the goon squad let us loose we're safe." Dar gave the man a brief nod. They passed the desk and exited the front of the small terminal and back out into the muggy sunshine. The drive in front was full of empty cars. Military vehicles were lined up against the curb and some pulled up randomly. "Must be using the Coast Guard base here."

"Sure." Alastair took advantage of a small bench and sat down on it, glancing at his watch. "Hope that car's fast," he said. "Or he'll end up pouring me into the back seat." He rested his elbows on his knees. "I'm too old for all this crap."

Dar took a seat on the concrete, leaning against one of the support posts that held up the seventies era concrete overhang that would, in a rainstorm, almost completely fail in protecting anyone from getting wet. She could smell newly cut grass, and the dusty pavement, and drawing a breath of warm damp air, admitted privately to herself that no matter how uncomfortable it was, it was home.

She'd been in prettier places, with better weather, and nicer scenery but there was something in her that only relaxed, only felt 'right' when she was in this air, with these colors and the distinctive tropical sunlight around her.

She wondered if Alastair felt like that too. "Were you born in Houston, Alastair?"

"About an hour north of there," Alastair replied. "Little place called Coldspring, near Lake Livingston." He glanced at her. "Why?"

"Just curious," Dar said. "You ever want to live anywhere else?"

Alastair leaned back and let his arms rest on the bench, extending his legs and crossing them at the ankles. "Y'know, I never did," he admitted. "When I was younger, I traveled a lot and saw a lot of places. I thought about moving, maybe to Colorado. It's pretty there."

"Mm."

"But I'd come back, and look around, and say, well, why move?" he continued. "Every place has its peculiar problems. Nothing is a paradise. I like Texas. I like the people, I like the attitude. It fits me."

"That's how I feel about here." Dar watched a lizard scamper down the pylon she was leaning against and regard her suspiciously. "I bitch about the traffic and the politics but it's home." She glanced at her watch, then turned and looked at the long, tree lined approach to the terminal. "Here we go."

Alastair leaned forward and spotted the car approaching. "Well that wasn't too bad, now was it?"

"No." Dar got up off the ground. "I wanted to wait until we were rolling before I started yelling at people on the phone." She studied the big Lincoln Town Car that was rapidly approaching them. "Hope they remembered the YooHoo."

"Eh?"

The driver stopped the car and got out, coming around the front of the car rapidly. "Afternoon, folks," he said. "I had a little trouble getting past the police barricade, and I don't think they want me in here so we should make a little haste." He reached for their bags, popping the trunk with his remote in his other hand.

"Police?"   Alastair frowned, handing his bag over. "Place is closed...why do they need police?"

The driver threw his bag in the trunk and grabbed Dar's. "I guess you haven't heard what's been going on here, huh? I was real surprised to get a note to pick up here, tell you that."

"No, we haven't." Dar headed for the now open back door. "We've been in the air for nine hours."

Alastair was getting in the other side as the driver slammed the trunk and trotted for the front seat. "Something going on here in Florida? More terrorist activity?" He got in and joined Dar, as the driver slid behind the wheel and threw the car into gear.   "There's not a problem here, is there?"

"Problem?" The driver turned the car in a tight U, heading back down the approach as six police cars came rolling down the opposite lane. "Lady, they're arresting people and kicking down doors right and left around town." He watched intently in the rear view mirror as he drove, turning it so he could see the police cars. "My brother works for Dade County and he just told me the guys who took over those planes lived down here."

"Here?" Alastair asked. "What the hell?" He looked at Dar. "They lived here? I thought they were saying on the news before we left this was from some group outside?"

"Who knows at this point," the driver said. "Hey, I'm Dave, by the way," he added. "You gave me an address off Brickell, right?"   He looked quickly behind him. "Guess those guys forgot about me."

"Right," Dar murmured. "This all doesn't make sense."

"Nothing's made sense since yesterday morning," Dave said. "That cooler in the back has got the drinks you asked for. They aren't very cold yet, I had to stop by Publix to get them." He glanced at them in the rearview. "How'd you folks end up landing here anyway? We heard there were no planes allowed to land. It's been real dry for us. I sure was glad to get the call. You need to go anyplace else? Want to stop and pick up some java?"

Dar met his eyes in the mirror. "Do we look like we need it?" she asked, wryly.

"Anyone flying for nine hours needs it." He neatly sidestepped the question. "You a Starbucks or Versailles kinda lady?"

"Versailles, please," Dar had to smile. "I promised my boss here a café cubano."

"You got it," the driver said. "Sit back and relax, and I'll get you right there. I figured you were local."

"Thanks." Dar did, in fact, sit back in her seat. She opened her

PDA and looked up a number. "Might as well get this started." She was about to dial, when the phone rang. "Dar Roberts," she answered it, only to have it beep for a second incoming call.

Alastair was already on the phone, waiting for it to be answered. "Does that java come in buckets?" he asked. "I think we're going to need it."

Chapter Seventeen

KERRY FELT A sense of odd déjà vu as she took her bottle of ice tea and settled down in one of the thick leather chairs in the courtesy bus. "Gentlemen, thank you very much for taking time out of your day to talk with me for a minute."

The facilities chief, an older man with a bristly gray buzz cut and a weathered face, dropped into the chair across from her with a tired grunt. "Any excuse to sit down." He glanced up as one of the bus workers approached him and offered a tray. "What's that?"

"Roast beef sandwich, sir," the young woman supplied. "And we have chips and fresh potato salad."

The chief didn't hesitate, reaching over to envelop one of the rolls in a large, callused hand. "Hand them over. First thing I had since dark of the clock this a.m."

Having supplied herself with spicy chicken, Kerry was content to watch as the military men were served, Danny and two of the other techs were already busy at the nearby counter chowing down. She opened her bottle of ice tea and sipped from it, jerking just a bit as her PDA went off. She pulled it out and opened it, unable to repress a smile when she saw the message's sender.

Hey.

We're out of the airport and heading for coffee. Did you know all hell's breaking loose down here? People getting arrested and all that?

Jet lag sucks.

We are going to the office after this. I'm working on your gear. I got two calls from clients up in New York who complained they were down and told them off. I think I scared Alastair. Some guy from the NSA called me, but hung up before he could tell me what he wanted.

Left a message for Gerry. Maybe he can get me up there tonight.

Kerry's eyes widened. "Tonight?"

"Ma'am?" The bus attendant was in front of her. "Would you like a sandwich?"

Tonight? Kerry blinked at the tray, completely distracted. "Uh...no." She held up her tea. "I'm fine thanks. I stopped and had lunch on the way here." She waited for the server to move away, and then looked down again at her PDA.

I need a good night's sleep with you wrapped around me.

"So now, what's this all about?" the chief asked, wiping his lips with a company logo napkin. "You people the computer people?"

Kerry hesitated, then closed the PDA. "Yes, we're the computer people." She fought the urge to go back to Dar's note. "But we work with a lot more than computers. We handle the systems that let you communicate with the rest of the military infrastructure, and run most of the programs that bring in information and send out things like accounting and payroll."

The chief chewed his sandwich, studying her with faded blue eyes. "So what you're saying is you're important."

Kerry shook her head. "No. You're important," she disagreed. "The people here working their tails off to get things back up and going are important. Our mission here is to help you do that."

One gray eyebrow cocked. "Good answer."

The CO, a tall, lanky man with straight, dark hair chuckled softly under his breath. "Ms. Stuart, I've been trying to get hold of your management since yesterday," he said. "You don't need to sweet talk me into pushing to get you what you need."

"Well," Kerry paused, "we had to evacuate our commercial operations center and they took the brunt of that over in Houston. I know they were slammed. I was traveling here yesterday, Dar Roberts, our CIO and our CEO Alastair McLean were in transit back from England."

"Seems like you were putting together a plan to come help us anyway," the CO said. "But then, you people always do. I hate computers," he said. "I wish I could throw the lot of them into the Potomac, but at least you make ours work."

"Most of the time." Kerry accepted the compliment with a smile. "They're machines. They break." She paused a moment. "So what I need-to bring this conversation to a point—is power in our backup core space."

"One that ain't finished yet?" the chief asked.

"Sure," Kerry replied. "We never do things the easy way."

"What's the point of that, Ms. Stuart?" the CO asked.

"Please, call me Kerry," Kerry said. She stood up and went to the side mounted white board and picked up a marker. "Your systems are laid out like this. " She quickly sketched in the five sided building and its rings, putting squares in place rooted out of her memory of Dar's planning sessions. "Each area has a wiring closet, and those closets are connected with a fiber backbone."

She glanced behind her, finding the military men watching her intently. "Eventually, everything has to come back to one place, so we can take it out of the building. In this case, for this facility, we had two central locations for redundancy."

"Ah huh," the chief said. "Remember you all bitching about all that space it took up?" He turned and looked at the CO. "Had to hear that from you for a month."

"You did," the CO agreed. "Thought it was a waste of time until I got told I didn't know my ass from a teakettle and to leave the IT stuff to the IT people."

Kerry eyed him. "Talked to Dar, huh?"

"Certainly has a smart mouth," the CO said. "I was about to kick up when she went off talking for about twenty minutes, and I have to admit to you I did not understand one single word she said. Might as well have been speaking Turkish."

"The mouth goes with the rest of her," Kerry said, in a mild tone. "She's brilliant. Sometimes she goes on for twenty minutes and I don't understand a word."

"Yes, well, I realized that when we went through the plan for the reconstruction of the wing there, and figured out if we hadn't had a spare, we'd have been in a world of hurt trying to work around that. So all's good," the CO said. "But here we are and nothing's working."

"Right." Kerry went back to the diagram. "There is no way we can quickly recover the destroyed room." She looked over at the chief. "I think you probably realize that."

The man nodded. "Find all your folks?" he asked, the tone of the conversation suddenly growing quiet, and grim.

"Not all of them," Kerry said. "We're still missing a few."

The chief studied her. "Might have been in there. Your folks were, a lot."

There was an awkward silence. Kerry folded her arms, gripping the marker in her right hand. "That had occurred to me," she said. "But I hope that's not the case. I hope they're just out of touch and we'll hear from them today."

The CO cleared his throat. "So you need power in this new space," he said. "Chief, can we do that?"

The chief chewed his sandwich thoughtfully as they waited in silence for his answer. Kerry went over to the table and got her ice tea, leaning an elbow on the counter as she gave in and opened her PDA again.

I need a good night's sleep with you wrapped around me.

"I need that too," Kerry muttered under her breath. "Maybe I can call Gerry and ask him."

"How much power you need?" the chief spoke up suddenly.

Kerry glanced over at Danny. "Do you have that handy, or do I need to get it from the master document server?"

Danny stopped in mid chew. "Uh..."

"Ah hah." Kerry went over to where her laptop was resting on the counter and unlocked it. She opened a browser and typed in an address, waiting for the page to display over the satellite link before she entered a request. "Hang on."

She glanced back at the PDA on the counter.

We're driving through little Havana now. There are a lot people on the street talking. Want some café con leche? Alastair's trying a croqueta.

"Okay." Kerry reviewed the list on the screen. "Boy, there was a lot of stuff in there." She ran the calculations. "Ten racks at sixty amps per rack." She looked up at the chief. "Six hundred amps, twenty 30 amp lines."

The chief stopped chewing and stared at her. "In that little room?"

Kerry nodded wryly. "We also need AC."

"Son of a bitch!"

"Can we do it, chief?" the CO broke in. "Who the hell cares how much it is? It's not like we have a budget for it. What does it mean a bigger cable? C'mon now, you know what's at stake here. We're blind without that equipment."

"You don't even have equipment for me to plug in there," the chief turned around and said to him. "I know it ain't here because I heard those IT people talking about it."

The CO looked over at Kerry. "What's the story with that?"

Kerry leaned against the counter. "Dar's working on it," she said. "It'll be here. Our racking vendor is already preparing a truck heading here with the framework."

The chief looked around at her. "We can do it," he said, surprisingly. "I'll have power pulled in there by tonight. That do it for you?"

"Thank you." Kerry smiled warmly at him. "Yes, that takes a big weight off my shoulders. I wouldn't want to call in the markers I'm calling in just to get everything here and not be able to use it."

There was a little silence. The military men subsided into pensive thought, and Kerry took a sip of her ice tea. She took a breath, and from one moment to the next, seeing those tired faces, they changed from a problem she had to solve to human beings she just wanted to help.

She'd never felt a kinship to the military. She'd always regarded that world with a wary respect, not understanding it or the people who chose to be a part of it. Getting a closer look had never really been in her plans, right up until her partnership with Dar.

Dar had been her window into that world, however unexpected that had been. She still wasn't sure she understood most of it, but having talked with Ceci, and knowing and loving both her and Andrew, she'd gained, at least, sympathy for those people who chose to serve.

"What else can we do?" Kerry asked, gazing at them. "Can we get something or do something for the people here? Do people need help? Access to their systems for emergencies? We're bringing up an internet hotspot here and if you send your financial people to see me, I can get them into workstations here on the bus, or in our Herndon center."

The chief leaned forward, resting his elbows on his knees. "Can you take back yesterday?"

Kerry put her tea down and went over to where he was sitting, taking a seat on the couch next to him. "I wish I could," she said. "I think every single person I know would."

The chief looked at her. "Have you ever wanted to hit someone but you ain't got a target, young lady? I just want to find the people who thought this was a great and noble thing to do and keep hitting them until their guts come out on the floor."

"We all feel that way," the CO put a hand on the chief's shoulder. Billy remained silent, eyes wide, just watching behind them. "We all lost friends. We all have people in the hospital, and families hurting." He looked at Kerry. "But we have a job to do. We have jobs that only we can do, so we can turn this around."

Kerry nodded. "We'll get you back in operation," she stated. "We'll get everything fixed. We have the resources and the will to make it happen."

The bus attendants came back in, with chocolate cupcakes and hot coffee. The scents filled the interior, and the men all looked up, visibly brightening as the women came over.

"I know you're not part of the military," the CO addressed Kerry.

"No, I'm not. But my father in law is retired Navy, and my partner grew up on a Navy base down in south Florida," Kerry replied. "I won't pretend to understand your world, but I dearly love people who are a part of it."

The CO nodded after a pause. "Good enough," he said. "We'll get you what you need, Kerry. You get us what we need."

"Hey, boss?" Mark entered, then stopped, and sniffed. "Ooo...chocolate." He looked hopefully at the trays. "Got extra?"

Kerry patted the chief's knee and stood. "What's up?"

"ETA six hours for the sat trucks," Mark said, succinctly.

"Six hours? For the trucks that came from Houston?" Kerry asked, in disbelief. "What the hell did they do, put afterburners on the pickup trucks?"

"Didn't ask," Mark said, through a mouthful of cupcake. "Dar taught me sometimes it's better not to ask stuff like that."

The CO's eyes swung from one to the other. "What does that get us?"

Mark licked his fingers. "Couple of long ass cables and it gets your critical systems back online in slow motion," he said. "But it'll work. I've got enough gear in the back of my truck to get rudimentary routing moving as long as we can bring Newark back up."

"In six hours?" The CO's eyes lit up. "You're serious?"

"Sure." Mark nodded. "They said the power generator trucks would be there by then, didn't they?"

"They did," Kerry said. "They sure did."

"Great. We'll start cabling up the gear and running the lines in," Mark said. "I'm gonna need juice though. I can't run those enterprise switches and routers off my truck battery."

The chief stood up and latched on to his arm. "C'mon boy," he said. "I got your power for you. Come with me."

The CO and Billy got up and started after them. "Let's see what we can do to help," the CO said. "Billy round up some of those carts of yours."

"Sure thing." Billy turned and waved at Kerry. "Thanks, ma'am. For everything."

"Bwf..." Mark grabbed another cupcake as he was hauled bodily out of the bus. "Later boss!"

"Later." Kerry went back to the counter and picked up her tea, her eyes flicking to the PDA waiting on the shiny surface. She sat down on the stool nearby and took a cupcake from the tray, unwrapping it as she went back to her message.

She had a lot to do. There were things to arrange, and the conference call to get back to, her mother to call, the government to worry about...but she blocked out a space of time to sit, and have her cupcake, and recover her equilibrium.

Time for a Dar break.

DAR LED THE way toward the front doors to the office, better for a handful of croquettes and a large Styrofoam cup of café con leche inside her. "Know what?" she asked suddenly. "I forgot to tell them you were with me."

Alastair chuckled deep in his throat. "As though the world isn't topsy turvy enough, I show up you mean." He glanced up at the tall building. "Weren't you going to move out of this place?"

"I still might." Dar waved at the guard as the doors slid open, releasing a blast of cold air at them. "Afternoon, gentlemen."

"Ms. Roberts!" The guard nearest the door came around the desk and approached her. "Boy are we glad to see you," he said. "They said you were overseas! We had the building management here five times already today asking for plans, and emergency authorizations."

"I bet." Dar paused and clipped her badge to her T-shirt. "Give me a half hour to get into my office upstairs then send them up to me." She spotted a few familiar faces crossing the floor, and with an effort, wrenched her brain back into place to deal with being back at the office. "C'mon."

"Right behind you." Alastair had regained his cheerful good nature. "You know, that was some damn good coffee, Dar. You were right."

Mariana had just exited the elevator. Dar put two fingers between her teeth and let out a loud whistle, making Mariana stop in her tracks and look quickly around, scanning over them twice before she stopped and stared, then let out a yelp. "AH!"

Heads turned. Dar caught the looks of recognition and then the double takes as Alastair was spotted at her side. She waited for Mariana to reach them, and was surprised almost beyond speech when the woman threw her arms around her and gave her a hug. "Uh."

"Thank god you're safe." Mariana released her. "Alastair, you too," she added hastily. "Great to see you!"

Alastair burst into laughter. "Oh hell." He chuckled. "Nice to see you to, Mari." He patted her on the shoulder. "It ain't home, but it's damn nice to be on home soil again."

"Why didn't you tell me you were back?" Mariana turned on Dar. "Does Kerry know? Of course she knows you're here."

"She knows I'm in Miami, sure," Dar said. "But she didn't know until I landed because we didn't know until we landed. We were supposed to still be in the air heading to Mexico right now." She looked up as a group of people surrounded them. "Hey o..."

Later on, she had time to reflect on the fact that her relationship with Kerry had slowly, but surely, gotten her used to physical contact and how lucky that was for her co workers.

Jose grabbed her arm, and got a hand around her back. "Shit! You're here! Jesus, thank you." He wrung her neck a little then grabbed Alastair's hand. "Boss, good to see you."

Eleanor gave her a quick hug. "No bull, Dar," she said in a quieter tone. "Glad you're safe."

More hands. More voices.

"Jefa!"

Dar turned and found herself enveloped by Maria. This at least she welcomed. "Hey Maria." She returned her admin's hug. "Glad to be back."

Maria released her. "But not for so long, no?" she asked. "I think you will go find Kerrisita and help her. She is doing so much."

"I think you're right." Dar smiled.

"Hey Dar!" Duks elbowed in and got an arm around her shoulders. "Now things are looking up," he announced, giving Alastair a pat on the shoulder. "Sir. Welcome to our banana republic."

"Thanks." Alastair patted him on the side. "Good to see you Louis." He glanced at the crowd. "I think we should move this upstairs, folks. We're blocking the lobby."

"Hey, Ms. Roberts. Welcome home." One of the ops techs timidly clasped her hand. "Boy, we're glad you're here."

Dar felt a little overwhelmed.

"All right everyone, to what our friends in England call the lifts." Alastair took charge. He handed off his bag to a willing Jose. "Someone want to get Dar's roller here? Let's go, march people. We've got work to do." He put his hand on Dar's elbow and started herding people simply by the act of moving and presenting them with the choice of moving with him or being bowled over.

Mariana fell in next to Dar. "Did you get any rest at all since yesterday? Doesn't look like it."

"Not a lot." Dar collected herself. "Cat naps. I was covering for Kerry while she was traveling."

"We know." Mari gave her a sympathetic look. "And Mark was covering for you both while he was traveling. You know, we recorded the entire global meeting place, Dar. One day, a long time from now you should sit down and listen to it."

"That was something, wasn't it?" Alastair had been listening with one ear, apparently, carrying on two other conversations with the other.

"I think it was the finest moment this company ever had," Mari said, simply.

"Well." Dar reached the elevator and got in, going to the back corner and turning to face those following her in. "Maybe we can look at it sometime. Right now, it's a drop in the bucket." She clasped her briefcase in both hands as the elevator filled, and they started up.

"Alastair, I'll have an office set up for you," Mari said. "Just give me a few minutes when we get upstairs."

"Oh please," Alastair said. "What in blazes do you think I'm going to do here? Just give me a damn phone and a chair so I can let people bitch at me." He glanced sideways at Dar. "Keep them off the back of the people who do the real stuff."

"Well..."

"Shut up, Alastair. You do plenty," Dar said, in a loud enough voice to cut through the chatter in the elevator. "Cut the BS."

Her boss looked over at her, both gray eyebrows hiking.

Dar mirrored his expression right back at him.

The doors slid open, and everyone escaped out of the car into the hallway, pouring into the gray and maroon space as they cleared the way for Dar and Alastair to exit. Dar turned and headed toward her office, and after a second, her boss followed her.

Maria also followed her. "Jefa, do you want something from the café?"

"More coffee," Dar said, "and some of the cheese pastalitos. They make them better here than at Versailles." She glanced back at Alastair. "Want coffee?"

"Sure," Alastair agreed. "I'm just going to borrow your outside office to make a call until they finish setting up whatever poobah area they've come up with for me."

Dar snorted. "You can go work in Kerry's office if you want. She's got a boxing dummy in there if you get bored." She led the way into her office, pushing the door open and feeling a sense of relief as her eyes took in the familiar surroundings.

It was all a little too much, coming back like this. It had been too long a day, too long a flight, too many strange happenings to end with this clamor of familiarity rubbing her nerves so raw.

She opened the door to her inner office and went through, slowing down a little as she took in the plate glass walls, and the view of the ocean. Her desk was clean, as always, only the fighting fish and her monitor disturbing the sleek wooden surface.

"Well, you do have a couch in here. What do ya know." Alastair poked his head in.

"Yes, I do." Dar put her briefcase down and settled into her comfortable leather chair, its cool surface chilling her back a little through her thin T-shirt.   She reached under her desk to boot her computer, giving the trackball a spin as it started up. "Okay."

"Okay." Alastair came inside. "I'll take you up on that office offer. Just tell me where it is and I'll get out of your hair.'

Dar gave him a wry look, and pointed at the back door. "Go down that hall, door at the other end is Ker's."

Alastair looked at the door, then at her. "You've got to be kidding me."

Dar lifted both hands up in sheepish acknowledgement. "You can go out in the hall, turn left, find the kitchen, and go in the front way if you want to. Don't scare her admin though."

"The two of you, I swear." Alastair chuckled, making his way to the door and passing through it.

At last it was quiet. Dar sat back then turned her chair around to face the water. The surface was ruffled with white waves, a cavalcade of boats heading up into the bay and reminding her of yet another potential issue. "First things first."

She turned back around and tapped her speaker phone, dialing Gerry's phone number. Her desktop came up, and she typed her password in, watching as her backdrop came up, along with the global meeting place login box. She logged in, and changed her status.

Login: Roberts, Dar
Location: Miami Operations Center
Role: Miami operations executive.
Status: Missing my wife.

She backspaced over the last, and typed in *good* instead, and sent the box on its way.

The phone range twice, then was answered. "General Easton's office. Can I help you?" a woman's voice answered, sounding harried and a touch out of breath.

"I'd like to speak to the General please," Dar said. "It's Dar Roberts. He's expecting my call."

"One moment."

Dar scanned the screen as the status boards popped up, and there was a soft crackle that warned her the conference bridge was starting. She lowered the volume, as the phone came off hold.

"Hello, Ms. Roberts?" The woman's voice came back. "Hold on a moment, the General is getting to his desk."

"Sure. Tell him to take his time. I bet he's as tired as I am," Dar remarked.

"You know it," the woman said, her tone warming. "Hang on, I'm transferring."

A click, and then Gerry's voice boomed over the line. "Dar? That you?"

"It's me," Dar acknowledged. "How's it going there, Gerry? I'm in Miami."

"Miami! What the hell? I thought you were heading for Houston!"

"Me too. Long story."

There was a rustling noise and the sound of a door closing, then Gerry cleared his throat. "Well, I'm damn glad to hear you're back and on the ground safe," he said. "Things are a little better today. Had everyone on my backside this morning until I got a call from the fellas trying to make sense out of this place and found out your people are already moving on everything. Wonderful!"

Dar smiled. "I sent the best I have there, Gerry," she said. "Mark Polenti, my chief tech head, and Kerry's there, too."

"Y'know, that's what my fella said," Easton agreed. "Said your people are the best. Bringing in cupcakes and fixing everything. I really appreciate that, Dar."

"Anytime," Dar said. "So does that mean you don't need my ass up there? I'm sure Ker's got it under control."

"Ah," Gerry sighed. "Well, no."

Dar knew a moment of perfectly balanced conflict, as her desire to be where Kerry was battled against her knowledge that whatever Gerry was going to ask of her was, by definition, worse than what she was dealing with there already. "What's up?"

"You someplace quiet?"

"I'm in my office," Dar said. "The only thing listening is my fish."

"Right," Gerry said. "Listen, Dar I don't usually get involved in the civilian side of things, I've got more than enough on my plate right now, you see?"

"Sure."

"Just had the head of the White House financial office in here kicking me in the kiester," Gerry said. "Thing is, they lost a lot of facility there in New York."

"I know," Dar said. "We have a lot of customers down."

"Well, you'd know more about that than I would. Anyway, you know they shut down the Stock exchanges, right?" Gerry asked. "All the financial stuff down in the south tip of Manhattan?" He paused. "You knew about that right?"

"I didn't...well, I probably heard that in all the clamor yesterday but didn't pay that much attention," Dar admitted. "There was so much going on."

"Well, don't you know? Here too," Gerry said. "Feller from the White House seemed to say I'd been derelict in my duty because I didn't know a bull from a bear." He sighed aggrievedly. "So this guy comes over here and tells me it's a national emergency about those stock houses. Have to get them back working. Government is counting on it. World stability is at stake."

Dar's brows contracted. "Granted," she said. "Having the markets down sucks but didn't they say yesterday they shut them down on purpose to stop a run on them? I thought I heard that in a sound bite."

"Pish tosh," Easton said. "I got an earful about keeping consumer confidence up and all that, but the fact is all the blinking things and doodads in there can't work because of all the damage. They don't want to admit it, trying to make everything seem like it wasn't that much. You see?"

"Ah," Dar murmured. "I see." She paused. "Why the hell are they after you for that, Gerry? Since when is the Joint Chiefs in charge of telecommunications repair?"

"We aren't," Gerry stated, with a snort. "Which is what I told this feller, and he told me he didn't want to hear my problems. He wanted me to get his solved." The general cleared is throat. "Apparently because I," he said, "know you."

"Me?"

"You," Easton confirmed. "Someone told this guy that you'd be able to fix this thing."

"Me?" Dar repeated. "Gerry, they're not customers of ours. We have nothing to do with the Exchanges. That's all private line work," she protested. "I don't even know anyone down there."

"Well, Dar, I don't know what to tell you, but this guy said I should get hold of you and make you fix this problem for the White House," Gerry said. "Now, he said I wasn't suppose to tell you it was for the White House, but I told him if he wanted me to ask you to do something you had to know why or you'd tell them to...ah..."

"Kiss my ass?" Dar exhaled. "To be honest, Gerry, I really wouldn't tell the White House that, even though I think the current occupant has the mental capacity of a woodchuck, and the personality of what it excretes."

General Easton cleared his throat.

"I just don't know what we can do about it," she went on. "Honestly. None of that is ours, and they lost so much infras..."

She paused, thinking hard.

"Dar?"

"Yeah, sorry," Dar said. "I was just considering something. So what do they want me to do, Gerry?"

A soft buzzing sound came through the phone. "Damn thing," Gerry sighed. "Dar, honest, I don't know because all that whoohah you do is just so much mumbo jumbo to me. I think you need to come up to talk to this guy. Tell him the straight facts. If you can't do it, you can't."

"Okay," Dar agreed. "Can you get me a lift? I'll do him one better, I'll bring my boss with me so we can dispense with the 'let me talk to your boss' routine right off."

"Sure can." Easton sounded pleased. "Let me get my girl on it, and she'll call you with the scoop," he said. "Listen, Dar..." He hesitated. "If you can do anything for this guy, you might want to think about it. He's big. He can cause you a lot of trouble, if you catch my drift."

"Yeah," Dar murmured. "I catch your drift."

"Good. See you tonight then," Easton said. "Later, Dar."

"Later." Dar hung up the phone, leaning back in her chair with her hands laced behind her head. "Well, shit."

The door opened, and Maria poked her head in. "Ready for café, jefa?"

Dar looked at her. "Oh yeah," she said. "I sure am." She waited for Maria to enter. "Looks like I'll be flying out to DC tonight, Maria. Any chance of getting someone to run by my place and grab another overnight bag?"

"Of course," Maria said. "Mayte has already mentioned she would be glad to do that if you needed her to, and also to bring anything Kerrisita might need. We want to do our part as well."

Dar smiled at her. "This is a hell of a time, isn't it, Maria?"

Her admin set her coffee and pastries down and came around to the back side of the desk, leaning against the edge of it as she studied Dar. "I was crying so much, all day," Maria said. "I was so scared, for everything."

"Me too," Dar replied.

"Listening to Kerrisita, she sounded so upset also," Maria said. "But you know when you came on to the big conference, and what Kerrista said? We all said the same thing, all of us. Everyone."

Dar cocked her head in puzzlement. "Oh, you mean about being glad to hear my voice."

"Si." Maria nodded.

Dar exhaled. "Now that yesterday is over though, it's hard to know where we go from here," she said. "It all just makes so little sense."

"My Tomas says the same," Maria said. "Let me leave you to get your things done. I will send Mayte over to your house right away."

"I'll call my folks and have them get a bag ready," Dar said, leaning forward and reaching for the phone. "And I guess I better warn Alastair."

"Como?"

"I think I got us into a hell of a situation."

KERRY LEANED ON the steering wheel, waiting for the lights to change so she could continue her slow progress toward the Capital. She glanced at her watch, then pulled through the intersection and continued along her way.

She checked her watch. Thirty minutes until the time she'd told her mother she'd be there, and she figured she would even have time to find her way without having to run through the hallowed halls.

"Talk to Congress." She drummed her fingers on her steering wheel. "How completely freaky that I'm considering taking a break from what I was doing all day."

She picked up a bottle of juice from the cup holder and unscrewed the top, tossing a few tablets into her mouth and washing them down as she found the cross street she was looking for and turned down it. On one side was a stately office complex, its limestone front the same sedate cream she remembered.

The first time she visited the Russell building to see her father in his offices there, she'd been about eight. Kerry remembered, dimly, the feeling of wonder as she walked at her mother's side between the trees and up into the solemnly colonnaded rotunda.

Now she took a moment as she got out of the SUV to collect herself, and tug her jacket sleeves straight before she shouldered her brief case and closed the door. The cool air puffed against her hair as she crossed the road and walked down the sidewalk, giving the armed soldiers there a brief smile.

They glanced at her, but none of them made a motion to stop her. Apparently blond haired, Midwestern looking chicks weren't on the watch list. Kerry reached the visitors entrance and went inside, not surprised to see more armed soldiers there.

She approached the visitor's desk and stood quietly, waiting her turn as two men ahead of her spoke to the receptionist. The room was quiet, several people sitting in chairs on one side, one or two people working at tables, and the soldiers looking shockingly out of place in their field uniforms with guns slung over their shoulders.

What exactly, she wondered, were the soldiers supposed to do in case someone wanted to blow themselves up in the room? Jump on them? Surely not. Shoot them? Would that stop whoever it was from pressing a button?

Technology moved faster than people. Kerry knew that better than most. If someone in the room had explosives strapped to their chests and pressed a button, there was nothing on earth that could stop that signal from reaching its target.

Security, men with guns, presupposed the threat they were guarding against could be reasoned with or intimidated. If your aim was killing yourself and everyone around you, like those pilots, how secure could you really make anything outside? Require people to go around naked and putting them through plastic explosive detectors every six feet?

Bad. Kerry exhaled. Violence never really was the answer, was it? At best, it was a temporary roll of duct tape in a series of escalating contests of humanities drive to claw its way to the top of whatever anthill they occupied. "As a species, we sure suck sometimes."

"Ma'am?" The woman behind the desk was looking at her, one eyebrow lifted.

The men had left, and Kerry apologetically stepped forward to the edge of the table. "Sorry," she murmured. "I have an appointment with

Senator Stuart."

The woman studied the book in front of her. "Your name, please?"

"Kerrison Stuart."

The receptionist glanced up and studied her face for a moment. "Yes, she's expecting you," she said, after a pause. "Sergeant, can you please escort this lady to suite 356?"

The nearest soldier came over, and gave Kerry the once over, then nodded. "Yes, ma'am," he said. "Come with me please."

Kerry obediently circled the table and followed the soldier through the back door and into the building. The hallways too, were quiet. She could hear the far off sound of typing, something that had become an alien sound in the office buildings she now frequented.

It smelled of stone, and polish, and old wood. The buildings were from the early 1900's, and you could sense the history in the place as they walked along the wide corridor.

"Ma'am?" The soldier glanced sideways at her.

"Yes?"

"Do you know where you're going?"

Kerry repressed a smile. "Yes, I do," she said.

"That's a good thing. We just got here this morning, and I don't know even where the bathroom is. The soldier confessed. "There are a lot of little rooms around here."

"There are," Kerry agreed. "It used to hold around ninety different senator's offices, but now it's only about thirty of them, since everyone needs more people, more computers, more conference tables...it's a warren with all the interconnections now."

"Yeah," the soldier said. "You know the senator? I met her this morning. Seems like a nice lady."

"She's my mother,," Kerry replied.

"Oh, wow. That's cool." The man seemed to relax a little. "My mother would come in this place and want to right off paint it some other color. Put some plants around, you know?"

Kerry chuckled. "I know," she said. "This is more or less the same color as the walls in the house I grew up in, unfortunately. I'd go for a nice teal myself."

She led the way to the doors to her mother's offices. "Well, here we are."

"Okay. Thanks for showing me," the soldier said. "You have a good day now, okay ma'am?"

"Thanks." Kerry pushed the door open, giving the man a smile. "By the way, the bathrooms are down the next corridor, on the left." She winked at him, and ducked inside the office, closing the door behind her.

The soldier digested that information, and nodded. "That was a nice woman. Wish we had more people around like that."

He turned and started back toward the reception area, whistling softly under his breath.

Kerry was spared the need to interrupt the harried looking staff when her mother came out of one of the side doors, and spotted her.

"Ah, Kerry." Cynthia Stuart looked relieved. "I'm glad you could make it over here. Please, come inside and tell me how it is over at the Pentagon."

Kerry followed her back into what she remembered had been her father's office and knew a very strange moment of skewed déjà vu as she crossed to a chair across from the desk and set her briefcase down. "How are things going here today?"

Cynthia seated herself behind the desk. "Troubling," she said. "I hardly know where to start in addressing all of these issues. I just am quite glad my home area was not one of the ones affected."

Kerry sat down. "I'm sure you heard Florida was."

Her mother blinked a little. "I had heard. Yes. That's so very strange," she said. "I remember your father saying so many times how he felt uneasy about Miami, and now to hear all this makes me wonder if he didn't somehow know more than he realized."

"I don't think that's what he had in mind," Kerry said, after a brief pause. "I always got the sense he didn't trust Miami because of all the immigrants there. Hispanics are a majority. But I never got the idea that they were part of anything dangerous to the country."

"Perhaps," her mother said. "We will have to see what it is they found there. Maybe those men felt they could blend in more there than in other places."

Kerry half shrugged. "Like any other major city," she said. "We're working with the people at the Pentagon to get their systems back up. We should have some basic connectivity back in a few hours."

"I see." Her mother folded her hands. "Or, well, let me not lie about it. I assume that means something positive since I don't really understand what it is you mean."

Kerry relaxed a trifle in her seat. "It is." She paused. "They depend on computers to exchange information with everyone and everything. Right now, they have some dialup ability with a few servers, but it's very limited. What we'll do tonight is get their main computers to talk to the rest of the world using a portable satellite truck while my team is rebuilding the pieces that were destroyed in the attack."

"I see," Cynthia said, again. "Has Dar returned? I know you were concerned about her."

Kerry's face broke into a grin. "Believe it or not, she's home in Miami," she said. "I heard from her around one thirty or so. She may be heading up here tonight. It's a big load off my shoulders, that's for sure."

"How lovely," Cynthia said, with sincere warmth. "I'm so glad she's back safely. It's impossible to believe how dangerous simple travel now is. I was talking to one of my colleagues today about it, and he's terribly worried about tourism, and how that will affect the economy."

Kerry blinked. "Because people will be afraid to fly?"

"Yes," her mother nodded. "You may not realize it, but many of our airlines are on the borderline in terms of being profitable. This sort of thing devastates them. It's a domino also, as so many state economies depend on tourism, you know."

"Like Florida's." Kerry nodded. "Maybe people will just start staying closer to home. Travel in a car." Her brows twitched. "I always wondered what that was like. The longest car trip I've made is from Miami to Orlando."

Her mother looked thoughtful. "We never did have time for that as a family," she allowed. "I think I would have enjoyed driving through the Grand Canyon area. It's so beautiful."

"It's on our list too."

"Well, at any rate," Cynthia sighed. "Several of the intelligence committee would like to meet up with us in the caucus room at four. Does that suit you?" She watched Kerry's face carefully. "It shouldn't take more than perhaps an hour, and then I thought we could have some dinner."

"Sure," Kerry agreed readily. "That's fine by me. I was actually grateful for a reason to get out from under my staff at the Pentagon and let them do their jobs. When I'm around they tend to hover." She smiled briefly. "And really, there wasn't much for me to do there once I got the facilities straightened out and arranged for power and air conditioning."

"Excellent," her mother said.

"Senator?" One of the aides stuck their head in the door, and paused as they spotted Kerry. "Oh, hello there."

"Hi." Kerry smiled at the aide, the older man who'd been with them the night before. "How are you doing?"

"Much better for not having slept in the car, thanks." The aide briefly smiled. "Senator, they've confirmed it. It was the White House and Air Force One that was targeted. No doubt at all."

"Goodness." The senator frowned. "Then that last plane in Pennsylvania, it was headed there?"

"They think so, yes." The aide nodded. "I'm not sure how they were going to target Air Force One, but it was flying all over the place yesterday so..." He shrugged, and ducked back out.

"Thank goodness that came to nothing," Cynthia said. "What a horrible thing this is. So many people hurt. So many people killed." She looked up as her phone rang then glanced at Kerry. "Excuse me, Kerry. I have to take this." She picked up the phone. "Hello?"

"Sure." Kerry checked her PDA, gratified to find a note from Dar waiting for her like the fudge at the bottom of a sundae. She leaned on one arm of the chair and opened the note, half listening to her mother's end of the conversation.

Hey babe.

Kerry smiled, hearing Dar's voice saying the salutation. That was a recent development too.

I'm sitting here at my desk trying to get over being hugged by Eleanor.

Kerry stopped reading, her eyes going wide. She leaned closer to the PDA and reread the line, not quite able to believe what she was seeing. "Huh?"

"I'm sorry. Did you say something, Kerry?" her mother asked, putting her hand over the receiver.

"Uh?" Kerry looked up. "No, sorry. I was just reading something here." She indicated the PDA. "Status report from Dar."

"Ah, good." Cynthia went back to the phone. "Edgar, I'm sure you're concerned, and I know we have a somewhat large community of...well, yes, I agree it's possible. People are very upset."

Kerry wrenched her eyes back to the PDA.

I definitely have to head up there. I talked to Gerry, and I need to fill you in, but I'd rather do it in person.

Me too, Kerry agreed readily. I don't frankly care why he wants you up here, matter of fact. They could want us to light the White House with double redundant tin cans and strings and I wouldn't care.

So I'm waiting to hear from Gerry's secretary about flights. I'll drop you a note or call you when I find out anything. Alastair's got everyone in a twitter–he's working out of your office.

Kerry stopped again. My office? She ran quickly over what she'd left on her desk, relaxing when she remembered cleaning it off before she'd traveled. "They couldn't find him an office in that mausoleum?" she muttered. "Sheesh."

Mari wanted to get him space, but I told him he could work out of there and punch your dummy if he got frustrated.

Oh. Kerry scratched her nose. "Hope he likes having you looking back at him, sweetie. That's a big picture of you on my desk."

Anyway. I hope things are settling out there for you. I'd rather not spend the night configuring routers again.

Nope. Kerry could think of much better things to spend the night doing.

I'm going to go grab a sandwich. My body's all screwed up from the damn time change.

Later DD.

"Well, thanks for keeping me informed, Edgar," Cynthia sighed. "Please tell the chief to keep his eyes out for anything. I understand how people feel, but we have to uphold the law." She listened and put the phone back in its cradle. "Well. That's worrying."

"What's up?" Kerry gazed across the desk.

"You know, there are quite some numbers of Muslims that live in Michigan," her mother said. "Edgar Braces, one of the commissioners in Dearborn, is afraid there might be some repercussions against them."

"Ah," Kerry grunted. "I hope people don't react like that."

"I hope so too," Cynthia said. "But you know anger makes people so unreasonable sometimes."

How true that was. Kerry felt a sting of possibly unintended reproach in the words. She decided the retort that was in the back of her throat wasn't appropriate and her mother didn't deserve to hear it. She was being as gracious as Kerry had ever seen her, and she, herself had the inner grace to feel a little abashed for her previous behavior. "It kind of proves the theory though, that violence usually breeds nothing but more violence, doesn't it?"

Cynthia nodded. "We learn from our Lord Jesus that we must turn the other cheek, and love our neighbor, but sometimes I think that lesson stops when our neighbor does not share our values, or our faith, or our history." She studied her hands. "At times, it doesn't even extend to our families."

"Sometimes it doesn't." Kerry gazed back at her evenly. "It doesn't even take much of a difference."

Her mother's face wrinkled a little then she nodded. "Very true." She looked at her watch. "It's time to go down to the caucus room. Are you ready?"

"As I will ever be." Kerry closed her PDA and tucked it into her briefcase. "Let's go." She stood up and locked the tab on the case. "Okay to leave this here?"

Cynthia paused in the act of standing up. "Of course," she said. "We won't be long." She gestured toward the door, and followed Kerry. "Did you have something in mind that you would like for dinner?"

"How do you feel about sushi?"

"Sushi," Cynthia murmured. "I suppose I could try that. It certainly can't be any worse than the Samoan cultural dinner I attended last month."

Chapter Eighteen

ALASTAIR TOOK A moment to stroll around his borrowed office space. The room was neat, but he noticed at once that there were more personal items in it than there were in Dar's. Certificates on the walls, for one thing. He examined them.

Dar most likely had the same, and probably more, but he decided she was so secure in her technical reputation she found no use for the things as wall hangings. Kerry hadn't been at it as long, so she probably felt she had something to prove.

Both attitudes worked, he decided. He moved along to the front of the office, pausing to study the full size boxing dummy complete with what were obviously used gloves. Was it something he expected to find in a vice president's office?

Probably not. He turned and wandered back to the desk, pulling the chair out and taking a seat in it. The first thing he noticed was the pictures near the monitor. One big one of Dar, another of her and Kerry together, and one of Dar's parents with a small one next to it of the dog.

Not very different at all from his own desk. Alastair tapped his thumbs together. Then he pressed the speakerphone's button and dialed the extension to his office in Houston.

"Alastair McLean's office."

"Who the hell's that?" Alastair inquired. "Some old crackpot?"

Bea chuckled. "Hello, boss," she said. "Where are you now?"

"Caribbean Hell," Alastair answered. "I just got introduced to a demon's brew of coffee and sugar they suck down here by the gallon and my eyeballs are bouncing off the walls."

"Well that explains a lot about Dar," Bea said. "I just got off the phone with John Peter at travel, and he said he heard they'll let planes start flying again tomorrow. You want me to book you home?"

Alastair exhaled. "See what you can arrange," he said. "I've got a feeling I'm not going to make it back there before I have to go talk to some double breasted pair of wingtips in Washington, but it pays to be prepared."

"Will do," Bea said. "How's Dar?"

"Typically Dar," her boss said. "Y'know though, I'm glad I got to travel with her for a few days. I've come to the conclusion I think I like her," he added. "As a person, I mean, not as my top ass coverer."

"You're deciding this now?" his admin asked, in a puzzled tone. "I always thought you liked Dar."

"I always liked Dar Roberts, my often pain in the ass but frequently brilliant beyond belief employee," Alastair clarified. "I didn't really know Dar the karate expert who does handstands on airplanes for fun."

"Ahh."

"She's neat."

Bea started laughing. "Oh, Alastair."

Alastair chuckled along with her. "What a stinking damned mess this all is," he said, after a moment. "I have to say, though, Bea, I honestly couldn't ask for a better response than we had from everyone in the company. Across the board."

"Absolutely," Bea agreed. "Jacques was just here, and he was saying the same thing. Horrific situation, absolutely, but we did the right things so far."

"Yup." Alastair glanced up as he heard someone coming down the back hallway. "Hang on, I think I'll know in a minute if you can book those flights or not."

A moment later, the door opened and Dar's tall form eased inside. She had a look on her face that Alastair had come to characterize as *here comes trouble.* "Hi there. Bea's on the line."

"Hi Bea," Dar responded promptly. "How are you?"

"I've had better weeks, Paladar," Bea said. "I'm sure you have too."

"Ain't that the truth," Dar sighed. "Alastair, how do you feel about ending up in Washington tonight? Gerry's offering a flight for us. I got hold of him."

"Yeah?" Alastair's brows twitched. "What's the scoop?"

Dar sat down in one of Kerry's visitors chairs. "It's...at first I thought he needed to pressure me to get the systems back up there, but he said he's been in touch with the folks on the ground and he's very happy with our response."

Alastair smiled. "That's what I like to hear." He watched Dar's face, its sharp planes twitching into a wry acknowledgement. "But?"

"But," Dar repeated. "The loss of facility down in the tip of Manhattan has knocked out the financial sector."

"Well, sure."

"They seem to think we can fix that," Dar said. "I explained to him that it's not our piece of business. We don't deal with Wall Street, that's all private service."

"Hm." Alastair looked thoughtful. "No, it's not our piece of business," he agreed. "Yet."

Dar tilted her head in acknowledgement of the unspoken words. "The government people put pressure on Gerry to get me involved, because they've got some idea I can do a fast fix, and that's their interest. They don't much care, I got the feeling, of whose business that really is, they just need it taken care of because they need to open the markets."

"Ahh." Her boss nodded sagely. "I was wondering about that. I know they closed the indexes with some mention of market stability, but knowing where they are...yes, I see their point. They can't let the bastards know they hit us that hard in the monetary groin." He nodded.

"Get in there, Dar. That's not only important to them, it's also important to us. Our liquidity is tied up in those markets."

Dar gave him a look. "Gee, thanks." She groaned. "What in the hell do you expect me to do, go to New York and start running balls of twine and tin cans? Alastair, that's a lot of destruction in someplace we usually have to unearth hundred year old conduit to run through and have thirty seven pissed off unions to deal with."

"And?" Alastair inquired. "We lost a lot of facility there too, Dar. You were going to have to have people in there fixing things anyway. This is just one more tick on the task list. Call AT&T and Verizon, find out what their plan is, you know the drill."

"I know the drill," Dar said. "So back to my question. You ready to fly up and talk to the White House about all this?"

Alastair leaned back and folded his arms across his chest. "Unlooked for, Dar, and I hate to sound so mercenary given the circumstances, but this a first class opportunity for us. Of course I'll head up there with you. Are you kidding?"

Dar nodded. "Okay. I told Gerry you would," she acknowledged. "I'm waiting to hear back from his people on the pick up details."

"Great." Her boss seemed quite pleased. "Bea, can you write up something about this just to keep the board informed?"

"Absolutely," Bea responded. "So I won't bother trying to book you a flight then, I guess. You going to break the news to your wife or you want me to?"

"How big of a chicken do you think I am?" Alastair spluttered. "Good grief!"

Dar started laughing.

"Stop that." Alastair pointed at her. "You'd be a basket case if you had to tell Kerry you weren't coming up there and you know it."

Dar blushed visibly, but kept laughing.

"Pah." Her boss finally chuckled too. "I'll call her, Bea. I think she suspected it would end this way, after I told her about the Pentagon," he said. "I think I'll have to end up holding the fort there while our dynamic duo here go take on the real work."

"Dar, I have an ear in to the global conference," Bea said. "It's getting a little hectic in there. You might need to drop in–they're asking for Miami ops and I don't think Mark's on. His representative is getting squashed."

Dar got up. "Will do," she said. "I'll leave you to beg for your forgiveness in private." She sauntered over to the door and disappeared through it as her boss searched for something to throw at her. "Forget it." She stuck her head back inside the office. "Kerry doesn't leave trash around...whoa!"

A rubber ball bounced off the wall, deflected by a rapid motion of Dar's hand. "Watch it. I have darts in my office." She warned, pulling her head back in and closing the door.

Alastair chuckled then sighed. "Oh boy," he said. "I wasn't really ready to go up and duke it out with the White House this week. Bea, do me a favor and fill Ham in, will ya, while I call my wife"

"Sure," Bea said. "You tell Dar to take care of you, okay? No stabbing you with darts."

"With the amount of coffee I've had so far, I'd probably be better off with a pair of darts in my ass," her boss informed her. "Call you back, Bea."

"Will do, boss. Talk to you soon."

DAR DROPPED BACK into her seat, and gave her trackball a spin. She barely had a moment to review the information on the screen when her phone buzzed. "Yes, Maria?"

"Jefa, I have your papa on the phone for you. Line uno."

Dar pressed the key. "Hey Dad."

"Lo there, Dar." Her father's deep voice arose from the speaker. "That little girl helper of Kerry's just done left here."

"That was fast," Dar said. "Thanks for pulling a bag together for me. I'm waiting to hear back from Gerry."

"Don't they need you two in this here office?" Andy Roberts asked. "Seems like you'd be more use here then messing with those crazy people up north."

Dar leaned on her elbows, regarding the phone with some puzzled bemusement. "Well," she said. "I'm sure Kerry would much rather be here than in Washington, and I'd rather not get on a military transport when I've been up for what feels like three days but we don't really have a lot of choice."

"Why not?"

"Because it's our job, Dad."

"Silly ass company."

Dar chuckled a little. "Hey, the White House is calling for me, " she said. "What I am I supposed to say, no, I'd rather go lay in the sun with my partner?"

Andrew sighed. "World's just gone nuts," he said. "Ah just heard on the television that some of them people who took them planes down got trained to fly here."

"Here?" Dar asked. "In the states?"

"Here in this here town," her father corrected her. "They arrested some folks, and rousted a bunch more and they ain't finished yet."

Dar scanned the news ticker, seeing the confirmation there. "Crap," she muttered. "Like we aren't called a banana republic already."

"Anyhow," Andy said. "You kids be careful with them govmint people. Worse than alligators sometimes. Don't let Gerry get you into nothing, Dar. He candy assed his way out of that last damned mess we did get into."

Dar had to privately admit that was true. "I know," she said. "I don't think this really involves Gerry though, Dad. He was just passing along the message. I'm taking my boss with me, so we should be okay."

"That Alastair feller?

"Yeah," she said. "And our corporate lawyer is going to be up there too."

"That coon ass?"

Dar snorted, and started laughing. She covered her mouth to stifle it. "Ah...yes." She cleared her throat. "Hamilton is not that backwoods, Dad. He's lived in Boston for years."

"Coon ass," Andrew grumbled.

The speaker buzzed a little. "Miami exec, this is Newark Earth."

"Hang on Dad." Dar opened her mic. "Go ahead Newark. Did you get cell back?"

"For the moment, Miami–just wanted to let you know the trucks just got here from APC. They're setting up now to generate some power for us. We just sent some of the ops staff out to get...uh..supplies."

"Get them an entire barbeque with beer on me," Dar replied. "We have a dependency on your birds coming live for the uplink at the Pentagon," she said. "When that happens, that traffic takes priority. Tell everyone else to contact me if they have a problem with that."

"Yes ma'am!" The voice sounded exhaustedly ecstatic. "I sure will tell them that."

Dar clicked off. "So anyway, Dad," she said. "My plan is to get everything squared away, get the teams working, and then get my and Kerry's ass back here and out of it. You get too close if you're on the ground sometimes."

"Good girl," Andrew said. "Too damned easy to get sucked in. Had me a call from some old buddies before all hopped up and pissed. All'em off telling them to just sit and wait for the arm waving to settle down some."

Dar studied the phone somberly. "This isn't going to end here."

"Naw," her father grunted. "Ain't going to end no where, long as folks got what other folks want and everybody hates everybody." He paused. "Politics fight."

"True," Dar murmured. "There aren't any real winners anywhere in this."

"Ain't my fight," Andrew stated. "Got my fill the last time. Nobody damned learned nothing out of that and a lot of good people ended up losing from it." He sounded pissed off. "Jackasses."

"You tell Mom that?"

"Woman has been listening to me holler about it since dark," her father said.

"Yes," Ceci's voice broke in from the background. "It's nice not to be the anti-government radical in the family for twenty minutes. Novel experience. I'm enjoying it a lot."

Dar laughed softly. "I bet." She laced her fingers together and studied them. "Hey Dad?"

"Yeap?"

"Want to come with me?"

There was a slight pause. "What in the hell do you think I am on this damn phone for?" Andrew queried. "That button down feller and that coon ass ain't going to do squat with them people."

"Okay," Dar smiled. "I'll let them know, and call you when the arrangements are done."

"Thank you, rugrat."

"I love you too, Dad," Dar replied. "See you soon." She hung up the phone and considered her decision, then after a minute she nodded. "Yeah," she said. "Another pair of strong hands never hurts." She went back to the conference call, turning up the volume a little as she let herself absorb the flickering information. "Never hurts."

KERRY WAS CONSCIOUS of the eyes on her as she entered the caucus room, a step or two behind her mother. The last time she'd seen some of these men and women, she realized, was at her father's hearing. A few, at her father's funeral reception.

She resisted the urge to fuss with her hair and merely followed her mother across the floor to one of the desks, letting her hands rest on the back of the chair behind it as the room started to fill with harried, upset, and tired looking people.

She sat down and rested her forearms on the table, having a vague memory of her father showing her this room, impressing on her the history behind it. The investigation of the sinking of the Titanic had been held in this room, for instance, along with Watergate to put an alpha and an omega on the room's dignity.

She tried to imagine what it would have been like to stand in a corner, and listen to men in handlebar moustaches and top hats argue about icebergs and lifeboats in a matter where the vessel was British and the seas international.

The senators were still gathering. Her mother wandered over to talk to one of the newcomers and she took a moment to lean back in her chair and stretch, easing her shoulders back and popping them into place to relieve the stress.

Long day. Kerry exhaled, wishing her sleep had been better. Her eyes felt sore around the edges, and she blinked, rubbing them as she straightened up and rested her elbows on the table again. She checked her watch, wishing the session was already over so she could hurry the evening along, get past dinner, and then with any luck end her day in Dar's arms.

Just the thought made her eyes sting just a bit more. She glanced down at the table, rubbing her thumb over the lightly scarred wooden surface that reminded her faintly of the old pews in the church she'd grown up going to.

"Ms. Stuart?"

Kerry looked up, to find an older woman standing in front of the table where she was seated. "Yes?" she responded politely.

"Alicia Woodsworth." The woman extended a hand. "I'm Senator Marco's security analyst. Can I have a word with you before we start?"

"Sure." Kerry indicated a chair nearby. "I just hope I'm not going to have to say all this more than once. It's been a long day," she cautioned, in a mild tone. "I'll extend the courtesy to you though, since the Senator's from my state."

Alicia perched on the edge of the next table instead of taking a chair. She was a ginger haired woman with an athletic frame, a bit taller than Kerry was. "Thanks," she said. "I understand, and I'll be brief." She paused. "That's right. You do live in Florida, don't you?"

"I do." Kerry nodded. "Wish I was there right now, in fact." She studied her unexpected inquisitor, deciding her often off kilter gaydar was possibly accurate this time and she was in good family company. "But I'm sure everyone feels that way."

The woman nodded. "I'm sure the Senator does," she commented. "He was scheduled to fly home to attend his daughter's quinces this coming weekend." She cleared her throat. "Anyway." She folded her hands. "I'll leave the why and how and when to my boss's esteemed colleagues. My question for you is this."

Quinces. Kerry felt her attention drift a little, the word bringing back the memory of her and Dar attending Maria's daughter's quinces, there in the heart of conservative Little Havana surrounded by the scent of saffron and mint and the buzz of passionate Latin speech. "Boy I'd love a Mojito right now."

"So given that...excuse me?" Alicia paused and stared at her. "Did you say something?"

"Just clearing my throat." Kerry rested her chin on her fist. "Go on."

"As I was saying, given that your company is so integral to national security, what security processes do you have in place to keep terrorists from getting a job with you?" she asked. "That's my concern. Especially after what's been going on down in Miami."

"Well." Kerry leaned back and propped her knee up against the table, her peripheral vision watching the room fill behind them. "I don't think there's really a way to prevent that, honestly," she admitted. "How do you filter for someone who did what those men did?"

"They didn't come from Idaho."

Kerry studied her face. "We're an international company," she stated. "Most of our employees don't come from Idaho. I don't come from Idaho." She considered. "We run a reasonable battery of background checks. Our staff that works in secure facilities have to undergo security clearance processes."

"Would you have hired one of those men who piloted those planes?"

Pointless question. "If they were a skilled IT worker with no criminal background, they filled a job need and could legally work wherever they were applying, we might," Kerry said. "I don't think any company can say differently. Heck, I don't think the military can say differently."

"We have to do something," Alicia said. "We have to protect ourselves from these people. That's the trouble down in Miami. That's why they hid down there. Too many people from other places." She frowned, glancing around as the senators started to take seats. "I can't say that to my boss. But you understand."

Kerry's pale green eyes narrowed a little. She straightened up in her chair, her body coiling up a little as she brought her feet under her.

A man walked to the dais in the front and knocked a wooden gavel against it. "Ladies and gentlemen, please sit. This is an informal session, but given the circumstances we should keep it a short one."

Alicia stood up, and nodded slightly at Kerry. "Later then. Thanks." She walked over to where Alejandro Marcos was settling himself down, and bent over him, talking in a low voice.

"Good heavens, Kerry." Her mother was back, taking the chair next to her. "I wasn't expecting so many people to still be here. They must have gotten tied up in committee."

"Mm," her daughter grunted. "Just my luck."

Cynthia gave her a half nervous look. "I'm sure it won't be that bad," he said. "Really, it's just a few questions."

"At father's hearing, they just had a few questions." Kerry pronounced the words carefully. "That ended up with me escaping in a cab from a mob."

Her mother didn't say anything.

Kerry laced her fingers together and rested her chin against them. She didn't really feel that intimidated, somewhat to her surprise. She was more annoyed to have to face questioning about a company she knew was performing as well as anyone had any reason to expect.

"All right." A tall, distinguished looking man stepped to the dais. He had gray hair and an impeccably cut suit, He glanced over at Kerry for a long moment before he donned a pair of reading glasses and studied the contents of a folder he opened.

Alan Markhaus. Kerry drew in a little breath, remembering him from numerous visits in her younger years. An ally of her fathers, and always a welcome guest to her parents. Son of a Presbyterian minister she recalled, the senior senator from Minnesota and as conservative as they came.

Great. Kerry sighed silently, and waited, hoping her father's old friend would keep his questions to the emergency at hand.

"Let me start off then." The Senator removed his glasses. "Thank you all for attending. I know we're all tired, and I hope this won't take long." He waited for the murmuring to die down. "Based on the information we received from my esteemed colleague from Michigan..." He gave Cynthia a nod. "I thought it would be a good idea for us to get some clarification before things started running away from us again."

Several of the group nodded.

Kerry stayed where she was, aware of the eyes watching her. She was conscious of her own breathing, a little faster than normal and the uneasy knot in her gut as she sensed the edginess in the room. "Now I really wish I had that Mojito."

"Kerry?" Her mother leaned closer. "What was that?"

"Just clearing my throat." Kerry lowered her hands and folded them. "Wish I'd brought my briefcase."

"Ms. Stuart." Senator Markhaus half turned to face her. "It's come to our attention that during the crisis yesterday, when attacks were being made in various places, that you had a good deal of information, immediate information, as things were happening." He paused and waited.

"Yes, I did," Kerry answered.

The Senator waited, but when it was obvious nothing more was coming, he glanced back at his notes. "It's been suggested that you had more accurate information than we were provided." He returned his eyes to her. "Is that true?"

"I have no idea," Kerry replied. "I don't know what you were being told."

Markhaus nodded briefly. "Fair enough," he commented. "Suppose you tell us then, what your experience was, and how this information was provided to you."

Kerry stood up, always more comfortable standing when she had to address others. Part of that, she suspected, was her relatively short stature, but she also found it easier to project her voice that way. "Certainly."

Chairs shifted and she waited for everyone to turn to face her. She took a moment to collect her thoughts then returned the gazes evenly. "It's fairly simple," she said. "Let me give you some background on what my company does, however, so you will all understand the context of the information we gathered."

She stepped around the table and put her fingertips together in front of her, putting out of her mind her history with some of the people in the room not the least of which was her mother. "ILS has been contracted by a number of government agencies, including the military services, the general accounting office, the logistics office, among others to provide information technology services."

"What does that actually mean?" an older woman asked. "Information technology services?"

"It depends," Kerry backtracked. "We provide a wide range of services ranging from onsite help desks to programming, to network management." She paused, but the woman didn't speak up again. "We also manage a wide area network that carries most of the data between government agencies, and from the government and military to the public internet."

"What kind of data?" Markhaus asked. "Confidential data?"

"Again, it depends," Kerry said. "A large percentage of the data we carry is confidential at the least, and up to top secret encrypted on the other end of the scale. Accounting traffic. Payroll for the civil service. Command and control data streams for the armed forces."

She could see eyeballs starting to roll back in some heads. "In any case," she said. "We do a lot of work for the country. We have a presence in most military bases, in the Pentagon, at Cheyenne Mountain, and we maintain a good percentage of the computers all of our tax dollars pay for."

"Incredible. One company?" The woman turned toward Markhaus. "How was this allowed?"

Markhaus merely looked at Kerry, raising his eyebrows.

"It's called the free market," Kerry dryly informed her. "The government sends requests for pricing. We bid on them. So do a number of other companies."

"Ms. Stuart," Markhaus said. "Let's get off the subject of contracts. I am sure this is interesting to my colleagues, but frankly, I know all about your company's portfolio so please move on to the information we asked."

Kerry studied him for a moment. "I'm sure you are aware," she said, with a faint smile. "In any case, during the attacks yesterday we instituted a process we have for crisis management that involves the widespread communication of all of our resources."

She walked toward the dais. "One of the components of this process is the rapid collection of observations, information, and statistics between all parts of our company."

"But how did you get the information?" the woman asked. "That's what I am interested in. I understand passing it among yourselves, though I have to question the security around that."

"Boots on the ground," Kerry replied, in a mild tone. "The information comes from the people who were there. It doesn't take a rocket scientist to describe what you're seeing with your own eyes. We had people in the Pentagon when that plane hit. We had people handling data centers who were affected by the buildings collapsing. We handle the telecommunications for the airlines so of course we knew what was going on." She lifted her hands a little and let them drop. "We were in the middle of all of it. When the planes were rerouted to Canada, and they needed extra bandwidth to send reports and let people call home...we get that request."

A soft buzz of conversation followed her statement. Kerry watched the faces opposite her carefully, seeing surprise, doubt, suspicion, and boredom facing her. "I get that request," she clarified. "We spent most of the day dog paddling like a Chihuahua on Cuban coffee trying to keep things going."

"Who did you inform of all this?" a man asked.

"Inside our company? Everyone," Kerry said.

"In the government," the man said. "Who knew what you were doing?"

"No one," Kerry replied. "That's not what we're paid for. We get paid to know what to do and do it."

"What?" Another man stood up. "No wonder no one could tell us what was going on. How could you work in a vacuum like that?"

"There was no vacuum." Kerry felt her body tense, as she reacted to the rising emotion in the room.

"You were meddling in the government during a disaster!" The woman stood up, clearly outraged. "What do you mean, you didn't tell anyone what was going on?"

Cynthia stood as well. "Now, please," ahe said. "I did not ask..."

"Oh shut up!" the man said. "We know where your part is..."

"HEY!" Kerry startled even herself, as a loud bark erupted from her chest. She took a step toward the man as he whirled to face her. "Keep a civil tongue in your head to my mother." She glared at him. "Or you can take your questions and shove them up your ass."

There was a moment of utter, total silence after her yell's echoes faded.

"Sit down!" Kerry followed that up with another bark. "Who in the hell do you people think you are to be questioning me?" She felt the anger surging through her, making her vision lose a little color and bringing a flush to her skin. "Of course we didn't tell anyone. Why should we? What in the hell use would that have been? No one had any control over what was happening, least of all the people in this room."

"Ms. Stuart," Markhaus said. "Please recall where you are."

"I know where I am," Kerry retorted.

"Then please act like it," the Senator said. "We're due respect. I know you were raised knowing that."

Kerry turned her head and looked at him. She put her hands on her hips. "Someone once told me," she said. "Those who can, do. Those who can't, become consultants. Those who have no clue at all run for Congress."

Markhaus' lips twitched, his eyes narrowing a little.

"I can, and I do," Kerry said. "If you people did not have proper information from your regular channels, take that up with them. Don't stand here asking me why I didn't stop what I was doing to send updates to anyone." She spoke slowly and forcefully. "That is what my customers, who happen to include the government, pay me for."

Markhaus studied her, as the rest of the room shifted angrily. Uncomfortably. "So let me understand," he said. "All these people calling, all this chaos going on. People needing information, needing whatever it is...what did you call it, bandwidth?"

Kerry nodded.

"Who decides what takes priority?" the woman asked. "I know my offices were down. Why weren't they considered?"

"I make those decisions," Kerry stated. "Based on a set of priorities we catalog and adjust to fit the circumstances."

"You?" Markhaus asked.

"Me." Kerry's green eyes took on just a hint of wry amusement. "Now, let's not get too dramatic about it. We're a very large company. We have a very large number of contracts and customers and worldwide resources. We handle minor emergencies all the time. We plan for this." She paused. "We know what the priorities are."

"I am very disturbed." Cynthia Stuart came out from behind the table and joined Kerry. "Kerrison and her colleagues performed amazingly yesterday. I heard quite some parts of what they were doing. They deserve our thanks not this horrific inquisition."

"Cynthia, we just..." Markhaus waved a hand. "Please."

"Please nothing." Kerry's mother frowned at him. "I am sorry I asked Kerrison to appear here. I am even sorrier that I confided how competent her staff was yesterday. You make me very ashamed, as though you asked me to do this so you could take out your frustrations, our frustrations, on my daughter."

"Maybe we did," Markhaus agreed. "Welcome to the Hill." He didn't look apologetic at all. "You're damn right I'm frustrated. Standing up in front of the rest of the world with my pants around my ankles makes me that way."

"Then why not take that out on someone who deserves it?" Cynthia asked. "It seems to me that we have spent the day in ridiculous debate about how terrible this was, and we have not even discussed the fact that someone allowed it to happen."

Go Mom. Kerry eyed her mother with wry surprise.

Markhaus grunted, and shook his head.

"The question is," the woman next to her spoke up, but in a quieter tone. "Why did they know so much, and no one else seemed to?" She eyed Kerry briefly. "I didn't mean to be rude."

Kerry altered her body posture, removing her hands from her hips and sticking them in her pockets instead. "Well," she said. "It's called Information Technology for a reason. Knowing what's going on is what my business is. We have a good communication plan, we all speak the same language, and we're used to passing data to each other without the constraints of different agencies, different politics, or different chains of command."

Markhaus grunted. "Probably got a point there," he admitted. "I just heard the police and firemen in Manhattan couldn't even talk to each other because their radios were incompatible."

Everyone got quiet again.

"Did you hear, on CNN earlier, those sounds?" the woman asked. "All those chirps, from the firefighter's pagers they said."

Kerry let her eyes drop to the ground, as the silence lengthened after that. She jerked a little then when her cell phone buzzed softly, and she looked up in apology before she removed it form her belt. "I'm sorry, excuse me."

Mark's cell phone. "Hey." Kerry kept her voice low. "What's up?" She moved away from the now whispering Senators, and turned her back to them.

"Hey." Mark sounded subdued. "Listen, I was just listening in on the bridge. They found our big guy in NY."

"Bob? Where?" Kerry murmured.

Mark hesitated. "He's um...he didn't make it."

Kerry's heart sank. "Damn." She exhaled. "Does Dar know?"

"She was on the bridge," Mark said. "She went to go tell the big cheese. The NY people are pretty slammed."

"Damn it," Kerry sighed. "He and Alastair were good friends."

"Yeah," Mark murmured. "How's it going there?"

"I'm about to kick box a few senators and get my ass thrown in jail," Kerry admitted. "Tell Dar to bring cash."

That got a tiny laugh out of Mark. "Hey, listen. Good news is they got the Newark E up. Birds are synced, and I'm doing some bandwidth hacking while I wait for power here."

"Good job, Mark." Kerry sighed, and glanced over her shoulder. Some of the people were moving toward the door, and she realized the session seemed to be over. "Let me wrap this up, and I'll get back to you. The boss said she'd be heading out here tonight."

"Woo fucking hoo. I'll be glad to see her," Mark said.

"Me too," Kerry agreed. "Me too," she repeated, closing the cell phone. She turned and walked back to where her mother was standing, talking to Senator Markhaus. "Sorry."

"Is everything all right, Kerry?" her mother asked. "You look upset."

Kerry gazed past them. "One of our people in New York was killed in the attack," she said. "They just confirmed it."

"Oh dear. I'm so sorry." Cynthia put her hand on Kerry's shoulder. "Was it someone you knew well?"

"No." She shook her head. "But we've been trying to support our people there, and it's very hard news for them." Her eyes flicked to the door. "Are we done here?"

"For now," Senator Markhaus said. "Nice bit of fencing, by the way. Quoting your father back at me." He studied her coolly. "Wonder what he'd say if he'd heard you do that."

Kerry stared right back at him. "He'd tell you not to piss me off."
She glanced at her mother. "Excuse me. I'll wait outside." She eased
past them and made for the door, twitching her jacket across her
shoulders as she cleared it and went out.

"Was that called for, Alan?" Cynthia asked. "Please don't expect
me to ask Kerry to come in here again."

Markhaus put his hands in his pockets, regarding the now empty
doorframe. "Interesting kid," he said. "Turned out more like him than
he ever dreamed," he said. "He'd have popped a button listening to her
tell us off like that."

"Kerry has quite a temper," her mother agreed. "But in this case, I
agree with her. She did our country good service, and was rewarded
with accusations and your mean tongue. Why not turn that on your
dear friends in the administration instead? Is it just so much easier to
yell at a young woman?"

Markhaus gave her a sour look.

"Perhaps Roger was right." Cynthia straightened up. "We are ruled
by fools and cowards. Fortunately for me, my daughter is neither." She
turned and marched out, slamming the door with a resounding bang
behind her.

DAR SAT QUIETLY in the chair in Kerry's office, listening to the
quiet conversation on the speaker phone. Across the desk from her,
Alastair was crouched, leaning forward toward the phone with his head
resting on both fists.

She'd had to deliver bad news more than once in her lifetime, but
usually it was bad news of an impersonal sort. Telling Alastair about
Bob's death had been anything but impersonal. It made her feel sad,
and angry all over again at the senselessness of it all.

Her guts were in knots. She could see how upset Alastair really
was, though his expression was merely somber and his voice even as he
spoke into the phone to the devastated New York office.

"They're sure, John?" Alastair said.

"Yes, boss," a somber voice came back. "I got a call from St.
Vincent's. They thought they were going to get swamped, but they
didn't. Only a few...ah. Anyway, one of the doctors there knew him."

"Damn it."

"Most of the people here are in the big room. They're pretty upset. I
came in the conference room to talk to you," John Brenner added. "I
think we're all still in shock."

Alastair sighed. "Has anyone called his family?"

"No sir."

Dar watched her boss's face tense into a grimace, and she felt a
wallop of sympathy for him. She'd known Bob in a casual way, met him
once or twice, and argued with him extensively, but Alastair had been a

personal friend.

"All right. I will," Alastair said. "Damn, I'm sorry to hear it. John, is there anything I can do for the folks there? I know they must be taking it hard."

John Brenner sighed. "We all hoped everyone made it," he said. "After people started showing up today, we all thought, hey, we'll get through this and it'll just be getting things moving again."

"Yeah, I know," Alastair murmured. "We all hoped that."

"He stopped to help some people. It must have taken too long, I guess."

Alastair glanced across the desk, watching Dar's somber eyes watch him. "Sometimes I'd rather our people be a little less heroic," he said. "But he did what he had to. "

"Yes, sir. He did."

"All right. Whatever the folks there need-people, alcohol, whatever-make sure they get it John," Alastair said. "I'll get hold of Mari here and see if we can get a counselor down there."

John hesitated. "I think we'd appreciate it," he said. "It would be good to have someone to talk to," he admitted. "I'll call you later, boss, if we hear anything else. I'm going to go back inside with the rest of them."

"Okay John. Take care." Alastair exhaled, reaching forward to release the speakerphone. He then settled back in Kerry's chair and gazed across at Dar. "Goddamn it."

"Sorry," Dar murmured. "I know he was a friend, Alastair."

"He was," her boss said, in a sad tone. "His family are old friends of mine for a couple generations back, matter of fact. My Granddad and his Great Granddad were business partners." He shook his head. "What a damn shame."

"Yeah," Dar nodded quietly. "They were all down there Alastair. The odds weren't great in our favor to begin with."

Alastair gazed past her. "How many times in bad odds did you bring us out without a scratch? Maybe I got used to thinking we were just lucky that way."

Dar didn't know what to answer to that, so she just sat there quietly, wincing at the upset in her stomach.

"Damn it," Alastair whispered. "Damn it, damn it, damn it."

Dar jumped a bit, as her cell phone rang. She unclipped it and checked the caller ID, then opened it. "Gerry," she warned Alastair, before she answered. "Dar Roberts."

"Hello, Dar. Gerry Easton here," the General said. "We've got you all set up. They want to grab you in a helo. You have space for that there?"

Dar's brows creased. "Ah...a helicopter?" she asked. "Gerry, we can drive to the damn airport. I'd have to clear half the parking lot to get one in here unless it was the size of one of those traffic copters."

"Well, hang on a minute." Gerry put her on hold.

Dar looked across at Alastair and shook her head. "Helicopter. Jesus."

Alastair pressed his fingertips against his lips. "Y'know Dar," he said. "Given the news, I think I'd better renege on my offer to go with you."

Dar's eyes opened wide. "What?"

"I think I'd better get Bea to book me to New York tomorrow morning," Alastair said. "Those people need support. Bob's family needs support. The government can wait."

"Hello, Dar?" Gerry came back on. "They'd rather pick you up. Got their pants on fire, now they're scuttling I guess. Man said he can put the chopper down near by you. Fifteen minutes," he said. "Hate to push the point, Dar, but we've got several hells in hand baskets around here and everyone's in a rush."

Dar studied her boss. "I'll be ready," she said. "See you soon, Gerry."

"Well done. Good job," the General said. "Talk to you later."

He hung up. Dar closed the phone and held it in her hands, her expression thoughtful. Then she opened the phone again and dialed. "Dad? Hey. Last minute crap. They want to helo me out of here in fifteen. Can you...ah, you are. Okay, see you in a few."

She closed the phone again with a wry grimace. Then she cocked her head and looked over at the man behind her lover's desk. "So."

"Think I'm throwing you to the wolves again?" Alastair asked.

"No," she answered. "But does this give you a better perspective on why I went to be with Kerry when you needed me in Houston that time?" she asked. "When she was in Michigan?"

Alastair tilted his head, and frowned. "Was I mad about that?" he queried. "I wasn't, was I?" He watched Dar's brows lift. "I was, now that I think about it. That General of yours was threatening God only knows what, wasn't he?"

Dar nodded.

"Scared the pants off me." Her boss mused. "Then Bea came in and told me what a jackass I was to even think about yelling at you," he admitted. "With Kerry's father passing on. I just let that get lost in all the craziness. Shouldn't have pushed you."

"We did all right out of it." Dar half shrugged. "But there wasn't any way I was leaving. So I understand. Family comes first. Friends come first. Business is just business."

"It is," her boss agreed, mildly. "But I am sorry about that, Dar."

"Ah." Dar cast her mind back to that dark time, when Kerry's father had passed away and everything seemed to be turned against them. She never regretted getting on the plane to Michigan. "I didn't care."

"About me yelling?"

"Yeah. I felt bad about selling a piece of my soul to Gerry but it didn't matter. Kerry needed me there," Dar remarked. "Everyone else could have gotten screwed three ways in a leaky raft, as my father says, for all I cared."

Alastair nodded. "People matter. Glad you understand, Dar. I don't want to pitch you into the fire, but I know you can handle it."

"I can," Dar agreed. "It's my infrastructure anyway. I grew out of needing a buffer a long time ago." She eyed her boss. "You've been stepping in front of trucks for me for a week. I could get insulted. Let me go bust my own balls for a while."

Her boss managed a half grin. "I am throwing you to the wolves, Dar," he said. "I'm sorry. But I can't go dick around with a bunch of politicians when I know those people in New York are hurting. I gotta go."

"I know." Dar got up. "I'm going to grab my stuff and go say hi to my Dad. He's on the way up to my office," she said. "Go take care of those people, Alastair. They need it. We'll be fine." She circled the desk and put a hand on Alastair's shoulder. "Leave the politicians to me."

Alastair's pale eyes met hers. "That's supposed to make me feel better?"

Dar chuckled. "Think of how they'll feel." She gave her boss's shoulder a squeeze. "Maria will take care of a hotel for you for tonight and getting you to the airport. Just let her know what the details are."

Alastair reached up and clasped her hand with his own. "Thanks. I will," he said. "Be careful, willya? Having you get dinged again because of this place ain't worth it, lady."

"You too." Dar smiled her voice warm with affection. "Give the people in Manhattan my regards. I have a feeling I'll be seeing them soon myself." She straightened up and headed for the door, slipping through it and closing it behind her.

Alastair exhaled, letting his elbows rest on the chair arms. Then he reached out and punched Bea's extension again, waiting for her to answer. "It's me."

"I heard, Alastair. I'm so sorry," Bea said. "What a shame. Do you know if there are any arrangements yet? What can I do for the family...for you?"

Alastair closed his eyes, reaching up to pinch the bridge of his nose for a long moment before he answered. "Don't know yet," he answered, briefly. "Haven't talked to the family." He fell silent, biting the inside of his lip.

Bea was quiet for a moment. "Tough day, boss," she said, eventually.

"Yeah," he agreed. "Just got a whole lot tougher."

"Dar's admin just messaged me with your hotel details," Bea said. "She's such a sweetheart. I'll start working on getting you a flight up tomorrow morning. You want the first one out, I guess?"

"Yeah." Alastair cleared his throat. "Sounds fine. Early as you can."

"You want to stay somewhere near the office there? I can try getting something close. Hard to say what's available though."

"Get me whatever you can," her boss answered quietly. "Doesn't matter."

The inner door opened, and he looked up quickly, to find Dar coming into the room again with a set of keys in her hand. "Ah." He cleared his throat again. "Thought you were out of here."

"Almost." Dar set the keys down. "I know you can get a ride from anyone here, or a cab, but sometimes it's good to have your own transport. Just leave it at the hotel, and I'll get it picked up." She knelt down and put her hand on his knee. "Pick a causeway and find a beach. That's where I go to chill out."

His eyes met hers, and he managed a faint smile. "Thanks, Paladar. I'll try not to crash into any palm trees."

Dar patted his leg then stood up. "Later." She disappeared again, leaving silence and the faint scent of leather in her wake.

Alastair jingled the keys lightly in his fingers. "Y'know, Bea, if I was thirty years younger, Kerry would have a fight on her hands," he chuckled wryly. "No offense to my wife."

"You know, Alastair, you're right," Bea said, after a pause and a long sigh. "She is really neat. How did we miss seeing this side of her all these years?"

"Don't know, and really don't care. I'm just glad we have her because she's damn good people." Alastair regarded the pictures facing him. "I'm going to get out of here, Bea. Arrange what you can, just drop me the details."

"Will do, boss. Have a margarita for me."

Alastair stood up. "You can bet on it," he said. "Who knows? Maybe I'll go get myself a tattoo. It's been that kind of week."

"Alastair."

"Yeah, I know. My wife would kill me." Alastair sighed. "Talk to you later, Bea." He hung up the phone and circled the desk, heading for the door. Just short of it, he stopped and regarded the boxing dummy.

Its face, what there was of it, was scuffed. He picked up one of the gloves and looked at it, the laces loosened from the last hand it fit over. He put it over his fingers and slid it on, finding the inside of it snug, but well worn.

Did Kerry really spend that much time beating the daylights out of something? Was the stress here as bad as all that?

Experimentally, he faced off against the dummy and socked it one in the puss, making the spring loaded torso rock back and forth energetically. Its stolid face looked back at him as it wobbled back and forth.

He hit it again. "Huh." He was faintly surprised at how satisfying it felt. Then, after a moment's thought, he wasn't surprised. Quietly, he removed the glove and hung it back next to its mate, giving the dummy a pat on the head.

The corridor was empty when he left the office, and he took advantage of that to stroll to the elevator, slowing when he spotted Maria approaching him. "Hello, Maria."

"Senor McLean," Maria responded politely. "Dar has asked me to make sure your bag is put in her car, yes? I sent Mayte down to take care of that for you," she said. "I think the army has come for her and her papa out in the parking lot. I was going to go see that."

"I'll join you." Alastair punched the elevator button. "Thanks for grabbing my things. Does Dar always think of everything?"

Maria merely looked at him, both her dark eyebrows lifting.

"Silly question. I know she does." Alastair held the elevator door and followed Maria inside. "She's thought of everything ever since I've known her."

The door closed and they rode down in companionable silence.

Chapter Nineteen

KERRY HELD THE door for her mother as they entered the small, typically decorated Japanese restaurant. It was quiet inside, too late for the happy hour crowd, and she was glad enough to settle in a comfortable banquette to one side of the sushi bar.

It felt very good to simply sit, even with her mother across from her. "Ugh." She leaned back and let her arms rest on her thighs. "What a bunch of posers."

Cynthia looked up from examining the menu, peering at Kerry across a pair of half glasses. "Are you speaking of my colleagues?"

"Yes." Kerry lifted her hand a rubbed the back of her neck, too tired to worry about being rude.

"Well, I have to agree," her mother said. "I can't believe they disregarded all of the things we discussed earlier in favor of a senseless attack on your company."

A waiter came by, bowing to them and waiting in silence.

"Can I get a Kirin, please?" Kerry asked. "Mother, would you like a drink?"

Cynthia pondered a moment. "I would." She decided. "Could I perhaps get a glass of white wine?"

"Yes of course," the waiter said. "You want something to start?"

Kerry glanced at the menu. "Trust me to order?" she asked.

Cynthia hesitated then nodded. "Of course," she said.

The waiter turned to Kerry, his eyebrows cocking.

"Ah...two orders of the edamame, please, two of the watercress salads...Mother, I think you'd like the tuna tataki roll, and I'd like the sushi and tempura plate, please." Kerry glanced across the table. "All right with you?"

Her mother looked a touch nonplussed. "Well, certainly. That sounds lovely." She handed her menu back and settled back in her seat. "I can't say I've tried sushi. Your father wasn't partial to oriental food."

Kerry remembered that. "Strictly old fashioned American food. I recall," she said. "I didn't acquire a taste for it until I moved down to Florida. It's too hot to eat that heavy all the time." She played with her fork. "Japanese food is usually cool or room temperature, looks great on the plate, and it's good for you on top of it."

"Hm," Cynthia murmured. She glanced up as the waiter returned, bearing a tray with Kerry's beer, her wine, and two plates of green pods. He put the pods and the drinks down, gave them another little bow, and retreated.

Kerry picked up her glass and took a sip of her beer. It was cold and light, and it went down easy. She leaned back against the padded surface and relaxed, glad the day was almost over.

Almost. She had this dinner to get through, drop her mother off back at her office, then make the drive back to her hotel and wait for the crowning end to her day that, with any luck, would involve her, Dar, and being naked.

Or her, Dar, and footy pajamas. Or her, Dar, and remaining fully clothed. She really didn't care as long as the her and the Dar part were in there. She missed her partner something fierce, and now the constant strain and aggravation were starting to wear on her.

"Are these like peas?" her mother asked, studying the edamame.

"Soy beans." Kerry put her beer down and picked one up, squeezing it and popping the resulting bean into her mouth. "With a little salt."

"Oh." Cynthia picked one up and examined it, then put pressure on the end and started a bit as the pod split and the bean almost went across the table. "My goodness." She captured it and put it cautiously to her lips, chewing it as though it might explode.

Kerry finished her pod and went on to the next one. "Dar and I play games with these," she related. "I can squeeze one into her mouth from across the table."

Her mother stared at her. "Kerrison," she said, after a moment. "You don't really."

Kerry smiled wryly. "Yeah, I do," she said. "It's our neighborhood joint near the office. They all know us there. They don't care if we throw food at each other." She picked up another pod. "We do lunch there a lot. It gets so hectic and stressful at the office, it's nice to just sit and blow off steam sometimes."

"That seems very strange," her mother said then sighed. "But really, what isn't strange these days. I don't understand what the world is coming to."

True. Kerry felt like the world had stopped and started spinning the opposite direction. So much had changed in so few days, and looking forward she saw only more change ahead of them. Not good change, either.

It was an uncharacteristically pessimistic feeling. She didn't much like it.

Cynthia ate another bean slowly. She picked up her glass and sipped her wine, watching Kerry over the rim. "It's been a terrible day, hasn't it?"

"Lousy," her daughter agreed. "Lousy couple of days. The only bright spot for me today was Dar telling me she's heading up here." She paused. "Well, that and you telling the other senators off."

Cynthia blinked. "Well, I don't think..." She stopped. "On the other hand, perhaps I did. They made me very upset."

"Me too."

"I am sorry about that," Cynthia said, in a sincere tone. "I really did not expect them to do what they did. I knew they had questions, but I thought they were more interested in finding a way to better communicate. Not..."

"Not find someone to blame?" Kerry half shrugged. "Well, it's over. I hope they learned something from it, but if they didn't, they didn't. I don't have time to worry about it." She gave the waiter a smile, as he returned with their salads. "Thanks."

Cynthia picked up her fork and investigated the watercress. "Oh, this is lovely," she said, after tasting a bite. "Quite delightful."

Kerry maneuvered her chopsticks expertly and spent a quiet moment ingesting the greens. They were crisp and fresh, the dressing a touch spicy, and with more than a hint of citrus. "That is good," she said, after wiping her lips.

Her mother took another sip of wine. "This is really very nice, Kerry," she said. "Is this some place you plan to bring Dar to, when she arrives?"

Kerry slowly finished her salad, considering the question. "Maybe. She loves sushi." She allowed. "I don't think we're going to be here long though. "

"Oh, really?"

"Yes." Kerry wiped her lips on her napkin. "Soon as we get the backups running here, my guess is we'll both be needed in New York." She studied her glass. "There's a lot more to do there." Her brows knit a little. "So many people. So much damage. What a total waste."

Slowly, her mother nodded. "I was very sorry to hear about your colleague. Did you know him well?"

Bob. She hadn't really known him at all. He'd been a name on an email, a voice on the phone. He'd been the guy Dar had been with when Kerry's plane had gotten in trouble, and that was the one set of personal memories she had of him.

He'd been touring Dar around the city, so very proud of it, her partner had said.

Now, being in that city had ended in his death. Kerry was sure he'd never even considered having something like that happen to him. No one did.

Just a routine day for them. Just a regular visit to clients, a bid in process, a day that had probably started with coffee at the deli across from the office at Rockefeller Center, and plans for lunch down in the business district.

"He was our senior sales executive in the Northeast," Kerry said. "I spoke to him often. He was a nice guy." She paused. "He loved New York."

Cynthia shook her head. "Terrible."

"He was a good friend of our CEO's." Kerry went on. "Dar had to tell him they found his body."

"Oh my." Her mother put a hand to her mouth. "How terrible for her. "

Kerry nodded, taking a swallow of her beer. "I'm sure it was tough. She and Alastair are pretty close." She leaned back again, stretching her back out a little. She felt stiff, and her body felt tired, a bone deep ache that made her hope she wasn't coming down with something.

"Really?" Cynthia took a sip of her wine. "I thought he was an older man."

"He is," Kerry agreed. "But Dar's worked for him for a long time. She's pretty much his right hand. He depends on her all the time to get things right." She smiled as the waiter returned, placing their plates down with a flourish. "Thanks. That looks really great."

"Ma'am, excellent. Can I get you another beer?"

"Sure," Kerry readily agreed. "Mother?"

"Well, yes." Cynthia handed over her empty glass. "This looks lovely, and smells delicious," she concluded. "Really, I can't think why I haven't tried this before. Certainly we have plenty of oriental places here in Washington."

Kerry was busy with her sushi, mixing her soy sauce and wasabi just so, and adding a bit of the pickled ginger to it. "Dar tricked me into trying it the first time," she related. "She said I could have teriyaki chicken and a salad, and she had this big plate of really gorgeous colorful sushi in front of her.

"Oh my."

"I ended up eating half of it." Kerry selected a piece of her meal and dipped a bit of it into the soy sauce then popped it into her mouth and chewed contentedly.

"This is wonderful." Cynthia tried her tuna. "So light."

Kerry merely nodded. It had been a long time since her spicy chicken sandwich and the cupcakes hadn't done anything to stabilize her blood sugar. She had a nagging headache, and she just hoped the sushi would settle her body down and let her get through the rest of the night and back to her hotel.

Last thing she needed was a migraine.

"Angela was telling me you have a vacation cabin?" her mother asked. "It sounded lovely."

Kerry swallowed, glad of the subject change to safer and less tense waters. "We do," she said. "Dar and I decided we liked spending time down in the Keys, so we found a place just south of Key Largo and restored a cabin down there."

"How charming!" Cynthia smiled. "I know you and your brother and sister both used to love the cabins down by the lake in the summer."

"Yes, we did." Kerry took a sip of her freshly filled beer. "It's really cute. It has a kitchen, and a nice big living room, a bedroom, and two offices that also have pull down beds," she said. "It's right on the water. We love watching sunsets from the porch."

"You always sound so busy. I'm so glad you take time out to relax," her mother said. "It was so hard for us to take family vacations with your father so occupied all the time. I know you children went to camp, but it's not the same thing."

Kerry chuckled. "I told Dar about my camp experiences a few times and we had to laugh because her idea of camp and my idea of camp were way far apart. "

"Really? But of course, she grew up in Florida, didn't she? I'm sure it's very different there than up in the mountains."

"She grew up on a navy base," Kerry said, quietly. "I think she wanted to be in the navy until she was in high school. So yes, it was very different."

Cynthia glanced at her. "Goodness. What on earth would she have done in the navy? She's far too clever for that."

What would Dar have done in the navy? Kerry used the excuse of ingesting more sushi to give her a moment to ponder the question. She knew Dar had wanted to be a Seal, like Andrew had been, but if not that then what?

"I'm sure she'd have ended up in some position in intelligence, or planning." Kerry wiped her lips. "But I'm very glad she decided to go into IT instead, since I don't think I'd have had a chance to meet her if she'd gone into the service."

There was a small silence. "Well," Cynthia said, after a pause. "I'm glad too."

Kerry looked up from her plate in surprise.

"I am glad," her mother said. "That you found someone who makes you so happy, Kerry. No matter whom that person turned out to be."

Kerry studied her mother's face reflected in the sedate light of the restaurant. "Thanks," she replied in a quiet tone. "I never had a choice about loving Dar and I never wanted one, but losing my family because of it really hurt."

"I know," Cynthia said. "It hurt your father and me too, though I know you probably find that hard to believe. We did things that I look back on now and wonder how I could have thought they were right. They weren't."

Kerry exhaled. "I did some of those things too," she admitted. "I think I figured if you hated me anyway, it didn't matter what I did."

Her mother reached over and touched her hand. "We never hated you," she said. "As angry and frustrated as your father was, he truly felt in his heart what he did he did because he loved you."

"You know." Kerry studied her mother's face again. "I believe that."

"Do you?" Cynthia seemed surprised.

Her daughter nodded. "Because despite everything that happened, I didn't hate either of you." She fiddled with her chopsticks. "I didn't expect you to like or accept what my choices were."

Her mother ate quietly for a few minutes, giving Kerry the chance to do the same. The air had lightened though, and Kerry felt a wary sense of relief along with a hope that the thaw would continue.

She didn't really like conflict. Dar reveled in it, taking every opportunity she could to dive into the deep end of the combative pool, relishing the challenge of going head to head with anyone who cared to argue with her.

Except Kerry. Dar didn't like arguing between them any more than Kerry did.

"We didn't really understand, " her mother said, after a while. "I don't think your father ever did, really, though I believe he did come to respect Dar and her family." She took a sip of her wine. "I decided after he passed away that I would educate myself and try to gain an understanding of how you have chosen to live and really, Kerry, it's not terribly different than anyone else."

Kerry felt like a Martian had just taken a seat at the table and was asking for popcorn. "Ah...you're right. It's not," she managed to respond. "We wake up, go to work, hang out, go to the gym, come home, balance the checkbook, watch television, and go to bed. It's not any different from anyone else. We just both happen to be women."

Her mother nodded. "So it seems. I cannot pretend I do not wish it was otherwise, but I have come to accept that it is your choice, and that is all right with me," she said. "I like Dar and her family very much. They seem like very sincere people, and I do not find much of that around here. I often wish I hadn't decided to take this task on."

"You'd rather be home?" Kerry guessed.

"I would, yes," her mother replied. "I understand the politics around me, but I truly do not like them. It often makes me quite disgusted with humanity."

Kerry nodded wryly, knowing a moment of personal growth she hadn't expected. "I hear you." She could almost hear Dar's knowing chuckle. "Maybe you can come with Angie and Mike and visit us. We'll give you a ride in our boat, and you can meet my dog."

Her mother was quiet for a long moment. "I would like that," she said. "After this horrible emergency is over, we shall make plans to do so."

Kerry smiled and lifted her beer glass, waiting for her mother to hesitantly do the same before she reached over and clinked them together. Then she put the glass down and went back to her sushi, determined not to waste a single bite.

IT WAS LATE when they pulled back into the parking lot outside Cynthia's offices. Kerry briefly regretted the need to retrieve her briefcase then shrugged and shut the SUV's engine off, opening the door to hop out of it.

She took a moment, as her mother got out of the other side, to check her cell phone. Again. "Darn it." She frowned at the instrument, conspicuously lacking in messages from Dar. "Where are you, Dixiecup?"

With a sigh, she returned the phone to her belt and circled the front of the SUV, joining her mother as they walked across the still half full parking lot in the brassy glare of the security lights.

"What are your plans now?" her mother asked. "It's a shame your things are at the hotel, you could easily have stayed in the townhouse."

Kerry stifled a yawn. "Best laid plans," she remarked. "In any case, Dar will probably come in late tonight and she knows to go there."

"Ah, yes. Of course. Well..." Cynthia lifted a hand. "If you stay over another night, please, both of you are more than welcome to stay at our home here."

Kerry appreciated the offer, honestly. However, she remembered the somewhat cramped and often busy confines of the townhouse and knew her partner would appreciate the space and hot tubs of the hotel instead. "Thanks very much," she replied. "I really appreciate that, Mother, and I know Dar will too. Hotels can get old after a while. "

Her mother smiled.

"It just will depend on our task list once Dar gets here," Kerry demurred. "I think I mentioned that she's got some confidential information she didn't want to discuss over the phone, no telling what that involves."

"Of course," Cynthia nodded. "I've had a lovely time tonight. I'm so glad we got a chance to visit a little."

They entered the door, and got only the briefest of looks from the soldiers standing guard, all of them looking tired and more than a little discouraged.

"Good evening," Cynthia greeted them.

"Ma'am," one of the soldiers responded. "Do you know how late everyone's supposed to be here?"

Kerry's mother paused. "Well, it's hard to say," she said. "Usually, perhaps nine, perhaps ten p.m., but with the extraordinary events going on, possibly people will be staying later. I myself am leaving as soon as my daughter here retrieves her things from my office."

The soldier sighed. "Thanks ma'am," he said. "Wish they'd put some vending machines in," he muttered. "They even turned off the coffee pot."

Cynthia looked around the small reception room. The soldiers were the only occupants, the receptionists having long gone home for the day. "Are you staying here all night?" she asked. "My goodness."

"Yes, ma'am," the soldier agreed. "Long as you all are."

"I vote we pull a fire alarm and clear the building then," Kerry spoke up for the first time. "I think you all need your sleep more than the senators need to grouse and wring their hands."

"Kerry." Her mother eyed her. "I'm sure everyone here has a good reason to be at work."

Kerry exchanged wry glances with the soldier, who reached up and touched the brim of his camo cap. She pulled her cell phone from her belt and dialed a number. "Hey Mark, it's Kerry."

"Hey boss," Mark said. "We're in the trailer, chilling."

"If you're chilling, that must be good news." Kerry smiled. "Newark up?"

"Yeah, and soon as they finish the power feed we can do something for this place, at least barebones," Mark replied. "You're gonna have to come play ref on them though, everyone's a priority one in their own minds around here."

Kerry nodded. "Yeah, I know. Anyone there free to take a little ride?" she asked. "If you've got some spare chow, the poor guys down here guarding my mother's office could use some."

"Hang on." Mark put the line on hold.

Kerry looked at the soldiers, who were now focused on her with imperfectly hidden hopefulness.

"So...you want stuff over at your mom's office?" Mark got back on the phone. "I got a couple of volunteers here to bring it. How many guys?"

"Six." Kerry smiled. "Six big, hungry Marines."

"Can do, boss," Mark said. "You sticking around there? Be cool if you could make sure they get in all right."

Kerry's brows twitched. "Ah...sure," She said. "But tell them not to sightsee on the way over. I'm about out of steam."

"No problem," Mark replied. "They'll be right over. You just hang tight."

"Thanks Mark," Kerry said. "You get some rest, okay? Let me know when the power gets put in."

"Sure will. Later, boss."

"Isn't that lovely," Cynthia said.

Kerry replaced the phone on her belt. "Okay guys," she said. "It'll probably be sandwiches and chips, but at least it's better than a vending machine. A couple of our guys will bring it over in a company truck."

The Marines grinned. "Now that's service. Thank you ma'am," the senior one said. "We were supposed to get a relief three hours ago, but they've got our whole platoon out all over the place."

"My pleasure," Kerry said.

Cynthia clasped her hands. "Shall we go to my office? I'm sure it won't take them long to get here. For once the traffic is not so abominable." She gestured toward the inner door, then followed Kerry as she eased past and headed for it. "Gentlemen."

"Ma'am." The soldiers all smiled at her, more cheerful now.

Kerry exhaled as she walked along the marble floor. The building was quieter now, some offices showing lights and shadows, others quiet and dark. She wondered, briefly, what the difference was, between those who'd gone home, and those who'd stayed.

"Kerry, that was wonderful of you," her mother said. "So thoughtful, to take care of those soldiers. Tomorrow, I will find out why they were left there like that, to be sure."

"No problem," Kerry said. "I was pretty sure we had extra. We always order enough food for three times the people we have."

"Really?"

"Nerds eat anything and everything as much as you'll give them." Her daughter chuckled a little. "When we have lunch meetings we put the extras in the break room and get out of the way. It's like locusts descending."

Cynthia made a small sound of surprise. "In any case, it was a lovely gesture. I know they appreciated it."

The door to the Senator's office was closed, and the panel dark behind it. Cynthia removed a key from her purse and unlocked the door, pushing it open and reaching inside to turn the lights on. "I see everyone's left."

"They had a long day." Kerry entered and moved past the quiet desks, and now silent computers. She entered her mother's office and went to her briefcase, fishing her PDA out of it and opening it up.

Three messages, none from Dar. She frowned, and glanced briefly at the ones that were there, finding nothing more than automatic notifications. After a moment, Kerry closed the device and took out her cell phone again, dialing the first speed entry with impatient motions.

Her mother entered. "The intelligence committee is still meeting," she commented. "I'm sure they're trying to make sense out of everything that's going on. I wonder...perhaps I will join them for a few minutes to see what's happening."

Kerry listened to the ringing on the other end. "Sounds like a good idea," she said, scowling as the phone went to voice mail. She listened to Dar's gruff message, waiting for the beep.

"This is Dar Roberts. If I am not answering, I'm probably too busy for a message, but you can leave one at the beep."

At other times, it would have made her chuckle. But Kerry was starting to get a knot in her gut, a shadow of worry over the absence of any sign of her partner. "Hey hon," she said into the phone. "Where are you? Give me a buzz, huh?" She closed the phone. "Damn it."

Cynthia blinked. "Something wrong?"

Kerry tossed her phone up and caught it as it fell. "I can't reach Dar, and I don't know where she is," she said. "She said they were trying to fly her up here tonight, but I haven't heard anything since." She leaned on the back of the chair. "So I'm a little worried."

Her mother went behind her desk and sat down. "Is there someone we can call?" she asked, practically. "Surely if as you say, the military was allowing her to fly on one of their planes, someone must know about it."

Kerry sat down in the chair, setting her briefcase on the floor. "I'm sure someone does," she said. "I just don't know how to get in touch with anyone. It was probably General Easton, and he's a family friend of Dar's. I don't have his direct number here."

Her mother frowned, and sat back. "General Easton?" she asked. "Gerald Easton, you mean? From the Joint Chief's?"

"Yes." Kerry nodded. "Our dog Cappuccino came from one of his Labrador Alabaster's litters." She paused. "She was a gift."

"Oh." Cynthia didn't seem to know what to make of that. "How lovely." She pondered that. "I have to admit, I am not terribly fond of dogs, " she said. "Is yours large?"

Kerry nodded. "She's beautiful," she replied. "She's so smart, and so funny. She's almost human." A thought occurred to her. "Here, let me show you." She opened her briefcase and removed her laptop, opening it and starting it booting. "I've got pictures."

"Wonderful," Cynthia said. She got up and went to a small, wood paneled refrigerator in one corner of the office. "I have some water here, would you like some?"

"Sure." Kerry put her laptop on the desk and waited for it to finish starting up. "I've always liked dogs."

"I know." Her mother came back with two glasses, and two small bottles of Perrier. "I remember how terribly upset you were when your little pet passed on. I felt terrible for you even though as I say, I am not fond of them myself."

Kerry gazed at her slowly forming screen then looked up over it at her mother as she seated herself. "Did you know Kyle had her put down?"

Caught right in the act of sitting down, Cynthia stopped, half standing, one hand on the desk and the other on the bottle of water. She stared back at Kerry.

She didn't Kerry felt an odd wash of relief as her skill at reading body language detected the honest shock in her mother's posture. "He paid off an intern at the hospital," she added quietly. "He ended up working for us and came in and confessed to me two or three months ago. Said it haunted him."

Kerry paused, blinking a few times. Then she shook her head and concentrated on her laptop, calling up her photo albums as she pushed aside the memories. "Haunted me too."

The sound of a body hitting a leather seat was loud in the room as she clicked. "My god," Cynthia finally said. "No, I did not know that...what a b..." she stopped. "Certainly, your father didn't know."

Kerry looked up at her, one brow lifting.

"We spoke of it." Her mother seemed to sense the skepticism. "He wanted to get you another one." She watched Kerry's face. "I'm afraid I talked him out of it. But if I'd known...ugh!" She got up, visibly agitated. "I look back and wonder how we could have been so unaware."

She turned back around. "Kerrison, are you sure? This is true?"

Kerry nodded. "I'm sure," she said. "Hell, Mother, he killed my fish when he broke into my apartment in Miami and searched it. The man was a psychopath."

Cynthia's jaw dropped slightly. 'W...what?"

"You knew he visited me there." Kerry felt an odd mixture of regret, relief, and curiosity. "Father sent him. Don't tell me now he was acting all on his own. I won't believe it."

Her mother blinked. "Yes," she said. "Your father sent him. He sent him to find out how you really were doing. He thought you were perhaps not doing well, but too proud to tell us," she murmured. "Kyle said nothing about a fish, or breaking into anyplace, he just...he told us he felt you were hiding something from us."

"Well," Kerry exhaled. "I was."

"But he said he spoke with you." Cynthia sat down. "Didn't he?"

"He did. He came back the next day," Kerry said. "He started to threaten me but Dar was there." She shook her head. "Anyway." She got up and turned her laptop around, coming to kneel next to her mother's chair. "Here's Cappuccino."

With a visible effort, Cynthia focused on the screen. "Oh," she murmured. "She is quite large." She studied the profile on the screen. "But quite attractive, as well. Lovely color, almost white, isn't it?"

"Cream," Kerry agreed, calling up a second picture. "This is our cabin."

Relieved as the subject changed, her mother leaned forward. "Charming," she said. "Is that stained glass? How lovely with the sun coming in."

"That's our bedroom." Kerry's lips twitched a little. "Here's the kitchen, and that's the view out the bay window in the living room."

"Stunning."

"That's our motorcycle."

"Oh my."

"Stay with me, Mom." Kerry had to fight to stifle a laugh. "It's a Honda." She heard the sound of footsteps, and looked up, as the inner door opened. "Ah."

Cynthia also looked up. "Hello Alan," she said. "I didn't realize you were still here. It's late."

Markhaus entered, pausing when he spotted Kerry behind the desk. "I was hoping to discuss some matters with you in private." He removed half glasses from his eyes and gave Kerry a disapproving look. "We have a serious situation here."

Cynthia merely gazed back at him. "I'm afraid my family is quite the most serious matter in my life at the moment. Whatever it is, Alan, can wait until tomorrow. "

"It can't," he said.

"Then feel free to discuss it in front of my daughter," Cynthia replied. "I believe she's cleared for this sort of thing, Aren't you, Kerrison?"

"Yes," Kerry confirmed briefly. "But I'll be glad to step out, Mother. I wouldn't want to add any of our confidential information into the mix."

Markhaus openly glared at her.

"Certainly not," her mother said. "Alan, please be brief. Kerrison has been kind enough to provide a meal for our guards since no one else seems to have remembered them. We are merely waiting for that to arrive then we are going home for the evening."

"Cynthia, are you not aware of what's going on here?" Markhaus came closer to the desk. "This country's been attacked. We are effectively at war. I realize you have no experience in any international matters, but at least pretend to give a damn."

Kerry slowly stood up.

"I do." Her mother folded her hands on her desk. "I just seem to have the sense to know that all of us sitting here burning the midnight oil, so to speak, and talking about it is simply pointless. We do not have any information. All we have is speculation, and rumor. Or has the White House responded to your questions?"

"They were trying to kill the President."

"At least he's a valid target," Kerry said quietly.

"What?" The man looked at her. "What kind of nonsense talk is that? These people are insane!" He waved his free hand. "We have to have plans. We have to find out how this happened. We have to put together a strategy to get back at them, and make sure this never happens again."

"Do you know why they did it?" Kerry countered.

"It doesn't matter!" Markhaus shot back. "I don't care why they did it."

"Then you won't ever keep them from doing it again." Kerry folded her arms over her chest. "What are you going to do, send bombers over there and blow them up?"

"That's an option," Markhaus said. "If it were up to me, I'd have them send a nuke over there and just sterilize the whole damn region."

"Alan!" Cynthia stood up. "What are you saying?"

"No bleeding hearts here," he said. "Or pansies." He looked directly at Kerry. "That's what the problem is. We don't have enough right thinking people. Just perverts and peaceniks."

"Are you calling me a pervert?" Kerry asked, sharply. "Hold on a minute, mister. Who the hell do you think you are?"

"Now, hold on." Cynthia stood up. "This is ridiculous. Please!"

"Ridiculous?" Markhaus pointed at Kerry. "How do we know you didn't help them, since you had all that information? How do we know you didn't sell us out?"

"Alan!"

"Oh yeah sure," Kerry shot back. "I sold out to a fundamentalist organization that probably prefers to have gay people euthanized. Yeah. I'm into that. "She put her hands on her hips. "If anyone sold this country out it's you. It's this damn government."

"Kerrison!"

"That's the kind of patriot you raised." Markhaus pointed at Cynthia. "That's what the biggest problem this country has. Sick minds!" He turned and left. Cynthia chased after him in furious silence, leaving Kerry to stand bristling in the middle of the room with no place for her anger to go but inside.

"Shit." Abruptly she sat down, her temples threatening to explode. She could hear her heart hammering in her chest, and the throbbing was making red streaks against the inside of her eyes as she sat there with them closed.

It was too much. She wanted to throw up, every inch of her body twitching with unreleased anger. It was hard to think.

Hard to breathe.

Then a hand gripped her knee, warm and sure, a casual familiarity in the touch that made her eyes blink open. "Uh?"

"Hey beautiful," Dar's voice tickled her ears. "Can I buy you a drink?"

She felt a moment of tingling shock then the anger and frustration evaporated as she took in the twinkle in those blue eyes and felt a smile replacing the grimace on her face.

Heaven.

Kerry exhaled audibly, slumping sideways against the tall figure kneeling at her side, her head coming to rest on Dar's shoulder as she felt Dar's hand come up and cradle the side of her face, the warmth against her skin intoxicating in its own right. "Oh thank God!"

"Thank Gerry, a couple of Air Force pilots, and six big hungry Marines," her partner said. "We're your volunteers."

"Ungh." Kerry captured Dar's hand and kissed it relentlessly. "Mark is dead for not telling me you were there. You're dead for not telling me you were there. I was a nervous wreck wondering where you were."

"Sorry." Dar kissed her on the forehead. "I idiotically left my cell and PDA in my briefcase that is sitting back in Miami. I figured another ten minutes wouldn't matter after that and I wanted to surprise you."

"You did."

"Didn't mean to stress you."

"Don't care." Kerry closed her eyes, absorbing her partner's scent, and the sound of her voice and the gentle touch stroking her hair. "All better now."

The inner door closed. Kerry heard footsteps and the sound of a chair squeaking nearby. She opened one eye to see her mother looking back at her, her expression distressed. "Sorry."

"Don't be," Cynthia said. "The man is an ass."

Kerry felt Dar's body jerk with silent laughter. She smiled in reaction, feeling a physical sense of relief it was hard to quantify or describe. "Dar's here."

"Yes, I did notice that," Cynthia said. "I'm glad."

"My Dad's outside talking to the Marines," Dar said. "Alastair went on to New York."

"Awesome," Kerry mumbled. "Can I have that drink now?"

Dar stroked her hair. "Sure." She glanced over at Kerry's mother. "Want a drink too?"

"Absolutely," Cynthia Stuart said. "I think we should get out of here at once."

"Best idea I've heard all day." Kerry managed to stand as Dar rose to her feet, wrapped her arms around her partner and hugged her as hard as she could. "Unnngh."

Dar returned the hug fully. "Damn I missed you," she said, in an undertone. "Damn, damn, damn."

"Damn, damn, damn," Kerry repeated, rocking them both back and forth. "You got that right."

Chapter Twenty

"YOU MUST BE exhausted." Kerry nevertheless was content to sprawl half across Dar's lap in the back of the SUV, her head resting on her partner's thigh as Dar's hands worked the kinks out of her neck. "Do you even know what time it is?"

"Do you even think I care?" Dar glanced at the driver's seats, where her father was ensconced at the wheel with Kerry's mother directing him. It gave her a Twilight Zone feeling and she quickly returned her attention to Kerry.

"Probly not."

"You're probly right." Dar was tired, but not sleepy. In truth, given all the travel, she really had no sense of what time her body thought it was, but regardless, she was looking forward to a dark hotel room and a nice soft bed with her partner in it. "Mark made some good progress over there."

"I know," Kerry said. "I really wanted to get out of there because I was more in their way than anything once I'd gotten the brass on the same page as us."

Dar chuckled. "Our technology bus has become the social center onsite. If the PR department were here they'd be pissing in their pants at all the good press they didn't arrange or pay for."

Kerry smiled, her fingertips tracing the seam line of Dar's jeans. Then her smile faded. "It's awful about Bob."

"Yeah," Dar exhaled. "Alastair's pretty shaken up over it. I think he really wanted to be here with us, but his family is old friends of Bob's." She kneaded Kerry's shoulders, feeling the tension in the tight muscles there. "I think the rest of the staff there will be glad to see him though."

"Ungh."

"How's your headache?"

"Better," Kerry murmured. "Just having you here makes me feel better. Why is that? You always do that to me."

Dar gazed quietly down at her. "I don't know," she said, after a pause. "I know I feel better just being here. You think we're nuts?"

"Probably," Kerry acknowledged. "Do you care?"

"Nope."

"Me either."

"I need to call Gerry in the morning," Dar said. "I'm sure he tried to call me tonight but the only place I have his private number is in my cell." She sighed. "I'll have to have Maria get it for me."

"I can't believe you forgot your briefcase," Kerry mumbled. "Jesus, Dar. That has your laptop in it."

"Also had my wallet in it," her partner informed her. "Luckily for me I did remember to bring my father."

"What's that, Dardar?" Andrew asked, from the driver's seat. "You kids all right back there? We're almost to that there hotel of yours."

"I was just telling Kerry about our trip," Dar said. "I hear that hotel has a nice bar."

"With leather chairs," Kerry supplied. "The big cushy ones."

"Ah do believe a beer would be right nice about now," Andrew allowed. "Been one hell of a day after another damn hell of a day."

"It was so nice of you to come along, commander," Cynthia said. "You have always been so supportive," she added. "I believe you need to turn...ah, no left there. Ah. Oh."

"Hold on there." Andrew directed the SUV across several lanes of traffic. "Jest be a minute."

"Keep your eyes closed," Dar advised her partner, who had stirred and started to get up. "Don't look. I just got that knot out of your back."

"Mmph." Kerry grunted and relaxed again. "Company has insurance on this thing, right?" She had her knee braced against the back of the front passenger seat, and with Dar's grip on her, and her hold on Dar's leg, she figured she was pretty safe.

It was getting late, and she was really feeling it. She wished she could ask Andrew to just drop them off.

"Thank you again for bringing all those supplies for our poor guards," Cynthia went on. "They were very happy with what you brought I believe."

"Damn sure shoulda been," Andrew said. "That was some nice roast beef, Dardar. You all sure don't fool around with grub, do ya?"

"Nerds require a lot of protein liberally applied," Dar said. "Keeps the brain cells running." She riffled through Kerry's pale hair, as one eyeball appeared and rotated up to watch her. "So yeah, we don't eat quiche."

Andrew chuckled.

"Have you ever eaten quiche?" Kerry asked, in a low mutter.

"Not knowingly," Dar confided. "Have you?"

Kerry nodded mournfully.

Dar leaned closer. "What is quiche?" she whispered.

"Overcooked egg omelette in a cake pan with a bunch of weird stuff it in and not enough egg."

Dar made a face. "Ew." She leaned back against the seat and peered through the front windshield, spotting their hotel rapidly approaching. She could feel a vague disassociation clouding her senses, a product of the long day's worth of overwhelming input. Though she knew there were lists of things she should be doing right at the moment she also knew she wasn't going to do them.

People made mistakes when they were as tired as she was. Like leaving briefcases full of important documents, machines, and credit cards somewhere. Dar gently kneaded the back of Kerry's neck with one hand as she watched the streetlamps go by in silence.

They pulled into the hotel valet lobby, and reluctantly Dar released her partner and gave her a scratch on the back. "Here we are."

With an audible sigh, Kerry pushed herself up and sat back, running the fingers of one hand through her hair. She waited for the valet to open the door and hopped out blinking a little in the cool air as the sounds of the hotel surrounded her.

It all looked a little different. She glanced around her as they walked up the steps and into the lobby, wondering if she was just not remembering what it had been like or if she was imagining differences. She followed Andrew into the big bar, among only a few other patrons, most gathered at the bar watching the television.

She sat down in one of the comfortable looking chairs, and extended her legs as the rest of them settled around her, a waitress in an impeccably cut suit gliding their way at once.

Bad day for business, she guessed. Or, maybe they recognized her mother. She glanced to one side. Or maybe the tall, scarred Andrew caught their eye.

"Ms. Stuart, welcome back," the waitress addressed her directly. "What is your pleasure?"

"Uh?" Kerry felt her brain wrench off onto a siding. She turned her head and looked at Dar just long enough for her partner to start snickering.

"I think she means to drink, hon," Dar drawled. "I'll take an Irish coffee, thanks," she told the waitress. "And she'd probably like a Mojito if you can manage it."

Kerry got lightheaded, as the blood rushed to her face. "Thank you. Yes. That will be fine," she muttered, rubbing her face. "Sorry, it's been a long day."

"Of course." The waitress didn't even turn a hair. She swiveled and addressed Cynthia. "Ma'am?"

Dar patted Kerry's knee. "Sorry." She leaned on the chair arm. "You okay?"

Kerry slouched back into her chair, and simply took a moment to study the angular face across the chair from her. That's what was different, she realized. Dar was here, and that made everything different.

She felt different, having her partner here. She felt less defensive, less on edge. Her eyes met Dar's and she tried to quantify the change, seeing both exhaustion and happiness reflected back at her.

"I'm really glad you're here," she said, watching the smile appear on Dar's lips.

"I'm not glad I'm here," Dar replied. "But I'm really glad we're together."

Ah. Yes. Kerry felt that nailed down her feelings completely. "Yeah." She felt the blush finally fade, and she was able to glance across the low table at her mother and Dar's father. "That's exactly what I meant."

"Kerry," Cynthia said. "I have to say I'm terribly sorry for what happened at my office. I was wrong. I should not have involved you at all," she said. "I thought I was doing a good thing, bringing information to my colleagues. Instead, it seems to have only made them angry."

"Jackasses," Andrew commented. "Gov'mint people got caught with their shorts round their ankles now they're hollering foul."

Cynthia half turned and regarded him. "Are you saying they should have known this was going to occur, Commander?"

"Anybody with an eyeball and half an ear knew that," the ex SEAL responded mildly. "Them folks tried to blow up them buildings before. They ain't got no voice. That's how they talk. Blow things up. Blow up buildings, blow up police stations, blow up their own folks."

Cynthia blinked at him. "Oh. My."

"Ah been there," Andrew added, almost as an afterthought. "Ain't no love there for us. Only thing we got between us is money."

A silence fell, as the waitress returned with a tray full of drinks. She set down Kerry's first then went around the table, her motions quick and efficient. "Ms. Stuart, would you like something sent to your suite? I brought your tea up last night."

Oh. "Um.. I think I'm okay for now, thanks." Kerry finally made the connection as to why she'd been addressed first. Her waking in the palatial suite seemed to be from another time, and had happened to another person. "But do you have a dessert menu from the restaurant?"

"Of course." The waitress smiled at her. "Here you are." She handed Kerry a leather bound folio. "I'll be right back."

Kerry leaned on the chair arm and opened the menu, immediately gaining a dark head resting on her shoulder as Dar peered at it as well. "What do I want?" she mused.

"That." Dar pointed at the brownie sundae. "Get it twice the size and I'll share it with you," she suggested, her shoulder bumping Kerry's. "Either that or this." She pointed next at a peach cobbler with ice cream.

"We're going to be bouncing off the walls all night," Kerry said. She turned her head to see that tiny bit of mischief erupt in her partner's eyes just a moment too late. "Jesus. Don't say it." She sighed. "Not twice in ten minutes."

Dar snickered, but held her silence.

"Well," Cynthia sighed. "I'm not sure really what to do at this point. What I am truly afraid of is that some of my colleagues will use this as an excuse to put in place some ideas that might not have found wide acceptance before."

Kerry put the menu down and sat back, picking up her Mojito and taking a sip of it. The cool minty sweetness almost hid the bite of rum and she licked her lips and put it back down on the table. The waitress came back, and Kerry pointed at both herself and Dar. "Sundae." She glanced at Andrew, who nodded, then at her mother. "Mother?"

Cynthia frowned then shrugged. "Why not?"

"Four." Kerry felt her second wind kicking in. Or perhaps it was her third or fourth by this time. "Dar, can you let us in on what the issue is with Gerry?"

Dar glanced at Kerry's mother, then at Kerry. One brow twitched then she half shrugged. "Sure," she said. "Take this with a grain of salt, since I haven't talked to anyone but Gerry about this, and he was pretty vague."

She paused, and glanced around, but they were quite alone in their corner of the bar, the television providing an irresistible draw to everyone else including the staff. "The problem is they lost all the local feeds into the stock exchanges and the banking centers down on the tip of Manhattan."

Kerry nodded. Cynthia nodded. Andrew grunted. "Okay," Kerry added, after Dar paused. "And?"

"And, they need to get them back online, and not let out how damaging that is to our financial infrastructure," Dar supplied.

Everyone nodded again. "Well, that's understandable," Cynthia ventured. "But I'm not quite sure...I mean, surely everyone knows that, and by now it's being worked on," she paused. "Isn't it?"

Kerry folded her arms across her chest. "Probably not yet," she said. "The place where all those connections were is buried under the debris from the South tower."

"Oh," Kerry's mother murmured. "Well, then..."

"Where do we come in to this?" Kerry looked at Dar. "None of that's ours," she added. "We've got some customers down there, sure, and I'm already working on plans to get them rerouted, but we don't touch the markets. I remember them saying how we were locked out of those contracts."

"Someone told someone we could fix it," Dar said, succinctly. "That's what Gerry wants me to talk to that someone about. "

Cynthia was looking from one of them to the other. "I don't understand. What is this about locked contracts? "

"Politics," Dar and Kerry said together. Then Kerry half turned to face her partner. "They think we can fix it? Dar that makes no sense. We don't have anything down there. No contacts, nothing. You remember what happened the last time we tried to put a bid in?"

"It doesn't make sense," Dar agreed. "That's why we need to talk to them. Find out why they think that. Alastair said I should get in and do whatever I needed to...but Ker, he doesn't get it. He doesn't know what the score is there. I think he's just not thinking straight."

Kerry shook her head. "Well, okay," she said. "On one hand we've got part of the government pissed off because we know everything, and on the other, we've got part of the government thinking we're Thor, god of the Internets. Who knows what's going to happen tomorrow."

"Thor, god of the internet," Dar mused. "I'm going to get a T-shirt that says that."

Andrew chuckled. Cynthia paused, then she laughed as well, and the mood lightened a little.

"Really, it should wait for tomorrow," Kerry's mother said. "It's very late, and I'm sure we're all very tired. I hope the morning will bring some return to normal. I hear airplane flights are resuming." She looked over at Dar. "I am glad you arranged to arrive this evening, however, Dar. I know Kerrison missed you terribly."

"Mother," Kerry sighed.

"Didn't you?" Dar reached over and took Kerry's hand in her own. "I sure as hell missed you."

"Of course I did." Kerry felt a little flustered. "But sheesh...you came for other reasons." She eyed her partner, who had a faint smile on her face. "Didn't you?"

Dar shook her head.

"Dar."

Dar shrugged. "I'm too tired to lie," she said. "It just so happened that Gerry's plan coincided with where I needed to be. If it hadn't, I'd have told him he had to wait." She gazed back at three sets of eyes then looked over at Kerry. "Don't give me that look. You were going to start driving for Houston yesterday."

Kerry scratched her nose, and looked faintly abashed.

"Anyway..." Dar sipped her coffee with her free hand, the fingers of the other tangled with Kerry's. "You and I will go down to the offices of whoever it is Gerry talked to and straighten it all out tomorrow. "

"The other sat trucks are holding outside Newark," Kerry informed her. "Not sure if you got that on the call. They won't let anyone down into lower Manhattan yet."

Dar nodded. "We can compare notes tomorrow morning. See where we want the plan to go from here."

"I know what my intentions are," Cynthia spoke up suddenly. "I have decided to return home, as early as I can. We have many things back in Michigan that I'm worried about," she said. "I realize there is much debate going on here, but there are people there that might be in danger."

Kerry nodded. "I think that's a good decision."

"I already know what will happen here," her mother said, in a quieter tone. "I already know speaking against it will do nothing. One of my colleagues spoke with me earlier today, she's afraid even to ask questions. Everyone is so angry."

"Ah get that," Andrew said. "Ah know what that feels like. Someone done kicked you and all you want to do is get up and kick back." He folded both arms over his broad chest. "That whole turn t'other cheek business never did much take hold in this here country."

Cynthia sighed.

Kerry took a swallow of her Mojito, glad of the warmth of Dar's fingers around hers. From the corner of her eye she could see ice cream heading their way, and she could sense the end of the evening coming as well, when she'd walk with Dar across the lobby and take the elevator to her-no their-suite.

Everything was changing around her. The world, her family, her relationships with people...the one constant being the hand holding hers, the steady confidence in Dar's eyes, the knowledge that she would sleep tonight wrapped in the warm comfort of love.

She had no idea what tomorrow would bring. But for tonight, life was doing the best it could and she was glad enough to take what she could get.

"Want my cherry?"

And then again.

KERRY LAY FLAT on her back on the bed, her arms outstretched and her legs hanging off the edge with her bare feet on the floor. She wasn't doing much of anything except listening to Dar prowl around the suite, the faint snickers and sounds of things moving making her smile.

She'd teased Dar, of course, about the suite. Dar had scoffed at her, accusing her of blowing the place out of proportion until she opened the door and stepped back to let her skeptical partner enter.

Dar had, stopping in the lobby and looking around with an honestly startled expression. "Holy crap."

Kerry had merely smirked and strolled past her, securing a piece of chocolate from the waiting basket before heading for the bedroom and the waiting, already turned down, comfortable looking bed leaving her partner to explore their miniature palace. "Tolja."

"Holy crap."

Kerry smiled benignly at the ceiling. She was totally spaced, and totally exhausted. She studied the tiles for a while, then drifted off for a while, then started as a sound at the doorway made her turn her head and lift it up off the surface to look toward the opening. "Uh?"

Dar was in it, leaning casually against the frame, her body now draped in a clean T-shirt and a glass of milk in her hand. "Okay, you're right," her partner said. "You're going to have to bust your ass to beat this one," she said. "It's got three bathrooms. I had an entire shower and didn't make enough noise to wake you up."

Kerry smiled, and lifted one hand, curling her finger in a come hither gesture. "Glad I did now. C'mere."

Dar obliged, setting the glass down on the bedside table before she launched herself into the bed next to Kerry, making the smaller woman bounce. She rolled onto her side and settled down, taking hold of

Kerry's hand and bringing it to her lips for a kiss.

Now that they were alone, and they could say anything to each other, she really didn't feel like saying anything at all. Kerry angled her head and pulled Dar closer, reveling in the tingle in her guts as Dar abandoned her fingers and kissed her lips instead.

She looked up and found Dar looking back at her at close range, her partner's slightly bloodshot eyes expressing gentle affection that seemed to seep right through her. "I shouldn't have had that second Mojito," Kerry murmured mournfully. "I see three of you."

Dar grinned, the skin around her eyes crinkling up and glints of mischief coming into them. She leaned forward and kissed Kerry again, then rolled over and captured her partner's body, tangling her legs with Kerry's and pulling her over until they were in an untidy squash in the middle of the bed.

"Urgh." Kerry reveled in the heat where their bodies were pressed against each other. Dar's skin felt typically warm, and her skin held a hint of the apricot scrub from her shower. It was utterly familiar, and comforting. "You smell good."

"Do I?" Dar bit her ear gently. "I'm just glad to get the smell of airplane off me."

"What kind of plane did you come here on?" Kerry eased up onto her elbows, the air conditioning suddenly cold against the spot on her ear Dar had been suckling. "Did you have lots of Marines with you?"

"Nah. It was a transport." Dar slid her arms around Kerry's waist and studied her face. "Lots of nervous looking guys in suits. I'd have rather had the Marines. The ones in your mom's office were nice guys."

"They were," Kerry nodded. "I liked them."

"They really liked you." Dar's eyes twinkled. "One of them said he was going to try and get a job with us after his hitch was up, and find you again."

"Oh for Pete's sake." Kerry started laughing. "All I did was get them freaking sandwiches." She let her head drop, and they kissed for a few minutes, ending with heightened breathing as they paused, and Kerry let her forehead rest against Dar's. "Mm."

"Keeerrrry," Dar warbled in her ear. "I mmmiiisssed you."

"Sweetie, I sure as hell missed you too." Kerry nibbled at her partner's neck. "I think more than anything I missed being able to talk to you."

"More than anything?" Dar gently cupped one of Kerry's breasts, rubbing her thumb teasingly over the nipple.

"Heheh," Kerry chortled softly. "Okay, point taken."

"I can do that too." Dar tweaked her. "But yeah, it was frustrating as hell for me to have to listen to you on that call and not be able to just talk back however I wanted to," she admitted, closing her eyes a little as Kerry's hands slid across her hips. "I felt so far away."

Kerry leaned forward and kissed her again, her hand slipping under Dar's shirt. She felt her ribs move as she inhaled and a warm surge of desire flushed her skin as she felt Dar's thigh ease between hers. "You sure don't feel far away now."

Dar cupped her hand behind Kerry's neck and drew her down again. She rolled onto her side and took Kerry with her, as she felt her shirt peeled up and the cool air hit her skin. She felt flushed and the chill felt good, goose bumps raising as Kerry ducked her head down and kissed her breast. "Hope not."

Kerry smiled. She felt the exhaustion lifting as her body reacted to her partner's touch, a burning in her guts igniting as Dar unbuttoned her shirt and slid the bottom of it up, glad she'd already shed her jeans.

Impatiently, she ducked her head as Dar pulled her shirt off She was busy herself with doing the same to her partner. A moment of chill, then Dar pressed against her and all she could feel was a burn that felt like it was washing her clean.

Washing the last two days out. Washing out the tension of dealing with her family. Driving aside the memories of the destruction and the accusations at her mother's office.

Dar's hand slid over her hip and down the outside of her thigh. Kerry abandoned herself to the growing tension in her guts and simply lived in the moment, savoring the ragged edge to her breathing as the light touch became more deliberate and her body arched, wanting the release.

Wanting that deep burn, and the knowing jolt. "God, I love you," she breathed, just as the sensations became too intense for words and her body shuddering in reaction, her arms clamping around Dar's as she let out a yell.

Dar chuckled, breathing hard as Kerry's weight bore down on her, pushing her back over onto her back as she nuzzled the side of her neck. "Love you too." She closed her eyes as Kerry started her attack. "Specially when you do that."

Kerry laughed on an irregular breath, as she felt tears sting her eyes at the same time. "That?"

"Ungh."

"Thought so."

KERRY WAS CONTENT to lay where she was, her body relaxed as she gently traced an imaginary line across Dar's bare skin. It was hard to keep her eyes open, but the steady light stroking on the inside of her thigh was stoking a lazy desire and keeping her from dropping off into sleep.

She didn't mind. It felt good. It wasn't too demanding, just a teasing sensuality that made her very aware of Dar's near presence and focused her on the sound of her partner's breathing and the scent of her skin.

Dar kissed her shoulder.

"Hey Dar?" Kerry returned the kiss, letting her fingers trace her partner's nipple. "Were you really serious?"

Dar's eyes opened. "About what?" her voice rose. "This? Hello? Earth to Kerry?"

Kerry leaned forward and kissed her on the lips. "No." She rested her elbows on either side of Dar's head, and gently rubbed noses with her. "About coming here."

Dar looked up at her for a long moment. "Duh," she said. "Give me a break, willya?"

"I feel so crummy then." Kerry ducked her head for another kiss. "I should have tried harder to go to you."

"I was in England, Ker."

"I can swim."

Dar chuckled, and wrapped her arms around her partner. She felt Kerry's body shift against hers and she savored the moment. "You had a lot to deal with here. I'll cut you some slack," she advised. "Besides, if you had paddled over we'd just have had to fly right back here. "

"I know." Kerry kissed her neck, nipping her collarbone a bit. "It's been crazy," she admitted, resting her head against Dar's shoulder as she felt Dar's hand resume its stroking. "First my family, then yesterday. Just nuts."

"You seem to be getting on okay with your Mom," Dar ventured cautiously. "At least based on tonight anyway."

Kerry was silent for a moment. "Yeah," she said. "Once we got a few things out of the way. It hasn't been that bad, really. I took her for sushi tonight."

"Radical."

"No, she liked it." Kerry smiled, nestling closer. "I had her get the safe stuff, like what you did to me the first time."

Dar chuckled softly. "You ended up eating most of mine that night."

"I told her that," Kerry admitted. "I talked about you a lot." She rubbed the edge of her thumb against Dar's breastbone. "She said she was glad we met."

Dar's eyebrows hiked up. She studied the curve of Kerry's jaw, seeing the muscles move under the skin. "You think she meant it?"

Kerry was silent for a bit then exhaled. "You know, it's so hard for me to tell. I want to think she did, because she said that and some other stuff about how she and my father really weren't aware of stuff Kyle did...but I don't know whether she's saying it because it's true, or because she wants it to be true, and she wants me to stop being so damned pissed off."

Dar started gently massaging her partner's neck again. "Do you want to stop being pissed off?" she asked. "You know when I finally got back together with mine that's what I decided. I'd just blow off the past thirty years of my life, and start fresh. Too much crap to dig through."

"Is that really fair?"

Dar shrugged. "Is life really fair?" she countered. "What makes you feel good inside, to let that all go, or just let it fester?" She felt the warmth as Kerry exhaled, her breath warming the skin over Dar's breast.

"Well, duh," Kerry murmured. "Who'd feel good festering? It just seems so...I don't know, wussy to just say, okay, forget it, let's just move on." She pondered a bit more, feeling her body slowly relaxing again, the room around her retreating a little. "That whole turn the other cheek thing is a really tough sell."

Dar hugged her. "For what it's worth, I think your Mom's legit," she said. "I think she was a chickenshit when your father was alive, but she's got to live with that. Life's short enough."

Kerry remained silent for a few minutes then stifled a yawn, and wrapped herself firmly around her partner. "Save it," she said. "I just want a nice long night of listening to your crazy heartbeat. To heck with everything else."

"Works for me." Dar squirmed backwards, hauling Kerry with her until they hit the pillows. "Let it wait for tomorrow along with all the other problems." She tugged the covers loose, helped more or less by a silently giggling Kerry, and managed to get them wrapped over without rolling them both out of the bed.

That left only the light, and that was a short matter, well within Dar's long reach. She slapped the button and they were in darkness. The sound proofed windows blocked the noise from the street, and only the soft hum from the air conditioning and two simultaneous sighs were heard.

"That hole in the side of the building is pretty terrible, isn't it?" Kerry asked, softly.

'Yeah," Dar whispered back. "Surreal. Seeing the flag draped there made me tear up."

"Me too. They said it happened so fast no one had a chance to get away." Kerry took a little tighter hold. "Must have been horrible."

"Like in the hospital, for us."

"Yeah." The silence lengthened a bit. "We were really lucky that night,weren't we?"

"Very," Dar replied, in a soft voice. "Very, very lucky."

Kerry thought about that for a long moment. Then she pressed her body against Dar's, lifting herself up a trifle and kissing her with simple passion. She rode the surge of energy and felt Dar respond, their bodies tangling again as the covers became irrelevant.

It was a moment to just live life, without regard to what happened next.

AMAZING WHAT A difference a day made. Kerry whistled under her breath as she settled her headset on her ears, her laptop already alive with information. She was seated in front of the window with a view of a breezy fall day outside.

At her side rested a cup of steaming coffee and a croissant neatly piled with eggs and Swiss cheese. She picked up a slice of strawberry and ate it, her eyes scanning the screen as she tried to assess what the status.

Behind her, Dar's low burr was audible as she talked to Maria, and behind her partner the big television was on showing CNN's screen complete with its new ticker scrawl and live footage behind the announcer.

"Good morning, this is Miami Exec currently in Washington," Kerry announced as the conference line connected. "Hope everyone is doing well."

A brief crackle, then a host of voices responded. "Morning, ma'am." "Morning Kerry." "Hello, Miami...welcome back. " "Glad to hear you on, Exec."

"Morning boss," Mark's voice echoed slightly a little afterward, sounding tired. "Now that you're on I'm gonna go catch a few z's. Is the big kahuna there?"

"She is," Kerry smiled as she said it, glancing up to see Dar framed in the entranceway, leaning back against the stately dining table dressed in just her T-shirt. "You sneaky little bugger. I'll get you for that."

"Hey, she told me not to say anything," Mark protested. "You think I'm dumb enough to not listen?"

Kerry chuckled, a warm, rich sound that echoed a little on the call. "So where are we? Give me a status then go get some rest." She picked up her coffee and took a sip, stretching one leg out and flexing her toes against the thick carpet.

Unlike the previous day when she'd woken up tired and tense, defensive in the presence of her mother. Today she felt a resurgence of her usual optimistic nature and a sense of animal well being.

"Well, we got some good stuff to tell and some bad stuff," Mark said. "The good stuff is Newark's up, and they've stopped beating up on the LA Earthstation."

"Miami ops, that's almost true," a voice interrupted. "We just had a request from the governor here to belay a full 24 channels for the National Guard."

Mark sighed. "Hold up a sec, LA," he said. "Anyway, they got the power up here about two hours ago, and I was able to get a link up to Newark, but holy molasses, boss, it's like shoving an elephant through a punch down. We ain't doing crap for traffic."

"Latency?" Kerry asked.

"Not just that, everyone wants to put up on the wire. I can't get a priority list out of anybody cause they all think they're the most important."

"Not like we never heard that before," Kerry said. "Okay, hang tight and tell Newark to hang tight. I'll be over there to beat back the arm wavers shortly."

"Miami exec, this is Newark," the Earthstation spoke up. "We're fully online now. Please tell those folks at APC we're all going to buy stock in them."

"Me too," Kerry agreed, smiling again. "They really came through for us. So now we have to turn that around and come through for everyone else. Just prioritize best you can until I can sort everyone out."

A window popped up, and she glanced at it. *Good morning. You sound more chipper today.*

"Duh, Mari." Kerry switched to the window. *Yeah and I even got some sleep. Did Alastair get off okay?*

Jose and Eleanor took him to the airport and said they'd stay with him until his flight at 8. He said he took Dar's advice last night down on South Beach. Dare I ask?

Kerry glanced at her partner. *Hopefully she just gave him the name of a good steakhouse.* She typed back. *Otherwise I don't wanna know.*

"Miami exec, this is Lansing."

"Go ahead, Lansing." Kerry got back to business.

"Ma'am, we had six installs due today, but we have them all on standby. FedEx advised us they don't know yet when they are going to be able to come off ground hold and deliver anything."

Ugh. Kerry picked up her croissant and took a bite as she thought. She chewed and swallowed before she answered. "That's a problem," she acknowledged. "Anyone from Logistics in Miami on?"

"It's Dogbert here, ma'am," a voice answered. "They're telling us the same thing. We were expecting a lot of stuff today."

Dogbert. Kerry repressed a smile. "Can you get me a manifest of what we've got held up in FedEx, UPS and DHL?" she asked. "Logistics in Houston?"

"Here," a gruffer voice answered. "My brother's a director in DHL. He told me they're not even allowed to open the warehouses. They've got soldiers crawling all over them with dogs."

Kerry exhaled. "Okay, everyone out there, whoever's in operations for your respective areas, I need a list of activities in jeopardy due to non delivery, please. Let's get a calendar up and running and on the desktop so we can see the impact."

"Miami Exec, this is Herndon." Another voice. "We got word flights will take off this morning, but passenger only, and there's a lot of activity on the wire."

"Miami, this is Lansing again. The two installs we had gear for, the guys are telling us they're being denied access to proceed."

Dar came over and sat down next to her, resting her chin on one hand. "This is gonna be like a slow motion train wreck," she commented. "Our ops schedule is not designed to just stop for a few days."

Kerry knew that was true. The intricate web work of installers and technicians, product deployments and implementation scheduling was designed to be flexible, but only up to a point. She often had to shift resources around if a facility wasn't ready in time, or if a part was on backorder.

This was a completely different scope of interruption. "Okay, once we get a schedule up I need someone to run a match against the equipment we have tied up in transit against our distributed inventory. We may need to start driving."

"Maria says she's getting a lot of calls from clients," Dar said. "She's been in the office since five thirty. I'm waiting on a callback from Gerry now."

"Clients from New York and around here?" Kerry asked, clicking her mic off. "Sheesh...don't they know what's going on?"

Dar shook her head. "From all over. I'm not really sure why they're calling. Maria said it was almost like they just wanted to know everything was all right."

Kerry's brows knit. "Huh?"

Dar shrugged. "She's pulling my address book off the phone and she'll email it to you for me," she said.

"Can't she just..." Kerry let the thought trail off. "No, I guess she can't just FedEx everything to you. Damn. You don't realize how dependent you are on some things until they don't exist."

"She offered to fly with it," Dar said.

Kerry studied her face. "She hates flying."

"I know." Her partner smiled briefly. "I told her I'd wait. You're here. It's not like I'm out wandering the streets sleeping under a bench."

"That's true." Kerry covered Dar's free hand with her own and squeezed her fingers. "I'll definitely take care of you."

"Miami exec, this is Houston logistics," the gruff voice came back. "We just got notified we can't move tapes to storage. Facilities been ordered closed by the Feds."

"Oh god." Kerry covered her eyes. "Thanks, Houston. For how long?"

"No idea."

Dar shook her head. "Everyone's running scared now," she said. "I'll order up some storage containers for them and us. Keep working it." She got up and headed back to the room phone, the early rays of sun splashing over her bare legs.

"Okay, Houston. We got that. We'll see what we can do to help," Kerry said. "Newark, have you had any indication on an ETA for your city power? I have a feeling we're going to need those trucks in

Manhattan."

"Wish I could say yes, Miami exec." The Earthstation sounded apologetic. "My boss called this morning, and ConEd had a message on saying to try calling in a couple days."

"Nice." Kerry took another bite of her croissant. "Well, I'm sure they've got a ton of other issues. Doesn't help us much though."

"Miami exec, this is the Air Hub," a woman's voice broke in. "Air traffic control is back online." Her voice held a note of excitement. "We just got a request to host a big share for them for repositioning."

"Go ahead," Kerry said. "Houston ops watch the links and make sure they get space."

"On it," a male voice answered. "We are running a little hot across the board."

Kerry glanced over at Dar, who was on the phone, cupping one hand over her free ear. "I'll get the pipe meister to look at it in a minute. She's on another call."

Kerry?

Kerry looked at the popup then clicked on it. *Go ahead Mar.*

I heard from our office in Springfield. They had a big riot up there last night, apparently people protesting against people from the Middle East.

Oh great. Kerry remembered what her mother had said, and exhaled. *Knee jerk.*

Agreed. Should I send an alert out though? People don't stop to think sometimes.

"Hey Dar?" Kerry turned her head as she heard her partner hang up. "Mari said they had some anti-Arab ugliness in Illinois last night. She's asking if she should send out a bulletin."

Dar came over and sat back down, taking a sip of Kerry's coffee. "To do what? Tell our employees who happen to be Middle Eastern they should hide in the office?" she asked, practically. "I'm sure CNN is covering it, and I'm sure they're watching CNN. "

Kerry studied her face. "What pissed you off?"

Dar put the cup down. "Did I say I was pissed off?" she asked, arching her brow as Kerry continued to look at her. Her lips twitched. "I just got yelled at by Gerry for ten minutes for being the forgetful nitwit I know I was yesterday."

"Well, sweetie..."

"I know." Dar set the cup down. "Yes, she should send out a note. I think people are just starting to be stupid and I don't know where it's going to end."

Kerry turned back to her keyboard. *Dar says yes. Everyone should be very aware of what is going on around them.*

"We have to go to the White House."

Kerry stopped typing in mid word, going very still, before she turned her head and looked at her partner. "Excuse me?"

"Hope you brought your rainbow nerd T-shirt." Dar got up. "I'm going to take a shower. Let's hope they don't want to see my driver's license before they let us in."

Kerry stared at the retreating figure in somewhat stunned silence for a long moment before she wrenched her attention back to the laptop. "Ah...I'm going to have to go offline for a few minutes," she managed to get out. "Everyone just hang tight."

"Will do." "Sure." "No problem Miami exec."

Kerry got up and headed for the bathroom, hoping Dar hadn't really said what she thought she'd heard her say. She ducked inside the door, already hearing the water running, to find Dar in the middle of taking her shirt off. "The White House?"

"They're sending a car." Dar tossed her shirt on the counter. "C'mon. We don't have a lot of time. Apparently we've pissed a lot of people off and we've got a lot of explaining to do." She opened the shower door, allowing a healthy blast of steam to enter the room. "Dad's already down at the Pentagon helping."

"Helping to do what?" Kerry hurriedly got out of her shirt and joined her partner in the shower. "Dar, what the hell...the White House? What did we do? Who did we piss off?"

"Wish I knew." Dar squirted gel on a scrubby and started indiscriminately washing both herself and Kerry. "But I'm guessing we'll soon find out."

"Ugh."

Chapter Twenty-one

DAR FOLDED HER arms and glanced out the tinted window as the car sped through the streets. Kerry was sitting next to her, ear buds planted firmly in her ears as she directed the conference call in muted tones.

"Dar?" Kerry looked up. "Hamilton Baird just dropped into the call, said he'd meet us."

Dar nodded. "Good," she said. "Never thought I'd be glad to see his puss, but annoying as he is he's a first rate lawyer."

"Your father is listening from the RV," Kerry said. "What's a coon ass?"

Dar snorted in laughter, covering her mouth and then her eyes with one hand. "He didn't say that on the call, did he?"

"Um. Well, actually..."

"It's slang for someone from Cajun Louisiana. It's not really a compliment." Dar peered through her fingers. "Sort of like being called a hillbilly. Only worse."

"He laughed."

"My father?"

"Hamilton," Kerry said. "Then he called your Dad a redneck. I think the entire company's stunned to complete silence."

"Mari must be on the floor behind her desk out cold," Dar sighed. "Round out the electroshock therapy by calling Dad and telling them to behave."

"Whatever you say, boss." Kerry went back to her headset with a grin on her face.

Dar returned her gaze to the streets of Washington, working to ignore the twisting in her guts and faintly envying Kerry the distraction of her current task. She'd been in many high profile situations for the company and certainly she had a lot of confidence both in herself and her organization, but being called to the carpet at the White House was both a new and very nerve wracking experience for her.

She didn't like politics. Based on her previous experience, she didn't much like politicians. Dar felt that in order to be elected by a majority, politicians had to become the lowest common denominator and promise everything to everyone, delivering not much to anyone in the end.

Except in South Florida, to their relatives. Dar unfolded her arms and let her hands rest on her denim covered knees. Corruption wasn't viewed so much as a scandal in Miami but, as a bit of entertainment for the residents to discuss over café along with the latest news of Castro, the traffic, and whether or not hurricanes would be heavy or light this season.

Expected. Politicians were wheelers and dealers where she lived, and while it did earn Miami the banana republic reputation it had, Dar also found the up front acknowledgement quite a bit more refreshing. Straightforward, and local. The county and city leaders didn't much give a rat's ass about the rest of the state, or in fact, the rest of the country. Their focus was on drawing people and businesses in, pushing development to its limits, scooping in as much in taxes as they could, and spending money on whoever's pet project they got the most kickbacks for.

No euphemisms about bettering humanity. No long harangues about family values. Very commercial, very crass, very ethnic. Dar liked that. She remembered hearing one local politico talking to some moral values types at a fundraiser she'd been roped into attending, and they'd asked him about the dangers of a gay neighborhood springing up in a certain area.

"Let them come," the politico had said. "They improve any area they live in. Property value goes up, taxes go up. Show me that around a soup kitchen."

Blunt. Shocking. Very Miami. Dar remembered after Hurricane Andrew, when there had been hundreds of thousands of tons of debris to get rid of, and the state and federal government citing pollution regulations, had forbid burning to get rid of it.

They'd burned it anyway. The county manager had told the regulators to come arrest him if they didn't like it.

Dar felt a certain sympathy with the attitude.

The car turned into a long driveway, and pulled to a halt at a large iron guarded gate. "Ma'am, I'll need to show them your identification." Their driver half turned to look at her. "Can you pass it up please?"

"No." Dar laced her fingers. "Actually, I can give you Kerry's. Not mine."

The driver looked at her.

"I'm not deliberately being an asshole." Dar correctly interpreted his expression. "I just don't have it. My wallet and ID is back in Miami."

The driver continued to stare at her. "Ma'am, they won't let you in there without ID."

"Well," his passenger cleared her throat. "That could be true. But the government paid a lot of money to bring me up here from Florida on a military airplane and then send you to fetch me to the White House. Chances are someone in there knows who I am or at least will trust that I am who they think I am."

The driver shrugged, and turned back around. "See what they say." He drove the car forward a space, waiting for the rest of the line to clear the gate. Dar took the opportunity to fish inside Kerry's briefcase, bringing out her ID and holding it in one hand.

Kerry glanced up at her in question, one hand still cupped over her ear. Dar held up her passport folio, and she nodded, then went back to her conversation, reaching out with her other hand to pat Dar's knee.

The car pulled forward, and the driver opened the door, putting one leg out and standing up to talk to the guard rather than opening the window. Dar didn't much envy him, since she figured he was probably telling this armed, anxious, hyper alert man that he had some chick in the car who wanted in to the White House without even a driver's license.

"Dar, Houston's saying they're running really high on usage across the net," Kerry said. "You probably need to check it out."

Dar wiggled her fingers, and looked down at her empty lap, raising her brows at her partner. "They haven't put the chip in yet, hon. Can I borrow your laptop?"

"Of course." Kerry nudged her briefcase over with her foot. "You have to ask?"

"I have to ask because I'll need to sign in with your cached credentials and then rig the VPN system to ask for mine." Dar was drawing the machine out and putting in on her lap. "I usually ask nicely when I'm hacking my SO's system."

Kerry gave her a fond smile. "I love you," she said, then paused, and looked down at her mic, cursing silently. "What's that? No, no, I was... okay, never mind. Who has the name of the guy I need to talk to?"

Dar chuckled under her breath.

"You get me in so much damn trouble." Kerry obviously keyed the mic off this time, scribbling on a pad with her other hand. "Jesus."

The driver dropped back into the car. "Ma'am, they need to verify with the folks inside. I'm going to pull off over here so we don't block the gate."

"Sure." Dar clicked away at the keyboard. "I'll just be back here rerouting all of your paychecks to the French Foreign Legion." She inserted the cellular card and waited for the computer to fully boot, then opened a command line window and started typing.

"Didn't you rig the VPN system so no one could log in with someone else's laptop?" Kerry asked, idly.

"Yes."

"Mm." Kerry paused then cleared her throat. "Yes, Mr. Mitchell? This is Kerry Stuart from ILS." She paused again, listening. "Yes, I understand. Mr. Mitchell, I do un...sir," Kerry's voice lifted. "That's not correct. I do understand what has been going on the past two days, since I'm sitting in a car outside the gate to the White House right now waiting to talk to the folks inside about it."

Dar finished her typing then triggered the VPN connection. It obediently presented her with a login box, which she entered her credentials into and sent it on its way. "Problem?" she asked, in a casual tone.

"Not Dar level yet." Kerry covered the mouthpiece then removed her hand. "Right. So explain to me now why my technicians, who are busting their asses to try and keep their schedules on track, aren't being allowed to complete your install? The one you contracted for? You did ask us to do this, didn't you?"

Dar drummed her fingers on the palm rest, as her desktop formed itself in front of her. She could have actually used Kerry's, but their working style was so different it drove her crazy trying to find things on it.

She opened her custom monitoring application, glancing over the top of the laptop screen toward the driver. He was sitting quietly, relaxed and reading a notepad, occasionally looking up to watch the guards at the gate to see if they were going to come over to them.

Dar pondered what to do if they got turned away. Go to the Pentagon? Maybe Gerry could get her some temporary credentials. "I'm such an idiot." She sighed, as the gages formed up and she studied the results.

"Okay, then we have an understanding," Kerry said. "I'll send my team back up there, and they'll get on with the work. It shouldn't take long," she added. "Thanks." She hung up and went back to the conference call. "Jerk."

Dar keyed on the government routers that were managed from Houston, separating them out in a window and reviewing their statistics. "You're such a hardass, Ker."

"Pfft." Kerry keyed her mic. "Okay, I'm back," she said. "Lansing, this is Miami Exec. Please resend the techs up to Browerman and Fine, they're cleared to enter."

"This is Lansing, will do."

Dar heard the driver shift, and she peered past him to see the guards approaching. She put her head back down and typed quickly, her eyes flicking over the sets of numbers that flashed on and off the screen.

The window opened and the guard leaned down to peer in at them. "Good morning."

"Good morning." Kerry closed her mic.

"Which one of you is Paladar Roberts?" the guard asked.

"That'd be me." Dar glanced up, but kept typing. "I'm the jerk who showed up with no ID," she added. "And I am sorry about that."

The guard nodded. "That's posing a big problem for us." He watched Dar nod back. "But the people inside said to let you in with an escort, so I'm going to let you in, with an escort." He patted the window on the driver's side door. "Go on, Jack. We'll send two guys with you, and two guys will meet you at the stairs."

Kerry regarded him with a touch of concern. "Are we that dangerous looking?" she asked.

The guard just shook his head and waved, and the window closed as the driver put the car in gear and edged his way between two other vehicles toward the gates.

"Houston's right." Dar was clicking away. "They're eating up the wires. I'm going to throw some reserve at them."

"Without finding out why?" Kerry questioned.

"Wouldn't even know where to start asking," her partner admitted. "I'm sure it's all TCP/IP encapsulated frantic arm waving and ass covering mixed with legitimate intelligence movement, but there's really no way for me to step in and question it."

Kerry nodded, and went back to the call. "Folks, I'm going to have to drop offline in a few minutes here. If anything comes up, just call my cell and get me back on."

"There." Dar finished her configuration changes, saving them and cutting and pasting a large swath of tiny text into an email message. "I'll tell Houston I did that, but they need to keep it under their hat. I don't want anyone getting the idea we have inexhaustible bandwidth."

"Okay, I'm out," Kerry said, then she closed the phone, peering out of the window. They were pulling past a line of trees, liberally guarded by machine gun toting soldiers. Ahead there was a small parking area, in front of a huge, almost gothic looking building she only vaguely remembered. "Ah. The old executive."

Dar glanced up from her keyboard and looked out the window, peering at the large structure. Then she shook her head and went back to her keyboard. "Almost done."

Kerry ran her fingers through her hair. "There's Hamilton." She indicated the tall, urban figure leaning on the gate in a posture of bored waiting. "I have to admit, I'm pretty glad to see him given where we are."

Dar shut the laptop and leaned over to slide it into Kerry's briefcase. "Me too," she admitted briefly. "But don't let him know that."

The car pulled to a halt, and two soldiers approached immediately, signaling the vehicle following them. "Please wait and don't open the doors," the driver warned. "Let the soldiers do it."

"Sure." Dar leaned back and twiddled her fingers, as she watched the soldiers approach cautiously as though she was some sort of hyper technical land shark. It kept her mind off what waited for them though, and she only smiled at the man who opened the door, staying still until he realized she was pretty much harmless.

"Thank you ma'am, you can get out," the soldier said, courteously. "Sorry about that, we're a little tense here today."

"I completely understand." Dar swung her legs out and got up, surprising the soldier when she straightened to her full height that topped his by a few inches. She closed the door and paused, as Kerry made her way around behind the car to join her, then they started off toward the gates and their waiting corporate lawyer.

The two soldiers walked along side them. Both were young, but not too young, and they both had five o'clock shadows that probably had started sometime the previous afternoon. They looked tired. Dar suddenly felt empathy for them that she hadn't expected. "Hang in there guys." She told the one to her right. "I know it's been rough."

The soldier looked at her, his shoulders shifting into a more relaxed posture. "Thanks, ma'am."

They crossed the street and Hamilton pushed off his post and came to meet them. "Well, hello there ladies."

"Good morning, Mr. Baird," Kerry greeted him politely.

"Hamilton. Good to see you," Dar chimed in. "Thanks for coming down."

The lawyer seemed to be more subdued than usual. "Good to see you both," he said. "Let's go see what this hoohah is all about."

They started up the steps. "Sorry about my father," Dar commented. "I'm not sure he realized how big his audience was."

Hamilton chuckled. "Darlin', he's your father. Of course he realized. But he's a gorgeous old salt so it didn't bother me a bit." He glanced to either side at their silent escort. "Ain't enough like him and any how my mama raised me to be proud of being a coon ass."

"I don't think he meant it as an insult," Dar smiled. "Not from where we came from."

The lawyer laughed. "Lord I hope they don't regret asking us into this place." He waited for Dar and Kerry to enter the big doorway then followed before the soldiers could. "Sorry boys, beauty and treachery before virtue. "

The soldiers bumped into the frame in their haste to follow. "Sir! Ma'am! Wait!"

Kerry shifted the strap on her briefcase and shook her head, resisting the urge to move faster just to get to the end of the waiting. "Going to be one of those mornings."

DAR HAD HER hands stuck in her pockets, her head tipped back a little as she studied the shelves full of books in the room they'd been shuffled off to.

Kerry was sitting at a mahogany table behind her, working on her laptop as Hamilton spoke softly into his cell phone on the other side of the room.

Hurry up and wait, was that the tactic? Dar rocked up and down on her heels. In the distance, she could hear the muffled sounds of activity, the halls they'd been walked through to this waiting room had been full of men and women rapidly moving from one place to another, all with grim, intent faces.

Hamilton joined her at the shelves. "Al just buzzed me. He's still hanging around in that lovely airport of yours," he informed her. "But he does think he's going to get to sit on an airplane in the next twenty minutes."

Dar glanced at him. "Given how screwed up everything is, can't really expect flights to be taking off on schedule. He's probably going to get on something that's supposed to be in New York."

The corporate lawyer nodded. "It's a fine mess," he agreed. "But listen, thanks by the by for taking care of old Al through all this. He said you were just a peach."

Dar's brow lifted sharply.

"In an Al sort of way," Hamilton conceded, with a smile. "And speaking of, shall we play this as a bad cop with a worse cop routine? Neither you, nor I, are going to be mistaken for a good cop any time soon."

Dar pointed over her own shoulder with her thumb. "Brought the good cop," she explained succinctly. "Though the way she was telling off some senior senator last night I'm not sure they want to piss her off."

"With any luck they'll all realize they've got a lunch date and leave us alone," Hamilton said. "I do think what I am hearing about them being all up in their shorts at us is making me itch in places men should not."

Dar folded her arms. "I gotta agree with that. I don't know what the hell they think they're mad at. I've had a thousand people working round the clock for two days busting their asses to keep everyone's pie plates spinning. What damn more do they want?"

They both turned as the door opened, and a lot of footsteps echoed into the room just ahead of a crowd of men. "I do believe we're going to find out," Hamilton said. "C'mon, Igor. Let's go be bad."

Dar was already heading toward the table where Kerry was seated, since the group of men who had entered the room were also headed in that direction. She got in front of them before they reached her partner, bringing them up short as she simply stepped into the way and blocked it. "Gentlemen."

She missed the sweetly amused expression on Kerry's face as she looked up and observed this bit of unconscious chivalry, and it only lasted a moment before Kerry removed her ear buds and stood up as Hamilton joined her.

The man in the lead, a slim, tall, dark haired guy in a suit in his mid forties or so, took a step back and held his hand up to stop the crowd. "Are you Roberts?"

"Yes." Dar stuck her hands in her pockets and regarded him. "And you are?"

"John Franklin," the man said. "I'm from the NSA. Now, you listen to me..."

"Hold up." Dar didn't raise her voice. She put her hands back in her pockets and tilted her head a little, regarding the man carefully. "Can we discuss a few ground rules before we start swinging?"

Franklin frowned. "I don't think you understand the situation here."

"I do." Dar answered, in the same even, almost gentle tone. "You obviously want something from me. Since I'm as horrified as any other American over what happened two days ago, and since I'm from a military family, chances are I want to do whatever's in my power to help you in whatever your problem is."

"Well, okay." Franklin's posture moderated. He leaned back a trifle, shifting his weight to his back foot.

"So please don't start out by yelling and trying to browbeat me," Dar said. "I don't respond well to threats, so chances are you'll have a lot faster results if you just tell me what you need, let me see what I can do to give it to you."

Franklin motioned the rest of his group to sit down. He put his briefcase on the table across from where Kerry was standing and rested his hands on the handle of it. "All right, Ms. Roberts we can try that route."

"Great." Dar pulled a chair out and sat down, patting the one next to her which Kerry promptly took. "This is our vice president of operations, Kerrison Stuart, and our senior corporate legal counsel, Hamilton Baird."

Franklin nodded at them. "Mr. Baird. Ms. Stuart." He opened his briefcase, as the rest of the men with him settled at tables nearby. One stayed by the door, as though guarding it. "This is what we need." He took out a folder and opened it. "We need you to turn over the operation of all your computer systems to us."

Dar didn't answer. She tipped her head back and looked at Hamilton, one of her eyebrows lifting. "I think this is your gig."

"I think you're right," the lawyer agreed, with a smile. "Mr. Franklin." He leaned forward and rested his forearms on the table, clasping his hands. "If that was, in fact, a serious request, we can end this discussion right now, and I'll go call my office so they can start burping up little baby lawyers to handle all the paperwork for the lawsuits."

Kerry folded her hands together and kept quiet. She watched Franklin's face as he stared at Hamilton, and noted that neither the lawyer nor her partner appeared in any way tense.

Amazing. Mostly because Kerry knew Dar was strung up like a horse about to start the Kentucky Derby, and she could feel the faint vibration of her muscles through the kneecap that was firmly in contact with her own.

"What on earth would make you even think we'd consider that?" Kerry asked, to break the silence. "Mr. Franklin, the government pays us a lot of money to do what we do. What makes you think that we would betray that trust and those contracts, and that you have anyone who could take over them even if we would?"

"Look," he said. "They're just computers. You're not rocket scientists."

Dar rolled her head to one side, and chuckled. Kerry turned and regarded her. "You could be a rocket scientist," she remarked. "But in answer to your statement, Mr. Franklin, no. They're not just computers. You don't really even understand what we do."

"I understand very well what you do," Franklin protested. "We need to have those computers. We have to be able to see everything."

Dar stood up, and rested her fingers on the desk. "Are you talking about the Virginia facility?"

"Yes," Franklin said. "We went there. We were supposed to meet Ms. Stuart there, but she never showed up."

"I did," Kerry said. "I was there for hours. You were the ones who never showed up."

The tension was rising. Hamilton lazily removed his hand from his pocket, displaying a tape recorder. "Just so we're all on the same page."

"We don't have any government computers in the Virginia facility," Dar said. "What we do there is move data traffic between a number of government offices, mostly for the purposes of accounting. Can you explain to me what the national security need is to see that?"

"Okay," Franklin remained calm. "We think there are people, maybe a lot of people, here in the United States who have been here for a while, and who are working behind the scenes to promote terrorist activities."

Hamilton cleared his throat. "I do have to remind you there have always been people inside these United States who work behind the scenes to promote all kinds of agendas."

"This is not a joke," Franklin frowned at him.

"That's a fine thing, because I am not joking Those very same people, starting way back in the 1700's, have included the Continental Congress and lots of crazy half frozen men up in Massachusetts who used to run around in wigs and short pants setting fire to Tory underwear and dumping tea in Boston Harbor."

"Sir."

"That is not a joke, mister," Hamilton's voice got louder. "In case you grew up in Arkansas and didn't get history books in school, this country was born in terrorism. It ain't nothing new." He leaned forward on the table. "So please don't start waving the flag at me saying my company's got to do this illegal thing and that illegal thing because of this new fangled scary threat. "

"What we're asking is certainly not illegal. I have the request right here, signed by the president's Chief of Staff." Franklin took out a paper and pushed it across the desk. "We are to be given access to everything."

Dar let Hamilton take the paper and study it. "Who is performing the access?" she asked.

Franklin turned, and indicated the men with him. "This is my team," he said, with a hint of a smile.

Dar studied the first of them. "What do you do?"

"Data analysis," he responded promptly. "Myself, David, and Carl here are senior data analysts."

"Robert and I are database specialists," the man next to him promptly supplied.

Dar nodded slowly. "Any of you network engineers?" she asked. "Infrastructure specialists? Layer 3 people?"

The men looked at each other, then at Franklin.

"No," Franklin said. "We don't do that."

"We do that." Kerry picked up the ball from her partner. "That's what we do in the Virginia facility. "

"Gentlemen and beautiful ladies." Hamilton pushed the paper back over. "That's legally worth about as much as a one legged man in an ass kicking contest," he stated bluntly. "Nothing in there applies to us. We're not letting you put a pinky in the door."

Kerry could sense an explosion waiting to happen. She put her hand out, and touched Franklin's arm. "What actually are you looking for?" she asked. "Accounting records? You know it's probably going to be easier if you apply directly to the offices that generate them."

"That takes too long," Franklin said. "We don't have time for all the red tape."

Hamilton looked at him. "Are you saying it's just easier to browbeat a contractor?"

"I can get the president to write an executive order to have the army take over your office," Franklin said. "I don't really care what you say at this meeting, we'll get in there, and we'll get what we want. If you want to end up in jail today, that's okay with me. I don't like you. You people are just trash, and you're in my way. "

Hamilton looked over at Dar. "Darlin', I think this is your gig."

"I think you're right," Dar agreed. She turned back to Franklin. "Okay, jackass," she said. "I don't give a shit whose weenie you're swinging off of. Jesus Christ couldn't get into my systems unless I wanted him to, so you go ahead, and go get whatever orders your heart desires because trust me buddy, they mean jack nothing to me."

"You really don't understand," Franklin said. "I'm going to have you arrested."

"For what?" Dar asked.

"I don't need anything specific. Not anymore," the NSA man said. "You don't get it. The rules all changed. We don't care if what we're doing is illegal, we'll just change the laws." He stared at Dar. "We don't care. I will wreck you, and wreck your family, and wreck your company if you don't do what I want, because I can. I can do anything. So you better decide you're going to take us back to that office, open up everything, and just get the hell out of my way or..."

"Or," Dar said, a short explosion of sound. "Arrest me, Comrade. Take me to the gulag."

Both Kerry and Hamilton remained absolutely silent.

"That's not funny."

"Neither is what you just said," Dar shot back. "That I have no rights? That as an American citizen I can be tossed in jail for no reason, with no charges, with no recourse because I won't break the law for you? That's your new world? Someone point me out the nearest foreign embassy. I've got a passport to burn."

Franklin was breathing hard. "We're at war," he said.

"My father is a retired Navy Seal," Dar said. "What the hell do you know about war he didn't teach me before I was out of grade school?" She leaned on her hands on the table, looking him right in the eye. "You can arrest me, you can toss me in the gulag, you can scream and rant and rave and weenie waggle right across the White House lawn. You will not get into those systems."

Franklin stood, and they stared at each other.

"Excuse me." Kerry held up her hand. "Can I ask a question here?" She didn't wait for permission, suspecting correctly it wouldn't be forthcoming. "If you're looking for terrorist financial activities, why are you looking for them in the records of the civil service health plan, or the department of state payroll instead of asking the credit card companies to help you?"

Everyone turned around and looked at Kerry.

"Do you really think the general accounting office is full of Taliban?" Kerry persisted. "Or NASA's website?"

"What did you say about the credit card companies?" Franklin asked, slowly.

"Lord, I swear." Hamilton sighed, and put his head down on one fist. "It's enough to make a man want to move to Japan."

"If you really want to find people who are trying to do bad things, then you should look at things they buy. I don't think people can bring things like bombs into the country," Kerry said. "But they can buy things to make bombs and those places they buy them have to have records of it."

"We understand that," Franklin said. "We know more about it than you apparently give us credit for."

"Okay," Kerry said. "Then I'm sure you're already in touch with the major retailers and the credit card clearinghouses, right? I'm sure you've asked them to cross reference charges for whatever it is that interests you? Like phosphorous or whatever."

"Or flight lessons," Dar chimed in. "I'm sure they've already thought of that Kerry, if they're here asking us to review the traffic to the National Park service."

"Stay here." Franklin got up and motioned for a man to follow him, as he left the room, walking quickly.

There was a small silence after he left. Dar bumped Kerry on the shoulder then turned to Hamilton. "Now what?"

The lawyer was already on his cell phone. "I'm calling in some backup. This ain't even slightly funny."

KERRY CLASPED HER hands, wishing she could continue working just to pass the time if nothing else. But Dar and Hamilton had told her to close her laptop down and get off the call, both of them keyed and nervous in front of the eyes of the watching men around them.

Dar was pacing around in back of her. Hamilton was across the room, his head bent over his cell phone, muttering in a low Louisiana accent that obscured all meaning from whatever it was he was saying.

Kerry sighed and looked around the room again, her irritation at the whole situation creeping slowly toward a breaking point.

She could feel Dar's agitation, and her nape hairs prickled just as she sensed her partner turning and heading toward her seat, the rush of energy making her eyes blink a little.

"Okay," Dar's voice lifted, catching everyone's attention. "That's long enough. We've got work to do."

Kerry gathered herself up, getting her hiking boots under her as she prepared to stand up, guessing rightly that Dar intended on leaving.

"I don't think that's a good idea," one of the men said.

"I don't think you think," Dar shot right back. "So unless you're going to pull a gun and keep us here, move the hell out of the way." She tapped Kerry on the back and waited for her to rise, then started for the door

"And if you all are going to pull that gun, you better make sure you shoot to kill and hide the bodies," Hamilton joined Dar as she got to the aisle. "Because you ain't ever going to get loose of the legal trouble if you don't, I guarantee it."

"Listen Mister..."

"Listen Mister is a Louisiana lawyer, son." Hamilton waved a hand in his direction. "I ain't fooling with you. I have half the legal staff of ILS, which is bigger than most of your government departments heading here with torts and complaints enough to half bury this building. We ain't talking any more to you. Tell your lawyers to call me."

Kerry decided she really didn't have much to add to the conversation. She merely shouldered her briefcase and stuck close to her partner, resisting the urge to latch on to the back of Dar's belt. The whole situation was scaring her, and she felt very glad to be tucked behind Dar's tall form in relative safety.

"Agent Franklin said for you to stay here," the man said. "I think it's a good idea for you to do that. You don't want to get him pissed off at you." He was standing in their path, both hands raised, palms outward. "We're not going to do anything ridiculous like take guns out, but this is a serious situation, and it's in your best interests just to stay put until he gets back."

"No." Dar kept going. "It's in the best interests of our customers, which includes a lot of you, for us to get out of here and get on with doing our jobs." She squared her shoulders and looked the man right in the eye. "We're not going to do what you asked us to, no matter how long we stay."

"Well, now, just think about this a minute..." The man took a step backwards, toward the door as the three of them bore down on him. "We're not asking."

The door opened behind him before Dar could come up with any more bullshit responses. She looked past the man to see Franklin entering, but from the expression on his face, she wasn't sure now what was going on.

"Sir, but...let me explain." Franklin was coming in sideways. "I have a mandate!" He tried to hold the door shut but someone was pushing it open from the other side. "Sir!"

"Get the hell out of my way you little weasel!" a gruff, older voice answered. "Take your useless bunch of yuppies with you."

Hamilton and Dar exchanged glances. "This is getting ticklier than an octopus with athlete's foot," Hamilton said. "It's never boring around you, is it? Now I know why Al went to New York and sent me here. The man was probably exhausted."

Kerry edged up next to her partner for a better view. The NSA agents had stood and now they were milling a little, looking nervously at the door.

It was shoved open, and Franklin got out of the way as a tall, grizzled haired man entered, sweeping the room with his eyes.

"Ah." He put his hands on his hips. "Which one of you is Roberts?"

Dar lifted her hand and let it fall.

"You stupid bastard." The older man turned on Franklin. "We've been waiting on this damned person since yesterday, and you're dicking around with her in here? Get the hell out of my sight."

"SIR!" Franklin bravely raised his voice. "I have a MANDATE."

"I don't give a damn!" the man shouted right back. "You had a mandate to keep the country safe too, and you didn't do that either! Now get out!"

"Oo." Kerry muttered under her breath.

"You've got no right to say that!" Franklin stood up to him. "You didn't do anything either!"

Hamilton leaned closer. "Ya'll think we should take this opportunity to skedaddle?"'

"I dunno," Dar whispered back. "I think that's the guy who told Gerry to find me."

"That's enough," the older man said. "You folks, you IT people. Come with me." He gestured to Dar and company. "Franklin, I'd start packing. Take your hair brained schemes somewhere else."

Selecting the better part of valor, Dar led the way to the door, passing behind the older man and escaping out into the hallway with a sense of relief. Even if it was momentary, and she was about to dive from the pan into the fire.

"Absolute disaster." The older man slammed the door and turned to them. "Michael Bridges, advisor to the President," he said. "Where the hell have you people been? We expected you last night."

Dar studied him. "Long story," she said. "You want to hear it, or just get down to business?"

Bridges studied her in return. Then he snorted a little. "Let's go." He pointed down the hallway. They walked along, moving from side to side to avoid the throngs of busy people who seemed to be going in every direction possible.

"So you're a friend of Easton's, eh?" Bridges asked.

"Family friend, yes," Dar agreed. "This is my vice president of operations, Kerrison Stuart, by the way, and our senior corporate legal council, Hamilton Baird."

Bridges spared them a bare glance. "Had to bring a lawyer with you? I told Easton I only wanted you here. Bastard."

"Mamma always called me a son of a bitch, matter of fact." Hamilton smiled at him. "But thanks for the compliment."

"Meant Easton." The older man frowned at him. "Don't get all smartass with me."

"Based on the conversation in that room, I don't intend on going to the bathroom here without a lawyer." Dar interjected, suspecting their legal council was about to get downright Cajun on the man. "I've had people from the government asking me to break contracts and break laws for two days."

"Hmph." Bridges indicated a door, and shoved his way through it scattering secretaries on the other side like birds before a cat. "Move it! Get that damn conference room cleared!"

Dar paused before she entered the room, letting her eyes flick over it and noting the smoked glass panels in the ceiling. In the center of the room was a large, oval wooden conference table, with comfortable leather chairs surrounding it.

In the back of the room was a mahogany credenza, looking completely out of place against the lighter wood of the conference table, and the cream leather of the chairs. It had doors in it that were flung back to reveal a large screen television, and playing on the screen, unsurprisingly, was CNN.

Dar wondered, briefly, if most of the government didn't get their information from the same place its citizens did. "All hail Ted Turner."

"What was that?" Bridges got to the head of the table and dropped into the seat there, conspicuously larger and more comfortable looking than the rest. He was dressed in a pair of pleated slacks and had a white button down shirt on, but the sleeves were rolled up and his tie was loose enough to reveal an open top neck button. "Sit. Margerie, close the damn door."

One of the secretaries looked inside and nodded, then shut the door behind her. It blocked out most of the noise in the office, but not all of it.

"All right." Bridges leaned on his forearms. He was probably in his sixties, and had a long, lined face with thick gray eyebrows and light hazel eyes. "I'm not sure if you people know how the government works."

Kerry held her hand up. "I have some idea," she remarked, in a quiet tone. "But you know, Mr. Bridges, I don't think this situation has anything to do with how the government works," she went on. "Mr. Franklin told us the rule book got thrown out the window. Is that true?"

Bridges looked at Dar, then at Hamilton, then he studied Kerry. "Where the hell do I know you from?" He asked, instead of answering the question. "You look familiar."

"Thanksgivings at my parent's house," Kerry replied. "We didn't sit at the same table though."

Bridges blinked then his brows knit. "Oh, son of a bitch. You're Roger's kid, aren't you?" He asked sounding surprised. "What in the hell are you doing here? Ah, never mind." He turned back to Dar. "We're wasting time. Here's the deal."

Kerry settled back in her seat, lacing her fingers together. She remembered Bridges, all right. A mover and shaker that even her father had respected, rude and brash to her mother, a most unwelcome guest.

Not someone she'd really wanted to get involved with.

"I imagine you know all about the damage to all that technical stuff in New York," Bridges said. "That's all your company's business."

"Not exactly," Hamilton broke in. "Just want to get that cleared up. That ain't all ours."

"That's right," Dar agreed. "We do have some customers affected there, but most of the business infrastructure there isn't ours."

"You finished talking?" Bridges asked. "Yes? Good." He leaned on his forearms again. "I don't give a damn if it was yours or Martha Stewarts to begin with. The problem is it's broke."

Dar shrugged, and nodded. "It's broken," she agreed. "What does that have to do with us?"

"Well, I'll tell you," Bridges said. "I called all those bastard phone company people into this office, and they all told me the same thing. Sure, they can fix it, but it's going to take time." He studied Dar's face intently. "They gave me all kinds of BS excuses why. Now..." He held up a hand as Dar started to speak. "I'm not an idiot. I know two goddamn buildings at least fell on top of all that stuff. Don't bother saying it."

Dar subsided, then lifted both her hands and let them drop. "Okay.

So they told you it would take time to fix. It will. They're not lying about that."

"I know," the president's advisor said. "The issue is it can't."

Kerry rubbed her temples. "Mr. Bridges, that's like saying the sun can't rise tomorrow because it would be inconvenient. There's a physical truth to this. It takes time to build rooms, and run wires, and make things work."

"I know," Bridges said. "But the fact is it can't take time. I have to open the markets on Monday. That stuff has to work by Sunday so those idiot bankers can test everything. We have to do it, Ms. Roberts. I'm not being an asshole for no purpose here. If we don't restore confidence in the financial system, we stand to lose a hell of a lot more than a couple hundred stories of office space housed in ugly architecture."

There was a small silence after that. Bridges voice faded off into faint echoes. Dar tapped her thumbs together and pondered, reading through the lines and in between his gruff tones and seeing a truth there she understood.

Alastair had understood, immediately. There was a lot at stake.

"Why me?" Dar asked, after a long moment. "You had all the Telco's in here. It's their gear. It's their pipe. It's their equipment. They have to do the work. What the hell do you want from me in all this? I don't have a damn magic wand."

"Ah." Bridges pursed his lips. "Well, fair enough. You're right. It's not your stuff. Your company has nothing to do with the whole thing, other than being a customer of those guys who were in here. But the fact of the matter is, when I squeezed their balls hard enough, what popped out of the guys from AT&T was that if I wanted this done in that amount of time, come see you."

"Me." Dar started laughing. "Oh shit. Give me a break."

Hamilton had his chin resting on one hand, and he was simply watching and listening, the faintest of twitches at the corners of his lips.

"Why is that, Ms. Roberts?" Bridges asked. "I don't really know who the hell you are, or what your company does, except that it keeps coming up in the oddest conversations around here about who knew what when and how people who work for you keep showing up in the right places with the right stuff."

"Well now," Hamilton spoke up for the first time. "What old Dar here's going to say is she's damned if she knows why, but fact is, I do," he drawled. "It's in our portfolio, matter of fact. "

"Hamilton." Dar eyed him. "Shut up."

"Dar, you know I love you more than my luggage." The lawyer chuckled. "Mr. Bridges." He turned to the advisor. "Those gentlemen from our old friends American Telegraph and Telephone told you that because they know from experience standing in front of hurricane Dar here is one way to get your shorts blown right off your body and get strangled by them." He ignored Dar's murderous look. "She just doesn't take no for an answer."

Bridges got up and went to the credenza, removing a pitcher and pouring himself a glass from it. "I see." He turned. "Is that true, Ms. Roberts?"

Dar drummed her fingers on the table. "When it suits my goals, yes," she said, finally. "I've been known to be somewhat persistent."

Kerry covered her eyes with one hand, biting the inside of her lip hard to keep from laughing. She could sense Dar peeking over at her and worked hard to regain her composure.

"All right." Bridges sat back down. "So. What's it going to cost me then? I won't waste my time appealing to your patriotism."

Dar was silent for a long moment again. "You could," she said, looking him right in the eye. "Appeal to my patriotism. What makes you think I don't have any?"

"Just a hunch," Bridges said. "You don't seem the type."

Dar's eyes narrowed a trifle. "Do the country a favor," she said. "Flush your hunches down the toilet if they're all that worthless." She got up. "Unfortunately for everyone, my patriotism doesn't count in this case. There is nothing I can do to fix what's broken. I don't own any of the infrastructure, none of those companies has any reason to do me any favors, and that union tangled century's old mess down at the tip of Manhattan is way beyond my skills to sort out in three days no matter who says yes or no. It can't be done."

Bridges leaned on his knuckles and stared at her. "Can't be done?"

"Can't be done," Dar said. "But for a price, I'll give it my best try."

The advisor sat down.

Kerry felt like she was watching a game of tennis, where the volley was getting faster and faster and the ball was a small thermonuclear device. She had no idea where Dar was going with all this, and it had been a while since she'd seen her partner in this kind of a mood.

It was almost like watching a stranger. Dar was focused, and her eyes were like chips of crystal, with no emotion at all in them.

"What's your price?" Bridges asked, in a sardonic tone. "Maybe I'll try to pay it if you're only going to try and do what I'm asking."

"Get the NSA off my ass," Dar said, ticking one finger off. "Give my people clearance to get into the city." She ticked a second finger off. "Give me some kind of leverage to get through the politics. I'll give it my best shot. You get whatever you get out of it. Maybe it'll work. Maybe it won't."

The advisor rested his forearms on the table again and gazed at her, with a slightly puzzled look. "What's in it for you, then?" he asked. "What do you get out of it?"

Dar managed the faintest of smiles. "Service to my country," she answered, in a quiet tone. "It's the right thing to do, no matter how impossible it is."

"You really don't think it's possible," Bridges mused. "Everyone agrees with that, even the president. He wanted me to find some way to fake it." He looked up to find three sets of eyes staring at him in disbelief, and he shrugged in response. "Ms. Stuart will tell you just how much of the government is smoke and mirrors, I'm sure."

Kerry cleared her throat gently. "That's true," she said. "But we aren't smoke and mirrors. If Dar commits us to this, we'll go at it a hundred percent."

Bridges nodded. "Cheap enough price," he said. "All right, Ms. Roberts, do we have a deal? "

"I guess we do." Dar looked at Hamilton, who burst into laughter.

That seemed to strike Bridges funny too, and he chuckled. "Now I understand what Easton told me." He stood up. "Get out of here, people. I have an unending pile of crap to put on a potter's wheel and make into china."

They were glad enough to escape, slipping out the door and evading the flock of secretaries, emerging into the hallway where the pace hadn't slowed a bit. Hamilton steered them over to a corner out of the flow and they all took a minute to catch their breaths.

"That," Kerry finally said, "was seriously freaky."

"Got us out of the way of the spooks," Hamilton commented. "And Dar, no jokes here, darling. That was some good shuck and jive in that room. I couldn't have negotiated a better deal."

Dar exhaled, and shook her head. "Let's get out of here," she said. "I don't know what the hell I just got us into, but I sure don't want to spend any more time in this place. Let's go somewhere and scratch together a plan."

Kerry spotted Franklin heading down the hall in their direction. She grabbed Dar's arm. "Great idea. C'mon He hadn't had a chance to talk to Bridges yet."

They did, heading around a corner, and down a hall, hoping they ended up somehow at an outside door without getting into any more trouble.

Chapter Twenty-two

"OKAY." KERRY LED the way through the visitor's entrance to their offices. "Dar, I'm going to have to sign you in." She could feel her partner silently snickering. "Do you know what a pile of paperwork that's going to be?"

"Sorry," Dar said, with not a lot of sincerity. "Hey, if they won't let me in, we can go work out of the nerd bus. Dad's there and I hear the foods pretty good."

"Dar." Kerry eyed the receptionist as they approached. "How about we get you a loaner laptop and just push your image down to it? I'm sure we've got one in this place that can handle it."

"Bet they don't."

"Good morning, Ms. Stuart." The receptionist greeted her with a smile. "A lot of people were asking after you inside. I'm sure they'll be glad to see you."

Kerry set her briefcase down and removed her sunglasses. "Yeah, it's been that kind of morning," she agreed. "I need to sign in a corporate employee that doesn't have a badge with them."

The woman glanced past Kerry at the tall, lanky figure behind her. "That's no problem, ma'am, I just need to see some ID and I can process that for you."

"She doesn't have that either," Kerry said. "And we haven't installed integrated biometrics here yet, have we? Everyone needs a card." She took the visitor form that had been held out to her and passed it back. "Fill this out, hon."

Dar took the form with its clipboard and started obediently scribbling. "What's my purpose for visiting? Anarchy and general disruption of the business?"

The receptionist frowned. "If you mean the government handprint thing, no ma'am. But I can't issue a visitor pass without seeing some identification."

"You're just going to have to take my word for who this is," Kerry told her. "I'll authorize it...no wait." She turned and glanced at her partner. "I'm the requester, I can't also authorize. Shoot. I think you have to authorize it since you're my up chain."

Dar chuckled and kept writing.

The receptionist caught the clue. "Oh," she said. "Sorry, Ms. Roberts. We weren't expecting you."

"No one ever is." Dar produced a reasonably sexy grin. "I'm the Spanish Inquisition of ILS." She handed back the clipboard and the pen. "There you go."

The receptionist took it and studied the paper then pulled out a visitor pass and punched in the programming for it. "One of the people from the NSA was here yesterday looking for you, Ms. Stuart, after you left."

"I know. We found them." Kerry said, leaning against the counter as she watched Dar wander around the lobby examining it. "I think we got that all sorted out. Hopefully they won't be bothering us again."

"Okay, here you go ma'am." The receptionist handed over the visitor badge. "Should I let them know you're here?"

"And spoil my fun?" Dar took the badge from her and winked. "Nah."

"Thanks." Kerry smiled at the woman and led her troublemaking spouse toward the inner door. "We can use that office they assigned to me. It's big enough to party in." She scanned the door open and held it as Dar went past her. "So what's the plan?"

"What's the plan? " Dar sighed, as they walked down the hallway side by side. "I wish I knew what the plan was. I need to sit down and think for a few minutes and try to figure out where the hell to start." She said. "Want to stop in at ops first? You said they were a little rattled at my locking them down."

"Good idea." Kerry led the way to the security door and swiped through it, leading Dar into the inner operations center. Their entry caught the group by surprise, and voices fell off as people's heads turned as they spotted Kerry.

Kerry watched their eyes, as they shifted to her companion and stayed there, putting two and two together a lot faster than the receptionist did. "Good morning folks," she said. "As you can see, I called in the cavalry. Dar and I have just gotten back from the White House, and I think we've gotten a few things worked out that will take some of the stress off you all."

No one said anything for a very long moment. Then the shift supervisor, a different man than the previous day, came over. "Oh, well. Wow. That wasn't expected. Ms. Roberts, it's an honor." He timidly extended a hand, which Dar clasped in a genial manner. "Don Abernathy. We've been on conference calls a few times."

"We have," Dar agreed. "Someone want to vacate a seat so I can check things out in here?"

Kerry took a step back and amused herself in watching the staff as they scrambled around to make space for Dar on both the government and commercial side of the monitors. They had all been extremely respectful to her the previous day, but their attitude toward her partner was one of utter awe, and completely different in scope.

People usually did react to Dar differently. Kerry expected that. But she spent so much time around her at their Miami office that she often forgot how the rest of the company viewed her, since everyone in Miami was pretty much used to having her around.

Dar slid into an emptied chair and rested her long forearms on the console surface, pausing a moment to review the screen before she logged the user out and logged herself in with a patter of rapid keystrokes that sounded ridiculously loud in the suddenly quiet room.

Dar seemed to realize it. She stopped, and looked slowly around, first one way then the other. "People, sit the hell down. They don't pay me to teach typing."

Kerry chuckled under her breath, as the staff sidled back to their seats, save Don, who had an excuse to remain standing near the front of the console. "Dar, be nice." She chastised her. She walked over and put her hands on her partner's shoulders. "I'm going to go get some work done. Come get me when you're done showing off."

Dar leaned back, her head thumping gently against Kerry's chest. "Get me that laptop if you can. We're also going to need a video conference with Hamilton and his friends about what contacts we have in New York."

"Okay." Kerry just barely resisted the urge to give her a kiss on the top of her head. "I'll get that set up and let you know when it's ready."

Dar winked at her.

Kerry squeezed her boss's shoulders and then she stepped back and headed for the door, leaving a lot of bemused faces behind her.

She was used to that too. She made her way through the hall to the office she'd been issued and shouldered her way into it, crossing the carpet and putting her briefcase down on the desk. Before she opened it though, she went over and used the hot water dispenser tucked in one corner, getting a cup and a teabag sorted and steeping in short order.

A soft knock came at the door. "C'mon in." Kerry looked over her shoulder as the door opened, and Nan's dark head poked itself in. "Good morning, Nan," she greeted the woman. "How are you doing today?"

"Oh, hi. You are here. I'm doing okay, thanks." Nan slipped in. "Everyone's looking for you, though." She told Kerry. "In a bad way."

"Not the NSA again?" Kerry slipped her laptop out and opened it.

"No. Everyone but them," Nan said, frankly. "We're getting pounded for resources from all sides. I've been here since six and the phone hasn't stopped ringing off the hook."

That sounded a little strange. While the center did house a lot of systems, both government and civil, Kerry didn't really understand why the overall need would have surged now. "Okay," she said. "Let me get booted up, and I'll get on the bridge. You can also have them transfer any real trouble to the phone here." She circled the desk and slid into the chair. "And if it gets too scary, we'll throw Dar at them."

Nan cocked her head. "Literally?"

Kerry glanced up and grinned over the top of her screen. "She's in the ops center. If they all know what's good for them, they'll just be understanding and reasonable."

"Wow. I didn't realize she was here," Nan said. "I don't think anyone did...er, does." She put her hands in her pockets. "I'm sure I'd have heard if they did."

"We just got here." Kerry logged in as her laptop finished booting. She reached for her ear buds as she waited for the desktop to launch and key in the conference bridge. "We had a meeting we had to go to earlier."

"Okay, well, I'll let everyone know you're here then," Nan said. "I know they'll be glad to hear it. Anything else you need?"

Kerry paused before hitting the mic. "Matter of fact there is," she said. "I need to get my hands on the highest end laptop you've got here," she said. "Biggest hard drive, biggest chunk of RAM, highest screen resolution."

Intrigued, Nan removed her hands from her pockets and crossed the office, taking a seat in the visitor chair across from Kerry. "Okay," she said. "Most of the staff uses the standard type."

"I figured." Kerry started scanning the screen. "But that won't do, unfortunately. What else do we have here?" She read down the list of requests posted on the desktop, grimacing a little at the blinking red lines that had moved from requests to demands.

"Well." Nan frowned. "You want something like what you're using? I think we have one or two of that model around, maybe in the test center. I'd have to check on the RAM though. Mine's last year's model and it's got a gig."

Kerry glanced at the opposite wall briefly. "No. Has to be more horsepower than this one," she said.

"Would a server work?" Nan suggested. "I'm pretty sure we don't have anything even close to that in a laptop."

Kerry imagined her partner tucking one of the big suitcase size items under her arm to walk out with. "Ah...no...hang on," She clicked the mic on. "Miami ops, this is Miami exec. You on?"

"Go ahead boss," Mark answered. "You still with the goons?"

"In Herndon," Kerry answered. "You have any laptops with you?"

"Sure."

"Big enough to take the Godzilla image?"

"Miami exec, this is Newark Earthstation," a voice broke in. "We're maxed here, and I have the city of New York on the line demanding we give them priority on the birds."

"Hang on Newark. Mark, do you or not?" Kerry repeated.

"Yowp hang on one sec, Boss, we're checking the back tank," Mark called out, his voice obviously away from the mic. "Big Kahuna's box take a dive?"

"It's in Miami."

"Crap."

"Newark, this is Miami exec," Kerry said. "What traffic are they asking priority for?"

"Boss, we don't have anything close," Mark said. "Not that'll take the image for that beast without rolling over and crying, even mine."

"Miami exec, this is Newark. Some kind of telecommunications relay. City business they said." the Earthstation informed her. "They're getting pretty pushy, even for New Yorkers."

Kerry tapped on the desk. "They're under a lot of stress, guys. Cut them a little slack." She glanced at Nan and cut the mic off. "Where's the nearest hard core gaming shop?"

Nan blinked. "What?"

"Miami exec, we are, we are," Newark answered. "I told them we could only give them maybe 256, and they went off on me."

"Yeah?" Kerry asked. "Okay, well get them on the line, and I'll conference." She put the mic on hold again. "A gamer shop. You know, PC games. First person shooters? 3D gaming world sims?"

Nan stared at her. "You mean, like video games?" she queried. "Sonic the Hedgehog? That stuff?"

"Okay, Miami exec, hold on a few." Newark clicked off.

"Miami exec, this is Miami ops," Mark broke in. "Nego on anything we can give big D outside maybe my setup server. They got anything there?"

"They don't Mark. Can you find me a gamer hack shop around here?" Kerry asked. "I'll send someone to get whatever their top of the line is."

"Sweet. Hang on."

Kerry picked up her tea and sipped it, taking advantage of the moment's lull. "Okay, while that's going on, Lansing, how's it looking there today?"

"Miami, we have a lot of cellular backhaul hitting us today," her hometown local office said. "Also, it looks like VOIPs getting hit pretty hard in the Northeast. I'm running hot across the board."

"Confirm that, Miami, this is Herndon ops," another voice added. "We've seen building traffic since about seven and...eh? Oh, ah yes. Ah, someone's looking at it."

Kerry muffled a grin, knowing full well who that someone was. "Thanks, Herndon. Lansing, keep the shaping in. We don't know what we're going to be called on to move today with all that's going on.'

"Yes, ma'am."

"Miami, this is LA Earthstation."

Kerry checked her watch. "Good morning, LA."

"Ma'am, we've got Intelsat on the line. They've got a software issue on one of their control systems and they want to know if we've got anybody there that can look at it. They're tapped for resources."

"Okay poquito boss, I got a place for ya." Mark came back on. "Got a pencil?"

Nan quickly grabbed a pad and a pen. "How do you keep up with all this?"

"Acquired attention deficit disorder. Comes with the job." Kerry was scribbling something herself. "Hang on LA. Miami applications support, you on?"

"We're here," a male voice answered. "I think we're the only ones not that busy today, Ms. Stuart. Would you like us to call Intelsat and engage them?"

"I would. Go ahead Mark. We've got a pen waiting," Kerry said. "Apps, see what you can do to back up ops there too, I know folks must be pretty tired in the center."

"Will do."

Mark's voice rapidly recited an address that Nan just as rapidly copied down. She finished and looked at it. "You want me to go get the biggest thing they got, right?" she asked. "Max RAM, max storage, max pixel."

"You got it," Kerry said, busy making notes. "Shoot, we've got some stuff hitting the fan here...damn it, I can't get deliveries in freaking Iowa. How in the hell are we supposed to go fix New York?"

"Any particular color?"

Kerry looked up and over her laptop screen for a long moment of silence. Then her eyes twinkled a little. "Not. Pink," she enunciated very carefully.

"You got it." Nan got up and headed for the door. "Be back in a flash." Behind her, a burst of chatter erupted, as issues suddenly scaled over each other, and the tempo rose.

"Miami exec, this is Lansing, we just got an alert from Citibank they're spooling backups from Buffalo," Lansing broke in. "They're pushing the shaping profile."

"Miami, exec this is Newark, I have the Governor of New York on the line for you."

"Miami exec, this is the Air Hub, we're seeing a lot of congestion. We've got packets dropping here."

A loud whistle suddenly cut through all the chatter. Nan paused at the open door and stared back at the desk, but Kerry merely smiled.

"All right," Dar's voice briskly followed the whistle. "Thor, god of the internets is here. Kerry, go handle the Governor. I'll start squeezing the pipes. Everybody just relax. This is where we earn our reputation."

"Dar, what about..." Kerry paused, the time limit and the commitment they'd made weighing on her suddenly. Yes, they told the government they'd go try and fix their problem but what about all of their own?

"Already doing the prep," Dar answered. "I've got about a dozen reports running that are going to need my algorithms. Hope you find that laptop."

"Hope you find room in your pipes for me to pull your image," Kerry remarked wryly.

"First things first," her partner said, with easy confidence. "See what we can do over at Newark. We're going to need the leverage."

Ah. Kerry punched in the conference line for the Earthstation. Complications. "Will do, boss, will do."

DAR LEANED AGAINST the console, bracing her elbows on the surface and folding her hands together as she studied the screen. She was aware, in a disconnected way, that there were a lot of people watching her, but her attention was absorbed by the thin tracing lines and flickering statistics in front of her.

The barebones diagram she was studying was a scaled down version of what she was used to looking at in her office, with fewer colors and sketchier details. It was enough, though, for her to see the imbalances caused by the outages and the need to route around them.

Any individual outage was not a problem. Dar had built more than enough redundancy into her design to cope with that. In fact, multiple outages were usually not a problem either. But the combination of multiple outages of their own, and the suddenly heavy demand from everyone trying to route around outages themselves was giving her usually robust network fits.

Giving Dar fits. "Damn it." She put her hands back on the keyboard and rattled off a few commands. "We need to get those damn nodes reconnected north of the city," she muttered. "I've got everything coming south and it's crunching the hell out of us."

"Ma'am?" One of the console techs timidly leaned closer. "Are you talking to us, or just to you?"

Dar glanced up, watching everyone quickly pretend to look at something else. "Well." She drummed her fingers. "I was talking to myself, but if you've got any good ideas cough them up." She waited, but the crowd remained respectfully silent. "C'mon, people. I don't bite."

Don came forward, with an air of martyred bravery. "Well, uh, ma'am..."

"Whoa." Dar held her hand up. "First of all, I'm going to be around for a while. Stop the ma'am crap and call me by my name, please."

Don's eyes widened, and his nostrils flared visibly. "Uh," he said. "Okay, Ms. Roberts. If you say so."

Dar gave him a wry look.

"Anyway." Don glanced at the big board behind them. "Um, what exactly are you doing? It's hard for us to make suggestions when we don't really have a clue what's going on."

Everyone held their breath when he finished, but Dar merely chuckled. "Good point," she agreed, settling back in her chair. "The network is imbalanced because of the outages. We're pulling too much, especially on the commercial side." She pointed at the big board. "That's why all the lines are purple tending to red, instead of blue like they usually are."

Heads swung toward the board, then back to her. "That makes sense," one of the techs said. "But what can we do about it?"

"I think a lot of people are using more data bandwidth than usual too," one of the female techs added. "Sending emails, and listening to the internet with all that streaming video going on."

"Agreed," Dar said. "Same thing we're doing, since some of the traffic is us on the big bridge," she said. "That global meeting place isn't a text screen and a bunch of black and white pixels."

"Wow," the woman said. "I never even thought of that."

"Can we ask our customers not to do that?" Don spoke up. "How can we? This is something where people really need to communicate with each other, like what we're doing. That global meeting is an amazing thing."

Dar folded her hands. "Very true. So no, we really can't ask them not to reach out to each other. So that's why I'm rooting around in the bits and bytes to see if there's anything I can do to optimize what's going through." She went back to the screen and reviewed the results of her last command. "Let's see..."

She focused on the black screen again, studying the flows. Then a memory surfaced, and she cursed to herself, flipping through parts of the configuration, searching through the code with rapid, impatient flicks of her mouse.

"Boy it's really getting stuffed," Don remarked. "I bet we get calls any minute."

"You'd think folks would just remember what's going on," the female tech on Dar's other side muttered.

Ah. Dar found what she was looking for. "I'm such a jerk sometimes."

"Ma'am?" Don turned and looked at her.

Dar sniffed and rattled her keyboard, muttering under her breath.

"Air Hub, are you picking up the feed from the ATC? They're on the line here saying you're dropping it." Kerry's voice crackled over the speakers. "And, LA Earthstation, stand by, I managed another 24 transponder channels for you from Hughes."

"Miami exec, this is LA Earth. We're standing by. We've got half dozen requests for upgrades from the government side."

"Miami exec, this is the Air Hub. Stand by please we're checking."

"LA Earth, this is Newark Earth, save a few for us, please. We have two dozen to your half," a harried voice answered. "Miami exec, any extra for us?"

Kerry's voice sounded apologetic. "Newark, we're trying. They're absolutely saturated The only reason we got west coast space is the airlines are moving again and the requests from Vancouver have slacked off."

"Miami exec, understood. Also be advised we were asked about our power trucks. The City wanted to know where we got them from. I told them they would need to talk to you."

Dar kept typing, one ear twitching at the flow of complaints. She could hear the strain starting again in her partner's voice, and resolved to attend to that critical issue next.

"Miami exec, this is Roosevelt Island," a new voice interrupted. "I have a cross-connect request here for new service? They said it was priority."

"Roosevelt, it is. Please provide them service at my request," Kerry answered. "We've provisioned a ten mg slice for them. It's data services for AT&T. Tunnel them through to our common carrier point in Philly, please. They're expecting it."

Dar looked up at the big board, her eyes lifting a little.

"Okay, ma'am, will do."

Dar wrenched her attention back to the screen, a set of changes already inputted, waiting for her confirmation. She hesitated then saved the changes without executing, and stood up. "Be right back."

"THEY THOUGHT I was crazy. " Nan set a large cardboard box down on the desk Kerry was using, as its occupant was retrieving another cup of tea. "They were saying what are you going to play with it…is it for a LAN party? Can you tell us where?"

Kerry chuckled as she returned, dropping back into her chair and rocking her head back and forth to loosen the tightening muscles in her neck. She glanced at her screen, then shifted her attention to the box and watched as it was opened releasing the scent of new computer equipment into the air.

Plastic off gassing mostly, but also a hint of the chemicals inside. As distinctive as a new car, and occasionally as expensive. "Bet they did," Kerry said. "If they only knew."

"If only," Nan agreed. "I told them I was buying it for my brother for his birthday," she admitted. "They wanted me to adopt them."

Kerry chuckled. "Nerds."

"They were glad for the sale." Nan opened the Styrofoam bag the machine was carefully encased in and slid it free, lifting it with both hands and placing it on the desk. "I was the only one in there."

Kerry folded her hands together and peered at the laptop. "Sexy," she said. "I think she'll like it."

"Like what?" a voice at the door surprised both of them.

Kerry looked across the room to see Dar entering, a cup in her hand. "Hey boss," she said. "How's it going?"

"It's going." Dar's nose twitched and she made a beeline for the desk as she spotted the boxes. "What do we have here?"

Nan's eyes widened and she stepped back from the desk, picking up the boxes and wrapping and getting hastily out of the way.

"Hm. I like the color." Dar hitched one knee up and took a seat on the desk, handing her cup over to Kerry as she reached over to take hold of the laptop. "Drink that. You're froggy again." She picked up the laptop with one hand and set it on her thigh, opening the latch and lifting the screen.

"Thanks." Kerry accepted the cup. "I've been drinking tea but it's not helping." She sipped the cold chocolate milk as she watched her partner. Then she shook her head a little, and glanced up at Nan. "Sorry. My manners went south there for a minute. Nan, this is Dar Roberts."

Nan cleared her throat. "Hello."

"Nan's been nice enough to run around for us the past two days. She went out to get your new toy, hon." Kerry unobtrusively gave her partner a nudge, distracting her from an apparently fascinating encounter with the laptop's BIOS.

Dar's eyes lifted and met the woman's. "We've spoken on the phone," she said after a moment. "You do the inventory recaps."

Nan blinked. "Um...yes, yes I do. Nice to meet you in person finally," she stammered a little. "I hope the machine's okay. It's pretty much the best they had."

Dar bent her head to study the machine's screen briefly. "I think it'll be fine," she said. "Good choice," she added, with a smile. "Thanks for doing my shopping for me. "

Nan smiled back. "Anytime."

"Okay." Dar got up and circled the desk, dropping to her knees and peering under it. "Got a cable, Ker?"

"Oh, wait, hang on... I can do that..." Nan scrambled forward, hauling up as Kerry lifted her hand and waved her back. "But..."

Dar's head popped up over the desk's surface, and her eyebrows hiked. "What?" She rummaged in Kerry's briefcase and disappeared again, with a grunt. "I hate these kinds of jacks. What moron had them installed here?"

Kerry scooted out of her way a bit, and leaned on the top of the desk. "Miami ops, this is Miami exec. How are those transfers coming?"

"Miami exec, this is Houston Ops," another voice broke in. "We have a bulk backup request from Cheyenne Mountain to secure storage, and a database parse. "

"Acknowledged," Kerry said. "Are you mentioning it just because it's out of time range?" She almost bit her tongue when she suddenly felt warmth against the side of her knee and realized it was Dar's breath.

"Yes, ma'am," Houston answered. "We can give them their standard bandwidth but if something comes up while it's transferring we're tapped."

Kerry glanced down, to see twinkling blue eyes looking back up at her. "What do you think?"

"What do I think?" Dar drawled, pressing her cheek against the outside of Kerry's leg. "Hm..." She watched the light blush climb up her throat before she relented, moving away and coming back up from under the desk with the end of an ethernet cable in her fingers. "Houston, let them go for it. I'll keep an eye on the pipe and if you start stressing it I can throw some compression on it."

"Okay, uh...ma'am," Houston said. "Will do."

Dar remained on her knees, plugging the laptop into the ethernet cable after she scribbled some numbers off the bottom of it. "Let me get at your session for a minute," she told her partner. "Miami ops, this is Miami exec. Stand by for a high speed encrypted image transfer. You're going to redline. No one freak out please."

"Copy that, Miami exec," Mark's voice broke in. "I tanked the alerter."

"All yours." Kerry slipped out of her seat and took her milk, retreating around the side of the desk to where Nan was somewhat awkwardly standing. She took up a spot next to the woman and sipped from the cup.

"Thanks. So is the computer." Dar dropped into the chair and flexed her hands, cracking the knuckles of her fingers before she started typing on Kerry's laptop. "Hope to hell this thing isn't different enough hardware for the image to choke."

"Dar's machine image is a one of a kind," Kerry said, conversationally to Nan. "She goes through laptops like popcorn, so we always have a snapshot ready. "

"Oh," Nan murmured. "What's so different about it?"

"Programs," Dar answered without looking up. "A handful of cranky, self written piles of code that do analytics on pretty much everything." She glanced at the paper, and then back at the screen. "Along with consolidated control consoles for the majority of the infrastructure."

"And Gopher Dar," Kerry commented.

"And Gopher Dar," her partner agreed. "Okay, Mark, here it comes, I ran it by mac."

"Gotcha."

"I'm going to clear out my inbox," Nan said. "If you all need anything, give me a ring." She backed away from the desk and escaped out the door, closing it quickly behind her.

Kerry watched her go, then turned back to her partner. "I think you're scaring her, hon."

Dar's brows twitched. "Me? I didn't do anything," she protested. "I thought I was being nice."

Kerry gave her an affectionate smile.

Dar hit a few more keys then turned to watch the newly purchased laptop. It blinked, then the screen shivered and blanked out, replaced by a spinning pirate flag. "Nice touch." She drummed her fingertips on the desktop. "This snap is from before I left for London, but I didn't have time to do much with it there so it should be all right."

"Holy crap!" a voice echoed on the line through Kerry's laptop.

"Didn't I tell everyone not to freak out?" Dar frowned, and tapped the mic. "Hold tight, people. This won't take long." She muted. "I hope." She leaned on the desk and tilted her head, peering over at Kerry. "We're going to have an issue."

Kerry blinked mildly at her. "Another one?" she asked. "Dar, we've got a metric ton of them now, you're sitting there thinking of more?" She perched on the edge of the desk, swirling her milk in its cup.

"Paradox," Dar said, succinctly. "We're going to need to be in lower Manhattan to make things happen."

"Sure."

"There's no damn comms or cell service in lower Manhattan. How do we make things happen if we can't communicate?"

"Ah." Kerry frowned. "We have to bring comms with us then, I guess."

"Miami exec, this is Miami ops, we just got a call from the banking center. They're saying they're seeing degraded response," a voice interrupted them.

"Shoot." Kerry leaned over and hit the mic. "Miami ops, tell them we're aware, and we're working to clear space. Please remind them we have a lot going on."

"Yes'm."

'We've moved big chunks of data before, and not caused that." Kerry looked at her partner. "Is that you, really?"

"Me, really," Dar admitted. "I prioritized the stream. Sixty more seconds and we're done. It would have taken a half hour otherwise." She drummed her fingers on the desk again. "I need those damn programs. I have structure diagrams from New York in one of them that might help us."

"Do we have anyone local we can call..." Kerry let her voice trail off. "Boy, that was stupid. Sorry," she muttered. She got up and went around the desk, coming to kneel next to Dar so she could see the laptop screen a little better. There was a black window open, full of Dar's cryptic typing and she rested her chin on her fist for a minute, releasing a long sigh.

Dar's hand immediately settled on the back of her neck, the strong fingers kneading the skin there with gentle sureness. "God, Dar. There's so much to do."

"I know," Dar responded. "I just feel like taking off and going to the beach when I think about all the crap we've got to get through." She kept rubbing Kerry's neck, feeling the bones move under her fingers. "Not looking forward to it."

"Me either."

Dar reached over and hit a few keys. "Done," she said, keying the mic. "Miami ops, Miami exec. Transfers complete." She draped her arm over Kerry's shoulders then leaned closer and kissed her on the back of her neck, just above her collar. "Let's hope I don't have to do that again."

"Honey, you can do that whenever you want." Kerry was content to remain where she was, one elbow resting on Dar's thigh as she listened to the chatter on the bridge call. To one side, she could hear the laptop rebooting and she struggled to gather her thoughts and go back to work as soon as she knew the machine was ready.

"That's not a bad idea,' Dar said, suddenly.

Kerry paused then cleared her throat gently. "What isn't?"

"Getting someone local," her partner replied. "We need someone really local. Someone who knows people."

They were both quiet. "I think Bob probably really knew people," Kerry said, finally.

"Yeah."

"Hello, hello, Miami?" Sherren's voice broke in. "Are you there?"

Kerry reached over and hit the mic. "We're here. How are things there, Sherren?"

"The phones came back on," the woman said. "We were all sitting in the boardroom just keeping each other company, and all of a sudden the phones started ringing off the hook in here. It's a madhouse now."

"Sorry about that, Sherren," Kerry sighed. "I did ask AT&T to try and work us into their priority schedule."

"No, hey, it's great," Sherren protested. "You don't know we couldn't make calls here or nothing, and now everyone can talk to their families. It's...that's the calls. People trying to talk to us, find out if we're okay."

"Oh."

"It's good. We're okay," Sherren said. "And oh my gosh. Oh, look. Mr. McLean just got here. I didn't know he was coming!"

Dar leaned forward. "He wanted to be with you all there. He thought you could use some support, Sherren. He knows you all have had a terrible time."

There was a long silence. Then Sherren's voice came back on, she was clearly in tears. "Oh," she gasped. "Oh, that's so wonderful. It's so wonderful people care about us." She sniffled. "We're trying to take care of each other."

Behind her, Dar could faintly hear Alastair's voice, sounding quiet and sad. "Sherren, tell him we're doing fine here, okay?" she said. "You all just hang in there."

"We will. We will. We're tough people," Sherren said. "I'll tell him. I'll be back."

"Miami exec, this is Combus 2." A low, deep voice took advantage of the break in the chatter. "We're in bound from Albany and I have Combus 3 about two miles behind me."

"Will they let them in?" Kerry whispered.

"From the north, maybe," Dar murmured back. She keyed the mic. "Combus 2, you and 3 try to get as far down toward the Rock as you can."

"Roger that, Ms. Roberts," the deep voice said. "Anything we need to stop and pick up?"

Dar glanced over at the monitor that was showing desperate scenes of men digging in debris, a pall of smoke hanging over the air. "Find a medical supply warehouse," she said. "Get breathing masks, filters, whatever you can. Suits," she added. "Miami exec, Miami Financial, you on?"

"Right here, my friend," Duks answered. "I will have my purchasing people find such a place, and let the good drivers know where it is. We will handle the payment for it."

"Thanks Duks," Dar said. "Combus, see if you can pick up bottled water or Gatorade, too."

"Will do ma'am."

Dar signed into her new laptop and got up, clearing Kerry's chair for her. "Let me get out of your way. I think I can..." She stopped, as Kerry put a hand on her arm. "What?"

"Stay here," Kerry said. "Just bring that chair around to this side. I want you here." She got up off her knees and settled into the chair. "Please?"

Dar studied her for a moment then smiled. "Works for me." She dragged the other chair over and settled back down. "Let's get back to business."

THE RV AND bus had, in fact, become the social center of their piece of the parking lot. Dar was glad enough to stick her hands in the pockets of her jacket and head toward the crowd, shifting her shoulders to settle the weight of a company issued backpack that held her new laptop in it.

It was almost dark. The lot was bright with emergency lights, though, and activity was plentiful and obvious. Kerry walked quietly at her side, speaking in an undertone to Nan, her own briefcase slung over her shoulder.

Dar was tired. It had been a long day, and she hadn't quite caught up to her jet lag, her body grumbling at her and wanting that soft hotel bed they'd left so early that morning. She glanced at the bus, seeing a swarm of activity around it and found herself resenting the need to be in the middle of that.

"Dar?" Kerry put a hand on her elbow.

"Hm?" She turned her head and peered at her partner. She noted the furrow in Kerry's brow, and realized she wasn't the only one tired.

"What's our plan here?"

"That's a damn good question." Dar sighed.

"Have you heard from Justin? I know that's the first question I'll get when we reach the bus."

"Maria said he hadn't called me back when I talked to her before we left the office," Dar said. "Gimme your cell and I'll call him again." She waited for Kerry to fish her phone from its clip on her belt. "He might actually answer the phone if he sees your name."

"Not after what I did during that whole ship thing." Kerry handed the device over. "He hasn't forgiven me for that one yet."

Dar paused to recall the number then dialed it, putting the phone to her ear as they walked between the parked trucks toward their little compound.

The bus was in the back, its extended sections fully extended, and its roof thick with antennas and the satellite dish that provided the transport with television and data. In front of it there was a work area with tables covered with various bits of technology on one side, and tables covered with various bits of daily living on the other.

There were camping chairs scattered around, and the bus's integrated barbeque grill was out and being used.

On the far side of the bus was the RV and Mark's truck with the big satellite trailer parked in a clear spot nearby with its dish fully extended. There were thick, black power cables snaking everywhere, and a large LCD television was fixed to the side of the trailer, showing CNN.

Their techs were busy around the tables, but they were mixed with a plethora of military in several different kinds of uniforms. The combination of high tech and post Apocalyptic camping made Kerry's eyebrows twitch.

"Justin, don't give me that," Dar was saying. "I'm not asking for extra equipment, just what you have scheduled for us. What's the damn problem?"

"Uh oh," Kerry muttered. "That doesn't sound good."

Nan glanced past her at the scowling CIO. "Who's she talking to?" she whispered.

"Our network equipment account manager," Kerry said, as they crossed the last line of cars and entered their space. "Hey guys. How's it going?"

The techs looked up, and their eyes brightened immediately. "Hey, Ms. Stuart. Mark was just asking for you," one said, "Lemme go get him."

"No need...we're heading for the bus ourselves," Kerry demurred. "We'll find him."

"If you don't cut the crap, I'm going to...what? No, you idiot, I'm not going to threaten you with pulling the contract, I'm just going to tell my customer here you're sitting on his goddamned gear for no good reason!" Dar's voice lifted into a familiar bark.

Kerry patted her back comfortingly, and gave the staff a smile. She spotted Andrew crossing between the RV and the bus, and waved to him as he saw them and changed direction.   He had on an ILS sweatshirt and dark carpenter pants with tools poking from every pocket, and just seeing him made Kerry feel better. "Hey Dad." She opened her arms and gave him a hug that he returned warmly. "What a day, huh?"

"Justin, stop being a moron. Where in the hell do you think I am? Did you even look at what order I was talking about?" Dar asked. "Don't give me that crap! He did? Then let me talk to him. Put his ass on the phone!"

"lo there kumquat," Andrew greeted her, giving his growling offspring a wary look. "Dar got problems?"

Kerry gave him a wry look. Then she half turned. "Nan, this is Andrew Roberts, Dar's father. Dad, this is Nan. She's from our Virginia office and has been giving us a big hand in getting things done."

"Lo there," Andrew greeted Nan amiably.

"Nice to meet you," Nan said.

"Got some folks inside I think want to talk to you two," Andrew informed Kerry, as Dar stepped to one side and half turned, lowering her voice. "Seems like they got some kinda issue they just come up with. That Mark feller just kept saying Dardar's name over and over again."

"Uh oh," Kerry winced. "Well, let's go see what that's all about while Dar straightens out our gear issues. She touched Dar's arm and pointed to the bus, waiting for her partner to nod before she started off in that direction.

Andrew paused then followed her, evidently figuring his daughter didn't need any help in yelling.

The bus was a beehive of activity, and they had to dodge a flurry of moving bodies in uniform until they finally made it to the steps and up into the courtesy bus. Kerry almost stopped short at the mild chaos inside, but after a brief pause she edged her way in and got into enough of a corner space to turn and look around.

Mark was in one corner with three techs, and four or five military men. Others were spread around the inside of the bus, working on clipboards, standing over the fax machine in the corner, and munching on some of the snacks laid out on platters in the service area.

One whole wall had been taken up by a whiteboard covered in scribbles. Kerry was glad to see so much apparent progress, but slightly overwhelmed at the amount of people stuffed in the bus. "Evening everyone."

Heads turned. "Hey, Kerry. Glad you're here," Mark said. "I hope you brought big D with you, cause we need her like crazy."

Know the feeling. Kerry nodded. "She's outside yelling. What's up?" She edged to one side a little to give Andrew room to stand, as Nan plastered her slim figure against the back wall. "This place is nuts."

"Tell me about it," Mark said wryly. "They got me power in the comms space. I got a truck with the racks due in like six hours, and what equipment I have I can throw in there since they got me aircon too."

"Good job," Kerry said. "Did you get the demarc installed?"

"If that's them plywood things, I done it," Andrew spoke up. "That's some damn hard concrete in that room I will tell you that."

"Yeah, I can still hear you drilling," Mark said. "But that's the problem, poquito boss. We got the blocks installed and we're ready to punch down."

"Great." Kerry smiled in relief. "So that's a problem?"

"Nu, uh." Mark shook his dark head. "I could tell you, but it's gonna be easier to show you. Can we grab big D and go look?"

"Well..." Kerry turned as the door to the bus opened, and Dar entered, her powerful charisma clearing space for her as she made her way over to where they were standing. She was juggling the cell phone in one hand, but looked moderately triumphant. "How'd it go?"

"What a moron," Dar said. "They put a hold on everyone's damn orders because they're scared to death they're going to get a call from the government asking for all their inventory." She lifted her hands and let them drop. "I had to yell at some executive vice president of something or other and threaten to put Gerry on the phone before they got it through their heads where I was calling from."

Everyone nodded in agreement. "And?" Kerry added, after a pause.

"Truck is leaving Chicago in ten minutes," Dar replied, glancing around and spotting a tray nearby. She reached one long arm over and snagged a brownie. "I told him they better be flooring it all the way here." She bit into the brownie and chewed it. "So how are things going here?"

They all looked over at Mark, who grimaced.

"Uh oh. Maybe I should have some milk first," Dar saw the expressions. "What's wrong?"

"Let's go take a ride," Mark said. "That's what I and the dudes were just talking about before you guys got here. We just found out."

"Found out what?" Dar grabbed another brownie as she followed Mark out the door.

"C'mon. I'd rather you just see it. Maybe you can tell me it's not as bad as I think it is."

Dar snorted. "If you're looking to me for optimism we're seriously in the weeds." She handed Kerry half the brownie. "This could require more than chocolate."

They trooped down the steps to the bus and around the side, where there was a six seater golf cart parked somewhat haphazardly, draped in cables and other bits of nerd paraphernalia. Dar cleared a termination kit out of the way and slid into the front passenger seat, setting her backpack down between her feet. "Let's go."

Mark took the wheel and started off, turning the cart in a tight circle and nearly flinging them out in all directions. "Whoops. Sorry."

"Wow. This has got a hell of a lot more kick than the one at our place." Kerry grabbed hold of the sides of the cart. "Jesus!"

"Gas powered." Mark threaded the cart through the parked cars and headed for the side of the damaged building. "Pretty cool though. I never realized how freaking big this place was until we had to hump all our crap out to that room."

They rode around the side of the building the cool night air making them blink a little as Mark maneuvered through the grounds. There was still smoke smoldering up from the destroyed area, and as they moved erratically along, the air would bring shocking hints of death that made them all go silent.

Save Andrew. "Big ass place," he commented. "Built like a damn brick. Ain't nothing left of what hit it."

There was an awkward silence. "Airplane is just an aluminum shell," Dar eventually commented. "Dangerous part was the aviation fuel. "

"Did you hear what people were saying though?" Nan spoke up from the rear seat. "People were saying that there wasn't any airplane that hit the building. That it was a bomb, or something else and that the government was lying."

Andrew turned around and peered at her. "Gov'mint's always lying," he said. "But that's just foolish talking. People don't know squat yapping on the television. I heard that."

Kerry frowned. "Why in the heck would they lie about that?" she wondered. "I mean yes, I agree with Dad, but sheesh. There's a hole in the side of the building. What difference would it make what made it?"

Dar cleared her throat as Mark aimed for a square of light. "Probably because it's easier to excuse not being able to get out of the way of an airplane than allowing some bunch of jackasses to plant a bomb in the biggest military office building in the continent."

Mark pulled the cart to a halt and put on the parking break. "You think that's what happened, boss?" he asked, hesitantly. "I mean, that's a pretty big hole."

"No." Dar got out. "I think a goddamned plane hit the side of the building. I can see where the tin foil hat brigade pulled that rumor from, that's all." She shouldered her backpack and followed Mark between two huge personnel carriers and over to a door in the side of the building.

It was open, spilling a bright yellow incandescence out across the ground and there was motion and voices just beyond it. Mark walked through without hesitation and turned to the left, moving along a hallway filled with boxes to a brightly lit space that smelled of concrete and plywood. "Here we go."

Dar entered the comms room, pausing to look around before she cleared the doorway and let the rest of them follow her. Inside, the big square space was lit by hanging florescent lamps, and the floor was obviously freshly swept.

Power cables were hanging everywhere from the ceiling, and the entire back wall had been covered in sheets of treated, three quarter inch plywood surmounted by rows and rows of circuit patch down blocks. "Nice," Dar commented.

The floor was already marked out for racks, and half the floor tiles were missing with most of the holes containing a tech and a spool of cabling. The smell of plastic and copper were sharp in the air. "Mark, you made amazing progress," Kerry added. "Great job."

"Thanks. My guys did most of the humping." Mark led them to the corner of the room, which had a large cabinet set in one wall. "And speaking of humps, here's my problem." He opened the double doors to the cabinet and stepped back, clearing the way for the rest of them. "That."

There was a long moment of silence. Then, as if by common accord, everyone looked over at Dar, who was standing closest to it, her hands planted on her hips.

Dar studied the huge mass of cabling, all a uniform size, and dull gray terminating in an absolute hairball of multicolor strands. "I take it none of this is tagged?" she asked, finally.

"Nope." Mark shook his head. "I guess they had a project planned to come in here before the room went live to straighten it all out." He glanced around at the little group. "Sucks, huh?"

Dar rubbed her forehead. "Shit," she said. "There is a thousand pair there at least."

"Wow," Nan murmured.

"Some are phones, some data, some WAN..." Mark agreed. "I had the local Telco guys here, but they say most of it's not theirs so they're not touching it."

Dar turned and looked at him. Mark shrugged.

"Let me see if I can leverage our relationship with the local." Kerry pulled her phone out. "At least they can give us a list of the circuits in here other than ours." She paged through her directory. "It's Verizon, isn't it?"

"And Qwest," Nan murmured.

"Doesn't really help us find our stuff though," Mark commented. "Man, I'd hate to break my ass for two days and get this space up only to have to stay on that freaking sat."

"We can't handle the traffic they're going to ask for over that," Dar said. "How many WAN people do we have here, Mark?" She shrugged her pack off her back and set it on the floor. "We're going to have to do this the hard way."

She looked over at him after he didn't answer. "Well?"

"You mean, besides you and me?" he answered wryly. "Dar, the two WAN techs I had up here are in the missing group."

The room was now conspicuously quiet, as the techs busy wiring in the floor turned to listen. Dar leaned back against the punch down, letting her hands fall to her thighs. She was quiet for a long moment then exhaled. "Going to be a long damn night then, I guess," she said, at last. "Do we have kits?"

"Yeah," Mark responded glumly.

"Break them out. Let's get started." Dar shoved away from the wall and flexed her hands, turning to face the mess with an air of grim determination. "Bring all the punch down kits you have. Might as well do some on the job training while I'm at it."

"You got it boss." Mark turned and trotted out, shaking his head a little.

"Bring some of that damn barbeque with you!" Dar yelled after him. "And all the Jolt you got."

Chapter Twenty-three

"KERRY, THE GOVERNOR of New York is on the line for you again." A quiet, apologetic voice broke into the chatter. "I told him you were working at the Pentagon, but he wants to talk to you anyway."

Kerry rested her head against her fist, her body curled up in one of the bus's leather chairs, finally vacated by one of the busy military officers. "No problem, give me a minute." She clicked her mic on, resisting the urge to rub her eyes. "Believe me, Newark, we're going to the wall here to pull the Pentagon traffic off your grid and put it back where it belongs."

"We know that, ma'am. I tried to explain that. I just..." The satellite supervisor sounded as exhausted as Kerry felt. "He just doesn't want to take that answer. I think he's as frustrated as we are."

Kerry reviewed the status on her teams. "Maybe he'll let me send the remote sat trucks in then," she mused.

"Would you like some coffee, ma'am?" One of the bus's seemingly tireless attendants stopped by with a tray. "We have some fresh cookies baking too."

"Sure." Kerry checked her watch, wincing a little at the time. "Strong as you got it. Thanks." She rattled at her keyboard and settled her ear buds more firmly. "Okay, go ahead and call my cell, Newark. Patch me into the governor."

"Stand by, ma'am."

Nearly midnight. Kerry leaned against the chair arm, glad it was big enough for her to curl up in, tucking her tired legs up under her in relative comfort. She knew herself to be far luckier than her partner. Dar was half buried in cables in that dry and dusty room faced with an almost never-ending task before her.

Kerry felt a little abashed, in fact, that she was here in the bus instead of at Dar's side, but there wasn't any way for her to connect to the conference in there and there was just so damned much to do.

So damned much. Her cell phone rang, and she closed the mic off to open it up. "Kerry Stuart," she announced quietly, turning her head a little as the attendant came back with a big, steaming mug that smelled of hazelnut.

"Hello, Kerry?"

Poised to deal with an annoyed politician, Kerry had to rapidly ratchet through her mental gears to deal with another one altogether. "Hello, Mother," she said. "Sorry, I was expecting the governor. "

"Oh. Well, of course, I'm sorry I disturbed you, ah..."

Kerry smiled, and picked up her coffee cup. "No problem. I'd rather be talking to you since you probably aren't going to ask me to do something impossible."

Dead silence for a moment. "Ah, well, yes, I see. Of course," Cynthia spluttered. "My goodness, that sounds terrible. Are you still working? It's so late. I just wanted to find out where you and Dar ended up this evening."

Was I supposed to call her? Kerry suddenly wondered. "Right now, we're at the Pentagon," she said. "Dar is hip deep in cables and I'm still working on issues from our bus."

"Oh my!" her mother said. "Kerry, it's midnight!"

"I know," Kerry acknowledged. "It feels like it's midnight. But we don't really have a choice. We have to get things fixed here, so we can get things moving for the governor, so we can get out of here and head to New York where apparently we're needed to save the Western world." She paused. "Or something like that."

"My goodness."

"By Monday," Kerry added. "So anyway. How was your day? When do you head back home?"

Her cell phone buzzed a second incoming call. She briefly toyed with the idea of letting it go to voice mail then sighed. "Hold on a minute, okay? I think that's the governor."

"Of course."

Kerry put the call on hold and answered the second. "Hello?"

"Ms, Stuart, I have the governor for you." The sound of the Newark ops manager's voice echoed softly in her ear. "Okay to conference?"

"Sure." Kerry sipped her coffee and waited for the click. "Good..." She checked her watch. "Morning, governor. What can I do for you?"

"Yes, Ms. Stuart, good morning to you too. Now listen, I know we spoke earlier but things are getting fairly critical here and..."

"Governor." Kerry interrupted him gently, but with force in her tone. "Things are critical here, too."

"I do understand that," the governor said. "But here's the situation. Our emergency command center was in 7 World Trade. Never even been used. We're working to set up a center to replace it but without being connected to anything we might as well be setting it up on a boat on the Niagara River."

Kerry closed her eyes in frustration. "I know...please understand sir I do know you need to..." She stopped and took a breath. Stop, think, then act, Ker. "Where are you setting up a command center, sir?"

"Pier 92," the governor said. "It's the old passenger cruise terminal. Right on the Hudson."

On the Hudson. Kerry racked her brains for a long moment. "I don't think we..." She paused. "Wait. That's right next to the Intrepid Air museum, isn't it?"

"Yes, yes it is," the Governor agreed. "Just down from there. Does that help? Is there something you can do? Come on, Ms. Stuart. We contracted with you because you people were supposed to be the best.

Now, I need the best. We don't have a choice."

"We might be able to," Kerry said, after a pause. "I need to pull up our schematics in that area. I will have to get back to you on it."

"I need an answer, Ms. Stuart."

"You need an answer that's meaningful and correct, Governor. Not bullshit I'm pulling out of my ass just to make you get off the phone." Kerry could scarcely believe she'd just said that. "I'll do my best. That's all I can give you right now."

The man sighed. "When can I expect to hear from you? We're running out of time."

"As soon as I have the answer, you'll hear from me. That could be in ten minutes, or it could be tomorrow morning. Depends on how much detail I need, and if I can get hold of someone on the ground there," Kerry said. "You may need to clear some obstacles for us."

"Obstacles?" the governor asked. "You mean people? Ms. Stuart, you find obstacles, you call me. Understand?"

"I do."

"Hope to hear from you soon. Goodbye." The governor hung up.

Kerry took another sip of her coffee, before she clicked back to her call on hold. "Hello, Mother." She looked up as a wonderful scent of fresh cookies came close, and found a platter almost at eye level to her. "Thank you," she mouthed at the attendant, capturing three of the cookies, their warmth stinging her skin a little.

"Dear, I don't mean to keep you. I hope things are going better," Cynthia said. "I have a flight back to Michigan tomorrow. Is there anything I can do for you here before I go?"

"Hold that thought a minute, Mother." Kerry motioned to the attendant, taking a bite of the warm cookie as the woman came back over. "Could you please have a tray of those and a gallon of cold milk with cups taken to the work site?"

"Absolutely, ma'am. Let me get one of the guys to ride me over," the attendant said. "Not a problem at all."

"Thanks." Kerry smiled at her, then shifted her attention back to the phone. "Mother," she said. "Thanks for hanging on. It's a little crazy here."

"I can hear that," Cynthia said. "Are you going to get some rest? What about poor Dar? She must be exhausted after all that traveling."

Dar must be. Kerry felt faintly abashed. "I'm going to go see if I can get her to take a break right now, matter of fact," she said. "But we've got a lot on our plates and getting more every time the phone rings."

"My."

"Anyway," Kerry sighed. "Thanks for offering. Just travel safe, and give Angie and Mike a hug for me."

"Well, I'm sure they'd be happier if you were coming back with me, but I will give them your best wishes. Try to get some rest," her mother said. "If there's anything I can do to help, just call."

"I will," Kerry said. "Good night, Mother."

"Goodnight."

Kerry closed the phone and gazed at it, as she broke off a cookie half and chewed. That had ended pretty much all right, she figured. If one reasonable thing had to come out of the disaster she was living, maybe it was that she, and her mother, could at least talk again.

She wasn't ready to let it all go. But she also didn't feel like she wanted to hold the rage inside her so much anymore. She was content to think that if things hadn't really moved forward, they also hadn't moved backwards, and she was in a place where she actually wouldn't mind having her mother visit their home.

She chewed her cookie, getting up and making her way through the much smaller crowd to the galley area to find herself some milk. She spotted Nan curled up in a chair near the back of the bus sleeping, and she felt a little bad about keeping the woman around so long.

"Hello, Ms. Stuart" Danny appeared, his sling covered in concrete dust. "Boy, we're sure getting things done here today, aren't we?"

Kerry leaned against the counter as she poured her cup of milk. "You know, we are," she admitted. "It doesn't seem like that to me, because there's so much left to do, but you guys are doing an amazing job."

Danny took a root beer from the small refrigerator and opened it, sucking down half the bottle in a gulp before he answered. "It's dry as heck in that room," he explained. "But let me tell you, Ms. Roberts is amazing."

Kerry felt a smile stretch her face muscles out. "She is."

"I mean…I know you know that." Danny blushed, just a little. "But we never got to work with her before, and you hear all kinds of stories from people but in reality, wow."

"Dar is an amazing person," Kerry said. "And I'm not just saying that because she's my boss, or because we're partners. She really is. In fact, I was about to head over there and see if I could get her to take a break for a few minutes. I know you guys have been at it for hours."

"It's tough work," Danny agreed mournfully. "I just came back to pick up more zip ties. The other guys don't want to take a break while Ms. Roberts is there cause she hasn't."

"Oh for heaven's sake." Kerry drained her milk and set the cup down in the small sink. "C'mon. Let's go back over there. Those poor guys." She dusted her hands off and wiped her lips on a napkin, as Danny hurried to finish his root beer. "I'm going to tell the bridge I'm going offline."

She walked back over to her laptop and put her ear buds in again. The chatter had faded off the last hour or so, only a few sporadic voices coming back on at intervals. Kerry keyed her mic and cleared her throat a little. "Folks, this is Miami exec. Just want to advise I'm going offline for a little while. I'll have my cell if anything's urgent."

"Noted, Miami exec," a soft voice answered. "This is Houston night ops. Everything's pretty quiet right now."

"Great. Check in with you later." Kerry unplugged herself and shrugged her jacket on, then she met Danny at the door and they exited the bus into the chilly night air.

DAR WAS PRETTY well convinced she'd actually died and gone to hell. She braced her tester with its one attached wire and reached for yet another dangling strand, bringing it over to touch it against the probe.

The tester lit up, surprising her. "Son of a bitch," she muttered, unclipping the wires and twisting them together. "Gimme a tag."

Mark handed over a piece of cardboard with a string. "Here you go," he said, his voice slightly hoarse. "Hey, that's ten, isn't it?"

Dar shook her head, re-clipping the wires and reading off the identifier. She scribbled it on the tag then tied the tag firmly to the twisted cables. "First person who gets our circuits gets a 200 percent raise and a month vacation."

A soft chorus of voices answered back. Dar glanced to either side of her, where techs were almost covered in the prickly, copper mass of wiring, testing patiently cable by cable looking for a match.

It was like finding a bird feather, and catching each one you saw to see if it was the one who lost it. Frustrating, maddening, aggravating, uncomfortable...if Dar had possessed a machete the chances were, she decided, that she'd have just gone amok with it and ended the problem in a mass of copper fragments.

There was no place to sit, no place to relax. You had to stand almost inside the cabinet to reach the wires, and the ones you weren't testing were poking through your clothes like tiny needles.

She and Mark had started off doing the testing. They'd managed to show three other techs how to use the testing sets, but though there were four other units, there wasn't any more space in front of the cabling cabinet so they'd just started plugging through it.

Dar knew she could get someone else to take over her set, and do the testing. She was, after all, their ultimate boss. But she felt all the eyes on her, and understood she had to live up to her reputation, and so she kept slogging.

Her eyes burned. She blinked a little, then a very different odor penetrated all the concrete and plastic and she turned to look over her shoulder as a woman entered the room with a tray and a pitcher. "What do we have here?"

"Cookies and milk," the bus attendant smiled. "Ms. Stuart told me to bring them over here."

Dar could smell the chocolate all the way in the back of the room.

"Are those just baked?"

"They are," the woman affirmed.

"Is that cold milk?" Dar asked, as she saw the techs all starting to turn around, faces covered in smudges of dust and eyes exhausted.

"Yes, it is," the attendant said.

Dar held her hands up, letting the tester fall against her thigh. "Did you bring towels?" She displayed her grunge covered palms with a wry expression.

"Ah." The attendant had to admit to being at a loss. "Well, we can go get some."

"Cookies will get cold." Dar eased away from the cabinet, carefully extracting her boots from the snarls of cable. "Take a break, boys. Let's not waste good, warm cookies."

The techs needed no further prompting. They laid their tools down and scrambled out of holes in the floor, stretching out sore backs and shaking out stiffened fingers. "Man, what time is it?" one asked. "I feel like I've been doing this for three days."

Dar wiped her fingers on her shirt to get the worst of the dust off, before she selected a cookie from the tray and accepted a cup of milk from the smiling attendant. "Thank you."

"You should really thank Ms. Stuart," the woman chuckled.

"She'll get hers later," Dar responded, with a somewhat rakish grin, which grew even more wry as a short, blond woman appeared in the doorway, leaning against it as she looked inside. "Well well. Speak of the devil."

Kerry entered, waving at the techs who all called out greetings. "How are you guys doing? Is Dar running you into the ground yet?"

"Hey." Dar seated herself against the bare wall, extending her legs out as she took a sip of her milk. "I'm working here too."

"I know." Kerry sat down next to her, the entire reason for her coming over now moot, but she didn't care in the least. "I came over to see how you were doing." She glanced up at the crowd, but they were clustered around the cookies, moving away once they'd gotten their share and settling down on the other side of the room.

Or wandering outside in the hall. Kerry wondered if they were being given space out of courtesy or just coincidence.

"I'm doing complete and utter suckitude." Dar gazed down at her now empty hand, its palm scraped and reddened. "We've found ten circuits out of a thousand in six hours."

"Jesus."

"If he was here, I'd give him a phone tester and tell him to get his ass working," Dar said. "Ker, this is insane. "

Kerry took hold of Dar's hand and stroked it, clasping her fingers around her partner's. "Can I help?" she asked. "I'm tired of yapping on the bridge. Why don't you go yap for a while, and I'll do this."

"And make me feel like a total zero for sticking you with this nightmare while I lounge in the bus?" Dar eyed her. "I don't think so."

"Are you saying that's what I was doing?"

Dar saw the quirk of Kerry's eyebrows, and the sudden bunching of her jaw. The last thing she really wanted to do this late in this crappy a situation was trigger her partner's temper. Kerry was tired. She was tired. No way she wanted a squabble. "No, hon. I sent you to the bus, remember?" she replied. "Is there any sense in both of us being miserable?"

Kerry studied her face. "Yes." She laced her fingers with Dar's. "Because I was just in that damn bus thinking I was a creep for not being out here with you," she admitted. "I'm tired of people telling me all their problems, and politicians calling to yell at me. The governor of New York wants his new office connected."

"You have got to be kidding me."

"Well, it's their disaster response office," Kerry said. "Long story, and anyway, we can't even look at that until we get through this. So teach me to use one of those things and let me suffer here with you like the sappy love struck goofball I really am."

Dar sighed, looking across at the cabinet with its morass of wires. "I feel like just quitting and going to bed," she admitted, in a soft voice. "Ker, I don't want to sit here and do this. It's going to take days. We don't have days."

Kerry gently rubbed the side of her hand. "Is there any other way to do it?"

"No."

"Can we get the vendor in here to do it? It's really their hairball," Kerry asked, reasonably. "Let me call them again."

Dar was silent for a moment then nodded. "Call them," she said. "I've had enough of this."

Kerry leaned over and rested her head against Dar's shoulder for a brief moment then straightened up and pulled her cell phone out. "You got it, boss."

"Ten freaking lines in six hours." Dar sighed, letting her head rest against the wall. "Most moronic thing I've ever done."

"WHAT DO I want? I want your technicians standing in front of me ready to go help, that's what I want." Kerry heard the sharpness in her own tone, and knew she was close to losing her temper.

"Ms. Stuart, I don't have anyone to send you." The male voice on the other end of the line sounded as harassed as she felt. "I'm not trying to blow you off. I just don't have anyone. We sent everyone...everyone we had to New York."

Kerry felt her neck start to get hot. "So what am I supposed to tell the generals here at the Pentagon?" she asked. "And by the way, let me make sure I have the spelling of your name right."

"Ms. Stuart, please. Don't think threats are going to get you anywhere."

"I'm not threatening anyone," Kerry said. "I just have to know what the hell I am supposed to say to the military leadership of this country when they ask me why they have no communications."

The man sighed. "Look, we're under a lot of pressure from the political people. They told us to send everyone to New York, and damn it, that's what we did."

"They told us the same thing," Kerry shot back. "But we're intelligent people, and we know better. So fine. That's what I'll tell the people here. That your company abandoned them to go hook the mayor's phone back up and make sure the stock traders can make money."

"Oh come on," the man said, in exasperation. "Would you please cut the crap? This isn't a stupid game anymore."

"I'm not playing anything. That's exactly what I am going to go tell the Joint Chiefs of Staff," Kerry said, in an inflexible tone. "And trust me, when we pull everyone's ass out of the fire here, we're going to take every bit of business you had and make it ours, because that's my CIO in that demarc room punching down your lousy circuits."

The tension and the exhaustion were getting to her. Kerry was on the verge of just hanging up.

"What is it you want from me, Ms Stuart?" the man asked, after a pause.

"I want linemen in here, sorting out your part of the fucking hairball someone left in this facility," Kerry responded, in soft, precise tones. "And if you can't do that, I guarantee not only will the Pentagon not do any more business with you, we won't either and we're a hell of a lot bigger."

A click sounded down the line, and she was listening to nothing but a busy tone. Kerry closed the phone and exhaled, letting her head rest against her hand. She was sitting in the hallway, lit by orange fluorescent lights that made her head pound all the harder.

She checked her watch. Two a.m. "Jesus." She leaned back against the wall, feeling the hard surface cold against her skin. Her skin was covered in dust, and her lack of progress in getting help for Dar and the rest of their crew made her feel covered in dust inside as well.

She heard a sound, and turned her head to see a tall figure approaching her, a little too tall, and too broad to be Dar, but with the same bouncy stride. "Hey Dad."

"Hey there kumquat." Andrew came over and slid down the wall to settle next to her. "You don't look so hot."

"I feel crummy," Kerry agreed. "I can't get anyone to come here and help us. It's so frustrating"

Andrew absorbed this, drawing his knees up and resting his forearms on them. "Hell of a lot of work," he agreed. "Ah was watching

Dar do that for a while, made my eyeballs ache."

"Me too. She won't let me take over for her," Kerry said. "We've rotated the other techs in at least once. But she won't stop."

"Stubborn kid," Her father-in-law agreed. "Gets that from me, I do believe."

Kerry leaned over and rested her head against his shoulder. "Can you go talk her into taking a break?"

Andrew's brows quirked. "Ah could try," he said. "But she's out stubborned me before now."

Kerry sighed, and straightened. Then she gathered herself up and climbed to her feet. "C'mon. Let's both try," she said. "Maybe that'll work." She waited for Andrew to stand and then she led the way back to the demarc room, pausing in the doorway to look inside.

Most of the pockets in the floor were now closed. The majority of the techs were now clustered around the back of the room, where four were stolidly at Dar's side working on the cables, and the rest were doing busy work waiting their turn.

Everyone looked utterly exhausted. No one was even trying to leave. Kerry felt a tiny prickle of pride, the hint of a lifting of her nape hairs at the understated loyalty of their staff and the stolid, equally understated leadership of her steadily working partner.

She started across the room, gathering her arguments, steeling herself to maybe even get Dar mad at her, as she straightened her shoulders and sucked in a lungful of air.

"Oh!" One of the techs yelped, as though he'd been bitten. "Ms. Roberts...Ms Roberts...I think this is one of ours!" The man froze in place, gripping the wires in a deathly tight clutch and not taking his eyes off them. "Holy cow!"

Dar clipped her kit to the wall and crawled over the pile of cabling to where he was standing, the rest of the techs edging out of her way as fast as they could. She peered over his shoulder at the readout then she clapped him on the shoulder. "It is."

"Oh holy Christ." Mark came in on the other side. "Dude, you just won the brass ring. That's the fucking backbone management uplink." He looked at Dar. "We can bring up services on this, boss. It's only a T1.5, but it's a hell of a lot better than that portable sat."

Kerry sidled up in back of Dar and looked over the man's shoulder too, her arm slipping around her partner's waist and giving it a squeeze. "Wow. Nice job, Ken."

The tech looked around, and smiled at her. "I feel like I won the lottery," he confessed.

"You did," Dar said. "I promised a 200 percent raise and a month vacation. You got it." She took the cables from him and carefully routed them, winding them through the spools on the top of the punch down and seating them with a double punch of her tool. "Little bastard."

She removed a pen from her pocket and scribbled a mark on the punch down. "Someone cross connect that over to the temp rack please."

"Right on that ma'am." A tech was already routing wires from the other side of the room.

Ken looked around at Kerry. "Is she serious, ma'am?"

"Absolutely," Kerry answered immediately. "She never promises anything she won't deliver on." She waited for her partner to come back over and bump her lightly, stopping next to her instead of going back to the hairball. "Dar, if we've got basic comms back, I think we should let these folks take a break and get some sleep. "

"You think so, huh?" Dar rested her elbow on Kerry's shoulder.

"I do," Kerry said. "I know it's just a drop in the bucket, but you all can't keep this up all night and expect to also keep working again tomorrow. Which we have to do," she reminded her partner.

Dar slowly looked around the room. Three of the techs were busy running cables and making connections to the thick panel that then ran out of the room and around the corner, ending at the satellite rig Mark had set up.

The rest were sitting quietly, just watching her and waiting. Everyone would continue working if she said to, and Dar knew that. They were nowhere near in the clear, and stopping now would probably be a mistake, and certainly would lose them time they could not afford.

However.

"I think you're right," Dar said, after a pause. "Moving the management traffic off the sat will get me enough wiggle room to work with. We can take a break."

She could see the utter relief on everyone's faces. A glance to her right showed a similar expression on Kerry's face, and the shoulder she was resting her arm on relaxed. "Let's go hijack one of those SUVs." She turned to the rest of the techs. "Take a break, people. Get some rest. You all did great work here tonight, and it'll make tomorrow a lot easier.

"Back at you boss," Mark said. "I've got two or three guys in reserve, bunking out waiting for the rack truck to get here. Should be any time, so it's a good deal we're gonna take a break to get out of their way."

Dar nodded. "Let's go." She slipped her arm around Kerry's shoulders and steered her toward the door. "C'mon, Dad. Time to go back to that scandalous hotel of ours."

Andrew had his hands in his pockets, and was nodding slowly. "Been a damn long day," he agreed, as he joined them in leaving the room. "Ah will be glad to wave bye to this here rock pile for today."

"Me too," Dar exhaled, as they exited the door and walked outside into the night air. It was much quieter now, though work was going on at the impact site as they passed it, cranes removing debris, and people moving in and out, there was a hush over everything that let them hear the flutter of the big American flag draped over the building with startling clarity.

A cluster of motion drew their attention, and they turned their heads to watch a group of six people leading dogs fanning out to enter the destroyed area.

"Are those search dogs?" Kerry asked.

"Looks like it." Dar stifled a yawn. "Guess it's safe enough for them to go in now," she added. "So no luck with the Telco vendors?"

"Ugh."

Dar gave her shoulders a squeeze. "Don't stress over it. They really can't do any more than we're doing, Ker. At least we can prioritize what circuits come up if we're the ones punching them down."

Andrew grunted, and waggled his head back and forth. "Them people should be helping though," he disagreed. "Not right for you all to be doing their work."

"Exactly," Kerry said. "I know we can do it. The point is we shouldn't have to. Dar shouldn't have to be standing there for what...eight, ten hours sorting through that mess."

Dar chuckled. "Eh." She shrugged. "At least it was doing something productive. I'm about out of options relieving all the throttle points until we relieve some of the congestion in Newark. There's just too much routing that way."

"Ugh," Kerry repeated. "You know, I gave that guy such a hard time too, about sending everyone to New York. But we're going to have to do that too, Dar. I don't know how we're going to do all that work there, and still get stuff here all going."

They stepped over the dividers into the parking area and headed for the bus. This late, most of the activity had settled down, but still there were techs gathered around the satellite rig, and two unfamiliar ones at the work tables setting up cable rigs. "Good morning all," Kerry called out, as they arrived.

The techs at the table looked up, then went still, their eyes widening as they recognized the figures appearing out of the darkness. "Oh, hell. It's the big cheezes!"

"Big mangos," Dar disagreed, with a wry grin. "You folks getting ready to cut some traffic over? We got one link up in that hell hole in there."

The techs around the sat hurried over. "That's what we heard," one said. "Mark called us on the radio. A T1 he said? That's going to be a lot better than the rig here. We're so maxed on it we can barely get management traffic through."

The door to the RV opened, and two more techs climbed out, rubbing their eyes. "Hey, what's the scoop out here?" one asked. "Anything interesting...oh. Hi Ms. Roberts."

"Ah will go get that car," Andrew decided. "Be right back." He ambled off disappearing between the RV and the bus before they could stop him.

"Guess he figures we'll never get loose of here given our own devices." Kerry whispered. "Want a cup of coffee?"

"Nah." Dar waited for the new techs to join them. "Randy, the most interesting thing that happened is that after ten hours of cable wrangling we got one circuit up. They're moving traffic off the sat."

"Hot damn," Randy stretched. "We're waiting for the rack truck. Mark said it should be here any time. We'll get them in and constructed and the power distribution units in and, hopefully, tomorrow morning the gear will get here."

Dar checked her watch. "Sounds right," she said. "Should be about twelve, fourteen hours from there to here. So we're right on track." She turned to Kerry. "Remind me to talk to Mariana about bonus packages for everyone here, will you?"

"Sure will." Kerry didn't miss the veritable forest of pricked ears suddenly around her. "Even though I know everyone's pitching in because that's the kind of people we have, we need to reward the really spectacular performance we've seen the last few days."

"Yup." Dar looked around, nodding in satisfaction. "We're on the right track here for sure. I think we can schedule ourselves to move on to New York tomorrow. I hope we're as lucky there in terms of staffing."

The moonlight shone down on a small group of smiling faces, as the techs enjoyed the praise. "You know," Randy said, "we don't usually get a chance to really make a difference like this. It's kind of cool."

The techs nodded. "Yeah," another one said. "It sucks big time that this happened, but coming here, and doing this stuff...it makes me feel good. My parents are all excited back home that I'm here, helping the country out."

"Better than being stuck in the configuration room in Miami?" Kerry smiled warmly at them.

"Heck yeah. Plus the bus is here," Randy said, with a rakish grin. "We don't get brownies made for us back home."

Everyone laughed, and both Dar and Kerry joined in. "We'll have to look at that when we get back." Kerry mused. "And those fresh cookies were pretty good too."

"Fresh cookies," Randy said. "Where? In the bus? Man, let's go get some and some coffee before that truck shows up and we've got to hump all that tonnage inside." He trotted toward the bus with his partner chasing after him. "Thanks Ms. Stuart!"

"Anytime," Kerry called after him.

A low rumble caught their attention, and they turned to see one of the company SUVs trundling its way toward them. "Our chariot," Dar said, with a sigh. "Damn, I'm so tired I actually don't mind my father driving it."

A cheer went up from the sat rig. "Circuit's up! Yeah! I'm seeing frames from our net!" One of the techs almost yodeled his excitement. "Boy is it great to see that router again!!"

Dar unwound her arm from Kerry's shoulder and walked over to them, peering over their shoulders at the laptop propped up on one end of the sat rig. "That's ours, all right," she commented. "Good."

"We did it." The tech shook his head a little. "On tin cans and strings and a lot of duct tape, but man, we did it."

Standing there, in the fluorescent lit glare, in the shadows of so much destruction, Kerry knew a moment of relieved triumph. They had done it. No one would ever probably know they'd done anything, no one would probably care, save those few people who had worked with them, but here in the chill of an early morning she knew they'd surmounted a lot of odds in a single facet of the total disaster.

One small step. One small achievement, but in all the chaos and all the grief surrounding them it felt good.

"Hey, Ms. Stuart!"

Kerry turned, to see Billy approaching. "Well, hello there," she greeted the captain.

"My guys told me something just happened," Billy said. "All of a sudden, our stuff's moving."

Kerry indicated the sat rig. "We got one of our circuits up," she said. "Only one, but it's a start." She smiled as the techs all started cheering, and doing a little nerd dance around the rig. "I think they're as excited as your guys are."

The captain had been talking into a mouthpiece, a cable trailing down from his ear to a radio rig clipped to his shoulder. "That is one fantastic piece of news." He put his hands on his hips and exhaled. "We've been feeling a little like second class citizens around here. Everyone's focused on New York."

Kerry nodded in understanding. "I got that sense also. But you know Dar and her father are personal friends of Gerald Easton's. They understand how important it is to get you up and running again even if other people don't."

"That's what I heard," Billy said. "You're good people, Ms. Stuart. Thank you."

Kerry felt tears sting her eyes. "You're good people here too, Billy. Thanks for putting it on the line for us."

He blinked, and Kerry saw his jaw muscles clench.

"Ready to go, Ker?" Dar came up next to her. "Hello there. Guess you heard the good news."

Billy nodded. He held his hand out to them. "Thanks." He gripped Dar's and then Kerry's. "Get some rest, you all. That's what I'm going to do now." He walked off, pausing to rub his face on his sleeve before he disappeared between two trucks and into the shadows.

Kerry looked very thoughtful as they walked toward the waiting SUV. "You really giving Ken a 200 percent raise?"

"Yep."

"You realize he'll make more than most of our VP's."

"Don't give a damn. It's my budget, I'll be glad to be on the line for it." Dar rocked her head from side to side, exhaling. "It's worth it. I'm so tired I can't see straight. He probably saved me from cross-connecting an electrical lead into my damn navel."

Kerry put an arm around her waist. "Me personally, I'd be more excited about the month vacation."

"We get that too. Everyone involved in this gets that."

"After we fix New York."

"Yeah." Dar opened the door and climbed in, surprised when Kerry climbed right after her, and settled squished in the seat half sprawled over her lap. Then she laughed faintly and shut the door, burying her face in Kerry's shirt and letting the tension roll out of her. "Let's go."

"You got that right, rugrat." Andrew started the SUV forward. "This here be the end of this day."

CRAWLING INTO BED was an exquisite relief. Kerry felt sore and exhausted, her legs aching from the constant activity they'd been experiencing since early the previous morning. She lay there limp in the middle of the bed, dressed in just a T-shirt.

It felt amazing to be laying still. But in the back of her mind, the press of all the things that she knew still needed doing, needed checking up on, needed arranging for was making her head hurt and her stomach queasy. "Hey, Dar?"

"Uh huh?" Dar entered the bedroom, rubbing her eyes. She dropped onto the bed with atypical gracelessness and exhaled audibly stretching her long body out before she rolled over and pulled Kerry into an embrace. "I think I want to stop time for a few hours."

"Only a few?" Kerry silently savored the heat of the contact. "I just want to go home."

"Do you?" Dar reached over and turned the bedside light off, leaving them in darkness. She settled her arms back around Kerry and lightly rubbed her back. "We're caught in a pretty tough situation here."

Kerry draped her arm across Dar's waist and sighed. "I feel so crappy."

"Tired? Me too." Dar nestled closer and nibbled her ear.

"Frustrated," Kerry admitted. "Besides being tired. I feel like we're just starting to climb a really tall mountain full of angry people and bad situations.'

"Yeah, we are," Dar agreed. "But y'know, Ker, I decided tonight when I felt like taking a weed whacker to that panel that we just have to look at the whole damn thing as one big challenge. We can't freak out, and we can't just chuck it."

"Even if we're being asked to do the impossible?" Kerry felt her body relaxing, Dar's light touch on her back easing away the aggravation of the day.

"Sure. What fun would it be if it was easy?"

Kerry looked up at Dar, her eyes adjusting and seeing the angular profile tilted toward her. "You amaze me sometimes."

"Do I?" Dar smiled.

"Yes, you do." Kerry kissed her on the shoulder, pulling the fabric of her shirt down a little so she hit skin instead of cotton. "I think you did a fantastic job of leadership tonight. I was so proud of you, and the rest of our guys."

"I was just glad that line tech found that damn circuit," Dar admitted. "I don't know how much more of that I was going to be able to take. Talk about timing." She nibbled Kerry's ear again. "The only worse thing I could think of happening was starting my period."

Kerry blinked, feeling her lashes brush against Dar's skin as she silently called up a mental picture of their joint calendar. After a moment she thumped her forehead against Dar's shoulder. "Oh mushrooms. We're both due." She exhaled in aggravation. "Did you even bring..."

"I'm sure this swanky hotel has a concierge who'd love to go shopping for supplies for the owner of the penthouse mansion in the morning," Dar reassured her. "I was just glad to get out of there before anything started. My bleeding on those cables woulda thrown every damn thing into a royal spin."

"Yikes," Kerry said, after a moment's reflection. "I don't think I'd want that to end up in the departmental newsletter."

"Me either," her partner stated firmly.

"No wonder I've been in such a pissy mood all day." Kerry now, belatedly, recognized the symptoms. "Jesus I wish you'd said something before."

"I was busy," Dar reminded her.

"I know. Me too." Kerry sorted through what she had packed, and sighed in relief when she realized pain reliever was among the items. "Damn we're going to have to run around all day tomorrow too." She closed her eyes, as the nibbling moved around the edge of her ear to her earlobe.

Hard to stay in a bad mood with that sensation, she reckoned. Hard to stay in a bad mood when the warmth of their bodies pressing against each other penetrated all the aches and the stiffness, and she felt her breathing slow.

Felt her breathing come to match Dar's rhythm, an odd synergy she'd started to notice more and more lately.

Tomorrow might be hell. Kerry let the worry slip from her, savoring instead the immediate reality of this comfortable bed and the intrinsically greater comfort of Dar's embrace. "Mm."

"Mm." Dar exhaled against the skin on Kerry's neck. "I've been dreaming all day of this moment."

Kerry felt a little happy chill go up her back. She slid her arms around Dar and gave her a hug then relaxed against her body with a satisfied wriggle. "I always dream of this," she admitted. "Especially during sucky days."

Dar chuckled softly, almost soundlessly, more a motion than a sound.

"I have the weirdest dreams with you and me in them." Kerry closed her eyes. "Did I ever tell you about the one with a penguin?" She took a breath to go on then found she couldn't because Dar's lips were blocking the sound.

But that was all right too.

AS IT TURNED out, it wasn't quite their time the next morning. Kerry was glad enough for any reprieve. She started eating her blueberry pancakes, listening to the conference bridge with one ear and to Dar's pacing ramblings with the other.

It was just seven o'clock. Getting up that early had been painful, but Dar had gotten a call from the board, and her consolation prize had been this plate of excellent pancakes and acceptably crisp bacon.

"Hello, is Kerrisita there?"

Kerry swallowed her mouthful hastily and switched on the mic. "Right here, Maria," she said. "Is there a problem?"

"No, no problema, Kerrisita. The FedEx says they can come pick up Dar's package. I was wanting to make sure where to send it."

Ah. "So, FedEx is flying again," Kerry said. "Miami ops, did you hear that?"

"Boo yah!" Mark's voice erupted, sounding a touch sleepy. "Right from the RV, boss. I hear it. That's great news. Hang on, let me get status here."

Kerry took a sip of her coffee. "Hang on for me too, Maria. Let me talk to Dar and see where we're going to be." She clicked off and got up, putting her ear buds down as she went into the next room where Dar was using the room's speakerphone. "Hey."

Dar had stopped and was leaning over the phone with both hands braced. She glanced up at Kerry, her dark bangs falling into her eyes. "Hold up, people. I need to check something." She put the call on hold. "Que Paso?"

"FedEx is moving again," Kerry said. "Maria wants to send your ID and phone."

"Great."

"Where?" Kerry held still as Dar circled the desk and nuzzled against her, licking a drop of syrup from her lips in a miniature cascade of sensuality. "Ah." She closed her eyes and they kissed again, the silence going on for quite some time.

"What was the question?" Dar asked, opening one eye and peering down at her.

Kerry had to admit her mind had gone completely blank. "I have no idea," she muttered. "I'm sure it was important. I came all the way out here about it."

"I remember." Dar rested her forearms on Kerry's shoulders. "Where to send my damn wallet," she said. "Paradox, again. I'd say here, since it'll be easier to get here at the hotel, but we need to go to New York and it'll probably be this afternoon. So to the Rock, please."

"Okay." Kerry obediently nodded. "I'll tell Maria. Do you think you'll be able to fly though, without ID?"

"Guess we'll find out." Dar gave her a kiss then bumped her toward the other room. "Go finish your breakfast before it gets cold."

"I'd rather finish you before you get cold," Kerry responded, with a rakish grin, as her partner's brows lifted and her eyes widened. "But I guess I'll settle for pancakes for now." She winked at Dar and ambled back into the other room, taking a moment to drink half her glass of orange juice before she got back on the phone. "Phew."

She clicked the mic. "Maria? You there?"

"Si, Kerrisita. I am here. "

"Dar says to have it sent to the New York office, please. She's expecting us to leave from here today and head up there," Kerry said. "I'm just hoping they'll let her on the plane with no ID."

"Jesu," Maria said. "They were just saying here on the television how strict it is now. Kerrisita, did you hear all the things going on? They went and took someone off one of the cruise ships even!"

Having been involved in cruise ships in the not so distant past, Kerry somehow didn't find that surprising. "One of the terrorists was on a cruise?" she asked.

"They did not say." Maria sounded disappointed. "They found something in the Europe too, in some countries in the north. People they had arrested."

Kerry sat down and cut a forkful of pancakes. "Unreal," she said, before ingesting them. She chewed and swallowed. "Maria, call the airline, would you? Let's find out what Dar's supposed to do so we don't get surprised at the airport."

"Si, I will do that."

"Hey, poquito boss." Mark got back on. "Man, we got good news here. Truck just pulled up with the gear, and the racks are ready and humming for them, and...wait for it...we found another circuit!"

Kerry put her fork down and clapped, hearing the echo in her ear buds. "Nice work!" She complimented her team. "Go go go."

"Miami exec, this is Newark." The earth station reported in. "We do see a decrease in saturation today. Boy. Is that a welcome sight. Good work, you guys." She paused, and studied her plate. "Mark, can you just run down where we are, overall."

"Sure."

Kerry clicked her mic off, nodding a little as she listened and ate more pancakes.

DAR SPRAWLED IN the leather desk chair, her bare feet propped up against the desk and her elbow resting on its surface. She listened to the voices on the conference call with barely contained aggravation, shifting forward suddenly only to relax again, as another voice took up the argument.

She picked up her glass of grapefruit juice and sipped from it. The astringent beverage was cold, and she swallowed a few mouthfuls before there was a gap in the discussion and she saw her chance to dive in. "Hey!"

The phone almost visibly shuddered. "Yes, Dar," Alastair said, after a moment. "Listen, I know things are tough where you are, but we're getting a lot of pressure here from a lot of people."

"Too bad," Dar said. "Have any of you been listening to what I've said the past twenty minutes? It's 8:00 a.m. I got back from the work site at 3:00 a.m. We just got things moving there."

"Now Dar," Hamilton chimed in. "Settle your shorts. Nobody said you weren't working hard. We just made some promises to the government and they want to know when we're gonna keep them."

"I can't see why we're delaying," another voice chimed in. "This is big. We've got a great opportunity here."

Dar glanced plaintively at the ceiling. "What the hell's wrong with you people?" she asked. "Did you not see the hole in the side of the Pentagon on CNN? Do you not know what goes on in that building?"

"Now Dar,"Alastair sighed. "Well listen folks. Today they're doing a big ceremony, and I've got to go get ready for it," he said. "I know your people there are working like anything, Dar. I understand it's important to get things going there. I know you've got a personal responsibility for the place. But damn it, I need you here."

Dar turned her head and glared at the phone. "So, what part of yes, I'm making arrangements to get to the city today wasn't clear?" she asked. "Did that whole five minute spiel from me at the beginning of this call not mean anything to anyone there?"

Alastair sighed. "I was hoping you'd be here this morning."

"I was sleeping this morning," Dar said. "And frankly, you all can kiss my ass. Anyone who thinks they can do this better, c'mon. Bring it."

"Dar, no one said that."

"Then everyone just shut up and do something productive." Dar turned and slammed her hand on the desk, raising her voice to a loud yell. "Instead of tying me up when I should be!" She turned, to find

Kerry unexpectedly standing behind her. "Yeop."

"What was that, Dar?" Hamilton asked. "Cat get your tongue?"

"Nothing." Dar leaned back in the chair and let Kerry rub her shoulders. "Are we done?"

Long silence. "Well, I guess I'll see you here later today, huh Dar?" Alastair asked. "The mayor was just on the line, something about an office at the pier...any chance of looking at that first?"

"Sure," Dar said. "Done now?"

"Good bye, all," her boss sighed and gave in. "I'll do what I can here. Going to be a rough day." He clicked off the phone and it echoed a little, then the room was once again silent.

"He sounds pissed."

"He wants me to be there making him look good," Dar said. "Screw that, Kerry. We had work to do here. "

"Uh huh. And we'd better be taking a train to go there," Kerry informed her. "Cause sweetheart, they're not letting anyone fly without ID," she said. "If we get packing, we can catch a train in an hour, and be in New York in three more after that. We end up in Penn Station. "

"A train," Dar mused. "Think we can get tickets? Probably pretty busy. No one wants to fly."

"Already got them." Kerry kissed the top of her head. "C'mon. Let's just get there. I'll give Dad a call." She held a hand out to Dar. "Shower? We'll save time together."

"Hedonist."

"Takes one to know one."

To be continued...

OTHER MELISSA GOOD TITLES

Tropical Storm

From bestselling author Melissa Good comes a tale of hearta
longing, family strife, lust for love, and redemption. *Tropical S*
took the lesbian reading world by storm when it was first v
ten...now read this exciting revised "author's cut" edition.

Dar Roberts, corporate raider for a multi-national tech comp
is cold, practical, and merciless. She does her job with a razor-sh
accuracy. Friends are a luxury she cannot allow herself, and lov
something she knows she'll never attain.

Kerry Stuart left Michigan for Florida in an attempt to get a
from her domineering politician father and the constraints of
overly conservative life her family forced upon her. After college
worked her way into supervision at a small tech company, onl
have it taken over by Dar Roberts' organization. Her associa
with Dar begins in disbelief, hatred, and disappointment, but w
Dar unexpectedly hires Kerry as her work assistant, the dynamic
their relationship change. Over time, a bond begins to form.

But can Dar overcome years of habit and conditioning to o
herself up to the uncertainty of love? And will Kerry escape from
clutches of her powerful father in order to live a better life?

ISBN 978-1-932300-60-4

Hurricane Watch

In this sequel to "Tropical Storm," Dar and Kerry are back
making their relationship permanent. But an ambitious
colleague threatens to divide them --- and out them. He wants D
head and her job, and he's willing to use Kerry to do it. Can t
home life survive the office power play?

Dar and Kerry are redefining themselves and their prioritie
build a life and a family together. But with the scheming colleag
and old flames trying to drive them apart and bring them down,
two women must overcome fear, prejudice, and their own past
protect the company and each other. Does their relationship h
enough trust to survive the storm?

Enter the lives of two captivating characters and their world
Melissa Good's thousands of fans already know and love. Your h
will be touched by the poignant realism of the story. Your senses
emotions will be electrified by the intensity of their problems.
will care about these characters before you get very far into the st

ISBN 978-1-935053-00-2

Eye of the Storm

Eye of the Storm picks up the story of Dar Roberts and Kerry Stu-
few months after Hurricane Watch ends. At first it looks like
are settling into their lives together but, as readers of this series
learned, life is never simple around Dar and Kerry. Surrounded
ndless corporate intrigue, Dar experiences personal discoveries
force her to deal with issues that she had buried long ago and
y finally faces the consequences of her own actions. As always,
help each other through these personal challenges that, in the
strengthen them as individuals and as a couple.

ISBN 978-1-932300-13-0

Red Sky At Morning

A connection others don't understand...
A love that won't be denied...
Danger they can sense but cannot see...

Dar Roberts was always ruthless and single-minded...until she
Kerry Stuart.
Kerry was oppressed by her family's wealth and politics. But
saved her from that.
Now new dangers confront them from all sides. While traveling
Chicago, Kerry's plane is struck by lightning. Dar, in New York
a stockholders' meeting, senses Kerry is in trouble. They simulta-
usly experience feelings that are new, sensations that both are
ictant to admit when they are finally back together. Back in
mi, a cover-up of the worst kind, problems with the military, and
xpected betrayals will cause more danger. Can Kerry help as Dar
to examine her life and loyalties and call into question all she's
ieved in since childhood? Will their relationship deepen through
ll? Or will it be destroyed?

ISBN 978-1-932300-80-2

Thicker Than Water

This fifth entry in the continuing saga of Dar Roberts and ▮ Stuart starts off with Kerry involved in mentoring a church gro▮ girls. Kerry is forced to acknowledge her own feelings toward experiences with her own parents as she and Dar assist a teer from the group who gets jailed because her parents tossed he onto the streets when they found out she is gay. While trying to the teenagers adjust to real world situations, Kerry gets a call cerning her father's health. Kerry flies to her family's side a▮ father dies, putting the family in crisis. Caught up in an internat problem, Dar abandons the issue to go to Michigan, determin▮ support Kerry in the face of grief and hatred. Dar and Kerry down Kerry's extended family with a little help from their own, return home, where they decide to leave work and the world be for a while for some time to themselves.

ISBN 978-1-932300-24-6

Terrors of the High Seas

After the stress of a long Navy project and Kerry's fat▮ death, Dar and Kerry decide to take their first long vacation toge▮ A cruise in the eastern Caribbean is just the nice, peaceful time need — until they get involved in a family feud, an old murder, come face to face with pirates as their vacation turns into a rac find the key to a decades old puzzle.

ISBN 978-1-932300-45-1

Tropical Convergence

There's trouble on the horizon for ILS when a rival challer them head on, and their best weapons, Dar and Kerry, are distrac by life instead of focusing on the business. Add to that an old fla and an aggressive entreprenaur throwing down the gauntlet and at least is ready to throw in the towel. Is Kerry ready to follow s or will she decide to step out from behind Dar's shadow and step to the challenges they both face?

ISBN 978-1-935053-18-7

FORTHCOMING TITLES
from Yellow Rose Books

A Long Time Coming
by Cate Swannell

A Long Time Coming tells the story of Sarah and Shelby, two
⟨w⟩en who meet as therapist and client, but whose friendship
⟨mo⟩ves beyond that into something much deeper. They see each
⟨othe⟩r through break-ups, deaths, trauma and depression and fight
⟨thro⟩ugh each obstacle, including the ethical constraints imposed by
⟨thei⟩r professional relationship. Through 16 years of life experience,
⟨can⟩ their relationship stay strong and able to withstand all life
⟨thro⟩ws at them?

Available January 2011
ISBN 978-1-935053-42-2

The Other Mrs. Champion
by Brenda Adcock

Sarah Champion, 55, of Massachusetts, was leading the perfect
⟨life⟩ with Kelley, her partner and wife of twenty-five years. That is,
⟨unti⟩l Kelley was struck down by an unexpected stroke away from
⟨hom⟩e. But Sarah discovers she hadn't known her partner and lover as
⟨wel⟩l as she thought.
  Accompanied by Kelley's long-time friend and attorney, Sarah
⟨and⟩ her children rush to Vancouver, British Columbia to say their
⟨goo⟩dbyes, only to discover another woman, Pauline, keeping a vigil
⟨ove⟩r Kelley in the hospital. Confronted by the fact that her wife also
⟨had⟩ a Canadian wife, Sarah struggles to find answers to resolve her
⟨em⟩otional and personal turmoil.
  Alone and lonely, Sarah turns to the only other person who
⟨kne⟩w Kelley as well as she did-Pauline Champion. Will the two
⟨wo⟩men be able to forge a friendship despite their simmering animos-
⟨ity⟩? Will their growing attraction eventually become Kelley's final
⟨gift⟩ to the women she loved?

ISBN 978-1-935053-46-0
Available March 2011

OTHER YELLOW ROSE PUBLICATIONS

ki Stevenson	Family Values	978-1-932300-89-5
ki Stevenson	Family Ties	978-1-935053-03-3
ki Stevenson	Certain Personal Matters	978-1-935053-06-4
te Swannell	Heart's Passage	978-1-932300-09-3
te Swannell	No Ocean Deep	978-1-932300-36-9

VISIT US ONLINE AT

www.regalcrest.biz

At the Regal Crest Website You'll Find

- The latest news about forthcoming titles and r
releases

- Our complete backlist of romance, myste
thriller and adventure titles

- Information about your favorite authors

- Current bestsellers

Regal Crest titles are available from all progress
booksellers including numerous sources online. C
distributors are Bella Distribution and Ingram.